Raymond Chandler was born in Chicago in 1888. He came to England at an early age and studied at Dulwich College, completing his education in France and Germany.

In addition to his service with a Canadian infantry regiment in the First World War, he worked in many trades and professions – teacher, book-reviewer, poet, paragraph writer, essayist, student pilot, accountant, oil executive and 'pulp' writer.

For the last forty years of his life he lived in the United States, largely in the Southern California region which provided the background for his classic series of Philip Marlowe crime novels. Raymond Chandler died in 1959.

Also by Raymond Chandler in Picador

The Chandler Collection
Volume 1
The Big Sleep
The Lady in the Lake
The Little Sister

The Chandler Collection
Volume 3
Pearls Are a Nuisance
Smart-Alec Kill
Killer in the Rain

# The
# Chandler
# Collection

## *Volume 2*

## The High Window

—✡—

## The Long Good-bye

—✡—

## Playback

published by Pan Books

*The High Window* first published in Great Britain 1943
by Hamish Hamilton Ltd
First Pan Books edition published 1979
© Raymond Chandler 1943
*The Long-Goodbye* first published in Great Britain 1953
by Hamish Hamilton Ltd
First Pan Books edition published 1979
© Raymond Chandler 1953
*Playback* first published in Great Britain 1958
Reissued 1973 by Hamish Hamilton Ltd
First Pan Books edition published 1980
© Raymond Chandler 1958
This collected Picador edition published 1983 by Pan Books Ltd,
Cavaye Place, London SW10 9PG
9 8 7 6 5 4 3 2
ISBN 0 330 28155 0
Printed and bound in Great Britain by
Cox & Wyman Ltd, Reading

# Contents

# The High Window

# One

The house was on Dresden Avenue in the Oak Knoll section of Pasadena, a big solid cool-looking house with burgundy brick walls, a terra-cotta tile roof, and a white stone trim. The front windows were leaded downstairs. Upstairs windows were of the cottage type and had a lot of rococo imitation stonework trimming around them.

From the front wall and its attendant flowering bushes a half-acre or so of fine green lawn drifted in a gentle slope down to the street, passing on the way an enormous deodar around which it flowed like a cool green tide around a rock. The sidewalk and the parkway were both very wide and in the parkway were three white acacias that were worth seeing. There was a heavy scent of summer on the morning and everything that grew was perfectly still in the breathless air they get over there on what they call a nice cool day.

All I knew about the people was that they were a Mrs Elizabeth Bright Murdock and family and that she wanted to hire a nice clean private detective who wouldn't drop cigar ashes on the floor and never carried more than one gun. And I knew she was the widow of an old coot with whiskers named Jasper Murdock who had made a lot of money helping out the community, and got his photograph in the Pasadena paper every year on his anniversary, with the years of his birth and death underneath, and the legend: *His Life Was His Service.*

I left my car on the street and walked over a few dozen stumble stones set into the green lawn, and rang the bell in the brick portico under a peaked roof. A low red brick wall ran along the front of the house the short distance from the door to the edge of the driveway. At the end of the walk, on a concrete block, there was a little painted negro in white riding-breeches and a green jacket and a red cap. He was holding a whip, and there was an iron hitching ring in the block at his feet. He looked a little sad, as if he had been waiting there a long time and was getting discouraged. I went over and patted his head while I was waiting for somebody to come to the door.

After a while a middle-aged sourpuss in a maid's costume

opened the front door about eight inches and gave me the beady eye.

'Philip Marlowe,' I said. 'Calling on Mrs Murdock. By appointment.'

The middle-aged sourpuss ground her teeth, snapped her eyes shut, snapped them open and said in one of those angular hardrock pioneer-type voices: 'Which one?'

'Huh?'

'Which Mrs Murdock?' she almost screamed at me.

'Mrs Elizabeth Bright Murdock,' I said. 'I didn't know there was more than one.'

'Well, there is,' she snapped. 'Got a card?'

She still had the door a scant eight inches open. She poked the end of her nose and a thin muscular hand into the opening. I got my wallet out and got one of the cards with just my name on it and put it in the hand. The hand and nose went in and the door slammed in my face.

I thought that maybe I ought to have gone to the back door. I went over and patted the little negro on the head again.

'Brother,' I said, 'you and me both.'

Time passed, quite a lot of time. I stuck a cigarette in my mouth, but didn't light it. The Good Humour man went by in his little blue and white wagon, playing 'Turkey in the Straw' on his music-box. A large black and gold butterfly fish-tailed in and landed on a hydrangea bush almost at my elbow, moved its wings slowly up and down a few times, then took off heavily and staggered away through the motionless hot scented air.

The front door came open again. The sourpuss said: 'This way.'

I went in. The room beyond was large and square and sunken and cool and had the restful atmosphere of a funeral chapel and something like the same smell. Tapestry on the blank roughened stucco walls, iron grilles imitating balconies outside high windows, heavy carved chairs with plush seats and tapestry backs and tarnished gilt tassels hanging down their sides. At the back a stained-glass window about the size of a tennis-court. Curtained french doors underneath it. An old musty, fusty, narrow-minded, clean and bitter room. It didn't look as if anybody ever sat in it or would ever want to. Marble-topped tables with crooked legs, gilt clocks, pieces of small statuary in two colours of marble. A lot of junk that would take a week to dust. A lot of money, and all wasted. Thirty years before, in the wealthy close-mouthed provincial town Pasedena then was, it must have seemed like quite a room.

We left it and went along a hallway and after a while the sourpuss opened a door and motioned me in.

'Mr Marlowe,' she said through the door in a nasty voice, and went away grinding her teeth.

# Two

It was a small room looking out on the back garden. It had an ugly red and brown carpet and was furnished as an office. It contained what you would expect to find in a small office. A thin, fragile-looking, blondish girl in shell glasses sat behind a desk with a typewriter on a pulled-out leaf at her left. She had her hands poised on the keys, but she didn't have any paper in the machine. She watched me come into the room with the stiff, half-silly expression of a self-conscious person posing for a snapshot. She had a clear, soft voice, asking me to sit down.

'I am Miss Davis. Mrs Murdock's secretary. She wanted me to ask you for a few references.'

'References?'

'Certainly. References. Does that surprise you?'

I put my hat on her desk and the unlighted cigarette on the brim of the hat. 'You mean she sent for me without knowing anything about me?'

Her lip trembled and she bit it. I didn't know whether she was scared or annoyed or just having trouble being cool and business-like. But she didn't look happy.

'She got your name from the manager of a branch of the California-Security Bank. But he doesn't know you personally,' she said.

'Get your pencil ready,' I said.

She held it up and showed me that it was freshly sharpened and ready to go.

I said: 'First off, one of the vice-presidents of that same bank. George S. Leake. He's in the main office. Then State Senator Huston Oglethorpe. He may be in Sacramento, or he may be at his office in the State Building in Los Angeles. Then Sidney Dreyfus, Jr, of Dreyfus, Turner & Swayne, attorneys in the Title-Insurance Building. Got that?'

She wrote fast and easily. She nodded without looking up. The light danced on her blonde hair.

'Oliver Fry of the Fry-Krantz Corporation, Oil Well Tools. They're over on East Ninth, in the industrial district. Then, if you would like a couple of cops, Bernard Ohls of the DA's staff, and Detective-Lieutenant Carl Randall of the Central Homicide Bureau. You think maybe that would be enough?'

'Don't laugh at me,' she said. 'I'm only doing what I'm told.'

'Better not call the last two, unless you know what the job is,' I said. 'I'm not laughing at you. Hot, isn't it?'

'It's not hot for Pasadena,' she said, and hoisted her phone book up on the desk and went to work.

While she was looking up the numbers and telephoning hither and yon I looked her over. She was pale with a sort of natural paleness and she looked healthy enough. Her coarse-grained coppery blonde hair was not ugly in itself, but it was drawn back so tightly over her narrow head that it almost lost the effect of being hair at all. Her eyebrows were thin and unusually straight and were darker than her hair, almost a chestnut colour. Her nostrils had the whitish look of an anaemic person. Her chin was too small, too sharp and looked unstable. She wore no make-up except orange-red on her mouth and not much of that. Her eyes behind the glasses were very large, cobalt blue with big irises and a vague expression. Both lids were tight so that the eyes had a slightly oriental look, or as if the skin of her face was naturally so tight that it stretched her eyes at the corners. The whole face had a sort of off-key neurotic charm that only needed some clever make-up to be striking.

She wore a one-piece linen dress with short sleeves and no ornament of any kind. Her bare arms had down on them, and a few freckles.

I didn't pay much attention to what she said over the telephone. Whatever was said to her she wrote down in shorthand, with deft easy strokes of the pencil. When she was through she hung the phone book back on a hook and stood up and smoothed the linen dress down over her thighs and said:

'If you will just wait a few moments—' and went towards the door.

Half-way there she turned back and pushed a top drawer of her desk shut at the side. She went out. The door closed. There was silence. Outside the window bees buzzed. Far off I heard the whine of a vacuum cleaner. I picked the unlighted cigarette off my hat, put it in my mouth and stood up. I went around the desk and pulled open the drawer she had come back to shut.

It wasn't any of my business. I was just curious. It wasn't any of my business that she had a small Colt automatic in the drawer. I shut it and sat down again.

She was gone about four minutes. She opened the door and stayed at it and said: 'Mrs Murdock will see you now.'

We went along some more hallway and she opened half of a double glass door and stood aside. I went in and the door was closed behind me.

It was so dark in there that at first I couldn't see anything but the outdoors light coming through thick bushes and screens. Then I saw that the room was a sort of sun porch that had been allowed to get completely overgrown outside. It was furnished with grass rugs and reed stuff. There was a reed chaise-longue over by the window. It had a curved back and enough cushions to stuff an elephant and there was a woman leaning back on it with a wine-glass in her hand. I could smell the thick scented alcoholic odour of the wine before I could see her properly. Then my eyes got used to the light and I could see her.

She had a lot of face and chin. She had pewter-coloured hair set in a ruthless permanent, a hard beak and large moist eyes with the sympathetic expression of wet stones. There was lace at her throat, but it was the kind of throat that would have looked better in a football sweater. She wore a greyish silk dress. Her thick arms were bare and mottled. There were jet buttons in her ears. There was a low glass-topped table beside her and a bottle of port on the table. She sipped from the glass she was holding and looked at me over it and said nothing.

I stood there. She let me stand while she finished the port

in her glass and put the glass down on the table and filled it again. Then she tapped her lips with a handkerchief. Then she spoke. Her voice had a hard baritone quality and sounded as if it didn't want any nonsense.

'Sit down, Mr Marlowe. Please do not light that cigarette. I'm asthmatic.'

I sat down in a reed rocker and tucked the still unlighted cigarette down behind the handkerchief in my outside pocket.

'I've never had any dealing with private detectives, Mr Marlowe. I don't know anything about them. Your references seem satisfactory. What are your charges?'

'To do what, Mrs Murdock?'

'It's a very confidential matter, naturally. Nothing to do with the police. If it had to do with the police, I should have called the police.'

'I charge twenty-five dollars a day, Mrs Murdock. And, of course, expenses.'

'It seems high. You must make a great deal of money.' She drank some more of her port. I don't like port in hot weather, but it's nice when they let you refuse it.

'No,' I said. 'It isn't. Of course, you can get detective work done at any price – just like legal work. Or dental work. I'm not an organization. I'm just one man and I work at just one case at a time. I take risks, sometimes quite big risks, and I don't work all the time. No, I don't think twenty-five dollars a day is too much.'

'I see. And what is the nature of the expenses?'

'Little things that come up here and there. You never know.'

'I should prefer to know,' she said acidly.

'You'll know,' I said. 'You'll get it all down in black and white. You'll have a chance to object, if you don't like it.'

'And how much retainer would you expect?'

'A hundred dollars would hold me,' I said.

'I should hope it would,' she said, and finished her port and poured the glass full again without even waiting to wipe her lips.

'From people in your position, Mrs Murdock, I don't necessarily have to have a retainer.'

'Mr Marlowe,' she said, 'I'm a strong-minded woman. But don't let me scare you. Because if you can be scared by me, you won't be much use to me.'

I nodded and let that one drift with the tide.

She laughed suddenly and then she belched. It was a nice light belch, nothing showy, and performed with easy unconcern. 'My asthma,' she said carelessly. 'I drink this wine as medicine. That's why I'm not offering you any.'

I swung a leg over my knee. I hoped that wouldn't hurt her asthma.

'Money,' she said, 'is not really important. A woman in my position is always overcharged and gets to expect it. I hope you will be worth your fee. Here is the situation. Something of considerable value has been stolen from me. I want it back, but I want more than that. I don't want anybody arrested. The thief happens to be a member of my family – by marriage.'

She turned the wine-glass with her thick fingers and smiled faintly in the dim light of the shadowed room. 'My daughter-in-law,' she said. 'A charming girl – and tough as an oak board.'

She looked at me with a sudden gleam in her eyes.

'I have a damn fool of a son,' she said. 'But I'm very fond of him. About a year ago he made an idiotic marriage, without my consent. This was foolish of him because he is quite incapable of earning a living and he has no money except what I give him, and I am not generous with money. The lady he chose, or who chose him, was a night-club singer. Her name, appropriately enough, was Linda Conquest. They have lived here in this house. We didn't quarrel because I don't allow people to quarrel with me in my own house, but there has not been good feeling between us. I have paid their expenses, given each of them a car, made the lady a sufficient but not gaudy allowance for clothes and so on. No doubt she found the life rather dull. No doubt she found my son dull. I find him dull myself. At any rate, she moved out, very abruptly, a week or so ago, without leaving a forwarding address or saying good-bye.'

She coughed, fumbled for a handkerchief, and blew her nose.

'What was taken,' she went on, 'was a coin. A rare gold coin called a Brasher Doubloon. It was the pride of my husband's collection. I care nothing for such things, but he did. I have kept the collection intact since he died four years ago. It is upstairs, in a locked fireproof room, in a set of fireproof cases. It is insured, but I have not reported the loss yet. I don't want to, if I

15

can help it. I'm quite sure Linda took it. The coin is said to be worth over ten thousand dollars. It's a mint specimen.'

'But pretty hard to sell,' I said.

'Perhaps. I don't know. I didn't miss the coin until yesterday. I should not have missed it then, as I never go near the collection, except that a man in Los Angeles named Morningstar called up, said he was a dealer, and was the Murdock Brasher, as he called it, for sale? My son happened to take the call. He said he didn't believe it was for sale, it never had been, but that if Mr Morningstar would call some other time, he could probably talk to me. It was not convenient then, as I was resting. The man said he would do that. My son reported the conversation to Miss Davis, who reported it to me. I had her call the man back. I was faintly curious.'

She sipped some more port, flopped her handkerchief about and grunted.

'Why were you curious, Mrs Murdock?' I asked, just to be saying something.

'If the man was a dealer of any repute, he would know that the coin was not for sale. My husband, Jasper Murdock, provided in his will that no part of his collection might be sold, loaned or hypothecated during my lifetime. Nor removed from this house, except in case of damage to the house necessitating removal, and then only by action of the trustees. My husband' – she smiled grimly – 'seemed to feel that I ought to have taken more interest in his little pieces of metal while he was alive.'

It was a nice day outside, the sun shining, the flowers blooming, the birds singing. Cars went by on the street with a distant comfortable sound. In the dim room with the hard-faced woman and the winy smell everything seemed a little unreal. I tossed my foot up and down over my knee and waited.

'I spoke to Mr Morningstar. His full name is Elisha Morningstar and he has offices in the Belfont Building on Ninth Street in downtown Los Angeles, I told him the Murdock collection was not for sale, never had been, and, so far as I was concerned, never would be, and that. I was surprised that he didn't know that. He hemmed and hawed and then asked me if he might examine the coin. I said certainly not. He thanked me rather dryly and hung up. He sounded like an old man. So I went upstairs to examine the coin myself, something I had not done in a year. It was gone from its place in one of the locked fireproof cases.'

I said nothing. She refilled her glass and played a tattoo with her thick fingers on the arm of the chaise-longue. 'What I thought then you can probably guess.'

I said: 'The part about Mr Morningstar, maybe. Somebody had offered the coin to him for sale and he had known or suspected where it came from. The coin must be very rare.'

'What they call a mint specimen is very rare indeed. Yes, I had the same idea.'

'How would it be stolen?' I asked.

'By anyone in this house, very easily. The keys are in my bag, and my bag lies around here and there. It would be a very simple matter to get hold of the keys long enough to unlock a door and a cabinet and then return the keys. Difficult for an outsider, but anybody in the house could have stolen it.'

'I see. How do you establish that your daughter-in-law took it, Mrs Murdock?'

'I don't – in a strictly evidential sense. But I'm quite sure of it. The servants are three women who have been here many, many years – long before I married Mr Murdock, which was only seven years ago. The gardener never comes in the house. I have no chauffeur, because either my son or my secretary drives me. My son didn't take it, first because he is not the kind of fool that steals from his mother, and second, if he had taken it, he could easily have prevented me from speaking to the coin dealer, Morningstar. Miss Davis – ridiculous. Just not the type at all. Too mousy. No, Mr Marlowe, Linda is the sort of lady who might do it just for spite, if nothing else. And you know what these night-club people are.'

'All sorts of people – like the rest of us,' I said. 'No signs of a burglar, I suppose? It would take a pretty smooth worker to lift just one valuable coin, so there wouldn't be. Maybe I had better look the room over, though.'

She pushed her jaw at me and muscles in her neck made hard lumps. 'I have just told you, Mr Marlowe, that Mrs Leslie Murdock, my daughter-in-law, took the Brasher Doubloon.'

I stared at her and she stared back. Her eyes were as hard as the bricks in her front walk. I shrugged the stare off and said:

'Assuming that is so, Mrs Murdock, just what do you want done?'

'In the first place I want the coin back. In the second place I want an uncontested divorce for my son. And I don't intend to buy it. I dare say you know how these things are arranged.'

She finished the current instalment of port and laughed rudely.

'I may have heard,' I said. 'You say the lady left no forwarding address. Does that mean you have no idea at all where she went?'

'Exactly that.'

'A disappearance then. Your son might have some ideas he hasn't passed along to you. I'll have to see him.'

The big grey face hardened into even ruggeder lines. 'My son knows nothing. He doesn't even know the doubloon has been stolen. I don't want him to know anything. When the time comes I'll handle him. Until then I want him left alone. He will do exactly what I want him to.'

'He hasn't always,' I said.

'His marriage,' she said nastily, 'was a momentary impulse. Afterwards he tried to act like a gentleman. I have no such scruples.'

'It takes three days to have that kind of momentary impulse in California, Mrs Murdock.'

'Young man, do you want this job or don't you?'

'I want it if I'm told the facts and allowed to handle the case as I see fit. I don't want it if you're going to make a lot of rules and regulations for me to trip over.'

She laughed harshly. 'This is a delicate family matter, Mr Marlowe. And it must be handled with delicacy.'

'If you hire me, you'll get all the delicacy I have. If I don't have enough delicacy, maybe you'd better not hire me. For instance, I take it you don't want your daughter-in-law framed. I'm not delicate enough for that.'

She turned the colour of a cold boiled beet and opened her mouth to yell. Then she thought better of it, lifted her port glass and tucked away some more of her medicine.

'You'll do,' she said dryly, 'I wish I had met you two years ago, before he married her.'

I didn't know exactly what this last meant, so I let it ride. She bent over sideways and fumbled with the key on a house telephone and growled into it when she was answered.

There were steps and the little copper-blonde came tripping into the room with her chin low, as if somebody might be going to take a swing at her.

'Make this man a cheque for two hundred and fifty dollars,' the old dragon snarled at her. 'And keep your mouth shut about it.'

The little girl flushed all the way to her neck. 'You know I never talk about your affairs, Mrs Murdock,' she bleated. 'You know I don't. I wouldn't dream of it, I—'

She turned with her head down and ran out of the room. As she closed the door I looked out at her. Her lip was trembling but her eyes were mad.

'I'll need a photo of the lady and some information,' I said when the door was shut again.

'Look in the desk drawer.' Her rings flashed in the dimness as her thick grey finger pointed.

I went over and opened the single drawer of the reed desk and took out the photo that lay all alone in the bottom of the drawer, face up, looking at me with cool dark eyes. I sat down again with the photo and looked it over. Dark hair parted loosely in the middle and drawn back loosely over a solid piece of forehead. A wide cool go-to-hell mouth with very kissable lips. Nice nose, not too small, not too large. Good bone all over the face. The expression of the face lacked something. Once the something might have been called breeding, but these days I didn't know what to call it. The face looked too wise and too guarded for its age. Too many passes had been made at it and it had grown a little too smart in dodging them. And behind this expression of wiseness there was the look of simplicity of the little girl who still believes in Santa Claus.

I nodded over the photo and slipped it into my pocket, thinking I was getting too much out of it to get out of a mere photo, and in a very poor light at that.

The door opened and the little girl in the linen dress came in with a three-decker cheque book and a fountain-pen and made a desk of her arm for Mrs Murdock to sign. She straightened up with a strained smile and Mrs Murdock made a sharp gesture towards me and the little girl tore the cheque out and gave it to me. She hovered inside the door, waiting. Nothing was said to her, so she went out softly again and closed the door.

I shook the cheque dry, folded it and sat holding it. 'What can you tell me about Linda?'

'Practically nothing. Before she married my son she shared an apartment with a girl named Lois Magic – charming names these people choose for themselves – who is an entertainer of some sort. They worked at a place called the Idle Valley Club, out Ventura Boulevard way. My son Leslie knows it far too well. I know nothing about Linda's family or origins. She said once she was born in Sioux Falls. I suppose she had parents. I was not interested enough to find out.'

Like hell she wasn't. I could see her digging with both hands, digging hard, and getting herself a double handful of gravel.

'You don't know Miss Magic's address?'

'No. I never did know.'

'Would your son be likely to know – or Miss Davis?'

'I'll ask my son when he comes in. I don't think so. You can ask Miss Davis. I'm sure she doesn't.'

'I see. You don't know of any other friends of Linda's?'

'No.'

'It's possible that your son is still in touch with her, Mrs Murdock – without telling you.'

She started to get purple again. I held my hand up and dragged a soothing smile over my face. 'After all he has been married to her a year,' I said. 'He must know something about her.'

'You leave my son out of this,' she snarled.

I shrugged and made a disappointed sound with my lips. 'Very well. She took her car, I suppose. The one you gave her?'

'A steel grey Mercury, 1940 model, a coupé. Miss Davis can give you the licence number, if you want that. I don't know whether she took it.'

'Would you know what money and clothes and jewels she had with her?'

'Not much money. She might have had a couple of hundred dollars at most.' A fat sneer made deep lines around her nose and mouth. 'Unless, of course, she has found a new friend.'

'There's that,' I said ... 'Jewellery?'

'An emerald and diamond ring of no very great value, a platinum Longines watch with rubies in the mounting, a very good cloudy amber necklace which I was foolish enough to give her myself. It has a diamond clasp with twenty-six small diamonds in the shape of a playing-card diamond. She had other things, of course. I never paid much attention to them. She dressed well but not strikingly. Thank God for a few small mercies.'

She refilled her glass and drank and did some more of her semi-social belching.

'That's all you can tell me, Mrs Murdock?'

'Isn't it enough?'

'Not nearly enough, but I'll have to be satisfied for the time being. If I find she did not steal the coin, that ends the investigation as far as I'm concerned. Correct?'

'We'll talk it over,' she said roughly. 'She stole it all right. And I don't intend to let her get away with it. Paste that in your hat, young man. And I hope you are even half as rough as you like to act, because these night-club girls are apt to have some very nasty friends.'

I was still holding the folded cheque by one corner down between my knees. I got my wallet out and put it away and stood up, reaching my hat off the floor.

'I like them nasty,' I said. 'The nasty ones have very simple minds. I'll report to you when there is anything to report, Mrs Murdock. I think I'll tackle this coin dealer first. He sounds like a lead.'

She let me get to the door before she growled at my back: 'You don't like me very well, do you?'

I turned to grin back at her with my hand on the knob. 'Does anybody?'

She threw her head back and opened her mouth wide and roared with laughter. In the middle of the laughter I opened the door and went out and shut the door on the rough mannish sound. I went back along the hall and knocked on the secretary's half-open door, then pushed it open and looked in.

She had her arms folded on her desk and her face down on the folded arms. She was sobbing. She screwed her head around and looked up at me with tear-stained eyes. I shut the door and went over beside her and put an arm around her thin shoulders.

'Cheer up,' I said. 'You ought to feel sorry for her. She thinks she's tough and she's breaking her back trying to live up to it.'

The little girl jumped erect, away from my arm. 'Don't touch me,' she said breathlessly. 'Please. I never let men touch me. And don't say such awful things about Mrs Murdock.'

Her face was all pink and wet from tears. Without her glasses her eyes were very lovely.

I stuck my long-waiting cigarette into my mouth and lit it.

'I – I didn't mean to be rude,' she snuffled. 'But she does humiliate me so. And I only want to do my best for her.' She snuffled some more and got a man's handkerchief out of her desk and shook it out and wiped her eyes with it. I saw on the hanging-down corner the initials L.M. embroidered in purple. I stared at it and blew cigarette smoke towards the corner of the room, away from her hair. 'Is there something you want?' she asked.

'I want the licence number of Mrs Leslie Murdock's car.'

'It's 2XIIII, a grey Mercury convertible, 1940 model.'

'She told me it was a coupé.'

'That's Mr Leslie's car. They're the same make and year and colour. Linda didn't take the car.'

'Oh. What do you know about a Miss Lois Magic?'

'I only saw her once. She used to share an apartment with Linda. She came here with a Mr – a Mr Vannier.'

'Who's he?'

She looked down at her desk. 'I – she just came with him. I don't know him.'

'Okay, what does Miss Lois Magic look like?'

'She's a tall handsome blonde. Very – very appealing.'

'You mean sexy?'

'Well—' she blushed furiously, 'in a nice well-bred sort of way, if you know what I mean.'

'I know what you mean,' I said, 'but I never got anywhere with it.'

'I can believe that,' she said tartly.

'Know where Miss Magic lives?'

She shook her head, no. She folded the big handkerchief very carefully and put it in the drawer of her desk, the one where the gun was.

'You can swipe another one when that's dirty,' I said.

She leaned back in her chair and put her small neat hands on her desk and looked at me levelly.

'I wouldn't carry that tough-guy manner too far, if I were you, Mr Marlowe. Not with me, at any rate.'

'No?'

'No. And I can't answer any more questions without specific instructions. My position here is very confidential.'

'I'm not tough,' I said. 'Just virile.'

She picked up a pencil and made a mark on a pad. She smiled faintly up at me, all composure again.

'Perhaps I don't like virile men,' she said.

'You're a screwball,' I said, 'if ever I met one. Good-bye.'

I went out of her office, shut the door firmly, and walked back along the empty halls through the big silent sunken funereal living-room and out of the front door.

The sun danced on the warm lawn outside. I put my dark glasses on and went over and patted the little negro on the head again.

'Brother, it's even worse than I expected,' I told him.

The stumble stones were hot through the soles of my shoes. I got into the car and started it and pulled away from the kerb.

A small sand-coloured coupé pulled away from the kerb behind me. I didn't think anything of it. The man driving it wore a dark porkpie type straw hat with a gay print band and dark glasses were over his eyes, as over mine.

I drove back towards the city. A dozen blocks later, at a traffic stop, the sand-coloured coupé was still behind me. I shrugged and just for the fun of it circled a few blocks. The coupé held its position. I swung into a street lined with immense pepper trees, dragged my car around in a fast U-turn and stopped against the kerbing.

The coupé came carefully around the corner. The blond head under the cocoa straw hat with the tropical print band didn't even turn my way. The coupé sailed on and I drove back to the Arroyo Seco and on towards Hollywood. I looked carefully several times, but I didn't spot the coupé again.

# Three

I had an office in the Cahuenga Building, sixth floor, two small rooms at the back. One I left open for a patient client to sit in, if I had a patient client. There was a buzzer on the door which I could switch on and off from my private thinking parlour.

I looked into the reception-room. It was empty of everything but the smell of dust. I threw up another window, unlocked the communicating door and went into the room beyond. Three hard chairs and a swivel chair, flat desk with a glass top, five green filing-cases, three of them full of nothing, a calendar and a framed licence bond on the wall, a phone, a washbowl in a stained wood cupboard, a hat-rack, a carpet that was just something on the floor, and two open windows with net curtains that puckered in and out like the lips of a toothless old man sleeping.

The same stuff I had had last year, and the year before that. Not beautiful, not gay, but better than a tent on the beach.

I hung my hat and coat on the hat-rack, washed my face and hands in cold water, lit a cigarette and hoisted the phone book on to the desk. Elisha Morningstar was listed at 824 Belfont Building, 422 West Ninth Street. I wrote that down and the phone number that went with it and had my hand on the instrument when I remembered that I hadn't switched on the buzzer of the reception-room. I reached over the side of the desk and clicked it on and caught it right in stride. Somebody had just opened the door of the outer office.

I turned my pad face down on the desk and went over to see who it was. It was a slim tall self-satisfied looking number in a tropical worsted suit of slate-blue, black and white shoes, a dull ivory-coloured shirt and a tie and display handkerchief the colour of jacaranda bloom. He was holding a long black cigarette-holder in a peeled back white pigskin glove and he was wrinkling his nose at the dead magazines on the library table and the chairs and the rusty floor covering and the general air of not much money being made.

As I opened the communicating door he made a quarter turn and stared at me out of a pair of rather dreamy pale eyes set close to a narrow nose. His skin was sun-flushed, his reddish hair was brushed back hard over a narrow skull, and the thin line of his moustache was much redder than his hair.

He looked me over without haste and without much pleasure. He blew some smoke delicately and spoke through it with a faint sneer.

'You're Marlowe?'

I nodded.

'I'm a little disappointed,' he said. 'I rather expected something with dirty fingernails.'

'Come inside,' I said, 'and you can be witty sitting down.'

I held the door for him and he strolled past me flicking cigarette-ash on the floor with the middle nail of his free hand. He sat down on the customer's side of the desk, took off the glove from his right hand and folded this with the other already off and laid them on the desk. He tapped the cigarette-end out of the long black holder, prodded the ash with a match until it stopped smoking, fitted another cigarette and lit it with a broad mahogany-coloured match. He leaned back in his chair with a smile of a bored aristocrat.

'All set?' I inquired. 'Pulse and respiration normal? You wouldn't like a cold towel on your head or anything?'

He didn't curl his lip because it had been curled when he came in. 'A private detective,' he said. 'I never met one. A shifty business, one gathers. Keyhole peeping, raking up scandal, that sort of thing.'

'You here on business,' I asked him, 'or just slumming?'

His smile was as faint as a fat lady at a fireman's ball.

'The name is Murdock. That probably means a little something to you.'

'You certainly made nice time over here,' I said, and started to fill a pipe.

He watched me fill the pipe. He said slowly: 'I understand my mother has employed you on a job of some sort. She has given you a cheque.'

I finished filling the pipe, put a match to it, got it drawing and leaned back to blow smoke over my right shoulder towards the open window. I didn't say anything.

He leaned forward a little more and said earnestly: ' I know being cagey is all part of your trade, but I am not guessing. A little worm told me, a simple garden worm, often trodden on, but still somehow surviving – like myself. I happened to be not far behind you. Does that help to clear things up?'

'Yeah,' I said. 'Supposing it made any difference to me.'

'You are hired to find my wife, I gather.'

I made a snorting sound and grinned at him over the pipe bowl.

'Marlowe,' he said, even more earnestly. 'I'll try hard, but I don't think I am going to like you.'

'I'm screaming,' I said. 'With rage and pain.'

'"And if you will pardon a homely phrase, your tough guy act stinks.'

'Coming from you, that's bitter.'

He leaned back again and brooded at me with pale eyes. He fussed around in the chair, trying to get comfortable. A lot of people had tried to get comfortable in that chair. I ought to try it myself sometime. Maybe it was losing business for me.

'Why should my mother want Linda found?' he asked slowly. 'She hated her guts. I mean my mother hated Linda's guts. Linda was quite decent to my mother. What do you think of her?'

'Your mother?'

'Of course. You haven't met Linda, have you?'

'That secretary of your mother's has her job hanging by a frayed thread. She talks out of turn.'

He shook his head sharply. 'Mother won't know. Anyhow, Mother couldn't do without Merle. She has to have somebody to bully. She might yell at her or even slap her face, but she couldn't do without her. What did you think of her?'

'Kind of cute – in an old-world sort of way.'

He frowned. 'I mean Mother. Merle's just a simple little girl, I know.'

'Your powers of observation startle me,' I said.

He looked surprised. He almost forgot to fingernail the ash of his cigarette. But not quite. He was careful not to get any of it in the ash-tray, however.

'About my mother,' he said patiently.

'A grand old war-horse,' I said. 'A heart of gold and the gold buried good and deep.'

'But why does she want Linda found? I can't understand it. Spending money on it, too. My mother hates to spend money. She thinks money is part of her skin. Why does she want Linda found?'

'Search me,' I said. 'Who said she did?'

'Why, you implied so. And Merle—'

'Merle's just romantic. She made it up. Hell, she blows her nose in a man's handkerchief. Probably one of yours.'

He blushed. 'That's silly. Look, Marlowe. Please, be reasonable and give me an idea what it's all about. I haven't much money, I'm afraid, but would a couple of hundred—'

'I ought to bop you,' I said. 'Besides, I'm not supposed to talk to you. Orders.'

'Why, for heaven's sake?'

'Don't ask me things I don't know. I can't tell you the answers. And don't ask me things I do know, because I won't tell you the answers. Where have you been all your life? If a man in my line of work is handed a job, does he go around answering questions about it to anyone that gets curious?'

'There must be a lot of electricity in the air,' he said nastily, 'for a man in your line of work to turn down two hundred dollars'.

There was nothing in that for me, either. I picked his broad mahogany match out of the tray and looked at it. It had thin yellow edges and there was white printing on it. ROSEMONT. H. RICHARDS '3 – the rest was burnt off. I doubled the match and squeezed the halves together and tossed it in the waste basket.

'I love my wife,' he said suddenly, and showed me the hard white edges of his teeth. 'A corny touch, but it's true.'

'The Lombardos are still doing all right.'

He kept his lips pulled back from his teeth and talked through them at me. 'She doesn't love me. I know of no particular reason why she should. Things have been strained between us. She was used to a fast-moving sort of life. With us, well, it has been pretty dull. We haven't quarrelled. Linda's the cool type. But she hasn't really had a lot of fun being married to me.'

'You're just too modest,' I said.

His eyes glinted, but he kept his smooth manner pretty well in place.

'Not good, Marlowe. Not even fresh. Look, you have the air of a decent sort of guy. I know my mother is not putting out two hundred and fifty bucks just to be breezy. Maybe it's not Linda. Maybe it's something else. Maybe—' he stopped and then said this very slowly watching my eyes, 'maybe it's Morny.'

'Maybe it is,' I said cheerfully.

He picked his gloves up and slapped the desk with them and put them down again. 'I'm in a spot there all right,' he said. 'But I didn't think she knew about it. Morny must have called her up. He promised not to.'

This was easy. I said: 'How much are you into him for?'

It wasn't so easy. He got suspicious again. 'If he called her up, he would have told her. And she would have told you,' he said thinly.

'Maybe it isn't Morny,' I said, beginning to want a drink very badly. 'Maybe the cook is with child by the iceman. But if it was Morny, how much?'

'Twelve thousand,' he said, looking down and flushing.

'Threats?'

He nodded.

'Tell him to go fly a kite,' I said. 'What kind of lad is he? Tough?'

He looked up again, his face being brave. 'I suppose he is. I suppose they all are. He used to be a screen heavy. Good-looking in a flashy way, a chaser. But don't get any ideas. Linda just worked there, like the waiters and the band. And if you are looking for her, you'll have a hard time finding her.'

I sneered at him politely.

'Why would I have a hard time finding her? She's not buried in the backyard, I hope.'

He stood up with a flash of anger in his pale eyes. Standing there leaning over the desk a little he whipped his right hand up in a neat enough gesture and brought out a small automatic, about .25 calibre, with a walnut grip. It looked like the brother of the one I had seen in the drawer of Merle's desk. The muzzle looked vicious enough pointing at me. I didn't move.

'If anybody tries to push Linda around, he'll have to push me around first,' he said tightly.

'That oughtn't be too hard. Better get more gun – unless you're just thinking of bees.'

He put the little gun back in his inside pocket. He gave me a straight hard look and picked his gloves up and started for the door.

'It's a waste of time talking to you,' he said. 'All you do is crack wise.'

I said: 'Wait a minute,' and got up and went around the desk. 'It might be a good idea for you not to mention this interview to your mother, if only for the little girl's sake.'

He nodded. 'For the amount of information I got, it doesn't seem worth mentioning.'

'That straight goods about your owing Morny twelve grand?'

He looked down, then up, then down again. He said: 'Anybody who could get into Alex for twelve grand would have to be a lot smarter than I am.'

I was quite close to him. I said: 'As a matter of fact, I don't even think you are worried about your wife. I think you know where she is. She didn't run away from you at all. She just ran away from your mother.'

He lifted his eyes and drew one glove on. He didn't say anything.

'Perhaps she'll get a job,' I said. 'And make enough money to support you.'

He looked down at the floor again, turned his body to the right a little and the gloved fist made a tight unrelaxed arc through the air upwards. I moved my jaw out of the way and caught his wrist and pushed it slowly back against his chest, leaning on it. He slid a foot back on the floor and began to breathe hard. It was a slender wrist. My fingers went around it and met.

We stood there looking into each other's eyes. He was breathing like a drunk, his mouth open and his lips pulled back. Small round spots of bright red flamed on his cheeks. He tried to jerk his wrist away, but I put so much weight on him that he had to take another short step back to brace himself. Our faces were now only inches apart.

'How come your old man didn't leave you some money?' I sneered. 'Or did you blow it all?'

He spoke between his teeth, still trying to jerk loose. 'If it's any of your rotten business and you mean Jasper Murdock, he wasn't my father. He didn't like me and he didn't leave me a cent. My father was a man named Horace Bright who lost his money in the crash and jumped out of his office window.'

'You milk easy,' I said, 'but you give pretty thin milk. I'm sorry for what I said about your wife supporting you. I just wanted to get your goat.'

I dropped his wrist and stepped back. He still breathed hard and heavily. His eyes on mine were very angry, but he kept his voice down.

'Well, you got it. If you're satisfied, I'll be on my way.'

'I was doing you a favour,' I said. 'A gun toter oughtn't to insult so easily. Better ditch it.'

'That's my business,' he said. 'I'm sorry I took a swing at you. It probably wouldn't have hurt much, if it had connected.'

'That's all right.'

He opened the door and went on out. His steps died along the corridor. Another screwball. I tapped my teeth with a knuckle in time to the sound of his steps as long as I could hear them. Then I went back to the desk, looked at my pad, and lifted the phone.

# Four

After the bell had rung three times at the other end of the line a light childish sort of girl's voice filtered itself through a hank of gum and said: 'Good morning. Mr Morningstar's office.'

'Is the old gentleman in?'

'Who is calling, please?'

'Marlowe.'

'Does he know you, Mr Marlowe?'

'Ask him if he wants to buy any early American gold coins.'

'Just a minute, please.'

There was a pause suitable to an elderly party in an inner office having his attention called to the fact that somebody on the telephone wanted to talk to him. Then the phone clicked and a man spoke. He had a dry voice. You might even call it parched.

'This is Mr Morningstar.'

'I'm told you called Mrs Murdock in Pasadena, Mr Morningstar. About a certain coin.'

'About a certain coin,' he repeated. 'Indeed. Well?'

'My understanding is that you wished to buy the coin in question from the Murdock collection.'

'Indeed? And who are you, sir?'

'Philip Marlowe. A private detective. I'm working for Mrs Murdock.'

'Indeed,' he said for the third time. He cleared his throat carefully. 'And what did you wish to talk to me about, Mr Marlowe?'

'About this coin.'

'But I was informed it was not for sale.'

'I still want to talk to you about it. In person.'

'Do you mean she has changed her mind about selling?'

'No.'

'Then I'm afraid I don't understand what you want, Mr Marlowe. What have we to talk about?' He sounded sly now.

I took the ace out of my sleeve and played it with a languid grace. 'The point is, Mr Morningstar, that at the time you called up you already knew the coin wasn't for sale.'

'Interesting,' he said slowly. 'How?'

'You're in the business, you couldn't help knowing. It's a matter of public record that the Murdock collection cannot be sold during Mrs Murdock's lifetime.'

'Ah,' he said. 'Ah.' There was a silence. Then, 'At three o'clock,' he said, not sharp, but quick. 'I shall be glad to see you here in my office. You probably know where it is. Will that suit you?'

'I'll be there,' I said.

I hung up and lit my pipe again and sat there looking at the wall. My face was stiff with thought, or with something that made my face stiff. I took Linda Murdock's photo out of my pocket, stared at it for a while, decided that the face was pretty commonplace after all, locked the photo away in my desk. I picked Murdock's second match out of my ashtray and looked it over. The lettering on this one read: TOP ROW W. D. WRIGHT '36.

I dropped it back in the tray, wondering what made this important. Maybe it was a clue.

I got Mrs Murdock's cheque out of my wallet, endorsed it, made out a deposit slip and a cheque for cash, got my bank-book out of the desk, and folded the lot under a rubber band and put them in my pocket.

Lois Magic was not listed in the phone book.

I got the classified section up on the desk and made a list of the half-dozen theatrical agencies that showed in the largest type and called them. They all had bright cheerful voices and wanted to ask a lot of questions, but they either didn't know or didn't care to tell me anything about a Miss Lois Magic, said to be an entertainer.

I threw the list in the waste-basket and called Kenny Haste, a crime reporter on the *Chronicle*.

'What do you know about Alex Morny?' I asked him when we were through cracking wise at each other.

'Runs a plushy night-club and gambling joint in Idle Valley, about two miles off the highway back towards the hills. Used to be in pictures. Lousy actor. Seems to have plenty of protection. I never heard of him shooting anybody on the public square at high noon. Or at any other time for that matter. But I wouldn't like to bet on it.'

'Dangerous?'

'I'd say he might be, if necessary. All those boys have been to picture shows and know how night-club bosses are supposed to act. He has a bodyguard who is quite a character. His name's Eddie Prue, he's about six feet five inches tall and thin as an honest alibi. He has a frozen eye, the result of a war wound.'

'Is Morny dangerous to women?'

'Don't be Victorian, old top. Women don't call it danger.'

'Do you know a girl named Lois Magic, said to be an entertainer. A tall gaudy blonde, I hear.'

'No. Sounds as though I might like to.'

'Don't be cute. Do you know anybody named Vannier? None of these people are in the phone book.'

'Nope. But I could ask Gertie Arbogast, if you want to call back. He knows all the night-club aristocrats. And heels.'

'Thanks, Kenny. I'll do that. Half an hour?'

He said that would be fine, and we hung up. I locked the office and left.

At the end of the corridor, in the angle of the wall, a youngish blond man in a brown suit and a cocoa-coloured straw hat with a brown and yellow tropical print band was reading the evening paper with his back to the wall. As I passed him he yawned and tucked the paper under his arm and straightened up.

He got into the elevator with me. He could hardly keep his eyes open he was so tired. I went out on the street and walked a block to the bank to deposit my cheque and draw out a little folding money for expenses. From there I went to the Tigertail Lounge and sat in a shallow booth and drank a martini and ate a sandwich. The man in the brown suit posted himself at the end of the bar and drank coca-colas and looked bored and piled pennies in front of him, carefully smoothing the edges. He had his dark glasses on again. That made him invisible.

I dragged my sandwich out as long as I could and then strolled back to the telephone booth at the inner end of the bar. The man in the brown suit turned his head quickly and then covered the motion by lifting his glass. I dialled the *Chronicle* office again.

'Okay,' Kenny Haste said. 'Gertie Arbogast says Morny married your gaudy blonde not very long ago. Lois Magic. He doesn't know Vannier. He says Morny bought a place out beyond Bel-Air, a white house on Stillwood Crescent Drive, about five blocks north of Sunset. Gertie says Morny took it over from a busted flush named Arthur Blake Popham who got caught in a mail fraud rap. Popham's initials are still on the gates. And probably on the toilet paper, Gertie says. He was that kind of a guy. That's all we seem to know.'

'Nobody could ask more. Many thanks, Kenny.'

I hung up, stepped out of the booth, met the dark glasses above the brown suit under the cocoa straw hat and watched them turn quickly away.

I spun around and went back through a swing door into the kitchen and through that to the alley and along the alley a quarter block to the back of the parking lot where I had put my car.

No sand-coloured coupé succeeded in getting behind me as I drove off, in the general direction of Bel-Air.

# Five

Stillwood Crescent Drive curved leisurely north from Sunset Boulevard, well beyond the Bel-Air Country Club golf-course. The road was lined with walled and fenced estates. Some had high walls, some had low walls, some had ornamental iron fences, some were a bit old-fashioned and got along with tall hedges. The street had no sidewalk. Nobody walked in that neighbourhood, not even the postman.

The afternoon was hot, but not hot like Pasadena. There was a drowsy smell of flowers and sun, a swishing of lawn sprinklers gentle behind hedges and walls, the clear ratchety sound of lawn mowers moving delicately over serene and confident lawns.

I drove up the hill slowly, looking for monograms on gates. Arthur Blake Popham was the name. A.B.P. would be the initials. I found them almost at the top, gilt on a black shield, the gates folded back on a black composition driveway.

It was a glaring white house that had the air of being brand new, but the landscaping was well advanced. It was modest enough for the neighbourhood, not more than fourteen rooms and probably only one swimming pool. Its wall was low, made of brick with the concrete all oozed out between and set that way and painted over white. On top of the wall a low iron railing painted black. The name A. P. Morny was stencilled on the large silver-coloured postbox at the service entrance.

I parked my car on the street and walked up the black driveway to a side door of glittering white paint shot with patches of colour from the stained-glass canopy over it. I hammered on a large brass knocker. Back along the side of the house a chauffeur was washing off a Cadillac.

The door opened and a hard-eyed Filipino in a white coat curled his lip at me. I gave him a card.

'Mrs Morny,' I said.

He shut the door. Time passed, as it always does when I go calling. The swish of water on the Cadillac had a cool sound. The chauffeur was a little runt in breeches and leggings and a sweat-stained shirt. He looked like an over-grown jockey and he made the same kind of hissing noise as he worked on the car that a groom makes rubbing down a horse.

A red-throated humming-bird went into a scarlet bush beside the door, shook the long tubular blooms around a little, and zoomed off so fast he simply disappeared in the air.

The door opened, the Filipino poked my card at me. I didn't take it.

'What you want?'

It was a tight crackling voice, like someone tiptoeing across a lot of eggshells.

'Want to see Mrs Morny.'

'She not at home.'

'Didn't you know that when I gave you the card?'

He opened his fingers and let the card flutter to the ground. He grinned, showing me a lot of cut-rate dental work.

'I know when she tell me.'

He shut the door in my face, not gently.

I picked the card up and walked along the side of the house to where the chauffeur was squirting water on the Cadillac sedan and rubbing the dirt off with a big sponge. He had red-rimmed eyes and a bang of corn-coloured hair. A cigarette hung exhausted at the corner of his lower lip.

He gave me the quick side glance of a man who is minding his own business with difficulty. I said:

'Where's the boss?'

The cigarette jiggled in his mouth. The water went on swishing gently on the paint.

'Ask at the house, Jack.'

'I done asked. They done shut the door in mah face.'

'You're breaking my heart, Jack.'

'How about Mrs Morny?'

'Same answer, Jack. I just work here. Selling something?'

I held my card so that he could read it. It was a business card this time. He put the sponge down on the running-board, and

35

the hose on the cement. He stepped around the water to wipe his hands on a towel that hung at the side of the garage doors. He fished a match out of his pants, struck it and tilted his head back to light the dead butt that was stuck in his face.

His foxy little eyes flicked around this way and that and he moved behind the car, with a jerk of the head. I went over near him.

'How's the little old expense account?' he asked in a small careful voice.

'Fat with inactivity.'

'For five I could start thinking.'

'I wouldn't want to make it that tough for you.'

'For ten I could sing like four canaries and a steel guitar.'

'I don't like these plushy orchestrations,' I said.

He cocked his head sideways. 'Talk English, Jack.'

'I don't want you to lose your job, son. All I want to know is whether Mrs Morny is home. Does that rate more than a buck?'

'Don't worry about my job, Jack. I'm solid.'

'With Morny – or somebody else?'

'You want that for the same buck?'

'Two bucks.'

He eyed me over 'You ain't working for him, are you?'

'Sure.'

'You're a liar.'

'Sure.'

'Gimme the two bucks,' he snapped.

I gave him two dollars.

'She's in the backyard with a friend,' he said. 'A nice friend. You got a friend that don't work and a husband that works, you're all set, see?' He leered.

'You'll be all set in an irrigation ditch one of these days.'

'Not me, Jack. I'm wise. I know how to play 'em. I monkeyed around these kind of people all my life.'

He rubbed the two dollar bills between his palms, blew on them, folded them longways and wideways and tucked them in the watch pocket of his breeches.

'That was just the soup,' he said. 'Now for five more—'

A rather large blond cocker spaniel tore around the Cadillac, skidded a little on the wet concrete, took off neatly, hit me in the stomach and thighs with all four paws, licked my face, dropped on the ground, ran around my legs, sat down between them, let his tongue out all the way and started to pant.

I stepped over him and braced myself against the side of the car and got my handkerchief out.

A male voice called: 'Here, Heathcliff. Here, Heathcliff.' Steps sounded on a hard walk.

'That's Heathcliff,' the chauffeur said sourly.

'Heathcliff?'

'Cripes, that's what they call the dog, Jack.'

'*Wuthering Heights?*' I asked.

'Now you're double-talking again,' he sneered. 'Look out – company.'

He picked up the sponge and the hose and went back to washing the car. I moved away from him. The cocker spaniel immediately moved between my legs again, almost tripping me.

'Here, Heathcliff,' the male voice called out louder, and a man came into view through the opening of a latticed tunnel covered with climbing roses.

Tall, dark, with a clear olive skin, brilliant black eyes, gleaming white teeth. Sideburns. A narrow black moustache. Sideburns too long, much too long. White shirt with embroidered initials on the pocket, white slacks, white shoes. A wrist-watch that curved half-way around a lean dark wrist, held on by a gold chain. A yellow scarf around a bronzed slender neck.

He saw the dog squatted between my legs and didn't like it. He snapped long fingers and snapped a clear hard voice:

'Here, Heathcliff. Come here at once!'

The dog breathed hard and didn't move, except to lean a little closer to my right leg.

'Who are you?' the man asked, staring me down.

I held out my card. Olive fingers took the card. The dog quietly backed out from between my legs, edged around the front end of the car, and faded silently into the distance.

'Marlowe,' the man said. 'Marlowe, eh? What's this? A detective? What do you want?'

'Want to see Mrs Morny.'

He looked me up and down, brilliant black eyes sweeping slowly and the silky fringes of long eyelashes following them.

'Weren't you told she was not in?'

'Yeah, but I didn't believe it. Are you Mr Morny?'

'No.'

'That's Mr Vannier,' the chauffeur said behind my back, in the drawled, over-polite voice of deliberate insolence. 'Mr Vannier's a friend of the family. He comes here quite a lot.'

Vannier looked past my shoulder, his eyes furious. The chauffeur came around the car and spat the cigarette-stub out of his mouth with casual contempt.

'I told the shamus the boss wasn't here, Mr Vannier.'

'I see.'

'I told him Mrs Morny and you was here. Did I do wrong?'

Vannier said: 'You could have minded your own business.'

The chauffeur said: 'I wonder why the hell I didn't think of that.'

Vannier said: 'Get out before I break your dirty little neck for you.'

The chauffeur eyed him quietly and then went back into the gloom of the garage and started to whistle. Vannier moved his hot angry eyes over to me and snapped:

'You were told Mrs Morny was not in, but it didn't take. Is that it? In other words the information failed to satisfy you.'

'If we have to have other words,' I said, 'those might do.'

'I see. Could you bring yourself to say what point you wish to discuss with Mrs Morny?'

'I'd prefer to explain that to Mrs Morny herself.'

'The implication is that she doesn't care to see you.'

Behind the car the chauffeur said: 'Watch his right, Jack. It might have a knife in it.'

Vannier's olive skin turned the colour of dried seaweed. He turned on his heel and rapped at me in a stifled voice: 'Follow me.'

He went along the brick path under the tunnel of roses and through a white gate at the end. Beyond was a walled-in garden containing flower-beds crammed with showy annuals, a badminton court, a nice stretch of greensward, and a small tiled pool glittering angrily in the sun. Beside the pool there was a flagged space set with blue and white garden furniture, low tables with composition tops, reclining chairs with foot-rests and enormous cushions, and over all a blue and white umbrella as big as a small tent.

A long-limbed languorous type of showgirl blonde lay at her ease in one of the chairs, with her feet raised on a padded rest and a tall misted glass at her elbow, near a silver ice bucket and a Scotch bottle. She looked at us lazily as we came over the grass. From thirty feet away she looked like a lot of class. From ten feet away she looked like something made up to be seen from thirty feet away. Her mouth was too wide, her eyes were too blue, her make-up was too vivid, the thin arch of her eyebrows was almost fantastic in its curve and spread, and the mascara was so thick on her eyelashes that they looked like miniature iron railings.

She wore white duck slacks, blue and white open-toed sandals over bare feet and crimson lake toenails, a white silk blouse and a necklace of green stones that were not square-cut emeralds. Her hair was as artificial as a night-club lobby.

On the chair beside her there was a white straw garden hat with a brim the size of a spare tyre and a white satin chin-strap. On the brim of the hat lay a pair of green sun-glasses with lenses the size of doughnuts.

Vannier marched over to her and snapped out: 'You've got to can that nasty little red-eyed driver of yours, but quick. Otherwise I'm liable to break his neck any minute. I can't go near him without getting insulted.'

The blonde coughed lightly, flicked a handkerchief around without doing anything with it, and said:

'Sit down and rest your sex appeal. Who's your friend?'

Vannier looked for my card, found he was holding it in his hand and threw it on her lap. She picked it up languidly, ran her eyes over it, ran them over me, sighed and tapped her teeth with her fingernails.

'Big, isn't he? Too much for you to handle, I guess.'

Vannier looked at me nastily. 'All right, get it over with, whatever it is.'

'Do I talk to her?' I asked. 'Or do I talk to you and have you put it in English?'

The blonde laughed. A silvery ripple of laughter that held

the unspoiled naturalness of a bubble dance. A small tongue played roughishly along her lips.

Vannier sat down and lit a gold-tipped cigarette and I stood there looking at them.

I said: 'I'm looking for a friend of yours, Mrs Morny. I understand that she shared an apartment with you about a year ago. Her name is Linda Conquest.'

Vannier flicked his eyes up, down, up, down. He turned his head and looked across the pool. The cocker spaniel named Heathcliff sat over there looking at us with the white of one eye.

Vannier snapped his fingers. 'Here, Heathcliff! Here, Heathcliff! Come here, sir!'

The blonde said: 'Shut up. The dog hates your guts. Give your vanity a rest, for heaven's sake.'

Vannier snapped: 'Don't talk like that to me.'

The blonde giggled and petted his face with her eyes.

I said: 'I'm looking for a girl named Linda Conquest, Mrs Morny.'

The blonde looked at me and said: 'So you said. I was just thinking I don't think I've seen her in six months. She got married.'

'You haven't seen her in six months?'

'That's what I said, big boy. What do you want to know for?'

'Just a private inquiry I'm making.'

'About what?'

'About a confidential matter,' I said.

'Just think,' the blonde said brightly. 'He's making a private inquiry about a confidential matter. You hear that, Lou? Busting in on total strangers that don't want to see him is quite all right, though, isn't it, Lou? On account of he's making a private inquiry about a confidential matter.'

'Then you don't know where she is, Mrs Morny?'

'Didn't I say so?' Her voice rose a couple of notches.

'No. You said you didn't think you had seen her in six months. Not quite the same thing.'

'Who told you I shared an apartment with her?' the blonde snapped.

'I never reveal a source of information, Mrs Morny.'

'Sweetheart, you're fussy enough to be a dance director. I

should tell you everything, you should tell me nothing.'

'The position is quite different,' I said. 'I'm a hired hand obeying instructions. The lady has no reason to hide out, has she?'

'Who's looking for her?'

'Her folk.'

'Guess again. She doesn't have any folks.'

'You must know her pretty well, if you know that,' I said.

'Maybe I did once. That don't prove I do now.'

'Okay,' I said. 'The answer is you know, but you won't tell.'

'The answer,' Vannier said suddenly, 'is that you're not wanted here and the sooner you get out the better we like it.'

I kept on looking at Mrs Morny. She winked at me and said to Vannier: 'Don't get so hostile, darling. You have a lot of charm, but you have small bones. You're not built for the rough work. That right, big boy?'

I said: 'I hadn't thought about it, Mrs Morny. Do you think Mr Morny could help me – or would?'

She shook her head. 'How would I know? You could try. If he don't like you, he has guys around that can bounce you.'

'I think you could tell me yourself, if you wanted to.'

'How are you going to make me want to?' Her eyes were inviting.

'With all these people around,' I said, 'how can I?'

'That's a thought,' she said, and sipped from her glass, watching me over it.

Vannier stood up very slowly. His face was white. He put his hand inside his shirt and said slowly, between his teeth: 'Get out, mug. While you can still walk.'

I looked at him in surprise. 'Where's your refinement?' I asked him. 'And don't tell me you wear a gun with your garden clothes.'

The blonde laughed, showing a fine strong set of teeth. Vannier thrust his hand under his left arm inside the shirt and set his lips. His black eyes were sharp and blank at the same time, like a snake's eyes.

'You heard me,' he said, almost softly. 'And don't write me off too quick. I'd plug you as soon as I'd strike a match. And fix it afterwards.'

I looked at the blonde. Her eyes were bright and her mouth looked sensual and eager, watching us.

I turned and walked away across the grass. About half-way across it I looked back at them. Vannier stood in exactly the same position, his hand inside his shirt. The blonde's eyes were still wide and her lips parted, but the shadow of the umbrella had dimmed her expression and at that distance it might have been either fear or pleased anticipation.

I went on over the grass, through the white gate and along the brick path under the rose arbour. I reached the end of it, turned, walked quietly back to the gate and took another look at them. I didn't know what there would be to see or what I cared about it when I saw it.

What I saw was Vannier practically sprawled on top of the blonde, kissing her.

I shook my head and went back along the walk.

The red-eyed chauffeur was still at work on the Cadillac. He had finished the wash job and was wiping off the glass and nickel with a large chamois. I went around and stood beside him.

'How you come out?' he asked me out of the side of his mouth.

'Badly. They tramped all over me,' I said.

He nodded and went on making the hissing noise of a groom rubbing down a horse.

'You better watch your step. The guy's heeled,' I said. 'Or pretends to be.'

The chauffeur laughed shortly. 'Under that suit? Nix.'

'Who is this guy Vannier? What does he do?'

The chauffeur straightened up, put the chamois over the sill of a window and wiped his hands on the towel that was now stuck in his waistband.

'Women, my guess would be,' he said.

'Isn't it a bit dangerous – playing with this particular woman?'

'I'd say it was,' he agreed. 'Different guys got different ideas of danger. It would scare me.'

'Where does he live?'

'Sherman Oaks. She goes over there. She'll go once too often.'

'Ever run across a girl named Linda Conquest? Tall, dark, handsome, used to be a singer with a band?'

'For two bucks, Jack, you expect a lot of service.'

'I could build it up to five.'

He shook his head. 'I don't know the party. Not by that name. All kinds of dames come here, mostly pretty flashy. I don't get introduced.' He grinned.

I got my wallet out and put three ones in his little damp paw. I added a business card.

'I like small close-built men,' I said. 'They never seem to be afraid of anything. Come and see me some time.'

'I might at that, Jack. Thanks. Linda Conquest, huh? I'll keep my ear-flaps off.'

'So long,' I said. 'The name?'

'They call me Shifty. I never knew why.'

'So long, Shifty.'

'So long. Gat under his arm – in them clothes? Not a chance.'

'I don't know,' I said. 'He made the motion. I'm not hired to gunfight with strangers.'

'Hell, that shirt he's wearing only got two buttons at the top. I noticed. Take him a week to pull a rod from under that.' But he sounded faintly worried.

'I guess he was just bluffing,' I agreed. 'If you hear mention of Linda Conquest, I'll be glad to talk business with you.'

'Okay, Jack.'

I went back along the black driveway. He stood there scratching his chin.


## Six

I drove along the block looking for a place to park so that I could run up to the office for a moment before going on downtown.

A chauffeur-driven Packard edged out from the kerb in front of a cigar store about thirty feet from the entrance to my building. I slid into the space, locked the car and stepped out. It was only then that I noticed the car in front of which I had parked was a familiar-looking sand-coloured coupé. It didn't have to be the same one. There were thousands of them. Nobody was in it. Nobody was near it that wore a cocoa straw hat with a brown and yellow band.

43

I went around to the street side and looked at the steering-post. No licence holder. I wrote the licence plate number down on the back of an envelope, just in case, and went on into my building. He wasn't in the lobby, or in the corridor upstairs.

I went into the office, looked on the floor for mail, didn't find any, bought myself a short drink out of the office bottle and left. I didn't have any time to spare to get downtown before three o'clock.

The sand-coloured coupé was still parked, still empty. I got into mine and started up and moved out into the traffic stream.

I was below Sunset on Vine before he picked me up. I kept on going, grinning, and wondering where he had hid. Perhaps in the car parked behind his own. I hadn't thought of that.

I drove south to Third and all the way downtown on Third. The sand-coloured coupé kept half a block behind me all the way. I moved over to Seventh and Grand, parked near Seventh and Olive, stopped to buy cigarettes I didn't need, and then walked east along Seventh without looking behind me. At Spring I went into the Hotel Metropole, strolled over to the big horse-shoe cigar counter to light one of my cigarettes and then sat down in one of the old leather chairs in the lobby.

A blond man in a brown suit, dark glasses and the now familiar hat, came into the lobby and moved unobtrusively among the potted palms and the stucco arches to the cigar counter. He bought a package of cigarettes and broke it open standing there, using the time to lean his back against the counter and give the lobby the benefit of his eagle eye.

He picked up his change and went over and sat down with his back to a pillar. He tipped his hat down over his dark glasses and seemed to go to sleep with an unlighted cigarette between his lips.

I got up and wandered over and dropped into the chair beside him. I looked at him sideways. He didn't move. Seen at close quarters his face seemed young and pink and plump and the blond beard on his chin was very carelessly shaved. Behind the dark glasses his eyelashes flicked up and down rapidly. A hand on his knee tightened and pulled the cloth into wrinkles. There was a wart on his cheek just below the right eyelid.

I struck a match and held the flame to his cigarette. 'Light?'

'Oh – thanks,' he said, very surprised. He drew breath in until the cigarette tip glowed. I shook the match out, tossed it into the sand jar at my elbow and waited. He looked at me sideways several times before he spoke.

'Haven't I seen you somewhere before?'

'Over on Dresden Avenue in Pasadena. This morning.'

I could see his cheeks get pinker than they had been. He sighed.

'I must be lousy,' he said.

'Boy, you stink,' I agreed.

'Maybe it's the hat,' he said.

'The hat helps,' I said. 'But you don't need it.'

'It's a pretty tough dollar in this town,' he said sadly. 'You can't do it on foot, you ruin yourself with taxi fares if you use taxis, and if you use your own car, it's always where you can't get to it fast enough. You have to stay too close.'

'But you don't have to climb in a guy's pocket,' I said. 'Did you want something with me or are you just practising?'

'I figured I'd find out if you were smart enough to be worth talking to.'

'I'm very smart,' I said. 'It would be a shame not to talk to me.'

He looked carefully around the back of his chair and on both sides of where we were sitting and then drew a small pigskin wallet out. He handed me a nice fresh card from it. It read: George Anson Phillips. Confidential Investigations. 212 Seneger Building, 1924 North Wilcox Avenue, Hollywood. A Glenview telephone number. In the upper left-hand corner there was an open eye with an eyebrow arched in surprise and very long eyelashes.

'You can't do that,' I said, pointing to the eye. 'That's the Pinkerton's. You'll be stealing their business.'

'Oh hell,' he said, 'what little I get wouldn't bother them.'

I snapped the card on my fingernail and bit down hard on my teeth and slipped the card into my pocket.

'You want one of mine – or have you completed your file on me?'

'Oh, I know all about you,' he said. 'I was a deputy at Ventura the time you were working on the Gregson case.'

Gregson was a con man from Oklahoma City who was followed all over the United States for two years by one of his victims until he got so jittery that he shot up a service station attendant who mistook him for an acquaintance. It seemed a long time ago to me.

I said: 'Go on from there.'

'I remembered your name when I saw it on your registration this a.m. So when I lost you on the way into town I just looked you up. I was going to come in and talk, but it would have been a violation of confidence. This way I kind of can't help myself.'

Another screwball. That made three in one day, not counting Mrs Murdock, who might turn out to be a screwball, too.

I waited while he took his dark glasses off and polished them and put them on again and gave the neighbourhood the once over again. Then he said:

'I figured we could, maybe, make a deal. Pool our resources, as they say. I saw the guy go into your office, so I figured he had hired you.'

'You knew who he was?'

'I'm working on him,' he said, and his voice sounded flat and discouraged. 'And where I am getting is no place at all.'

'What did he do to you?'

'Well, I'm working for his wife.'

'Divorce?'

He looked all around him carefully and said in a small voice: 'So she says. But I wonder.'

'They both want one,' I said. 'Each trying to get something on the other. Comical, isn't it?'

'My end I don't like so well. A guy is tailing me around some of the time. A very tall guy with a funny eye. I shake him but after a while I see him again. A very tall guy. Like a lamp-post.'

A very tall man with a funny eye. I smoked thoughtfully.

'Anything to do with you?' the blond man asked me a little anxiously.

I shook my head and threw my cigarette into the sand jar. 'Never saw him that I know of.' I looked at my strap watch. 'We better get together and talk this thing over properly, but I can't do it now. I have an appointment.'

'I'd like to,' he said. 'Very much.'

'Let's then. My office, my apartment, or your office, or where?'

He scratched his badly shaved chin with a well-chewed thumbnail.

'My apartment,' he said at last. 'It's not in the phone book. Give me that card a minute.'

He turned it over on his palm when I gave it to him and wrote slowly with a small metal pencil, moving his tongue along his lips. He was getting younger every minute. He didn't seem much more than twenty by now, but he had to be, because the Gregson case had been six years back.

He put his pencil away and handed me back the card. The address he had written on it was 204 Florence Apartments, 128 Court Street.

I looked at him curiously. 'Court Street on Bunker Hill?'

He nodded, flushing all over his blond skin. 'Not too good,' he said quickly. 'I haven't been in the chips lately. Do you mind?'

'No, why would I?'

I stood up and held a hand out. He shook it and dropped it and I pushed it down into my hip pocket and rubbed the palm against the handkerchief I had there. Looking at his face more closely I saw that there was a line of moisture across his upper lip and more of it along the side of his nose. It was not as hot as all that.

I started to move off and then I turned back to lean down close to his face and say: 'Almost anybody can pull my leg, but just to make sure, she's a tall blonde with careless eyes, huh?'

'I wouldn't call them careless,' he said.

I held my face together while I said: 'And just between the two of us this divorce stuff is a lot of hooey. It's something else entirely, isn't it?'

'Yes,' he said softly, 'and something I don't like more every minute I think about it. Here.'

He pulled something out of his pocket and dropped it into my hand. It was a flat key.

'No need for you to wait around in the hall, if I happen to be out. I have two of them. What time would you think you would come?'

'About four-thirty, the way it looks now. You sure you want to give me this key?'

'Why, we're in the same racket,' he said, looking up at me innocently, or as innocently as he could look through a pair of dark glasses.

At the edge of the lobby I looked back. He sat there peacefully, with the half-smoked cigarette dead between his lips and the gaudy brown and yellow band on his hat looking as quiet as a cigarette advertisement on the back page of the *Saturday Evening Post*.

We were in the same racket. So I wouldn't chisel him. Just like that. I could have the key to his apartment and go in and make myself at home. I could wear his slippers and drink his liquor and lift up his carpet and count the thousand-dollar bills under it. We were in the same racket.

# Seven

The Belfont Building was eight storeys of nothing in particular that had got itself pinched off between a large green and chromium cut-rate suit emporium and a three-storey and basement garage that made a noise like lion cages at feeding time. The small dark narrow lobby was as dirty as a chicken yard. The building directory had a lot of vacant space on it. Only one of the names meant anything to me and I knew that one already. Opposite the directory a large sign tilted against the fake marble wall said: *Space for Renting Suitable for Cigar Stand. Apply Room* 316.

There were two open-grille elevators but only one seemed to be running and that not busy. An old man sat inside it slack-jawed and watery-eyed on a piece of folded burlap on top of a wooden stool. He looked as if he had been sitting there since the Civil War and had come out of that badly.

I got in with him and said 'eight', and he wrestled the doors shut and cranked his buggy and we dragged upwards lurching. The old man breathed hard, as if he was carrying the elevator on his back.

I got out at my floor and started along the hallway and behind me the old man leaned out of the car and blew his nose with his fingers into a carton full of floor sweepings.

Elisha Morningstar's office was at the back, opposite the fire-door. Two rooms, both doors lettered in flaked black paint on pebbled glass. *Elisha Morningstar. Numismatist.* The one farther back said: *Entrance.*

I turned the knob and went into a small narrow room with two windows, a shabby little typewriter desk, closed, a number of wall cases of tarnished coins in tilted slots with yellowed typewritten labels under them, two brown filing-cases at the back against the wall, no curtains at the windows, and a dust-grey floor carpet so threadbare that you wouldn't notice the rips in it unless you tripped over one.

An inner wooden door was open at the back across from the filing-cases, behind the little typewriter desk. Through the door came the small sounds a man makes when he isn't doing anything at all. Then the dry voice of Elisha Morningstar called out:

'Come in, please. Come in.'

I went along and in. The inner office was just as small but had a lot more stuff in it. A green safe almost blocked off the front half. Beyond this a heavy old mahogany table against the entrance door held some dark books, some flabby old magazines, and a lot of dust. In the back wall a window was open a few inches, without effect on the musty smell. There was a hat-rack with a greasy black felt hat on it. There were three long-legged tables with glass tops and more coins under the glass tops. There was a heavy dark leather-topped desk midway of the room. It had the usual desk stuff on it, and in addition a pair of jeweller's scales under a glass dome and two large nickel-framed magnifying-glasses and a jeweller's eyepiece lying on a buff scratch pad, beside a cracked yellow silk handkerchief spotted with ink.

In the swivel chair at the desk sat an elderly party in a dark grey suit with high lapels and too many buttons down the front. He had some stringy white hair that grew long enough to tickle his ears. A pale grey bald patch loomed high up in the middle of it, like a rock above the timberline. Fuzz grew out of his ears, far enough to catch a moth.

He had sharp black eyes which had a pouch under each eye brownish purple in colour and traced with a network of wrinkles and veins. His cheeks were shiny and his short sharp nose looked as if it had hung over a lot of quick ones in its time. A Hoover collar which no decent laundry would have allowed on the premises nudged his Adam's apple and a black string tie poked a small hard knot out at the bottom of the collar, like a mouse getting ready to come out of a mousehole.

He said: 'My young lady had to go to the dentist. You are Mr Marlowe?'

I nodded.

'Pray, be seated.' He waved a thin hand at the chair across the desk. I sat down. 'You have some identification, I presume?'

I showed it to him. While he read it I smelled him from across the desk. He had a sort of dry musty smell, like a fairly clean Chinaman.

He placed my card face down on top of his desk and folded his hands on it. His sharp black eyes didn't miss anything in my face.

'Well, Mr Marlowe, what can I do for you?'

'Tell me about the Brasher Doubloon.'

'Ah, yes,' he said. 'The Brasher Doubloon. An interesting coin.' He lifted his hands off the desk and made a steeple of the fingers, like an old-time family lawyer getting set for a little tangled grammar. 'In some ways the most interesting and valuable of all early American coins. As no doubt you know.'

'What I don't know about early American coins you could almost crowd into the Rose Bowl.'

'Is that so?' he said. 'Is that so? Do you want me to tell you?'

'What I'm here for, Mr Morningstar.'

'It is a gold coin, roughly equivalent to a twenty-dollar gold piece, and about the size of a half-dollar. Almost exactly. It was made for the State of New York in the year 1787. It was not minted. There were no mints until 1793, when the first mint was opened in Philadelphia. The Brasher Doubloon was coined probably by the pressure moulding process and its maker was a private goldsmith named Ephraim Brasher, or Brashear. Where the names survives it is usually spelled Brashear, but not on the coin. I don't know why.'

I got a cigarette into my mouth and lit it. I thought it might do something to the musty smell. 'What's the pressure moulding process?'

'The two halves of the mould were engraved in steel, in intaglio, of course. These halves were then mounted in lead. Gold blanks were pressed between them in a coin press. Then the edges were trimmed for weight and smoothed. The coin was not milled. There were no milling machines in 1787.'

'Kind of a slow process,' I said.

He nodded his peaked white head. 'Quite. And, since the surface-hardening of steel without distortion could not be accomplished at that time, the dies wore and had to be re-made from time to time. With consequent slight variations in design which would be visible under strong magnification. In face, it would be safe to say no two of the coins would be identical, judged by modern methods of microscopic examination. Am I clear?'

'Yeah,' I said. 'Up to a point. How many of these coins are there and what are they worth?'

He undid the steeple of fingers and put his hands back on the desk top and patted them gently up and down.

'I don't know how many there are. Nobody knows. A few hundred, a thousand, perhaps more. But of these very few indeed are uncirculated specimens in what is called mint condition. The value varies from a couple of thousand on up. I should say that at the present time, since the devaluation of the dollar, an uncirculated specimen, carefully handled by a reputable dealer, might easily bring ten thousand dollars, or even more. It would have to have a history, of course.'

I said : 'Ah,' and let smoke out of my lungs slowly and waved it away with the flat of my hand, away from the old party across the desk from me. He looked like a non-smoker. 'And without a history and not so carefully handled – how much?'

He shrugged. 'There would be the implication that the coin was illegally acquired. Stolen, or obtained by fraud. Of course it might not be so. Rare coins do turn up in odd places at odd times. In old strong boxes, in the secret drawers of desks in old New England houses. Not often, I grant you. But it happens. I know of a very valuable coin that fell out of the stuffing of a horsehair sofa which had been restored by an antique dealer. The sofa had been in the same room in the same house in Fall River, Massachusetts, for ninety years. Nobody knew how the coin got there. But generally speaking, the implication of theft would be strong. Particularly in this part of the country.'

He looked at the corner of the ceiling with an absent stare. I looked at him with a not so absent stare. He looked like a man who could be trusted with a secret – if it was his own secret.

He brought his eyes down to my level slowly and said: 'Five dollars, please.'

I said: 'Huh?'

'Five dollars, please.'

'What for?'

'Don't be absurd, Mr Marlowe. Everything I have told you is available in the public library. In Fosdyke's *Register*, in particular. You choose to come here and take up my time relating it to you. For this my charge is five dollars.'

'And suppose I don't pay it,' I said.

He leaned back and closed his eyes. A faint smile twitched at the corners of his lips. 'You will pay it,' he said.

I paid it. I took the five out of my wallet and got up to lean over the desk and spread it out right in front of him, carefully. I stroked the bill with my fingertips, as if it was a kitten.

'Five dollars, Mr Morningstar,' I said.

He opened his eyes and looked at the bill. He smiled.

'And now,' I said, 'let's talk about the Brasher Doubloon that somebody tried to sell you.'

He opened his eyes a little wider. 'Oh, did somebody try to sell me a Brasher Doubloon? Now why would they do that?'

'They needed the money,' I said. 'And they didn't want too many questions asked. They knew or found out that you were in the business and that the building where you had your office was a shabby dump where anything could happen. They knew your office was at the end of a corridor and that you were an elderly man who would probably not make any false moves – out of regard for your health.'

'They seem to have known a great deal,' Elisha Morningstar said dryly.

'They knew what they had to know in order to transact their business. Just like you and me. And none of it was hard to find out.'

He stuck his little finger in his ear and worked it around and brought it out with a little dark wax on it. He wiped it off casually on his coat.

'And you assume all this from the mere fact that I called up Mrs Murdock and asked if her Brasher Doubloon was for sale?'

'Sure. She had the same idea herself. It's reasonable. Like I said over the phone to you, you would know that coin was not for sale. If you knew anything about the business at all. And I can see that you do.'

He bowed, about one inch. He didn't quite smile but he looked about as pleased as a man in a Hoover collar ever looks.

'You would be offered this coin for sale,' I said, 'in suspicious circumstances. You would want to buy it, if you could get it cheap and had the money to handle it. But you would want to know where it came from. And even if you were quite sure it was stolen, you could still buy it, if you could get it cheap enough.'

'Oh, I could, could I?' He looked amused, but not in a large way.

'Sure you could – if you are a reputable dealer. I'll assume you are. By buying the coin – cheap – you would be protecting the owner or his insurance carrier from complete loss. They'd be glad to pay you back your outlay. It's done all the time.'

'Then the Murdock Brasher has been stolen,' he said abruptly.

'Don't quote me,' I said. 'It's a secret.'

He almost picked his nose this time. He just caught himself. He picked a hair out of one nostril instead, with a quick jerk and a wince. He held it up and looked at it. Looking at me past it he said:

'And how much will your principal pay for the return of the coin?'

I leaned over the desk and gave him my shady leer. 'One grand. What did you pay?'

'I think you are a very smart young man,' he said. Then he screwed his face up and his chin wobbled and his chest began to bounce in and out and a sound came out of him like a convalescent rooster learning to crow again after a long illness.

He was laughing.

It stopped after a while. His face came all smooth again and his eyes, opened, black and sharp and shrewd.

'Eight hundred dollars,' he said. 'Eight hundred dollars for an uncirculated specimen of the Brasher Doubloon.' He chortled.

'Fine. Got it with you? That leaves you two hundred. Fair enough. A quick turnover, a reasonable profit and no trouble for anybody.'

'It is not in my office,' he said. 'Do you take me for a fool?' He reached an ancient silver watch out of his vest on a black fob. He screwed up his eyes to look at it. 'Let us say eleven in the morning,' he said. 'Come back with your money. The coin may or may not be here, but if I am satisfied with your behaviour, I will arrange matters.'

'That is satisfactory,' I said, and stood up. 'I have to get the money anyhow.'

'Have it in used bills,' he said almost dreamily. 'Used twenties will do. An occasional fifty will do no harm.'

I grinned and started for the door. Half-way there I turned around and went back to lean both hands on the desk and push my face over it.

'What did she look like?'

He looked blank.

'The girl that sold you the coin.'

He looked blanker.

'Okay,' I said. 'It wasn't a girl. She had help. It was a man. What did the man look like?'

He pursed his lips and made another steeple with his fingers. 'He was a middle-aged man, heavy set, about five feet seven inches tall and weighing around one hundred and seventy pounds. He said his name was Smith. He wore a blue suit, black shoes, a green tie and shirt, no hat. There was a brown bordered handkerchief in his outer pocket. His hair was dark brown sprinkled with grey. There was a bald patch about the size of a dollar on the crown of his head and a scar about two inches long running down the side of his jaw. On the left side, I think. Yes, on the left side.'

'Not bad,' I said. 'What about the hole in his right sock?'

'I omitted to take his shoes off.'

'Darn careless of you,' I said.

He didn't say anything. We just stared at each other, half

curious, half hostile, like new neighbours. Then suddenly he went into his laugh again.

The five-dollar bill I had given him was still lying on his side of the desk. I flicked a hand across and took it.

'You won't want this now,' I said. 'Since we started talking in thousands.'

He stopped laughing very suddenly. Then he shrugged.

'At eleven a.m.,' he said. 'And no tricks, Mr Marlowe. Don't think I don't know how to protect myself.'

'I hope you do,' I said, 'because what you are handling is dynamite.'

I left him and tramped across the empty outer office and opened the door and let it shut, staying inside. There ought to be footsteps outside in the corridor, but his transom was closed and I hadn't made much noise coming on crepe rubber soles. I hoped he would remember that. I sneaked back across the threadbare carpet and edged in behind the door, between the door and the little closed typewriter desk. A kid trick, but once in a while it will work, especially after a lot of smart conversation, full of wordliness and sly wit. Like a sucker play in football. And if it didn't work this time, we would just be there sneering at each other again.

It worked. Nothing happened for a while except that a nose was blown. Then all by himself in there he went into his sick rooster laugh again. Then a throat was cleared. Then a swivel chair squeaked, and feet walked.

A dingy white head poked into the room, about two inches past the end of the door. It hung there suspended and I went into a state of suspended animation. Then the head was drawn back and four unclean fingernails came around the edge of the door and pulled. The door closed, clicked, was shut. I started breathing again and put my ear to the wooden panel.

The swivel-chair squeaked once more. The threshing sound of a telephone being dialled. I lunged across to the instrument on the little typewriter desk and lifted it. At the other end of the line the bell had started to ring. It rang six times. Then a man's voice said: 'Yeah?'

'The Florence Apartments?'

'Yeah.'

'I'd like to speak to Mr Anson in Apartment two-o-four.'

'Hold the wire. I'll see if he's in.'

Mr Morningstar and I held the wire. Noise came over it, the blaring sound of a loud radio broadcasting a baseball game. It was not close to the telephone, but it was noisy enough.

Then I could hear the hollow sound of steps coming nearer and the harsh rattle of the telephone receiver being picked up and the voice said:

'Not in. Any message?'

'I'll call later,' Mr Morningstar said.

I hung up fast and did a rapid glide across the floor to the entrance door and opened it very silently, like snow falling, and let it close the same way, taking its weight at the last moment, so that the click of the catch would not have been heard three feet away.

I breathed hard and tight going down the hall, listening to myself I pushed the elevator button. Then I got out the card which Mr George Anson Phillips had given me in the lobby of the Hotel Metropole. I didn't look at it in any real sense. I didn't have to look at it to recall that it referred to Apartment 204, Florence Apartments, 128 Court Street. I just stood there flicking it with a fingernail while the old elevator came heaving up in the shaft, straining like a gravel truck on a hairpin turn.

The time was three-fifty.

# Eight

Bunker Hill is old town, lost town, shabby town, crook town. Once, very long ago, it was the choice residential district of the city, and there are still standing a few of the jigsaw Gothic mansions with wide porches and walls covered with round-end shingles and full corner bay windows with spindle turrets. They are all rooming houses now, their parquetry floors are scratched and worn through the once glossy finish and the wide sweeping staircases are dark with time and with cheap varnish laid on over generations of dirt. In the tall rooms haggard landladies bicker with shifty tenants. On the wide cool front porches, reaching their cracked shoes into the sun and staring at nothing, sit the old men with faces like lost battles.

In and around the old houses there are flyblown restaurants and Italian fruit-stands and cheap apartment houses and little candy stores where you can buy even nastier things than their candy. And there are ratty hotels where nobody except people named Smith and Jones sign the register and where the night clerk is half watchdog and half pander.

Out of the apartment houses come women who should be young but have faces like stale beer; men with pulled-down hats and quick eyes that look the street over behind the cupped hand that shields the match flame; worn intellectuals with cigarette coughs and no money in the bank; fly cops with granite faces and unwavering eyes: cokies and coke peddlers; people who look like nothing in particular and know it, and once in a while even men that actually go to work. But they come out early, when the wide cracked sidewalks are empty and still have dew on them.

I was earlier than four-thirty getting over there, but not much. I parked at the end of the street, where the funicular railway comes struggling up the yellow clay bank from Hill Street, and walked along Court Street to the Florence Apartments. It was dark brick in front, three storeys, the lower windows at sidewalk level and masked by rusted screens and dingy net curtains. The entrance door had a glass panel and enough of the name left to be read. I opened it and went down three brass-bound steps into a hallway you could touch on both sides without stretching. Dim doors painted with numbers in dim paint. An alcove at the foot of the stairs with a pay telephone. A sign: *Manager Apt. 106.* At the back of the hallway a screen-door and in the alley beyond it four tall battered garbage pails in a line, with a dance of flies in the sunlit air above them.

I went up the stairs. The radio I had heard over the telephone was still blatting the baseball game. I read numbers and went up front. Apartment 204 was on the right side and the baseball game was right across the hall from it. I knocked, got no answer and knocked louder. Behind my back three Dodgers struck out against a welter of synthetic crowd noise. I knocked a third time and looked out of the front hall window while I felt in my pocket for the key George Anson Phillips had given me.

Across the street was an Italian funeral home, neat and quiet and reticent, white painted brick, flush with the side-walk. Pietro Palermo Funeral Parlours. The thin green script of a neon sign lay across its façade, with a chaste air. A tall man in dark clothes came out of the front door and leaned against the white wall. He looked very handsome. He had dark skin and a handsome head of iron-grey hair brushed back from his fore-head. He got out what looked at that distance to be a silver or platinum and black enamel cigarette case, opened it languidly with two long brown fingers and selected a gold-tipped cigarette. He put the case away and lit the cigarette with a pocket lighter that seemed to match the case. He put that away and folded his arms and stared at nothing with half-closed eyes. From the tip of his motionless cigarette a thin wisp of smoke rose straight up past his face, as thin and straight as the smoke of a dying campfire at dawn.

Another batter struck out or flew out behind my back in the recreated ball game. I turned from watching the tall Italian, put the key into the door of Apartment 204 and went in.

A square room with a brown carpet, very little furniture and that not inviting. The wall bed with the usual distorting mirror faced me as I opened the door and made me look like a two-time loser sneaking home from a reefer party. There was a birch-wood easy-chair with some hard-looking upholstery beside it in the form of a davenport. A table before the window held a lamp with a shirred paper shade. There was a door on either side of the bed.

The door to the left led into a small kitchenette with a brown woodstone sink and a three-burner stove and an old electric icebox that clicked and began to throb in torment just as I pushed the door open. On the woodstone drainboard stood the remains of somebody's breakfast, mud at the bottom of a cup, a burnt crust of bread, crumbs on a board, a yellow slime of melted butter down the slope of a saucer, a smeared knife and a granite coffee-pot that smelt like sacks in a hot barn.

I went back around the wall bed and through the other door.

It gave on a short hallway with an open space for clothes and a built-in dresser. On the dresser was a comb and a black brush with a few blond hairs in its black bristles. Also a can of talcum, a small flashlight with a cracked lens, a pad of writing-paper, a bank pen, a bottle of ink on a blotter, cigarettes and matches in a glass ashtray that contained half a dozen stubs.

In the drawers of the dresser were about what one suitcase would hold in the way of socks and underclothes and handkerchiefs. There was a dark grey suit on a hanger, not new but still good, and a pair of rather dusty black brogues on the floor under it.

I pushed the bathroom door. It opened about a foot and then stuck. My nose twitched and I could feel my lips stiffen and I smelled the harsh, sharp bitter smell from beyond the door. I leaned against it. It gave a little but came back, as though somebody was holding it against me. I poked my head through the opening.

The floor of the bathroom was too short for him, so his knees were poked up and hung outwards slackly and his head was pressed against the woodstone baseboard at the other end, not tilted up, but jammed tight. His brown suit was rumpled a little and his dark glasses stuck out of his breast-pocket at an unsafe angle. As if that mattered. His right hand was thrown across his stomach, his left hand lay on the floor, palm up, the fingers curled a little. There was a blood-caked bruise on the right side of his head, in the blond hair. His open mouth was full of shiny crimson blood.

The door was stopped by his leg. I pushed hard and edged around it and got in. I bent down to push two fingers into the side of his neck against the big artery. No artery throbbed there, or even whispered. Nothing at all. The skin was icy. It wouldn't have been icy. I just thought it was. I straightened up and leaned my back against the door and made hard fists in my pockets and smelled the cordite fumes. The baseball game was still going on, but through two closed doors it sounded remote.

I stood and looked down at him. Nothing in that, Marlowe, nothing at all. Nothing for you here, nothing. You didn't even know him. Get out, get out fast.

I pulled away from the door and pulled it open and went back through the hall into the living-room. A face in the mirror looked at me. A strained, leering face. I turned away from it quickly and took out the flat key George Anson Phillips had given me and rubbed it between my moist palms and laid it down beside the lamp.

I smeared the doorknob opening the door and the outside knob closing the door. The Dodgers were ahead seven to three, the first half of the eighth. A lady who sounded well on with her drinking was singing Frankie and Johnny, the roundhouse version, in a voice that even whisky had failed to improve. A deep man's voice growled to her to shut up and she kept on singing and there was a hard quick movement across the floor and a smack and a yelp and she stopped singing and the baseball game went right on.

I put the cigarette in my mouth and lit it and went back down the stairs and stood in the half dark of the hall angle looking at the little sign that read: *Manager, Apt. 106.*

I was a fool even to look at it. I looked at it for a long minute, biting the cigarette hard between my teeth.

I turned and walked down the hallway towards the back. A small enamelled plate on a door said: *Manager.* I knocked on the door.

# Nine

A chair was pushed back, feet shuffled, the door opened.

'You the manager?'

'Yeah.' It was the same voice I had heard over the telephone. Talking to Elisha Morningstar.

He held an empty, smeared glass in his hand. It looked as if somebody had been keeping goldfish in it. He was a lanky man with carroty short hair growing down to a point on his forehead. He had a long narrow head packed with shabby cunning. Greenish eyes stared under orange eyebrows. His ears were large and might have flapped in a high wind. He had a long nose that would be into things. The whole face was a trained face, a face that would know how to keep a secret, a face that held the effortless composure of a corpse in the morgue.

He wore his vest open, no coat, a woven hair watchguard, and round blue sleeve garters with metal clasps.

I said: 'Mr Anson?'

'Two-o-four.'

'He's not in.'

'What should I do – lay an egg?'

'Neat,' I said. 'You have them all the time, or is this your birthday?'

'Beat it,' he said. 'Drift.' He started to close the door. He opened it again to say: 'Take the air. Scram. Push off.' Having made his meaning clear he started to close the door again.

I leaned against the door. He leaned against it on his side. That brought our faces close together. 'Five bucks,' I said.

It rocked him. He opened the door very suddenly and I had to take a quick step forward in order not to butt his chin with my head.

'Come in,' he said.

A living-room with a wall-bed, everything strictly to specifications, even to the shirred paper lampshade and the glass ashtray. This room was painted egg-yolk yellow. All it needed was a few fat black spiders painted on the yellow to be anybody's bilious attack.

'Sit down,' he said, shutting the door.

I sat down. We looked at each other with the clear innocent eyes of a couple of used-car salesmen.

'Beer?' he said.

'Thanks.'

He opened two cans, filled the smeared glass he had been holding, and reached for another like it. I said I would drink out of the can. He handed me the can.

'A dime,' he said.

I gave him a dime.

He dropped it into his vest and went on looking at me. He pulled a chair over and sat in it and spread his bony up-jutting knees and let his empty hand droop between them.

'I ain't interested in your five bucks,' he said.

'That's fine,' I said. 'I wasn't really thinking of giving it to you.'

61

'A wisey,' he said. 'What gives? We run a nice respectable place here. No funny stuff gets pulled.'

'Quiet, too,' I said. 'Upstairs you could almost hear an eagle scream.'

His smile was wide, about three-quarters of an inch. 'I don't amuse easy,' he said.

'Just like Queen Victoria,' I said.

'I don't get it.'

'I don't expect miracles,' I said. The meaningless talk had a sort of cold bracing effect on me, making a mood with a hard, gritty edge.

I got my wallet out and selected a card from it. It wasn't my card. It read: *James B. Pollock, Reliance Indemnity Company, Field Agent.* I tried to remember what James B. Pollock looked like and where I had met him. I couldn't. I handed the carroty man the card.

He read it and scratched the end of his nose with one of the corners. 'Wrong john?' he asked, keeping his green eyes plastered to my face.

'Jewellery,' I said, and waved a hand.

He thought this over. While he thought it over I tried to make up my mind whether it worried him at all. It didn't seem to.

'We get one once in a while,' he conceded. 'You can't help it. He didn't look like it to me, though. Soft looking.'

'Maybe I got a bum steer,' I said. I described George Anson Phillips to him, George Anson Phillips alive, in his brown suit and his dark glasses and his cocoa straw hat with the brown and yellow print band. I wondered what had happened to the hat. It hadn't been up there. He must have got rid of it, thinking it was too conspicuous. His blond head was almost, but not quite, as bad.

'That sound like him?'

The carroty man took his time making up his mind. Finally he nodded yes, green eyes watching me carefully, lean hard hand holding the card up to his mouth and running the card along his teeth like a stick along the palings of a picket fence.

'I didn't figure him for no crook,' he said. 'But, hell, they come all sizes and shapes. Only been here a month. If he looked like a wrong gee, wouldn't have been here at all.'

I did a good job of not laughing in his face. 'What say we frisk the apartment while he's out?'

He shook his head. 'Mr Palermo wouldn't like it.'

'Mr Palermo?'

'He's the owner. Across the street. Owns the funeral parlours. Owns this building and a lot of other buildings. Practically owns the district, if you know what I mean.' He gave me a twitch of the lip and a flutter of the right eyelid. 'Gets the vote out. Not a guy to crowd.'

'Well, while he's getting the vote out or playing with a stiff or whatever he's doing at the moment, let's go up and frisk the apartment.'

'Don't get me sore at you,' the carroty man said briefly.

'That would bother me like two per cent of nothing at all,' I said. 'Let's go up and frisk the apartment.' I threw my empty beer can at the waste basket and watched it bounce back and roll half-way across the room.

The carroty man stood up suddenly and spread his feet apart and dusted his hands together and took hold of his lower lip with his teeth.

'You said something about five,' he shrugged.

'That was hours ago,' I said. 'I thought better of it. Let's go up and frisk the apartment.'

'Say that just once more—' his right hand slid towards his lip.

'If you're thinking of pulling a gun, Mr Palermo wouldn't like it,' I said.

'To hell with Mr Palermo,' he snarled, in a voice suddenly furious, out of a face suddenly charged with dark blood.

'Mr Palermo will be glad to know that's how you feel about him,' I said.

'Look,' the carroty man said very slowly, dropping his hand to his side and leaning forward from the hips and pushing his face at me as hard as he could. 'Look. I was sitting here having myself a beer or two. Maybe three. Maybe nine. What the hell? I wasn't bothering anybody. It was a nice day. It looked like it might be a nice evening – then you come in.' He waved a hand violently.

'Let's go up and frisk the apartment,' I said.

He threw both fists forward in tight lumps. At the end of the motion he threw his hands wide open, straining the fingers as far as they would go. His nose twitched sharply.

'If it wasn't for the job,' he said.

I opened my mouth. 'Don't say it!' he yelled.

He put a hat on, but no coat, opened a drawer and took out a bunch of keys, walked past me to open the door and stood in it, jerking his chin at me. His face still looked a little wild.

We went out into the hall and along it and up the stairs. The ball game was over and dance music had taken its place. Very loud dance music. The carroty man selected one of his keys and put it in the lock of Apartment 204. Against the booming of the dance band behind us in the apartment across the way a woman's voice suddenly screamed hysterically.

The carroty man withdrew the key and bared his teeth at me. He walked across the narrow hallway and banged on the opposite door. He had to knock hard and long before any attention was paid. Then the door was jerked open and a sharp-faced blonde in scarlet slacks and a green pullover stared out with sultry eyes, one of which was puffed and the other had been socked several days ago. She also had a bruise on her throat and her hand held a tall cool glass of amber fluid.

'Pipe down, but soon,' the carroty man said. 'Too much racket. I don't aim to ask you again. Next time I call some law.'

The girl looked back over her shoulder and screamed against the noise of the radio: 'Hey, Del! The guy says to pipe down! You wanna sock him?'

A chair squeaked, the radio noise died abruptly and a thick, bitter-eyed dark man appeared behind the blonde, yanked her out of the way with one hand and pushed his face at us. He needed a shave. He was wearing trousers, street shoes and an undershirt.

He settled his feet in the doorway, whistled a little breath in through his nose and said:

'Buzz off. I just come in from lunch. I had a lousy lunch. I wouldn't want nobody to push muscle at me.' He was very drunk, but in a hard practised sort of way.

The carroty man said: 'You heard me, Mr Hench. Dim that radio and stop the rough-house in here. And make it sudden.'

The man addressed as Hench said: 'Listen, pickle-puss—'

and heaved forward with his right foot in a hard stamp.

The carroty man's left foot didn't wait to be stamped on. The lean body moved back quickly and the thrown bunch of keys hit the floor behind, and clanked against the door of Apartment 204. The carroty man's right hand made a sweeping movement and came up with a woven leather blackjack.

Hench said: 'Yah!' and took two big handfuls of air in his two hairy hands, closed the hands into fists and swung hard at nothing.

The carroty man hit him on the top of his head and the girl screamed again and threw a glass of liquor in her boy friend's face. Whether because it was safe to do it now or because she made an honest mistake, I couldn't tell.

Hench turned blindly with his face dripping, stumbled and ran across the floor in a lurch that threatened to land him on his nose at every step. The bed was down and tumbled. Hench made the bed on one knee and plunged a hand under the pillow.

I said: 'Look out – gun.'

'I can fade that, too,' the carroty man said between his teeth and slid his right hand, empty now, under his open vest.

Hench was down on both knees. He came up on one and turned and there was a short black gun in his right hand and he was staring down at it, not holding it by the grip at all, holding it flat on his palm.

'Drop it!' the carroty man's voice said tightly and he went on into the room.

The blonde promptly jumped on his back and wound her long green arms around his neck, yelling lustily. The carroty man staggered and swore and waved his gun around.

'Get him, Del!' the blonde screamed. 'Get him good!'

Hench, one hand on the bed and one foot on the floor, both knees doubled, right hand holding the black gun flat on his palm, eyes staring down at it, pushed himself slowly to his feet and growled deep in his throat:

'This ain't my gun.'

I relieved the carroty man of the gun that was not doing him any good and stepped around him, leaving him to shake the blonde off his back as best he could. A door banged down the hallway and steps came along towards us.

65

I said: 'Drop it, Hench.'

He looked up at me, puzzled dark eyes suddenly sober.

'It ain't my gun,' he said and held it out flat. 'Mine's a Colt .32 – belly gun.'

I took the gun off his hand. He made no effort to stop me. He sat down on the bed, rubbed the top of his head slowly, and screwed his face up in difficult thought. 'Where the hell—' his voice trailed off and he shook his head and winced.

I sniffed the gun. It had been fired. I sprang the magazine out and counted the bullets through the small holes in the side. There were six. With one in the magazine, that made seven. The gun was a Colt .32, automatic, eight shot. It had been fired. If it had not been reloaded, one shot had been fired from it.

The carroty man had the blonde off his back now. He had thrown her into a chair and was wiping a scratch on his cheek. His green eyes were baleful.

'Better get some law,' I said. 'A shot has been fired from this gun and it's about time you found out there's a dead man in the apartment across the hall.'

Hench looked up at me stupidly and said in a quiet, reasonable voice: 'Brother, that simply ain't my gun.'

The blonde sobbed in a rather theatrical manner and showed me an open mouth twisted with misery and ham-acting. The carroty man went softly out of the door.


# Ten


'Shot in the throat with a medium-calibre gun and a soft-nosed bullet,' Detective-Lieutenant Jesse Breeze said. 'A gun like this and bullets like is in here.' He danced the gun on his hand, the gun Hench had said was not his gun. 'Bullet ranged upwards and probably hit the back of the skull. Still inside his head. The man's dead about two hours. Hand and face cold, but body still warm. No rigor. Was sapped with something hard before being shot. Likely with a gun butt. All that mean anything to you boys and girls?'

The newspaper he was sitting on rustled. He took his hat off and mopped his face and the top of his almost bald head. A fringe of light-coloured hair around the crown was damp and dark with sweat. He put his hat back on, a flat-crowned panama, burned dark by the sun. Not this year's hat, and probably not last year's.

He was a big man, rather paunchy, wearing brown and white shoes and sloppy socks and white trousers with thin black stripes, an open-neck shirt showing some ginger-coloured hair at the top of his chest, and a rough sky-blue sports-coat not wider at the shoulders than a two-car garage. He would be about fifty years old and the only thing about him that very much suggested cop was the calm unwinking, unwavering stare of his prominent pale-blue eyes, a stare that had no thought of being rude, but that anybody but a cop would feel to be rude. Below his eyes across the top of his cheeks and the bridge of his nose there was a wide path of freckles, like a mine-field on a war map.

We were sitting in Hench's apartment and the door was shut. Hench had his shirt on and he was absently tying a tie with thick blunt fingers that trembled. The girl was lying on the bed. She had a green wrap-around thing twisted about her head, a purse by her side and a short squirrel coat across her feet. Her mouth was a little open and her face was drained and shocked.

Hench said thickly: 'If the idea is the guy was shot with the gun under the pillow, okay. Seems like he might have been. It ain't my gun and nothing you boys can think up is going to make me say it's my gun.'

'Assuming that to be so,' Breeze said, 'how come? Somebody swiped your gun and left this one. When, how, what kind of gun was yours?'

'We went out about three-thirty or so to get something to eat at the hashhouse around the corner,' Hench said. 'You can check that. We must have left the door unlocked. We were kind of hitting the bottle a little. I guess we were pretty noisy. We had the ball game going on the radio. I guess we shut it off when we went out. I'm not sure. You remember?' He looked at the girl lying white-faced and silent on the bed. 'You remember, sweet?'

The girl didn't look at him or answer him.

'She's pooped,' Hench said. 'I had a gun, a Colt .32, same calibre as that, but a belly gun. A revolver, not an automatic. There's a piece broken off the rubber grip. A Jew named Morris gave it to me three, four years ago. We worked together in a bar. I don't have no permit, but I don't carry the gun neither.'

Breeze said: 'Hitting the hooch like you birds been and having a gun under the pillow sooner or later somebody was going to get shot. You ought to know that.'

'Hell, we didn't even know the guy,' Hench said. His tie was tied now, very badly. He was cold sober and very shaky. He stood up and picked a coat off the end of the bed and put it on and sat down again. I watched his fingers tremble lighting a cigarette. 'We don't know his name. We don't know anything about him. I see him maybe two, three times in the hall, but he don't even speak to me. It's the same guy, I guess. I ain't even sure of that.'

'It's the fellow that lived there,' Breeze said. 'Let me see now, this ball game is a studio re-broadcast, huh?'

'Goes on at three,' Hench said. 'Three to say four-thirty, or sometimes later. We went out about the last half the third. We was gone about an inning and a half, maybe two. Twenty minutes to half an hour. Not more.'

'I guess he was shot just before you went out,' Breeze said. 'The radio would kill the noise of the gun near enough. You must of left your door unlocked. Or even open.'

'Could be,' Hench said wearily. 'You remember, honey?'

Again the girl on the bed refused to answer him or even look at him.

Breeze said: 'You left your door open or unlocked. The killer heard you go out. He got into your apartment, wanting to ditch his gun, saw the bed down, walked across and slipped his gun under the pillow, and then imagine his surprise. He found another gun there waiting for him. So he took it along. Now if he meant to ditch his gun, why not do it where he did his killing? Why take the risk of going into another apartment to do it? Why the fancy pants?'

I was sitting in the corner of the davenport by the window. I put in my nickel's worth, saying: 'Suppose he had locked himself out of Phillips's apartment before he thought of ditch-ing the gun? Suppose coming out of the shock of his murder, he found himself in the hall still holding the murder gun. He would want to ditch it fast. Then if Hench's door was open and he had heard them go out along the hall—'

Breeze looked at me briefly and grunted: 'I'm not saying it isn't so. I'm just considering.' He turned his attention back to Hench. 'So now, if this turns out to be the gun that killed Anson, we got to try and trace *your* gun. While we do that we got to have you and the young lady handy. You understand that, of course?'

Hench said: 'You don't have any boys that can bounce me hard enough to make me tell it different.'

'We can always try,' Breeze said mildly. 'And we might just as well get started.'

He stood up, turned and swept the crumpled newspapers off the chair on to the floor. He went over to the door, then turned and stood looking at the girl on the bed. 'You all right, sister, or should I call for a matron?'

The girl on the bed didn't answer him.

Hench said: 'I need a drink. I need a drink bad.'

'Not while I'm watching you,' Breeze said, and went out of the door.

Hench moved across the room and put the neck of a bottle into his mouth and gurgled liquor. He lowered the bottle, looked at what was left in it and went over to the girl. He pushed her shoulder.

'Wake up and have a drink,' he growled at her.

The girl stared at the ceiling. She didn't answer him or show that she had heard him.

'Let her alone,' I said. 'Shock.'

Hench finished what was in the bottle, put the empty bottle down carefully and looked at the girl again, then turned his back on her and stood frowning at the floor. 'Jeeze, I wish I could remember better,' he said under his breath.

Breeze came back into the room with a young fresh-faced plainclothes detective. 'This is Lieutenant Spangler,' he said. 'He'll take you down. Get going, huh?'

Hench went back to the bed and shook the girl's shoulder. 'Get on up, babe. We gotta take a ride.'

The girl turned her eyes without turning her head, and looked at him slowly. She lifted her shoulders off the bed and put a hand under her and swung her legs over the side and stood up, stamping her right foot, as if it was numb.

'Tough, kid – but you know how it is,' Hench said.

The girl put a hand to her mouth and bit the knuckle of her little finger, looking at him blankly. Then she swung the hand suddenly and hit him in the face as hard as she could. Then she half ran out of the door.

Hench didn't move a muscle for a long moment. There was a confused noise of men talking outside, a confused noise of cars down below in the street. Hench shrugged and cocked his heavy shoulders back and swept a slow look around the room, as if he didn't expect to see it again very soon, or at all. Then he went out past the young fresh-faced detective.

The detective went out. The door closed. The confused noise outside was dimmed a little and Breeze and I sat looking at each other heavily.


# Eleven

After a while Breeze got tired of looking at me and dug a cigar out of his pocket. He slit the cellophane band with a knife and trimmed the end of the cigar and lit it carefully, turning it around in the flame, and holding the burning match away from it while he stared thoughtfully at nothing and drew on the cigar and made sure it was burning the way he wanted it to burn.

Then he shook the match out very slowly and reached over to lay it on the sill of the open window. Then he looked at me some more.

'You and me,' he said, 'are going to get along.'

'That's fine,' I said.

'You don't think so,' he said. 'But we are. But not because I took any sudden fancy to you. It's the way I work. Everything in the clear. Everything sensible. Everything quiet. Not like that dame. That's the kind of dame that spends her life looking for trouble and when she finds it, it's the fault of the first guy she can get her finger-nails into.'

'He gave her a couple of shiners,' I said. 'That wouldn't make her love him too much.'

'I can see,' Breeze said, 'that you know a lot about dames.'

'Not knowing a lot about them has helped me in my business,' I said. 'I'm open-minded.'

He nodded and examined the end of his cigar. He took a piece of paper out of his pocket and read from it. 'Delmar B. Hench, 45, bar-tender, unemployed. Maybelle Masters, 26, dancer. That's all I know about them. I've got a hunch there ain't a lot more to know.'

'You don't think he shot Anson?' I asked.

Breeze looked at me without pleasure. 'Brother, I just got here.' He took a card out of his pocket and read from that. 'James B. Pollock, Reliance Indemnity Company, Field Agent. What's the idea?'

'In a neighbourhood like this it's bad form to use your own name,' I said. 'Anson didn't either.'

'What's the matter with the neighbourhood?'

'Practically everything,' I said.

'What I would like to know,' Breeze said, 'is what you know about the dead guy?'

'I told you already.'

'Tell me again. People tell me so much stuff I get it all mixed up.'

'I know what it says on his card, that his name is George Anson Phillips, that he claimed to be a private detective. He was outside my office when I went to lunch. He followed me downtown, into the lobby of the Hotel Metropole. I led him there. I spoke to him and he admitted he had been following me and said it was because he wanted to find out if I was smart enough to do business with. That's a lot of baloney, of course. He probably hadn't quite made up his mind what to do and was waiting for something to decide him. He was on a job – he said – he had got leery of and he wanted to join up with somebody, perhaps somebody with a little more experience than he had, if he had any at all. He didn't act as if he had.'

Breeze said: 'And the only reason he picked on you is that

71

six years ago you worked on a case in Ventura while he was a deputy up there.'

I said: 'That's my story.'

'But you don't have to get stuck with it,' Breeze said calmly. 'You can always give us a better one.'

'It's good enough,' I said. 'I mean it's good enough in the sense that it's bad enough to be true.'

He nodded his big slow head.

'What's your idea of all this?' he asked.

'Have you investigated Phillips's office address?'

He shook his head, no.

'My idea is you will find out he was hired because he was simple. He was hired to take this apartment here under a wrong name, and to do something that turned out to be not what he liked. He was scared. He wanted a friend, he wanted help. The fact that he picked me after so long a time and such little knowledge of me showed he didn't know many people in the detective business.'

Breeze got his handkerchief out and mopped his head and face again. 'But it don't begin to show why he had to follow you around like a lost pup instead of walking right up to your office door and in.'

'No,' I said, 'it doesn't.'

'Can you explain that?'

'No. Not really.'

'Well, how would you try to explain it?'

'I've already explained it in the only way I know how. He was undecided whether to speak to me or not. He was waiting for something to decide him. I decided by speaking to him.'

Breeze said: 'That is a very simple explanation. It is so simple it stinks.'

'You may be right,' I said.

'And as the result of this little hotel lobby conversation this guy, a total stranger to you, asks you to his apartment and hands you his key. Because he wants to talk to you.'

I said: 'Yes.'

'Why couldn't he talk to you then?'

'I had an appointment,' I said.

'Business?'

I nodded.

'I see. What you working on?'

I shook my head and didn't answer.

'This is murder,' Breeze said. 'You're going to have to tell me.'

I shook my head again. He flushed a little.

'Look,' he said tightly, 'you got to.'

'I'm sorry, Breeze,' I said. 'But so far as things have gone, I'm not convinced of that.'

'Of course you know I can throw you in the can as a material witness,' he said casually.

'On what grounds?'

'On the grounds that you are the one who found the body, that you gave a false name to the manager here, and that you don't give a satisfactory account of your relations with the dead guy.'

I said: 'Are you going to do it?'

He smiled bleakly. 'You got a lawyer?'

'I know several lawyers. I don't have a lawyer on a retainer basis.'

'How many of the commissioners do you know personally?'

'None. That is, I've spoken to three of them, but they might not remember me.'

'But you have good contacts in the mayor's office and so on?'

'Tell me about them,' I said. 'I'd like to know.'

'Look, buddy,' he said earnestly, 'you must got some friends somewhere. Surely.'

'I've got a good friend in the Sheriff's office, but I'd rather leave him out of it.'

He lifted his eyebrows. 'Why? Maybe you're going to need friends. A good word from a cop we know to be right might go a long way.'

'He's just a personal friend,' I said. 'I don't ride around on his back. If I get in trouble, it won't do him any good.'

'How about the homicide bureau?'

'There's Randall,' I said. 'If he's still working out of Central Homicide. I had a little time with him on a case once. But he doesn't like me too well.'

Breeze sighed and moved his feet on the floor, rustling the

newspapers he had pushed down out of the chair.

'Is all this on the level – or are you just being smart? I mean about all the important guys you don't know?'

'It's on the level,' I said. 'But the way I am using it is smart.'

'It ain't smart to say so right out.'

'I think it is.'

He put a big freckled hand over the whole lower part of his face and squeezed. When he took the hand away there were round red marks on his cheeks from the pressure of thumb and fingers. I watched the marks fade.

'Why don't you go on home and let a man work?' he asked crossly.

I got up and nodded and went towards the door. Breeze said to my back: 'Gimme your home address.'

I gave it to him. He wrote it down. 'So long,' he said drearily; 'don't leave town. We'll want a statement – maybe tonight.'

I went out. There were two uniformed cops outside on the landing. The door across the way was open and a fingerprint man was still working inside. Downstairs I met two more cops in the hallway, one at each end of it. I didn't see the carroty manager. I went out the front door. There was an ambulance pulling away from the kerb. A knot of people hung around on both sides of the street, not as many as would accumulate in some neighbourhoods.

I pushed along the sidewalk. A man grabbed me by the arm and said: 'What's the damage, Jack?'

I shook his arm off without speaking or looking at his face and went on down the street to where my car was.


# Twelve


It was a quarter to seven when I let myself into the office and clicked the light on and picked a piece of paper off the floor. It was a notice from the Green Feather Messenger Service saying that a package was held awaiting my call and would be delivered upon request at any hour of the day or night. I put it on the desk, peeled my coat off and opened the windows. I got a half-bottle of Old Taylor out of the deep drawer of the desk and drank a short drink, rolling it around on my tongue. Then I sat there holding the neck of the cool bottle and wondering how it would feel to be a homicide dick and find bodies lying around and not mind at all, not have to sneak out wiping doorknobs, not have to ponder how much I could tell without hurting a client and how little I could tell without too badly hurting myself. I decided I wouldn't like it.

I pulled the phone over and looked at the number on the slip and called it. They said my package could be sent right over. I said I would wait for it.

It was getting dark outside now. The rushing sound of the traffic had died a little and the air from the open window, not yet cool from the night, had that tired end-of-day smell of dust, automobile exhaust, sunlight rising from hot walls and sidewalks, the remote smell of food in a thousand restaurants, and perhaps, drifting down from the residential hills above Hollywood – if you had a nose like a hunting dog – a touch of that peculiar tomcat smell that eucalyptus trees give off in warm weather.

I sat there smoking. Ten minutes later the door was knocked on and I opened it to a boy in a uniform cap who took my signature and gave me a small square package, not more than two and a half inches wide, if that. I gave the boy a dime and listened to him whistling his way back to the elevators.

The label had my name and address printed on it in ink, in a quite fair imitation of typed letters, larger and thinner than pica. I cut the string that tied the label to the box and unwound the thin brown paper. Inside was a thin cheap cardboard box pasted over with brown paper and stamped *Made in Japan* with a rubber stamp. It would be the kind of box you would get in a Jap store to hold some small carved animal or a small piece of jade. The lid fitted down all the way and tightly. I pulled it off and saw tissue paper and cotton-wool.

Separating these I was looking at a gold coin about the size of a half-dollar, bright and shining as if it had just come from the mint.

The side facing me showed a spread eagle with a shield for a breast and the initials E.B. punched into the left wing. Around these was a circle of beading, between the beading and the smooth unmilled edge of the coin, the legend E PLURIBUS UNUM. At the bottom was the date 1787.

I turned the coin over on my palm. It was heavy and cold and my palm felt moist under it. The other side showed a sun rising or setting behind a sharp peak of mountain, then a double circle of what looked like oak leaves, then more Latin, NOVA EBORACA COLUMBIA EXCELSIOR. At the bottom of this side, in smaller capitals, the name BRASHER.

I was looking at the Brasher Doubloon.

There was nothing else in the box or in the paper, nothing on the paper. The hand-written printing meant nothing to me. I didn't know anybody who used it.

I filled an empty tobacco-pouch half full, wrapped the coin up in tissue-paper, snapped a rubber band around it and tucked it into the tobacco in the pouch and put more in on top. I closed the zipper and put the pouch in my pocket. I locked the paper and string and box and label up in a filing cabinet, sat down again and dialled Elisha Morningstar's number on the phone. The bell rang eight times at the other end of the line. It was not answered. I hardly expected that. I hung up again, looked Elisha Morningstar up in the book and saw that he had no listing for a residence phone in Los Angeles or the outlying towns that were in the phone book.

I got a shoulder holster out of the desk and strapped it on and slipped a Colt .32 automatic into it, put on hat and coat, shut the windows again, put the whisky away, clicked the lights off and had the office door unlatched when the phone rang.

The ringing bell had a sinister sound, for no reason of itself, but because of the ears to which it rang. I stood there braced and tense, lips tightly drawn back in a half grin. Beyond the closed windows the neon lights glowed. The dead air didn't move. Outside the corridor was still. The bell rang in darkness, steady and strong.

I went back and leaned on the desk and answered. There was a click and a droning on the wire and beyond that nothing. I depressed the connection and stood there in the dark, leaning over, holding the phone with one hand and holding the flat riser on the pedestal down with the other. I didn't know what I was waiting for.

The phone rang again. I made a sound in my throat and put it to my ear again, not saying anything at all.

So we were there silent, both of us, miles apart maybe, each one holding a telephone and breathing and listening and hearing nothing, not even the breathing.

Then after what seemed a very long time there was the quiet remote whisper of a voice saying dimly, without any tone:

'Too bad for you, Marlowe.'

Then the click again and the droning on the wire and I hung up and went back across the office and out.


# Thirteen


I drove west on Sunset, fiddled around a few blocks without making up my mind whether anyone was trying to follow me, then parked near a drug-store and went into its phone booth. I dropped my nickel and asked the O-operator for a Pasadena number. She told me how much money to put in.

The voice which answered the phone was angular and cold. 'Mrs Murdock's residence.'

'Philip Marlowe here. Mrs Murdock, please.'

I was told to wait. A soft but very clear voice said: 'Mr Marlowe? Mrs Murdock is resting now. Can you tell me what it is?'

'You oughtn't to have told him.'

'I – who—?'

'That loopy guy whose handkerchief you cry into.'

'How dare you?'

'That's fine,' I said. 'Now let me talk to Mrs Murdock. I have to.'

'Very well. I'll try.' The soft clear voice went away and I waited a long wait. They would have to lift her up on the pillows and drag the port bottle out of her hard grey paw and feed her the telephone. A throat was cleared suddenly over the wire. It sounded like a freight train going through a tunnel.

'This is Mrs Murdock.'

'Could you identify the property we were talking about this morning, Mrs Murdock? I mean, could you pick it out from others just like it?'

'Well – are there others just like it?'

'There must be. Dozens, hundreds for all I know. Anyhow, dozens. Of course, I don't know where they are.'

She coughed. 'I don't really know much about it. I suppose I couldn't identify it then. But in the circumstances—'

'That's what I'm getting at, Mrs Murdock. The identification would seem to depend on tracing the history of the article back to you. At least to be convincing.'

'Yes. I suppose it would. Why? Do you know where it is?'

'Morningstar claims to have seen it. He says it was offered to him for sale – just as you suspected. He wouldn't buy. The seller was not a woman, he says. That doesn't mean a thing, because he gave me a detailed description of the party which was either made up or was a description of somebody he knew more than casually. So the seller may have been a woman.'

'I see. It's not important now.'

'Not important?'

'No. Have you anything else to report?'

'Another question to ask. Do you know a youngish blond fellow named George Anson Phillips? Rather heavy set, wearing a brown suit and a dark pork-pie hat with a gay band. Wearing that today. Claimed to be a private detective.'

'I do not. Why should I?'

'I don't know. He enters the picture somewhere. I think he was the one who tried to sell the article. Morningstar tried to call him up after I left. I snuck back into his office and overheard.'

'You what?'

'I snuck.'

'Please do not be witty, Mr Marlowe. Anything else?'

'Yes, I agreed to pay Morningstar one thousand dollars for the return of the – the article. He said he could get it for eight hundred ...'

'And where were you going to get the money, may I ask?'

'Well, I was just talking. This Morningstar is a downy bird. That's the kind of language he understands. And then again you might have wanted to pay it. I wouldn't want to persuade you. You could always go to the police. But if for any reason you didn't want to go to the police, it might be the only way you could get it back – buying it back.'

I would probably have gone on like that for a long time, not knowing just what I was trying to say, if she hadn't stopped me with a noise like a seal barking.

'This is all very unnecessary now, Mr Marlowe. I have decided to drop the matter. The coin has been returned to me.'

'Hold the wire a minute,' I said.

I put the phone down on the shelf and opened the booth door and stuck my head out, filling my chest with what they were using for air in the drug-store. Nobody was paying any attention to me. Up front the druggist, in a pale-blue smock, was chatting across the cigar counter. The counter boy was polishing glasses at the fountain. Two girls in slacks were playing the pinball machine. A tall, narrow party in a black shirt and a pale yellow scarf was fumbling magazines at the rack. He didn't look like a gunman.

I pulled the booth shut and picked up the phone and said: 'A rat was gnawing my foot. It's all right now. You got it back. you said. Just like that. How?'

'I hope you are not too disappointed,' she said in her uncompromising baritone. 'The circumstances are a little difficult. I may decide to explain and I may not. You may call at the house tomorrow morning. Since I do not wish to proceed with the investigation, you will keep the retainer as payment in full.'

'Let me get this straight,' I said. 'You actually got the coin back – not a promise of it, merely?'

'Certainly not. And I'm getting tired. So, if you—'

'One moment, Mrs Murdock. It isn't going to be as simple as all that. Things have happened.'

'In the morning you may tell me about them,' she said sharply, and hung up.

I pushed out of the booth and lit a cigarette with thick awkward fingers. I went back along the store. The druggist was alone now. He was sharpening a pencil with a small knife, very intent, frowning.

'That's a nice sharp pencil you have there,' I told him.

He looked up, surprised. The girls at the pinball machine looked at me, surprised. I went over and looked at myself in the mirror behind the counter. I looked surprised.

I sat down on one of the stools and said: 'A double Scotch, straight.'

The counter man looked surprised. 'Sorry, this isn't a bar, sir. You can buy a bottle at the liquor counter.'

'So it is,' I said. 'I mean, so it isn't. I've had a shock. I'm a little dazed. Give me a cup of coffee, weak, and a very thin ham sandwich on stale bread. No, better not eat yet, either. Good-bye.'

I got down off the stool and walked to the door in a silence that was as loud as a ton of coal going down a chute. The man in the black shirt and yellow scarf was sneering at me over the *New Republic*.

'You ought to lay off that fluff and get your teeth into something solid, like a pulp magazine,' I told him, just to be friendly.

I went on out. Behind me somebody said: 'Hollywood's full of them.'


# Fourteen


The wind had risen and had a dry taut feeling, tossing the tops of trees, and making the swung arc-light up the side street cast shadows like crawling lava. I turned the car and drove east again.

The hock shop was on Santa Monica, near Wilcox, a quiet old-fashioned little place, washed gently by the lapping waves of time. In the front window there was everything you could think of, from a set of trout flies in a thin wooden box to a portable organ, from a folding baby carriage to a portrait camera with a four-inch lens, from a mother-of-pearl lorgnette in a faded plush case to a single action Frontier Colt, .44 calibre, the model they still make for Western peace officers whose grandfathers taught them how to file the trigger and shoot by fanning the hammer back.

I went into the shop and a bell jangled over my head and somebody shuffled and blew his nose far at the back and steps came. An old Jew in a tall black skull-cap came along behind the counter, smiling at me over cut-out glasses.

I got my tobacco-pouch out, got the Brasher Doubloon out of that and laid it on the counter. The window in front was clear glass and I felt naked. No panelled cubicles with hand-carved spittoons and doors that locked themselves as you closed them.

The Jew took the coin and lifted it on his hand. 'Gold, is it? A gold hoarder you are, maybe,' he said, twinkling.

'Twenty-five dollars,' I said. 'The wife and the kiddies are hungry.'

'Oi, that is terrible. Gold, it feels, by the weight. Only gold and, maybe, platinum it could be.' He weighed it casually on a pair of small scales. 'Gold it is,' he said. 'So ten dollars you are wanting?'

'Twenty-five dollars.'

'For twenty-five dollars what would I do with it? Sell it, maybe? For fifteen dollars worth of gold is maybe in it. Okay. Fifteen dollars.'

'You got a good safe?'

'Mister, in this business are the best safes money can buy. Nothing to worry about here. It is fifteen dollars, is it?'

'Make out the ticket.'

He wrote it out partly with his pen and partly with his tongue. I gave my true name and address. Bristol Apartments, 1634 North Bristol Avenue, Hollywood.

'You are living in that district and you are borrowing fifteen dollars,' the Jew said sadly, and tore off my half of the ticket and counted out the money.

I walked down to the corner drug-store and bought an envelope and borrowed a pen and mailed the pawn-ticket to myself.

I was hungry and hollow inside. I went over to Vine to eat, and after that I drove downtown again. The wind was still rising and it was drier than ever. The steering-wheel had a gritty feeling under my fingers and the inside of my nostrils felt tight and drawn.

The lights were on here and there in the tall buildings. The green and chromium clothier's store on the corner of Ninth and Hill was a blaze of light. In the Belfont Building a few windows glowed here and there, but not many. The same old plough-horse sat in the elevator on his piece of folded burlap, looking straight in front of him, blank-eyed, almost gathered to history.

I said: 'I don't suppose you know where I can get in touch with the building superintendent?'

He turned his head slowly and looked past my shoulder. 'I hear how in Noo York they got elevators that just whiz. Go thirty floors at a time. High speed. That's in Noo York.'

'The hell with New York,' I said. 'I like it here.'

'Must take a good man to run them fast babies.'

'Don't kid yourself, dad. All those cuties do is push buttons, say "Good morning, Mr Whoosis," and look at their beauty spots in the car mirror. Now you take a Model T job like this – it takes a man to run it. Satisfied?'

'I work twelve hours a day,' he said. 'And glad to get it.'

'Don't let the union hear you.'

'You know what the union can do?' I shook my head. He told me. Then he lowered his eyes until they almost looked at me. 'Didn't I see you before somewhere?'

'About the building super,' I said gently.

'Year ago he broke his glasses,' the old man said. 'I could of laughed. Almost did.'

'Yes. Where could I get in touch with him this time of the evening?'

He looked at me a little more directly.

'Oh, the building super? He's home, ain't he?'

'Sure. Probably. Or gone to the pictures. But where is home? What's his name?'

'You want something?'

'Yes.' I squeezed a fist in my pocket and tried to keep from yelling. 'I want the address of one of the tenants. The tenant I want the address of isn't on the phone book – at his home. I mean where he lives when he's not in his office. You know, home.' I took my hands out and made a shape in the air, writing the letters slowly, h-o-m-e.

The old man said: 'Which one?' It was so direct that it jarred me.

'Mr Morningstar.'

'He ain't home. Still in his office.'

'Are you sure?'

'Sure I'm sure. I don't notice people much. But he's old like me and I notice him. He ain't been down yet.'

I got into the car and said: 'Eight.'

He wrestled the doors shut and we ground our way up. He didn't look at me any more. When the car stopped and I got out he didn't speak or look at me again. He just sat there blank-eyed, hunched on the burlap and the wooden stool. As I turned the angle of the corridor he was still sitting there. And the vague expression was back on his face.

At the end of the corridor two doors were alight. They were the only two in sight that were. I stopped outside to light a cigarette and listen, but I didn't hear any sound of activity. I opened the door marked *Entrance* and stepped into the narrow office with the small closed typewriter desk. The wooden door was still ajar. I walked along to it and knocked on the wood and said: 'Mr Morningstar.'

No answer. Silence. Not even a sound of breathing. The hairs moved on the back of my neck. I stepped around the door. The ceiling light glowed down on the glass cover of the jeweller's scales, on the old polished wood around the leather desk top, down the side of the desk, on a square-toed, elastic-sided black shoe, with a white cotton sock above it.

The shoe was at the wrong angle, pointing to the corner of the ceiling. The rest of the leg was behind the corner of the big safe. I seemed to be wading through mud as I went on into the room.

He lay crumpled on his back. Very lonely, very dead.

The safe door was wide open and keys hung in the lock of the inner compartment. A metal drawer was pulled out. It was empty now. There may have been money in it once.

Nothing else in the room seemed to be different.

The old man's pockets had been pulled out, but I didn't touch

83

him except to bend over and put the back of my hand against his livid, violet-coloured face. It was like touching a frog's belly. Blood had oozed from the side of his forehead where he had been hit. But there was no powder smell on the air this time, and the violet colour of his skin showed that he had died of a heart stoppage, due to shock and fear, probably. That didn't make it any less murder.

I left the lights burning, wiped the doorknobs, and walked down the fire stairs to the sixth floor. I read the names on the doors going along, for no reason at all. *H. R. Teager, Dental Laboratories, L. Pridview, Public Accountant, Dalton and Rees Typewriting Service, Dr E. J. Blaskowitz,* and underneath the name in small letters: *Chiropractic Physician.*

The elevator came growling up and the old man didn't look at me. His face was as empty as my brain.

I called the Receiving Hospital from the corner, giving no name.

# Fifteen

The chessmen, red and white bone, were lined up ready to go and had that sharp, competent and complicated look they always have at the beginning of a game. It was ten o'clock in the evening, I was home at the apartment, I had a pipe in my mouth, a drink at my elbow and nothing on my mind except two murders and the mystery of how Mrs Elizabeth Bright Murdock had got her Brasher Doubloon back while I still had it in my pocket.

I opened a little paper-bound book of tournament games published in Leipzig, picked out a dashing-looking Queen's Gambit, moved the white pawn to Queen's four, and the bell rang at the door.

I stepped around the table and picked the Colt .38 off the drop-leaf of the oak desk and went over to the door holding it down beside my right leg.

'Who is it?'

'Breeze.'

I went back to the desk to lay the gun down again before I opened the door. Breeze stood there looking just as big and sloppy as ever, but a little more tired. The young, fresh-faced dick named Spangler was with him.

They rode me back into the room without seeming to and Spangler shut the door. His bright young eyes flicked this way and that while Breeze let his older and harder ones stay on my face for a long moment, then he walked around me to the davenport.

'Look around,' he said out of the corner of his mouth.

Spangler left the door and crossed the room to the dinette, looked in there, recrossed and went into the hall. The bathroom door squeaked, his steps went farther along.

Breeze took his hat off and mopped his semi-bald dome. Doors opened and closed distantly. Closets. Spangler came back.

'Nobody here,' he said.

Breeze nodded and sat down, placing his panama beside him. Spangler saw the gun lying on the desk. He said: 'Mind if I look?'

I said: 'Phooey on both of you.'

Spangler walked to the gun and held the muzzle to his nose, sniffing. He broke the magazine out, ejected the shell in the chamber, picked it up and pressed it into the magazine. He laid the magazine on the desk and held the gun so that light went into the open bottom of the breech. Holding it that way he squinted down the barrel.

'A little dust,' he said. 'Not much.'

'What did you expect?' I said. 'Rubies?'

He ignored me, looked at Breeze and added: 'I'd say this gun has not been fired within twenty-four hours. I'm sure of it.'

Breeze nodded and chewed his lip and explored my face with his eyes. Spangler put the gun together neatly and laid it aside and went and sat down. He put a cigarette between his lips and lit it and blew smoke contentedly.

'We know damn well it wasn't a long .38 anyway,' he said. 'One of those things will shoot through a wall. No chance of the slug staying inside a man's head.'

'Just what are you guys talking about?' I asked.

Breeze said: 'The usual thing in our business. Murder. Have

a chair. Relax. I thought I heard voices in here. Maybe it was the next apartment.'

'Maybe,' I said.

'You always have a gun lying around on your desk?'

'Except when it's under my pillow,' I said. 'Or under my arm. Or in the drawer of the desk. Or somewhere I can't just remember where I happened to put it. That help you any?'

'We didn't come here to get tough, Marlowe.'

'That's fine,' I said. 'So you prowl my apartment and handle my property without asking my permission. What do you do when you get tough – knock me down and kick me in the face?'

'Aw hell,' he said and grinned. I grinned back. We all grinned. Then Breeze said: 'Use your phone?'

I pointed to it. He dialled a number and talked to someone named Morrison, saying: 'Breeze at' – he looked down at the base of the phone and read the number off – 'any time now. Marlowe is the name that goes with it. Sure. Five or ten minutes is okay.'

He hung up and went back to the davenport.

'I bet you can't guess why we're here.'

'I'm always expecting the brothers to drop in,' I said.

'Murder ain't funny, Marlowe.'

'Who said it was?'

'Don't you kind of act as if it was?'

'I wasn't aware of it.'

He looked at Spangler and shrugged. Then he looked at the floor. Then he lifted his eyes slowly, as if they were heavy, and looked at me again. I was sitting down by the chess table now.

'You play a lot of chess?' he asked, looking at the chessmen.

'Not a lot. Once in a while I fool around with a game here, thinking things out.'

'Don't it take two guys to play chess?'

'I play over tournament games that have been recorded and published. There's a whole literature about chess. Once in a while I work out problems. They're not chess, properly speaking. What are we talking about chess for? Drink?'

'Not right now,' Breeze said. 'I talked to Randall about you. He remembers you very well, in connection with a case down at the beach.' He moved his feet on the carpet, as if they were very tired. His solid old face was lined and grey with fatigue. 'He said you wouldn't murder anybody. He says you are a nice guy, on the level.'

'That was friendly of him,' I said.

'He says you make good coffee and you get up kind of late in the mornings and are apt to run to a very bright line of chatter and that we should believe anything you say, provided we can check it by five independent witnesses.'

'To hell with him,' I said.

Breeze nodded exactly as though I had said just what he wanted me to say. He wasn't smiling and he wasn't tough, just a big solid man working at his job. Spangler had his head back on the chair and his eyes half closed and was watching the smoke from his cigarette.

'Randall says we should look out for you. He says you are not as smart as you think you are, but that you are a guy things happen to, and a guy like that could be a lot more trouble than a very smart guy. That's what he says, you understand. You look all right to me. I like everything in the clear. That's why I'm telling you.'

I said it was nice of him.

The phone rang. I looked at Breeze, but he didn't move, so I reached for it and answered it. It was a girl's voice. I thought it was vaguely familiar, but I couldn't place it.

'Is this Mr Philip Marlowe?'

'Yes.'

'Mr Marlowe, I'm in trouble, very great trouble. I want to see you very badly. When can I see you?'

I said: 'You mean tonight? Who am I talking to?'

'My name is Gladys Crane. I live at the Hotel Normandy on Rampart. When can you—'

'You mean you want me to come over there tonight?' I asked, thinking about the voice, trying to place it.

'I—' The phone clicked and the line was dead. I sat there holding it, frowning at it, looking across it at Breeze. His face was quietly empty of interest.

'Some girl says she's in trouble,' I said. 'Connection broken.'

I held the plunger down on the base of the phone waiting for it to ring again. The two cops were completely silent and motionless. Too silent, too motionless.

The bell rang again and I let the plunger up and said: 'You want to talk to Breeze, don't you?'

'Yeah.' It was a man's voice and it sounded a little surprised.

'Go on, be tricky,' I said, and got up from the chair and went out to the kitchen. I heard Breeze talking very briefly then the sound of the phone being returned to the cradle.

I got a bottle of Four Roses out of the kitchen closet and three glasses. I got ice and ginger-ale from the icebox and mixed three highballs and carried them in on a tray and sat the tray down on the cocktail table in front of the davenport where Breeze was sitting. I took two of the glasses, handed one to Spangler, and took the other to my chair.

Spangler held the glass uncertainly, pinching his lower lip between thumb and finger, looking at Breeze to see whether he would accept the drink.

Breeze looked at me very steadily. Then he sighed. Then he picked the glass up and tasted it and sighed again and shook his head sideways with a half smile; the way a man does when you give him a drink and he needs it very badly and it is just right and the first swallow is like a peek into a cleaner, sunnier, brighter world.

'I guess you catch on pretty fast, Mr Marlowe,' he said, and leaned back on the davenport completely relaxed. 'I guess now we can do some business together.'

'Not that way,' I said.

'Huh?' He bent his eyebrows together. Spangler leaned forward in his chair and looked bright and attentive.

'Having stray broads call me up and give me a song and dance so you can say they said they recognized my voice somewhere, sometime.'

'The girl's name is Gladys Crane,' Breeze said.

'So she told me. I never heard of her.'

'Okay,' Breeze said. 'Okay.' He showed me the flat of his freckled hand. 'We're not trying to pull anything that's not legitimate. We only hope you ain't, either.'

'Ain't either what?'

'Ain't either trying to pull anything not legitimate. Such as holding out on us.'

'Just why shouldn't I hold out on you, if I feel like it?' I asked. 'You're not paying my salary.'

'Look, don't get tough, Marlowe.'

'I'm not tough. I don't have any idea of being tough. I know enough about cops not to get tough with them. Go ahead and speak your piece and don't try to pull any more phonies like that telephone call.'

'We're on a murder case,' Breeze said. 'We have to try to run it the best we can. You found the body. You had talked to the guy. He had asked you to come to his apartment. He gave you his key. You said you didn't know what he wanted to see you about. We figured that maybe with time to think back you could have remembered.'

'In other words I was lying the first time,' I said.

Breeze smiled a tired smile. 'You been around enough to know that people always lie in murder cases.'

'The trouble with that is how are you going to know when I stop lying?'

'When what you say begins to make sense, we'll be satisfied.'

I looked at Spangler. He was leaning forward so far he was almost out of his chair. He looked as if he was going to jump. I couldn't think of any reason why he should jump, so I thought he must be excited. I looked back at Breeze. He was about as excited as a hole in the wall. He had one of his cellophane-wrapped cigars between his thick fingers and he was slitting the cellophane with a penknife. I watched him get the wrapping off and trim the cigar end with the blade and put the knife away, first wiping the blade carefully on his trousers. I watched him strike a wooden match and light the cigar carefully, turning it around in the flame, then hold the match away from the cigar, still burning, and draw on the cigar till he decided it was properly lighted. Then he shook the match out and laid it down beside the crumpled cellophane on the glass top of the cocktail table. Then he leaned back and pulled up one leg of his trousers and smoked peacefully. Every motion had been exactly as it had been when he lit a cigar in Hench's apartment, and exactly as it always would be whenever he lit a cigar. He was that kind of man, and that made him dangerous. Not as dangerous as a brilliant man, but much more dangerous than a quick excitable one like Spangler.

'I never saw Phillips before today,' I said. 'I don't count that he said he saw me up in Ventura once, because I don't remember him. I met him just the way I told you. He tailed me around and I braced him. He wanted to talk to me, he gave me his key, I went to his apartment, used the key to let myself in when he didn't answer – as he had told me to do. He was dead. The police were called and through a set of events or incidents that had nothing to do with me, a gun was found under Hench's pillow. A gun that had been fired. I told you this and it's true.'

Breeze said: 'When you found him you went down to the apartment manager, guy named Passmore, and got him to go up with you without telling him anybody was dead. You gave Passmore a phony card and talked about jewellery.'

I nodded. 'With people like Passmore and apartment houses like that one, it pays to be a little on the cagey side. I was interested in Phillips. I thought Passmore might tell me something about him, if he didn't know he was dead, that he wouldn't be likely to tell me if he knew the cops were going to bounce in on him in a brief space of time. That's all there was to that.'

Breeze drank a little of his drink and smoked a little of his cigar and said: 'What I'd like to get in the clear is this. Everything you just told us might be strictly the truth, and yet you might not be telling us the truth. If you get what I mean.'

'Like what?' I asked, getting perfectly well what he meant.

He tapped on his knee and watched me with a quiet up from under look. Not hostile, not even suspicious. Just a quiet man doing his job.

'Like this. You're on a job. We don't know what it is. Phillips was playing at being a private dick. He was on a job. He tailed you around. How can we know, unless you tell us, that his job and your job don't tie in somewhere? And if they do, that's our business. Right?'

'That's one way to look at it,' I said. 'But it's not the only way, and it's not my way.'

'Don't forget this is a murder case, Marlowe.'

'I'm not. But don't you forget I've been around this town a

90

long time, more than fifteen years. I've seen a lot of murder cases come and go. Some have been solved, some couldn't be solved, and some could have been solved that were not solved. And one or two or three of them have been solved wrong. Somebody was paid to take a rap, and the chances are it was known or strongly suspected. And winked at. But skip that. It happens, but not often. Consider a case like the Cassidy case. I guess you remember it, don't you?'

Breeze looked at his watch. 'I'm tired,' he said. 'Let's forget the Cassidy case. Let's stick to the Phillips case.'

I shook my head. 'I'm going to make a point, and it's an important point. Just look at the Cassidy case. Cassidy was a very rich man, a multi-millionaire. He had a grown-up son. One night the cops were called to his home and young Cassidy was on his back on the floor with blood all over his face and a bullet-hole in the side of his head. His secretary was lying on *his* back in an adjoining bathroom, with his head against the second bathroom door, leading to a hall, and a cigarette burned out between the fingers of his left hand, just a short burned-out stub that had scorched the skin between his fingers. A gun was lying by his right hand. He was shot in the head, not a contact wound. A lot of drinking had been done. Four hours had elapsed since the deaths and the family doctor had been there for three of them. Now, what did you do with the Cassidy case?'

Breeze sighed. 'Murder and suicide during a drinking spree. The secretary went haywire and shot young Cassidy. I read it in the papers or something. Is that what you want me to say?'

'You read it in the papers,' I said, 'but it wasn't so. What's more, you knew it wasn't so and the DA knew it wasn't so and the DA's investigators were pulled off the case within a matter of hours. There was no inquest. But every crime reporter in town and every cop on every homicide detail knew it was Cassidy that did the shooting, that it was Cassidy that was crazy drunk, that it was the secretary who tried to handle him and couldn't and at last tried to get away from him, but wasn't quick enough. Cassidy's was a contact wound and the secretary's was not. The secretary was left-handed and he had a cigarette in his left hand when he was shot. Even if you are right-handed, you don't change a cigarette over to your other hand and shoot a man while casually holding the cigarette. They might do that on *Gang Busters*, but rich men's secretaries don't do it. And what were the family and the family doctor doing during the four hours they didn't call the cops? Fixing it so there would only be a superficial investigation. And why were no tests of the hands made for nitrates? Because you didn't want the truth. Cassidy was too big. But this was a murder case, too, wasn't it?'

'The guys were both dead,' Breeze said. 'What the hell difference did it make who shot who?'

'Did you ever stop to think,' I said, 'that Cassidy's secretary might have had a mother or a sister or a sweetheart – or all three? That they had their pride and their faith and their love for a kid who was made out to be a drunken paranoiac because his boss's father had a hundred million dollars?'

Breeze lifted his glass slowly and finished his drink slowly and put it down slowly and turned the glass slowly on the glass top of the cocktail table. Spangler sat rigid, all shining eyes and lips parted in a sort of rigid half smile.

Breeze said: 'Make your point.'

I said: 'Until you guys own your own souls you don't own mine. Until you guys can be trusted every time and always, in all times and conditions, to seek the truth out and find it and let the chips fall where they may – until that time comes, I have a right to listen to my conscience, and protect my client the best way I can. Until I'm sure you won't do him more harm than you'll do the truth good. Or until I'm hauled before somebody that can make me talk.'

Breeze said: 'You sound to me just a little like a guy who is trying to hold his conscience down.'

'Hell,' I said. 'Let's have another drink. And then you can tell me about that girl you had me talk to on the phone.'

He grinned: 'That was a dame that lives next door to Phillips. She heard a guy talking to him at the door one evening. She works days as an usherette. So we thought maybe, she ought to hear your voice. Think nothing of it.'

'What kind of voice was it?'

'Kind of a mean voice. She said she didn't like it.'

'I guess that's what made you think of me,' I said.

I picked up the three glasses and went out to the kitchen with them.

# Sixteen

When I got there I had forgotten which glass was which, so I rinsed them all out and dried them and was starting to make more drinks when Spangler strolled out and stood just behind my shoulder.

'It's all right,' I said. 'I'm not using any cyanide this evening.'

'Don't get too foxy with the old guy,' he said quietly to the back of my neck. 'He knows more angles than you think.'

'Nice of you,' I said.

'Say, I'd like to read up on that Cassidy case,' he said. 'Sounds interesting. Must have been before my time.'

'It was a long time ago,' I said. 'And it never happened. I was just kidding.' I put the glasses on the tray and carried them back into the living-room and set them around. I took mine over to my chair behind the chess table.

'Another phony,' I said. 'Your sidekick sneaks out to the kitchen and gives me advice behind your back about how careful I ought to keep on account of the angles you know that I don't think you know. He has just the right face for it. Friendly and open and an easy blusher.'

Spangler sat down on the edge of his chair and blushed. Breeze looked at him casually, without meaning.

'What did you find out about Phillips?' I asked.

'Yes,' Breeze said. 'Phillips. Well, George Anson Phillips is a kind of pathetic case. He thought he was a detective, but it looks as if he couldn't get anybody to agree with him. I talked to the sheriff at Ventura. He said George was a nice kid, maybe a little too nice to make a good cop, even if he had any brains. George did what they said and he would do it pretty well, provided they told him which foot to start on and how many steps to take which way and little things like that. But he didn't develop much, if you get what I mean. He was the sort of cop who would be likely to hang a pinch on a chicken thief, if he saw the guy steal the chicken and the guy fell down running away and hit his head on a post or something and knocked himself out. Otherwise it might get a little tough and George would have to go back to the office for instructions. Well, it wore the sheriff down after a while and he let George go.'

Breeze drank some more of his drink and scratched his chin with a thumbnail like the blade of a shovel.

'After that George worked in a general store at Simi for a man named Sutcliff. It was a credit business with little books for each customer and George would have trouble with the books. He would forget to write the stuff down or write it in the wrong book and some of the customers would straighten him out and some would let George forget. So Sutcliff thought maybe George would do better at something else, and he came to Los Angeles. He had come into a little money, not much, but enough for him to get a licence and put up a bond and get himself a piece of an office. I was over there. What he had was desk room with another guy who claims he is selling Christmas cards. Name of Marsh. If George had a customer, the arrangement was Marsh would go for a walk. Marsh says he didn't know where George lived and George didn't have any customers. That is, no business came into the office that Marsh knows about. But George put an advertisement in the paper and he might have got a customer out of that. I guess he did, because about a week ago Marsh found a note on his desk that George would be out of town for a few days. That's the last he heard of him. So George went over to Court Street and took an apartment under the name of Anson and got bumped off. And that's all we know about George so far. Kind of a pathetic case.'

He looked at me with a level, uncurious gaze and raised his glass to his lips.

'What about this advertisement?'

Breeze put the glass down and dug a thin piece of paper out of his wallet and put it down on the cocktail table. I went over and picked it up and read it. It said:

*Why worry? Why be doubtful or confused? Why be gnawed by suspicion? Consult cool, careful, confidential, discreet investigator. George Anson Phillips. Glenview 9521.*

I put it down on the glass again.

'It ain't any worse than lots of business personals,' Breeze said. 'It don't seem to be aimed at the carriage trade.'

Spangler said: 'The girl in the office wrote it for him. She said she could hardly keep from laughing, but George thought it was swell. The Hollywood Boulevard office of the *Chronicle*.'

'You checked that fast,' I said.

'We don't have any trouble getting information,' Breeze said. 'Except maybe from you.'

'What about Hench?'

'Nothing about Hench. Him and the girl were having a liquor party. They would drink a little and sing a little and scrap a little and listen to the radio and go out to eat once in a while, when they thought of it. I guess it had been going on for days. Just as well we stopped it. The girl has two bad eyes. The next round Hench might have broken her neck. The world is full of bums like Hench – and his girl.'

'What about the gun Hench said wasn't his?'

'It's the right gun. We don't have the slug yet, but we have the shell. It was under George's body and it checks. We had a couple more fired and compared the ejector marks and the firing-pin dents.'

'You believe someone planted it under Hench's pillow?'

'Sure. Why would Hench shoot Phillips? He didn't know him.'

'How do you know that?'

'I know it,' Breeze said, spreading his hands. 'Look, there are things you know because you have them down in black and white. And there are things you know because they are reasonable and have to be so. You don't shoot somebody and then make a lot of racket calling attention to yourself, and all the time you have the gun under your pillow. The girl was with Hench all day. If Hench shot anybody, she would have some idea. She doesn't have any such idea. She would spill, if she had. What is Hench to her? A guy to play around with, no more. Look, forget Hench. The guy who did the shooting hears the loud radio and knows it will cover a shot. But all the same he saps Phillips and drags him into the bathroom and shuts the door before he shoots him. He's not drunk. He's minding his own business, and careful. He goes out, shuts the bathroom door, the radio stops, Hench and the girl go out to eat. Just happens that way.'

'How do you know the radio stopped?'

'I was told,' Breeze said calmly. 'Other people live in that dump. Take it the radio stopped and they went out. Not quiet. The killer steps out of the apartment and Hench's door is open. That must be because otherwise he wouldn't think anything about Hench's door.'

'People don't leave their doors open in apartment houses. Especially in districts like that.'

'Drunks do. Drunks are careless. Their minds don't focus well. And they only think of one thing at a time. The door was open – just a little maybe, but open. The killer went in and ditched his gun on the bed and found another gun there. He took that away, just to make it look worse for Hench.'

'You can check the gun,' I said.

'Hench's gun? We'll try to, but Hench says he doesn't know the number. If we find it, we might do something there. I doubt it. The gun we have we will try to check, but you know how those things are. You get just so far along and you think it is going to open up for you, and then the trail dies out cold. A dead end. Anything else you can think of that we might know that might be a help to you in your business?'

'I'm getting tired,' I said. 'My imagination isn't working very well.'

'You were doing fine a while back,' Breeze said. 'On the Cassidy case.'

I didn't say anything. I filled my pipe up again but it was too hot to light. I laid it on the edge of the table to cool off.

'It's God truth,' Breeze said slowly, 'that I don't know what to make of you. I can't see you deliberately covering up on any murder. And neither can I see you knowing as little about all this as you pretend to know.'

I didn't say anything, again.

Breeze leaned over to revolve his cigar butt in the tray until he had killed the fire. He finished his drink, put on his hat and stood up.

'How long you expect to stay dummied up?' he asked.

'I don't know.'

'Let me help you out. I give you till tomorrow noon, a little better than twelve hours. I won't get my post-mortem report before that anyway. I give you till then to talk things over with your party and decide to come clean.'

'And after that?'

'After that I see the Captain of Detectives and tell him a private eye named Philip Marlowe is withholding information which I need in a murder investigation, or I'm pretty sure he is. And what about it? I figure he'll pull you in fast enough to singe your breeches.'

I said: 'Uh-huh. Did you go through Phillips's desk?'

'Sure. A very neat young feller. Nothing in it at all, except a little kind of diary. Nothing in that either, except about how he went to the beach or took some girl to the pictures and she didn't warm up much. Or how he sat in the office and no business come in. One time he got a little sore about his laundry and wrote a whole page. Mostly it was just three or four lines. There was only one thing about it. It was all done in a kind of printing.'

I said: 'Printing?'

'Yeah, printing in pen and ink. Not big block caps like people trying to disguise things. Just neat fast little printing as if the guy could write that way as fast and easy as any way.'

'He didn't write like that on the card he gave me,' I said.

Breeze thought about that for a moment. Then he nodded. 'True. Maybe it was this way. There wasn't any name in the diary either, in the front. Maybe the printing was just a little game he played with himself.'

'Like Pepys's shorthand,' I said.

'What was that?'

'A diary a man wrote in a private shorthand, a long time ago.'

Breeze looked at Spangler, who was standing up in front of his chair, tipping the last few drops of his glass.

'We better beat it,' Breeze said. 'This guy is warming up for another Cassidy case.'

Spangler put his glass down and they both went over to the door. Breeze shuffled a foot and looked at me sideways, with his hand on the doorknob.

'You know any tall blondes?'

'I'd have to think,' I said. 'I hope so. How tall?'

'Just tall. I don't know how tall that is. Except that it would be tall to a guy who is tall himself. A wop named Palermo owns that apartment house on Court Street. We went across to see him in his funeral parlours. He owns them too. He says he saw a tall blonde come out of the apartment house about three-thirty. The manager, Passmore, don't place anybody in the joint that he would call a tall blonde. The wop says she was a looker. I give some weight to what he says because he give us a good description of you. He didn't see this tall blonde go in, just saw her come out. She was wearing slacks and a sports jacket and a wrap-around. But she had light blonde hair and plenty of it under the wrap-around.'

'Nothing comes to me,' I said. 'But I just remembered something else. I wrote the licence number of Phillips's car down on the back of an envelope. That will give you his former address, probably. I'll get it.'

They stood there while I went to get it out of my coat in the bedroom. I handed the piece of envelope to Breeze and he read what was on it and tucked it into his billfold.

'So you just thought of this, huh?'

'That's right.'

'Well, well,' he said. 'Well, well.'

The two of them went along the hallway towards the elevator, shaking their heads.

I shut the door and went back to my almost untasted second drink. It was flat. I carried it to the kitchen and hardened it up from the bottle and stood there holding it and looking out of the window at the eucalyptus trees tossing their limber tops against the bluish dark sky. The wind seemed to have risen again. It thumped at the north window and there was a heavy slow pounding noise on the wall of the building, like a thick wire banging the stucco between insulators.

I tasted my drink and wished I hadn't wasted the fresh whisky on it. I poured it down the sink and got a fresh glass and drank some ice water.

Twelve hours to tie up a situation which I didn't even begin to understand. Either that or turn up a client and let the cops go to work on her and her whole family. Hire Marlowe and get your house full of law. Why worry? Why be doubtful and confused? Why be gnawed by suspicion? Consult cock-eyed, care-less, clubfooted, dissipated investigator. Philip Marlowe, Glenview 7537. See me and you meet the best cops in town. Why despair? Why be lonely? Call Marlowe and watch the wagon come.

This didn't get me anywhere either. I went back to the living-room and put a match to the pipe that had cooled off now on the edge of the chess table. I drew the smoke in slowly, but it still tasted like the smell of hot rubber. I put it away and stood in the middle of the floor, pulling my lower lip out and letting it snap against my teeth.

The telephone rang. I picked it up and growled into it.

'Marlowe?'

The voice was a harsh low whisper. It was a harsh low whisper I had heard before.

'All right,' I said. 'Talk it up whoever you are. Whose pocket have I got my hand in now?'

'Maybe you're a smart guy,' the harsh whisper said. 'Maybe you would like to do yourself some good.'

'How much good?'

'Say about five C's worth of good.'

'That's grand,' I said. 'Doing what?'

'Keeping your nose clean,' the voice said. 'Want to talk about it?'

'Where, when, and who to?'

'Idle Valley Club. Morny. Anytime you get here.'

'Who are you?'

A dim chuckle came over the wire. 'Just ask at the gate for Eddie Prue.'

The phone clicked dead. I hung it up.

It was near eleven-thirty when I backed my car out of the garage and drove towards Cahuenga Pass.


# Seventeen


About twenty miles north of the pass a wide boulevard with flowering moss in the parkways turned towards the foothills. It ran for five blocks and died – without a house in its entire length. From its end a curving asphalt road dived into the hills. This was Idle Valley.

Around the shoulder of the first hill there was a low white building with a tiled roof beside the road. It had a roofed porch and a floodlighted sign on it read: *Idle Valley Patrol.* Open gates were folded back on the shoulders of the road, in the middle of which a square white sign standing on its point said STOP in letters sprinkled with reflector buttons. Another floodlight blistered the space of road in front of the sign.

I stopped. A uniformed man with a star and a strapped-on gun in a woven leather holster looked at my car, then at a board on a post.

He came over to the car. 'Good evening. I don't have your car. This is a private road. Visiting?'

'Going to the club.'

'Which one?'

'Idle Valley Club.'

'Eighty-seven seventy-seven. That's what we call it here. You mean Mr Morny's place?'

'Right.'

'You're not a member, I guess.'

'No.'

'I have to check you in. To somebody who is a member or to somebody who lives in the valley. All private property here, you know.'

'No gate crashers, huh?'

He smiled. 'No gate crashers.'

'The name is Philip Marlowe,' I said. 'Calling on Eddie Prue.'

'Prue?'

'He's Mr Morny's secretary. Or something.'

'Just a minute, please.'

He went to the door of the building, and spoke. Another uniformed man inside plugged in on a PBX. A car came up behind me and honked. The clack of the typewriter came from the open door of the patrol office. The man who had spoken to me looked at the honking car and waved it in. It slid around me and scooted off into the dark, a green long open convertible sedan with three dizzy-looking dames in the front seat, all cigarettes and arched eyebrows and go-to-hell expressions. The car flashed around a curve and was gone.

The uniformed man came back to me and put a hand on the car door. 'Okay, Mr Marlowe. Check with the officer at the club, please. A mile ahead on your right. There's a lighted parking lot and the number on the wall. Just the number. Eighty-seven seventy-seven. Check with the officer there, please.'

I said: 'Why would I do that?'

He was very calm, very polite, and very firm. 'We have to know exactly where you go. There's a great deal to protect in Idle Valley.'

'Suppose I don't check with him?'

'You kidding me?' His voice hardened.

'No. I just wanted to know.'

'A couple of cruisers would start looking for you.'

'How many are you in the patrol?'

'Sorry,' he said. 'About a mile ahead on the right, Mr Marlowe.'

I looked at the gun strapped to his hip, the special badge pinned to his shirt. 'And they call this a democracy,' I said.

He looked behind him and then spat on the ground and put a hand on the sill of the car door. 'Maybe you got company,' he said. 'I knew a fellow belonged to the John Reed Club. Over in Boyle Heights, it was.'

'Tovarich,' I said.

'The trouble with revolutions,' he said, 'is that they get in the hands of the wrong people.'

'Check,' I said.

'On the other hand,' he said, 'could they be any wronger than the bunch of rich phonies that live around here?'

'Maybe you'll be living in here yourself some day,' I said.

He spat again. 'I wouldn't live in here if they paid me fifty thousand a year and let me sleep in chiffon pyjamas with a string of matched pink pearls around my neck.'

'I'd hate to make you the offer,' I said.

'You make me the offer any time,' he said. 'Day or night. Just make me the offer and see what it gets you.'

'Well, I'll run along now and check with the officer of the club,' I said.

'Tell him to go spit up his left trousers leg,' he said. 'Tell him I said so.'

'I'll do that,' I said.

A car came up behind and honked. I drove on. Half a block of dark limousine blew me off the road with its horn and went past me making a noise like dead leaves falling.

The wind was quiet out here and the valley moonlight was so sharp that the black shadows looked as if they had been cut with an engraving tool.

Around the curve the whole valley spread out before me. A thousand white houses built up and down the hills, ten thousand lighted windows and the stars hanging down over them politely, not getting too close, on account of the patrol.

The wall of the club building that faced the road was white and blank, with no entrance door, no windows on the lower floor. The number was small but bright in violet-coloured neon. 8777. Nothing else. To the side, under rows of hooded, downward-shining lights, were even rows of cars, set out in the white lined slots on the smooth black asphalt. Attendants in crisp clean uniforms moved in the lights.

The road went around to the back. A deep concrete porch there, with an overhanging canopy of glass and chromium, but very dim lights. I got out of the car and received a check with the licence number on it, carried it over to a small desk where a uniformed man sat and dumped it in front of him.

'Philip Marlowe,' I said. 'Visitor.'

'Thank you, Mr Marlowe.' He wrote the name and number down, handed me back my check and picked up a telephone.

A negro, in a white linen double-breasted guards' uniform, gold epaulettes, a cap with a broad gold band, opened the door to me.

The lobby looked like a high-budget musical. A lot of light and glitter, a lot of scenery, a lot of clothes, a lot of sound, an all-star cast, and a plot with all the originality and drive of a split fingernail. Under the beautiful soft indirect lighting the wall seemed to go up for ever and, to be lost in soft lascivious stars that really twinkled. You could just manage to walk on the carpet without waders. At the back was a free-arched stairway with a chromium and white enamel gangway going up in wide shallow carpeted steps. At the entrance to the dining-room a chubby captain of waiters stood negligently with a two-inch satin stripe on his pants and a bunch of gold-plated menus under his arm. He had the sort of face that can turn from a polite simper to cold-blooded fury almost without moving a muscle.

The bar entrance was to the left. It was dusky and quiet and a bartender moved moth-like against the faint glitter of piled glassware. A tall handsome blonde, in a dress that looked like sea-water sifted over with gold dust, came out of the Ladies' Room touching up her lips and turned towards the arch, humming.

The sound of rumba music came through the archway and she nodded her gold head in time to it, smiling. A short fat man with a red face and glittering eyes waited for her with a white wrap over his arm. He dug his thick fingers into her bare arm and leered up at her.

A check girl in peach-bloom Chinese pyjamas came over to take my hat and disapprove of my clothes. She had eyes like strange sins.

A cigarette girl came down the gangway. She wore an egret plume in her hair, enough clothes to hide behind a toothpick, one of her long beautiful naked legs was silver, and one was gold. She had the utterly disdainful expression of a dame who makes her dates by long distance.

I went into the bar and sank into a leather bar seat packed with down. Glasses tinkled gently, lights glowed softly, there were quiet voices whispering of love, or ten per cent, or whatever they whisper about in a place like that.

A tall, fine-looking man in a grey suit cut by an angel suddenly stood up from a small table by the wall and walked over to the bar and started to curse one of the barmen. He cursed him in a loud clear voice for a long minute, calling him about nine names that are not usually mentioned by tall, fine-looking men in well-cut grey suits. Everybody stopped talking and looked at him quietly. His voice cut through the muted rumba music like a shovel through snow.

The barman stood perfectly still, looking at the man. The barman had curly hair and a clear warm skin and wide-set careful eyes. He didn't move or speak. The tall man stopped

103

talking and stalked out of the bar. Everybody watched him out except the barman.

The barman moved slowly along the bar to the end where I sat and stood looking away from me, with nothing in his face but pallor. Then he turned to me and said:

'Yes, sir?'

'I want to talk to a fellow named Eddie Prue.'

'So?'

'He works here,' I said.

'Works here doing what?' His voice was perfectly level and as dry as dry sand.

'I understand he's the guy that walks behind the boss. If you know what I mean.'

'Oh. Eddie Prue.' He moved one lip slowly over the other and made small tight circles on the bar with his bar cloth. 'Your name?'

'Marlowe.'

'Marlowe. Drink while waiting?'

'A dry martini will do.'

'A martini. Dry. Veddy, veddy dry.'

'Okay.'

'Will you eat it with a spoon or a knife and fork?'

'Cut it in strips,' I said. 'I'll just nibble it.'

'On your way to school,' he said. 'Should I put the olive in a bag for you?'

'Sock me on the nose with it,' I said. 'If it will make you feel any better.'

'Thank you, sir,' he said. 'A dry martini.'

He took three steps away from me and then came back and leaned across the bar and said: 'I made a mistake in a drink. The gentleman was telling me about it.'

'I heard him.'

'He was telling me about it as gentlemen tell you about things like that. As big shot directors like to point out to you your little errors. And you heard him.'

'Yeah,' I said, wondering how long this was going to go on.

'He made himself heard – the gentleman did. So I come over here and practically insult you.'

'I got the idea,' I said.

He held up one of his fingers and looked at it thoughtfully.

'Just like that,' he said. 'A perfect stranger.'

'It's my big brown eyes,' I said. 'They have that gentle look.'

'Thanks, chum,' he said, and quietly went away.

I saw him talking into a phone at the end of the bar. Then I saw him working with a shaker. When he came back with the drink he was all right again.

# Eighteen

I carried the drink over to a small table against the wall and sat down there and lit a cigarette. Five minutes went by. The music that was coming through the fret had changed in tempo without my noticing it. A girl was singing. She had a rich deep down around the ankles contralto that was pleasant to listen to. She was singing 'Dark Eyes' and the band behind her seemed to be falling asleep.

There was a heavy round of applause and some whistling when she ended.

A man at the next table said to his girl: 'They got Linda Conquest back with the band. I heard she got married to some rich guy in Pasadena, but it didn't take.'

The girl said: 'Nice voice. If you like female crooners.'

I started to get up but a shadow fell across my table and a man was standing there.

A great long gallows of a man with a ravaged face and a haggard frozen right eye that had a clotted iris and the steady look of blindness. He was so tall that he had to stoop to put his hand on the back of the chair across the table from me. He stood there sizing me up without saying anything and I sat there sipping the last of my drink and listening to the contralto voice singing another song. The customers seemed to like corny music in there. Perhaps they were all tired out trying to be ahead of the minute in the place where they worked.

'I'm Prue,' the man said in his harsh whisper.

'So I gathered. You want to talk to me, I want to talk to you, and I want to talk to the girl that just sang.'

'Let's go.'

There was a locked door at the back end of the bar. Prue unlocked it and held it for me and we went through that and up a flight of carpeted steps to the left. A long straight hallway with several closed doors. At the end of it a bright star cross-wired by the mesh of a screen. Prue knocked on a door near the screen and opened it and stood aside for me to pass him.

It was a cosy sort of office, not too large. There was a built-in upholstered corner seat by the french windows and a man in a white dinner-jacket was standing with his back to the room, looking out. He had grey hair. There was a large black and chromium safe, some filing-cases, a large globe in a stand, a small built-in bar, and the usual broad heavy executive desk with the usual high-backed padded leather chair behind it.

I looked at the ornaments on the desk. Everything standard and all copper. A copper lamp, pen set and pencil tray, a glass and copper ashtray with a copper elephant on the rim, a copper letter opener, a copper thermos bottle on a copper tray, copper corners on the blotter holder. There was a spray of almost copper-coloured sweet peas in a copper vase.

It seemed like a lot of copper.

The man at the window turned around and showed me that he was going on fifty and had soft ash-grey hair and plenty of it, and a heavy handsome face with nothing unusual about it except a short puckered scar in his left cheek that had almost the effect of a deep dimple. I remembered the dimple. I would have forgotten the man. I remembered that I had seen him in pictures a long time ago, at least ten years ago. I didn't remember the pictures or what they were about or what he did in them, but I remembered the dark heavy handsome face and the puckered scar. His hair had been dark then.

He walked over to his desk and sat down and picked up his letter opener and poked at the ball of his thumb with the point. He looked at me with no expression and said: 'You're Marlowe?'

I nodded.

'Sit down.' I sat down. Eddie Prue sat in a chair against the wall and tilted the front legs off the floor.

'I don't like peepers,' Morny said.

I shrugged.

'I don't like them for a lot of reasons,' he said. 'I don't like them in any way or at any time. I don't like them when they bother my friends. I don't like them when they bust in on my wife.'

I didn't say anything.

'I don't like them when they question my driver or when they get tough with my guests,' he said.

I didn't say anything.

'In short,' he said. 'I just don't like them.'

'I'm beginning to get what you mean,' I said.

He flushed and his eyes glittered. 'On the other hand,' he said, 'just at the moment I might have a use for you. It might pay you to play ball with me. It might be a good idea. It might pay you to keep your nose clean.'

'How much might it pay me?' I asked.

'It might pay you in time and health.'

'I seem to have heard this record somewhere,' I said. 'I just can't put a name to it.'

He laid the letter-opener down and swung open a door in the desk and got a cut-glass decanter out. He poured liquid out of it in a glass and drank it and put the stopper back in the decanter and put the decanter back in the desk.

'In my business,' he said, 'tough boys come a dime a dozen. And would-be tough boys come a nickel a gross. Just mind your business and I'll mind my business and we won't have any trouble.' He lit a cigarette. His hand shook a little.

I looked across the room at the tall man sitting tilted against the wall, like a loafer in a country store. He just sat there without motion, his long arms hanging, his lined grey face full of nothing.

'Somebody said something about some money,' I said to Morny. 'What's that for? I know what the bawling out is for. That's you trying to make yourself think you can scare me.'

'Talk like that to me,' Morny said, 'and you are liable to be wearing lead buttons on your vest.'

'Just think,' I said. 'Poor old Marlowe with lead buttons on his vest.'

Eddie Prue made a dry sound in his throat that might have been a chuckle.

'And as for me minding my own business and not minding yours,' I said, 'it might be that my business and your business would get a little mixed up together. Through no fault of mine.'

'It better not,' Morny said. 'In what way?' He lifted his eyes quickly and dropped them again.

'Well, for instance, your hard boy here calling me up on the phone and trying to scare me to death. And later in the evening calling me up and talking about five C's and how it would do me some good to drive out here and talk to you. And, for instance, that same hard boy or somebody who looks just like him – which is a little unlikely – following around after a fellow in my business who happened to get shot this afternoon, on Court Street on Bunker Hill.'

Morny lifted his cigarette away from his lips and narrowed his eyes to look at the tip. Every motion, every gesture, right out of the catalogue.

'Who got shot?'

'A fellow named Phillips, a youngish blond kid. You wouldn't like him. He was a peeper.' I described Phillips to him.

'I never heard of him,' Morny said.

'And also, for instance, a tall blonde who didn't live there was seen coming out of the apartment house just after he was killed,' I said.

'What tall blonde?' His voice had changed a little. There was urgency in it.

'I don't know that. She was seen and the man who saw her could identify her, if he saw her again. Of course, she need not have anything to do with Phillips.'

'This man Phillips was a shamus?'

I nodded. 'I told you that twice.'

'Why was he killed, and how?'

'He was sapped and shot in his apartment. We don't know why he was killed. If we knew that, we would likely know who killed him. It seems to be that kind of a situation.'

'Who is "we"?'

'The police and myself. I found him dead. So I had to stick around.'

Prue let the front legs of his chair down on the carpet very

108

quietly and looked at me. His good eye had a sleepy expression I didn't like.

Morny said: 'You told the cops what?'

I said: 'Very little. I gather from your opening remarks to me here that you know I am looking for Linda Conquest. Mrs Leslie Murdock. I've found her. She's singing here. I don't know why there should have been any secret about it. It seems to me that your wife or Mr Vannier might have told me. But they didn't.'

'What my wife would tell a peeper,' Morny said, 'you could put in a gnat's eye.'

'No doubt she has her reasons,' I said. 'However that's not very important now. In fact, it's not very important that I see Miss Conquest. Just the same I'd like to talk to her a little. If you don't mind.'

'Suppose I mind,' Morny said.

'I guess I would like to talk to her, anyway,' I said. I got a cigarette out of my pocket and rolled it around in my fingers and admired his thick and still-dark eyebrows. They had a fine shape, an elegant curve. Prue chuckled. Morny looked at him and frowned and looked back at me, keeping the frown on his face.

'I asked you what you told the cops,' he said.

'I told them as little as I could. This man Phillips asked me to come and see him. He implied he was too deep in a job he didn't like, and needed help. When I got there he was dead. I told the police that. They didn't think it was quite the whole story. It probably isn't. I have until tomorrow noon to fill it out. So I'm trying to fill it out.'

'You wasted your time coming here,' Morny said.

'I got the idea that I was asked to come here.'

'You can go to hell back any time you want to,' Morny said. 'Or you can do a little job for me – for five hundred dollars. Either way you leave Eddie and me out of any conversations you might have with the police.'

'What's the nature of the job?'

'You were at my house this morning. You ought to have an idea.'

'I don't do divorce business,' I said.

His face turned white. 'I love my wife,' he said. 'We've only been married eight months. I don't want any divorce. She's a swell girl and she knows what time it is, as a rule. But I think she's playing with a wrong number at the moment.'

'Wrong in what way?'

'I don't know. That's what I want found out.'

'Let me get this straight,' I said. 'Are you hiring me on a job – or off a job I already have?'

Prue chuckled again against the wall.

Morny poured himself some more brandy and tossed it quickly down his throat. Colour came back into his face. He didn't answer me.

'And let me get another thing straight,' I said. 'You don't mind your wife playing around, but you don't want her playing with somebody named Vannier. Is that it?'

'I trust her heart,' he said slowly. 'But I don't trust her judgement. Put it that way.'

'And you want me to get something on this man Vannier?'

'I want to find out what he is up to.'

'Oh. Is he up to something?'

'I think he is. I don't know what.'

'You think he is – or you want to think he is?'

He stared at me levelly for a moment, then he pulled the middle drawer of his desk out, reached in and tossed a folded paper across to me. I picked it up and unfolded it. It was a carbon copy of a grey billhead. *Cal-Western Dental Supply Company*, and an address. The bill was for *30 lb Kerr's Crystobolite $15.75*, and *25 lb White's Albastone*, *$7.75*, plus tax. It was made out to *H. R. Teager, Will Call*, and stamped *Paid* with a rubber stamp. It was signed for in the corner: *L. G. Vannier*.

I put it down on the desk.

'That fell out of his pocket one night when he was here,' Morny said. 'About ten days ago. Eddie put one of his big feet on it and Vannier didn't notice he had dropped it.'

I looked at Prue, then at Morny, then at my thumb. 'Is this supposed to mean something to me?'

'I thought you were a smart detective. I figured you could find out.'

I looked at the paper again, folded it and put it in my pocket. 'I'm assuming you wouldn't give it to me unless it meant something,' I said.

Morny went to the black and chromium safe against the wall and opened it. He came back with five new bills spread out in his fingers like a poker hand. He smoothed them edge to edge, riffled them lightly, and tossed them on the desk in front of me.

'There's your five C's,' he said. 'Take Vannier out of my wife's life and there will be the same again for you. I don't care how you do it and I don't want to know anything about how you do it. Just do it.'

I poked at the crisp new bills with a hungry finger. Then I pushed them away. 'You can pay me when – and if – I deliver,' I said. 'I'll take my payment tonight in a short interview with Miss Conquest.'

Morny didn't touch the money. He lifted the square bottle and poured himself another drink. This time he poured one for me and pushed it across the desk.

'And as for this Phillips murder,' I said, 'Eddie here was following Phillips a little. You want to tell me why?'

'No.'

'The trouble with a case like this is that the information might come from somebody else. When a murder gets into the papers you never know what will come out. If it does, you'll blame me.'

He looked at me steadily and said : 'I don't think so. I was a bit rough when you came in, but you shape up pretty good. I'll take a chance.'

'Thanks,' I said. 'Would you mind telling me why you had Eddie call me up and give me the shakes?'

He looked down and tapped on the desk. 'Linda's an old friend of mine. Young Murdock was out here this afternoon to see her. He told her you were working for old lady Murdock. She told me. I didn't know what the job was. You say you don't take divorce business, so it couldn't be that the old lady hired you to fix anything like that up.' He raised his eyes on the last words and stared at me.

I stared back at him and waited.

'I guess I'm just a fellow who likes his friends,' he said. 'And doesn't want them bothered by dicks.'

'Murdock owes you some money, doesn't he?'

He frowned. 'I don't discuss things like that.'

He finished his drink, nodded and stood up. 'I'll send Linda up to talk to you. Pick your money up.'

He went to the door and out. Eddie Prue unwound his long body and stood up and gave me a dim grey smile that meant nothing and wandered off after Morny.

I lit another cigarette and looked at the dental supply company's bill again. Something squirmed at the back of my mind, dimly. I walked to the window and stood looking out across the valley. A car was winding up a hill towards a big house with a tower that was half glass brick with light behind it. The headlights of the car moved across it and turned in towards a garage. The lights went out and the valley seemed darker.

It was very quiet and quite cool now. The dance band seemed to be somewhere under my feet. It was muffled, and the tune was indistinguishable.

Linda Conquest came in through the open door behind me and shut it and stood looking at me with a cold light in her eyes.

# Nineteen

She looked like her photo and not like it. She had the wide cool mouth, the short nose, the wide cool eyes, the dark hair parted in the middle and the broad white line between the parting. She was wearing a white coat over her dress, with the collar turned up. She had her hands in the pockets of the coat and a cigarette in her mouth.

She looked older, her eyes were harder, and her lips seemed to have forgotten to smile. They would smile when she was singing, in that staged artificial smile. But in repose they were thin and tight and angry.

She moved over to the desk and stood looking down, as if counting the copper ornaments. She saw the cut-glass decanter, took the stopper out, poured herself a drink and tossed it down with a quick flip of the wrist.

'You're a man named Marlowe?' she asked, looking at me. She put her hips against the end of the desk and crossed her ankles.

I said I was a man named Marlowe.

'By and large,' she said, 'I am quite sure I am not going to like you one damned little bit. So speak your piece and drift away.'

'What I like about this place is everything runs so true to type,' I said. 'The cop on the gate, the shine on the door, the cigarette and check girls, the fat greasy sensual Jew with the tall stately bored showgirl, the well-dressed, drunk and horribly rude director cursing the barman, the silent guy with the gun, the night-club owner with the soft grey hair and the B-picture mannerisms, and now you – the tall dark torcher with the negligent sneer, the husky voice, the hard-boiled vocabulary.'

She said: 'Is that so?' and fitted her cigarette between her lips and drew slowly on it. 'And what about the wise-cracking snooper with the last year's gags and the come-hither smile?'

'And what gives me the right to talk to you at all?' I said.

'I'll bite. What does?'

'She wants it back. Quickly. It has to be fast or there will be trouble.'

'I thought—' she started to say and stopped cold. I watched her remove the sudden trace of interest from her face by monkeying with her cigarette and bending her face over it. 'She wants what back, Mr Marlowe?'

'The Brasher Doubloon.'

She looked up at me and nodded, remembering – letting me see her remembering.

'Oh, the Brasher Doubloon.'

'I bet you completely forgot it,' I said.

'Well, no. I've seen it a number of times,' she said. 'She wants it back, you said. Do you mean she thinks I took it?'

'Yeah. Just that.'

'She's a dirty old liar,' Linda Conquest said.

'What you think doesn't make you a liar,' I said. 'It only sometimes makes you mistaken. Is she wrong?'

'Why would I take her silly old coin?'

'Well – it's worth a lot of money. She thinks you might need

113

money. I gather she was not too generous.'

She laughed, a tight sneering little laugh. 'No,' she said. 'Mrs Elizabeth Bright Murdock would not rate as very generous.'

'Maybe you just took it for spite, kind of,' I said hopefully.

'Maybe I ought to slap your face.' She killed her cigarette in Morny's copper goldfish bowl, speared the crushed stub absently with the letter opener and dropped it into the wastebasket.

'Passing on from that to perhaps more important matters,' I said, 'will you give him a divorce?'

'For twenty-five grand,' she said, not looking at me, 'I should be glad to.'

'You're not in love with the guy, huh?'

'You're breaking my heart, Marlowe.'

'He's in love with you,' I said. 'After all, you did marry him.'

She looked at me lazily. 'Mister, don't think I didn't pay for that mistake.' She lit another cigarette. 'But a girl has to live. And it isn't always as easy as it looks. And so a girl can make a mistake, marry the wrong guy and the wrong family, looking for something that isn't there. Security, or whatever.'

'But not needing any love to do it,' I said.

'I don't want to be too cynical, Marlowe. But you'd be surprised how many girls marry to find a home, especially girls whose arm muscles are all tired out fighting off the kind of optimists that come into these gin and glitter joints.'

'You had a home and you gave it up.'

'It got to be too dear. That port-sodden old fake made the bargain too tough. How do you like her for a client?'

'I've had worse.'

She picked a shred of tobacco off her lip. 'You notice what she's doing to that girl?'

'Merle? I noticed she bullied her.'

'It isn't just that. She has her cutting out dolls. The girl had a shock of some kind and the old brute has used the effect of it to dominate the girl completely. In company she yells at her but in private she's apt to be stroking her hair and whispering in her ear. And the kid sort of shivers.'

'I didn't quite get all that,' I said.

'The kid's in love with Leslie, but she doesn't know it.

Emotionally she's about ten years old. Something funny is going to happen in that family one of these days. I'm glad I won't be there.

I said: 'You're a smart girl, Linda. And you're tough and you're wise. I suppose when you married him you thought you could get your hands on plenty.'

She curled her lip. 'I thought it would at least be a vacation. It wasn't even that. That's a smart, ruthless woman, Marlowe. Whatever she's got you doing, it's not what she says. She's up to something. Watch your step.'

'Would she kill a couple of men?'

She laughed.

'No kidding,' I said. 'A couple of men have been killed and one of them at least is connected with rare coins.'

'I don't get it,' she looked at me levelly. 'Murdered, you mean?'

I nodded.

'You tell Morny all that?'

'About one of them.'

'You tell the cops?'

'About one of them. The same one.'

She moved her eyes over my face. We stared at each other. She looked a little pale, or just tired. I thought she had grown a little paler than before.

'You're making that up,' she said between her teeth.

I grinned and nodded. She seemed to relax then.

'About the Brasher Doubloon?' I said. 'You didn't take it. Okay. About the divorce, what?'

'That's none of your affair.'

'I agree. Well, thanks for talking to me. Do you know a fellow named Vannier?'

'Yes.' Her face froze hard now. 'Not well. He's a friend of Lois.'

'A very good friend.'

'One of these days he's apt to turn out to be a small quiet funeral, too.'

'Hints,' I said, 'have sort of been thrown in that direction. There's something about the guy. Every time his name comes up the party freezes.'

She stared at me and said nothing. I thought that an idea was stirring at the back of her eyes, but if so it didn't come out. She said quietly:

'Morny will sure as hell kill him, if he doesn't lay off Lois.'

'Go on with you. Lois flops at the drop of a hat. Anybody can see that.'

'Perhaps Alex is the one person who can't see it.'

'Vannier hasn't anything to do with my job, anyway. He has no connection with the Murdocks.'

She lifted a corner of her lip at me and said: 'No? Let me tell you something. No reason why I should. I'm just a great big open-hearted kid. Vannier knows Elizabeth Bright Murdock and well. He never came to the house but once while I was there, but he called on the phone plenty of times. I caught some of the calls. He always asked for Merle.'

'Well – that's funny,' I said. 'Merle, huh?'

She bent to crush out her cigarette and again she speared the stub and dropped it into the waste-basket.

'I'm very tired,' she said suddenly. 'Please go away.'

I stood there for a moment, looking at her and wondering. Then I said: 'Good night, and thanks. Good luck.'

I went out and left her standing there with her hands in the pockets of the white coat, her head bent and her eyes looking at the floor.

It was two o'clock when I got back to Hollywood and put the car away and went upstairs to my apartment. The wind was all gone but the air still had that dryness and lightness of the desert. The air in the apartment was dead and Breeze's cigar butt had made it a little worse than dead. I opened windows and flushed the place through while I undressed and stripped the pockets of my suit.

Out of them with other things came the dental supply company's bill. It still looked like a bill to one H. R. Teager for 30 lb of crystobolite and 25 lb of albastone.

I dragged the phone book up on the desk in the living-room and looked up Teager. Then the confused memory clicked into place. His address was 422 West Ninth Street. The address of the Belfont Building was 422 West Ninth Street.

H. R. Teager Dental Laboratories had been one of the names

on doors on the sixth floor of the Belfont Building when I did my backstairs crawl away from the office of Elisha Morningstar.

But even the Pinkertons have to sleep, and Marlowe needed far, far more sleep than the Pinkertons. I went to bed.


# Twenty

It was just as hot in Pasadena as the day before and the big dark red brick house on Dresden Avenue looked just as cool and the little painted negro waiting by the hitching block looked just as sad. The same butterfly landed on the same hydrangea bush – or it looked like the same one – the same heavy scent of summer lay on the morning, and the same middle-aged sourpuss with the frontier voice opened to my ring.

She led me along the same hallways to the same sunless sunroom. In it Mrs Elizabeth Bright Murdock sat in the same reed chaise-longue and as I came into the room she was pouring herself a slug from what looked like the same port bottle but was more probably a grandchild.

The maid shut the door, I sat down and put my hat on the floor, just like yesterday, and Mrs Murdock gave me the same hard level stare and said:

'Well?'

'Things are bad,' I said. 'The cops are after me.'

She looked as flustered as a side of beef. 'Indeed. I thought you were more competent than that.'

I brushed it off. 'When I left here yesterday morning a man followed me in a coupé. I don't know what he was doing here or how he got here. I suppose he followed me here, but I feel doubtful about that. I shook him off, but he turned up again in the hall outside my office. He followed me again, so I invited him to explain why and he said he knew who I was and he needed help and asked me to come to his apartment on Bunker Hill and talk to him. I went, after I had seen Mr Morningstar, and found the man shot to death on the floor of his bathroom.'

Mrs Murdock sipped a little port. Her hand might have

shaken a little, but the light in the room was too dim for me to be sure. She cleared her throat.

'Go on.'

'His name is George Anson Phillips. A young, blond fellow, rather dumb. He claimed to be a private detective.'

'I never heard of him,' Mrs Murdock said coldly. 'I never saw him to my knowledge and I don't know anything about him. Did you think I employed him to follow you?'

'I didn't know what to think. He talked about pooling our resources and he gave me the impression that he was working for some member of your family. He didn't say so in so many words.'

'He wasn't. You can be quite definite on that.' The baritone voice was as steady as a rock.

'I don't think you know quite as much about your family as you think you do, Mrs Murdock.'

'I know you have been questioning my son – contrary to my orders,' she said coldly.

'I didn't question him. He questioned me. Or tried to.'

'We'll go into that later,' she said harshly. 'What about this man you found shot? You are involved with the police on account of him?'

'Naturally. They want to know why he followed me, what I was working on, why he spoke to me, why he asked me to come to his apartment and why I went. But that is only half of it.'

She finished her port and poured herself another glass.

'How's your asthma?' I asked.

'Bad,' she said. 'Get on with your story.'

'I saw Morningstar. I told you about that over the phone. He pretended not to have the Brasher Doubloon, but admitted it had been offered to him and said he could get it. As I told you. Then you told me it had been returned to you, so that was that.'

I waited, thinking she would tell me some story about how the coin had been returned, but she just stared at me bleakly over the wineglass.

'So, as I had made a sort of arrangement with Mr Morningstar to pay him a thousand dollars for the coin—'

'You had no authority to do anything like that,' she barked.

I nodded, agreeing with her.

'Maybe I was kidding him a little,' I said. 'And I know I was kidding myself. Anyway, after what you told me over the phone I tried to get in touch with him to tell him the deal was off. He's not in the phone book except at his office. I went to his office. This was quite late. The elevator man said he was still in his office. He was lying on his back on the floor, dead. Killed by a blow on the head and shock, apparently. Old men die easily. The blow might not have been intended to kill him. I called the Receiving Hospital, but didn't give my name.'

'That was wise of you,' she said.

'Was it? It was considerate of me, but I don't think I'd call it wise. I want to be nice, Mrs Murdock. You understand that in your rough way, I hope. But two murders happened in the matter of hours and both the bodies were found by me. And both the victims were connected – in some manner – with your Brasher Doubloon.'

'I don't understand. This other, younger man also?'

'Yes. Didn't I tell you over the phone? I thought I did.' I wrinkled my brow, thinking back. I knew I had.

She said calmly: 'It's possible. I wasn't paying a great deal of attention to what you said. You see, the doubloon had already been returned. And you sounded a little drunk.'

'I wasn't drunk. I might have felt a little shock, but I wasn't drunk. You take all this very calmly.'

'What do you want me to do?'

I took a deep breath. 'I'm connected with one murder already, by having found the body and reported it. I may presently be connected with another, by having found the body and not reported it. Which is much more serious for me. Even as far as it goes, I have until noon today to disclose the name of my client.'

'That,' she said, still much too calm for my taste, 'would be a breach of confidence. You are not going to do that, I'm sure.'

'I wish you'd leave that damn port alone and make some effort to understand the position,' I snapped at her.

She looked vaguely surprised and pushed her glass away – about four inches away.

'This fellow Phillips,' I said, 'had a licence as a private detective. How did I happen to find him dead? Because he followed

119

me and I spoke to him and he asked me to come to his apartment. And when I got there he was dead. The police know all this. They may even believe it. But they don't believe the connection between Phillips and me is quite that much of a coincidence. They think there is a deeper connection between Phillips and me and they insist on knowing what I am doing, who I am working for. Is that clear?'

'You'll find a way out of all that,' she said. 'I expect it to cost me a little more money, of course.'

I felt myself getting pinched around the nose. My mouth felt dry. I needed air. I took another deep breath and another dive into the tub of blubber that was sitting across the room from me on the reed chaise-longue, looking as unperturbed as a bank president refusing a loan.

'I'm working for you,' I said, 'now, this week, today. Next week I'll be working for somebody else, I hope. And the week after that for still somebody else. In order to do that I have to be on reasonably good terms with the police. They don't have to love me, but they have to be fairly sure I am not cheating on them. Assume Phillips knew nothing about the Brasher Doubloon. Assume, even, that he knew about it, but that his death had nothing to do with it. I still have to tell the cops what I know about him. And they have to question anybody they want to question. Can't you understand that?'

'Doesn't the law give you the right to protect a client?' she snapped. 'If it doesn't, what is the use of anyone's hiring a detective?'

I got up and walked around my chair and sat down again. I leaned forward and took hold of my kneecaps and squeezed them until my knuckles glistened.

'The law, whatever it is, is a matter of give-and-take, Mrs Murdock. Like most other things. Even if I had the legal right to stay clammed-up – refuse to talk – and got away with it once, that would be the end of my business. I'd be a guy marked for trouble. One way or another they would get me. I value your business, Mrs Murdock, but not enough to cut my throat for you and bleed in your lap.'

She reached for her glass and emptied it.

'You seem to have made a nice mess of the whole thing,' she

said. 'You didn't find my daughter-in-law and you didn't find my Brasher Doubloon. But you found a couple of dead men that I have nothing to do with and you have neatly arranged matters so that I must tell the police all my private and personal business in order to protect you from your own incompetence. That's what I see. If I am wrong, pray correct me.'

She poured some more wine and gulped it too fast and went into a paroxysm of coughing. Her shaking hand slid the glass on to the table, slopping the wine. She threw herself forward in her seat and got purple in the face.

I jumped up and went over and landed one on her beefy back that would have shaken the City Hall.

She let out a long strangled wail and drew her breath in rackingly and stopped coughing. I pressed one of the keys on her dictaphone-box and when somebody answered, metallic and loud, through the metal disc, I said: 'Bring Mrs Murdock a glass of water, quick!' and then let the key up again.

I sat down again and watched her pull herself together. When her breath was coming evenly and without effort, I said: 'You're not tough. You just think you're tough. You been living too long with people that are scared of you. Wait'll you meet up with some law. Those boys are professionals. You're just a spoiled amateur.'

The door opened and the maid came in with a pitcher of ice-water and a glass. She put them down on the table and went out.

I poured Mrs Murdock a glass of water and put it in her hand.

'Sip it, don't drink it. You won't like the taste of it, but it won't hurt you.'

She sipped, then drank half of the glass, then put the glass down and wiped her lips.

'To think,' she said raspingly, 'that out of all the snoopers for hire I could have employed, I had to pick out a man who would bully me in my own home.'

'That's not getting you anywhere, either,' I said. 'We don't have a lot of time. What's our story to the police going to be?'

'The police mean nothing to me. Absolutely nothing. And if you give them my name, I shall regard it as a thoroughly disgusting breach of faith.'

That put me back where we started.

'Murder changes everything, Mrs Murdock. You can't dummy up on a murder case. We'll have to tell them why you employed me and what to do. They won't publish it in the papers, you know. That is, they won't if they believe it. They certainly won't believe you hired me to investigate Elisha Morningstar just because he called up and wanted to buy the doubloon. They may not find out that you couldn't have sold the coin, if you wanted to, because they might not think of that angle. But they won't believe you hired a private detective just to investigate a possible purchaser. Why should you?'

'That's my business, isn't it?'

'No. You can't fob the cops off that way. You have to satisfy them that you are being frank and open and have nothing to hide. As long as they think you are hiding something they never let up. Give them a reasonable and plausible story and they go away cheerful. And the most reasonable and plausible story is always the truth. Any objection to telling it?'

'Every possible objection,' she said. 'But it doesn't seem to make much difference. Do we have to tell them I suspected my daughter-in-law of stealing the coin and that I was wrong?'

'It would be better.'

'And that it has been returned and how?'

'It would be better.'

'That is going to humiliate me very much.'

I shrugged.

'You're a callous brute,' she said. 'You're a cold-blooded fish. I don't like you. I deeply regret ever having met you.'

'Mutual,' I said.

She reached a thick finger to a key and barked into the talking-box. 'Merle. Ask my son to come in here at once. And I think you may as well come in with him.'

She released the key, pressed her broad fingers together and let her hands drop heavily to her thighs. Her bleak eyes went up to the ceiling.

Her voice was quiet and sad, saying: 'My son took the coin, Mr Marlowe. My son. My own son.'

I didn't say anything. We sat there glaring at each other. In a couple of minutes they both came in and she barked at them to sit down.

# Twenty-one

Leslie Murdock was wearing a greenish slack suit and his hair looked damp, as if he had just been taking a shower. He sat hunched forward, looking at the white buck shoes on his feet, and turning a ring on his finger. He didn't have his long black cigarette-holder and he looked a little lonely without it. Even his moustache seemed to droop a little more than it had in my office.

Merle Davis looked just the same as the day before. Probably she always looked the same. Her copper blonde hair was dragged down just as tight, her shell-rimmed glasses looked just as large and empty, her eyes behind them just as vague. She was even wearing the same one-piece linen dress with short sleeves and no ornament of any kind, not even earrings.

I had the curious feeling of re-living something that had already happened.

Mrs Murdock sipped her port and said quietly:

'All right, son. Tell Mr Marlowe about the doubloon. I'm afraid he has to be told.'

Murdock looked up at me quickly and then dropped his eyes again. His mouth twitched. When he spoke his voice had the toneless quality, a flat tired sound, like a man making a confession after an exhausting battle with his conscience.

'As I told you yesterday in your office, I owe Morny a lot of money. Twelve thousand dollars. I denied it afterwards, but it's true. I do owe it. I didn't want mother to know. He was pressing me pretty hard for payment. I suppose I knew I would have to tell her in the end, but I was weak enough to want to put it off. I took the doubloon, using her keys one afternoon when she was asleep and Merle was out. I gave it to Morny and he agreed to hold it as security because I explained to him that he couldn't get anything like twelve thousand dollars for it unless he could give its history and show that it was legitimately in his possession.'

He stopped talking and looked up at me to see how I was taking it. Mrs Murdock had her eyes on my face, practically puttied there. The little girl was looking at Murdock with her lips parted and an expression of suffering on her face.

Murdock went on. 'Morny gave me a receipt, in which he agreed to hold the coin as collateral and not to convert it without notice and demand. Something like that. I don't profess to know how legal it was. When this man Morningstar called up and asked about the coin I immediately became suspicious that Morny either was trying to sell it or that he was at least thinking of selling it and was trying to get a valuation on it from somebody who knew about rare coins. I was badly scared.'

He looked up and made a sort of face at me. Maybe it was the face of somebody being badly scared. Then he took his handkerchief out and wiped his forehead and sat holding it between his hands.

'When Merle told me mother had employed a detective – Merle ought not to have told me, but mother has promised not to scold her for it.' He looked at his mother. The old warhorse clamped her jaws and looked grim. The little girl had her eyes still on his face and didn't seem to be very worried about the scolding. He went on: 'Then I was sure she had missed the doubloon and had hired you on that account. I didn't really believe she had hired you to find Linda. I knew where Linda was all the time. I went to your office to see what I could find out. I didn't find out very much. I went to see Morny yesterday afternoon and told him about it. At first he laughed in my face, but when I told him that even my mother couldn't sell the coin without violating the terms of Jasper Murdock's will and that she would certainly set the police on him when I told her where the coin was, then he loosened up. He got up and went to the safe and got the coin out and handed it to me without a word. I gave him back his receipt and he tore it up. So I brought the coin home and told mother about it.'

He stopped talking and wiped his face again. The little girl's eyes moved up and down with the motions of his hand.

In the silence that followed I said: 'Did Morny threaten you?'

He shook his head. 'He said he wanted his money and he needed it and I had better get busy and dig it up. But he wasn't threatening. He was very decent, really. In the circumstances.'

'Where was this?'

'At the Idle Valley Club, in his private office.'

'Was Eddie Prue there?'

The little girl tore her eyes away from his face and looked at me. Mrs Murdock said thickly: 'Who is Eddie Prue?'

'Morny's bodyguard,' I said. 'I didn't waste *all* my time yesterday, Mrs Murdock.' I looked at her son, waiting.

He said: 'No, I didn't see him. I know him by sight, of course. You would only have to see him once to remember him. But he wasn't around yesterday.'

I said: 'Is that all?'

He looked at his mother. She said harshly: 'Isn't it enough?'

'Maybe,' I said. 'Where is the coin now?'

'Where would you expect it to be?' she snapped.

I almost told her, just to see her jump. But I managed to hold it in. I said: 'That seems to take care of that, then.'

Mrs Murdock said heavily: 'Kiss your mother, son, and run along.'

He got up dutifully and went over and kissed her on the forehead. She patted his hand. He went out of the room with his head down and quietly shut the door. I said to Merle: 'I think you had better have him dictate that to you just the way he told it and make a copy of it and get him to sign it.'

She looked startled. The old woman snarled:

'She certainly won't do anything of the sort. Go back to your work, Merle. I wanted you to hear this. But if I ever again catch you violating my confidence, you know what will happen.'

The little girl stood up and smiled at her with shining eyes. 'Oh, yes, Mrs Murdock. I never will. Never. You can trust me.'

'I hope so,' the old dragon growled. 'Get out.'

Merle went out softly.

Two big tears formed themselves in Mrs Murdock's eyes and slowly made their way down the elephant hide of her cheeks, reached the corners of her fleshy nose and slid down her lip. She scrabbled around for a handkerchief, wiped them off and then wiped her eyes. She put the handkerchief away, reached for her wine and said placidly:

'I'm very fond of my son, Mr Marlowe. Very fond. This grieves me deeply. Do you think he will have to tell this story to the police?'

'I hope not,' I said. 'He'd have a hell of a time getting them to believe it.'

Her mouth snapped open and her teeth glinted at me in the dim light. She closed her lips and pressed them tight, scowling at me with her head lowered.

'Just what do you mean by that?' she snapped.

'Just what I said. The story doesn't ring true. It has a fabricated, over-simple sound. Did he make it up himself or did you think it up and teach it to him?'

'Mr Marlowe,' she said in a deadly voice, 'you are treading on very thin ice.'

I waved a hand. 'Aren't we all? All right, suppose it's true. Morny will deny it, and we'll be right back where we started. Morny will have to deny it, because otherwise it would tie him to a couple of murders.'

'Is there anything so unlikely about that being the exact situation?' she blared.

'Why would Morny, a man with backing, protection and some influence, tie himself to a couple of small murders in order to avoid tying himself to something trifling, like selling a pledge? It doesn't make sense to me.'

She stared, saying nothing. I grinned at her, because for the first time she was going to like something I said.

'I found your daughter-in-law, Mrs Murdock. It's a little strange to me that your son, who seems so well under your control, didn't tell you where she was.'

'I didn't ask him,' she said in a curiously quiet voice, for her.

'She's back where she started, singing with the band at the Idle Valley Club. I talked to her. She's a pretty hard sort of girl in a way. She doesn't like you very well. I don't find it impossible to think that she took the coin all right, partly from spite. And I find it slightly less impossible to believe that Leslie knew it or found it out and cooked up that yarn to protect her. He says he's very much in love with her.'

She smiled. It wasn't a beautiful smile, being on slightly the wrong kind of face. But it was a smile.

'Yes,' she said gently. 'Yes. Poor Leslie. He would do just that. And in that case' – she stopped and her smile widened until

126

it was almost ecstatic – 'in that case my dear daughter-in-law may be involved in murder.'

I watched her enjoying the idea for a quarter of a minute. 'And you'd just love that,' I said.

She nodded, still smiling, getting the idea she liked before she got the rudeness in my voice. Then her face stiffened and her lips came together hard. Between them and her teeth she said:

'I don't like your tone. I don't like your tone at all.'

'I don't blame you,' I said. 'I don't like it myself. I don't like anything. I don't like this house or you or the air of repression in the joint, or the squeezed down face of the little girl or that twerp of a son you have, or this case or the truth I'm not told about it and the lies I am told about it and—'

She started yelling then, noise out of a splotched furious face, eyes tossing with fury, sharp with hate:

'Get out! Get out of this house at once! Don't delay one instant! Get out!'

I stood up and reached my hat off the carpet and said:

'I'll be glad to.'

I gave her a sort of tired leer and picked my way to the door and opened it and went out. I shut it quietly, holding the knob with a stiff hand and clicking the lock gently into place.

For no reason at all.


# Twenty-two

Steps gibbered along after me and my name was called and I kept on going until I was in the middle of the living-room. Then I stopped and turned and let her catch up with me, out of breath, her eyes trying to pop through her glasses and her shining copper-blonde hair catching funny little lights from the high windows.

'Mr Marlowe? Please! Please, don't go away. She wants you. She really does!'

127

'I'll be darned. You've got Sub-deb Bright on your mouth this morning. Looks all right, too.'

She grabbed my sleeve. 'Please!'

'The hell with her,' I said. 'Tell her to jump in the lake. Marlowe can get sore, too. Tell her to jump in two lakes, if one won't hold her. Not clever, but quick.'

I looked down at the hand on my sleeve and patted it. She drew it away swiftly and her eyes looked shocked.

'Please, Mr Marlowe. She's in trouble. She needs you.'

'I'm in trouble, too,' I growled. 'I'm up to my earflaps in trouble. What are you crying about?'

'Oh, I'm really very fond of her. I know she's rough and blustery, but her heart is pure gold.'

'To hell with her heart, too,' I said. 'I don't expect to get intimate enough with her for that to make any difference. She's a fat-faced old liar. I've had enough of her. I think she's in trouble all right, but I'm not in the excavating business. I have to get told things.'

'Oh, I'm sure if you would only be patient—'

I put my arm around her shoulders, without thinking. She jumped about three feet and her eyes blazed with panic.

We stood there staring at each other, making breath noises, me with my mouth open as it too frequently is, she with her lips pressed tight and her little pale nostrils quivering. Her face was as pale as the unhandy make-up would let it be.

'Look,' I said slowly, 'did something happen to you when you were a little girl?'

She nodded, very quickly.

'A man scared you or something like that?'

She nodded again. She took her lower lip between her little white teeth.

'And you've been like this ever since?'

She just stood there, looking white.

'Look,' I said, 'I won't do anything to you that will scare you. Not ever.'

Her eyes melted with tears.

'If I touched you,' I said, 'it was just like touching a chair or a door. It didn't mean anything. Is that clear?'

'Yes.' She got a word out at last. Panic still twitched in the

128

depths of her eyes, behind the tears. 'Yes.'

'That takes care of me,' I said. 'I'm all adjusted. Nothing to worry about in me any more. Now take Leslie. He has his mind on other things. You know he's all right – in the way we mean. Right?'

'Oh, yes,' she said. 'Yes, indeed.' Leslie was aces. With her. With me he was a handful of bird gravel.

'Now take the old wine barrel,' I said. 'She's rough and she's tough and she thinks she can eat walls and spit bricks, and she bawls you out, but she's fundamentally decent to you, isn't she?'

'Oh, she is, Mr Marlowe. I was trying to tell you—'

'Sure. Now why don't you get over it? Is he still around – this other one that hurt you?'

She put her hand to her mouth and gnawed the fleshy part at the base of the thumb, looking at me over it, as if it was a balcony.

'He's dead,' she said. 'He fell out of a – out of a – a window.'

I stopped her with my big right hand. 'Oh, that guy. I heard about him. Forget it, can't you?'

'No,' she said, shaking her head seriously behind the hand. 'I can't. I can't seem to forget it at all. Mrs Murdock is always telling me to forget it. She talks to me for the longest times telling me to forget it. But I just can't.'

'It would be a darn sight better,' I snarled, 'if she would keep her fat mouth shut about it for the longest times. She just keeps it alive.'

She looked surprised and rather hurt at that. 'Oh, that isn't all,' she said. 'I was his secretary. She was his wife. He was her first husband. Naturally she doesn't forget it either. How could she?'

I scratched my ear. That seemed sort of noncommittal. There was nothing much in her expression now except that I didn't really think she realized that I was there. I was a voice coming out of somewhere, but rather impersonal. Almost a voice in her own head.

Then I had one of my funny and often unreliable hunches. 'Look,' I said, 'is there someone you meet that has that effect on you? Some one person more than another?'

She looked all around the room. I looked with her. Nobody

129

was under a chair or peeking at us through a door or a window.

'Why do I have to tell you?' she breathed.

'You don't. It's just how you feel about it.'

'Will you promise not to tell anybody – anybody in the whole world, not even Mrs Murdock?'

'Her last of all,' I said. 'I promise.'

She opened her mouth and put a funny little confiding smile on her face, and then it went wrong. Her throat froze up. She made a croaking noise. Her teeth actually rattled.

I wanted to give her a good hard squeeze but I was afraid to touch her. We stood. Nothing happened. We stood. I was about as much use as a humming-bird's spare egg would have been.

Then she turned and ran. I heard her steps going along the hall. I heard a door close.

I went after her along the hall and reached the door. She was sobbing behind it. I stood there and listened to the sobbing.

There was nothing I could do about it. I wondered if there was anything anybody could do about it.

I went back to the glass porch and knocked on the door and opened it and put my head in. Mrs Murdock sat just as I had left her. She didn't seem to have moved at all.

'Who's scaring the life out of that little girl?' I asked her.

'Get out of my house,' she said between her fat lips.

I didn't move. Then she laughed at me hoarsely.

'Do you regard yourself as a clever man, Mr Marlowe?'

'Well, I'm not dripping with it,' I said.

'Suppose you find out for yourself.'

'At your expense?'

She shrugged her heavy shoulders. 'Possibly. It depends. Who knows?'

'You haven't bought a thing,' I said. 'I'm still going to have to talk to the police.'

'I haven't bought anything,' she said, 'and I haven't paid for anything. Except the return of the coin. I'm satisfied to accept that for the money I have already given you. Now go away. You bore me. Unspeakably.'

I shut the door and went back. No sobbing behind the door. Very still. I went on.

I let myself out of the house. I stood there, listening to the

130

sunshine burn the grass. A car started up in back and a grey Mercury came drifting along the drive at the side of the house. Mr Leslie Murdock was driving it. When he saw me he stopped.

He got out of the car and walked quickly over to me. He was nicely dressed; all fresh clothes now, cream-coloured gaberdine slacks, black and white shoes, with polished black toes, a sport coat of very small black and white check, black and white handkerchief, cream shirt, no tie. He had a pair of green sun-glasses on his nose.

He stood close to me and said in a low timid sort of voice: 'I guess you think I'm an awful heel.'

'On account of that story you told about the doubloon?'

'Yes.'

'That didn't affect my way of thinking about you in the least,' I said.

'Well—'

'Just what do you want me to say?'

He moved his smoothly tailored shoulders in a deprecatory shrug. His silly little reddish-brown moustache glittered in the sun.

'I suppose I like to be liked,' he said.

'I'm sorry, Murdock. I like your being that devoted to your wife. If that's what it is.'

'Oh. Didn't you think I was telling the truth? I mean, did you think I was saying all that just to protect her?'

'There was that possibility.'

'I see.' He put a cigarette into the long black holder, which he took from behind his display handkerchief. 'Well – I guess I can take it that you don't like me.' The dim movement of his eyes was visible behind the green lenses, fish moving in a deep pool.

'It's a silly subject,' I said. 'And damned unimportant. To both of us.'

He put a match to the cigarette and inhaled. 'I see,' he said quietly. 'Pardon me for being crude enough to bring it up.'

He turned on his heel and walked back to his car and got in. I watched him drive away before I moved. Then I went over and patted the little painted negro boy on the head a couple of times before I left.

'Son,' I said to him, 'you're the only person around this house that's not nuts.'

## Twenty-three

The police loudspeaker-box on the wall grunted and a voice said: 'KGPL. Testing.' A click and it went dead.

Detective-Lieutenant Jesse Breeze stretched his arms high in the air and yawned and said: 'Couple of hours late, ain't you?'

I said: 'Yes. But I left a message for you that I would be. I had to go to the dentist.'

'Sit down.'

He had a small littered desk across one corner of the room. He sat in the angle behind it, with a tall bare window to his left and a wall with a large calendar about eye height to his right. The days that had gone down to dust were crossed off carefully in soft black pencil, so that Breeze glancing at the calendar always knew exactly what day it was.

Spangler was sitting sideways at a smaller and much neater desk. It had a green blotter and an onyx pen set and a small brass calendar and an abalone shell full of ashes and matches and cigarette-stubs. Spangler was flipping a handful of bank pens at the felt back of a seat cushion on end against the wall, like a Mexican knife-thrower flipping knives at a target. He wasn't getting anywhere with it. The pens refused to stick.

The room had that remote, heartless, not quite dirty, not quite clean, not quite human smell that such rooms always have. Give a police department a brand new building and in three months all its rooms will smell like that. There must be something symbolic in it.

A New York police reporter wrote once that when you pass in beyond the green lights of the precinct station you pass clear out of this world into a place beyond the law.

I sat down. Breeze got a cellophane-wrapped cigar out of his pocket and the routine with it started. I watched it detail by detail, unvarying, precise. He drew in smoke, shook his match

132

out, laid it gently in the black glass ashtray, and said: 'Hi, Spangler.'

Spangler turned his head and Breeze turned his head. They grinned at each other. Breeze poked the cigar at me.

'Watch him sweat,' he said.

Spangler had to move his feet to turn far enough around to watch me sweat. If I was sweating, I didn't know it.

'You boys are as cute as a couple of lost golf-balls,' I said. 'How in the world do you do it?'

'Skip the wisecracks,' Breeze said. 'Had a busy little morning?'

'Fair,' I said.

He was still grinning. Spangler was still grinning. Whatever it was Breeze was tasting he hated to swallow it.

Finally he cleared his throat, straightened his big freckled face out, turned his head enough so that he was not looking at me but could still see me and said in a vague empty sort of voice:

'Hench confessed.'

Spangler swung clear around to look at me. He leaned forward on the edge of his chair and his lips were parted in an ecstatic half-smile that was almost indecent.

I said: 'What did you use on him – a pickaxe?'

'Nope.'

They were both silent, staring at me.

'A wop,' Breeze said.

'A what?'

'Boy, are you glad?' Breeze said.

'You are going to tell me or are you just going to sit there looking fat and complacent and watch me being glad?'

'We like to watch a guy being glad,' Breeze said. 'We don't often get a chance.'

I put a cigarette in my mouth and jiggled it up and down.

'We used a wop on him,' Breeze said. 'A wop named Palermo.'

'Oh. You know something?'

'What?' Breeze asked.

'I just thought of what is the matter with policeman's dialogue.'

'What?'

133

'They think every line is a punch line.'

'And every pinch is a good pinch,' Breeze said calmly. 'You want to know – or you want to just crack wise?'

'I want to know.'

'Was like this, then. Hench was drunk. I mean he was drunk deep inside, not just on the surface. Screwy drunk. He'd been living on it for weeks. He'd practically quit eating and sleeping. Just liquor.. He'd got to the point where liquor wasn't making him drunk, it was keeping him sober. It was the last hold he had on the real world. When a guy gets like that and you take his liquor away and don't give him anything to hold him down, he's a lost cuckoo.'

I didn't say anything. Spangler still had the same erotic leer on his young face. Breeze tapped the side of his cigar and no ash fell off and he put it back in his mouth and went on.

'He's a psycho case, but we don't want any psycho case made out of our pinch. We made that clear. We want a guy that don't have any psycho record.'

'I thought you were sure Hench was innocent.'

Breeze nodded vaguely. 'That was last night. Or maybe I was kidding a little. Anyway in the night, bang, Hench is bugs. So they drag him over to the hospital ward and shoot him full of hop. The jail doc. does. That's between you and me. No hop in the record. Get the idea?'

'All too clearly,' I said.

'Yeah.' He looked vaguely suspicious of the remark, but he was too full of his subject to waste time on it. 'Well, this a.m. he is fine. Hop still working, the guy is pale but peaceful. We go see him. How you doing, kid? Anything you need? Any little thing at all? Be glad to get it for you. They treating you nice in here? You know the line.'

'I do,' I said. 'I know the line.'

Spangler licked his lips in a nasty way.

'So after a while he opens his trap just enough to say "Palermo." Palermo is the name of the wop across the street that owns the funeral home and the apartment house and stuff. You remember? Yeah, you remember. On account of he said something about a tall blonde. All hooey. Them wops got tall blondes on the brain. In sets of twelve. But this Palermo is important. I asked around. He gets the vote out up there. He's a guy that can't be pushed around. Well, I don't aim to push him around. I say to Hench, "You mean Palermo's a friend of yours?" He says, "Get Palermo." So we come back here to the hutch and phone Palermo, and Palermo says he will be right down. Okay. He is here very soon. We talk like this: Hench wants to see you, Mr Palermo. I wouldn't know why. He's a poor guy, Palermo says. A nice guy. I think he's okay. He wanta see me, that's a fine. I see him. I see him alone. Without any coppers. I say, Okay, Mr Palermo, and we go over to the hospital ward and Palermo talks to Hench and nobody listens. After a while Palermo comes out and he says, Okay, copper. He make the confess. I pay the lawyer, maybe. I like the poor guy. Just like that. He goes away.'

I didn't say anything. There was a pause. The loudspeaker on the wall put out a bulletin and Breeze cocked his head and listened to ten or twelve words and then ignored it.

'So we go in with a steno and Hench gives us the dope. Phillips made a pass at Hench's girl. That was day before yesterday, out in the hall. Hench was in the room and he saw it, but Phillips got into his apartment and shut the door before Hench could get out. But Hench was sore. He socked the girl in the eye. But that didn't satisfy him. He got to brooding, the way a drunk will brood. He says to himself, that guy can't make a pass at my girl. I'm the boy that will give him something to remember me by. So he keeps an eye open for Phillips. Yesterday afternoon he sees Phillips go into his apartment. He tells the girl to go for a walk. She don't want to go for a walk, so Hench socks her in the other eye. She goes for a walk. Hench knocks on Phillips's door and Phillips opens it. Hench is a little surprised at that, but I told him Phillips was expecting you. Anyway, the door opens and Hench goes in and tells Phillips how he feels and what he is going to do and Phillips is scared and pulls a gun. Hench hits him with a sap. Phillips falls down and Hench ain't satisfied. You hit a guy with a sap and he falls down and what have you? No satisfaction, no revenge. Hench picks the gun off the floor and he is very drunk there being dissatisfied and Phillips grabs for his ankle. Hench doesn't know why he did what he did then. He's all fuzzy in the head. He drags

Phillips into the bathroom and gives him the business with his own gun. You like it?'

'I love it,' I said. 'But what is the satisfaction in it for Hench?'

'Well, you know how a drunk is. Anyway, he gives him the business. Well it ain't Hench's gun, you see, but he can't make a suicide out of it. There wouldn't be any satisfaction for him in that. So Hench takes the gun away and puts it under his pillow and takes his own gun out and ditches it. He won't tell us where. Probably passes it to some tough guy in the neighbourhood. Then he finds the girl and they eat.'

'That was a lovely touch,' I said. 'Putting the gun under his pillow. I'd never in the world have thought of that.'

Breeze leaned back in his chair and looked at the ceiling. Spangler, the big part of the entertainment over, swung around in his chair and picked up a couple of bank pens and threw one at the cushion.

'Look at it this way,' Breeze said. 'What was the effect of that stunt? Look how Hench did it. He was drunk, but he was smart. He found that gun and showed it before Phillips was found dead. First we get the idea that a gun is under Hench's pillow that killed a guy – been fired anyway – and then we get the stiff. We believed Hench's story. It seemed reasonable. Why would we think any man would be such a sap as to do what Hench did? It doesn't make any sense. So we believed somebody put the gun under Hench's pillow and took Hench's gun away and ditched it. And suppose Hench ditched the death gun instead of his own, would he have been any better off? Things being what they were we would be bound to suspect him. And that way he wouldn't have started our minds thinking any particular way about him. The way he did he got us thinking he was a harmless drunk that went out and left his door open and somebody ditched a gun on him.'

He waited, with his mouth a little open and the cigar in front of it, held up by a hard freckled hand, and his pale blue eyes full of dim satisfaction.

'Well,' I said, 'if he was going to confess anyway, it wouldn't have made very much difference. Will he cop a plea?'

'Sure. I think so. I figure Palermo could get him off with manslaughter. Naturally, I'm not sure.'

'Why would Palermo want to get him off with anything?'

'He kind of likes Hench. And Palermo is a guy we can't push around.'

I said: 'I see.' I stood up. Spangler looked at me sideways along glistening eyes. 'What about the girl?'

'Won't say a word. She's smart. We can't do anything to her. Nice neat little job all around. You wouldn't kick, would you? Whatever your business is, it's still your business. Get me?'

'And the girl is a tall blonde,' I said. 'Not of the freshest, but still a tall blonde. Although only one. Maybe Palermo doesn't mind.'

'Hell, I never thought of that,' Breeze said. He thought about it and shook it off. 'Nothing in that, Marlowe. Not enough class.'

'Cleaned up and sober, you never can tell,' I said. 'Class is a thing that has a way of dissolving rapidly in alcohol. That all you want with me?'

'Guess so.' He slanted the cigar up and aimed it at my eye. 'Not that I wouldn't like to hear your story. But I don't figure I have an absolute right to insist on it the way things are.'

'That's white of you, Breeze,' I said. 'And you, too, Spangler. A lot of the good things in life to both of you.'

They watched me go out, both with their mouths a little open.

I rode down to the big marble lobby and went and got my car out of the official parking lot.

# Twenty-four

Mr Pietro Palermo was sitting in a room which, except for a mahogany roll-top desk, a sacred triptych in gilt frames and a large ebony and ivory crucifixion, looked exactly like a Victorian parlour. It contained a horseshoe sofa and chairs with carved mahogany frames and antimacassars of fine lace. There was an ormolu clock on the grey-green marble mantel, a grandfather clock ticking lazily in the corner, and some wax flowers under a glass dome on an oval table with a marble top and curved elegant legs. The carpet was thick and full of gentle sprays of flowers. There was even a cabinet for bric-a-brac and there was plenty of bric-a-brac in it, little cups in fine china, little figurines in glass and porcelain, odds and ends of ivory and dark rosewood, painted saucers, an early American set of swan salt-cellars, stuff like that.

Long lace curtains hung across the windows, but the room faced south and there was plenty of light. Across the street I could see the windows of the apartment where George Anson Phillips had been killed. The street between was sunny and silent.

The tall Italian with the dark skin and the handsome head of iron grey hair read my card and said:

'I got business in twelve minutes. What you want, Meester Marlowe?'

'I'm the man that found the dead man across the street yesterday. He was a friend of mine.'

His cold black eyes looked me over silently. 'That'sa not what you tell Luke.'

'Luke?'

'He manage the joint for me.'

'I don't talk much to strangers, Mr Palermo.'

'That'sa good. You talk to me, huh?'

'You're a man of standing, an important man. I can talk to you. You saw me yesterday. You described me to the police. Very accurately, they said.'

'Si. I see much,' he said without emotion.

'You saw a tall blonde woman come out of there yesterday.'

He studied me. 'Not yesterday. Wasa two three days ago. I tell the coppers yesterday.' He snapped his long dark fingers. 'The coppers, bah!'

'Did you see any strangers yesterday, Mr Palermo?'

'Is back way in and out,' he said. 'Is stair from second floor also.' He looked at his wrist-watch.

'Nothing there then,' I said. 'This morning you saw Hench.'

He lifted his eyes and ran them lazily over my face.

'The coppers tell you that, huh?'

'They told me you got Hench to confess. They said he was a friend of yours. How good a friend they didn't know, of course.'

'Hench make the confess, huh?' He smiled, a sudden brilliant smile.

'Only Hench didn't do the killing,' I said.

'No?'

'No.'

'That'sa interesting. Go on, Meester Marlowe.'

'The confession is a lot of baloney. You got him to make it for some reason of your own.'

He stood up and went to the door and called out: 'Tony.'

He sat down again. A short, tough-looking wop came into the room, looked at me and sat down against the wall in a straight chair.

'Tony, thees man a Meester Marlowe. Look, take the card.'

Tony came to get the card and sat down with it. 'You look at thees man very good, Tony. Not forget him, huh?'

Tony said: 'Leave it to me, Mr Palermo.'

Palermo said: 'Was a friend to you, huh? A good friend, huh?'

'Yes.'

'That'sa bad. Yeah. That'sa bad. I tell you something. A man's friend is a man's friend. So I tell you. But you don' tell anybody else. Not the damn coppers, huh?'

'No.'

'That'sa promise, Meester Marlowe. That'sa something not to forget. You not forget?'

'I won't forget.'

'Tony, he not forget you. Get the idea?'

'I gave you my word. What you tell me is between us here.'

'That'sa fine. Okay. I come of large family. Many sisters and brothers. One brother very bad. Almost so bad as Tony.'

Tony grinned.

'Okay, thees brother live very quiet. Across the street. Gotta move. Okay, the coppers fill the joint up. Not so good. Ask too many questions. Not good for business, not good for thees bad brother. You get the idea?'

'Yes,' I said. 'I get the idea.'

'Okay, thees Hench no good, but poor guy, drunk, no job. Pay no rent, but I got lotsa money. So I say, Look, Hench, you make the confess. You sick man. Two three weeks sick. You go into court. I have a lawyer for you. You say to hell with the confess. I was drunk. The damn coppers are stuck. The judge he turn you loose and you come back to me and I take care of you. Okay? So Hench say okay, make the confess. That'sa all.'

I said: 'And after two or three weeks the bad brother is a long way from here and the trail is cold and the cops will likely just write the Phillips killing off as unsolved. Is that it?'

'Si.' He smiled again. A brilliant warm smile, like the kiss of death.

'That takes care of Hench, Mr Palermo,' I said. 'But it doesn't help me much about my friend.'

He shook his head and looked at his watch again. I stood up. Tony stood up. He wasn't going to do anything, but it's better to be standing up. You move faster.

'The trouble with you birds,' I said, 'is you make mystery of nothing. You have to give the password before you bite a piece of bread. If I went down to headquarters and told the boys everything you have told me, they would laugh in my face. And I would be laughing with them.'

'Tony don't laugh much,' Palermo said.

'The earth is full of people who don't laugh much, Mr Palermo,' I said. 'You ought to know. You put a lot of them where they are.'

'Is my business,' he said, shrugging enormously.

'I'll keep my promise,' I said. 'But in case you should get to doubting that, don't try to make any business for yourself out of me. Because in my part of town I'm a pretty good man and if the business got made out of Tony instead, it would be strictly on the house. No profit.'

Palermo laughed. 'That'sa good,' he said. 'Tony. One funeral – on the house. Okay.'

He stood up and held his hand out, a fine strong warm hand.

# Twenty-five

In the lobby of the Belfont Building, in the single elevator that had light in it, on the piece of folded burlap, the same watery-eyed relic sat motionless, giving his imitation of the forgotten man. I got in with him and said: 'Six.'

The elevator lurched into motion and pounded its way upstairs. It stopped at six, I got out, and the old man leaned out of the car to spit and said in a dull voice:

'What's cookin'?'

I turned around all in one piece, like a dummy on a revolving platform. I stared at him.

He said: 'You got a grey suit on today.'

'So I have,' I said. 'Yes.'

'Looks nice,' he said. 'I like the blue you was wearing yesterday, too.'

'Go on,' I said. 'Give out.'

'You rode up to eight,' he said. 'Twice. Second time was late. You got back on at six. Shortly after that the boys in blue came bustlin' in.'

'Any of them up there now?'

He shook his head. His face was like a vacant lot. 'I ain't told them anything,' he said. 'Too late to mention it now. They'd eat my ass off.'

I said: 'Why?'

'Why I ain't told them? The hell with them. You talked to me civil. Damn few people do that. Hell, I know you didn't have nothing to do with that killing.'

'I played you wrong,' I said. 'Very wrong.' I got a card out and gave it to him. He fished a pair of metal-framed glasses out of his pocket, perched them on his nose and held the card a foot away from them. He read it slowly, moving his lips, looked at me over the glasses, handed me back the card.

'Better keep it,' he said. 'Case I get careless and drop it. Mighty interestin' life yours, I guess.'

'Yes and no. What was the name?'

'Grandy. Just call me Pop. Who killed him?'

'I don't know. Did you notice anybody going up there or

coming down – anybody that seemed out of place in this building, or strange to you?'

'I don't notice much,' he said. 'I just happened to notice you.'

'A tall blonde, for instance, or a tall slender man with side-
burns, about thirty-five years old.'

'Nope.'

'Everybody going up or down about then would ride in your
car.'

He nodded his worn head. ''Less they used the fire stairs.
They come out in the alley, bar-lock door. Party would have to
come in this way, but there's stairs back of the elevator to the
second floor. From there they can get to the fire stairs. Nothing
to it.'

I nodded. 'Mr Grandy, could you use a five-dollar bill – not
as a bribe in any sense, but as a token of esteem from a sincere
friend?'

'Son, I could use a five-dollar bill so rough Abe Lincoln's
whiskers would be all lathered up with sweat.'

I gave him one. I looked at it before I passed it over. It was
Lincoln on the five, all right.

He tucked it small and put it away deep in his pocket. 'That's
right nice of you,' he said. 'I hope to hell you didn't think I was
fishin'.'

I shook my head and went along the corridor, reading the
names again. *Dr E. J. Blaskowitz, Chiropractic Physician. Dalton and Rees Typewriting Service. L. Pridview, Public Accountant.* Four blank doors. *Moss Mailing Company.* Two more
blank doors. *H. R. Teager, Dental Laboratories.* In the same
relative position as the Morningstar office two floors above, but
the rooms were cut up differently. Teager had only one door
and there was more wall space in between his door and the next
one.

The knob didn't turn. I knocked. There was no answer. I
knocked harder, with the same result. I went back to the elevator. It was still at the sixth floor. Pop Grandy watched me come
as if he had never seen me before.

'Know anything about H. R. Teager?' I asked him.

He thought. 'Heavy-set, oldish, sloppy clothes, dirty fingernails, like mine. Come to think I didn't see him in today.'

142

'Do you think the super would let me into his office to look around?'

'Pretty nosey, the super is. I wouldn't recommend it.'

He turned his head very slowly and looked up the side of the car. Over his head on a big metal ring a key was hanging. A pass-key. Pop Grandy turned his head back to normal position, stood up off his stool and said: 'Right now I gotta go to the can.'

He went. When the door had closed behind him I took the key off the cage wall and went back along to the office of H. R. Teager, unlocked it and went in.

Inside was a small windowless ante-room on the furnishings of which a great deal of expense had been spared. Two chairs, a smoking-stand from a cut-rate drug-store, a standing lamp from the basement of some borax emporium, a flat stained wood table with some old picture magazines on it. The door closed behind me on the door-closer and the place went dark except for what little light came through the pebbled glass panel. I pulled the chain switch of the lamp and went over to the inner door in a wall that cut across the room. It was marked: *H. R. Teager. Private.* It was not locked.

Inside it there was a square office with two uncurtained east windows and very dusty sills. There was a swivel-chair and two straight chairs, both plain hard stained wood, and there was a squarish flat-topped desk. There was nothing on the top of it except an old blotter and a cheap pen set and a round glass ash-tray with cigar ash in it. The drawers of the desk contained some dusty paper linings, a few wire clips, rubber bands, worn-down pencils, pens, rusty pen points, used blotters, four uncancelled two-cent stamps, and some printed letterheads, envelopes and bill forms.

The wire paper-basket was full of junk. I almost wasted ten minutes going through it rather carefully. At the end of that time I knew what I was pretty sure of already: that H. R. Teager carried on a small business as a dental technician doing laboratory work for a number of dentists in unprosperous sections of the city, the kind of dentists who have shabby offices on second floor walk-ups over stores, who lack both the skill and the equipment to do their own laboratory work, and who like to send it out to men like themselves, rather than to the big efficient hard-boiled laboratories who wouldn't give them any credit.

I did find one thing. Teager's home address at 1354B Toberman Street on the receipted part of a gas bill.

I straightened up, dumped the stuff back into the basket and went over to the wooden door marked *Laboratory*. It had a new Yale lock on it and the pass-key didn't fit it. That was that. I switched off the lamp in the outer office and left.

The elevator was downstairs again. I rang for it and when it came up I sidled in around Pop Grandy, hiding the key, and hung it up over his head. The ring tinkled against the cage. He grinned.

'He's gone,' I said. 'Must have left last night. Must have been carrying a lot of stuff. His desk is cleaned out.'

Pop Grandy nodded. 'Carried two suitcases. I wouldn't notice that, though. Most always does carry a suitcase. I figure he picks up and delivers his work.'

'Work such as what?' I asked as the car growled down. Just to be saying something.

'Such as makin' teeth that don't fit,' Pop Grandy said. 'For poor old bastards like me.'

'You wouldn't notice,' I said, as the doors struggled open on the lobby. 'You wouldn't notice the colour of a humming-bird's eye at fifty feet. Not much you wouldn't.'

He grinned. 'What's he done?'

'I'm going over to his house and find out,' I said. 'I think most likely he's taken a cruise to nowhere.'

'I'd shift places with him,' Pop Grandy said. 'Even if he only got to Frisco and got pinched there, I'd shift places with him.'

## Twenty-six

Toberman Street. A wide dusty street, off Pico. No. 1354B was an upstairs flat, south, in a yellow and white frame building. The entrance door was on the porch, beside another marked

144

1352B. The entrances to the downstairs flats were at right angles, facing each other across the width of the porch. I kept on ringing the bell, even after I was sure that nobody would answer it. In a neighbourhood like that there is always an expert window-peeker.

Sure enough the door of 1354A was pulled open and a small bright-eyed woman looked out at me. Her dark hair had been washed and waved and was an intricate mass of bobby pins.

'You want Mrs Teager?' she shrilled.

'Mr or Mrs.'

'They gone away last night on their vacation. They loaded up and gone away late. They had me stop the milk and the paper. They didn't have much time. Kind of sudden, it was.'

'Thanks. What kind of car do they drive?'

The heart-rending dialogue of some love serial came out of the room behind her and hit me in the face like a wet dish-towel.

The bright-eyed woman said: 'You a friend of theirs?' In her voice, suspicion was as thick as the ham in her radio.

'Never mind,' I said in a tough voice. 'All we want is our money. Lots of ways to find out what car they were driving.'

The woman cocked her head, listening. 'That's Beula May,' she told me with a sad smile. 'She won't go to the dance with Doctor Myers. I was scared she wouldn't.'

'Aw hell,' I said, and went back to my car and drove on home to Hollywood.

The office was empty. I unlocked my inner room and threw the windows up and sat down.

Another day drawing to its end, the air dull and tired, the heavy growl of homing traffic on the boulevard, and Marlowe in his office nibbling a drink and sorting the day's mail. Four advertisements; two bills; a handsome coloured postcard from a hotel in Santa Rosa where I had stayed for four days last year, working on a case; a long, badly typed letter from a man named Peabody in Sausalito, the general and slightly cloudy drift of which was that a sample of the handwriting of a suspected person would, when exposed to the searching Peabody examination, reveal the inner emotional characteristics of the individual, classified according to both the Freudian and Jung systems.

There was a stamped addressed envelope inside. As I tore the stamp off and threw the letter and envelope away I had a vision of a pathetic old rooster in long hair, black felt hat and black bow tie, rocking on a rickety porch in front of a lettered window, with the smell of ham hocks and cabbage coming out of the door at his elbow.

I sighed, retrieved the envelope, wrote its name and address on a fresh one, folded a dollar bill into a sheet of paper and wrote on it: 'This is positively the last contribution.' I signed my name, sealed the envelope, stuck a stamp on it and poured another drink.

I filled and lit my pipe and sat there smoking. Nobody came in, nobody called, nothing happened, nobody cared whether I died or went to El Paso.

Little by little the roar of the traffic quieted down. The sky lost its glare. Over in the west it would be red. An early neon light showed a block away, diagonally over roofs. The ventilator churned dully in the wall of the coffee shop down in the alley. A truck filled and backed and growled its way out on to the boulevard.

Finally the telephone rang. I answered it and the voice said: 'Mr Marlowe? This is Mr Shaw. At the Bristol.'

'Yes, Mr Shaw. How are you?'

'I'm very well, thanks, Mr Marlowe. I hope you are the same. There's a young lady here asking to be let into your apartment. I don't know why.'

'Me neither, Mr Shaw. I didn't order anything like that. Does she give a name?'

'Oh yes. Quite. Her name is Davis. Miss Merle Davis. She is – what shall I say? – quite verging on the hysterical.'

'Let her in,' I said, rapidly. 'I'll be there in ten minutes. She's the secretary of a client. It's a business matter entirely.'

'Quite. Oh yes. Shall I – er – remain with her?'

'Whatever you think,' I said and hung up.

Passing the open door of the wash cabinet I saw a stiff excited face in the glass.

# Twenty-seven

As I turned the key in my door and opened it Shaw was already standing up from the davenport. He was a tall man with glasses and a high-domed bald head that made his ears look as if they had slipped down on his head. He had the fixed smile of polite idiocy on his face.

The girl sat in my easy-chair behind the chess table. She wasn't doing anything, just sitting there.

'Ah, there you are, Mr Marlowe,' Shaw chirped. 'Yes. Quite. Miss Davis and I have been having such an interesting little conversation. I was telling her I originally came from England. She hasn't – er – told me where she came from.' He was half-way to the door saying this.

'Very kind of you, Mr Shaw,' I said.

'Not at all,' he chirped. 'Not at all. I'll just run along now. My dinner, possibly—'

'It's very nice of you,' I said, 'I appreciate it.'

He nodded and was gone. The unnatural brightness of his smile seemed to linger in the air after the door closed, like the smile of a Cheshire cat.

I said: 'Hello, there.'

She said: 'Hello.' Her voice was quite calm, quite serious. She was wearing a brownish linen coat and skirt, a broad-brimmed low-crowned straw hat with a brown velvet band that exactly matched the colour of her shoes and the leather trimming on the edges of her linen envelope bag. The hat was tilted rather daringly for her. She was not wearing her glasses.

Except for her face she would have looked all right. In the first place her eyes were quite mad. There was white showing all around the iris and they had a sort of fixed look. When they moved the movement was so stiff that you could almost hear something creak. Her mouth was in a tight line at the corners, but the middle part of her upper lip kept lifting off her teeth, upwards and outwards as if fine threads attached to the edge of the lip were pulling it. It would go up so far that it didn't seem possible, and then the entire lower part of her face would go into a spasm and when the spasm was over her mouth would be tight shut, and then the process would slowly start all over again. In addition to this there was something wrong with her neck, so that very slowly her head was drawn around to the left about forty-five degrees. It would stop there, her neck would twitch, and her head would slide back the way it had come.

The combination of these two movements, taken with the immobility of her body, the tight-clasped hands in her lap, and the fixed stare of her eyes, was enough to start anybody's nerves backfiring.

There was a can of tobacco on the desk, between which and her chair was the chess table with the chessmen in their box. I got the pipe out of my pocket and went over to fill it at the can of tobacco. That put me just on the other side of the chess table from her. Her bag was lying on the edge of the table, in front of her and a little to one side. She jumped a little when I went over there, but after that she was just like before. She even made an effort to smile.

I filled the pipe and struck a paper match and lit it and stood there holding the match after I had blown it out.

'You're not wearing your glasses,' I said.

She spoke. Her voice was quiet, composed. 'Oh, I only wear them around the house and for reading. They're in my bag.'

'You're in the house now,' I said. 'You ought to be wearing them.'

I reached casually for the bag. She didn't move. She didn't watch my hands. Her eyes were on my face. I turned my body a little as I opened the bag. I fished the glass case out and slid it across the table.

'Put them on,' I said.

'Oh, yes, I'll put them on,' she said. 'But I'll have to take my hat off, I think ...'

'Yes, take your hat off,' I said.

She took her hat off and held it on her knees. Then she remembered about the glasses and forgot about the hat. The hat fell on the floor while she reached for the glasses. She put them on. That helped her appearance a lot, I thought.

While she was doing this I got the gun out of her bag and slid it into my hip pocket. I didn't think she saw me. It looked like the same Colt .25 automatic with the walnut grip that I had seen in the top right-hand drawer of her desk the day before.

I went back to the davenport and sat down and said: 'Well, here we are. What do we do now? Are you hungry?'

'I've been over to Mr Vannier's house,' she said.

'Oh.'

'He lives in Sherman Oaks. At the end of Escamillo Drive. At the very end.'

'Quite, probably,' I said without meaning, and tried to blow a smoke ring, but didn't make it. A nerve in my cheek was trying to twang like a wire. I didn't like it.

'Yes,' she said in her composed voice, with her upper lip still doing the hoist and flop movement, and her chin still swinging around at anchor and back again. 'It's very quiet there. Mr Vannier has been living there three years now. Before that he lived up in the Hollywood hills, on Diamond Street. Another man lived with him there, but they didn't get along very well, Mr Vannier said.'

'I feel as if I could understand that, too,' I said. 'How long have you known Mr Vannier?'

'I've known him eight years. I haven't known him very well. I have had to take him a – a parcel now and then. He liked to have me bring it myself.'

I tried again with a smoke ring. Nope.

'Of course,' she said, 'I never liked him very well. I was afraid he would – I was afraid he—'

'But he didn't,' I said.

For the first time her face got a human natural expression – surprise.

'No,' she said. 'He didn't. That is, he didn't really. But he had his pyjamas on.'

'Taking it easy,' I said. 'Lying around all afternoon with his pyjamas on. Well, some guys have all the luck, don't they?'

'Well you have to know something,' she said seriously. 'Something that makes people pay you money. Mrs Murdock has been wonderful to me, hasn't she?'

'She certainly has,' I said. 'How much were you taking him today?'

'Only five hundred dollars. Mrs Murdock said that was all she could spare, and she couldn't really spare that. She said it

149

would have to stop. It couldn't go on. Mr Vannier would always promise to stop, but he never did.'

'It's a way they have,' I said.

'So there was only one thing to do. I've known that for years, really. It was all my fault and Mrs Murdock has been so wonderful to me. It couldn't make me any worse than I was already, could it?'

I put my hand up and rubbed my cheek hard, to quiet the nerve. She forgot that I hadn't answered her and went on again.

'So I did it,' she said. 'He was there in his pyjamas, with a glass beside him. He was leering at me. He didn't even get up to let me in. But there was a key in the front door. Somebody had left a key there. It was – it was—' her voice jammed in her throat.

'It was a key in the front door,' I said. 'So you were able to get in.'

'Yes.' She nodded and almost smiled again. 'There wasn't anything to it, really. I don't even remember hearing the noise. But there must have been a noise, of course. Quite a loud noise.'

'I suppose so,' I said.

'I went over quite close to him, so I couldn't miss,' she said.

'And what did Mr Vannier do?'

'He didn't do anything at all. He just leered, sort of. Well, that's all there is to it. I didn't like to go back to Mrs Murdock and make any more trouble for her. And for Leslie.' Her voice hushed on the name, and hung suspended, and a little shiver rippled over her body. 'So I came here,' she said. 'And when you didn't answer the bell, I found the office and asked the manager to let me in and wait for you. I knew you would know what to do.'

'And what did you touch in the house while you were there?' I asked. 'Can you remember at all? I mean, besides the front door. Did you just go in at the door and come out without touching anything in the house?'

She thought and her face stopped moving. 'Oh, I remember one thing,' she said. 'I put the light out. Before I left. It was a lamp. One of these lamps that shine upwards, with big bulbs. I put that out.'

I nodded and smiled at her. Marlowe, one smile, cheerful.

'What time was this – how long ago?'

'Oh, just before I came over here. I drove. I had Mrs Murdock's car. The one you asked about yesterday. I forgot to tell you that she didn't take it when she went away. Or did I? No, I remember now I did tell you.'

'Let's see,' I said. 'Half an hour to drive here, anyway. You've been here close to an hour. That would be about five-thirty when you left Mr Vannier's house. And you put the light off.'

'That's right.' She nodded again, quite brightly. Pleased at remembering. 'I put the light out.'

'Would you care for a drink?' I asked her.

'Oh, no.' She shook her head quite vigorously. 'I never drink anything at all.'

'Would you mind if I had one?'

'Certainly not. Why should I?'

I stood up, gave her a studying look. Her lip was still going up and her head was still going around, but I thought not so far. It was like a rhythm which is dying down.

It was difficult to know how far to go with this. It might be that the more she talked, the better. Nobody knows very much about the time of absorption of a shock.

I said: 'Where is your home?'

'Why – I live with Mrs Murdock. In Pasadena.'

'I mean, your real home. Where your folks are.'

'My parents live in Wichita,' she said. 'But I don't go there – ever. I write once in a while, but I haven't seen them for years.'

'What does your father do?'

'He has a dog and cat hospital. He's a veterinarian. I hope they won't have to know. They didn't about the other time. Mrs Murdock kept it from everybody.'

'Maybe they won't have to know,' I said. 'I'll get my drink.'

I went out around the back of her chair to the kitchen and poured it and I made it a drink that was a drink. I put it down in a lump and took the little gun off my hip and saw that the safety was on. I smelled the muzzle, broke out the magazine. There was a cartridge in the chamber, but it was one of those guns that won't fire when the magazine is out. I held it so that I could look into the breech. The cartridge in there was the wrong size and was crooked against the breech block. It looked

151

like a .32. The cartridges in the magazine were the right size, .25's. I fitted the gun together again and went back to the living-room.

I hadn't heard a sound. She had just slid forward in a pile in front of the chair, on top of her nice hat. She was as cold as a mackerel.

I spread her out a little and took her glasses off and made sure she hadn't swallowed her tongue. I wedged my folded handkerchief into the corner of her mouth so that she wouldn't bite her tongue when she came out of it. I went to the phone and called Carl Moss.

'Phil Marlowe, Doc. Any more patients or are you through?'

'All through,' he said. 'Leaving. Trouble?'

'I'm home,' I said. 'Four-o-eight Bristol Apartments, if you don't remember. I've got a girl here who has pulled a faint. I'm not afraid of the faint, I'm afraid she may be nuts when she comes out of it.'

'Don't give her any liquor,' he said. 'I'm on my way.'

I hung up and knelt down beside her. I began to rub her temples. She opened her eyes. The lip started to lift. I pulled the handkerchief out of her mouth. She looked up at me and said: 'I've been over to Mr Vannier's house. He lives in Sherman Oaks. I—'

'Do you mind if I lift you up and put you on the davenport? You know me – Marlowe, the big boob that goes around asking all the wrong questions.'

'Hello,' she said.

I lifted her. She went stiff on me, but she didn't say anything. I put her on the davenport and tucked her skirt down over her legs and put a pillow under her head and picked her hat up. It was as flat as a flounder. I did what I could to straighten it out and laid it aside on the desk.

She watched me sideways, doing this.

'Did you call the police?' she asked softly.

'Not yet,' I said. 'I've been too busy.'

She looked surprised. I wasn't quite sure, but I thought she looked a little hurt, too.

I opened up her bag and turned my back to her to slip the gun back into it. While I was doing that I took a look at what else was in the bag. The usual oddments, a couple of handker-chiefs, lipstick, a silver and red enamel compact with powder in it, a couple of tissues, a purse with some hard money and a few dollar bills, no cigarettes, no matches, no tickets for the theatre.

I pulled open the zipper pocket at the back. That held her driver's licence and a flat packet of bills, ten fifties. I riffled them. None of them brand new. Tucked into the rubber band that held them was a folded paper. I took it out and opened it and read it. It was neatly typewritten, dated that day. It was a common receipt form and it would, when signed, acknowledge the receipt of $500. 'Payment on Account.'

It didn't seem as if it would ever be signed now. I slipped money and receipt into my pocket. I closed the bag and looked over at the davenport.

She was looking at the ceiling and doing that with her face again. I went into my bedroom and got a blanket to throw over her.

Then I went to the kitchen for another drink.

# Twenty-eight

Dr Carl Moss was a big burly Jew with a Hitler moustache, pop eyes and the calmness of a glacier. He put his hat and bag in a chair and went over and stood looking down at the girl on the davenport inscrutably.

'I'm Dr Moss,' he said. 'How are you?'

She said: 'Aren't you the police?'

He bent down and felt her pulse and then stood there watch-ing her breathing. 'Where does it hurt, Miss—'

'Davis,' I said. 'Miss Merle Davis.'

'Miss Davis.'

'Nothing hurts me,' she said, staring up at him. 'I – I don't even know why I'm lying here like this. I thought you were the police. You see, I killed a man.'

'Well, that's a normal human impulse,' he said. 'I've killed dozens.' He didn't smile.

She lifted her lip and moved her head around for him.

'You know you don't have to do that,' he said, quite gently. 'You feel a twitch of the nerves here and there and you proceed to build it up and dramatize it. You can control it, if you want to.'

'Can I?' she whispered.

'If you want to,' he said. 'You don't have to. It doesn't make any difference to me either way. Nothing pains at all, eh?'

'No.' She shook her head.

He patted her shoulder and walked out to the kitchen. I went after him. He leaned his hips against the sink and gave me a cool stare. 'What's the story?'

'She's the secretary of a client. A Mrs Murdock in Pasadena. The client is rather a brute. About eight years ago a man made a hard pass at Merle. How hard I don't know. Then – I don't mean immediately – but around that time he fell out of a window or jumped. Since then she can't have a man touch her – not in the most casual way, I mean.'

'Uh-huh.' His pop eyes continued to read my face. 'Does she think he jumped out of the window on her account?'

'I don't know. Mrs Murdock is the man's widow. She married again and her second husband is dead too. Merle has stayed with her. The old woman treats her like a rough parent treats a naughty child.'

'I see. Regressive.'

'What's that?'

'Emotional shock, and the subconscious attempt to escape back to childhood. If Mrs Murdock scolds her a good deal, but not too much, that would increase the tendency. Identification of childhood subordination with childhood protection.'

'Do we have to go into that stuff?' I growled.

He grinned at me calmly. 'Look, pal. The girl's obviously a neurotic. It's partly induced and partly deliberate. I mean to say that she really enjoys a lot of it. Even if she doesn't realize that she enjoys it. However, that's not of immediate importance. What's this about killing a man?'

'A man named Vannier who lives in Sherman Oaks. There seems to be some blackmail angle. Merle had to take him his

154

money, from time to time. She was afraid of him. I've seen the guy. A nasty type. She went over there this afternoon and she says she shot him.'

'Why?'

'She says she didn't like the way he leered at her.'

'Shot him with what?'

'She had a gun in her bag. Don't ask me why. I don't know. But if she shot him, it wasn't with that. The gun's got a wrong cartridge in the breech. It can't be fired as it is. Also it hasn't been fired.'

'This is too deep for me,' he said. 'I'm just a doctor. What did you want me to do with her?'

'Also,' I said, ignoring the question, 'she said the lamp was turned on and it was about five-thirty of a nice summery afternoon. And the guy was wearing his sleeping-suit and there was a key in the lock of the front door. And he didn't get up to let her in. He just sort of sat there sort of leering.'

He nodded and said: 'Oh.' He pushed a cigarette between his heavy lips and lit it. 'If you expect me to tell you whether she really thinks she shot him, I can't do it. From your description I gather that the man is shot. That so?'

'Brother, I haven't been there. But that much seems pretty clear.'

'If she thinks she shot him and isn't just acting – and, God, how these types do act! – that indicates it was not a new idea to her. You say she carried a gun. So perhaps it wasn't. She may have a guilt complex. Wants to be punished, wants to expiate some real or imaginary crime. Again I ask what do you want me to do with her? She's not sick, she's not loony.'

'She's not going back to Pasadena.'

'Oh.' He looked at me curiously. 'Any family?'

'In Wichita. Father's a vet. I'll call him, but she'll have to stay here tonight.'

'I don't know about that. Does she trust you enough to spend the night in your apartment?'

'She came here of her own free will, and not socially. So I guess she does.'

He shrugged and fingered the sidewall of his coarse black

155

moustache. 'Well, I'll give her some nembutal and we'll put her to bed. And you can walk the floor wrestling with your conscience.'

'I have to go out,' I said. 'I have to go over there and see what has happened. And she can't stay here alone. And no man, not even a doctor, is going to put her to bed. Get a nurse. I'll sleep somewhere else.'

'Phil Marlowe,' he said. 'The shop-soiled Galahad. Okay. I'll stick around until the nurse comes.'

He went back into the living-room and telephoned the Nurses' Registry. Then he telephoned his wife. While he was telephoning, Merle sat up on the davenport and clasped her hands primly in her lap.

'I don't see why the lamp was on,' she said. 'It wasn't dark in the house at all. Not that dark.'

I said: 'What's your dad's first name?'

'Dr Wilbur Davis. Why?'

'Wouldn't you like something to eat?'

At the telephone Carl Moss said to me: 'Tomorrow will do for that. This is probably just a lull.' He finished his call, hung up, went to his bag and came back with a couple of yellow capsules in his hand on a fragment of cotton. He got a glass of water, handed her the capsules and said: 'Swallow.'

'I'm not sick, am I?' she said, looking up at him.

'Swallow, my child, swallow.'

She took them and put them in her mouth and took the glass of water and drank.

I put my hat on and left.

On the way down in the elevator I remembered that there hadn't been any keys in her bag, so I stopped at the lobby floor and went out through the lobby to the Bristol Avenue side. The car was not hard to find. It was parked crookedly about two feet from the kerb. It was a grey Mercury convertible and its licence number was 2XIII. I remembered that this was the number of Linda Murdock's car.

A leather keyholder hung in the lock. I got into the car, started the engine, saw that there was plenty of gas, and drove it away. It was a nice eager little car. Over Cahuenga Pass it had the wings of a bird.

# Twenty-nine

Escamillo Drive made three jogs in four blocks, for no reason that I could see. It was very narrow, averaged about five houses to a block and was overhung by a section of shaggy brown foot-hill on which nothing lived at this season except sage and manzanita. In its fifth and last block, Escamillo Drive did a neat little curve to the left, hit the base of the hill hard, and died without a whimper. In this last block were three houses, two on the opposite entering corners, one at the dead end. This was Vannier's. My spotlight showed the key still in the door.

It was a narrow English type bungalow with a high roof, leaded front windows, a garage to the side, and a trailer parked beside the garage. The early moon lay quietly on its small lawn. A large oak tree grew almost on the front porch. There was no light in the house now, none visible from the front at least.

From the lay of the land a light in the living-room in the day-time did not seem utterly improbable. It would be a dark house except in the morning. As a love-nest the place had its points, but as a residence for a blackmailer I didn't give it very high marks. Sudden death can come to you anywhere, but Vannier had made it too easy.

I turned into his driveway, backed to get myself pointed out of the dead end, and then drove down to the corner and parked there. I walked back in the street because there was no sidewalk. The front door was made of iron-bound oak planks, bevelled where they joined. There was a thumb latch instead of a knob. The head of the flat key projected from the lock. I rang the bell, and it rang with that remote sound of a bell ringing at night in an empty house. I walked around the oak tree and poked the light of my pencil flash between the leaves of the garage door. There was a car in there. I went back around the house and looked at a small flowerless yard, walled in by a low wall of fieldstone. Three more oak trees, a table and a couple of all-metal chairs under one of them. A rubbish burner at the back. I shone my light into the trailer before I went back to the front. There didn't seem to be anybody in the trailer. Its door was locked.

I opened the front door, leaving the key in the lock. I wasn't going to work any dipsy-doodle in this place. What ever was, was. I just wanted to make sure. I felt around on the wall inside the door for a light switch, found one and tilted it up. Pale flame bulbs in pairs in wall brackets went on all around the room, showing me the big lamp Merle had spoken of, as well as other things. I went over to switch the lamp on, then back to switch the wall light off. The lamp had a big bulb inverted in a porcelain glass bowl. You could get three different intensities of light. I clicked the button switch around until I had all there was.

The room ran from front to back, with a door at the back and an arch up front to the right. Inside that was a small dining-room. Curtains were half-drawn across the arch, heavy pale green brocade curtains, far from new. The fireplace was in the middle of the left wall, bookshelves opposite and on both sides of it, not built in. Two davenports angled across the corners of the room and there was one gold chair, one pink chair, one brown chair, one brown and gold jacquard chair with footstool.

Yellow pyjama legs were on the footstool, bare ankles, feet in dark green morocco leather slippers. My eyes ran up from the feet, slowly, carefully. A dark green figured silk robe, tied with a tasselled belt. Open above the belt showing a monogram on the pocket of the pyjamas. A handkerchief neat in the pocket, two stiff points of white linen. A yellow neck, the face turned sideways, pointed at a mirror on the wall. I walked around and looked in the mirror. The face leered all right.

The left arm and hand lay between a knee and the side of the chair, the right arm hung outside the chair, the ends of the fingers touching the rug. Touching also the butt of a small revolver, about .32 calibre, a belly gun, with practically no barrel. The right side of the face was against the back of the chair, but the right shoulder was dark brown with blood and there was some on the right sleeve. Also on the chair. A lot of it on the chair.

I didn't think his head had taken that position naturally. Some sensitive soul had not liked the right side of it.

I lifted my foot and gently pushed the footstool sideways a few inches. The heels of the slippers moved reluctantly over the jacquard surface, not with it. The man was as stiff as a board.

So I reached down and touched his ankle. Ice was never half as cold.

On a table at his right elbow was half of a dead drink, an ashtray full of butts and ash. Three of the butts had lipstick on them. Bright Chinese-red lipstick. What a blonde would use.

There was another ashtray beside another chair. Matches in it and a lot of ash, but no stubs.

On the air of the room a rather heavy perfume struggled with the smell of death, and lost. Although defeated, it was still there.

I poked through the rest of the house, putting lights on and off. Two bedrooms, one furnished in light wood, one in red maple. The light one seemed to be a spare. A nice bathroom with tan and mulberry tiling and a stall shower with a glass door. The kitchen was small. There were a lot of bottles on the sink. Lots of bottles, lots of glass, lots of fingerprints, lots of evidence. Or not, as the case might be.

I went back to the living-room and stood in the middle of the floor, breathing with my mouth as far as possible and wondering what the score would be when I turned this one in. Turn this one in and report that I was the fellow who had found Morningstar and run away. The score would be low, very low. Marlowe, three murders. Marlowe practically knee-deep in dead men. And no reasonable, logical, friendly account of himself whatsoever. But that wasn't the worst of it. The minute I opened up I would cease to be a free agent. I would be through with doing whatever it was I was doing and with finding out whatever it was I was finding out.

Carl Moss might be willing to protect Merle with the mantle of Aesculapius, up to a point. Or he might think it would do her more good in the long run to get it all off her chest, whatever it was.

I wandered back to the jacquard chair and set my teeth and grabbed enough of his chair to pull the head away from the chair back. The bullet had gone in at the temple. The set-up could be for suicide. But people like Louis Vannier do not commit suicide. A blackmailer, even a scared blackmailer, has a sense of power, and loves it.

I let the head go back where it wanted to go and leaned down to scrub my hand on the nap of the rug. Leaning down I saw the

159

corner of a picture frame under the lower shelf of the table at Vannier's elbow. I went around and reached for it with a handkerchief.

The glass was cracked across. It had fallen off the wall. I could see the small nail. I could make a guess how it had happened. Somebody standing at Vannier's right, even leaning over him, somebody he knew and had no fear of, had suddenly pulled a gun and shot him in the right temple. And then, startled by the blood or the recoil of the shot, the killer had jumped back against the wall and knocked the picture down. It had landed on a corner and jumped under the table. And the killer had been too careful to touch it, or too scared.

I looked at it. It was a small picture, not interesting at all. A guy in doublet and hose, with lace at his sleeve ends, and one of those round puffy velvet hats with a feather, leaning far out of a window and apparently calling out to somebody downstairs. Downstairs not being in the picture. It was a colour reproduction of something that had never been needed in the first place.

I looked around the room. There were other pictures, a couple of rather nice water-colours, some engravings – very old-fashioned this year, engravings, or are they? Half a dozen in all. Well, perhaps the guy liked the picture, so what? A man leaning out of a high window. A long time ago.

I looked at Vannier. He wouldn't help me at all. A man leaning out of a high window, a long time ago.

The touch of the idea at first was so light that I almost missed it and passed on. A touch of a feather, hardly that. The touch of a snowflake. A high window, a man leaning out – a long time ago.

It snapped in place. It was so hot it sizzled. Out of a high window a long time ago – eight years ago – a man leaning – too far – a man falling – to his death. A man named Horace Bright.

'Mr Vannier,' I said with a little touch of admiration, 'you played that rather neatly.'

I turned the picture over. On the back dates and amounts of money were written. Dates over almost eight years amounts mostly of $500, a few $750, two for $1,000. There was a running total in small figures. It was $11,100. Mr Vannier had not received the latest payment. He had been dead when it arrived.

It was not a lot of money, spread over eight years. Mr Vannier's customer had bargained hard.

The cardboard back was fastened into the frame with steel gramophone needles. Two of them had fallen out. I worked the cardboard loose and tore it a little getting it loose. There was a white envelope between the back and the picture. Sealed, blank. I tore it open. It contained two square photographs and a negative. The photos were just the same. They showed a man leaning far out of a window with his mouth open yelling. His hands were on the brick edges of the window-frame. There was a woman's face behind his shoulder.

He was a thinnish dark-haired man. His face was not very clear, nor the face of the woman behind him. He was leaning out of a window and yelling or calling out.

There I was holding the photograph and looking at it. And so far as I could see, it didn't mean a thing. I knew it had to. I just didn't know why. But I kept on looking at it. And in a little while something was wrong. It was a very small thing, but it was vital. The position of the man's hands, lined against the corner of the wall where it was cut out to make the window-frame. The hands were not holding anything, they were not touching anything. It was the inside of his wrists that lined against the angle of the bricks. The hands were in air.

The man was not leaning. He was falling.

I put the stuff back in the envelope and folded the cardboard back and stuffed that into my pocket also. I hid frame, glass and picture in the linen closet under towels.

All this had taken too long. A car stopped outside the house. Feet came up the walk.

I dodged behind the curtains in the archway.


# Thirty


The front door opened and then quietly closed.

There was a silence, hanging in the air like a man's breath in frosty air, and then a thick scream, ending in a wail of despair.

Then a man's voice, tight with fury, saying: 'Not bad, not good. Try again.'

The woman's voice said: 'My God, it's Louis! He's dead!'

The man's voice said: 'I may be wrong, but I still think it stinks.'

'My God! He's dead, Alex. Do something for God's sake – do something!'

'Yeah,' the hard, tight voice of Alex Morny said. 'I ought to. I ought to make you look just like him. With blood and everything. I ought to make you just as dead, just as cold, just as rotten. No, I don't have to do that. You're that already. Just as rotten. Eight months married and cheating on me with a piece of merchandise like that. My God! What did I ever think of to put in with a chippy like you?'

He was almost yelling at the end of it.

The woman made another wailing noise.

'Quit stalling,' Morny said bitterly. 'What do you think I brought you over here for? You're not kidding anybody. You've been watched for weeks. You were here last night. I've been here already today. I've seen what there is to see. Your lipstick on cigarettes, your glass that you drank out of. I can see you now, sitting on the arm of his chair, rubbing his greasy hair, and then feeding him a slug while he was still purring. Why?'

'Oh, Alex – darling – don't say such awful things.'

'Early Lillian Gish,' Morny said. 'Very early Lillian Gish. Skip the agony, Toots. I have to know how to handle this. What the hell you think I'm here for? I don't give one little flash in hell about you any more. Not any more, Toots, not any more, my precious darling angel blonde mankiller. But I do care about myself and my reputation and my business. For instance, did you wipe the gun off?'

Silence. Then the sound of a blow. The woman wailed. She was hurt, terribly hurt. Hurt in the depths of her soul. She made it rather good.

'Look, angel,' Morny snarled. 'Don't feed me the ham. I've been in pictures. I'm a connoisseur of ham. Skip it. You're going to tell me how this was done if I have to drag you around the room by your hair. Now – did you wipe off the gun?'

Suddenly she laughed. An unnatural laugh, but clear and with a nice tinkle to it. Then she stopped laughing, just as suddenly.

Her voice said: 'Yes.'

'And the glass you were using?'

'Yes.' Very quiet now, very cool.

'And you put his prints on the gun?'

'Yes.'

He thought in the silence. 'Probably won't fool them.' he said. 'It's almost impossible to get a dead man's prints on a gun in a convincing way. However. What else did you wipe off?'

'N-nothing. Oh, Alex. Please don't be so brutal.'

'Stop it. *Stop it?* Show me how you did it, how you were standing, how you held the gun.'

She didn't move.

'Never mind about the prints,' Morny said. 'I'll put better ones on. Much better ones.'

She moved slowly across the opening of the curtains and I saw her. She was wearing pale-green gaberdine slacks, a fawn-coloured leisure jacket with stitching on it, a scarlet turban with a gold snake in it. Her face was smeared with tears.

'Pick it up,' Morny yelled at her. 'Show me!'

She bent beside the chair and came up with the gun in her hand and her teeth bared. She pointed the gun across the opening in the curtains, towards the space of room where the door was.

Morny didn't move, didn't make a sound.

The blonde's hand began to shake and the gun did a queer up and down dance in the air. Her mouth trembled and her arm fell.

'I can't do it,' she breathed. 'I ought to shoot you, but I can't.'

The hand opened and the gun thudded to the floor.

Morny went swiftly past the break in the curtains, pushed her out of the way and with his foot pushed the gun back to about where it had been.

'You couldn't do it,' he said thickly. 'You couldn't do it. Now watch.'

He whipped a handkerchief out and bent to pick the gun up again. He pressed something and the gate fell open. He reached his right hand into his pocket and rolled a cartridge in his fingers, moving his fingertips on the metal, pushed the cartridge into a cylinder. He repeated the performance four times more, snapped the gate shut, then opened it and spun it a little to set it in a certain spot. He placed the gun down on the floor, withdrew his hand and handkerchief and straightened up.

'You couldn't shoot me,' he sneered, 'because there was nothing in the gun but one empty cartridge. Now it's loaded again. The cylinders are in the right place. One shot has been fired. And your fingerprints are on the gun.'

The blonde was very still, looking at him with haggard eyes.

'I forgot to tell you,' he said softly, '*I* wiped the gun off. I thought it would be so much nicer to be *sure* your prints were on it. I was pretty sure they were – but I felt as if I would like to be *quite* sure. Get it?'

The girl said quietly: 'You're going to turn me in?'

His back was towards me. Dark clothes. Felt hat pulled low. So I couldn't see his face. But I could just about see the leer with which he said:

'Yes, angel, I am going to turn you in.'

'I see,' she said, and looked at him levelly. There was a sudden grave dignity in her over-emphasized chorus-girl's face.

'I'm going to turn you in, angel,' he said slowly, spacing his words as if he enjoyed his act. 'Some people are going to be sorry for me and some people are going to laugh at me. But it's not going to do my business any harm. Not a bit of harm. That's one nice thing about a business like mine. A little notoriety won't hurt it at all.'

'So I'm just publicity value to you, now,' she said. 'Apart, of course, from the danger that you might have been suspected yourself.'

'Just so,' he said. 'Just so.'

'How about my motive?' she asked, still calm, still level-eyed and so gravely contemptuous that he didn't get the expression at all.

'I don't know,' he said. 'I don't care. You were up to something with him. Eddie tailed you downtown to a street on Bunker Hill where you met a blond guy in a brown suit. You gave him something. Eddie dropped you and tailed the guy to an apartment house near there. He tried to tail him some more, but he had a hunch the guy spotted him, and he had to drop it. I don't know what it was all about. I know one thing, though. In that apartment house a young guy named Phillips was shot yesterday. Would you know anything about that, my sweet?'

The blonde said: 'I wouldn't know anything about it. I don't know anybody named Phillips and strangely enough I didn't just run up and shoot anybody out of sheer girlish fun.'

'But you shot Vannier, my dear,' Morny said almost gently.

'Oh yes,' she drawled. 'Of course. We were wondering what my motive was. You get it figured out yet?'

'You can work that out with the johns,' he snapped. 'Call it a lovers' quarrel. Call it anything you like.'

'Perhaps,' she said, 'when he was drunk he looked just a little like you. Perhaps that was the motive.'

He said: 'Ah,' and sucked his breath in.

'Better-looking,' she said. 'Younger, with less belly. But with the same god-damned self-satisfied smirk.'

'Ah,' Morny said, and he was suffering.

'Would that do?' she asked him softly.

He stepped forward and swung a fist. It caught her on the side of the face and she went down and sat on the floor, a long leg straight out in front of her, one hand to her jaw, her very blue eyes looking up at him.

'Maybe you oughtn't to have done that,' she said. 'Maybe I won't go through with it, now.'

'You'll go through with it, all right. You won't have any choice. You'll get off easy enough. Christ, I know that. With your looks. But you'll go through with it, angel. Your fingerprints are on that gun.'

She got to her feet slowly, still with the hand to her jaw.

Then she smiled. 'I knew he was dead,' she said. 'That is my key in the door. I'm quite willing to go downtown and say I shot him. But don't lay your smooth white paw on me again – if you want my story. Yes. I'm quite willing to go to the cops. I'll feel a lot safer with them than I feel with you.'

Morny turned and I saw the hard white leer of his face and the scar dimple in his cheek twitching. He walked past the opening in the curtains. The front door opened again. The blonde stood still a moment, looked back over her shoulder at the corpse, shuddered slightly, and passed out of my line of vision.

The door closed. Steps on the walk. Then car doors opening and closing. The motor throbbed, and the car went away.


# Thirty-one

After a long time I moved out from my hiding-place and stood looking around the living-room again. I went over and picked the gun up and wiped it off very carefully and put it down again. I picked the three rouge-stained cigarette-stubs out of the tray on the table and carried them into the bathroom and flushed them down the toilet. Then I looked around for the second glass with her fingerprints on it. There wasn't any second glass. The one that was half full of a dead drink I took to the kitchen and rinsed out and wiped on a dish-towel.

Then the pasty part. I knelt on the rug by his chair and picked up the gun and reached for the trailing bone-stiff hand. The prints would not be good, but they would be prints and they would not be Lois Morny's. The gun had a checked rubber grip, with a piece broken off on the left side below the screw. No prints on that. An index print on the right side of the barrel, two fingers on the trigger guard, a thumb print on the flat piece on the left side, behind the chambers. Good enough.

I took one more look around the living-room.

I put the lamp down to a lower light. It still glared too much on the dead yellow face. I opened the front door, pulled the key out and wiped it off and pushed it back into the lock. I shut the door and wiped the thumb-latch off and went my way down the block to the Mercury.

I drove back to Hollywood and locked the car up and started along the sidewalk past the other parked cars to the entrance of the Bristol.

A harsh whisper spoke to me out of darkness, out of a car. It spoke my name. Eddie Prue's long blank face hung somewhere up near the roof of a small Packard, behind its wheel. He was alone in it. I leaned on the door of the car and looked in at him.

'How you making out, shamus?'

I tossed a match down and blew smoke at his face. I said: 'Who dropped that dental supply company's bill you gave me last night? Vannier, or somebody else?'

'Vannier.'

'What was I supposed to do with it – guess the life history of a man named Teager?'

'I don't go for dumb guys,' Eddie Prue said.

I said: 'Why would he have it in his pocket to drop? And if he did drop it, why wouldn't you just hand it back to him? In other words, seeing that I'm a dumb guy, explain to me why a bill for dental supplies should get anybody all excited and start trying to hire private detectives. Especially gents like Alex Morny, who don't like private detectives.'

'Morny's a good head,' Eddie Prue said coldly.

'He's the fellow for whom they coined the phrase, "as ignorant as an actor."'

'Skip that. Don't you know what they use that dental stuff for?'

'Yeah. I found out. They use albastone for making moulds of teeth and cavities. It's very hard, very fine grain and retains any amount of fine detail. The other stuff, crystobolite, is used to cook out the wax in an invested wax model. It's used because it stands a great deal of heat without distortion. Tell me you don't know what I'm talking about.'

'I guess you know how they make gold inlays,' Eddie Prue said. 'I guess you do, huh?'

'I spent two of my hours learning today. I'm an expert. What does it get me?'

He was silent for a little while, and then he said: 'You ever read the paper?'

'Once in a while.'

'It couldn't be you read where an old guy named Morningstar was bumped off in the Belfont Building on Ninth Street, just two floors above where this H. R. Teager had his office. It couldn't be you read that, could it?'

I didn't answer him. He looked at me for a moment longer, then he put his hand forward to the dash and pushed the starter-button. The motor of his car caught and he started to ease in the clutch.

'Nobody could be as dumb as you act,' he said softly. 'Nobody ain't. Good night to you.'

The car moved away from the kerb and drifted down the hill towards Franklin. I was grinning into the distance as it disappeared.

I went up to the apartment and unlocked the door and pushed it open a few inches and then knocked gently. There was movement in the room. The door was pulled open by a strong-looking girl with a black stripe on the cap of her white nurse's uniform.

'I'm Marlowe. I live here.'

'Come in, Mr Marlowe. Dr Moss told me.'

I shut the door quietly and we spoke in low voices. 'How is she?' I asked.

'She's asleep. She was already drowsy when I got here. I'm Miss Lymington. I don't know very much about her except that her temperature is normal and her pulse still rather fast, but going down. A mental disturbance, I gather.'

'She found a man murdered,' I said. 'It shot her full of holes. Is she hard enough asleep so that I could go in and get a few things to take to the hotel?'

'Oh, yes. If you're quiet. She probably won't wake. If she does, it won't matter.'

I went over and put some money on the desk. 'There's coffee and bacon and eggs and bread and tomato juice and oranges and liquor here,' I said. 'Anything else you'll have to phone for.'

'I've already investigated your supplies,' she said, smiling. 'We have all we need until after breakfast tomorrow. Is she going to stay here?'

'That's up to Dr Moss. I think she'll be going home as soon as she is fit for it. Home being quite a long way off, in Wichita.'

'I'm only a nurse,' she said. 'But I don't think there is anything the matter with her that a good night's sleep won't cure.'

'A good night's sleep and a change of company,' I said, but that didn't mean anything to Miss Lymington.

I went along the hallway and peeked into the bedroom. They had put a pair of my pyjamas on her. She lay almost on her back with one arm outside the bedclothes. The sleeve of the pyjama coat was turned up six inches or more. The small hand below the end of the sleeve was in a tight fist. Her face looked drawn and white and quite peaceful. I poked about in the closet and got a suitcase and put some junk in it. As I started back out I looked at Merle again. Her eyes opened and looked straight up at the ceiling. Then they moved just enough to see me and a faint little smile tugged at the corners of her lips.

'Hello.' It was a weak spent little voice, a voice that knew its owner was in bed and had a nurse and everything.

'Hello.'

I went around near her and stood looking down, with my polished smile on my clear-cut features.

'I'm all right,' she whispered. 'I'm fine. Aren't I?'

'Sure.'

'Is this your bed I'm in?'

'That's all right. It won't bite you.'

'I'm not afraid,' she said. A hand came sliding towards me and lay palm up, waiting to be held. I held it. 'I'm not afraid of you. No woman would ever be afraid of you, would she?'

'Coming from you,' I said, 'I guess that's meant to be a compliment.'

Her eyes smiled, then got grave again. 'I lied to you,' she said softly. 'I – I didn't shoot anybody.'

'I know. I was over there. Forget it. Don't think about it.'

'People are always telling you to forget unpleasant things. But you never do. It's so kind of silly to tell you to, I mean.'

'Okay,' I said, pretending to be hurt. 'I'm silly. How about making some more sleep?'

She turned her head until she was looking into my eyes. I sat on the edge of the bed, holding her hand.

'Will the police come here?' she asked.

'No. And try not to be disappointed.'

She frowned. 'You must think I'm an awful fool.'

'Well – maybe.'

A couple of tears formed in her eyes and slid out at the corners and rolled gently down her cheeks.

'Does Mrs Murdock know where I am?'

'Not yet. I'm going over to tell her.'

'Will you have to tell her – everything?'

'Yeah, why not?'

She turned the head away from me. 'She'll understand,' her

voice said softly. 'She knows the awful thing I did eight years ago. The frightful terrible thing.'

'Sure,' I said. 'That's why she's been paying Vannier money all this time.'

'Oh, dear,' she said, and brought her other hand out from under the bedclothes and pulled away the one I was holding so that she could squeeze them tightly together. 'I wish you hadn't had to know that. I wish you hadn't. Nobody ever knew but Mrs Murdock. My parents never knew. I wish you hadn't.'

The nurse came in at the door and looked at me severely.

'I don't think she ought to be talking like this, Mr Marlowe. I think you should leave now.'

'Look, Miss Lymington, I've known this little girl two days. You've only known her two hours. This is doing her a lot of good.'

'It might bring on another – er – spasm,' she said, severely avoiding my eyes.

'Well, if she has to have it, isn't it better for her to have it now, while you're here, and get it over with? Go on out to the kitchen and buy yourself a drink.'

'I never drink on duty,' she said coldly. 'Besides, somebody might smell my breath.'

'You're working for me now. All my employees are required to get liquored up from time to time. Besides, if you had a good dinner and were to eat a couple of the Chasers in the kitchen cabinet, nobody would smell your breath.'

She gave me a quick grin and went back out of the room. Merle had been listening to this as if it was a frivolous interruption to a very serious play. Rather annoyed.

'I want to tell you all about it,' she said breathlessly. 'I—'

I reached over and put a paw over her two locked hands. 'Skip it. I know. Marlowe knows everything – except how to make a decent living. It doesn't amount to beans. Now you're going back to sleep and tomorrow I'm going to take you on the way back to Wichita – to visit your parents. At Mrs Murdock's expense.'

'Why, that's wonderful of her,' she cried, her eyes opening wide and shining. 'But she's always been wonderful to me.'

I got up off the bed. 'She's a wonderful woman,' I said, grin-

170

ning down at her. 'Wonderful. I'm going over there now and we're going to have a perfectly lovely talk over the teacups. And if you don't go to sleep right now, I won't let you confess to any more murders.'

'You're horrid,' she said. 'I don't like you.' She turned her head away and put her arms back under the bedclothes and shut her eyes.

I went towards the door. At the door I swung around and looked back quickly. She had one eye open, watching me. I gave her a leer and it snapped shut in a hurry.

I went back to the living-room, gave Miss Lymington what was left of my leer, and went out with my suitcase.

I drove over to Santa Monica Boulevard. The hockshop was still open. The old Jew in the tall black skull-cap seemed surprised that I was able to redeem my pledge so soon. I told him that was the way it was in Hollywood.

He got the envelope out of the safe and tore it open and took my money and pawnticket and slipped the shining gold coin out on his palm.

'So valuable this is I am hating to give it back to you,' he said. 'The workmanship, you understand, the workmanship is beautiful.'

'And the gold in it must be worth all of twenty dollars,' I said.

He shrugged and smiled and I put the coin in my pocket and said good night to him.


# Thirty-two


The moonlight lay like a white sheet on the front lawn except under the deodar where there was the thick darkness of black velvet. Lights in two lower windows were lit and in one upstairs room visible from the front. I walked across the stumble-stones and rang the bell.

I didn't look at the little painted negro by the hitching-block. I didn't pat his head tonight. The joke seemed to have worn thin.

A white-haired, red-faced woman I hadn't seen before opened the door and I said: 'I'm Philip Marlowe. I'd like to see Mrs Murdock. Mrs Elizabeth Murdock.'

She looked doubtful. 'I think she's gone to bed,' she said. 'I don't think you can see her.'

'It's only nine o'clock.'

'Mrs Murdock goes to bed early.' She started to close the door.

She was a nice old thing and I hated to give the door the heavy shoulder. I just leaned against it.

'It's about Miss Davis,' I said. 'It's important. Could you tell her that?'

'I'll see.'

I stepped back and let her shut the door.

A mocking-bird sang in a dark tree nearby. A car tore down the street much too fast and skidded around the next corner. The thin shreds of a girl's laughter came back along the dark street as if the car had spilled them out in its rush.

The door opened after a while and the woman said: 'You can come in.'

I followed her across the big empty entrance room. A single dim light burned in one lamp, hardly reaching to the opposite wall. The place was too still, and the air needed freshening. We went along the hall to the end and up a flight of stairs with a carved handrail and newel post. Another hall at the top, a door open towards the back.

I was shown in at the open door and the door was closed behind me. It was a big sitting-room with a lot of chintz, a blue and silver wallpaper, a couch, a blue carpet and french windows open on a balcony. There was an awning over the balcony.

Mrs Murdock was sitting in a padded wing chair with a card-table in front of her. She was wearing a quilted robe and her hair looked a little fluffed out. She was playing solitaire. She had the pack in her left hand and she put a card down and moved another one before she looked up at me.

Then she said: 'Well?'

I went over by the card-table and looked down at the game. It was Canfield.

'Merle's at my apartment,' I said. 'She threw an ing-bing.'

172

Without looking up she said: 'And just what is an ing-bing, Mr Marlowe?'

She moved another card, then two more quickly.

'A case of the vapours, they used to call it,' I said. 'Ever catch yourself cheating at that game?'

'It's no fun if you cheat,' she said gruffly. 'And very little if you don't. What's this about Merle? She has never stayed out like this before. I was getting worried about her.'

I pulled a slipper chair over and sat down across the table from her. It put me too low down. I got up and got a better chair and sat in that.

'No need to worry about her,' I said. 'I got a doctor and a nurse. She's asleep. She was over to see Vannier.'

She laid the pack of cards down and folded her big grey hands on the edge of the table and looked at me solidly.

'Mr Marlowe,' she said, 'you and I had better have something out. I made a mistake calling you in the first place. That was my dislike of being played for a sucker, as you would say, by a hard-boiled little animal like Linda. But it would have been much better, if I had not raised the point at all. The loss of the doubloon would have been much easier to bear than you are. Even if I had never got it back.'

'But you did get it back,' I said.

She nodded. Her eyes stayed on my face. 'Yes. I got it back. You heard how.'

'I didn't believe it.'

'Neither did I,' she said calmly. 'My fool of a son was simply taking the blame for Linda. An attitude I find childish.'

'You have a sort of knack,' I said, 'of getting yourselves surrounded with people who take such attitudes.'

She picked her cards up again and reached down to put a black ten on a red jack, both cards that were already in the layout. Then she reached sideways to a small heavy table on which was her port. She drank some, put the glass down and gave me a hard, level stare.

'I have a feeling that you are going to be insolent, Mr Marlowe.'

I shook my head. 'Not insolent. Just frank. I haven't done so badly for you, Mrs Murdock. You did get the doubloon back.

173

I kept the police away from you – so far. I didn't do anything on the divorce, but I found Linda – your son knew where she was all the time – and I don't think you'll have any trouble with her. She knows she made a mistake marrying Leslie. However, if you don't think you got value—'

She made a humph noise and played another card. She got the ace of diamonds up to the top line. 'The ace of clubs is buried, darn it. I'm not going to get it out in time.'

'Kind of slide it out,' I said, 'when you're not looking.'

'Hadn't you better,' she said very quietly, 'get on with telling me about Merle? And don't gloat too much, if you have found out a few family secrets, Mr Marlowe.'

'I'm not gloating about anything. You sent Merle to Vannier's place this afternoon, with five hundred dollars.'

'And if I did?' She poured some of her port and sipped, eyeing me steadily over the glass.

'When did he ask for it?'

'Yesterday. I couldn't get it out of the bank until today. What happened?'

'Vannier's been blackmailing you for about eight years, hasn't he? On account of something that happened on 26th April 1933?'

A sort of panic twitched in the depths of her eyes, but very far back, very dim, and somehow as though it had been there for a long time and had just peeped out at me for a second.

'Merle told me a few things,' I said. 'Your son told me how his father died. I looked up the records and the papers today. Accidental death. There had been an accident in the street under his office and a lot of people were craning out of windows. He just craned out too far. There was some talk of suicide because he was broke and had fifty thousand life insurance for his family. But the coroner was nice and slid past that.'

'Well?' she said. It was a cold hard voice, neither a croak nor a gasp. A cold, hard, utterly composed voice.

'Merle was Horace Bright's secretary. A queer little girl in a way, over-timid, not sophisticated, a little-girl mentality, likes to dramatize herself, very old-fashioned ideas about men, all that sort of thing. I figure he got high one time and made a pass at her and scared her out of her socks.'

'Yes?' Another cold hard monosyllable prodding me like a gun-barrel.

'She brooded and got a little murderous inside. She got a chance and passed right back at him. While he was leaning out of a window. Anything in it?'

'Speak plainly, Mr Marlowe. I can stand plain talk.'

'Good grief, how plain do you want it? She pushed her employer out of a window. Murdered him, in two words. And got away with it. With your help.'

She looked down at the left hand clenched over her cards. She nodded. Her chin moved a short inch, down, up.

'Did Vannier have any evidence?' I asked. 'Or did he just happen to see what happened and put the bite on you and you paid him a little now and then to avoid scandal – and because you were really very fond of Merle?'

She played another card before she answered me. Steady as a rock.

'He talked about a photograph,' she said. 'But I never believed it. He couldn't have taken one. And if he had taken one, he would have shown it to me – sooner or later.'

I said: 'No, I don't think so. It would have been a very fluky shot, even if he happened to have the camera in his hand, on account of the doings down below in the street. But I can see he might not have dared to show it. You're a pretty hard woman, in some ways. He might have been afraid you would have him taken care of. I mean that's how it might look to him, a crook. How much have you paid him?'

'That's none—' she started to say, then stopped and shrugged her big shoulders. A powerful woman, strong, rugged, ruthless and able to take it. She thought. 'Eleven thousand one hundred dollars, not counting the five hundred I sent him this afternoon.'

'Ah. It was pretty darn nice of you, Mrs Murdock. Considering everything.'

She moved a hand vaguely, made another shrug. 'It was my husband's fault,' she said. 'He was drunk, vile. I don't think he really hurt her, but, as you say, he frightened her out of her wits. I – I can't blame her too much. She has blamed herself enough all these years.'

'She had to take the money to Vannier in person?'

'That was her idea of penance. A strange penance.'

I nodded. 'I guess that would be in character. Later you married Jasper Murdock and you kept Merle with you and took care of her. Anybody else know?'

'Nobody. Only Vannier. Surely he wouldn't tell anybody.'

'No. I hardly think so. Well, it's all over now. Vannier is through.'

She lifted her eyes slowly and gave me a long level gaze. Her grey head was a rock on top of a hill. She put the cards down at last and clasped her hands tightly on the edge of the table. The knuckles glistened.

I said: 'Merle came to my apartment when I was out. She asked the manager to let her in. He phoned me and I said yes. I got over there quickly. She told me she had shot Vannier.'

Her breath was a faint whisper in the stillness of the room.

'She had a gun in her bag, God knows why. Some idea of protecting herself against men, I suppose. But somebody – Leslie, I should guess – had fixed it to be harmless by jamming a wrong size cartridge in the breech. She told me she had killed Vannier and fainted. I got a doctor friend of mine. I went over to Vannier's house. There was a key in the door. He was dead in a chair, long dead, cold, stiff. Dead long before Merle went there. She didn't shoot him. Her telling me that was just drama. The doctor explained it after a fashion, but I won't bore you with it. I guess you understand all right.'

She said: 'Yes. I think I understand. And now?'

'She's in bed, in my apartment. There's a nurse there. I phoned Merle's father long-distance. He wants her to come home. That all right with you?'

She just stared.

'He doesn't know anything,' I said quickly. 'Not this or the other time. I'm sure of that. He just wants her to come home. I thought I'd take her. It seems to be my responsibility now. I'll need that last five hundred that Vannier didn't get – for expenses.'

'And how much more?' she asked brutally.

'Don't say that. You know better.'

'Who killed Vannier?'

'Looks like he committed suicide. A gun at his right hand. Temple contact wound. Morny and his wife were there while I was. I hid. Morny's trying to pin it on his wife. She was playing games with Vannier. So she probably thinks he did it, or had it done. But it shapes up like suicide. The cops will be there by now. I don't know what they will make of it. We just have to sit tight and wait it out.'

'Men like Vannier,' she said grimly, 'don't commit suicide.'

'That's like saying girls like Merle don't push people out of windows. It doesn't mean anything.'

We stared at each other, with that inner hostility that had been there from the first. After a moment I pushed my chair back and went over to the french windows. I opened the screen and stepped out on to the porch. The night was all around, soft and quiet. The white moonlight was cold and clear, like the justice we dream of but don't find.

The trees down below cast heavy shadows under the moon. In the middle of the garden there was a sort of garden within a garden. I caught the glint of an ornamental pool. A lawn swing beside it. Somebody was lying in the lawn swing and a cigarette-tip glowed as I looked down.

I went back into the room. Mrs Murdock was playing solitaire again. I went over to the table and looked down.

'You got the ace of clubs out,' I said.

'I cheated,' she said without looking up.

'There was one thing I wanted to ask you,' I said. 'This doubloon business is still cloudy, on account of a couple of murders which don't seem to make sense now that you have the coin back. What I wondered was if there was anything about the Murdock Brasher that might identify it to an expert – to a man like old Morningstar.'

She thought, sitting still, not looking up. 'Yes. There might be. The coinmaker's initials, E.B., are on the left wing of the eagle. Usually, I'm told, they are on the right wing. That's the only thing I can think of.'

I said: 'I think that might be enough. You did actually get the coin back, didn't you? I mean that wasn't just something said to stop my ferreting around?'

She looked up swiftly and then down. 'It's in the strong room at this moment. If you can find my son, he will show it to you.'

'Well, I'll say good night. Please have Merle's clothes packed and sent to my apartment in the morning.'

Her head snapped up again and her eyes glared. 'You're pretty high-handed about all this, young man.'

'Have them packed,' I said. 'And send them. You don't need Merle any more – now that Vannier is dead.'

Our eyes locked hard and held locked for a long moment. A queer stiff smile moved the corners of her lips. Then her head went down and her right hand took the top card off the pack held in her left hand and turned it and her eyes looked at it and she added it to the pile of unplayed cards below the layout, and then turned the next card, quietly, calmly, in a hand as steady as a stone pier in a light breeze.

I went across the room and out, closed the door softly, went along the hall, down the stairs, along the lower hall past the sun-room and Merle's little office, and out into the cheerless, stuffy, unused living-room that made me feel like an embalmed corpse just to be in it.

The french doors at the back opened and Leslie Murdock stepped in and stopped, staring at me.

## Thirty-three

His slack suit was rumpled and also his hair. His little reddish moustache looked just as ineffectual as ever. The shadows under his eyes were almost pits.

He was carrying his long black cigarette-holder, empty, and tapping it against the heel of his left hand as he stood, not liking me, not wanting to meet me, not wanting to talk to me.

'Good evening,' he said stiffly. 'Leaving?'

'Not quite yet. I want to talk to you.'

'I don't think we have anything to talk about. And I'm tired of talking.'

'Oh, yes we have. A man named Vannier.'

'Vannier? I hardly know the man. I've seen him around. What I know I don't like.'

'You know him a little better than that,' I said.

He came forward into the room and sat down in one of the I-dare-you-to-sit-in-me chairs and leaned forward to cup his chin in his left hand and look at the floor.

'All right,' he said wearily. 'Get on with it. I have a feeling you are going to be very brilliant. Remorseless flow of logic and intuition and all that rot. Just like a detective in a book.'

'Sure. Taking the evidence piece by piece, putting it all together in a neat pattern, sneaking in an odd bit I had on my hip here and there, analysing the motives and characters and making them out to be quite different from what anybody – or I myself for that matter – thought them to be up to this golden moment – and finally making a sort of world-weary pounce on the least promising suspect.'

He lifted his eyes and almost smiled. 'Who thereupon turns as pale as paper, froths at the mouth, and pulls a gun out of his right ear.'

I sat down near him and got a cigarette out. 'That's right. We ought to play it together some time. You got a gun?'

'Not with me. I have one. You know that.'

'Have it with you last night when you called on Vannier?'

He shrugged and bared his teeth. 'Oh. Did I call on Vannier last night?'

'I think so. Deduction. You smoke Benson & Hedges Virginia cigarettes. They leave a firm ash that keeps its shape. An ashtray at his house had enough of those little grey rolls to account for at least two cigarettes. But no stubs in the tray. Because you smoke them in a holder and a stub from a holder looks different. So you removed the stubs. Like it?'

'No.' His voice was quiet. He looked down at the floor again.

'That's an example of deduction. A bad one. For there might not have been any stubs, but if there had been and they had been removed, it might have been because they had lipstick on them. Of a certain shade that would at least indicate the colouring of the smoker. And your wife has a quaint habit of throwing her stubs into the waste-basket.'

'Leave Linda out of this,' he said coldly.

'Your mother still thinks Linda took the doubloon and that your story about taking it to give to Alex Morny was just a cover-up to protect her.'

'I said leave Linda out of it.' The tapping of the black holder against his teeth had a sharp quick sound, like a telegraph key.

'I'm willing to,' I said. 'But I didn't believe your story for a different reason. This.' I took the doubloon out and held it on my hand under his eyes.

He stared at it tightly. His mouth set.

'This morning when you were telling your story this was hocked on Santa Monica Boulevard for safe keeping. It was sent to me by a would-be detective named George Phillips. A simple sort of fellow who allowed himself to get into a bad spot through poor judgement and over-eagerness for a job. A thick-set blond fellow in a brown suit, wearing dark glasses and a rather gay hat. Driving a sand-coloured Pontiac, almost new. You might have seen him hanging about in the hall outside my office yesterday morning. He had been following me around and before that he might have been following you around.'

He looked genuinely surprised. 'Why would he do that?'

I lit my cigarette and dropped the match in a jade ashtray that looked as if it had never been used as an ashtray.

'I said he might have. I'm not sure he did. He might have just been watching this house. He picked me up here and I don't think he followed me here.' I still had the coin on my hand. I looked down at it, turned it over by tossing it, looked at the initials E.B. stamped into the left wing, and put it away. 'He might have been watching the house because he had been hired to peddle a rare coin to an old coin dealer named Morning-star. And the old coin dealer somehow suspected where the coin came from, and told Phillips, or hinted to him, and that the coin was stolen. Incidentally, he was wrong about that. If your Brasher Doubloon is really at this moment upstairs, then the coin Phillips was hired to peddle was not a stolen coin. It was a counterfeit.'

His shoulders gave a quick little jerk, as if he was cold. Otherwise he didn't move or change position.

'I'm afraid it's getting to be one of those long stories after all,' I said, rather gently. 'I'm sorry. I'd better organize it a little better. It's not a pretty story, because it has two murders in it, maybe three. A man named Vannier and a man named Teager had an idea. Teager is a dental technician in the Belfont Building, old Morningstar's building. The idea was to counterfeit a rare and valuable gold coin, not too rare to be marketable, but rare enough to be worth a lot of money. The method they thought of was about what a dental technician uses to make a gold inlay. Requiring the same materials, the same apparatus, the same skill. That is, to reproduce a model exactly, in gold, by making a matrix in a hard white fine cement called albastone, then making a replica of the model in that matrix in moulding-wax, complete in the finest detail, then investing the wax, as they call it, in another kind of cement called crystobolite, which has the property of standing great heat without distortion. A small opening is left from the wax to outside by attaching a steel pin which is withdrawn when the cement sets. Then the crystobolite casting is cooked over a flame until the wax boils out through this small opening, leaving a hollow mould of the original model. This is clamped against a crucible on a centrifuge and molten gold is shot into it by centrifugal force from the crucible. Then the crystobolite, still hot, is held under cold water and it disintegrates, leaving the gold core with a gold pin attached, representing the small opening. That is trimmed off, the casting is cleaned in acid and polished and you have, in this case, a brand new Brasher Doubloon, made of solid gold and exactly the same as the original. You get the idea?'

He nodded and moved a hand wearily across his head.

'The amount of skill this would take,' I went on, 'would be just what a dental technician would have. The process would be of no use for a current coinage, if we had a gold coinage, because the material and labour would cost more than the coin would be worth. But for a gold coin that was valuable through being rare, it would fit fine. So that's what they did. But they had to have a model. That's where you came in. You took the doubloon all right, but not to give to Morny. You took it to give to Vannier. Right?'

He stared at the floor and didn't speak.

'Loosen up,' I said. 'In the circumstances it's nothing very awful. I suppose he promised you money, because you needed

181

it to pay off gambling debts and your mother is close. But he had a stronger hold over you than that.'

He looked up quickly then, his face very white, a kind of horror in his eyes.

'How did you know that?' he almost whispered.

'I found out. Some I was told, some I researched, some I guessed. I'll get to that later. Now Vannier and his pal have made a doubloon and they want to try it out. They wanted to know their merchandise would stand up under inspection by a man supposed to know rare coins. So Vannier had the idea of hiring a sucker and getting him to try to sell the counterfeit to old Morningstar, cheap enough so the old guy would think it was stolen. They picked George Phillips for their sucker, through a silly ad. he was running in the paper for business. I think Lois Morny was Vannier's contact with Phillips, at first, anyway. I don't think she was in the racket. She was seen to give Phillips a small package. This package may have contained the doubloon Phillips was to try to sell. But when he showed it to old Morningstar he ran into a snag. The old man knew his coin collections and his rare coins. He probably thought the coin was genuine enough – it would take a lot of testing to show it wasn't – but the way the maker's initials were stamped on the coin was unusual and suggested to him that the coin might be the Murdock Brasher. He called up here and tried to find out. That made your mother suspicious and the coin was found to be missing and she suspected Linda, whom she hates, and hired me to get it back and put the squeeze on Linda for a divorce, without alimony.'

'I don't want a divorce,' Murdock said hotly. 'I never had any such idea. She had no right—' he stopped and made a despairing gesture and a kind of sobbing sound.

'Okay, I know that. Well, old Morningstar threw a scare into Phillips, who wasn't crooked, just dumb. He managed to get Phillips's phone number out of him. I heard the old man call that number, eavesdropping in his office after he thought I had left. I had just offered to buy the doubloon back for a thousand dollars and Morningstar had taken up the offer, thinking he could get the coin from Phillips, make himself some money and everything lovely. Meantime Phillips was watching this house, perhaps to see if any cops were coming and going. He saw me, saw my car, got my name off the registration and it just happened he knew who I was.

'He followed me around trying to make up his mind to ask me for help until I braced him in a downtown hotel and he mumbled about knowing me from a case in Ventura when he was a deputy up there, and about being in a spot he didn't like and about being followed around by a tall guy with a funny eye. That was Eddie Prue, Morny's side-winder. Morny knew his wife was playing games with Vannier and had her shadowed. Prue saw her make contact with Phillips near where he lived on Court Street, Bunker Hill, and then followed Phillips until he thought Phillips had spotted him, which he had. And Prue, or somebody working for Morny, may have seen me go to Phillips's apartment on Court Street. Because he tried to scare me over the phone and later asked me to come and see Morny.'

I got rid of my cigarette-stub in the jade ashtray, looked at the bleak, unhappy face of the man sitting opposite me, and ploughed on. It was heavy going, and the sound of my voice was beginning to sicken me.

'Now we come back to you. When Merle told you your mother had hired a dick, that threw a scare into *you*. You figured she had missed the doubloon and you came steaming up to my office and tried to pump me. Very debonair, very sarcastic at first, very solicitous for your wife, but very worried. I don't know what you think you found out, but you got in touch with Vannier. You now had to get the coin back to your mother in a hurry, with some kind of story. You met Vannier somewhere and he gave you a doubloon. Chances are it's another counterfeit. He would be likely to hang on to the real one. Now Vannier sees his racket in danger of blowing up before it gets started. Morningstar has called your mother and I have been hired. Morningstar has spotted something. Vannier goes down to Phillips's apartment, sneaks in the back way and has it out with Phillips, trying to find out where he stands.

'Phillips doesn't tell him he has already sent the counterfeit doubloon to me, addressing it in a kind of printing afterwards found in a diary in his office. I infer that from the fact Vannier didn't try to get it back from me. I don't know what Phillips told Vannier, of course, but the chances are he told him the job was crooked, that he knew where the coin came from, and that he was going to the police or to Mrs Murdock. And Vannier pulled a gun, knocked him on the head and shot him. He searched him and the apartment and didn't find the doubloon. So he went to Morningstar. Morningstar didn't have the counterfeit either, but Vannier probably thought he had. He cracked the old man's skull with a gun-butt and went through his safe, perhaps found some money, perhaps found nothing, at any rate left the appearance of a stick-up behind him. Then Mr Vannier breezed on home, still rather annoyed because he hadn't found the doubloon, but with the satisfaction of a good afternoon's work under his vest. A couple of nice neat murders. That left you.'

# Thirty-four

Murdock flicked a strained look at me, then his eyes went to the black cigarette-holder he still had clenched in his hand. He tucked it in his shirt pocket, stood up suddenly, ground the heels of his hands together and sat down again. He got a handkerchief out and mopped his face.

'Why me?' he asked in a thick strained voice.

'You knew too much. Perhaps you knew about Phillips, perhaps not. Depends how deep you were in it. But you knew about Morningstar. The scheme had gone wrong and Morningstar had been murdered. Vannier couldn't just sit back and hope you wouldn't hear about that. He had to shut your mouth, very, very tight. But he didn't have to kill you to do it. In fact, killing you would be a bad move. It would break his hold on your mother. She's a cold, ruthless, grasping woman, but hurting you would make a wildcat of her. She wouldn't care what happened.'

Murdock lifted his eyes. He tried to make them blank with astonishment. He only made them dull and shocked.

'My mother – what—?'

184

'Don't kid me any more than you have to,' I said. 'I'm tired to death of being kidded by the Murdock family. Merle came to my apartment this evening. She's there now. She had been over to Vannier's house to bring him some money. Blackmail money. Money that had been paid to him off and on for eight years. I know why.'

He didn't move. His hands were rigid with strain on his knees. His eyes had almost disappeared into the back of his head. They were doomed eyes.

'Merle found Vannier dead. She came to me and said she had killed him. Let's not go into why she thinks she ought to confess to other people's murders. I went over there and he had been dead since last night. He was as stiff as a wax dummy. There was a gun lying on the floor by his right hand. It was a gun I had heard described, a gun that belonged to a man named Hench, in an apartment across the hall from Phillips's apartment. Somebody ditched the gun that killed Phillips and took Hench's gun. Hench and his girl were drunk and left their apartment open. It's not proved that it was Hench's gun, but it will be. If it is Hench's gun, and Vannier committed suicide, it ties Vannier to the death of Phillips. Lois Morny also ties him to Phillips, in another way. If Vannier didn't commit suicide – and I don't believe he did – it might still tie him to Phillips. Or it might tie somebody else to Phillips, somebody who also killed Vannier. There are reasons why I don't like that idea.'

Murdock's head came up. He said: 'No?' in a suddenly clear voice. There was a new expression on his face, something bright and shining and at the same time just a little silly. The expression of a weak man being proud.

I said: 'I think you killed Vannier.'

He didn't move and the bright shining expression stayed on his face.

'You went over there last night. He sent for you. He told you he was in a jam and that if the law caught up with him, he would see that you were in the jam with him. Didn't he say something like that?'

'Yes,' Murdock said quietly. 'Something exactly like that. He was drunk and a bit high and he seemed to have a sense of power. He gloated, almost. He said if they got him in the gas

185

chamber I would be sitting right beside him. But that wasn't all he said.'

'No. He didn't want to sit in the gas chamber and he didn't at the time see any very good reason why he should, if you kept your mouth good and tight. So he played his trump card. His first hold on you, what made you take the doubloon and give it to him, even if he did promise you money as well, was something about Merle and your father. I know about it. Your mother told me what little I hadn't put together already. That was his first hold and it was pretty strong. Because it would let you justify yourself. But last night he wanted something still stronger. So he told you the truth and said he had proof.'

He shivered, but the light clear proud look managed to stay on his face.

'I pulled a gun on him,' he said, almost in a happy voice. 'After all, she is my mother.'

'Nobody can take that away from you.'

He stood up, very straight, very tall. 'I went over to the chair he sat in and reached down and put the gun against his face. He had a gun in the pocket of his robe. He tried to get it, but he didn't get it in time. I took it away from him. I put my gun back in my pocket. I put the muzzle of the other gun against the side of his head and told him I would kill him, if he didn't produce his proof and give it to me. He began to sweat and babble that he was just kidding me. I clicked back the hammer on the gun to scare him some more.'

He stopped and held a hand out in front of him. The hand shook but as he stared down at it it got steady. He dropped it to his side and looked me in the eye.

'The gun must have been fired or had a very light action. It went off. I jumped back against the wall and knocked a picture down. I jumped from surprise that the gun went off, but it kept the blood off me. I wiped the gun off and put his fingers around it and then put it down on the floor close to his hand. He was dead at once. He hardly bled except the first spurt. It was an accident.'

'Why spoil it?' I half sneered. 'Why not make it a nice clean honest murder?'

'That's what happened. I can't prove it, of course. But I think

I might have killed him anyway. What about the police?'

I stood up and shrugged my shoulders. I felt tired, spent, drawn out and sapped. My throat was sore from yapping and my brain ached from trying to keep my thoughts orderly.

'I don't know about the police,' I said. 'They and I are not very good friends, on account of they think I am holding out on them. And God knows they are right. They may get to you. If you weren't seen, if you didn't leave any fingerprints around, and even if you did, if they don't have any other reason to suspect you and get your fingerprints to check, then they may never think of you. If they find out about the doubloon and that it was the Murdock Brasher, I don't know where you stand. It all depends on how well you stand up to them.'

'Except for mother's sake,' he said, 'I don't very much care. I've always been a flop.'

'And on the other hand,' I said, ignoring the feeble talk, 'if the gun really has a very light action and you get a good lawyer and tell an honest story and so on, no jury will convict you. Juries don't like blackmailers.'

'That's too bad,' he said. 'Because I am not in a position to use that defence. I don't know anything about blackmail. Vannier showed me where I could make some money, and I needed it badly.'

I said: 'Uh-huh. If they get you where you need the blackmail dope, you'll use it all right. Your old lady will make you. If it's her neck or yours, she'll spill.'

'It's horrible,' he said. 'Horrible to say that.'

'You were lucky about that gun. All the people we know have been playing with it, wiping prints off and putting them on. I even put a set on myself just to be fashionable. It's tricky when the hand is stiff. But I had to do it. Morny was over there having his wife put hers on. He thinks she killed Vannier, so she probably thinks he did.'

He just stared at me. I chewed my lip. It felt as stiff as a piece of glass.

'Well, I guess I'll just be running along now,' I said.

'You mean you are going to let me get away with it?' His voice was getting a little supercilious again.

'I'm not going to turn you in, if that's what you mean. Beyond that I guarantee nothing. If I'm involved in it, I'll have to face up to the situation. There's no question of morality involved. I'm not a cop nor a common informer nor an officer of the court. You say it was an accident. Okay, it was an accident. I wasn't a witness. I haven't any proof either way. I've been working for your mother and whatever right to my silence that gives her, she can have. I don't like her, I don't like you. I don't like this house. I didn't particularly like your wife. But I like Merle. She's kind of silly and morbid, but she's kind of sweet, too. And I know what has been done to her in this damn family for the past eight years. And I know she didn't push anybody out of any window. Does that explain matters?'

He gobbled, but nothing came that was coherent.

'I'm taking Merle home,' I said. 'I asked your mother to send her clothes to my apartment in the morning. In case she kind of forgets, being busy with her solitaire game, would you see that that is done?'

He nodded dumbly. Then he said in a queer small voice: 'You are going – just like that? I haven't – I haven't even thanked you. A man I hardly know, taking risks for me – I don't know what to say.'

'I'm going the way I always go,' I said. 'With an airy smile and a quick flip of the wrist. And with a deep and heartfelt hope I won't be seeing you in the fish-bowl. Good night.'

I turned my back on him and went to the door and out. I shut the door with a quiet, firm click of the lock. A nice, smooth exit, in spite of all the nastiness. For the last time I went over and patted the little painted negro on the head and then walked across the long lawn by the moon-drenched shrubs and the deodar tree to the street and my car.

I drove back to Hollywood, bought a pint of good liquor, checked in at the Plaza, and sat on the side of the bed staring at my feet and lapping the whisky out of the bottle.

Just like any common bedroom drunk.

When I had enough of it to make my brain fuzzy enough to stop thinking, I undressed and got into bed, and after a while, but not soon enough, I went to sleep.

# Thirty-five

It was three o'clock in the afternoon and there were five pieces of luggage inside the apartment door, side by side on the carpet. There was my yellow cowhide, well scraped on both sides from being pushed around in the boots of cars. There were two nice pieces of airplane luggage, both marked L.M. There was an old black imitation walrus thing marked M.D. and there was one of these little leatherette overnight cases which you can buy in drug-stores for a dollar forty-nine.

Dr Carl Moss had just gone out of the door cursing me because he had kept his afternoon class of hypochondriacs waiting. The sweetish smell of his Fatima poisoned the air for me. I was turning over in what was left of my mind what he had said when I asked him how long it would take Merle to get well.

'It depends what you mean by well. She'll always be high on nerves and low on animal emotion. She'll always breathe thin air and smell snow. She'd have made a perfect nun. The religious dream, with its narrowness, its stylized emotions and its grim purity, would have been a perfect release for her. As it is, she will probably turn out to be one of these acid-faced virgins that sit behind little desks in public libraries and stamp dates in books.'

'She's not that bad,' I had said, but he had just grinned at me with his wise Jew face and gone out of the door. 'And besides, how do you know they are virgins?' I added to the closed door, but that didn't get me any farther.

I lit a cigarette and wandered over to the window and after a while she came through the doorway from the bedroom part of the apartment and stood there looking at me with her eyes dark-ringed and a pale composed little face without any make-up except on the lips.

'Put some rouge on your cheeks,' I told her. 'You look like the snow maiden after a hard night with the fishing fleet.'

So she went back and put some rouge on her cheeks. When she came back again she looked at the luggage and said softly: 'Leslie lent me two of his suitcases.'

I said: 'Yeah,' and looked her over. She looked very nice. She had a pair of long-waisted, rust-coloured slacks on, and Bata shoes and a brown and white print shirt and an orange scarf. She didn't have her glasses on. Her large clear cobalt eyes had a slightly dopey look, but not more than you would expect. Her hair was dragged down tight, but I couldn't do anything much about that.

'I've been a terrible nuisance,' she said. 'I'm terribly sorry.'

'Nonsense. I talked to your father and mother both. They're tickled to death. They've only seen you twice in over eight years and they feel as if they almost lost you.'

'I'll love seeing them for a while,' she said, looking down at the carpet. 'It's very kind of Mrs Murdock to let me go. She's never been able to spare me for long.' She moved her legs as if she wondered what to do with them in slacks, although they were her slacks and she must have had to face the problem before. She finally put her knees close together and clasped her hands on top of them.

'Any little talking we might have to do,' I said, 'or anything you might want to say to me, let's get it over with now. Because I'm not driving half-way across the United States with a nervous breakdown in the seat beside me.'

She bit a knuckle and sneaked a couple of quick looks at me around the side of the knuckle. 'Last night—' she said, and stopped and coloured.

'Let's use a little of the old acid,' I said. 'Last night you told me you killed Vannier and then you told me you didn't. I know you didn't. That's settled.'

She dropped the knuckle, looked at me levelly, quiet, composed and the hands on her knees now not straining at all.

'Vannier was dead a long time before you got there. You went there to give him some money for Mrs Murdock.'

'No – for me,' she said. 'Although, of course, it was Mrs Murdock's money. I owe her more than I'll ever be able to repay. Of course, she doesn't give me much salary, but that would hardly—'

I said roughly: 'Her not giving you much salary is a characteristic touch and your owing her more than you can ever repay is more truth than poetry. It would take the Yankee outfield with two bats each to give her what she has coming from you. However, that's unimportant now. Vannier committed suicide because he had got caught out in a crooked job. That's flat and final. The way you behaved was more or less an act. You got a severe nervous shock seeing his leering dead face in a mirror and that shock merged into another one a long time ago and you just dramatized it in your screwy little way.'

She looked at me shyly and nodded her copper-blonde head, as if in agreement.

'And you didn't push Horace Bright out of any window,' I said.

Her face jumped then and turned startlingly pale. 'I – I—' her hand went to her mouth and stayed there and her shocked eyes looked at me over it.

'I wouldn't be doing this,' I said, 'if Dr Moss hadn't said it would be all right and we might as well hand it to you now. I think, maybe, you think you killed Horace Bright. You had a motive and an opportunity and just for a second I think you might have had the impulse to take advantage of the opportunity. But it wouldn't be in your nature. At the last minute you would hold back. But at that last minute probably something snapped and you pulled a faint. He did actually fall, of course, but you were not the one that pushed him.'

I held it a moment and watched the hand drop down again to join the other one and the two of them twine together and pull hard on each other.

'You were made to think you had pushed him,' I said. 'It was done with care, deliberation and the sort of quiet ruthlessness you only find in a certain kind of woman dealing with another woman. You wouldn't think of jealousy to look at Mrs Murdock now – but if that was a motive, she had it. She had a better one – fifty thousand dollars' life insurance – all that was left from a ruined fortune. She had the strange wild possessive love for her son such women have. She's cold, bitter, unscrupulous, and she used you without mercy or pity, as insurance, in case Vannier ever blew his top. You were just a scapegoat to her. If you want to come out of this pallid sub-emotional life you have been living, you have got to realize and believe what I am telling you. I know it's tough.'

'It's utterly impossible,' she said quietly, looking at the bridge of my nose, 'Mrs Murdock has been wonderful to me always. It's true I never remembered very well – but you shouldn't say such awful things about people.'

I got out the white envelope that had been in the back of Vannier's picture. Two prints in it and a negative. I stood in front of her and put a print on her lap.

'Okay, look at it. Vannier took it from across the street.'

She looked at it. 'Why, that's Mr Bright,' she said. 'It's not a very good picture, is it? And that's Mrs Murdock – Mrs Bright she was then – right behind him. Mr Bright looks mad.' She looked up at me with a sort of mild curiosity.

'If he looks mad there,' I said, 'you ought to have seen him a few seconds later, when he bounced.'

'When he what?'

'Look,' I said, and there was a kind of desperation in my voice now, 'that is a snapshot of Mrs Elizabeth Bright Murdock giving her first husband the heave out of his office window. He's falling. Look at the position of his hands. He's screaming with fear. She is behind him and her face is hard with rage – or something. Don't you get it at all? This is what Vannier has had for proof all these years. The Murdocks never saw it, never really believed it existed. But it did. I found it last night, by a fluke of the same sort that was involved in the taking of the picture. Which is a fair sort of justice. Do you begin to understand?'

She looked at the photo again and laid it aside. 'Mrs Murdock has always been lovely to me,' she said.

'She made you the goat,' I said, in the quietly strained voice of a stage manager at a bad rehearsal. 'She's a smart, tough, patient woman. She knows her complexes. She'll even spend a dollar to keep a dollar, which is what few of her type will do. I hand it to her. I'd like to hand it to her with an elephant gun, but my polite breeding restrains me.'

'Well,' she said, 'that's that.' And I could see she had heard one word in three and hadn't believed what she had heard. 'You must never show this to Mrs Murdock. It would upset her terribly.'

I got up and took the photo out of her hand and tore it into small pieces and dropped them in the waste-basket.

'Maybe you'll be sorry I did that,' I told her, not telling her I had another and the negative. 'Maybe some night – three months – three years from now – you will wake up in the night and realize I have been telling you the truth. And, maybe, then you will wish you could look at that photograph again. And, maybe, I am wrong about this, too. Maybe you would be very disappointed to find out you hadn't really killed anybody. That's fine. Either way it's fine. Now we are going downstairs and get in my car and we are going to drive to Wichita to visit your parents. And I don't think you are going back to Mrs Murdock, but it may well be that I am wrong about that, too. But we are not going to talk about this any more. Not any more.'

'I haven't any money,' she said.

'You have five hundred dollars that Mrs Murdock sent you. I have it in my pocket.'

'That's really awfully kind of her,' she said.

'Oh hell and fireflies,' I said and went out to the kitchen and gobbled a quick drink, before we started. It didn't do me any good. It just made me want to climb up the wall and gnaw my way across the ceiling.


# Thirty-six


I was gone ten days. Merle's parents were vague, kind, patient people, living in an old frame house in a quiet shady street. They cried when I told them as much of the story as I thought they should know. They said they were glad to have her back and they would take good care of her and they blamed themselves a lot, and I let them do it.

When I left, Merle was wearing a bungalow apron and rolling pie-crust. She came to the door wiping her hands on the apron and kissed me on the mouth and began to cry and ran back into the house, leaving the doorway empty until her mother came into the space with a broad homely smile on her face to watch me drive away.

I had a funny feeling as I saw the house disappear, as though

I had written a poem and it was very good and I had lost it and would never remember it again.

I called Lieutenant Breeze when I got back and went down to ask him how the Phillips case was coming. They had cracked it very neatly, with the right mixture of brains and luck you always have to have. The Mornys never went to the police after all, but somebody called and told about a shot in Vannier's house and hung up quickly. The fingerprint man didn't like the prints on the gun too well, so they checked Vannier's hand for powder nitrates. When they found them they decided it was suicide after all. Then a dick named Lackey working out of Central Homicide thought to work on the gun a little and he found that a description of it had been distributed, and a gun like it was wanted in connection with the Phillips killing. Hench identified it, but better than that they found a half-print of his thumb on the side of the trigger, which, not ordinarily being pulled back, had not been wiped off completely.

With that much in hand and a better set of Vannier's prints than I could make, they went over Phillips's apartment again and also over Hench's. They found Vannier's left hand on Hench's bed and one of his fingers on the underside of the toilet flush lever in Phillips's place. Then they got to work in the neighbourhood with photographs of Vannier, and proved he had been along the alley twice and on a side street at least three times. Curiously, nobody in the apartment house had seen him, or would admit it.

All they lacked now was a motive. Teager obligingly gave them that by getting himself pinched in Salt Lake City trying to peddle a Brasher Doubloon to a coin dealer who thought it was genuine but stolen. He had a dozen of them at his hotel, and one of them turned out to be genuine. He told them the whole story and showed a minute mark that he had used to identify the genuine coin. He didn't know where Vannier got it and they never found out because there was enough in the papers to make the owner come forward, if it had been stolen. And the owner never did. And the police didn't care any more about Vannier once they were convinced he had done murder. They left it at suicide, although they had a few doubts.

They let Teager go after a while, because they didn't think he had any idea of murder being done and all they had on him was attempted fraud. He had bought the gold legally and counterfeiting an obsolete New York State coin didn't come under the federal counterfeiting laws. Utah refused to bother with him.

They never believed Hench's confession. Breeze said he just used it for a squeeze on me, in case I was holding out. He knew I couldn't keep quiet if I had proof that Hench was innocent. It didn't do Hench any good, either. They put him in the line-up and pinned five liquor-store hold-ups on him and a wop named Gaetano Prisco, in one of which a man was shot dead. I never heard whether Prisco was a relative of Palermo's, but they never caught him, anyway.

'Like it?' Breeze asked me, when he had told me all this, or all that had then happened.

'Two points not clear,' I said. 'Why did Teager run away and why did Phillips live on Court Street under a phony name?'

'Teager ran away because the elevator man told him old Morningstar had been murdered and he smelled a hook-up. Phillips was using the name of Anson because the finance company was after his car and he was practically broke and getting desperate. That explains why a nice young boob like him could get roped in to something that must have looked shady from the start.'

I nodded and agreed that could be so.

Breeze walked to his door with me. He put a hard hand on my shoulder and squeezed.

'Remember that Cassidy case you were howling about to Spangler and me that night in your apartment?'

'Yes.'

'You told Spangler there wasn't any Cassidy case. There was – under another name. I worked on it.'

He took his hand off my shoulder and opened the door for me and grinned straight into my eyes.

'On account of the Cassidy case,' he said, 'and the way it made me feel, I sometimes give a guy a break he could perhaps not really deserve. A little something paid back out of the dirty millions to a working stiff – like me – or like you. Be good.'

It was night. I went home and put my old house clothes on and set the chessmen out and mixed a drink and played over another Capablanca. It went fifty-nine moves. Beautiful, cold, remorseless chess, almost creepy in its silent implacability.

When it was done I listened at the open window for a while and smelled the night. Then I carried my glass out to the kitchen and rinsed it and filled it with ice water and stood at the sink sipping it and looking at my face in the mirror.

'You and Capablanca,' I said.

# The Long Good-bye

# One

The first time I laid eyes on Terry Lennox he was drunk in a Rolls Royce Silver Wraith outside the terrace of The Dancers. The parking lot attendant had brought the car out and he was still holding the door open because Terry Lennox's left foot was still dangling outside, as if he had forgotten he had one. He had a young-looking face but his hair was bone white. You could tell by his eyes that he was plastered to the hairline, but otherwise he looked like any other nice young man in a dinner jacket who had been spending too much money in a joint that exists for that purpose and for no other.

There was a girl beside him. Her hair was a lovely shade of dark red and she had a distant smile on her lips and over her shoulders she had a blue mink that almost made the Rolls Royce look like just another automobile. It didn't quite. Nothing can.

The attendant was the usual half-tough character in a white coat with the name of the restaurant stitched across the front of it in red. He was getting fed up.

'Look, mister,' he said with an edge to his voice, 'would you mind a whole lot pulling your leg into the car so I can kind of shut the door? Or should I open it all the way so you can fall out?'

The girl gave him a look which ought to have stuck at least four inches out of his back. It didn't bother him enough to give him the shakes. At The Dancers they get the sort of people that disillusion you about what a lot of golfing money can do for the personality.

A low-slung foreign speedster with no top drifted into the parking lot and a man got out of it and used the dash lighter on a long cigarette. He was wearing a pullover check shirt, yellow slacks, and riding boots. He strolled off trailing clouds of incense, not even bothering to look towards the Rolls Royce. He probably thought it was corny. At the foot of the steps up to the terrace he paused to stick a monocle in his eye.

The girl said with a nice burst of charm: 'I have a wonderful idea darling. Why don't we just take the cab to your place and get your convertible out? It's such a wonderful night for a run up the coast to Montecito. I know some people there who are throwing a dance around the pool.'

The white-haired lad said politely: 'Awfully sorry, but I don't have it any more. I was compelled to sell it.' From his voice and articulation you wouldn't have known he had had anything stronger than orange juice to drink.

'Sold it, darling? How do you mean?' She slid away from him along the seat but her voice slid away a lot further than that.

'I mean I had to,' he said. 'For eating money.'

'Oh, I see.' A slice of spumoni wouldn't have melted on her now.

The attendant had the white-haired boy right where he could reach him – in a low income bracket. 'Look, buster,' he said, 'I've got to put a car away. See you some more some other time – maybe.'

He let the door swing open. The drunk promptly slid off the seat and landed on the blacktop on the seat of his pants. So I went over and dropped my nickel. I guess it's always a mistake to interfere with a drunk. Even if he knows and likes you he is always liable to haul off and poke you in the teeth. I got him under the arms and got him up on his feet.

'Thank you so very much,' he said politely.

The girl slid under the wheel. 'He gets so goddam English when he's loaded,' she said in a stainless-steel voice. 'Thanks for catching him.'

'I'll get him in the back of the car,' I said.

'I'm terribly sorry. I'm late for an engagement.' She let the clutch in and the Rolls started to glide. 'He's just a lost dog,' she added with a cool smile. 'Perhaps you can find a home for him. He's housebroken – more or less.'

And the Rolls ticked down the entrance driveway on to Sunset Boulevard, made a right turn, and was gone. I was looking after her when the attendant came back. And I was still holding the man up and he was now sound asleep.

'Well, that's one way of doing it,' I told the white coat.

'Sure,' he said cynically. 'Why waste it on a lush? Them curves and all.'

'You know him?'

'I heard the dame call him Terry. Otherwise I don't know him from a cow's caboose. But I only been here two weeks.'

'Get my car, will you?' I gave him the ticket.

By the time he brought my Olds over I felt as if I was holding up a sack of lead. The white coat helped me get him into the front seat. The customer opened an eye and thanked us and went to sleep again.

'He's the politest drunk I ever met,' I said to the white coat.

'They come all sizes and shapes and all kinds of manners,' he said. 'And they're all bums. Looks like this one had a plastic job one time.'

'Yeah.' I gave him a dollar and he thanked me. He was right about the plastic job. The right side of my new friend's face was frozen and whitish and seamed with thin, fine scars. The skin had a glossy look along the scars. A plastic job and a pretty drastic one.

'Whatcha aim to do with him?'

'Take him home and sober him up enough to tell me where he lives.'

The white coat grinned at me. 'Okay, sucker. If it was me, I'd just drop him in the gutter and keep going. Them booze hounds just make a man a lot of trouble for no fun. I got a philosophy about them things. The way the competition is nowadays a guy has to save his strength to protect hisself in the clinches.'

'I can see you've made a big success out of it,' I said.

He looked puzzled and then he started to get mad, but by that time I was in the car and moving.

He was partly right of course. Terry Lennox made me plenty of trouble. But after all that's my line of work.

I was living that year in a house on Yucca Avenue in the Laurel Canyon district. It was a small hillside house on a dead-end street with a long flight of redwood steps to the front door and a grove of eucalyptus trees across the way. It was furnished, and it belonged to a woman who had gone to Idaho to live with her widowed daughter for a while. The rent was low, partly because the owner wanted to be able to come back on short notice, and partly because of the steps. She was getting too old to face them every time she came home.

I got the drunk up them somehow. He was eager to help but his legs were rubber and he kept falling asleep in the middle of an apologetic sentence. I got the door unlocked and dragged him inside and spread him on the long couch, threw a rug over him and let him go back to sleep. He snored like a grampus for an hour. Then he came awake all of a sudden and wanted to go to the bathroom. When he came back he looked at me peeringly, squinting his eyes, and wanted to know where the hell he was. I told him. He said his name was Terry Lennox and that he lived in an apartment in Westwood and no one was waiting up for him. His voice was clear and unslurred.

He said he could handle a cup of black coffee. When I brought it he sipped it carefully, holding the saucer close under the cup.

'How come I'm here?' he asked, looking around.

'You squiffed out at The Dancers in a Rolls. Your girl friend ditched you.'

'Quite,' he said. 'No doubt she was entirely justified.'

'You English?'

'I've lived there. I wasn't born there. If I might call a taxi, I'll take myself off.'

'You've got one waiting.'

He made the steps on his own going down. He didn't say much on the way to Westwood, except that it was very kind of me and he was sorry to be such a nuisance. He had probably said it so often and to so many people that it was automatic.

His apartment was small and stuffy and impersonal. He might have moved in that afternoon. On a coffee table in front of a hard green davenport there was a half-empty Scotch bottle and melted ice in a bowl and three empty fizzwater bottles and two glasses and a glass ashtray loaded with stubs with and without lipstick. There wasn't a photograph or a personal article of any kind in the place. It might have been a hotel room rented for a meeting or a farewell, for a few drinks and a talk, for a roll in the hay. It didn't look like a place where anyone lived.

He offered me a drink, I said no thanks. I didn't sit down. When I left he thanked me some more, but not as if I had climbed a mountain for him, nor as if it was nothing at all. He was a little shaky and a little shy but polite as hell. He stood in the open door until the automatic elevator came up and I got into it. Whatever he didn't have he had manners.

He hadn't mentioned the girl again. Also, he hadn't mentioned that he had no job and no prospects and that almost his last dollar had gone into paying the check at The Dancers for a bit of high-class fluff that couldn't stick around long enough to make sure he didn't get tossed in the sneezer by some prowl car boys or rolled by a tough hackie and dumped out in a vacant lot.

On the way down in the elevator I had an impulse to go back up and take the Scotch bottle away from him. But it wasn't any of my business and it never does any good anyway. They always find a way to get it if they have to have it.

I drove home chewing my lip. I'm supposed to be tough but there was something about the guy that got to me. I didn't know what it was unless it was the white hair and the scarred face and the clear voice and the politeness. Maybe that was enough. There was no reason why I should ever see him again. He was just a lost dog, like the girl said.

# Two

It was the week after Thanksgiving when I saw him again. The stores along Hollywood Boulevard were already beginning to fill up with overpriced Christmas junk, and the daily papers were beginning to scream about how terrible it would be if you didn't get your Christmas shopping done early. It would be terrible anyway; it always is.

It was about three blocks from my office building that I saw a cop car double-parked and the two buttons in it staring at something over by a shop window on the sidewalk. The something was Terry Lennox – or what was left of him – and that little was not too attractive.

He was leaning against a store front. He had to lean against something. His shirt was dirty and open at the neck and partly outside his jacket and partly not. He hadn't shaved for four or five days. His nose was pinched. His skin was so pale that the long thin scars hardly showed. And his eyes were like holes poked in a snow bank. It was pretty obvious that the buttons in the prowl car were about ready to drop the hook on him, so I went over there fast and took hold of his arm.

'Straighten up and walk,' I said, putting on the tough. I winked at him from the side. 'Can you make it? Are you stinko?'

He looked me over vaguely and then smiled his little one-sided smile. 'I have been,' he breathed. 'Right now I guess I'm just a little – empty.'

'Okay, but make with the feet. You're half-way into the drunk tank already.'

He made the effort and let me walk him through the sidewalk loafers to the edge of the curb. There was a taxi stand there and I yanked open the door.

'He goes first,' the hackie said, jerking a thumb at the cab ahead. He swung his head around and saw Terry. 'If at all,' he added.

'This is an emergency. My friend is sick.'

'Yeah,' the hackie said. 'He could get sick somewheres else.'

'Five bucks,' I said, 'and let's see that beautiful smile.'

'Oh well,' he said, and stuck a magazine with a Martian on the cover behind his mirror. I reached in and got the door open. I got Terry Lennox in and the shadow of the prowl car blocked the far window. A grey-haired cop got out and came over. I went around the taxi and met him.

'Just a minute, Mac. What have we got here? Is the gentleman in the soiled laundry a real close friend of yours?'

'Close enough for me to know he needs a friend. He's not drunk.'

'For financial reasons, no doubt,' the cop said. He put his hand out and I put my licence in it. He looked at it and handed it back. 'Oh ho,' he said. 'A P.I. picking up a client.' His voice changed and got tough. 'That tells a little something about you, Mr Marlowe. What about him?'

'His name's Terry Lennox. He works in pictures.'

'That's nice,' the cop said sarcastically. He leaned into the taxi and stared at Terry back in the corner. 'I'd say he didn't work too lately. I'd say he didn't sleep indoors too lately. I'd even say he was a wag and so maybe we ought to take him in.'

'Your arrest record can't be that low,' I said. 'Not in Hollywood.'

He was still looking in at Terry. 'What's your friend's name, buddy?'

'Philip Marlowe,' Terry said slowly. 'He lives on Yucca Avenue, Laurel Canyon.'

The cop pulled his head out of the window space. He turned, and made a gesture with his hand. 'You could of just told him.'

'I could have, but I didn't.'

He stared at me for a second or two. 'I'll buy it this time,' he said. 'But get him off the street.' He got into the police car and the police car went away.

I got into the taxi and we went the three odd blocks to my parking lot and shifted to my car. I held out the five spot to the hackie. He gave me a stiff look and shook his head.

'Just what's on the meter, Jack, or an even buck if you feel like it. I been down and out myself. In Frisco. Nobody picked me up in no taxi either. There's one stony-hearted town.'

'San Francisco,' I said mechanically.

'I call it Frisco,' he said. 'The hell with them minority groups. Thanks.' He took the dollar and went away.

We went to a drive-in where they made hamburgers that didn't taste like something the dog wouldn't eat. I fed Terry Lennox a couple and a bottle of beer and drove him home. The steps were still tough on him but he grinned and panted and made the climb. An hour later he was shaved and bathed and he looked human again. We sat down over a couple of very mild drinks.

'Lucky you remembered my name,' I said.

'I made a point of it,' he said. 'I looked you up too. Could I do less?'

'So why not give me a ring? I live here all the time. I have an office as well.'

'Why should I bother you?'

'Looks like you had to bother somebody. Looks like you don't have many friends.'

'Oh I have friends,' he said, 'of a sort.' He turned his glass on the table top. 'Asking for help doesn't come easy – especially when it's all your own fault.' He looked up with a tired smile. 'Maybe I can quit drinking one of these days. They all say that, don't they?'

'It takes about three years.'

'Three years?' He looked shocked.

'Usually it does. It's a different world. You have to get used to a paler set of colours, a quieter lot of sounds. You have to allow for relapses. All the people you used to know well will get to be just a little strange. You won't even like most of them, and they won't like you too well.'

'That wouldn't be much of a change,' he said. He turned and looked at the clock. 'I have a two-hundred-dollar suitcase checked at the Hollywood bus station. If I could bail it out I could buy a cheap one and pawn the one that's checked for enough to get to Vegas on the bus. I can get a job there.'

I didn't say anything. I just nodded and sat there nursing my drink.

'You're thinking that idea might have come to me a little sooner,' he said quietly.

'I'm thinking there's something behind all this that's none of my business. Is the job for sure or just a hope?'

'It's for sure. Fellow I knew very well in the army runs a big club there, the Terrapin Club. He's part racketeer, of course, they all are – but the other part is a nice guy.'

'I can manage the bus fare and something over. But I'd just as soon it bought something that would stay bought for a while. Better talk to him on the phone.'

'Thank you, but it's not necessary. Randy Starr won't let me down. He never has. And the suitcase will pawn for fifty dollars. I know from experience.'

'Look,' I said, 'I'd put up what you need. I'm no big soft-hearted slob. So you take what's offered and be good. I want you out of my hair because I've got a feeling about you.'

'Really?' He looked down into his glass. He was only sipping the stuff. 'We've only met twice and you've been more than white to me both times. What sort of feeling?'

'A feeling that next time I'll find you in worse trouble than I can get you out of. I don't know just why I have the feeling, but I have it.'

He touched the right side of his face gently with two finger-tips. 'Maybe it's this. It does make me look a little sinister, I suppose. But it's an honourable wound – or anyhow the result of one.'

'It's not that. That doesn't bother me at all. I'm a private dick. You're a problem that I don't have to solve. But the problem is there. Call it a hunch. If you want to be extra polite, call it a sense of character. Maybe that girl didn't walk out on you at The Dancers just because you were drunk. Maybe she had a feeling too.'

He smiled faintly. 'I was married to her once. Her name is Sylvia Lennox. I married her for her money.'

I stood up scowling at him. 'I'll fix you some scrambled eggs. You need food.'

'Wait a minute, Marlowe. You're wondering why if I was down and out and Sylvia had plenty I couldn't ask her for a few bucks. Did you ever hear of pride?'

'You're killing me, Lennox.'

'Am I? My kind of pride is different. It's the pride of a man who has nothing else. I'm sorry if I annoy you.'

I went out to my kitchen and cooked up some Canadian bacon and scrambled eggs and coffee and toast. We ate in the breakfast nook. The house belonged to the period that always had one.

I said I had to go to the office and would pick up his suitcase on the way back. He gave me the check ticket. His face now had a little colour and the eyes were not so far back in his head that you had to grope for them.

Before I went out I put the whisky bottle on the table in front of the couch. 'Use your pride on that,' I said. 'And call Vegas, if only as a favour to me.'

He just smiled and shrugged his shoulders. I was still sore going down the steps. I didn't know why, any more than I knew why a man would starve and walk the streets rather than pawn his wardrobe. Whatever his rules were he played by them.

The suitcase was the damnedest thing you ever saw. It was bleached pigskin and when new had been a pale cream colour. The fittings were gold. It was English made and if you could buy it here at all, it would cost more like eight hundred than two.

I planked it down in front of him. I looked at the bottle on the cocktail table. He hadn't touched it. He was as sober as I was. He was smoking, but not liking that very well.

'I called Randy,' he said. 'He was sore because I hadn't called him before.'

'It takes a stranger to help you,' I said. 'A present from Sylvia?' I pointed at the suitcase.

He looked out of the window. 'No. That was given to me in England, long before I met her. Very long ago indeed. I'd like to leave it with you, if you could lend me an old one.'

I got five double sawbucks out of my wallet and dropped them in front of him. 'I don't need security.'

'That wasn't the idea at all. You're no pawnbroker. I just don't want it with me in Vegas. And I don't need this much money.'

'Okay. You keep the money and I'll keep the suitcase. But this house is easy to burgle.'

'It wouldn't matter,' he said indifferently. 'It wouldn't matter at all.'

He changed his clothes and we ate dinner at Musso's about five-thirty. No drinks. He caught the bus on Cahuenga and I drove home thinking about this and that. His empty suitcase was on my bed where he had unpacked it and put his stuff in a lightweight job of mine. His had a gold key which was in one of the locks. I locked the suitcase up empty and tied the key to the handle and put it on the high shelf on my clothes closet. It didn't feel quite empty, but what was in it was no business of mine.

It was a quiet night and the house seemed emptier than usual. I set out the chessmen and played a French defence against Steinitz. He beat me in forty-four moves, but I had him sweating a couple of times.

The phone rang at nine-thirty and the voice that spoke was one I had heard before.

'Is this Mr Philip Marlowe?'

'Yeah, I'm Marlowe.'

'This is Sylvia Lennox, Mr Marlowe. We met very briefly in front of The Dancers one night last month. I heard afterwards that you had been kind enough to see that Terry got home.'

'I did that.'

'I suppose you know that we are not married any more, but I've been a little worried about him. He gave up the apartment he had in Westwood and nobody seems to know where he is.'

'I noticed how worried you were the night we met.'

'Look, Mr Marlowe, I've been married to the man. I'm not

very sympathetic to drunks. Perhaps I was a little unfeeling and perhaps I had something rather important to do. You're a private detective and this can be put on a professional basis, if you prefer it.'

'It doesn't have to be put on any basis at all, Mrs Lennox. He's on a bus going to Las Vegas. He has a friend there who will give him a job.'

She brightened up very suddenly. 'Oh – to Las Vegas? How sentimental of him. That's where we were married.'

'I guess he forgot,' I said, 'or he would have gone somewhere else.'

Instead of hanging up on me she laughed. It was a cute little laugh. 'Are you always as rude as this to your clients?'

'You're not a client, Mrs Lennox.'

'I might be some day. Who knows? Let's say to your lady friends, then.'

'Same answer. The guy was down and out, starving, dirty, without a bean. You could have found him if it had been worth your time. He didn't want anything from you then and he probably doesn't want anything from you now.'

'That,' she said coolly, 'is something you couldn't possibly know anything about. Good night.' And she hung up.

She was dead right, of course, and I was dead wrong. But I didn't feel wrong. I just felt sore. If she had called up half an hour earlier I might have been sore enough to beat the hell out of Steinitz – except that he had been dead for fifty years and the chess game was out of a book.


# Three


Three days before Christmas I got a cashier's cheque on a Las Vegas bank for $100. A note written on hotel paper came with it. He thanked me, wished me a Merry Christmas and all kinds of luck and said he hoped to see me again soon. The kick was in a postscript. 'Sylvia and I are starting a second honeymoon. She says please don't be sore at her for wanting to try again.'

I caught the rest of it in one of those snob columns in the society section of the paper. I don't read them often, only when I run out of things to dislike.

'Your correspondent is all fluttery at the news that Terry and

Sylvia Lennox have rehitched at Las Vegas, the dears. She's the younger daughter of multimillionaire Harlan Potter of San Francisco and Pebble Beach, of course. Sylvia is having Marcel and Jeanne Duhaux redecorate the entire mansion in Encino from basement to roof in the most *devastatingly dernier cri*. Curt Westerheym, Sylvia's last but one, my dears, gave her the little eighteen-room shack for a wedding present, you may remember. And whatever happened to Curt, you ask? Or do you? St Tropez has the answer, and permanently, I hear. Also a certain very, *very* blue-blooded French duchess with two perfectly adorable children. And what does Harlan Potter think of the remarriage, you may also ask? One can only guess. Mr Potter is one person who but *never* gives an interview. How exclusive can you get, darlings?'

I threw the paper into the corner and turned on the TV set. After the society page dog vomit even the wrestlers looked good. But the facts were probably right. On the society page they better be.

I had a mental picture of the kind of eighteen-room shack that would go with a few of the Potter millions, not to mention decorations by Duhaux in the latest sub-phallic symbolism. But I had no mental picture at all of Terry Lennox loafing around one of the swimming pools in Bermuda shorts and phoning the butler by R/T to ice the champagne and get the grouse a-toasting. There was no reason why I should have. If the guy wanted to be somebody's woolly bear, it was no skin off my teeth. I just didn't want to see him again. But I knew I would – if only on account of his goddam gold-plated pigskin suitcase.

It was five o'clock of a wet March evening when he walked into my down-at-heels brain emporium. He looked changed. Older, very sober and severe and beautifully calm. He looked like a guy who had learned to roll with a punch. He wore an oyster-white raincoat and gloves and no hat, and his white hair was as smooth as a bird's breast.

'Let's go to some quiet bar and have a drink,' he said, as if he had been in ten minutes before. 'If you have the time, that is.'

We didn't shake hands. We never did. Englishmen don't shake hands all the time like Americans and although he wasn't English he had some of the mannerisms.

I said: 'Let's go by my place and pick up your fancy suitcase. It kind of worries me.'

He shook his head. 'It would be kind of you to keep it for me.'

'Why?'

'I just feel that way. Do you mind? It's a sort of link with a time when I wasn't a no-good waster.'

'Nuts to that,' I said. 'But it's your business.'

'If it bothers you because you think it might be stolen—'

'That's your business too. Let's go get that drink.'

We went to Victor's. He drove me in a rust-coloured Jowett Jupiter with a flimsy canvas rain top under which there was only just room for the two of us. It had pale leather upholstery and what looked like silver fittings. I'm not too fussy about cars, but the damn thing did make my mouth water a little. He said it would do sixty-five in second. It had a squatty little gear shift that barely came up to his knee.

'Four speeds,' he said. 'They haven't invented an automatic shift that will work for one of these jobs yet. You don't really need one. You can start it in third even uphill and that's as high as you can shift in traffic anyway.'

'Wedding present?'

'Just a casual "I happened to see this gadget in a window" sort of present. I'm a very pampered guy.'

'Nice,' I said. 'If there's no price tag.'

He glanced at me quickly and then put his eyes back on the wet pavement. Double wipers swished gently over the little windscreen. 'Price tag? There's always a price tag, chum. You think I'm not happy maybe?'

'Sorry. I was out of line.'

'I'm rich. Who the hell wants to be happy?' There was a bitterness in his voice that was new to me.

'How's your drinking?'

'Perfectly elegant, old top. For some strange reason I seem to be able to handle the stuff. But you never know, do you?'

'Perhaps you were never really drunk.'

We sat in a corner of the bar at Victor's and drank gimlets. 'They don't know how to make them here,' he said. 'What they call a gimlet is just some lime or lemon juice and gin with a dash of sugar and bitters. A real gimlet is half gin and half Rose's Lime Juice and nothing else. It beats martinis hollow.'

'I was never fussy about drinks. How did you get on with Randy Starr? Down my street he's called a tough number.'

He leaned back and looked thoughtful. 'I guess he is. I guess they all are. But it doesn't show on him. I could name you a couple of lads in the same racket in Hollywood that act the part. Randy doesn't bother. In Las Vegas he's a legitimate businessman. You look him up next time you're there. He'll be your pal.'

'Not too likely. I don't like hoodlums.'

'That's just a word, Marlowe. We have that kind of world. Two wars gave it to us and we are going to keep it. Randy and I and another fellow were in a jam once. It made a sort of bond between us.'

'Then why didn't you ask him for help when you needed it?'

He drank up his drink and signalled the waiter. 'Because he couldn't refuse.'

The waiter brought fresh drinks and I said: 'That's just talk to me. If by any chance the guy owed you something, think of *his* end. He'd like a chance to pay something back.'

He shook his head slowly. 'I know you're right. Of course I did ask him for a job. But I worked at it while I had it. As for asking favours or handouts, no.'

'But you'll take them from a stranger.'

He looked me straight in the eye. 'The stranger can keep going and pretend not to hear.'

We had three gimlets, not doubles, and it didn't do a thing to him. That much would just get a real souse started. So I guess maybe he was cured at that.

Then he drove me back to the office.

'We have dinner at eight-fifteen,' he said. 'Only millionaires can afford it. Only millionaires' servants will stand for it nowadays. Lots of lovely people coming.'

From then on it got to be a sort of habit with him to drop in around five o'clock. We didn't always go to the same bar, but oftener to Victor's than anywhere else. It may have had some association for him that I didn't know about. He never drank too much, and that surprised him.

'It must be something like the tertian ague,' he said. 'When it hits you its bad. When you don't have it, it's as though you never did have it.'

'What I don't get is why a guy with your privileges would want to drink with a down-at-heel private eye.'

'Are you being modest?'

'Nope. I'm just puzzled. I'm a reasonably friendly type but we don't live in the same world. I don't even know where you hang out except that it's Encino. I should guess your home life is adequate.'

'I don't have any home life.'

We were drinking gimlets again. The place was almost empty.

There was the usual light scattering of compulsive drinkers getting tuned up at the bar on the stools, the kind that reach very slowly 'for the first one and watch their hands so they won't knock anything over.

'I don't get that. Am I supposed to?'

'Big production, no story, as they say around the movie lots. I guess Sylvia is happy enough though not necessarily with me. In our circle that's not too important. There's always something to do if you don't have to work or consider the cost. It's no real fun but the rich don't know that. They never had any. They never want anything very hard except maybe somebody else's wife and that's a pretty pale desire compared with the way a plumber's wife wants new curtains for the living-room.'

I didn't say anything. I let him carry the ball.

'Mostly I just kill time,' he said, 'and it dies hard. A little tennis, a little golf, a little swimming and horseback riding, and the exquisite pleasure of watching Sylvia's friends trying to hold out to lunch time before they start killing their hangovers.'

'The night you went to Vegas she said she didn't like drunks.'

He grinned crookedly. I was getting so used to his scarred face that I only noticed it when some change of expression emphasized its one-sided woodenness.

'She meant drunks without money. With money they are just heavy drinkers. If they vomit in the lanai, that's for the butler to handle.'

'You didn't have to have it the way it is.'

He finished his drink at a gulp and stood up. 'I've got to run, Marlowe. Besides I'm boring you and God knows I'm boring myself.'

'You're not boring me. I'm a trained listener. Sooner or later I may figure out why you like being a kept poodle.'

He touched his scars gently with a fingertip. He had a remote little smile. 'You should wonder why she wants me around, not why I want to be there, waiting patiently on my satin cushion to have my head patted.'

'You like satin cushions,' I said, as I stood up to leave with him. 'You like silk sheets and bells to ring and the butler to come with his deferential smile.'

'Could be. I was raised in an orphanage in Salt Lake City.'

We went out into the tired evening and he said he wanted to walk. We had come in my car, and for once I had been fast enough to grab the check. I watched him out of sight. The light from a store window caught the gleam of his white hair for a moment as he faded into the light mist.

I liked him better drunk, down and out, hungry and beaten and proud. Or did I? Maybe I just liked being top man. His reasons for things were hard to figure. In my business there's a time to ask questions and a time to let your man simmer until he boils over. Every good cop knows that. It's a good deal like chess or boxing. Some people you have to crowd and keep off balance. Some you just box and they will end up beating themselves.

He would have told me the story of his life if I had asked him. But I never ever asked him how he got his face smashed. If I had and he told me, it just possibly might have saved a couple of lives. Just possibly, no more.

# Four

The last time we had a drink in a bar was in May and it was earlier than usual, just after four o'clock. He looked tired and thinner but he looked around with a slow smile of pleasure.

'I like bars just after they open for the evening. When the air inside is still cool and clean and everything is shiny and the barkeep is giving himself that last look in the mirror to see if his tie is straight and his hair is smooth. I like the neat bottles on the bar back and the lovely shining glasses and the anticipation. I like to watch the man mix the first one of the evening and put it down on a crisp mat and put the little folded napkin beside it. I like to taste it slowly. The first quiet drink of the evening in a quiet bar – that's wonderful.'

I agreed with him.

'Alcohol is like love,' he said. 'The first kiss is magic, the second is intimate, the third is routine. After that you take the girl's clothes off.'

'Is that bad?' I asked him.

'It's excitement of a high order, but it's an impure emotion – impure in the aesthetic sense. I'm not sneering at sex. It's necessary and it doesn't have to be ugly. But it always has to be managed. Making it glamorous is a billion-dollar industry and it costs every cent of it.'

He looked around and yawned. 'I haven't been sleeping well. It's nice in here. But after a while the lushes will fill the place up and talk loud and laugh and the goddam women will start waving their hands and screwing up their faces and tinkling their goddam bracelets and making up with the packaged charm which will later on in the evening have a slight but unmistakable odour of sweat.'

'Take it easy,' I said. 'So they're human, they sweat, they get dirty, they have to go to the bathroom. What did you expect – golden butterflies hovering in a rosy mist?'

He emptied his glass and held it upside down and watched a slow drop form on the rim and then tremble and fall.

'I'm sorry for her,' he said slowly. 'She's such an absolute bitch. Could be I'm fond of her too in a remote sort of way. Some day she'll need me and I'll be the only guy around not holding a chisel. Likely enough then I'll flunk out.'

I just looked at him. 'You do a great job of selling yourself,' I said after a moment.

'Yeah, I know. I'm a weak character, without guts or ambition. I caught the brass ring and it shocked me to find out it wasn't gold. A guy like me has one big moment in his life, one perfect swing on the high trapeze. Then he spends the rest of his time trying not to fall off the sidewalk into the gutter.'

'What's this in favour of?' I got out a pipe and started to fill it.

'She's scared. She's scared stiff.'

'What of?'

'I don't know. We don't talk much any more. Maybe of the old man. Harlan Potter is a cold-hearted son of a bitch. All Victorian dignity on the outside. Inside he's as ruthless as a Gestapo thug. Sylvia is a tramp. He knows it and he hates it and there's nothing he can do about it. But he waits and he watches and if Sylvia ever gets into a big mess of scandal he'll break her in half and bury the two halves a thousand miles apart.'

'You're her husband.'

He lifted the empty glass and brought it down hard on the edge of the table. It smashed with a sharp ring. The barman stared, but didn't say anything.

'Like that, chum. Like that. Oh sure, I'm her husband. That's what the record says. I'm the three white steps and the big green front door and the brass knocker you rap one long and two short and the maid lets you into the hundred-dollar whore-house.'

I stood up and dropped some money on the table. 'You talk too damn much,' I said, 'and it's too damn much about you. See you later.'

I walked out, leaving him sitting there shocked and white-faced as well as I could tell by the kind of light they have in bars. He called something after me, but I kept going.

Ten minutes later I was sorry. But ten minutes later I was somewhere else. He didn't come to the office any more. Not at all, not once. I had got to him where it hurt.

I didn't see him again for a month. When I did it was five o'clock in the morning and just beginning to get light. The persistent ringing of the doorbell yanked me out of bed. I ploughed down the hall and across the living-room and opened up. He stood there looking as if he hadn't slept for a week. He had a light topcoat on with the collar turned up and he seemed to be shivering. A dark felt hat was pulled down over his eyes.

He had a gun in his hand.

# Five

The gun wasn't pointed at me, he was just holding it. It was a medium-calibre automatic, foreign made, certainly not a Colt or a Savage. With the white face and the scars and the turned-up collar and the pulled-down hat and the gun, he could have stepped right out of an old-fashioned kick-'em-in-the-teeth gangster movie.

'You're driving me to Tijuana to get a plane at ten-fifteen,' he said. 'I have a passport and visa and I'm all set except for transportation. For certain reasons I can't take a train or a bus or a plane from L.A. Would five hundred bucks be a reasonable taxi fare?'

I stood in the doorway and didn't move to let him in. 'Five hundred plus the gat?' I asked.

He looked down at it rather absently. Then he dropped it into his pocket.

'It might be a protection,' he said, 'for you. Not for me.'

'Come on in then.' I stood to one side and he came in with an exhausted lunge and fell into a chair.

The living-room was still dark, because of the heavy growth of shrubbery the owner had allowed to mask the windows. I put a lamp on and mooched a cigarette. I lit it. I stared down at him. I rumpled my hair which was already rumpled. I put the old tired grin on to my face.

'What the hell's the matter with me – sleeping such a lovely morning away? Ten-fifteen, huh? Well, there's plenty of time. Let's go out to the kitchen and I'll brew some coffee.'

'I'm in a great deal of trouble, shamus.' Shamus, it was the first time he had called me that. But it kind of went with his style of entry, the way he was dressed, the gun and all.

'It's going to be a peach of a day. Light breeze. You can hear those tough old eucalyptus trees across the street whispering to each other. Talking about old times in Australia when the wallabies hopped about underneath the branches and the koala bears rode piggy back on each other. Yes, I got the general idea you were in some trouble. Let's talk about it after I've had a couple of cups of coffee. I'm always a little light-headed when I first wake up. Let us confer with Mr Huggins and Mr Young.'

'Look, Marlowe, this is not the time—'

'Fear nothing, old boy. Mr Huggins and Mr Young are two of the best. They make Huggins-Young Coffee for me. It's their life work, their pride and joy. One of these days I'm going to see that they get the recognition they deserve. So far all they're making is money. You couldn't expect that to satisfy them.'

I left him with that bright chatter and went out to the kitchen at the back. I turned the hot water on and got the coffee-maker down off the shelf. I wet the rod and measured the stuff into the top and by that time the water was steaming. I filled the lower half of the dingus and set it on the flame. I set the upper part on top and gave it a twist so it would bind.

By that time he had come in after me. He leaned in the doorway a moment and then edged across to the breakfast nook and slid into the seat. He was still shaking. I got a bottle of Old Grand-dad off the shelf and poured him a shot in a big glass. I knew he would need a big glass. Even with that he had to use both hands to get it to his mouth. He swallowed, put the glass down with a thud and hit the back of the seat with a jar.

'Almost passed out,' he muttered. 'Seems like I've been up for a week. Didn't sleep at all last night.'

The coffee-maker was almost ready to bubble. I turned the flame low and watched the water rise. It hung a little at the bottom of the glass tube. I turned the flame up just enough to get it over the hump and then turned it low again quickly. I stirred the coffee and covered it. I set my timer for three minutes. Very methodical guy, Marlowe. Nothing must interfere with his coffee technique. Not even a gun in the hand of a desperate character.

I poured him another slug. 'Just sit there,' I said. 'Don't say a word. Just sit.'

He handled the second slug with one hand. I did a fast wash-up in the bathroom and the bell of the timer went just as I got back. I cut the flame and set the coffee-maker on a straw mat on the table. Why do I go into such detail? Because the charged atmosphere made every little thing stand out as a performance, a movement distinct and vastly important. It was one of those hypersensitive moments when all your automatic movements, however long established, however habitual, become separate acts of will. You are like a man learning to walk after polio. You take nothing for granted, absolutely nothing at all.

The coffee was all down and the air rushed in with its usual fuss and the coffee bubbled and then became quiet. I removed the top of the maker and set it on the drainboard in the socket of the cover.

I poured two cups and added a slug to his. 'Black for you, Terry.' I added two lumps of sugar and some cream to mine. I was coming out of it by now. I wasn't conscious of how I opened the fridge and got the cream carton.

I sat down across from him. He hadn't moved. He was propped in the corner of the nook, rigid. Then without warning his head came down on the table and he was sobbing.

He didn't pay any attention when I reached across and dug the gun out of his pocket. It was a Mauser 7.65, a beauty. I sniffed it. Not fired. I sprang the magazine loose. It was full. Nothing in the breech.

He lifted his head and saw the coffee and drank some slowly, not looking at me. 'I didn't shoot anybody,' he said.

'Well – not recently anyhow. And the gun would have had to be cleaned. I hardly think you shot anybody with this.'

'I'll tell you about it,' he said.

'Wait just a minute.' I drank my coffee as quickly as the heat would let me. I refilled my cup. 'It's like this,' I said. 'Be very careful what you tell me. If you really want me to ride you down to Tijuana, there are two things I must not be told. One – are you listening?'

He nodded very slightly. He was looking blank-eyed at the wall over my head. The scars were very livid this morning. His skin was almost dead white but the scars seemed to shine out of it just the same.

'One,' I repeated slowly, 'if you have committed a crime or anything the law calls a crime – a serious crime, I mean – I can't be told about it. Two, if you have essential knowledge that such a crime has been committed, I can't be told about that either. Not if you want me to drive you to Tijuana. That clear?'

He looked me in the eye. His eyes focused, but they were lifeless. He had the coffee inside him. He had no colour, but he was steady. I poured him some more and loaded it in the same way.

'I told you I was in a jam,' he said.

'I heard you. I don't want to know what kind of jam. I have a living to earn, a licence to protect.'

'I could hold the gun on you,' he said.

I grinned and pushed the gun across the table. He looked down at it but didn't touch it.

'Not to Tijuana you couldn't hold it on me, Terry. Not across the border, not up the steps into a plane. I'm a man who occasionally has business with guns. We'll forget about the gun. I'd look great telling the cops I was so scared I just had to do what you told me to. Supposing, of course, which I don't know, that there was anything to tell the cops.'

'Listen,' he said, 'it will be noon or even later before anybody knocks at the door. The help knows better than to disturb her when she sleeps late. But by about noon her maid would knock and go in. She wouldn't be in her room.'

I sipped my coffee and said nothing.

'The maid would see that her bed hadn't been slept in,' he went on. 'Then she would think of another place to look. There's a big guest house pretty far back from the main house. It has its own driveway and garage and so on. Sylvia spent the night there. The maid would eventually find her there.'

I frowned. 'I've got to be very careful what questions I ask you, Terry. Couldn't she have spent the night away from home?'

'Her clothes would be thrown all over the room. She never hangs anything up. The maid would know she had put a robe over her pyjamas and gone out that way. So it would only be to the guest house.'

'Not necessarily,' I said.

'It would be to the guest house. Hell, do you think they don't know what goes on in the guest house? Servants always know.'

'Pass it,' I said.

He ran a finger down the side of his good cheek hard enough to leave a red streak. 'And in the guest house,' he went on slowly, 'the maid would find—'

'Sylvia dead drunk, paralysed, spifflicated, iced to the eyebrows,' I said harshly.

'Oh.' He thought about it. Big think. 'Of course,' he added, 'that's how it would be. Sylvia is not a souse. When she does get over the edge it's pretty drastic.'

'That's the end of the story,' I said. 'Or almost. Let me improvise. The last time we drank together I was a bit rough with you, walked out, if you recall. You irritated the hell out of me. Thinking it over afterwards I could see that you were just trying to sneer yourself out of a feeling of disaster. You say you have a passport and a visa. It takes a little time to get a visa to Mexico. They don't let just anybody in. So you've been planning to blow for some time. I was wondering how long you would stick '

'I guess I felt some vague kind of obligation to be around, some idea she might need me for something more than a front to keep the old man from nosing around too hard. By the way, I tried to call you in the middle of the night.'

'I sleep hard. I didn't hear.'

'Then I went to a Turkish bath place. I stayed a couple of hours, had a steam bath, a plunge, a needle shower, a rub-down and made a couple of phone calls from there. I left the car at Le Brea and Fountain. I walked from there. Nobody saw me turn into your street.'

'Do these phone calls concern me?'

'One was to Harlan Potter. The old man flew down to Pasadena yesterday, some business. He hadn't been to the house. I had a lot of trouble getting him. But he finally talked to me. I told him I was sorry, but I was leaving.' He was looking a little sideways when he said this, towards the window over the sink and the tecoma bush that fretted against the screen.

'How did he take it?'

'He was sorry. He wished me luck. Asked if I needed any money.' Terry laughed harshly. 'Money. Those are the first five letters of his alphabet. I said I had plenty. Then I called Sylvia's sister. Much the same story there. That's all.'

'I want to ask this,' I said. 'Did you ever find her with a man in that guest house?'

He shook his head. 'I never tried. It would not have been difficult. It never has been.'

'Your coffee's getting cold.'

'I don't want any more.'

'Lots of men, huh? But you went back and married her again. I realize that she's quite a dish, but all the same—'

'I told you I was no good. Hell, why did I leave her the first

219

time? Why after that did I get stinking every time I saw her? Why did I roll in the gutter rather than ask her for money? She's been married five times, not including me. Any one of them would go back at the crook of her finger. And not just for a million bucks.'

'She's quite a dish,' I said. I looked at my watch. 'Just why does it have to be ten-fifteen at Tijuana?'

'There's always space on that flight. Nobody from L.A. wants to ride a DC 3 over mountains when he can take a Connie and make it in seven hours to Mexico City. And the Connies don't stop where I want to go.'

I stood up and leaned against the sink. 'Now let's add it up and don't interrupt me. You came to me this morning in a highly emotional condition and wanted to be driven to Tijuana to catch an early plane. You had a gun in your pocket, but I needn't have seen it. You told me you had stood things as long as you could but last night you blew up. You found your wife dead drunk and a man had been with her. You got out and went to a Turkish bath to pass the time until morning and you phoned your wife's two closest relatives and told them what you were doing. Where you went was none of my business. You had the necessary documents to enter Mexico. How you went was none of my business either. We are friends and I did what you asked me without much thought. Why wouldn't I? You're not paying me anything. You had your car but you felt too upset to drive yourself. That's your business too. You're an emotional guy and you got yourself a bad wound in the war. I think I ought to pick up your car and shove it in a garage somewhere for storage.'

He reached into his clothes and pushed a leather key-holder across the table.

'How does it sound?' he asked.

'Depends who's listening. I haven't finished. You took nothing but the clothes you stood up in and some money you had from your father-in-law. You left everything she had given you including that beautiful piece of machinery you parked at La Brea and Fountain. You wanted to go away as clean as it was possible for you to go and still go. All right. I'll buy it. Now I shave and get dressed.'

'Why are you doing it, Marlowe?'

'Buy yourself a drink while I shave.'

I walked out and left him sitting there hunched in the corner of the nook. He still had his hat and light topcoat on. But he looked a lot more alive.

I went into the bathroom and shaved. I was back in the bed-room knotting my tie when he came and stood in the doorway. 'I washed the cups just in case,' he said. 'But I got thinking. Maybe it would be better if you called the police.'

'Call them yourself. I haven't anything to tell them.'

'You want me to?'

I turned around sharply and gave him a hard stare. 'Goddam it!' I almost yelled at him. 'Can't you for Chrissake just leave it lay?'

'I'm sorry.'

'Sure you're sorry. Guys like you are always sorry, and always too late.'

He turned and walked back along the hall to the living-room.

I finished dressing and locked up the back part of the house. When I got to the living-room he had fallen asleep in a chair, his head on one side, his face drained of colour, his whole body slack with exhaustion. He looked pitiful. When I touched his shoulder he came awake slowly as if it was a long way from where he was to where I was.

When I had his attention I said: 'What about a suitcase? I still got that white pigskin job on the top shelf in my closet.'

'It's empty,' he said without interest. 'Also it's too con-spicuous.'

'You'd be more conspicuous without any baggage.'

I walked back to the bedroom and stood up on the steps in the clothes closet and pulled the white pigskin job down off the high shelf. The square ceiling trap was right over my head, so I pushed that up and reached in as far as I could and dropped his leather key-holder behind one of the dusty tie beams or whatever they were.

I climbed down with the suitcase, dusted it off and shoved some things into it, a pair of pyjamas never worn, toothpaste, an extra toothbrush, a couple of cheap towels and washcloths, a package of cotton handkerchiefs, a fifteen-cent tube of shaving cream and one of those razors they give with a package of blades. Nothing used, nothing marked, nothing conspicuous except that his own stuff would be better. I added a pint of bourbon still in its wrapping paper. I locked the suitcase and left the key in one of the locks and carried it up front. He had gone to sleep again. I opened the door without waking him and carried the suitcase down to the garage and put it in the con-vertible behind the front seat. I got the car out and locked the garage and went up the steps to wake him. I finished locking up and we left.

I drove fast but not fast enough to get tagged. We hardly spoke on the way down. We didn't stop to eat either. There wasn't that much time.

The border people had nothing to say to us. Up on the windy mesa where the Tijuana Airport is I parked close to the office and just sat while Terry got his ticket. The propellers of the DC 3 were already turning over slowly, just enough to keep warm. A tall dreamboat of a pilot in a grey uniform was chatting with a group of four people. One was about six feet four and carried a gun case. There was a girl in slacks beside him, and a smallish middle-aged man and a grey-haired woman so tall that she made him look puny. Three or four obvious Mexicans were standing around as well. That seemed to be the load. The steps were at the door but nobody seemed anxious to get in. Then a Mexican flight steward came down the steps and stood waiting. There didn't seem to be any loudspeaker equipment. The Mexicans climbed into the plane but the pilot was still chatting with the Americans.

There was a big Packard parked next to me. I got out and took a gander at the licence on the post. Maybe some day I'll learn to mind my own business. As I pulled my head out I saw the tall woman staring in my direction.

Then Terry came across the dusty gravel.

'I'm all set,' he said. 'This is where I say good-bye.'

He put his hand out. I shook it. He looked pretty good now, just tired, just tired as all hell.

I lifted the pigskin suitcase out of the Olds and put it down on the gravel. He stared at it angrily.

'I told you I didn't want it,' he said snappishly.

'There's a nice pint of hooch in it, Terry. Also some pyjamas and stuff. And it's all anonymous. If you don't want it, check it. Or throw it away.'

'I have reasons,' he said stiffly.

'So have I.'

He smiled suddenly. He picked up the suitcase and squeezed my arm with his free hand. 'Okay, pal. You're the boss. And remember, if things get tough, you have a blank cheque. You don't owe me a thing. We had a few drinks together and got to be friendly and I talked too much about me. I left five C notes in your coffee can. Don't be sore at me.'

'I'd rather you hadn't.'

'I'll never spend half of what I have.'

'Good luck, Terry.'

The two Americans were going up the steps into the plane. A squatty guy with a wide-dark face came out of the door of the office building and waved and pointed.

'Climb aboard,' I said. 'I know you didn't kill her. That's why I'm here.'

He braced himself. His whole body got stiff. He turned slowly, then looked back.

'I'm sorry,' he said quietly. 'But you're wrong about that. I'm going to walk quite slowly to the plane. You have plenty of time to stop me.'

He walked. I watched him. The guy in the doorway of the office was waiting, but not too impatient. Mexicans seldom are. He reached down and patted the pigskin suitcase and grinned at Terry. Then he stood aside and Terry went through the door. In a little while Terry came out through the door on the other side, where the customs people are when you're coming in. He walked, still slowly, across the gravel to the steps. He stopped there and looked towards me. He didn't signal or wave. Neither did I. Then he went up into the plane, and the steps were pulled back.

I got into the Olds and started it and backed and turned and moved half-way across the parking space. The tall woman and the short man were still out on the field. The woman had a handkerchief out to wave. The plane began to taxi down to the end of the field, raising plenty of dust. It turned at the far end and the motors revved up in a thundering roar. It began to move forward, picking up speed slowly.

The dust rose in clouds behind it. Then it was airborne. I watched it lift slowly into the gusty air and fade off into the naked blue sky to the south-east.

Then I left. Nobody at the border gate looked at me as if my face meant as much as the hands on a clock.


# Six


It's a long drag back from Tijuana and one of the dullest drives in the state. Tijuana is nothing; all they want there is the buck. The kid who sidles over to your car and looks at you with big wistful eyes and says, 'One dime, please, mister,' will try to sell you his sister in the next sentence. Tijuana is not Mexico. No border town is anything but a border town, just as no waterfront in anything but a waterfront. San Diego? One of the most beautiful harbours in the world and nothing in it but navy and a few fishing boats. At night it is fairyland. The swell is as gentle as an old lady singing hymns. But Marlowe has to get home and count the spoons.

The road north is as monotonous as a sailor's chanty. You go through a town, down a hill, along a stretch of beach, through a town, down a hill, along a stretch of beach.

It was two o'clock when I got back and they were waiting for me in a dark sedan with no police tags, no red light, only the double antenna, and not only police cars have those. I was half-way up the steps before they came out of it and yelled at me, the usual couple in the usual suits, with the usual stony leisure of movement, as if the world was waiting hushed and silent for them to tell it what to do.

'Your name Marlowe? We want to talk to you.'

He let me see the glint of a badge. For all I caught of it he might have been Pest Control. He was grey-blond and looked sticky. His partner was tall, good-looking, neat, and had a precise nastiness about him, a goon with an education. They had watching and waiting eyes, patient and careful eyes, cool, disdainful eyes, cops' eyes. They get them at the passing-out parade at the police school.

'Sergeant Green, Central Homicide. This is Detective Dayton.'

I went on up and unlocked the door. You don't shake hands with big city cops. That close is too close.

They sat in the living-room. I opened the windows and the breeze whispered. Green did the talking.

'Man named Terry Lennox. Know him, huh?'

'We have a drink together once in a while. He lives in Encino, married money. I've never been where he lives.'

'Once in a while,' Green said. 'How often would that be?'

'It's a vague expression. I meant it that way. It could be once a week or once in two months.'

'Met his wife?'

'Once, very briefly, before they were married.'

'You saw him last when and where?'

I took a pipe off the end table and filled it. Green leaned forward close to me. The tall lad sat farther back holding a ball point poised over a red-edged pad.

'This is where I say, "What's this all about?" and you say, "We ask the questions."'

'So you just answer them, huh?'

I lit the pipe. The tobacco was a little too moist. It took me some time to light it properly and three matches.

'I got time,' Green said, 'but I already used up a lot of it waiting around. So snap it up, mister. We know who you are. And you know we ain't here to work up an appetite.'

'I was just thinking,' I said. 'We used to go to Victor's fairly often, and not so often to The Green Lantern and The Bull and Bear – that's the place down at the end of the Strip that tries to look like an English Inn—'

'Quit stalling.'

'Who's dead?' I asked.

Detective Dayton spoke up. He had a hard, mature, don't-try-to-fool-with-me voice. 'Just answer the questions, Marlowe. We are conducting a routine investigation. That's all you need to know.'

Maybe I was tired and irritable. Maybe I felt a little guilty. I could learn to hate this guy without even knowing him. I could just look at him across the width of a cafeteria and want to kick his teeth in.

'Shove it, Jack,' I said. 'Keep that guff for the juvenile bureau. It's a horse laugh even to them.'

Green chuckled. Nothing changed in Dayton's face that you could put a finger on but he suddenly looked ten years older and twenty years nastier. The breath going through his nose whistled faintly.

'He passed the bar examination,' Green said. 'You can't fool around with Dayton.'

I got up slowly and went over to the bookshelves. I took down the bound copy of the California Penal Code. I held it out to Dayton.

'Would you kindly find me the section that says I have to answer the questions?'

He was holding himself very still. He was going to slug me and we both knew it. But he was going to wait for the break. Which meant that he didn't trust Green to back him up if he got out of line.

He said: 'Every citizen has to co-operate with the police. In all ways, even by physical action, and especially by answering any questions of a non-incriminating nature the police think it necessary to ask.' His voice saying this was hard and bright and smooth.

'It works out that way,' I said. 'Mostly by a process of direct or indirect intimidation. In law no such obligation exists. Nobody has to tell the police anything, any time, anywhere.'

'Aw shut up,' Green said impatiently. 'You're crawfishing and you know it. Sit down. Lennox's wife has been murdered. In a guest house at their place in Encino. Lennox has skipped out. Anyway he can't be found. So we're looking for a suspect in a murder case. That satisfy you?'

I threw the book in a chair and went back to the couch across the table from Green. 'So why come to me?' I asked. 'I've never been near the house. I told you that.'

Green patted his thighs, up and down, up and down. He grinned at me quietly. Dayton was motionless in the chair. His eyes ate me.

'On account of your phone number was written on a pad in his room during the past twenty-four hours,' Green said. 'It's a date pad and yesterday was torn off but you could see the impression on today's page. We don't know when he called you up. We don't know where he went or why or when. But we got to ask, natch.'

'Why in the guest house?' I asked, not expecting him to answer, but he did.

He blushed a little. 'Seems she went there pretty often. At night. Had visitors. The help can see down through the trees where the lights show. Cars come and go, sometimes late, sometimes very late. Too much is enough, huh. Don't kid yourself. Lennox is our boy. He went down that way about one in the a.m. The butler happened to see. He came back alone, maybe twenty minutes later. After that nothing. The lights stayed on. This morning no Lennox. The butler goes down by the guest house. The dame is as naked as a mermaid on the bed and let me tell you he don't recognize her by her face. She practically ain't got one. Beat to pieces with a bronze statuette of a monkey.'

'Terry Lennox wouldn't do anything like that,' I said. 'Sure she cheated on him. Old stuff. She always had. They'd been divorced and remarried. I don't suppose it made him happy but why should he go crazy over it now?'

'Nobody knows that answer,' Green said patiently. 'It happens all the time. Men and women both. A guy takes it and takes it and takes it. Then he don't. He probably don't know why himself, why at that particular instant he goes berserk. Only he does, and somebody's dead. So we got business to do. So we ask you one simple question. So quit horsing around or we take you in.'

'He's not going to tell you, Sergeant,' Dayton said acidly. 'He read that law book. Like a lot of people that read a law book he thinks the law is in it.'

'You make the notes,' Green said, 'and leave your brains alone. If you're real good we'll let you sing Mother Machree at the police smoker.'

'The hell with you, Sarge, if I may say so with proper respect for your rank.'

'Let you and him fight,' I said to Green. 'I'll catch him when he drops.'

Dayton laid his note pad and ball point aside very carefully. He stood up with a bright gleam in his eyes. He walked over and stood in front of me.

'On your feet, bright boy. Just because I went to college don't make me take any guff from a nit like you.'

I started to get up. I was still off balance when he hit me. He hooked me with a neat left and crossed it. Bells rang, but not for dinner. I sat down hard and shook my head. Dayton was still there. He was smiling now.

'Let's try again,' he said. 'You weren't set that time. It wasn't really kosher.'

I looked at Green. He was looking at his thumb as if studying a hangnail. I didn't move or speak, waiting for him to look up. If I stood up again, Dayton would slug me again. He might slug me again anyhow. But if I stood up and he slugged me, I would take him to pieces, because the blows proved he was strictly a boxer. He put them in the right place but it would take a lot of them to wear me down.

Green said almost absently: 'Smart work, Billy boy. You gave the man exactly what he wanted. Clam juice.'

Then he looked up and said mildly: 'Once more, for the record, Marlowe. Last time you saw Terry Lennox, where and how and what was talked about, and where did you come from just now. Yes – or no?'

Dayton was standing loosely, nicely balanced. There was a soft, sweet sheen in his eyes.

'How about the other guy?' I asked, ignoring him.

'What other guy was that?'

'In the hay, in the guest house. No clothes on. You're not saying she had to go down there to play solitaire.'

'That comes later – when we get the husband.'

'Fine. If it's not too much trouble when you already have a patsy.'

'You don't talk, we take you in, Marlowe.'

'As a material witness?'

'As a material my foot. As a suspect. Suspicion of accessory after the fact of murder. Helping a suspect escape. My guess is you took the guy somewhere. And right now a guess is all I need. The skipper is tough these days. He knows the rule book but he gets absent-minded. This could be a misery for you. One way or another we get a statement from you. The harder it is to get, the surer we are we need it.'

'That's a lot of crap to him,' Dayton said. 'He knows the book.'

'It's a lot of crap to everybody,' Green said calmly. 'But it still works. Come on, Marlowe. I'm blowing the whistle on you.'

'Okay,' I said. 'Blow it. Terry Lennox was my friend. I've got a reasonable amount of sentiment invested in him. Enough not to spoil it just because a cop says come through. You've got a case against him, maybe far more than I hear from you. Motive, opportunity, and the fact that he skipped out. The motive is old stuff, long neutralized, almost part of the deal. I don't admire that kind of deal, but that's the kind of guy he is – a little weak and very gentle. The rest of it means nothing except that if he knew she was dead he knew he was a sitting duck for you. At the inquest if they have one and if they call me, I'll have to answer questions. I don't have to answer yours. I can see you're a nice guy, Green. Just as I can see your partner is just another goddam badge-flasher with a power complex. If you want to get me in a real jam, let him hit me again. I'll break his goddam pencil for him.'

Green stood up and looked at me sadly. Dayton hadn't moved. He was a one-shot tough guy. He had to have time out to pat his back.

'I'll use the phone,' Green said. 'But I know what answer I'll get. You're a sick chicken, Marlowe. A very sick chicken. Get the hell outa my way.' This last to Dayton. Dayton turned and went back and picked up his pad.

Green crossed to the phone and lifted it slowly, his plain face creased with the long, slow, thankless grind. That's the trouble with cops. You're all set to hate their guts and then you meet one that goes human on you.

The Captain said to bring me in, and rough.

They put handcuffs on me. They didn't search the house, which seemed careless of them. Possibly they figured I would be too experienced to have anything there that could be dangerous to me. In which they were wrong. An expert search would have turned up the car keys. And when the car was found, as it would be sooner or later, they would fit the keys to it and know he had been in my company.

Actually, as it turned out, that meant nothing. The car was never found by any police. It was stolen sometime in the night, driven most probably to El Paso, fitted with new keys and forged papers, and put on the market eventually in Mexico City. The procedure is routine. Mostly the money comes back in the form of heroin. Part of the good-neighbour policy, as the hoodlums see it.

# Seven

The homicide skipper that year was a Captain Gregorius, a type of copper that is getting rarer but by no means extinct, the kind that solves crimes with the bright light, the soft sap, the kick to the kidneys, the knee to the groin, the fist to the solar plexus, the night stick to the base of the spine. Six months later he was indicted for perjury before a grand jury, booted without trial, and later stamped to death by a big stallion on his ranch in Wyoming.

Right now I was his raw meat. He sat behind the desk with his coat off and his sleeves rolled almost to his shoulders. He was as bald as a brick and getting heavy around the waist like all hard-muscled men in middle age. His eyes were fish grey. His big nose was a network of burst capillaries. He was drinking coffee and not quietly. His blunt, strong hands had hairs thick on their backs. Grizzled tufts stuck out of his ears. He pawed something on his desk and looked at Green.

Green said: 'All we got on him is he won't tell us nothing, skipper. The phone number makes us look him up. He's out riding and don't say where. He knows Lennox pretty well and don't say when he saw him last.'

'Thinks he's tough,' Gregorius said indifferently. 'We could change that.' He said it as if he didn't care one way or another. He probably didn't. Nobody was tough to him. 'Point is the D.A. smells a lot of headlines on this one. Can't blame him, seeing who the girl's old man is. I guess we better pick this fellow's nose for him.'

He looked at me as if I was a cigarette stub, or an empty chair. Just something in his line of vision, without interest for him.

Dayton said respectfully: 'It's pretty obvious that his whole attitude was designed to create a situation where he could refuse to talk. He quoted law at us and needled me into socking him. I was out of line there, Captain.'

Gregorius eyed him bleakly. 'You must needle easy if this punk can do it. Who took the cuffs off?'

Green said he did. 'Put them back on,' Gregorius said. 'Tight. Give him something to brace him up.'

Green put the cuffs back on or started to. 'Behind the back,' Gregorius barked. Green cuffed my hands behind my back. I was sitting in a hard chair.

'Tighter,' Gregorius said. 'Make them bite.'

Green made them tighter. My hands started to feel numb.

Gregorius looked at me finally. 'You can talk now. Make it snappy.'

I didn't answer him. He leaned back and grinned. His hand went out slowly for his coffee cup and went around it. He leaned forward a little. The cup jerked but I beat it by going sideways out of the chair. I landed hard on my shoulder, rolled over and got up slowly. My hands were quite numb now. They didn't feel anything. The arms above the cuffs were beginning to ache.

Green helped me back into the chair. The wet smear of the coffee was over the back and some of the seat, but most of it was on the floor.

'He don't like coffee,' Gregorius said. 'He's a swifty. He moves fast. Good reflexes.'

Nobody said anything. Gregorius looked me over with fish eyes.

'In here, mister, a dick licence don't mean any more than a calling card. Now let's have your statement, verbal at first. We'll take it down later. Make it complete. Let's have, say, a full account of your movements since ten p.m. last night. I mean full. This office is investigating a murder and the prime suspect is missing. You connect with him. Guy catches his wife cheating and beats her head to raw flesh and bone and blood-soaked hair. Our old friend the bronze statuette. Not original but it works. You think any goddam private eye is going to quote law at me over this, mister, you got a hell of a tough time coming your way. There ain't a police force in the country could do its job with a law book. You got information and I want it. You could of said no and I could of not believed you. But you didn't even say no. You're not dummying up on me, my friend. Not six cents' worth. Let's go.'

'Would you take the cuffs off, Captain?' I asked. 'I mean if I made a statement?'

'I might. Make it short.'

'If I told you I hadn't seen Lennox within the last twenty-four hours, hadn't talked to him and had no idea where he might be – would that satisfy you, Captain?'

'It might – if I believed it.'

'If I told you I had seen him and where and when, but had no idea he had murdered anyone or that any crime had been committed, and further had no idea where he might be at this moment, that wouldn't satisfy you at all, would it?'

'With more detail I might listen. Things like where, when, what he looked like, what was talked about, where he was headed. It might grow into something.'

'With your treatment,' I said, 'it would probably grow into making me an accessory.'

His jaw muscles bulged. His eyes were dirty ice. 'So?'

'I don't know,' I said. 'I need legal advice. I'd like to co-operate. How would it be if we had somebody from the D.A.'s office here?'

He let out a short raucous laugh. It was over very soon. He got up slowly and walked around the desk. He leaned down close to me, one big hand on the wood, and smiled. Then without change of expression he hit me on the side of the neck with a fist like a piece of iron.

The blow travelled eight or ten inches, no more. It nearly took my head off. Bile seeped into my mouth. I tasted blood mixed with it. I heard nothing but a roaring in my head. He leaned over me still smiling, his left hand still on the desk. His voice seemed to come from a long way off.

'I used to be tough but I'm getting old. You take a good punch, mister, and that's all you get from me. We got boys over at the City Jail that ought to be working in the stockyards. Maybe we hadn't ought to have them because they ain't nice, clean powder-puff punchers like Dayton here. They don't have four kids and a rose garden like Green. They live for different amusements. It takes all kinds and labour's scarce. You got any more funny little ideas about what you might say, if you bothered to say it?'

'Not with the cuffs on, Captain.' It hurt even to say that much.

He leaned further towards me and I smelled his sweat and the gas of corruption. Then he straightened and went back around the desk and planted his solid buttocks in his chair. He picked up a three-cornered ruler and ran his thumb along one edge as if it was a knife. He looked at Green.

'What are you waiting for, Sergeant?'

'Orders.' Green ground out the word as if he hated the sound of his own voice.

'You got to be told? You're an experienced man, it says in the records. I want a detailed statement of this man's movements for the past twenty-four hours. Maybe longer, but that much at first. I want to know what he did every minute of the time. I want it signed and witnessed and checked. I want it in two hours. Then I want him back here clean, tidy and unmarked. And one thing more, Sergeant—'

He paused and gave Green a stare that would have frozen a fresh-baked potato.

'—next time I ask a suspect a few civil questions I don't want you standing there looking as if I had torn his ear off.'

'Yes sir.' Green turned to me. 'Let's go,' he said gruffly.

Gregorius bared his teeth at me. They needed cleaning – badly. 'Let's have the exit line, chum.'

'Yes, sir,' I said politely. 'You probably didn't intend it, but you've done me a favour. With an assist from Detective Dayton. You've solved a problem for me. No man likes to betray a friend but I wouldn't betray an enemy into your hands. You're not only a gorilla, you're an incompetent. You don't know how to operate a simple investigation. I was balanced on a knife edge and you could have swung me either way. But you had to abuse me, throw coffee in my face, and use your fists on me when I was in a spot where all I could do was take it. From now on I wouldn't tell you the time by the clock on your own wall.'

For some strange reason he sat there perfectly still and let me say it. Then he grinned. 'You're just a little old cop-hater, friend. That's all you are, shamus, just a little old cop-hater.'

'There are places where cops are not hated, Captain. But in those places you wouldn't be a cop.'

He took that too. I guess he could afford it. He'd probably taken worse many times. Then the phone rang on his desk. He looked at it and gestured. Dayton stepped smartly around the desk and lifted the receiver.

'Captain Gregorius' office. Detective Dayton speaking.'

He listened. A tiny frown drew his handsome eyebrows together. He said softly: 'One moment, please, sir.'

He held the phone out to Gregorius. 'Commissioner Allbright, sir.'

Gregorius scowled. 'Yeah? What's that snotty bastard want?' He took the phone, held it a moment and smoothed his face out. 'Gregorius, Commissioner.'

He listened. 'Yeah, he's here in my office, Commissioner. I been asking him a few questions. Not co-operative. Not co-operative at all ... How's that again?' A sudden ferocious scowl twisted his face into dark knots. The blood darkened his forehead. But his voice didn't change in tone by a fraction. 'If that's a direct order, it ought to come through the Chief of Detectives, Commissioner ... Sure, I'll act on it until it's confirmed. Sure. ... Hell, no. Nobody laid a glove on him ... Yes, sir. Right away.'

He put the phone back in its cradle. I thought his hand shook a little. His eyes moved up and across my face and then to Green. 'Take the cuffs off,' he said tonelessly.

Green unlocked the cuffs. I rubbed my hands together, waiting for the pins and needles of circulation.

'Book him in the County Jail,' Gregorius said slowly. 'Suspicion of murder. The D.A. has glommed the case right out of our hands. Lovely system we got around here.'

Nobody moved. Green was close to me, breathing hard. Gregorius looked up at Dayton.

'Whatcha waiting for, cream puff? An ice cream cone maybe?'

Dayton almost choked. 'You didn't give me any orders, skipper.'

'Say sir to me, damn you! I'm skipper to sergeants and better. Not to you, kiddo. Not to you. Out.'

'Yes, sir.' Dayton walked quickly to the door and went out. Gregorius heaved himself to his feet and moved to the window and stood with his back to the room.

'Come on, let's drift,' Green muttered in my ear.

'Get him out of here before I kick his face in,' Gregorius said to the window.

Green went to the door and opened it. I started through. Gregorius barked suddenly. 'Hold it! Shut that door!'

Green shut it and leaned his back to it.

'Come here you!' Gregorius barked at me.

I didn't move. I stood and looked at him. Green didn't move either. There was a grim pause. Then very slowly Gregorius walked across the room and stood facing me toe to toe. He put his big, hard hands in his pockets. He rocked on his heels.

'Never laid a glove on him,' he said under his breath, as if talking to himself. His eyes were remote and expressionless. His mouth worked convulsively.

Then he spat in my face.

He stepped back. 'That will be all, thank you.'

He turned and went back to the window. Green opened the door again.

I went through it reaching for my handkerchief.


# Eight


Cell No. 3 in the felony tank has two bunks, pullman style, but the tank was not very full and I had the cell to myself. In the felony tank they treat you pretty well. You get two blankets, neither dirty nor clean, and a lumpy mattress two inches thick which goes over criss-crossed metal slats. There is a flush toilet, a wash basin, paper towels and gritty grey soap. The cell block is clean and doesn't smell of disinfectant. The trusties do the work. The supply of trusties is always ample.

The jail deputies look you over and they have wise eyes. Unless you are drunk or a psycho or act like one you get to keep your matches and cigarettes. Until preliminary you wear your own clothes. After that you wear the jail denims, no tie, no belt, no shoelaces. You sit on the bunk and wait. There is nothing else to do.

In the drunk tank it is not so good. No bunk, no chair, no blankets, no nothing. You lie on the concrete floor. You sit on the toilet and vomit in your own lap. That is the depth of misery. I've seen it.

Although it was still daylight the lights were on in the ceiling. Inside the steel door of the cell block was a basket of steel bars around the Judas window. The lights were controlled from outside the steel door. They went out at nine p.m. Nobody came through the door or said anything. You might be in the middle of a sentence in a newspaper or magazine. Without any sound of a click or any warning – darkness. And there you were until the summer dawn with nothing to do but sleep if you could, smoke if you had anything to smoke, and think if you had anything to think about that didn't make you feel worse than not thinking at all.

In jail a man has no personality. He is a minor disposal problem and a few entries on reports. Nobody cares who loves or hates him, what he looks like, what he did with his life. Nobody reacts to him unless he gives trouble. Nobody abuses him. All that is asked of him is that he go quietly to the right cell and remain quiet when he gets there. There is nothing to fight against, nothing to be mad at. The jailers are quiet men without animosity or sadism. All this stuff you read about men yelling and screaming, beating against the bars, running spoons along them, guards rushing in with clubs – all that is for the big house. A good jail is one of the quietest places in the world. You could walk through the average cell block at night and look in through the bars and see a huddle of brown blanket, or a head of hair, or a pair of eyes looking at nothing. You might hear a snore. Once in a long while you might hear a nightmare. The life in a jail is in suspension, without purpose or meaning. In another cell you might see a man who cannot sleep or even try to sleep. He is sitting on the edge of his bunk doing nothing. He looks at you or doesn't. You look at him. He says nothing and you say nothing. There is nothing to communicate.

In the corner of the cell block there may be a second steel door that leads to the show-up box. One of its walls is wire mesh painted black. On the back wall are ruled lines for height. Overhead are floodlights. You go in there in the morning as a rule, just before the night captain goes off duty. You stand against the measuring lines and the lights glare at you and there is no light behind the wire mesh. But plenty of people are out there: cops, detectives, citizens who have been robbed or assaulted or swindled or kicked out of their cars at gun point or conned out of their life savings. You don't see or hear them. You hear the voice of the night captain. You receive him loud and clear. He puts you through your paces as if you were a performing dog. He is tired and cynical and competent. He is the stage manager of a play that has had the longest run in history, but it no longer interests him.

'All right, you. Stand straight. Pull your belly in. Pull your chin in. Keep your shoulders back. Hold your head level. Look straight front. Turn left. Turn right. Face front again and hold your hands out. Palms up. Palms down. Pull your sleeves back. No visible scars. Hair dark brown, some grey. Eyes brown. Height six feet, one-half inch. Weight about one-ninety. Name, Philip Marlowe. Occupation, private detective. Well, well, nice to see you, Marlowe. That's all. Next man.'

Much obliged, Captain. Thanks for the time. You forgot to have me open my mouth. I have some nice inlays and one very high-class porcelain jacket crown. Eighty-seven dollars' worth of porcelain jacket crown. You forgot to look inside my nose too, Captain. A lot of scar tissues in there for you. Septum operation and was that guy a butcher! Two hours of it in those days. I hear they do it in twenty minutes now. I got it playing football, Captain, a slight miscalculation in an attempt to block a punt. I blocked the guy's foot instead – after he kicked the ball. Fifteen yards penalty, and that's about how much stiff bloody tape they pulled out of my nose an inch at a time the day after the operation. I'm not bragging, Captain. I'm just telling you. It's the little things that count.

On the third day a deputy unlocked my cell in the middle of the morning.

'Your lawyer's here. Kill the butt – and not on the floor.'

I flushed it down the toilet. He took me to the conference room. A tall, pale, dark-haired man was standing there looking out of the window. There was a fat brown brief-case on the table. He turned. He waited for the door to close. Then he sat down near his brief-case on the far side of a scarred oak table that came out of the Ark. Noah bought it second-hand. The lawyer opened a hammered-silver cigarette case and put it in front of him and looked me over.

'Sit down, Marlowe. Care for a cigarette? My name is Endicott. Sewell Endicott. I've been instructed to represent you without cost or expense to you. I guess you'd like to get out of here, wouldn't you?'

I sat down and took one of the cigarettes. He held a lighter for me.

'Nice to see you again, Mr Endicott. We've met before – while you were D.A.'

He nodded. 'I don't remember, but it's quite possible.' He smiled faintly. 'That position was not quite in my line. I guess I don't have enough tiger in me.'

'Who sent you?'

'I'm not at liberty to say. If you accept me as your attorney, the fee will be taken care of.'

'I guess that means they've got him.'

He just stared at me. I puffed at the cigarette. It was one of those things with filters in them. It tasted like a high fog strained through cotton wool.

'If you mean Lennox,' he said, 'and of course you do, no – they haven't got him.'

'Why the mystery, Mr Endicott? About who sent you.'

'My principal wishes to remain anonymous. That is the privilege of my principal. Do you accept me?'

'I don't know,' I said. 'If they haven't got Terry, why are they holding me? Nobody has asked me anything, nobody has been near me.'

He frowned and looked down at his long white delicate fingers. 'District Attorney Springer has taken personal charge of this matter. He may have been too busy to question you yet. But you are entitled to arraignment and a preliminary hearing. I can get you out on bail on a habeas corpus preceeding. You probably know what the law is.'

'I'm booked on suspicion of murder.'

He shrugged impatiently. 'That's just a catch-all. You could have been booked in transit to Pittsburgh, or any one of a dozen charges. What they probably mean is accessory after the fact. You took Lennox somewhere, didn't you?'

I didn't answer. I dropped the tasteless cigarette on the floor and stepped on it. Endicott shrugged again and frowned.

'Assume you did then, just for the sake of argument. To make you an accessory they have to prove intent. In this case that would mean knowledge that a crime had been committed and that Lennox was a fugitive. It's bailable in any case. Of course what you really are is a material witness. But a man can't be held in prison as a material witness in this state except by court order. He's not a material witness unless a judge so declares. But the law enforcement people can always find a way to do what they want to do.'

'Yeah,' I said. 'A detective named Dalton slugged me. A homicide captain named Gregorius threw a cup of coffee at me, hit me in the neck hard enough to bust an artery – you can see it's still swollen, and when a call from Police Commissioner Allbright kept him from turning me over to the wrecking crew, he spat in my face. You're quite right, Mr Endicott. The law boys can always do what they want to do.'

He looked at his wristwatch rather pointedly. 'You want out on bail or don't you?'

'Thanks. I don't think I do. A guy out on bail is already half guilty in the public mind. If he gets off later on, he had a smart lawyer.'

'That's silly,' he said impatiently.

'Okay, it's silly. I'm silly. Otherwise I wouldn't be here. If you're in touch with Lennox, tell him to quit bothering about me. I'm not in here for him. I'm in here for me. No complaints.

It's part of the deal. I'm in a business where people come to me with troubles. Big troubles, little troubles, but always troubles they don't want to take to the cops. How long would they come if any bruiser with a police shield could hold me upside down and drain my guts?'

'I see your point,' he said slowly. 'But let me correct you on one point. I am not in touch with Lennox. I scarcely know him. I'm an officer of the court, as all lawyers are. If I knew where Lennox was, I couldn't conceal the information from the District Attorney. The most I could do would be to agree to surrender him at a specified time and place after I had had an interview with him.'

'Nobody else would bother to send you here to help me.'

'Are you calling me a liar?' He reached down to rub out his cigarette stub on the underside of the table.

'I seem to remember that you're a Virginian, Mr Endicott. In this country we have a sort of historical fixation about Virginians. We think of them as the flower of southern chivalry and honour.'

He smiled. 'That was nicely said. I only wish it was true. But we're wasting time. If you had had a grain of sense you'd have told the police you hadn't seen Lennox for a week. It didn't have to be true. Under oath you could always have told the real story. There's no law against lying to the cops. They expect it. They feel much happier when you lie to them than when you refuse to talk to them. That's a direct challenge to their authority. What do you expect to gain by it?'

I didn't answer. I didn't really have an answer. He stood up and reached for his hat and snapped his cigarette case shut and put it in his pocket.

'You had to play the big scene,' he said coldly. 'Stand on your rights, talk about the law. How ingenuous can a man get, Marlowe? A man like you who is supposed to know his way around. The law isn't justice. It's a very imperfect mechanism. If you press exactly the right buttons and are also lucky, justice may show up in the answer. A mechanism is all the law ever was ever intended to be. I guess you're not in any mood to be helped. So I'll take myself off. You can reach me if you change your mind.'

'I'll stick it out for a day or two longer. If they catch Terry they won't care how he got away. All they'll care about is the circus they can make of the trial. The murder of Mr Harlan Potter's daughter is headline material all over the country. A crowd pleaser like Springer could ride himself right into Attorney-General on that show, and from there into the governor's chair and from there—' I stopped talking and let the rest of it float in the air.

Endicott smiled a slow derisive smile. 'I don't think you know very much about Mr Harlan Potter,' he said.

'And if they don't get Lennox, they won't *want* to know how he got away, Mr Endicott. They'll just want to forget the whole thing fast.'

'Got it all figured out, haven't you, Marlowe?'

'I've had the time. All I know about Mr Harlan Potter is that he is supposed to be worth a hundred million bucks, and that he owns nine or ten newspapers. How's the publicity going?'

'The publicity?' His voice was ice-cold saying it.

'Yeah. Nobody's interviewed me from the press. I expected to make a big noise in the papers out of this. Get lots of business. Private eye goes to jail rather than split on a pal.'

He walked to the door and turned with his hands on the knob. 'You amuse me, Marlowe. You're childish in some ways. True, a hundred million dollars can buy a great deal of publicity. It can also, my friend, if shrewdly employed, buy a great deal of silence.'

He opened the door and went out. Then a deputy came in and took me back to Cell No. 3 in the felony block.

'Guess you won't be with us long, if you've got Endicott,' he said pleasantly as he locked me in. I said I hoped he was right.


# Nine

The deputy on the early night shift was a big blond guy with meaty shoulders and a friendly grin. He was middle-aged and had long since outlived both pity and anger. He wanted to put in eight easy hours and he looked as if almost anything would be easy down his street. He unlocked my door.

'Company for you. Guy from the the D.A.'s office. No sleep, huh?'

'It's a little early for me. What time is it?'

'Ten-fourteen.' He stood in the doorway and looked over the cell. One blanket was spread on the lower bunk, one was folded for a pillow. There were a couple of used paper towels in the trash bucket and a small wad of toilet paper on the edge of the wash basin. He nodded approval. 'Anything personal in here?'

'Just me.'

He left the cell door open. We walked along a quiet corridor to the elevator and rode down to the booking desk. A fat man in a grey suit stood by the desk smoking a corncob. His fingernails were dirty and he smelled.

'I'm Spranklin from the D.A.'s office,' he told me in a tough voice. 'Mr Grenz wants you upstairs.' He reached behind his hip and came up with a pair of bracelets. 'Let's try these for size.'

The jail deputy and the booking clerk grinned at him with deep enjoyment. 'What's the matter, Sprank? Afraid he'll mug you in the elevator?'

'I don't want no trouble,' he growled. 'Had a guy break from me once. They ate my ass off. Let's go, boy.'

The booking clerk pushed a form at him and he signed it with a flourish. 'I never take no unnecessary chances,' he said. 'Man never knows what he's up against in this town.'

A prowl car cop brought in a drunk with a bloody ear. We went towards the elevator. 'You're in trouble, boy,' Spranklin told me in the elevator. 'Heap bad trouble.' It seemed to give him a vague satisfaction. 'A guy can get hisself in a lot of trouble in this town.'

The elevator man turned his head and winked at me. I grinned.

'Don't try nothing, boy,' Spranklin told me severely. 'I shot a man once. Tried to break. They ate my ass off.'

'You get it coming and going, don't you?'

He thought it over. 'Yeah,' he said. 'Either way they eat your ass off. It's a tough town. No respect.'

We got out and went in through the double doors of the D.A.'s office. The switchboard was dead, with lines plugged in for the night. There was nobody in the waiting chairs. Lights were on in a couple of offices. Spranklin opened the door of a small, lighted room which contained a desk, a filing case, a hard chair or two, and a thick-set man with a hard chin and stupid eyes. His face was red and he was just pushing something into the drawer of his desk.

'You could knock,' he barked at Spranklin.

'Sorry, Mr Grenz,' Spranklin bumbled. 'I was thinkin' about the prisoner.'

He pushed me into the office. 'Should I take the cuffs off, Mr Grenz?'

'I don't know what the hell you put them on for,' Grenz said sourly. He watched Spranklin unlock the cuffs on my wrist. He had the key on a bunch the size of a grapefruit and it troubled him to find it.

'Okay, scram,' Grenz said. 'Wait outside to take him back.'

'I'm kind of off duty, Mr Grenz.'

'You're off duty when I say you're off duty.'

Spranklin flushed and edged his fat bottom out through the door. Grenz looked after him savagely, then when the door closed he moved the same look to me. I pulled a chair over and sat down.

'I didn't tell you to sit down,' Grenz barked.

I got a loose cigarette out of my pocket and stuck it in my mouth. 'And I didn't say you could smoke,' Grenz roared.

'I'm allowed to smoke in the cell block. Why not here?'

'Because this is my office. *I* make the rules here.' A raw smell of whisky floated across the desk.

'Take another quick one,' I said. 'It'll calm you down. You got kind of interrupted when we came in.'

His back hit the back of the chair hard. His face went dark red. I struck a match and lit my cigarette.

After a long minute Grenz said softly 'Okay, tough boy. Quite a man, aren't you? You know something? They're all sizes and shapes when they come in here, but they all go out the same size – small. And the same shape – bent.'

'What did you want to see me about, Mr Grenz? And don't mind me if you feel like hitting that bottle. I'm a fellow that will take a snort myself, if I'm tired and nervous and over-worked.'

'You don't seem much impressed by the jam you're in.'

'I don't figure I'm in any jam.'

'We'll see about that. Meantime I want a very full statement from you.' He flicked a finger at a recording set on a stand beside his desk. 'We'll take it now and have it transcribed tomorrow. If the Chief Deputy is satisfied with your statement, he may release you on your own undertaking not to leave town. Let's go.' He switched on the recorder. His voice was cold, decisive and as nasty as he knew how to make it. But his right hand kept edging towards the desk drawer. He was too young to have veins in his nose, but he had them, and the whites of his eyes were a bad colour.

'I get so tired of it,' I said.

'Tired of what?' he snapped.

'Hard little men in hard little offices talking hard little words that don't mean a goddam thing. I've had fifty-six hours in the felony block. Nobody pushed me around, nobody tried to prove he was tough. They didn't have to. They had it on ice for when they needed it. And why was I in there? I was booked on suspicion. What the hell kind of legal system lets a man be shoved in a felony tank because some cop didn't get an answer to some question? What evidence did he have? A telephone number on a pad. And what was he trying to prove by locking me up? Not a damn thing except that he had the power to do it. Now you're on the same pitch – trying to make me feel what a lot of power you generate in this cigar box you call your office. You send this scared babysitter over late at night to bring me in here. You think maybe sitting alone with my thoughts for fifty-six hours has made gruel out of my brains? You think I'm going to cry in your lap and ask you to stroke my head because I'm so awful goddam lonely in the great big jail? Come off it, Grenz. Take your drink and get human; I'm willing to assume you are just doing your job. But take the brass knuckles off before you start. If you're big enough you don't need them, and if you need them you're not big enough to push me around.'

He sat there and listened and looked at me. Then he grinned sourly. 'Nice speech,' he said. 'Now you've got the crap out of your system, let's get that statement. You want to answer specific questions or just tell it your own way?'

'I was talking to the birds,' I said. 'Just to hear the breeze blow. I'm not making any statement. You're a lawyer and you know I don't have to.'

'That's right,' he said coolly. 'I know the law. I know police work. I'm offering you a chance to clear yourself. If you don't want it, that's jake with me too. I can arraign you tomorrow morning at ten a.m. and have you set for a preliminary hearing. You may get bail, although I'll fight it, but if you do, it will be stiff. It'll cost you plenty. That's one way we can do it.'

He looked down at a paper on his desk, read it, and turned it face down.

'On what charge?' I asked him.

'Section Thirty-two. Accessory after the fact. A felony. It rates up to a five spot in Quentin.'

'Better catch Lennox first,' I said carefully. Grenz had something and I sensed it in his manner. I didn't know how much, but he had something all right.

He leaned back in his chair and picked up a pen and twirled it slowly between his palms. Then he smiled. He was enjoying himself.

'Lennox is a hard man to hide, Marlowe. With most people you need a photo and a good clear photo. Not with a guy that has scars all over one side of his face. Not to mention white hair, and not over thirty-five years old. We got four witnesses, maybe more.'

'Witnesses to what?' I was tasting something bitter in my mouth, like the bile I had tasted after Captain Gregorius slugged me. That reminded me that my neck was still sore and swollen. I rubbed it gently.

'Don't be a chump, Marlowe. A San Diego superior court judge and his wife happened to be seeing their son and daughter-in-law off on that plane. All four saw Lennox and the judge's wife saw the car he came in and who came with him. You don't have a prayer?'

'That's nice,' I said. 'How did you get to them?'

'Special bulletin on radio and TV. A full description was all it took. The judge called in.'

'Sounds good,' I said judicially. 'But it takes a little more than that, Grenz. You have to catch him and prove he committed a murder. Then you have to prove I knew it.'

He snapped a finger at the back of the telegram. 'I think I will take that drink,' he said. 'Been working nights too much.' He opened the drawer and put a bottle and a shot glass on the desk. He poured it full to the brim and knocked it back in a lump. 'Better,' he said. 'Much better. Sorry I can't offer you one while you're in custody.' He corked the bottle and pushed it away from him, but not out of reach. 'Oh yeah, we got to prove something, you said. Well, it could be we already got a confession, chum. Too bad, huh?'

A small but very cold finger moved the whole length of my spine, like an icy insect crawling.

'So why do you need a statement from me?'

He grinned. 'We like a tidy record. Lennox will be brought back and tried. We need everything we can get. It's not so much what we want from you, as what we might be willing to let you get away with – if you co-operate.'

I stared at him. He did a little paper-fiddling. He moved around in his chair, looked at his bottle, and had to use up a lot of will-power not grabbing for it. 'Maybe you'd like the whole libretto,' he said suddenly with an off-key leer. 'Well, smart guy, just to show you I'm not kidding here it is.'

I leaned across his desk and he thought I was reaching for his bottle. He grabbed it away and put it back in the drawer. I just

243

wanted to drop a stub in his ashtray. I leaned back again and lit another pill. He spoke rapidly.

'Lennox got off the plane at Mazatlan, an airline junction point and a town of about thirty-five thousand. He disappeared for two or three hours. Then a tall man with black hair and a dark skin and what might have been a lot of knife scars booked to Torreon under the name of Silvano Rodriguez. His Spanish was good but not good enough for a man of his name. He was too tall for a Mexican with such a dark skin. The pilot turned in a report on him. The cops were too slow at Torreon. Mex cops are no balls of fire. What they do best is shoot people. By the time they got going the man had chartered a plane and gone on to a little mountain town called Otatoclan, a small-time summer resort with a lake. The pilot of the charter plane had trained as a combat pilot in Texas. He spoke good English. Lennox pretended not to catch what he said.'

'If it *was* Lennox,' I put in.

'Wait a while, chum. It was Lennox all right. Okay, he gets off at Otatoclan and registers at the hotel there, this time as Mario de Cerva. He was wearing a gun, a Mauser 7.65, which doesn't mean too much in Mexico, of course. But the charter pilot thought the guy didn't seem kosher, so he had a word with the local law. They put Lennox under surveillance. They did some checking with Mexico City and then they moved in.'

Grenz picked up a ruler and sighted along it, a meaningless gesture which kept him from looking at me.

I said, 'Uh-huh. Smart boy, your charter pilot, and nice to his customers. The story stinks.'

He looked up at me suddenly. 'What we want,' he said dryly, 'is a quick trial, a plea of second degree, which we will accept. There are some angles we'd rather not go into. After all, the family is pretty influential.'

'Meaning Harlan Potter.'

He nodded briefly. 'For my money the whole idea is all wet. Springer could have a field day with it. It's got everything. Sex, scandal, money, beautiful unfaithful wife, wounded war-hero husband – I suppose that's where he got the scars – hell, it would be front page stuff for weeks. Every rag in the country would eat it up. So we shuffle it off to a fast fade.' He shrugged. 'Okay, if the chief wants it that way, it's up to him. Do I get that statement?' He turned to the recording machine which had been humming away softly all this time, with the light showing in front.

'Turn it off,' I said.

He swung around and gave me a vicious look. 'You like it in jail?'

'It's not too bad. You don't meet the best people, but who the hell wants to? Be reasonable, Grenz. You're trying to make a fink out of me. Maybe I'm obstinate, or even sentimental, but I'm practical too. Suppose you had to hire a private eye – yeah, yeah, I know how you would hate the idea – but just suppose you were where it was your only way out. Would you want one that finked on his friends?'

He stared at me with hate.

'A couple more points. Doesn't it strike you that Lennox's evasion tactics were just a little too transparent? If he wanted to be caught, he didn't have to go to all that trouble. If he didn't want to be caught, he had brains enough not to disguise himself as a Mexican in Mexico.'

'Meaning what?' Grenz was snarling at me now.

'Meaning you could just be filling me up with a lot of hooey you made up, that there wasn't any Rodriguez with dyed hair and there wasn't any Mario de Cerva at Otatoclan, and you don't know any more about where Lennox is than where Blackbeard the Pirate buried his treasure.'

He got his bottle out again. He poured himself a shot and drank it down quickly, as before. He relaxed slowly. He turned in his chair and switched off the recording machine.

'I'd like to have tried you,' he said gratingly. 'You're the kind of wise guy I like to work over. This rap will be hanging over you for a long, long time, cutie. You'll walk with it and eat with it and sleep with it. And next time you step out of line we'll murder you with it. Right now I got to do something that turns my guts inside out.'

He pawed on his desk and pulled the face-down paper to him, turned it over and signed it. You can always tell when a man is writing his own name. He has a special way of moving. Then he stood up and marched around the desk and threw the door of his shoe box open and yelled for Spranklin.

The fat man came in with his B.O. Grenz gave him the paper.

'I've just signed your release order,' he said. 'I'm a public servant and sometimes I have unpleasant duties. Would you care to know why I signed it?'

I stood up. 'If you want to tell me.'

'The Lennox case is closed, mister. There ain't any Lennox case. He wrote out a full confession this afternoon in his hotel room and shot himself. In Otatoclan, just like I said.'

I stood there looking at nothing. Out of the corner of my eye I saw Grenz back away slowly as if he thought I might be going to slug him. I must have looked pretty nasty for a moment. Then he was behind his desk again and Spranklin had grabbed on to my arm.

'Come on, move,' he said in a whining kind of voice. 'Man likes to get home nights once in a while.'

I went out with him and closed the door. I closed it quietly as if on a room where someone had just died.

# Ten

I dug out the carbon of my property slip and turned it over and receipted on the original. I put my belongings back in my pockets. There was a man draped over the end of the booking desk and as I turned away he straightened up and spoke to me. He was about six feet four inches tall and as thin as a wire.

'Need a ride home?'

In the bleak light he looked young-old, tired and cynical, but he didn't look like a grifter. 'For how much?'

'For free. I'm Lonnie Morgan of the *Journal*. I'm knocking off.'

'Oh, police beat,' I said.

'Just this week. The City Hall is my regular beat.'

We walked out of the building and found his car in the parking lot. I looked up at the sky. There were stars but there was too much glare. It was a cool, pleasant night. I breathed it in. Then I got into his car and he drove away from there.

'I live way out in Laurel Canyon,' I said. 'Just drop me anywhere.'

'They ride you in,' he said, 'but they don't worry how you get home. This case interests me, in a repulsive sort of way.'

'It seems there isn't any case,' I said. 'Terry Lennox shot himself this afternoon. So they say. So they say.'

'Very convenient,' Lonnie Morgan said, staring ahead through the windshield. His car drifted quietly along quiet streets. 'It helps them build their wall.'

'What wall?'

'Somebody's building a wall around the Lennox case, Marlowe. You're smart enough to see that, aren't you? It's not getting the kind of play it rates. The D.A. left town tonight for Washington. Some kind of convention. He walked out on the sweetest hunk of publicity he's had in years. Why?'

'No use to ask me. I've been in cold storage.'

'Because somebody made it worth his while, that's why. I don't mean anything crude like a wad of dough. Somebody promised him something important to him and there's only one man connected with the case in a position to do that. The girl's father.'

I leaned my head back in a corner of the car. 'Sounds a little unlikely,' I said. 'What about the press? Harlan Potter owns a few papers, but what about the competition?'

He gave me a brief amused glance and then concentrated on his driving. 'Ever been a newspaper man?'

'No.'

'Newspapers are owned and published by rich men. Rich men all belong to the same club. Sure, there's competition – hard, tough competition for circulation, for newsbeats, for exclusive stories. Just so long as it doesn't damage the prestige and privilege and position of the owners. If it does, down comes the lid. The lid, my friend, is down on the Lennox case. The Lennox case, my friend, properly built up, could have sold a hell of a lot of papers. It has everything. The trial would have drawn feature writers from all over the country. But there ain't going to be no trial. On account of Lennox checked out before it could get moving. Like I said – very convenient – for Harlan Potter and his family.'

I straightened up and gave him a hard stare.

'You calling the whole thing a fix?'

He twisted his mouth sardonically. 'Could just be Lennox had some help committing suicide. Resisting arrest a little. Mexican cops have very itchy trigger fingers. If you want to lay a little bet, I'll give you nice odds that nobody gets to count the bullet holes.'

'I think you're wrong,' I said. 'I knew Terry Lennox pretty well. He wrote himself off a long time ago. If they brought him back alive, he would have let them have it their way. He'd have copped a manslaughter plea.'

Lonnie Morgan shook his head. I knew what he was going to say and he said it. 'Not a chance. If he had shot her or cracked her skull, maybe yes. But there was too much brutality. Her face was beaten to a pulp. Second degree murder would be the

247

best he could get, and even that would raise a stink.'

I said: 'You could be right.'

He looked at me again. 'You say you knew the guy. Do you go for the set-up?'

'I'm tired. I'm not in a thinking mood tonight.'

There was a long pause. Then Lonnie Morgan said quietly: 'If I was a real bright guy instead of a hack newspaper man, I'd think maybe he didn't kill her at all.'

'It's a thought.'

He stuck a cigarette in his mouth and lit it by scratching a match on the dashboard. He smoked silently with a fixed frown on his thin face. We reached Laurel Canyon and I told him where to turn off the boulevard and where to turn again into my street. His car churned up the hill and stopped at the foot of my redwood steps.

I got out. 'Thanks for the ride, Morgan. Care for a drink?'

'I'll take a rain check. I figure you'd rather be alone.'

'I've got lots of time to be alone. Too damn much.'

'You've got a friend to say good-bye to,' he said. 'He must have been that if you let them toss you into the can on his account.'

'Who said I did that?'

He smiled faintly. 'Just because I can't print it don't mean I didn't know it, chum. So long. See you around.'

I shut the car door and he turned and drove off down the hill. When his tail lights vanished around the corner I climbed the steps, picked up newspapers and let myself into the empty house. I put all the lamps on and opened all the windows. The place was stuffy.

I made some coffee and drank it and took the five C notes out of the coffee can. They were rolled tight and pushed down into the coffee at the side. I walked up and down with a cup of coffee in my hand, turned the TV on, turned it off, sat, stood, and sat again. I read through the papers that had piled up on the front steps. The Lennox case started out big, but by that morning it was a Part Two item. There was a photo of Sylvia, but none of Terry. There was a snap of me that I didn't know existed. 'L.A. Private Detective Held for Questioning.' There was a large photo of the Lennox home in Encino. It was pseudo-English with a lot of peaked roof and it would have cost a hundred bucks to wash the windows. It stood on a knoll in a big two acres, which is a lot of real estate for the Los Angeles area. There was a photo of the guest house, which was a miniature of the main building. It was hedged in with trees. Both photos had obviously been taken from some distance off and then blown up and trimmed. There was no photo of what the papers called the 'death room'.

I had seen all this stuff before, in jail, but I read it and looked at it again with different eyes. It told me nothing except that a rich and beautiful girl had been murdered and the press had been pretty thoroughly excluded. So the influence had started to work very early. The crime beat boys must have gnashed their teeth and gnashed them in vain. It figured. If Terry talked to his father-in-law in Pasadena the very night she was killed, there would have been a dozen guards on the estate before the police were even notified.

But there was something that didn't figure at all – the way she had been beaten up. Nobody could tell me that Terry had done that.

I put the lamps out and sat by an open window. Outside in a bush a mocking bird ran through a few trills and admired himself before settling down for the night.

My neck itched, so I shaved and showered and went to bed and lay on my back listening, as if far off in the dark I might hear a voice, the kind of calm and patient voice that makes everything clear. I didn't hear it and I knew I wasn't going to. Nobody was going to explain the Lennox case to me. No explanation was necessary. The murderer had confessed and he was dead. There wouldn't even be an inquest.

As Lonnie Morgan of the *Journal* had remarked – very convenient. If Terry Lennox had killed his wife, that was fine. There was no need to try him and bring out all the unpleasant details. If he hadn't killed her, that was fine too. A dead man is the best fall guy in the world. He never talks back.

# Eleven

In the morning I shaved again and dressed and drove downtown in the usual way and parked in the usual place, and if the parking lot attendant happened to know that I was an important public character he did a top job in hiding it. I went upstairs and along the corridor and got keys out to unlock my door. A dark, smooth-looking guy watched me.

'You Marlowe?'

'So?'

'Stick around,' he said. 'A guy wants to see you.' He un-plastered his back from the wall and strolled off languidly.

I stepped inside the office and picked up the mail. There was more of it on the desk where the night cleaning woman had put it. I slit the envelopes after I opened windows and threw away what I didn't want, which was practically all of it. I switched on the buzzer to the other door and filled a pipe and lit it and then just sat there waiting for somebody to scream for help.

I thought about Terry Lennox in a detached sort of way. He was already receding into the distance, white hair and scarred face and weak charm and his peculiar brand of pride. I didn't judge him or analyse him, just as I had never asked him questions about how he got wounded or how he ever happened to get himself married to anyone like Sylvia. He was like somebody you meet on board ship and get to know very well and never really know at all. He was gone like the same fellow when he says good-bye at the pier and let's keep in touch, old man, and you know you won't and he won't. Likely enough you'll never even see the guy again. If you do he will be an entirely different person, just another Rotarian in a club car. How's business? Oh, not too bad. You look good. So do you. I've put on too much weight. Don't we all? Remember that trip in the *Franconia* (or whatever it was)? Oh sure, swell trip, wasn't it?

The hell it was a swell trip. You were bored stiff. You only talked to the guy because there wasn't anybody around that interested you. Maybe it was like that with Terry Lennox and me. No, not quite. I owned a piece of him. I had invested time and money in him, and three days in the ice-house, not to mention a slug on the jaw and a punch in the neck that I felt every time I swallowed. Now he was dead and I couldn't even give him back his five hundred bucks. That made me sore. It is always the little things that make you sore.

The door buzzer and the telephone rang at the same time. I answered the phone first because the buzzer meant only that somebody had walked into my pint-size waiting-room.

'Is this Mr Marlowe? Mr Endicott is calling you. One moment please.'

He came on the line. 'This is Sewell Endicott,' he said, as if he didn't know his goddam secretary had already fed me his name.

'Good morning, Mr Endicott.'

'Glad to hear they turned you loose. I think possibly you had the right idea not to build any resistance.'

'It wasn't an idea. It was just mulishness.'

'I doubt if you'll hear any more about it. But if you do and need help, let me hear from you.'

'Why should I? The man is dead. They'd have a hell of a time proving he ever came near me. Then they'd have to prove I had guilty knowledge. And then they'd have to prove he had committed a crime or was a fugitive.'

He cleared his throat. 'Perhaps,' he said carefully, 'you haven't been told he left a full confession.'

'I was told, Mr Endicott. I'm talking to a lawyer. Would I be out of line in suggesting that the confession would have to be proved too, both as to genuineness and as to veracity?'

'I'm afraid I have no time for a legal discussion,' he said sharply. 'I'm flying to Mexico with a rather melancholy duty to perform. You can probably guess what it is?'

'Uh-huh. Depends who you're representing. You didn't tell me, remember?'

'I remember very well. Well, good-bye, Marlowe. My offer of help is still good. But let me also offer you a little advice. Don't be too certain you're in the clear. You're in a pretty vulnerable business.'

He hung up. I put the phone back in its cradle carefully. I sat for a moment with my hand on it, scowling. Then I wiped the scowl off my face and got up to open the communicating door into my waiting-room.

A man was sitting by the window ruffling a magazine. He wore a bluish-grey suit with an almost invisible pale blue check. On his crossed feet were black moccasin-type ties, the kind with two eyelets that are almost as comfortable as strollers and don't wear your socks out every time you walk a block. His white handkerchief was folded square and the end of a pair of sunglasses showed behind it. He had thick, dark, wavy hair. He was tanned very dark. He looked up with bird-bright eyes and smiled under a hair-line moustache. His tie was a dark maroon tied in a pointed bow over a sparkling white shirt.

He threw the magazine aside. 'The crap these rags go for,' he said. 'I been reading a piece about Costello. Yeah, they know all about Costello. Like I know all about Helen of Troy.'

'What can I do for you?'

He looked me over unhurriedly. 'Tarzan on a big red scooter,' he said.

'What?'

'You, Marlowe. Tarzan on a big red scooter. They rough you up much?'

'Here and there. What makes it your business?'

'After Allbright talked to Gregorius?'

'No. Not after that.'

He nodded shortly. 'You got a crust asking Allbright to use ammunition on that slob.'

'I asked you what made it your business. Incidentally I don't know Commissioner Allbright and I didn't ask him to do anything. Why should he do anything for me?'

He stared at me morosely. He stood up slowly, graceful as a panther. He walked across the room and looked into my office. He jerked his head at me and went in. He was a guy who owned the place where he happened to be. I went in after him and shut the door. He stood by the desk looking around, amused.

'You're small-time,' he said. 'Very small-time.'

I went behind my desk and waited.

'How much you make in a month, Marlowe?'

I let it ride, and lit my pipe.

'Seven-fifty would be tops,' he said.

I dropped a burnt match into a tray and puffed tobacco smoke.

'You're a piker, Marlowe. You're a peanut grifter. You're so little it takes a magnifying glass to see you.'

I didn't say anything at all.

'You got cheap emotions. You're cheap all over. You pal around with a guy, eat a few drinks, talk a few gags, slip him a little dough when he's strapped, and you're sold out to him. Just like some school kid that read Frank Merriwell. You got no guts, no brains, no connections, no savvy, so you throw out a phony attitude and expect people to cry over you. Tarzan on a big red scooter.' He smiled a small weary smile. 'In my book you're a nickel's worth of nothing.'

He leaned across the desk and flicked me across the face backhanded, casually and contemptuously, not meaning to hurt me, and the small smile stayed on his face. Then, when I didn't even move for that, he sat down slowly and leaned an elbow on the desk and cupped his brown chin in his brown hand. The bird-bright eyes stared at me without anything in them but brightness.

'Know who I am, cheapie?'

'Your name's Menendez. The boys call you Mendy. You operate on the Strip.'

'Yeah? How did I get so big?'

'I wouldn't know. You probably started out as a pimp in a Mexican whorehouse.'

He took a gold cigarette case out of his pocket and lit a brown cigarette with a gold lighter. He blew acrid smoke and nodded. He put the gold cigarette case on the desk and caressed it with his fingertips.

'I'm a big bad man, Marlowe. I make lots of dough. I got to make lots of dough to juice the guys I got to juice in order to make lots of dough to juice the guys I got to juice. I got a place in Bel-Air that cost ninety grand and I already spent more than that to fix it up. I got a lovely platinum blonde wife and two kids in private schools back east. My wife's got a hundred and fifty grand in rocks and another seventy-five in furs and clothes. I got a butler, two maids, a cook, a chauffeur, not counting the monkey that walks behind me. Everywhere I go I'm a darling. The best of everything, the best food, the best drinks, the best clothes, the best hotel suites. I got a place in Florida and a sea-going yacht with a crew of five men. I got a Bentley, two Cadillacs, a Chrysler station wagon, and an MG for my boy. Couple of years my girl gets one too. What you got?'

'Not much,' I said. 'This year I have a house to live in – all to myself.'

'No woman?'

'Just me. In addition to that I have what you see here and twelve hundred dollars in the bank and a few thousand in bonds. That answer your question?'

'What's the most you ever made on a single job?'

'Eight-fifty.'

'Jesus, how cheap can a guy get?'

'Stop hamming and tell me what you want.'

He killed his cigarette half-smoked and immediately lit another. He leaned back in his chair. His lip curled at me.

'We were three guys in a foxhole eating,' he said. 'It was cold as hell, snow all around. We eat out of cans. Cold food. A little shelling, more mortar fire. We are blue with the cold, and I mean blue, Randy Starr and me and this Terry Lennox. A mortar shell plops right in the middle of us and for some reason it don't go off. Those Jerries have a lot of tricks. They got a twisted sense of humour. Sometimes you think it's a dud and three seconds later it ain't a dud. Terry grabs it and he's out of the foxhole before Randy and me can even start to get unstuck. But I mean quick, brother. Like a good ball handler. He throws himself face down and throws the thing away from him and it goes off in the air. Most of it goes over his head but a hunk gets the side of his face. Right then the krauts mount an attack and the next thing we know we ain't there any more.'

Menendez stopped talking and gave me the bright steady glare of his dark eyes.

'Thanks for telling me,' I said.

'You take a good ribbing, Marlowe. You're okay. Randy and me talked things over and we decided that what happened to Terry Lennox was enough to screw up any guy's brains. For a long time we figured he was dead but he wasn't. The krauts got him. They worked him over for about a year and a half. They did a good job but they hurt him too much. It cost us money to find out, and it cost us money to find him. But we made plenty in the black market after the war. We could afford it. All Terry gets out of saving our lives is half of a new face, white hair, and a bad case of nerves. Back east he hits the bottle, gets picked up here and there, kind of goes to pieces. There's something on his mind but we never know what. The next thing we know he's married to this rich dame and riding high. He unmarries her, hits bottom again, marries her again, and she gets dead. Randy and me can't do a thing for him. He won't let us except for that short job in Vegas. And when he gets in a real jam he don't come to us, he goes to a cheapie like you, a guy that cops can push around. So then *he* gets dead, and without telling us good-bye, and without giving us a chance to pay off. I got connections in Mexico that could have buried him for ever. I could have got him out of the country faster than a card sharp can stack a deck. But he goes crying to you. It makes me sore. A cheapie, a guy cops can push around.'

'The cops can push anybody around. What do you want me to do about it?'

'Just lay off,' Menendez said tightly.

'Lay off what?'

'Trying to make yourself dough or publicity out of the Lennox case. It's finished, wrapped up. Terry's dead and we don't want him bothered any more. The guy suffered too much.'

'A hoodlum with sentiment,' I said. 'That slays me.'

'Watch your lip, cheapie. Watch your lip. Mendy Menendez don't argue with guys. He tells them. Find yourself another way to grab a buck. Get me?'

He stood up. The interview was finished. He picked up his gloves. They were snow-white pigskin. They didn't look as if he had ever had them on. A dressy type, Mr Menendez. But very tough behind it all.

'I'm not looking for publicity,' I said. 'And nobody's offered me any dough. Why would they and for what?'

'Don't kid me, Marlowe. You didn't spend three days in the freezer just because you're a sweetheart. You got paid off. I ain't saying who by but I got a notion. And the party I'm thinking about has plenty more of the stuff. The Lennox case is closed and it stays closed even if—' he stopped dead and flipped his gloves at the desk edge.

'Even if Terry didn't kill her,' I said.

His surprise was as thin as the gold on a week-end wedding ring. 'I'd like to go along with you on that, cheapie. But it don't make any sense. But if it did make sense – and Terry wanted it the way it is – then that's how it stays.'

I didn't say anything. After a moment he grinned slowly. 'Tarzan on a big red scooter,' he drawled. 'A tough guy. Lets me come in here and walk all over him. A guy that gets hired for nickels and dimes and gets pushed around by anybody. No dough, no family, no prospects, no nothing. See you around, cheapie.'

I sat still with my jaws clamped, staring at the glitter of his gold cigarette case on the desk corner. I felt old and tired. I got up slowly and reached for the case.

'You forgot this,' I said, going around the desk.

'I got half a dozen of them,' he sneered.

When I was near enough to him I held it out. His hand reached for it casually. 'How about half a dozen of these?' I asked him and hit him as hard as I could in the middle of his belly.

He doubled up mewling. The cigarette case fell to the floor. He backed against the wall and his hands jerked back and forth convulsively. His breath fought to get into his lungs. He was sweating. Very slowly and with an intense effort he straightened up and we were eye to eye again. I reached out and ran a finger along the bone of his jaw. He held still for it. Finally he worked a smile on to his brown face.

'I didn't think you had it in you,' he said.

'Next time bring a gun – or don't call me cheapie.'

'I got a guy to carry the gun.'

'Bring him with you. You'll need him.'

'You're a hard guy to get sore, Marlowe.'

I moved the gold cigarette case to one side with my foot and bent and picked it up and handed it to him. He took it and dropped it into his pocket.

'I couldn't figure you,' I said. 'Why it was worth your time to come up here and ride me. Then it got monotonous. All tough guys are monotonous. Like playing cards with a deck that's all aces. You've got everything and you've got nothing. You're just sitting there looking at yourself. No wonder Terry didn't come to you for help. It would be like borrowing money from a whore.'

He pressed delicately on his stomach with two fingers. 'I'm sorry you said that, cheapie. You could crack wise once too often.'

He walked to the door and opened it. Outside the bodyguard straightened from the opposite wall and turned. Menendez jerked his head. The bodyguard came into the office and stood there looking me over without expression.

'Take a good look at him, Chick,' Menendez said. 'Make sure you know him just in case. You and him might have business one of these days.'

'I already saw him, Chief,' the smooth, dark, tight-lipped guy said in the tight-lipped voice they all affect. 'He wouldn't bother me none.'

'Don't let him hit you in the guts,' Menendez said with a sour grin. 'His right hook ain't funny.'

The bodyguard just sneered at me. 'He wouldn't get that close.'

'Well, so long, cheapie,' Menendez told me and went out.

'See you around,' the bodyguard told me coolly. 'The name's Chick Agostino. I guess you'll know me.'

'Like a dirty newspaper,' I said. 'Remind me not to step on your face.'

His jaw muscles bulged. Then he turned suddenly and went out after his boss.

The door closed slowly on the pneumatic gadget. I listened but I didn't hear their steps going down the hall. They walked as softly as cats. Just to make sure, I opened the door again after a minute and looked out. But the hall was quite empty.

I went back to my desk and sat down and spent a little time wondering why a fairly important local racketeer like Menendez would think it worth his time to come in person to my office and warn me to keep my nose clean, just minutes after I had received a similar though differently expressed warning from Sewell Endicott.

I didn't get anywhere with that, so I thought I might as well make it a perfect score. I lifted the phone and put in a call to the Terrapin Club at Las Vegas, person to person, Philip Marlowe calling Mr Randy Starr. No soap. Mr Starr was out of town, and would I talk to anyone else? I would not. I didn't even want to talk to Starr very badly. It was just a passing fancy. He was too far away to hit me.

After that nothing happened for three days. Nobody slugged me or shot at me or called me up on the phone and warned me to keep my nose clean. Nobody hired me to find the wandering daughter, the erring wife, the lost pearl necklace or the missing will. I just sat there and looked at the wall. The Lennox case died almost as suddenly as it had been born. There was a brief inquest to which I was not summoned. It was held at an odd hour, without previous announcement and without a jury. The coroner entered his own verdict, which was that the death of Sylvia Potter Westerheym di Giorgio Lennox had been caused with homicidal intent by her husband, Terence William Lennox, since deceased outside the jurisdiction of the coroner's office. Presumably a confession was read into the record. Presumably it was verified enough to satisfy the coroner.

The body was released for burial. It was flown north and buried in the family vault. The press was not invited. Nobody gave any interviews, least of all Mr Harlan Potter, who never gave interviews. He was about as hard to see as the Dalai Lama. Guys with a hundred million dollars live a peculiar life, behind a screen of servants, bodyguards, secretaries, lawyers and tame executives. Presumably they eat, sleep, get their hair cut and wear clothes. But you never know for sure. Everything you read or hear about them has been processed by a public relations gang of guys who are paid big money to create and maintain a usable personality, something simple and clean and sharp, like a sterilized needle. It doesn't have to be true. It just has to be consistent with the known facts, and the known facts you would count on your fingers.

Late afternoon of the third day the telephone rang and I was talking to a man who said his name was Howard Spencer, that he was a representative of a New York publishing house in California on a brief business trip, that he had a problem he would like to discuss with me and would I meet him in the bar of the Ritz-Beverly Hotel at eleven a.m. the next morning.

I asked him what sort of problem.

'Rather a delicate one,' he said, 'but entirely ethical. If we don't agree, I shall expect to pay you for your time, naturally.'

'Thank you, Mr Spencer, but that won't be necessary. Did someone I know recommend me to you?'

'Someone who knows about you – including your recent brush with the law, Mr Marlowe. I might say that that was what interested me. My business, however, has nothing to do with that tragic affair. It's just that – well, let's discuss it over a drink, rather than over the telephone.'

'You sure you want to mix it with a guy who has been in the cooler?'

He laughed. His laugh and his voice were both pleasant. He talked the way New Yorkers used to talk before they learned to talk Flatbush.

'From my point of view, Mr Marlowe, that is a recommendation. Not, let me add, the fact that you were, as you put it, in the cooler, but the fact, shall I say, that you appear to be extremely reticent, even under pressure.'

He was a guy who talked with commas, like a heavy novel. Over the phone anyway.

'Okay, Mr Spencer, I'll be there in the morning.'

He thanked me and hung up. I wondered who could have given me the plug. I thought it might be Sewell Endicott and called him to find out. But he had been out of town all week, and still was. It didn't matter much. Even in my business you occasionally get a satisfied customer. And I needed a job because I needed the money – or thought I did, until I got home that night and found the letter with a portrait of Madison in it.

# Twelve

The letter was in the red and white birdhouse mail box at the foot of my steps. A woodpecker on top of the box attached to the swing arm was raised and even at that I might not have looked inside because I never got mail at the house. But the woodpecker had lost the point of his beak quite recently. The wood was fresh broken. Some smart kid shooting off his atom gun.

The letter had Correo Aereo on it and a flock of Mexican stamps, and writing that I might or might not have recognized if Mexico hadn't been on my mind pretty constantly lately. I couldn't read the postmark. It was hand-stamped and the ink pad was pretty far gone. The letter was thick. I climbed my steps and sat down in the living-room to read it. The evening seemed very silent. Perhaps a letter from a dead man brings its own silence with it.

It began without date and without preamble.

'I'm sitting beside a second-floor window in a room in a not-too-clean hotel in a town called Otatoclan, a mountain town with a lake. There's a mail box just below the window and when the mozo comes in with some coffee I've ordered he is going to mail the letter for me and hold it up so that I can see it before he puts it in the slot. When he does that he gets a hundred-peso note, which is a hell of a lot of money for him.

'Why all the finagling? There's a swarthy character with pointed shoes and a dirty shirt outside the door watching it. He's waiting for something, I don't know what, but he won't let me out. It doesn't matter too much as long as the letter gets posted. I want you to have this money because I don't need it and the local gendarmerie would swipe it for sure. It is not intended to buy anything. Call it an apology for making you so much trouble and a token of esteem for a pretty decent guy. I've done everything wrong as usual, but I still have the gun. My hunch is that you have probably made up your mind on a certain point. I might have killed her and perhaps I did, but I never could have done the other thing. That kind of brutality is not in my line. So something is very sour. But it doesn't matter, not in the least. The main thing now is to save an unnecessary and useless scandal. Her father and her sister never did me any harm. They have their lives to live and I'm up to here in disgust with mine. Sylvia didn't make a bum out of me, I was one already. I can't give you any very clear answer about why she married me. I suppose it was just a whim. At least she died young and beauti-ful. They say lust makes a man old, but keeps a woman young. They say a lot of nonsense. They say the rich can always pro-tect themselves and that in their world it is always summer. I've lived with them and they are bored and lonely people.

'I have written a confession. I feel a little sick and more than a little scared. You read about these situations in books, but you don't read the truth. When it happens to you, when all you have left is the gun in your pocket, when you are cornered in a dirty little hotel in a strange country, and have only one way out – believe me, pal, there is nothing elevating or dramatic about it. It is just plain nasty and sordid and grey and grim.

'So forget it and me. But first drink a gimlet for me at Victor's. And the next time you make coffee, pour me a cup and put some bourbon in it and light me a cigarette and put it beside the cup. And after that forget the whole thing. Terry Lennox over and out. And so good-bye.

'A knock at the door. I guess it will be the mozo with the coffee. If it isn't, there will be some shooting. I like Mexicans, as a rule, but I don't like their jails. So long. Terry.'

That was all. I refolded the letter and put it back in the envelope. It had been the mozo with the coffee all right. Otherwise I would never have had the letter. Not with a portrait of Madison in it. A portrait of Madison is a $5,000 bill.

It lay in front of me green and crisp on the table top. I had never seen one before. Lots of people who work in banks haven't either. Very likely characters like Randy Starr and Menendez wear them for folding money. If you went to a bank and asked for one, they wouldn't have it. They'd have to get it for you from the Federal Reserve. It might take several days. There are only about a thousand of them in circulation in the whole USA. Mine had a nice glow around it. It created a little private sunshine all its own.

I sat there and looked at it for a long time. At last I put it away in my letter case and went out to the kitchen to make that coffee. I did what he asked me to, sentimental or not. I poured two cups and added some bourbon to his and set it down on the side of the table where he had sat the morning I took him to the plane. I lit a cigarette for him and set it in an ashtray beside the cup. I watched the steam rise from the coffee and the thin thread of smoke rise from the cigarette. Outside in the tecoma a bird was gussing around, talking to himself in low chirps, with an occasional brief flutter of wings.

Then the coffee didn't steam any more and the cigarette stopped smoking and was just a dead butt on the edge of an ashtray. I dropped it into the garbage can under the sink. I poured the coffee out and washed the cup and put it away.

That was that. It didn't seem quite enough to do for five thousand dollars.

I went to a late movie after a while. It meant nothing. I hardly saw what went on. It was just noise and big faces. When I got home again I set out a very dull Ruy Lopez and that didn't mean anything either. So I went to bed.

But not to sleep. At three a.m. I was walking the floor and listening to Katchaturian working in a tractor factory. He called it a violin concerto. I called it a loose fan belt and the hell with it.

A white night for me is as rare as a fat postman. If it hadn't been for Mr Howard Spencer at the Ritz-Beverly I would have killed a bottle and knocked myself out. And the next time I saw a polite character drunk in a Rolls Royce Silver Wraith, I would depart rapidly in several directions. There is no trap so deadly as the trap you set for yourself.

# Thirteen

At eleven o'clock I was sitting in the third booth on the right-hand side as you go in from the dining-room annex. I had my back against the wall and I could see anyone who came in or went out. It was a clear morning, no smog, no high fog even, and the sun dazzled the surface of the swimming-pool which began just outside the plate-glass wall of the bar and stretched to the far end of the dining-room. A girl in a white sharkskin suit and a luscious figure was climbing the ladder to the high board. I watched the band of white that showed between the tan of her thighs and the suit. I watched it carnally. Then she was out of sight, cut off by the deep overhang of the roof. A moment later I saw her flash down in a one and a half. Spray came high enough to catch the sun and make rainbows that were almost as pretty as the girl. Then she came up the ladder and unstrapped her white helmet and shook her bleach job loose. She wobbled her bottom over to a small white table and sat down beside a lumberjack in white drill pants and dark glasses and a tan so evenly dark that he couldn't have been anything but the hired man around the pool. He reached over and patted her thigh. She opened a mouth like a fire-bucket and laughed. That terminated my interest in her. I couldn't hear the laugh but the hole in her face when she unzipped her teeth was all I needed.

The bar was pretty empty. Three booths down a couple of sharpies were selling each other pieces of Twentieth Century-Fox, using double arm gestures instead of money. They had a telephone on the table between them and every two or three minutes they would play the match game to see who called Zanuck with a hot idea. They were young, dark, eager and full of vitality. They put as much muscular activity into a telephone conversation as I would put into carrying a fat man up four flights of stairs.

There was a sad fellow over on a bar stool talking to the bartender, who was polishing a glass and listening with that plastic smile people wear when they are trying not to scream. The customer was middle-aged, handsomely dressed, and drunk. He wanted to talk and he couldn't have stopped even if he hadn't really wanted to talk. He was polite and friendly and when I heard him he didn't seem to slur his words much, but you knew that he got up on the bottle and only let go of it when he fell asleep at night. He would be like that for the rest of his life and that was what his life was. You would never know how he got that way because even if he told you it would not be the truth. At the very best a distorted memory of the truth as he knew it. There is a sad man like that in every quiet bar in the world.

I looked at my watch and this high-powered publisher man was already twenty minutes late. I would wait half an hour and then I would leave. It never pays to let the customer make all the rules. If he can push you around, he will assume other people can too, and that is not what he hires you for. And right now I didn't need the work badly enough to let some fathead from back East use me for a horse-holder, some executive character in a panelled office on the eighty-fifth floor, with a row of pushbuttons and an intercom and a secretary in a Hattie Carnegie Career Girl's Special and a pair of those big, beautiful, promising eyes. This was the kind of operator who would tell you to be there at nine sharp and if you weren't sitting quietly with a pleased smile on your pan when he floated in two hours later on a double Gibson, he would have a paroxysm of outraged executive ability which would necessitate five weeks at Acapulco before he got back the hop on his high hard one.

The old bar waiter came drifting by and glanced softly at my weak Scotch and water. I shook my head and he bobbed his white thatch, and right then a dream walked in. It seemed to me for an instant that there was no sound in the bar, that the sharpies stopped sharping and the drunk on the stool stopped burbling away, and it was like just after the conductor taps on his music stand and raises his arms and holds them poised.

She was slim and quite tall in a white linen tailor-made with a black and white polka-dotted scarf around her throat. Her hair was the pale gold of a fairy princess. There was a small hat on it into which the pale gold hair nestled like a bird in its nest. Her eyes were cornflower blue, a rare colour, and the lashes were long and almost too pale. She reached the table across the way and was pulling off a white gauntleted glove and the old waiter had the table pulled out in a way no waiter will ever pull a table out for me. She sat down and slipped the gloves under the strap of her bag and thanked him with a smile so gentle, so exquisitely pure, that he was damn near paralysed by it. She said something to him in a very low voice. He hurried away, bending forward. There was a guy who really had a mission in life.

I stared. She caught me staring. She lifted her glance half an inch and I wasn't there any more. But wherever I was I was holding my breath.

There are blondes and blondes and it is almost a joke word nowadays. All blondes have their points, except perhaps the metallic ones who are as blond as a Zulu under the bleach and as to disposition as soft as a sidewalk. There is the small cute blonde who creeps and twitters, and the big statuesque blonde who straight-arms you with an ice-blue glare. There is the blonde who gives you the up-from-under look and smells lovely and shimmers and hangs on your arm and is always very, very tired when you take her home. She makes that helpless gesture and has that goddamned headache and you would like to slug her except that you are glad you found about the headache before you invested too much time and money and hope in her. Because the headache will always be there, a weapon that never wears out and is as deadly as the bravo's rapier or Lucrezia's poison vial.

There is the soft and willing and alcoholic blonde who doesn't care what she wears as long as it is mink or where she goes as long as it is the Starlight Roof and there is plenty of dry champagne. There is the small perky blonde who is a little pal and wants to pay her own way and is full of sunshine and common sense and knows judo from the ground up and can toss a truck driver over her shoulder without missing more than one sentence out of the editorial in the *Saturday Review*. There is the pale, pale blonde with anaemia of some non-fatal but incurable type. She is very languid and very shadowy and she speaks softly out of nowhere and you can't lay a finger on her because in the first place you don't want to and in the second place she is reading *The Waste Land* or Dante in the original, or Kafka or Kierkegaard or studying Provençal. She adores music and when the New York Philharmonic is playing Hindemith she can tell you which one of the six bass viols came in a quarter of a beat too late. I hear Toscanini can also. That makes two of them.

And lastly there is the gorgeous show piece who will outlast three kingpin racketeers and then marry a couple of millionaires at a million a head and end up with a pale rose villa at Cap d'Antibes, an Alfa Romeo town car complete with pilot and co-pilot, and a stable of shopworn aristocrats, all of whom she will treat with the affectionate absent-mindedness of an elderly duke saying good night to his butler.

The dream across the way was none of these, not even of that kind of world. She was unclassifiable, as remote and clear as mountain water, as elusive as its colour. I was still staring when a voice close to my elbow said:

'I'm shockingly late. I apologize. You must blame it on this. My name's Howard Spencer. You're Marlowe, of course.'

I turned my head and looked at him. He was middle-aged, rather plump, dressed as if he didn't give any thought to it, but well shaved and with thin hair smoothed back carefully over a head that was wide between the ears. He wore a flashy double-breasted vest, the sort of thing you hardly ever see in California except perhaps on a visiting Bostonian. His glasses were rimless and he was patting a shabby old dog of a brief-case which was evidently the 'this'.

'Three brand-new book-length manuscripts. Fiction. It would be embarrassing to lose them before we have a chance to reject them.' He made a signal to the old waiter who had just stepped back from placing a tall green something or other in front of the dream. 'I have a weakness for gin and orange. A silly sort of drink really. Will you join me? Good.'

I nodded and the old waiter drifted away.

Pointing to the brief-case I said: 'How do you know you are going to reject them?'

'If they were any good, they wouldn't be dropped at my hotel by the writers in person. Some New York agent would have them.'

'Then why take them at all?'

'Partly not to hurt feelings. Partly the thousand to one chance all publishers live for. But mostly you're at a cocktail party and get introduced to all sorts of people, and some of them have novels written and you are just liquored up enough to be benevolent and full of love for the human race, so you say you'd love to see the script. It is then dropped at your hotel with such sickening speed that you are forced to go through the motions of reading it. But I don't suppose you are much interested in publishers and their problems.'

The waiter brought the drinks. Spencer grabbed for his and took a healthy swig. He wasn't noticing the golden girl across the way. I had all his attention. He was a good contact man.

'If it's part of the job,' I said, 'I can read a book once in a while.'

'One of our most important authors lives around here,' he said casually. 'Maybe you've read his stuff. Roger Wade.'

'Uh-huh.'

'I see your point.' He smiled sadly. 'You don't care for historical romances. But they sell brutally.'

'I don't have any point, Mr Spencer. I looked at one of his books once. I thought it was tripe. Is that the wrong thing for me to say?'

He grinned. 'Oh no. There are many people who agree with you. But the point is at the moment that he's an automatic best-seller. And every publisher has to have a couple with the way costs are now.'

I looked across at the golden girl. She had finished her lime-ade or whatever it was and was glancing at a microscopic wristwatch. The bar was filling up a little, but not yet noisy. The two sharpies were still waving their hands and the solo drinker on the bar stool had a couple of pals with him. I looked back at Howard Spencer.

'Something to do with your problem?' I asked him. 'This fellow Wade, I mean.'

He nodded. He was giving me a careful once-over. 'Tell me a little about yourself, Mr Marlowe. That is, if you don't find the request objectionable.'

'What sort of thing? I'm a licensed private investigator and have been for quite a while. I'm a lone wolf, unmarried, getting middle-aged, and not rich. I've been in jail more than once and I don't do divorce business. I like liquor and women and chess and a few other things. The cops don't like me too well, but I know a couple I get along with. I'm a native son, born in Santa Rosa, both parents dead, no brothers or sisters, and when I get knocked off in a dark alley sometime, if it happens, as it could to anyone in my business, and to plenty of people in any business or no business at all these days, nobody will feel that the bottom has dropped out of his or her life.'

'I see,' he said. 'But all that doesn't exactly tell me what I want to know.'

I finished the gin and orange. I didn't like it. I grinned at him. 'I left out one item, Mr Spencer. I have a portrait of Madison in my pocket.'

'A portrait of Madison? I'm afraid I don't—'

'A five thousand dollar bill,' I said. 'Always carry it. My lucky piece.'

'Good God,' he said in a hushed voice. 'Isn't that terribly dangerous?'

'Who was it said that beyond a certain point all dangers are equal?'

'I think it was Walter Bagehot. He was talking about a steeplejack.' Then he grinned. 'Sorry, but I *am* a publisher. You're all right, Marlowe. I'll take a chance on you. If I didn't you would tell me to go to hell. Right?'

I grinned back at him. He called the waiter and ordered another pair of drinks.

'Here it is,' he said carefully. 'We are in bad trouble over Roger Wade. He can't finish a book. He's losing his grip and there's something behind it. The man seems to be going to pieces. Wild fits of drinking and temper. Every once in a while he disappears for days on end. Not very long ago he threw his wife downstairs and put her in the hospital with five broken ribs. There's no trouble between them in the usual sense, none at all. The man just goes nuts when he drinks.' Spencer leaned back and looked at me gloomily. 'We have to have that book finished. We need it badly. To a certain extent my job depends on it. But we need more than that. We want to save a very able writer who is capable of much better things than he has ever done. Something is very wrong. This trip he won't see me. I realize this sounds like a job for a psychiatrist. Mrs Wade disagrees. She is convinced that he is perfectly sane but that something is worrying him to death. A blackmailer, for instance. The Wades have been married five years. Something from his past may have caught up with him. It might even be – just as a wild guess – a fatal hit-and-run accident and someone has the goods on him. We don't know what it is. We want to know. And we are willing to pay well to correct the trouble. If it turns out to be a medical matter, well – that's that. If not, there has to be an answer. And in the meantime Mrs Wade has to be protected. He might kill her the next time. You never know.'

The second round of drinks came. I left mine untouched and watched him gobble half of his in one swallow. I lit a cigarette and just stared at him.

'You don't want a detective,' I said. 'You want a magician. What the hell could I do? If I happened to be there at exactly the right time, and if he isn't too tough for me to handle, I might knock him out and put him to bed. But I'd have to *be* there. It's a hundred to one against. You know that.'

'He's about your size,' Spencer said, 'but he's not in your condition. And you could be there all the time.'

'Hardly. And drunks are cunning. He'd be certain to pick a time when I wasn't around to throw his wingding. I'm not in the market for a job as a male nurse.'

'A male nurse wouldn't be any use. Roger Wade is not the kind of man to accept one. He is a very talented guy who has been jarred loose from his self-control. He has made too much money writing junk for halfwits. But the only salvation for a writer is to write. If there is anything good in him, it will come out.'

'Okay, I'm sold on him,' I said wearily. 'He's terrific. Also he's damn dangerous. He has a guilty secret and he tries to drown it in alcohol. It's not my kind of problem, Mr Spencer.'

'I see.' He looked at his wristwatch with a worried frown that knotted his face and made it look older and smaller. 'Well, you can't blame me for trying.'

He reached for his fat brief-case. I looked across at the golden girl. She was getting ready to leave. The white-haired waiter was hovering over her with the check. She gave him some money and a lovely smile and he looked as if he had shaken hands with God. She touched up her lips and put her white gauntlets on and the waiter pulled the table half-way across the room for her to stroll out.

I glanced at Spencer. He was frowning down at the empty glass on the table edge. He had the brief-case on his knees.

'Look,' I said. 'I'll go see the man and try to size him up, if you want me to. I'll talk to his wife. But my guess is he'll throw me out of the house.'

A voice that was not Spencer's said: 'No, Mr Marlowe, I don't think he would do that. On the contrary I think he might like you.'

I looked up into the pair of violet eyes. She was standing at the end of the table. I got up and canted myself against the back of the booth in that awkward away you have to stand when you can't slide out.

'Please don't get up,' she said in a voice like the stuff they use to line summer clouds with. 'I know I owe you an apology, but it seemed important for me to have a chance to observe you before I introduced myself. I am Eileen Wade.'

Spencer said grumpily: 'He's not interested, Eileen.'

She smiled gently. 'I disagree.'

I pulled myself together. I had been standing there off balance with my mouth open and me breathing through it like a sweet girl graduate. This was really a dish. Seen close up she was almost paralysing.

'I didn't say I wasn't interested, Mrs Wade. What I said or meant to say was that I didn't think I could do any good, and it might be a hell of a mistake for me to try. It might do a lot of harm.'

She was very serious now. The smile had gone. 'You are deciding too soon. You can't judge people by what they do. If you judge them at all, it must be by what they are.'

I nodded vaguely. Because that was exactly the way I had thought about Terry Lennox. On the facts he was no bargain, except for that one brief flash of glory in the foxhole – if Menendez told the truth about that – but the facts didn't tell the whole story by any means. He had been a man it was impossible to dislike. How many do you meet in a lifetime that you can say that about?'

'And you have to know them for that,' she added gently. 'Good-bye, Mr Marlowe. If you should change your mind—' She opened her bag quickly and gave me a card. 'And thank you for being here.'

She nodded to Spencer and walked away. I watched her out of the bar, down the glassed-in annex to the dining-room. She carried herself beautifully. I watched her turn under the arch-way that led to the lobby. I saw the last flicker of her white linen skirt as she turned the corner. Then I eased myself down into the booth and grabbed the gin and orange.

Spencer was watching me. There was something hard in his eyes.

'Nice work,' I said, 'but you ought to have looked at her once in a while. A dream like that doesn't sit across the room from you for twenty minutes without your even noticing.'

'Stupid of me, wasn't it?' He was trying to smile, but he didn't really want to. He didn't like the way I had looked at her. 'People have such queer ideas about private detectives. When you think of having one in your home—'

'Don't think of having this one in your home,' I said. 'Anyhow, think up another story first. You can do better than trying to make me believe anybody, drunk or sober, would throw that gorgeous downstairs and break five ribs for her.'

He reddened. His hands tightened on the brief-case. 'You think I'm a liar?'

'What's the difference? You've made your play. You're a little hot for the lady yourself, maybe.'

He stood up suddenly. 'I don't like your tone,' he said. 'I'm not sure I like *you*. Do me a favour and forget the whole idea. I think this ought to pay you for your time.'

He threw a twenty on the table, and then added some ones for the waiter. He stood a moment staring down at me. His eyes were bright and his face was still red. 'I'm married and have four children,' he said abruptly.

'Congratulations.'

He made a swift noise in his throat and turned and went. He went pretty fast. I watched him for a while and then I didn't. I drank the rest of my drink and got out my cigarettes and shook one loose and stuck it in my mouth and lit it. The old waiter came up and looked at the money.

'Can I get you anything else, sir?'

'Nope. The dough is all yours.'

He picked it up slowly. 'This is a twenty-dollar bill, sir. The gentleman made a mistake.'

'He can read. The dough is all yours, I said.'

'I'm sure I'm very grateful. If you are quite sure, sir—'

'Quite sure.'

He bobbed his head and went away, still looking worried. The bar was filling up. A couple of streamlined demi-virgins went by carolling and waving. They knew the two hotshots in the booth farther on. The air began to be spattered with darlings and crimson fingernails.

I smoked half of my cigarette, scowling at nothing and then got up to leave. I turned to reach back for my cigarettes and something bumped into me hard from behind. It was just what I needed. I swung round and I was looking at the profile of a broad-beamed crowd-pleaser in an overdraped Oxford flannel. He had the outstretched arm of the popular character and the two-by-six grin of the guy who never loses a sale.

I took hold of the outstretched arm and spun him around. 'What's the matter, Jack? Don't they make the aisles wide enough for your personality?'

He shook his arm loose and got tough. 'Don't get fancy, buster. I might loosen your jaw for you.'

'Ha, ha,' I said. 'You might play centre field for the Yankees and hit a home run with a breadstick.'

He doubled a meaty fist.

'Darling, think of your manicure,' I told him.

He controlled his emotions. 'Nuts to you, wise guy,' he sneered. 'Some other time, when I have less on my mind.'

'Could there be less?'

'G'wan, beat it,' he snarled. 'One more crack and you'll need new bridgework.'

I grinned at him. 'Call me up, Jack. But with better dialogue.'

His expression changed. He laughed. 'You in pictures, chum?'

'Only the kind they pin up in the post office.'

'See you in the mug book,' he said, and walked away, still grinning.

It was all very silly, but it got rid of the feeling. I went along the annex and across the lobby of the hotel to the main entrance. I paused inside to put on my sunglasses. It wasn't until I got into my car that I remembered to look at the card Eileen Wade had given me. It was an engraved card, but not a formal calling card, because it had an address and a telephone number on it. Mrs Roger Stearns Wade, 1247 Idle Valley Road. Tel. Idle Valley 5-6324.

I knew a good deal about Idle Valley, and I knew it had changed a great deal from the days when they had the gatehouse at the entrance and the private police force, and the gambling casino on the lake, and the fifty-dollar joy girls. Quiet money had taken over the tract after the casino was closed out. Quiet money had made it a subdivider's dream. A club owned the lake and the lake frontage and if they didn't want you in the club, you didn't get to play in the water. It was exclusive in the only remaining sense of the word that doesn't mean merely expensive.

I belonged in Idle Valley like a pearl onion on a banana split.

Howard Spencer called me up late in the afternoon. He had got over his mad and wanted to say he was sorry and he hadn't handled the situation very well, and had I perhaps any second thoughts.

'I'll go see him if he asks me to. Not otherwise.'

'I see. There would be a substantial bonus—'

'Look, Mr Spencer,' I said impatiently, 'you can't hire destiny. If Mrs Wade is afraid of the guy, she can move out. That's *her* problem. Nobody could protect her twenty-four hours a day from her own husband. There isn't that much protection in the world. But that's not all you want. You want to know why and how and when the guy jumped the rails, and then fix it so that he doesn't do it again – at least until he finishes that book. And that's up to him. If he wants to write the damn book bad enough, he'll lay off the hooch until he does it. You want too damn much.'

'They all go together,' he said. 'It's all one problem. But I guess I understand. It's a little over-subtle for your kind of operation. Well, good-bye. I'm flying back to New York tonight.'

'Have a smooth trip.'

He thanked me and hung up. I forgot to tell him I had given his twenty to the waiter. I thought of calling back to tell him, then I thought he was miserable enough already.

I closed the office and started off in the direction of Victor's to drink a gimlet, as Terry had asked me to in his letter. I changed my mind. I wasn't feeling sentimental enough. I went to Lowry's and had a martini and some prime ribs and Yorkshire pudding instead.

When I got home I turned on the TV set and looked at the fights. They were no good, just a bunch of dancing masters who ought to have been working for Arthur Murray. All they did was jab and bob up and down and feint one another off balance. Not one of them could hit hard enough to wake his grandmother out of a light doze. The crowd was booing and the referee kept clapping his hands for action, but they went right on swaying and jittering and jabbing long lefts. I turned to another channel and looked at a crime show. The action took place in a clothes closet and the faces were tired and over-familiar and not beautiful. The dialogue was stuff even Monogram wouldn't have used. The dick had a coloured houseboy for comic relief. He didn't need it, he was plenty comical all by himself. And the commercials would have sickened a goat raised on barbed wire and broken beer bottles.

I cut it off and smoked a long, cool, tightly packed cigarette. It was kind to my throat. It was made of fine tobacco. I forgot to notice what brand it was. I was about ready to hit the hay when Detective-Sergeant Green of homicide called me up.

'Thought you might like to know they buried your friend Lennox a couple of days ago right in that Mexican town where he died. A lawyer representing the family went down there and attended to it. You were pretty lucky this time, Marlowe. Next time you think of helping a pal skip the country, don't.'

'How many bullet holes did he have in him?'

'What's that?' he barked. Then he was silent for a space. Then he said rather too carefully: 'One, I should say. It's usually enough when it blows a guy's head off. The lawyer is bringing

271

back a set of prints and whatever was in his pockets. Anything more you'd like to know?'

'Yeah, but you can't tell me. I'd like to know who killed Lennox's wife.'

'Cripes, didn't Grenz tell you he left a full confession? It was in the papers, anyway. Don't you read the papers any more?'

'Thanks for calling me, Sergeant. It was real kind of you.'

'Look, Marlowe,' he said raspingly. 'You got any funny ideas about this case, you could buy yourself a lot of grief talking about them. The case is closed, finalized, and laid away in moth-balls. Damn lucky for you it is. Accessory after the fact is good for five years in this state. And let me tell you something else. I've been a cop a long time and one thing I've learned for sure is it ain't always what you do that gets you sent up. It's what it can be made to look like when it comes into court. Good night.'

He hung up in my ear. I replaced the phone, thinking that an honest cop with a bad conscience always acts tough. So does a dishonest cop. So does almost anyone, including me.

# Fourteen

Next morning the bell rang as I was wiping the talcum off an earlobe. When I got to the door and opened up I looked into a pair of violet-blue eyes. She was in brown linen this time, with a pimento-coloured scarf, and no earrings or hat. She looked a little pale, but not as though anyone had been throwing her downstairs. She gave me a hesitant little smile.

'I know I shouldn't have come here to bother you, Mr Marlowe. You probably haven't even had breakfast. But I had a reluctance to go to your office and I hate telephoning about personal matters.'

'Sure. Come in, Mrs Wade. Would you go for a cup of coffee?'

She came into the living-room and sat on the davenport with-out looking at anything. She balanced her bag on her lap and sat with her feet close together. She looked rather prim. I opened windows and pulled up venetian blinds and lifted a dirty ashtray off the cocktail table in front of her.

'Thank you. Black coffee, please. No sugar.'

I went out to the kitchen and spread a paper napkin on a green metal tray. It looked as cheesy as a celluloid collar. I crumpled it up and got out one of those fringed things that come in sets with little triangular napkins. They came with the house, like most of the furniture. I set out two Desert Rose coffee cups and filled them and carried the tray in.

She sipped. 'This is very nice,' she said. 'You make good coffee.'

'Last time anyone drank coffee with me was just before I went to jail,' I said. 'I guess you knew I'd been in the cooler, Mrs Wade.'

She nodded. 'Of course. You were suspected of having helped him escape, wasn't it?'

'They didn't say. They found my telephone number on a pad in his room. They asked me questions I didn't answer – mostly because of the way they were asked. But I don't suppose you are interested in that.'

She put her cup down carefully and leaned back and smiled at me. I offered her a cigarette.

'I don't smoke, thank you. Of course I'm interested. A neighbour of ours knew the Lennoxes. He must have been insane. He doesn't sound at all like that kind of man.'

I filled a bulldog pipe and lit it. 'I guess so,' I said. 'He must have been. He was badly wounded in the war. But he's dead and it's all done with. And I don't think you came here to talk about that.'

She shook her head slowly. 'He was a friend of yours, Mr Marlowe. You must have a pretty strong opinion. And I think you are a pretty determined man.'

I tamped the tobacco in my pipe and lit it again. I took my time and stared at her over the pipe bowl while I was doing it.

'Look, Mrs Wade,' I said finally. 'My opinion means nothing. It happens every day. The most unlikely people commit the most unlikely crimes. Nice old ladies poison whole families. Clean-cut kids commit multiple hold-ups and shootings. Bank managers with spotless records going back twenty years are found out to be long-term embezzlers. And successful and popular and supposedly happy novelists get drunk and put their wives in the hospital. We know damn little what makes even our best friends tick.'

I thought it would burn her up, but she didn't do much more than press her lips together and narrow her eyes.

'Howard Spencer shouldn't have told you that,' she said. 'It was my own fault. I didn't know enough to keep away from him. I've learned since that the one thing you can never do to a man

273

who is drinking too much is to try to stop him. You probably know that much better than I do.'

'You certainly can't stop him with words,' I said. 'If you're lucky, and *if* you have the strength, you can sometimes keep him from hurting himself or someone else. Even that takes luck.'

She reached quietly for her coffee cup and saucer. Her hands were lovely, like the rest of her. The nails were beautifully shaped and polished and only very slightly tinted.

'Did Howard tell you he hadn't seen my husband this time?'

'Yeah.'

She finished her coffee and put the cup carefully back on the tray. She fiddled with the spoon for a few seconds. Then she spoke without looking up at me.

'He didn't tell you why, because he didn't know. I am very fond of Howard but he is the managing type, wants to take charge of everything. He thinks he is very executive.'

I waited, not saying anything. There was another silence. She looked at me quickly then looked away again. Very softly she said: 'My husband has been missing for three days. I don't know where he is. I came here to ask you to find him and bring him home. Oh, it has happened before. One time he drove himself all the way to Portland and got sick in a hotel there and had to get a doctor to sober him up. It's a wonder how he ever got that far without getting into trouble. He hadn't eaten anything for three days. Another time he was in a Turkish bath in Long Beach, one of those Swedish places where they give high colonics. And the last time it was some sort of small private and probably not very reputable sanitarium. This was less than three weeks ago. He wouldn't tell me the name of it or where it was, just said he had been taking a cure and was all right. But he looked deadly pale and weak. I got a brief glimpse of the man who brought him home. A tall man dressed in the sort of over-elaborate cowboy outfit you would only see on the stage or in a Technicolor musical film. He let Roger out in the driveway and backed out and drove away at once.'

'Could have been a dude ranch,' I said. 'Some of these tame cowpunchers spend every dime they make on a fancy outfit like that. The women go crazy over them. That's what they're there for.'

She opened her bag and took out a folded paper. 'I've brought you a cheque for five hundred dollars, Mr Marlowe. Will you accept it as a retainer?'

She put the folded cheque down on the table. I looked at it, but didn't touch it. 'Why?' I asked her. 'You say he has been gone three days. It takes three or four to sober a man up and get some food into him. Won't he come back the way he did before? Or does something make this time different?'

'He can't stand much more of it, Mr Marlowe. It will kill him. The intervals are getting shorter. I'm badly worried. I'm more than worried, I'm scared. It's unnatural. We've been married for five years. Roger was always a drinker, but not a psychopathic drinker. Something is all wrong. I want him found. I didn't sleep more than an hour last night.'

'Any idea *why* he drinks?'

The violet eyes were looking at me steadily. She seemed a bit fragile this morning, but certainly not helpless. She bit her lower lip and shook her head. 'Unless it's me,' she said at last, almost in a whisper. 'Men fall out of love with their wives.'

'I'm only an amateur psychologist, Mrs Wade. A man in my racket has to be a little of that. I'd say it's more likely he has fallen out of love with the kind of stuff he writes.'

'It's quite possible,' she said quietly. 'I imagine all writers have spells like that. It's true that he can't seem to finish a book he is working on. But it isn't as if he had to finish it for the rent money. I don't think that is quite enough reason.'

'What sort of guy is he sober?'

She smiled. 'Well, I'm rather prejudiced. *I* think he is a very nice guy indeed.'

'And how is he drunk?'

'Horrible. Bright and hard and cruel. He thinks he is being witty when he is only being nasty.'

'You left out violent.'

She raised her tawny eyebrows. 'Just once, Mr Marlowe. And too much has been made of that. I'd never have told Howard Spencer. Roger told him himself.'

I got up and walked around in the room. It was going to be a hot day. It already was hot. I turned the blinds on one of the windows to keep the sun out. Then I gave it to her straight.

'I looked him up in *Who's Who* yesterday afternoon. He's forty-two years old, yours is his only marriage, no children. His people are New Englanders, he went to Andover and Princeton. He has a war record and a good one. He has written twelve of these fat sex and swordplay historical novels and every damn one of them has been on the bestseller lists. He must have made plenty of the folding. If he had fallen out of love with his wife, he sounds like the type who would say so and get a divorce. If he was haring around with another woman, you would probably know about it, and anyway he wouldn't have to get drunk just to prove he felt bad. If you've been married five years, then he was thirty-seven when that happened. I'd say he knew most of what there is to know about women by that time. I say most, because nobody ever knows all of it.'

I stopped and looked at her and she smiled at me. I wasn't hurting her feelings. I went on:

'Howard Spencer suggested – on what grounds I have no idea – that what's the matter with Roger Wade is something that happened a long time ago before you were married and that it has caught up with him now, and is hitting him harder than he can take. Spencer thought of blackmail. Would you know?'

She shook her head slowly. 'If you mean would I know if Roger had been paying out a lot of money to someone – no, I wouldn't know that. I don't meddle with his book-keeping affairs. He could give away a lot of money without my knowing it.'

'Okay then. Not knowing Mr Wade I can't have much idea how he would react to having the bite put on him. If he has a violent temper, he might break somebody's neck. If the secret, whatever it is, might damage his social or professional standing or even, to take an extreme case, made the law boys drop around, he might pay off – for a while anyhow. But none of this gets us anywhere. You want him found, you're worried, you're more than worried. So how do I go about finding him. I don't want your money, Mrs Wade. Not now, anyway.'

She reached into her bag again and came up with a couple of pieces of yellow paper. They looked like second sheets, folded, and one of them looked crumpled. She smoothed them out and handed them to me.

'One I found on his desk,' she said. 'It was very late, or rather early in the morning. I knew he had been drinking and I knew he hadn't come upstairs. About two o'clock I went down to see if he was all right – or comparatively all right, passed out on the floor or the couch or something. He was gone. The other paper was in the wastebasket or rather caught on the edge, so that it hadn't fallen in.'

I looked at the first piece, the one not crumpled. There was a short typewritten paragraph on it, no more. It read: 'I do not care to be in love with myself and there is no longer anyone else for me to be in love with. Signed: Roger (F. Scott Fitzgerald) Wade. PS This is why I never finished *The Last Tycoon*.'

276

'That mean anything to you, Mrs Wade?'

'Just attitudinizing. He has always been a great admirer of Scott Fitzgerald. He says Fitzgerald is the best drunken writer since Coleridge, who took dope. Notice the typing, Mr Marlowe. Clear, even, and no mistakes.'

'I did. Most people can't even write their names properly when soused.' I opened the crumpled paper. More typing, also without any errors or unevenness. This one read: 'I do not like you, Dr V. But right now you're the man for me.'

She spoke while I was still looking at it. 'I have no idea who Dr V. is. We don't know any doctor with a name beginning that way. I suppose he is the one who has that place where Roger was the last time.'

'When the cowpoke brought him home? Your husband didn't mention any names at all – even place names?'

She shook her head. 'Nothing. I've looked in the directory. There are dozens of doctors of one sort or another whose names begin with V. Also, it may not be his surname.'

'Quite likely he's not even a doctor,' I said. 'That brings up the question of ready cash. A legitimate man would take a cheque, but a quack wouldn't. It might turn into evidence. And a guy like that wouldn't be cheap. Room and board at his house would come high. Not to mention the needle.'

She looked puzzled. 'The needle?'

'All the shady ones use dope on their clients. Easiest way to handle them. Knock them out for ten or twelve hours and when they come out of it, they're good boys. But using narcotics without a licence can get you room and board with Uncle Sam. And that comes very high indeed.'

'I see. Roger probably would have several hundred dollars. He always keeps that much in his desk. I don't know why. I suppose it's just a whim. There's none there now.'

'Okay,' I said. 'I'll try to find Dr V. I don't know just how, but I'll do my best. Take the cheque with you, Mrs Wade.'

'But why? Aren't you entitled—'

'Later on, thanks. And I'd rather have it from Mr Wade. He's not going to like what I do in any case.'

'But if he's sick and helpless—'

'He could have called his own doctor or asked you to. He didn't. That means he didn't want to.'

She put the cheque back in her bag and stood up. She looked very forlorn. 'Our doctor refused to treat him,' she said bitterly.

'There are hundreds of doctors, Mrs Wade. Any one of them

would handle him once. Most of them would stay with him for some time. Medicine is a pretty competitive affair nowadays.'

'I see. Of course you must be right.' She walked slowly to the door and I walked with her. I opened it.

'You could have called a doctor on your own. Why didn't you?'

She faced me squarely. Her eyes were bright. There might have been a hint of tears in them. A lovely dish and no mistake.

'Because I love my husband, Mr Marlowe. I'd do anything in the world to help him. But I know what sort of man he is too. If I called a doctor every time he took too many drinks, I wouldn't have a husband very long. You can't treat a grown man like a child with a sore throat.'

'You can if he's a drunk. Often you damn well have to.'

She was standing close to me. I smelt her perfume. Or thought I did. It hadn't been put on with a spray gun. Perhaps it was just the summer day.

'Suppose there *is* something shameful in his past,' she said, dragging the words out one by one as if each of them had a bitter taste. 'Even something criminal. It would make no difference to me. But I'm not going to be the means of its being found out.'

'But it's all right if Howard Spencer hires me to find out?'

She smiled very slowly. 'Do you really think I expected you to give Howard any answer but the one you did – a man who went to jail rather than betray a friend?'

'Thanks for the plug, but that wasn't why I got jugged.'

She nodded after a moment of silence, said good-bye and started down the redwood steps. I watched her into her car, a slim, grey Jaguar, very new looking. She drove it up to the end of the street and swung around in the turning circle there. Her glove waved at me as she went by down the hill. The little car whisked around the corner and was gone.

There was a red oleander bush against part of the front wall of the house. I heard a flutter in it and a baby mocking-bird started cheeping anxiously. I spotted him hanging on to one of the top branches, flapping his wings as if he was having trouble keeping his balance. From the cypress trees at the corner of the wall there was a single harsh warning chirp. The cheeping stopped at once and the little fat bird was silent.

I went inside and shut the door and left him to his flying lesson. Birds have to learn too.

# Fifteen

No matter how smart you think you are, you have to have a place to start from; a name, an address, a neighbourhood, a background, an atmosphere, a point of reference of some sort. All I had was typing on a crumpled yellow page that said, 'I do not like you, Dr V. But right now you're the man for me.' With that I could pinpoint the Pacific Ocean, spend a month wading through the lists of half a dozen county medical associations, and end up with the big round O. In our town quacks breed like guinea pigs. There are eight counties within a hundred miles of the City Hall and in every town in every single one of them there are doctors, some genuine medical men, some just mail-order mechanics with a licence to cut corns or jump up and down on your spine. Of the real doctors some are prosperous and some poor, some ethical, others not sure they can afford it. A well-heeled patient with incipient DTs could be money from home to plenty of old geezers who have fallen behind in the vitamin and antibiotic trade. But without a clue there was no place to start. I didn't have the clue and Eileen Wade either didn't have it or didn't know she had it. And even if I found somebody that fitted and had the right initial, he might turn out to be a myth, so far as Roger Wade was concerned. The jingle might be something that just happened to run through his head while he was getting himself stewed up. Just as the Scott Fitzgerald allusion might be merely an off-beat way of saying good-bye.

In a situation like that the small man tries to pick the big man's brains. So I called up a man I knew in the Carne Organization, a flossy agency in Beverly Hills that specialized in protection for the carriage trade – protection meaning almost anything with one foot inside the law. The man's name was George Peters and he said he could give me ten minutes if I made it fast.

They had half the second floor of one of these candy pink four-storied buildings where the elevator doors open all by themselves with an electric eye, where the corridors are cool and quiet, and the parking lot has a name on every stall, and the druggist off the front lobby has a sprained wrist from filling bottles of sleeping pills.

The door was French grey outside and raised metal lettering, as clean and sharp as a new knife. THE CARNE ORGANIZATION, INC. GERALD C. CARNE, PRESIDENT. Below and smaller: ENTRANCE. It might have been an investment trust.

Inside was a small and ugly reception room, but the ugliness was deliberate and expensive. The furniture was scarlet and dark green, the walls were a flat Brunswick green, and the pictures hung on them were framed in a green about three shades darker than that. The pictures were guys in red coats on big horses that were just crazy to jump over high fences. There were two frameless mirrors tinted a slight but disgusting shade of rose pink. The magazines on the table of polished primavera were of the latest issue and each one was enclosed in a clear plastic cover. The fellow who decorated that room was not a man to let the colours scare him. He probably wore a pimento shirt, mulberry slacks, zebra shoes, and vermilion drawers with his initials on them in a nice friendly Mandarin orange.

The whole thing was just window-dressing. The clients of the Carne Organization were charged a minimum of one hundred fish per diem and they expected service in their homes. They didn't go sit in no waiting-room. Carne was an ex-colonel of military police, a big pink and white guy as hard as a board. He had offered me a job once, but I never got desperate enough to take it. There are one hundred and ninety ways of being a bastard and Carne knew all of them.

A rubbed glass partition slid open and a receptionist looked out at me. She had an iron smile and eyes that could count the money in your hip wallet.

'Good morning. May I help you?'

'George Peters, please. My name is Marlowe.'

She put a green leather book on the ledge. 'Is he expecting you, Mr Marlowe? I don't see your name on the appointment list.'

'It's a personal matter. I just talked to him on the phone.'

'I see. How do you spell your name, Mr Marlowe? And your first name, please?'

I told her. She wrote it down on a long narrow form, then slipped the edge under a clock punch.

'Who's that supposed to impress?' I asked her.

'We are very particular about details here,' she said coldly. 'Colonel Carne says you never know when the most trivial fact may turn out to be vital.'

'Or the other way around,' I said, but she didn't get it. When she had finished her bookwork she looked up and said:

'I will announce you to Mr Peters.'

I told her that made me very happy. A minute later a door in the panelling opened and Peters beckoned me into a battleship grey corridor lined with little offices that looked like cells. His office had sound proofing on the ceiling, a grey steel desk with two matching chairs, a grey dictating machine on a grey stand, a telephone and pen set of the same colour as the walls and floor. There were a couple of framed photographs on the walls, one of Carne in uniform, with his snowdrop helmet on, and one of Carne as a civilian seated behind a desk and looking inscrutable. Also framed on the wall was a small inspirational legend in steely letters on a grey background. It read:

*A Carne operative dresses, speaks and behaves like a gentleman*
*at all times and in all places. There are no exceptions to this rule*

Peters crossed the room in two long steps and pushed one of the pictures aside. Set into the grey wall behind it was a grey microphone pick-up. He pulled it out, unclipped a wire, and pushed it back in place. He moved the picture in front of it again.

'Right now I'd be out of a job,' he said, 'except that the son of a bitch is out fixing a drunk-driving rap for some actor. All the mike switches are in his office. He has the whole joint wired. The other morning I suggested to him that he have a microfilm camera installed with infra-red light behind a diaphanous mirror in the reception room. He didn't like the idea too well. Maybe because somebody else had it.'

He sat down in one of the hard grey chairs. I stared at him. He was a gawky, long-legged man with a bony face and receding hair. His skin had the worn, weathered look of a man who has been out of doors a great deal, in all kinds of weather. He had deep-set eyes and an upper lip almost as long as his nose. When he grinned the bottom half of his face disappeared into two enormous ditches that ran from his nostrils to the ends of his wide mouth.

'How can you take it?' I asked him.

'Sit down, pal. Breathe quietly, and keep your voice down and remember that a Carne operative is to a cheap shamus like you what Toscanini is to an organ grinder's monkey.' He paused and grinned. 'I take it because I don't give a damn. It's good money and any time Carne starts acting like he thought I was doing time in that maximum security prison he ran in England during the war, I'll pick up my cheque and blow. What's your trouble? I hear you had it rough a while back.'

'No complaints about that. I'd like to look at your file on the barred-window boys. I know you have one. Eddie Dowst told me after he quit here.'

He nodded. 'Eddie was just a mite too sensitive for the Carne Organization. The file you mention is top secret. In no circumstances must any confidential information be disclosed to outsiders. I'll get it at once.'

He went out and I stared at the grey wastebasket and the grey linoleum and the grey leather corners of the desk blotter. Peters came back with a grey cardboard file in his hand. He put it down and opened it.

'For Chrissake, haven't you got anything in this place that isn't grey?'

'The school colours, my lad. The spirit of the organization. Yeah, I have something that isn't grey.'

He pulled a desk drawer open and took out a cigar about eight inches long.

'An Upmann Thirty,' he said. 'Presented to me by an elderly gent from England who has been forty years in California and still says "wireless". Sober he is just an old swish with a good deal of superficial charm, which is all right with me, because most people don't have any, superficial or otherwise, including Carne. He has as much charm as a steel puddler's underpants. Not sober, the client has a strange habit of writing cheques on banks which never heard of him. He always makes good and with my fond help he has so far stayed out of the icebox. He gave me this. Should we smoke it together, like a couple of Indian chiefs planning a massacre?'

'I can't smoke cigars.'

Peters looked at the huge cigar sadly. 'Same here,' he said. 'I thought of giving it to Carne. But it's not really a one-man cigar, even when the one man is Carne.' He frowned. 'You know something? I'm talking too much about Carne. I must be edgy.' He dropped the cigar back in the drawer and looked at the open file. 'Just what do we want from this?'

'I'm looking for a well-heeled alcoholic with expensive tastes and money to gratify them. So far he hasn't gone in for cheque-bouncing. I haven't heard so anyway. He has a streak of violence and his wife is worried about him. She thinks he's hid out in some sobering-up joint but she can't be sure. The only clues we have is a jingle mentioning a Doctor V. Just the initial. My man is gone three days now.'

Peters stared at me thoughtfully. 'That's not too long,' he said. 'What's to worry about?'

'If I find him first, I get paid.'

He looked at me some more and shook his head. 'I don't get it, but that's okay. We'll see.' He began to turn the pages of the file. 'It's not too easy,' he said. 'These people come and go. A single letter ain't much of a lead.' He pulled a page out of the folder, turned some more pages, pulled another, and finally a third. 'Three of them here,' he said. 'Dr Amos Varley, an osteopath. Big place in Altadena. Makes or used to make night calls for fifty bucks. Two registered nurses. Was in a hassle with the State Narcotics people a couple of years back, and turned in his prescription book. This information is not really up to date.'

I wrote down the name and address in Altadena.

'Then we have Dr Lester Vukanich. Ear, Nose and Throat, Stockwell Building, on Hollywood Boulevard. This one's a dilly. Office practice mostly, and seems to sort of specialize in chronic sinus infections. Rather a neat routine. You go in and complain of a sinus headache and he washes out your antrums for you. First of course he has to anaesthetize with novocain. But if he likes your looks it don't have to be novocain. Catch?'

'Sure.' I wrote that down.

'This is good,' Peters went on, reading some more. 'Obviously his trouble would be supplies. So our Dr Vukanich does a lot of fishing off Ensenada and flies down in his own plane.'

'I wouldn't think he'd last long if he brings the dope in himself,' I said.

Peters thought about that and shook his head. 'I don't think I agree. He could last for ever if he's not too greedy. His only real danger is a discontented customer – pardon me, I mean patient – but he probably knows how to handle that. He's had fifteen years in the same office.'

'Where the hell do you get this stuff?' I asked him.

'We're an organization, my boy. Not a lone wolf like you. Some we get from the clients themselves, some we get from the inside. Carne's not afraid to spend money. He's a good mixer when he wants to be.'

'He'd love this conversation.'

'Screw him. Our last offering today is a man named Verringer. The operative who filed on him is long gone. Seems a lady poet suicided at Verringer's ranch in Sepulveda Canyon one time. He runs a sort of art colony for writers and such who want seclusion and a congenial atmosphere. Rates moderate. He sounds legit. He calls himself doctor, but doesn't practice medicine. Could be a PhD. Frankly, I don't know why he's in here. Unless there was something about this suicide.' He picked up a newspaper

283

clipping pasted to a blank sheet. 'Yeah, overdose of morphine. No suggestion Verringer knew anything about it.'

'I like Verringer,' I said. 'I like him very much.'

Peters closed the file and slapped it. 'You haven't seen this,' he said. He got up and left the room. When he came back I was standing up to leave. I started to thank him, but he shook it off.

'Look,' he said, 'there must be hundreds of places where your man could be.'

I said I knew that.

'And by the way, I heard something about your friend Lennox that might interest you. One of our boys ran across a fellow in New York five or six years ago that answers the description exactly. But the guy's name was not Lennox, he says. It was Marston. Of course he could be wrong. The guy was drunk all the time, so you couldn't really be sure.'

I said: 'I doubt if it was the same man. Why would he change his name? He had a war record that could be checked.'

'I didn't know that. Our man's in Seattle right now. You can talk to him when he gets back, if it means anything to you. His name is Ashterfelt.'

'Thanks for everything, George. It was a pretty long ten minutes.'

'I might need *your* help some day.'

'The Carne Organization,' I said, 'never needs anything from anybody.'

He made a rude gesture with his thumb. I left him in his metallic grey cell and departed through the waiting-room. It looked fine now. The loud colours made sense after the cell block.

# Sixteen

Back from the highway at the bottom of Sepulveda Canyon were two square yellow gateposts. A five-barred gate hung open from one of them. Over the entrance was a sign hung on wire: PRIVATE ROAD. NO ADMITTANCE. The air was warm and quiet and full of the tomcat smell of eucalyptus trees.

I turned in and followed a gravelled road round the shoulder of a hill, up a gentle slope, over a ridge and down the other side into a shadow valley. It was hot in the valley, ten or fifteen degrees hotter than on the highway. I could see now that the gravelled road ended in a loop around some grass edged with stones that had been lime-washed. Off to my left there was an empty swimming-pool, and nothing ever looks emptier than an empty swimming-pool. Around three sides of it there was what remained of a lawn dotted with redwood lounging chairs with badly faded pads on them. The pads had been of many colours, blue, green, yellow, orange, rust-red. Their edge bindings had come loose in spots, the buttons had popped, and the pads were bloated where this had happened. On the fourth side there was the high wire fence of a tennis court. The diving board over the empty pool looked knee-sprung and tired. Its matting covering hung in shreds and its metal fittings were flaked with rust.

I came to the turning loop and stopped in front of a redwood building with a shake roof and a wide front porch. The entrance had double screen doors. Large black flies dozed in the screens. Paths led off among the evergreen and always dusty California oaks and among the oaks there were rustic cabins scattered loosely over the side of the hill, some almost completely hidden. Those I could see had that desolate out-of-season look. Their doors were shut, their windows were blanked by drawn curtains of monkscloth or something of that order. You could almost feel the thick dust on their sills.

I switched off the ignition and sat there with my hands on the wheel listening. There was no sound. The place seemed to be as dead as Pharaoh, except that the doors behind the double screens were open and something moved in the dimness of the room beyond. Then I heard a light accurate whistling and a man's figure showed against the screen, pushed it open and strolled down the steps. He was something to see.

He wore a flat black gaucho hat with the woven strap under his chin. He wore a white silk shirt, spotlessly clean, open at the throat, with tight wristlets and loose puffed sleeves above. Around his neck a black fringed scarf was knotted unevenly so that one end was short and the other dropped almost to his waist. He wore a wide black sash and black pants, skin tight at the hips, coal black, and stitched with gold thread down the side to where they were slashed and belled out loosely with gold buttons along both sides of the slash. On his feet he wore patent-leather dancing pumps.

He stopped at the foot of the steps and looked at me, still whistling. He was as lithe as a whip. He had the largest and emptiest smoke-coloured eyes I had ever seen, under long, silky lashes. His features were delicate and perfect without being weak. His nose was straight and almost but not quite thin, his mouth was a handsome pout, there was a dimple in his chin, and his small ears nestled gracefully against his head. His skin had that heavy pallor which the sun never touches.

He struck an attitude with his left hand on a hip and his right made a graceful curve in the air.

'Greetings,' he said. 'Lovely day, isn't it?'

'Pretty hot in here for me.'

'I like it hot.' The statement was flat and final and closed the discussion. What I liked was beneath his notice. He sat down on a step, produced a long file from somewhere and began to file his fingernails. 'You from the bank?' he asked without looking up.

'I'm looking for Doctor Verringer.'

He stopped working with the file and looked off into the warm distance. 'Who's he?' he asked with no possible interest.

'He owns the place. Laconic as hell aren't you? As if you didn't know.'

He went back to his file and fingernails. 'You got told wrong, sweetie. The bank owns the place. They done foreclosed it or it's in escrow or something. I forget the details.'

He looked up at me with the expression of a man to whom details mean nothing. I got out of the Olds and leaned against the hot door, then I moved away from that to where there was some air.

'Which bank would that be?'

'You don't know, you don't come from there. You don't come from there, you don't have any business here. Hit the trail, sweetie. Buzz off but fast.'

'I have to find Dr Verringer.'

'The joint's not operating, sweetie. Like it says on the sign, this is a private road. Some gopher forgot to lock the gate.'

'You the caretaker?'

'Sort of. Don't ask any more questions, sweetie. My temper's not reliable.'

'What do you do when you get mad – dance a tango with a ground squirrel?'

He stood up suddenly and gracefully. He smiled a minute, an empty smile. 'Looks like I got to toss you back in your little old convertible,' he said.

'Later. Where would I find Dr Verringer about now?'

He pocketed his file in his shirt and something else took its

286

place in his right hand. A brief motion and he had a fist with shining brass knuckles on it. The skin over his cheekbones was tighter and there was a flame deep in his large smoky eyes.

He strolled towards me. I stepped back to get some room. He went on whistling but the whistle was high and shrill.

'We don't have to fight,' I told him. 'We don't have anything to fight about. And you might split those lovely britches.'

He was as quick as a flash. He came at me with a smooth leap and his left hand snaked out very fast. I expected a jab and moved my head well enough but what he wanted was my right wrist and he got it. He had a grip too. He jerked me off balance and the hand with the brass knucks came around in a looping bolo punch. A crack on the back of the head with those and I would be a sick man. If I pulled he would catch me on the side of the face or on the upper arm below the point of the shoulder. It would have been a dead arm or a dead face, whichever it happened to be. In a spot like that there is only one thing to do.

I went with the pull. In passing I blocked his left foot from behind, grabbed his shirt and heard it tear. Something hit me on the back of the neck, but it wasn't the metal. I spun to the left and he went over sideways and landed catlike and was on his feet again before I had any kind of balance. He was grinning now. He was delighted with everything. He loved his work. He came for me fast.

A strong beefy voice yelled from somewhere: 'Earl! Stop that at once! At once, do you hear me?'

The gaucho boy stopped. There was a sort of sick grin on his face. He made a quick motion and the brass knucks disappeared into the wide sash around the top of his pants.

I turned and looked at a solid chunk of man in a Hawaiian shirt hurrying towards us down one of the paths, waving his arms. He came up breathing a little fast.

'Are you crazy, Earl?'

'Don't ever say that, Doc,' Earl said softly. Then he smiled, turned away and went to sit on the steps of the house. He took off the flat crowned hat, produced a comb and began to comb his thick dark hair with an absent expression. In a second or two he started to whistle softly.

The heavy man in the loud shirt stood and looked at me. I stood and looked at him.

'What's going on here?' he growled. 'Who are you, sir?'

'Name's Marlowe. I was asking for Dr Verringer. The lad you call Earl wanted to play games. I figure it's too hot.'

'I am Dr Verringer,' he said with dignity. He turned his head. 'Go in the house, Earl.'

Earl stood up slowly. He gave Dr Verringer a thoughtful, studying look, his large smoky eyes blank of expression. Then he went up the steps and pulled the screen door open. A cloud of flies buzzed angrily and then settled on the screen again as the door closed.

'Marlowe?' Dr Verringer gave me his attention again. 'And what can I do for you, Mr Marlowe?'

'Earl says you are out of business here.'

'That is correct. I am just waiting for certain legal formalities before moving out. Earl and I are alone here.'

'I'm disappointed,' I said, looking disappointed. 'I thought you had a man named Wade staying with you.'

He hoisted a couple of eyebrows that would have interested a Fuller Brush man. 'Wade? I might possibly know somebody of that name – it's a common enough name – but why should he be staying with me?'

'Taking the cure.'

He frowned. When a guy has eyebrows like that he can really do you a frown. 'I am a medical man, sir, but no longer in practice. What sort of cure did you have in mind?'

'The guy's a wino. He goes off his rocker from time to time and disappears. Sometimes he comes home under his own power, sometimes he gets brought home, and sometimes he takes a bit of finding.' I got a business card out and handed it to him.

He read it with no pleasure.

'What goes with Earl?' I asked him. 'He think he's Valentino or something?'

He made with the eyebrows again. They fascinated me. Parts of them curled off all by themselves as much as an inch and a half. He shrugged his meaty shoulders.

'Earl is quite harmless, Mr Marlowe. He is – at times – a little dreamy. Lives in a play world, shall we say?'

'You say it, Doc. From where I stand he plays rough.'

'Tut, tut, Mr Marlowe. You exaggerate surely. Earl likes to dress himself up. He is childlike in that respect.'

'You mean he's a nut,' I said. 'This place some kind of sanitarium, isn't it? Or was?'

'Certainly not. When it was in operation it was an artists' colony. I provided meals, lodgings, facilities for exercise and entertainment, and above all, seclusion. And for moderate fees. Artists, as you probably know, are seldom wealthy people. In

288

the term artists I of course include writers, musicians and so on. It was a rewarding occupation for me – while it lasted.'

He looked sad when he said this. The eyebrows drooped at the outer corners to match his mouth. Give them a little more growth and they would be *in* his mouth.

'I know that,' I said. 'It's in the file. Also the suicide you had here a while back. A dope case, wasn't it?'

He stopped drooping and bristled. 'What file?' he asked sharply.

'We've got a file on what we call the barred window boys, Doctor. Places where you can't jump out of when the French fits take over. Small private sanitariums or what have you that treat alcoholics and dopers and mild cases of mania.'

'Such places must be licensed by law,' Dr Verringer said harshly.

'Yeah. In theory anyway. Sometimes they kind of forget about that.'

He drew himself up stiffly. The guy had a kind of dignity, at that. 'The suggestion is insulting, Mr Marlowe. I have no knowledge of why my name should be on any such list as you mention. I must ask you to leave.'

'Let's get back to Wade. Could he be here under another name, maybe?'

'There is no one here but Earl and myself. We are quite alone. Now if you will excuse me—'

'I'd like to look around.'

Sometimes you can get them mad enough to say something off-key. But not Dr Verringer. He remained dignified. His eyebrows went all the way with him. I looked towards the house. From inside there came a sound of music, dance music. And very faintly the snapping of fingers.

'I bet he's in there dancing,' I said. 'That's a tango. I bet you he's dancing all by himself in there. Some kid.'

'Are you going to leave, Mr Marlowe? Or shall I have to ask Earl to assist me in putting you off my property?'

'Okay, I'll leave. No hard feelings, Doctor. There were only three names beginning with V and you seemed the most promising of them. That's the only real clue we had – Dr V. He scrawled it on a piece of paper before he left. Doctor V.'

'There must be dozens,' Dr Verringer said evenly.

'Oh sure. But not dozens in our file of the barred window boys. Thanks for the time, Doctor. Earl bothers me a little.'

I turned and went over to my car and got into it. By the time

I had the door shut Dr Verringer was beside me. He leaned in with a pleasant expression.

'We need not quarrel, Mr Marlowe. I realize that in your occupation you often have to be rather intrusive. Just what bothers you about Earl?'

'He's so obviously a phony. Where you find one thing phony you're apt to expect others. The guy's a manic-depressive, isn't he? Right now he's on the upswing.'

He stared at me in silence. He looked grave and polite. 'Many interesting and talented people have stayed with me, Mr Marlowe. Not all of them were as level-headed as you may be. Talented people are often neurotic. But I have no facilities for the care of lunatics or alcoholics, even if I had the taste for that sort of work. I have no staff except Earl, and he is hardly the type to care for the sick.'

'Just what would you say he is the type for, Doctor? Apart from bubble-dancing and stuff?'

He leaned on the door. His voice got low and confidential. 'Earl's parents were dear friends of mine, Mr Marlowe. Someone has to look after Earl and they are no longer with us. Earl has to live a quiet life, away from the noise and temptations of the city. He is unstable but fundamentally harmless. I control him with absolute ease, as you saw.'

'You've got a lot of courage,' I said.

He sighed. His eyebrows waved gently, like the antennae of some suspicious insect. 'It has been a sacrifice,' he said. 'A rather heavy one. I thought Earl could help me with my work here. He plays beautiful tennis, swims and dives like a champion, and can dance all night. Almost always he is amiability itself. But from time to time there were – incidents.' He waved a broad hand as if pushing painful memories into the background. 'In the end it was either give up Earl or give up my place here.'

He held both hands palms up, spread them apart, turned them over and let them fall to his sides. His eyes looked moist with unshed tears.

'I sold out,' he said. 'This peaceful little valley will become a real estate development. There will be sidewalks and lamp posts and children with scooters and blatting radios. There will even' – he heaved a forlorn sigh – 'be Television.' He waved his hand in a sweeping gesture. 'I hope they will spare the trees,' he said, 'but I'm afraid they won't. Along the ridges there will be television aerials instead. But Earl and I will be far away, I trust.'

'Good-bye, Doctor. My heart bleeds for you.'

He put out his hand. It was moist but very firm. 'I appreciate your sympathy and understanding, Mr Marlowe. And I regret I am unable to help you in your quest for Mr Slade.'

'Wade,' I said.

'Pardon me, Wade, of course. Good-bye and good luck, sir.'

I started up and drove back along the gravelled road by the way I had come. I felt sad, but not quite as sad as Dr Verringer would have liked me to feel.

I came out through the gates and drove far enough around the curve of the highway to park out of sight of the entrance. I got out and walked back along the edge of the paving to where I could just see the gates from the barbed-wire boundary fence. I stood there under a eucalyptus and waited.

Five minutes or so passed. Then a car came down the private road churning gravel. It stopped out of sight from where I was. I pulled back still farther into the brush. I heard a creaking noise then the click of a heavy catch and the rattle of a chain. The car motor revved up and the car went back up the road.

When the sound of it had died I went back to my Olds and did a U-turn to face back towards town. As I drove past the entrance to Dr Verringer's private road I saw that the gate was fastened with a padlocked chain. No more visitors today, thank you.

# Seventeen

I drove the twenty-odd miles back to town and ate lunch. While I ate I felt more and more silly over the whole deal. You just don't find people the way I was going about it. You meet interesting characters like Earl and Dr Verringer, but you don't meet the man you are looking for. You waste tyres, gasoline, words and nervous energy in a game with no pay-off. You're not even betting table limit four ways on Black 28. With three names that started with V I had as much chance of paging my man as I had of breaking Nick the Greek in a crap game.

Anyway the first one is always wrong, a dead end, a promising lead that blows up in your face with no music. But he shouldn't have said Slade instead of Wade. He was an intelligent man. He wouldn't forget that easy, and if he did he would just forget.

Maybe, and maybe not. It had not been a long acquaintance. Over my coffee I thought about Drs Vukanich and Varley. Yes or no? They would kill most of the afternoon. By then I could call the Wade mansion in Idle Valley and be told the head of the household had returned to his domicile and all was gleaming bright for the time being.

Dr Vukanich was easy. He was only half a dozen blocks down the line. But Dr Varley was away to hell and gone in the Altadena hills, a long, hot, boring drive. Yes or no?

The final answer was yes. For three good reasons. One was that you can never know too much about the shadow line and the people who walk it. The second was that anything I could add to the file Peters had got out for me was just that much thanks and good will. The third reason was that I didn't have anything else to do.

I paid my check, left my car where it was and walked the north side of the street to the Stockwell Building. It was an antique with a cigar counter in the entrance and a manually operated elevator that lurched and hated to level off. The corridor of the sixth floor was narrow and the doors had frosted glass panels. It was older and much dirtier than my own building. It was loaded with doctors, dentists, Christian Science practitioners not doing too good, the kind of lawyers you hope the other fellow has, the kind of doctors and dentists who just scrape along. Not too skilful, not too clean, not too much on the ball, three dollars and please pay the nurse; tired, discouraged men who know just exactly where they stand, what kind of patients they can get and how much money they can be squeezed into paying. Please Do Not Ask For Credit. Doctor is In, Doctor is Out. That's a pretty shaky molar you have there, Mrs Kazinski. Now if you want this new acrylic filling, every bit as good as a gold inlay, I can do it for you for fourteen dollars. Novocain will be two dollars extra, if you wish it. Doctor is In, Doctor is Out. That will be Three Dollars. Please Pay the Nurse.

In a building like that there will always be a few guys making real money, but they don't look it. They fit into the shabby background, which is protective colouring for them. Shyster lawyers who are partners in a bail bond racket on the side (only about two per cent of all forfeited bail bonds are ever collected). Abortionists posing as anything you like that explains their furnishings. Dope pushers posing as urologists, dermatologists, or any branch of medicine in which the treatment can be frequent, and the regular use of local anaesthetics is normal.

Dr Lester Vukanich had a small and ill-furnished waiting-room in which there were a dozen people, all uncomfortable. They looked like anybody else. They had no signs on them. Anyway you can't tell a doper well under control from a vegetarian bookkeeper. I had to wait three-quarters of an hour. The patients went in through two doors. An active ear, nose and throat man can handle four sufferers at once, if he has enough room.

Finally I got in. I got to sit in a brown leather chair beside a table covered with a white towel on which was a set of tools. A sterilizing cabinet bubbled against the wall. Dr Vukanich came in briskly with his white smock and his round mirror strapped to his forehead. He sat down in front of me on a stool.

'A sinus headache, is it? Very severe?' He looked at a folder the nurse had given him.

I said it was awful. Blinding. Especially when I first got up in the morning. He nodded sagely.

'Characteristic,' he said, and fitted a glass cap over a thing that looked like a fountain pen.

He pushed it into my mouth. 'Close the lips but not the teeth, please.' While he said it he reached out and switched off the light. There was no window. A ventilating fan purred some-where.

Dr Vukanich withdrew his glass tube and put the lights back up. He looked at me carefully.

'No congestion at all, Mr Marlowe. If you have a headache, it is not from a sinus condition. I'd hazard a guess that you never had sinus trouble in your life. You had a septum operation sometime in the past, I see.'

'Yes, Doctor. Got a kick playing football.'

He nodded. 'There is a slight shelf of bone which should have been cut away. Hardly enough to interfere with breathing how-ever.'

He leaned back on the stool and held his knee. 'Just what did you expect me to do for you?' he asked. He was a thin-faced man with an uninteresting pallor. He looked like a tubercular white rat.

'I wanted to talk to you about a friend of mine. He's in bad shape. He's a writer. Plenty of dough, but bad nerves. Needs help. He lives on the sauce for days on end. He needs that little extra something. His own doctor won't co-operate any more.'

'Exactly what do you mean by co-operate?' Dr Vukanich asked.

'All the guy needs is an occasional shot to calm him down. I thought maybe we could work something out. The money would be solid.'

'Sorry, Mr Marlowe. It is not my sort of problem.' He stood up. 'Rather a crude approach, if I may say so. Your friend may consult me, if he chooses. But he'd better have something wrong with him that requires treatment. That will be ten dollars, Mr Marlowe.'

'Come off it, Doc. You're on the list.'

Dr Vukanich leaned against the wall and lit a cigarette. He was giving me time. He blew smoke and looked at it. I gave him one of my cards to look at instead. He looked at it.

'What list would that be?' he inquired.

'The barred window boys. I figure you might know my friend already. His name's Wade. I figure you might have him stashed away somewhere in a little white room. The guy is missing from home.'

'You are an ass,' Dr Vukanich told me. 'I don't go in for penny ante stuff like four-day liquor cures. They cure nothing in any case. I have no little white rooms and I am not acquainted with the friend you mention – even if he exists. That will be ten dollars – cash – right now. Or would you rather I called the police and made a complaint that you solicited me for narcotics?'

'That would be dandy,' I said. 'Let's.'

'Get out of here, you cheap grifter.'

I stood up off the chair. 'I guess I made a mistake, Doctor. The last time the guy broke parole he holed up with a doctor whose name began with a V. It was strictly an undercover operation. They fetched him late at night and brought him back the same way when he was over the jumps. Didn't even wait long enough to see him go in the house. So when he hops the coop again and don't come back for quite a piece, naturally we check over our files for a lead. We come up with three doctors whose names begin with V.'

'Interesting,' he said with a bleak smile. He was still giving me time. 'What is the basis of your selection?'

I stared at him. His right hand was moving softly up and down the upper part of his left arm on the inside of it. His face was covered with a light sweat.

'Sorry, Doctor. We operate very confidential.'

'Excuse me a moment. I have another patient that—'

He left the rest of it hanging in the air and went out. While

294

he was gone a nurse poked her head through the doorway, looked at me briefly and withdrew.

Then Dr Vukanich came back in strolling happily. He was smiling and relaxed. His eyes were bright.

'What? Are you still here?' He looked very surprised or pretended to. 'I thought our little visit had been brought to an end.'

'I'm leaving. I thought you wanted me to wait.'

He chuckled. 'You know something, Mr Marlowe? We live in extraordinary times. For a mere five hundred dollars I could have you put in the hospital with several broken bones. Comical, isn't it?'

'Hilarious,' I said. 'Shoot yourself in the vein, don't you, Doc? Boy, do you brighten up!'

I started out. '*Hasta luego, amigo,*' he chirped. 'Don't forget my ten bucks. Pay the nurse.'

He moved to an intercom, and was speaking into it as I left. In the waiting-room the same twelve people or twelve just like them were being uncomfortable. The nurse was right on the job.

'That will be ten dollars, please, Mr Marlowe. This office requires immediate cash payment.'

I stepped among the crowded feet to the door. She bounded out of her chair and ran around the desk. I pulled the door open.

'What happens when you don't get it?' I asked her.

'You'll find out what happens,' she said angrily.

'Sure. You're just doing your job. So am I. Take a gander at the card I left and you'll see what my job is.'

I went on out. The waiting patients looked at me with disapproving eyes. That was no way to treat Doctor.


# Eighteen


Dr Amos Varley was a very different proposition. He had a big old house in a big old garden with big old oak trees shading it. It was a massive frame structure with elaborate scrollwork along the overhang of the porches and the white porch railings had turned and fluted uprights like the legs of an old-fashioned grand piano. A few frail elderly people sat in long chairs on the porches with rugs tucked around them.

The entrance doors were double and had stained-glass panels.

The hall inside was wide and cool and the parquet floor was polished and without a single rug. Altadena is a hot place in summer. It is pushed back against the hills and the breeze jumps clear over it. Eighty years ago people knew how to build houses for this climate.

A nurse in crisp white took my card and after a wait Dr Amos Varley condescended to see me. He was a big, bald-headed guy with a cheery smile. His long white coat was spotless, he walked noiselessly on crêpe rubber soles.

'What can I do for you, Mr Marlowe?' He had a rich, soft voice to soothe the pain and comfort the anxious heart. Doctor is here, there is nothing to worry about, everything will be fine. He had that bedside manner, thick, honeyed layers of it. He was wonderful – and he was as tough as armour plate.

'Doctor, I am looking for a man named Wade, a well-to-do alcoholic who has disappeared from his home. His past history suggests that he is holed up in some discreet joint that can handle him with skill. My only lead is a reference to a Dr V. You're my third Dr V. and I'm getting discouraged.'

He smiled benignly. 'Only your third, Mr Marlowe? Surely there must be a hundred doctors in and around the Los Angeles area whose names begin with V.'

'Sure, but not many of them would have rooms with barred windows. I noticed a few upstairs here, on the side of the house.'

'Old people,' Dr Varley said sadly, but it was a rich full sadness. 'Lonely old people, depressed and unhappy old people, Mr Marlowe. Sometimes—' he made an expressive gesture with his hand, a curving motion outwards, a pause, then a gentle falling, like a dead leaf fluttering to the ground. 'I don't treat alcoholics here,' he added precisely. 'Now if you will excuse me—'

'Sorry, Doctor. You just happened to be on our list. Probably a mistake. Something about a run-in with the narcotics people a couple of years ago.'

'Is that so?' He looked puzzled, then the light broke. 'Ah, yes, an assistant I was unwise enough to employ. For a very short time. He abused my confidence badly. Yes, indeed.'

'Not the way I heard it,' I said. 'I guess I heard it wrong.'

'And how did you hear it, Mr Marlowe?' He was still giving me the full treatment with his smile and his mellow tones.

'That you had to turn in your narcotic prescription book.'

That got to him a little. He didn't quite scowl but he peeled off a few layers of the charm. His blue eyes had a chilly glint. 'And the source of this fantastic information?'

'A large detective agency that has had facilities for building files on that sort of thing.'

'A collection of cheap blackmailers, no doubt.'

'Not cheap, Doctor. Their base rate is a hundred dollars a day. It's run by a former colonel of military police. No nickel grabber, Doctor. He rates way up.'

'I shall give him a piece of my mind,' Dr Varley said with cool distaste. 'His name?' The sun had set in Dr Varley's manner. It was getting to be a chilly evening.

'Confidential, Doctor. But don't give it a thought. All in the day's work. Name of Wade doesn't ring a bell at all, huh?'

'I believe you know your way out, Mr Marlowe.'

The door of a small elevator opened behind him. A nurse pushed a wheel chair out. The chair contained what was left of a broken old man. His eyes were closed, his skin had a bluish tinge. He was well wrapped up. The nurse wheeled him silently across the polished floor and out of a side door. Dr Varley said softly:

'Old people. Sick old people. Lonely old people. Do not come back, Mr Marlowe. You might annoy me. When annoyed I can be rather unpleasant. I might even say *very* unpleasant.'

'Okay by me, Doctor. Thanks for the time. Nice little dying-in home you got here.'

'What was that?' He took a step towards me and peeled off the remaining layers of honey. The soft lines of his face set themselves into hard ridges.

'What's the matter?' I asked him. 'I can see my man wouldn't be here. I wouldn't look for anybody here that wasn't too frail to fight back. Sick old people. Lonely old people. You said it yourself, Doctor. Unwanted old people, but with money and hungry heirs. Most of them probably judged incompetent by the court.'

'I am getting annoyed,' Dr Varley said.

'Light food, light sedation, firm treatment. Put them out in the sun, put them back in the bed. Bar some of the windows in case there's a little spunk left. They love you, Doctor, one and all. They die holding your hand and seeing the sadness in your eyes. It's genuine, too.'

'It certainly is,' he said in a low throaty growl. His hands were fists now. I ought to knock it off. But he had begun to nauseate me.

'Sure it is,' I said. 'Nobody likes to lose a good paying customer. Especially one you don't even have to please.'

'Somebody has to do it,' he said. 'Somebody has to care for these sad old people, Mr Marlowe.'

'Somebody has to clean out cesspools. Come to think of it that's a clean honest job. So long, Dr Varley. When my job makes me feel dirty I'll think of you. It will cheer me up no end.'

'You filthy louse,' Dr Varley said between his wide white teeth. 'I ought to break your neck. Mine is an honourable branch of an honourable profession.'

'Yeah.' I looked at him wearily. 'I know it is. Only it smells of death.'

He didn't slug me, so I walked away from him and out. I looked back from the wide double doors. He hadn't moved. He had a job to do, putting back the layers of honey.

# Nineteen

I drove back to Hollywood feeling like a short length of chewed string. It was too early to eat, and too hot. I turned on the fan in my office. It didn't make the air any cooler, just a little more lively. Outside on the boulevard the traffic brawled endlessly. Inside my head thoughts stuck together like flies on fly paper.

Three shots, three misses. All I had been doing was seeing too many doctors.

I called the Wade home. A Mexican sort of accent answered and said that Mrs Wade was not at home. I asked for Mr Wade. The voice said Mr Wade was not home either. I left my name. He seemed to catch it without any trouble. He said he was the houseboy.

I called George Peters at The Carne Organization. Maybe he knew some more doctors. He wasn't in. I left a phony name and a right telephone number. An hour crawled by like a sick cockroach. I was a grain of sand on the desert of oblivion. I was a two-gun cowpoke fresh out of bullets. Three shots, three misses. I hate it when they come in threes. You call on Mr A. Nothing. You call on Mr B. Nothing. You call on Mr C. More of the same. A week later you find out it should have been Mr D. Only you didn't know he existed and by the time you found out the client had changed his mind and killed the investigation.

Drs Vukanich and Varley were scratched. Varley had it too rich to fool with hooch cases. Vukanich was a punk, a high-wire performer who hit the main line in his own office. The help must know. At least some of the patients must know. All it took to finish him was one sore head and one telephone call. Wade wouldn't have gone within blocks of him, drunk or sober. He might not be the brightest guy in the world – plenty of successful people are far from mental giants – but he couldn't be dumb enough to fool with Vukanich.

The only possible was Dr Verringer. He had the space and the seclusion. He probably had the patience. But Sepulveda Canyon was a long way from Idle Valley. Where was the point of contact, how did they know each other, and if Verringer owned that property and had a buyer for it, he was half-way to being pretty well heeled. That gave me an idea. I called a man I knew in a title company to find out the status of the property. No answer. The title company had closed for the day.

I closed for the day too, and drove over to La Cienaga to Rudy's Bar-B-Q, gave my name to the master of ceremonies and waited for the big moment on a bar stool with a whisky sour in front of me and Marek Weber's waltz music in my ears. After a while I got in past the velvet rope and ate one of Rudy's 'world-famous' salisbury steaks, which is hamburger on a slab of burnt wood, ringed with browned-over mashed potato, supported by fried onion rings and one of those mixed-up salads which men will eat with complete docility in restaurants, although they would probably start yelling if their wives tried to feed them one at home.

After that I drove home. As I opened the front door the phone started to ring.

'This is Eileen Wade, Mr Marlowe. You wanted me to call you.'

'Just to find out if anything had happened at your end. I have been seeing doctors all day and have made no friends.'

'No, I'm sorry. He still hasn't showed up. I can't help being rather anxious. Then you have nothing to tell me, I suppose.' Her voice was low and dispirited.

'It's a big crowded county, Mrs Wade.'

'It will be four whole days tonight.'

'Sure, but that's not too long.'

'For me it is.' She was silent for a while. 'I've been doing a lot of thinking, trying to remember something,' she went on. 'There must be something, some kind of hint or memory. Roger talks a great deal about all sorts of things.'

'Does the name Verringer mean anything to you, Mrs Wade?'

'No, I'm afraid not. Should it?'

'You mentioned that Mr Wade was brought home one time by a tall man dressed in a cowboy outfit. Would you recognize this tall man if you saw him again, Mrs Wade?'

'I suppose I might,' she said hesitantly, 'if the conditions were the same. But I only caught the merest glimpse of him. Was his name Verringer?'

'No, Mrs Wade. Verringer is a heavily built, middle-aged man who runs, or more accurately has run, some kind of guest ranch in Sepulveda Canyon. He has a dressed-up fancy boy named Earl working for him. And Verringer calls himself a doctor.'

'That's wonderful,' she said warmly. 'Don't you feel that you're on the right track?'

'I could be wetter than a drowned kitten. I'll call you when I know. I just wanted to make sure Roger hadn't come home and that you hadn't recalled anything definite.'

'I'm afraid I haven't been of much help to you,' she said sadly. 'Please call me at any time, no matter how late it is.'

I said I would do that and we hung up. I took a gun and a three-cell flashlight with me this time. The gun was a tough little short-barrelled .32 with flat-point cartridges. Dr Verringer's boy Earl might have other toys than brass knuckles. If he had, he was plenty goofy enough to play with them.

I hit the highway again and drove as fast as I dared. It was a moonless night, and would be getting dark by the time I reached the entrance to Dr Verringer's estate. Darkness was what I needed.

The gates were still locked with the chain and padlock. I drove on past and parked well off the highway. There was still some light under the trees but it wouldn't last long. I climbed the gate and went up the side of the hill looking for a hiking path. Far back in the valley I thought I heard a quail. A mourning dove exclaimed against the miseries of life. There wasn't any hiking path or I couldn't find one, so I went back to the road and walked along the edge of the gravel. The eucalyptus trees gave way to the oaks and I crossed the ridge and far off I could see a few lights. It took me three-quarters of an hour to work up behind the swimming-pool and the tennis courts to a spot where I could look down on the main building at the end of the road. It was lighted up and I could hear music coming from it. And farther off in the trees another cabin showed light. There were small dark cabins dotted all over the place in the trees. I went along a path now and suddenly a floodlight went on at the back of the main cabin. I stopped dead. The floodlight was not looking for anything. It pointed straight down and made a wide pool of light on the back porch and the ground beyond. Then a door banged open and Earl came out. Then I knew I was in the right place.

Earl was a cowpoke tonight, and it had been a cowpoke who brought Roger Wade home the time before. Earl was spinning a rope. He wore a dark shirt stitched with white and a polka-dot scarf knotted loosely round his neck. He wore a wide leather belt with a load of silver on it and a pair of tooled leather holsters with ivory-handled guns in them. He wore elegant riding pants and boots cross-stitched in white and glistening new. On the back of his head was a white sombrero and what looked like a woven silver cord hanging loosely down his shirt, the ends not fastened.

He stood there alone under the white floodlight, spinning his rope around him, stepping in and out of it, an actor without an audience, a tall, slender, handsome dude wrangler putting on a show all by himself and loving every minute of it. Two-Gun Earl, the Terror of Chochise County. He belonged on one of those guest ranches that are so all-fired horsey the telephone girl wears riding boots to work.

All at once he heard a sound, or pretended to. The rope dropped, his hands swept the two guns from the holsters and the crook of his thumbs was over the hammers as they came level. He peered into the darkness. I didn't dare move. The damn guns could be loaded. But the floodlight had blinded him and he didn't see anything. He slipped his guns back in the holsters, picked up the rope and gathered it loosely, went back into the house. The light went off, and so did I.

I moved around through the trees and got close to the small lighted cabin on the slope. No sound came from it. I reached a screened window and looked in. The light came from a lamp on a night table beside a bed. A man lay flat on his back in the bed, his body relaxed, his arms in pyjama sleeves outside the covers, his eyes wide open and staring at the ceiling. He looked big. His face was partly shadowed, but I could see that he was pale and that he needed a shave and had needed one for just about the right length of time. The spread fingers of his hands lay motionless on the outside of the bed. He looked as if he hadn't moved for hours.

I heard steps coming along the path at the far side of the cabin. A screen door creaked and then the solid shape of Dr

Verringer showed in the doorway. He was carrying what looked like a large glass of tomato juice. He switched on a standing lamp. His Hawaiian shirt gleamed yellowly. The man in the bed didn't even look at him.

Dr Verringer put the glass down on the night table and pulled a chair close and sat down. He reached for one of the wrists and felt a pulse. 'How are you feeling now, Mr Wade?' His voice was kindly and solicitous.

The man on the bed didn't answer him or look at him. He went on staring at the ceiling.

'Come, come, Mr Wade. Let us not be moody. Your pulse is only slightly faster than normal. You are weak, but otherwise—'

'Tejjy,' the man on the bed said suddenly, 'tell the man that if he knows how I am, the son of a bitch needn't bother to ask me.' He had a nice clear voice, but the tone was bitter.

'Who is Tejjy?' Dr Verringer asked patiently.

'My mouthpiece. She's up there in the corner.'

Dr Verringer looked up. 'I see a small spider,' he said. 'Stop acting, Mr Wade. It is not necessary with me.'

'*Tegenaria domestica*, the common jumping spider, pal. I like spiders. They practically never wear Hawaiian shirts.'

Dr Verringer moistened his lips. 'I have no time for playfulness, Mr Wade.'

'Nothing playful about Tejjy.' Wade turned his head slowly, as if it weighed very heavy, and stared at Dr Verringer contemptuously. 'Tejjy is dead serious. She creeps up on you. When you're not looking she makes a quick, silent hop. After a while she's near enough. She makes the last jump. You get sucked dry, Doctor. Very dry. Tejjy doesn't eat you. She just sucks the juice until there's nothing left but the skin. If you plan to wear that shirt much longer, Doctor, I'd say it couldn't happen too soon.'

Dr Verringer leaned back in the chair. 'I need five thousand dollars,' he said calmly. 'How soon could that happen?'

'You got six hundred and fifty bucks,' Wade said nastily. 'As well as my loose change. How the hell much does it cost in this bordello?'

'Chicken feed,' Dr Verringer said. 'I told you my rates had gone up.'

'You didn't say they had moved to Mount Wilson.'

'Don't fence with me, Wade,' Dr Verringer said curtly. 'You are in no position to get funny. Also you have betrayed my confidence.'

'I didn't know you had any.'

Dr Verringer tapped slowly on the arms of the chair. 'You called me up in the middle of the night,' he said. 'You were in a desperate condition. You said you would kill yourself if I didn't come. I didn't want to do it and you know why. I have no licence to practise medicine in this state. I am trying to get rid of this property without losing it all. I have Earl to look after and he was about due for a bad spell. I told you it would cost you a lot of money. You still insisted and I went. I want five thousand dollars.'

'I was foul with strong drink,' Wade said. 'You can't hold a man to that kind of bargain. You're damn well paid already.'

'Also,' Dr Verringer said slowly, 'you mentioned my name to your wife. You told her I was coming for you.'

Wade looked surprised. 'I didn't do anything of the sort,' he said. 'I didn't even see her. She was asleep.'

'Some other time then. A private detective has been here asking about you. He couldn't possibly have known where to come, unless he was told. I stalled him off, but he may come back. You have to go home, Mr Wade. But first I want my five thousand dollars.'

'You're not the brightest guy in the world, are you, Doc? If my wife knew where I was, why would she need a detective? She could have come herself – supposing she cared that much. She could have brought Candy, our houseboy. Candy would cut your Blue Boy into thin strips while Blue Boy was making up his mind what picture he was starring in today.'

'You have a nasty tongue, Wade. And a nasty mind.'

'I have a nasty five thousand bucks, too, Doc. Try and get it.'

'You will write me a cheque,' Dr Verringer said firmly. 'Now, at once. Then you will get dressed and Earl will take you home.'

'A cheque?' Wade was almost laughing. 'Sure I'll give you a cheque. Fine. How will you cash it?'

Dr Verringer smiled quietly. 'You think you will stop payment, Mr Wade. But you won't. I assure you that you won't.'

'You fat crook!' Wade yelled at him.

Dr Verringer shook his head. 'In some things, yes. Not in all. I am a mixed character like most people. Earl will drive you home.'

'Nix. That lad makes my skin crawl,' Wade said.

Dr Verringer stood up gently and reached over and patted the shoulder of the man on the bed. 'To me Earl is quite harmless, Mr Wade. I have ways of controlling him.'

'Name one,' a new voice said, and Earl came through the door in his Roy Rogers outfit. Dr Verringer turned, smiling.

'Keep that psycho away from me,' Wade yelled, showing fear for the first time.

Earl put his hands upon his ornamented belt. His face was deadpan. A light whistling noise came from between his teeth. He moved slowly into the room.

'You shouldn't have said that,' Dr Verringer said quickly, and turned towards Earl. 'All right, Earl. I'll handle Mr Wade my-self. I'll help him get dressed while you bring the car up here as close to the cabin as possible. Mr Wade is quite weak.'

'And he's going to be a lot weaker,' Earl said in a whistling kind of voice. 'Out of the way, fatso.'

'Now, Earl—' he reached out and grabbed the handsome young man's arm, 'you don't want to go back to Camarillo, do you? One word from me and—'

That was as far as he got. Earl jerked his arm loose and his right hand came up with a flash of metal. The armoured fist crashed against Dr Verringer's jaw. He went down as if shot through the heart. The fall shook the cabin. I started running.

I reached the door and yanked it open. Earl spun round, lean-ing forward a little, staring at me without recognition. There was a bubbling sound behind his lips. He started for me fast.

I jerked the gun out and showed it to him. It meant nothing. Either his own guns were not loaded or he had forgotten all about them. The brass knuckles were all he needed. He kept coming.

I fired through the open window across the bed. The crash of the gun in the small room seemed much louder than it should have been. Earl stopped dead. His head slewed around and he looked at the hole in the window screen. He looked back at me. Slowly his face came alive and he grinned.

'Wha' happen?' he asked brightly.

'Get rid of the knucks,' I said, watching his eyes.

He looked surprisedly down at his hand. He slipped the mauler off and threw it casually in the corner.

'Now the gun belt,' I said. 'Don't touch the guns, just the buckle.'

'They're not loaded,' he said, smiling. 'Hell, they're not even guns, just stage money.'

'The belt. Hurry it.'

He looked at the short-barrelled .32. 'That a real one? Oh, sure it is. The screen. Yeah, the screen.'

The man on the bed wasn't on the bed any more. He was behind Earl. He reached swiftly and pulled one of the bright guns loose. Earl didn't like this. His face showed it.

'Lay off him,' I said angrily. 'Put that back where you got it.'

'He's right,' Wade said. 'They're cap guns.' He backed away and put the shiny pistol on the table. 'Christ, I'm weak as a broken arm.'

'Take the belt off,' I said for the third time. When you start something with a type like Earl you have to finish it. Keep it simple and don't change your mind.

He did it at last, quite amiably. Then, holding the belt, he walked over to the table and got his other gun and put it in the holster and put the belt right back on again. I let him do it. It wasn't until then that he saw Dr Verringer crumpled on the floor against the wall. He made a sound of concern, went quickly across the room into the bathroom and came back with a glass jug of water. He dumped the water on Dr Verringer's head. Dr Verringer sputtered and rolled over. Then he groaned. Then he clapped a hand to his jaw. Then he started to get up. Earl helped him.

'Sorry, Doc. I must have just let fly without seeing who it was.'

'It's all right, nothing broken,' Verringer said, waving him away. 'Get the car up here, Earl. And don't forget the key for the padlock down below.'

'Car up here, sure. Right away. Key for the padlock. I got it. Right away, Doc.'

He went out of the room whistling.

Wade was sitting on the side of the bed, looking shaky. 'You the dick he was talking about?' he asked me. 'How did you find me?'

'Just asking around from people who know about these things,' I said. 'If you want to get home, you might get clothes on.'

Dr Verringer was leaning against the wall, massaging his jaw. 'I'll help him,' he said thickly. 'All I do is help people and all they do is kick me in the teeth.'

'I know just how you feel,' I said.

I went out and left them to work at it.

# Twenty

The car was close by when they came out, but Earl was gone. He had stopped the car, cut the lights and walked back towards the big cabin without saying anything to me. He was still whistling, groping for some half-remembered tune.

Wade climbed carefully into the back seat and I got in beside him. Dr Verringer drove. If his jaw hurt badly and his head ached, he didn't show it or mention it. We went over the ridge and down to the end of the gravelled drive. Earl had already been down and unlocked the gate and pulled it open. I told Verringer where my car was and he pulled up close to it. Wade got into it and sat silent, staring at nothing. Verringer got out and went round beside him. He spoke to Wade gently.

'About my five thousand dollars, Mr Wade. The cheque you promised me.'

Wade slid down and rested his head on the back of the seat. 'I'll think about it.'

'You promised it. I need it.'

'Duress, the word is, Verringer, a threat of harm. I have protection now.'

'I fed and washed you,' Verringer persisted. 'I came in the night. I protected you, I cured you – for the time being, at least.'

'Not five grand worth,' Wade sneered. 'You got plenty out of my pockets.'

Verringer wouldn't let go. 'I have a promise of a connection in Cuba, Mr Wade. You are a rich man. You should help others in their need. I have Earl to look after. To avail myself of this opportunity I need the money. I will pay it back in full.'

I began to squirm. I wanted to smoke, but I was afraid it would make Wade sick.

'Like hell you'd pay it back,' Wade said wearily. 'You won't live long enough. One of these night Blue Boy will kill you in your sleep.'

Verringer stepped back. I couldn't see his expression, but his voice hardened. 'There are more unpleasant ways to die,' he said. 'I think yours will be one of them.'

He walked back to his car and got into it. He drove in through his gates and was gone. I backed and turned and headed towards the city. After a mile or two Wade muttered: 'Why should I give that fat slob five thousand dollars?'

'No reason at all.'

'Then why do I feel like a bastard for not giving it to him?'

'No reason at all.'

He turned his head just enough to look at me. 'He handled me like a baby,' Wade said. 'He hardly left me alone for fear Earl would come in and beat me up. He took every dime I had in my pockets.'

'You probably told him to.'

'You on his side?'

'Skip it,' I said. 'This is just a job to me.'

Silence for a couple of miles more. We went past the fringe of one of the outlying suburbs. Wade spoke again.

'Maybe I'll give it to him. He's broke. The property is foreclosed. He won't get a dime out of it. All on account of that psycho. Why does he do it?'

'I wouldn't know.'

'I'm a writer,' Wade said. 'I'm supposed to understand what makes people tick. I don't understand one damn thing about anybody.'

I turned over the pass and after a climb the lights of the valley spread out endlessly in front of us. We dipped down to the highway north and west that goes to Ventura. After a while we passed through Encino. I stopped for a light and looked up towards the lights high on the hill where the big houses were. In one of them the Lennoxes had lived. We went on.

'The turn off is pretty close now,' Wade said. 'Or do you know it.'

'I know it.'

'By the way, you haven't told me your name.'

'Philip Marlowe.'

'Nice name.' His voice changed sharply, saying: 'Wait a minute. You the guy that was mixed up with Lennox?'

'Yeah.'

He was staring at me in the darkness of the car. We passed the last buildings on the main drag of Encino.

'I knew her,' Wade said. 'A little. Him I never saw. Queer business, that. The law boys gave you the rough edge, didn't they?'

I didn't answer him.

'Maybe you don't like to talk about it,' he said.

'Could be. Why would it interest you?'

'Hell, I'm a writer. It must be quite a story.'

'Take tonight off. You must be feeling pretty weak.'

'Okay, Marlowe. Okay. You don't like me. I get it.'

We reached the turn-off and I swung the car into it and towards the low hills and the gap between them that was Idle Valley.

'I don't either like you or dislike you,' I said. 'I don't know you. Your wife asked me to find you and bring you home. When I deliver you at your house I'm through. Why she picked on me I couldn't say. Like I said, it's just a job.'

We turned the flank of a hill and hit a wider more firmly paved road. He said his house was a mile farther on, on the right side. He told me the number, which I already knew. For a guy in his shape he was a pretty persistent talker.

'How much is she paying you?' he asked.

'We didn't discuss it.'

'Whatever it is, it's not enough. I owe you a lot of thanks. You did a great job, chum. I wasn't worth the trouble.'

'That's just the way you feel tonight.'

He laughed. 'You know something, Marlowe? I could get to like you. You're a bit of a bastard – like me.'

We reached the house. It was a two-storey overall shingle house with a small pillared portico and a long lawn from the entrance to a thick row of shrubs inside the white fence. There was a light in the portico. I pulled into the driveway and stopped close to the garage.

'Can you make it without help?'

'Of course.' He got out of the car. 'Aren't you coming in for a drink or something?'

'Not tonight, thanks; I'll wait here until you're in the house.'

He stood there breathing hard. 'Okay,' he said shortly.

He turned and walked carefully along a flagged path to the front door. He held on to a white pillar for a moment, then tried the door. It opened, he went in. The door stayed open and light washed across the green lawn. There was a sudden flutter of voices. I started backing from the driveway, following the back-up light. Somebody called out.

I looked and saw Eileen Wade standing in the open doorway. I kept going and she started to run. So I had to stop. I cut the lights and got out of the car. When she came up I said:

'I ought to have called you, but I was afraid to leave him.'

'Of course. Did you have a lot of trouble?'

'Well – a little more than ringing a doorbell.'

'Please come in the house and tell me all about it.'

'He should be in bed. By tomorrow he'll be as good as new.'

'Candy will put him to bed,' she said. 'He won't drink tonight, if that's what you are thinking of.'

'Never occurred to me. Good night, Mrs Wade.'

'You must be tired. Don't you want a drink yourself?'

I lit a cigarette. It seemed like a couple of weeks since I had tasted tobacco. I drank in the smoke.

'May I have just one puff?'

'Sure. I thought you didn't smoke.'

'I don't often.' She came close to me and I handed her the cigarette. She drew on it and coughed. She handed it back laughing. 'Strictly an amateur, as you see.'

'So you knew Sylvia Lennox,' I said. 'Was that why you wanted to hire me?'

'I knew who?' She sounded puzzled.

'Sylvia Lennox.' I had the cigarette back now. I was eating it pretty fast.

'Oh,' she said, startled. 'That girl that was – murdered. No, I didn't know her personally. I knew who she was. Didn't I tell you that?'

'Sorry, I'd forgotten just what you did tell me.'

She was still standing there quietly, close to me, slim and tall in a white dress of some sort. The light from the open door touched the fringe of her hair and made it glow softly.

'Why did you ask me if that had anything to do with my wanting to, as you put it, hire you?' When I didn't answer at once she added, 'Did Roger tell you he knew her?'

'He said something about the case when I told him my name. He didn't connect me with it immediately, then he did. He talked so damn much I don't remember half of what he said.'

'I see. I must go in, Mr Marlowe, and see if my husband needs anything. And if you won't come in—'

'I'll leave this with you,' I said.

I took hold of her and pulled her towards me and tilted her head back. I kissed her hard on the lips. She didn't fight me and she didn't respond. She pulled herself away quietly and stood there looking at me.

'You shouldn't have done that,' she said. 'That was wrong. You're too nice a person.'

'Sure. Very wrong,' I agreed. 'But I've been such a nice faithful well-behaved gun dog all day long, I got charmed into one of the silliest ventures I ever tackled, and damned if it didn't turn out just as though somebody had written a script for it. You know something? I believe you knew where he was all along – or at least knew the name of Dr Verringer. You just wanted to get me involved with him, tangled up with him so I'd feel a sense of responsibility to look after him. Or am I crazy?'

'Of course you're crazy,' she said coldly. 'That is the most outrageous nonsense I ever listened to.' She started to turn away.

'Wait a minute,' I said. 'That kiss won't leave a scar. You just think it will. And don't tell me I'm too nice a person. I'd rather be a heel.'

She looked back. 'Why?'

'If I hadn't been a nice guy to Terry Lennox, he would still be alive.'

'Yes?' she said quietly. 'How can you be so sure? Good night, Mr Marlowe. And thank you so very much for almost everything.'

She walked back along the edge of the grass. I watched her into the house. The door closed. The porch light went off. I waved at nothing and drove away.

# Twenty-one

Next morning I got up late on account of the big fee I had earned the night before. I drank an extra cup of coffee, smoked an extra cigarette, ate an extra slice of Canadian bacon, and for the three hundredth time I swore I would never again use an electric razor. That made the day normal. I hit the office about ten, picked up some odds and ends of mail, slit the envelopes and let the stuff lie on the desk. I opened the windows wide to let out the smell of dust and dinginess that collected in the night and hung in the still air, in the corners of the room, in the slats of the venetian blinds. A dead moth was spread-eagled on a corner of the desk. On the window-sill a bee with tattered wings was crawling along the woodwork, buzzing in a tired remote sort of way, as if she knew it wasn't any use, she was finished, she had flown too many missions and would never get back to the hive again.

I knew it was going to be one of those crazy days. Everyone has them. Days when nobody rolls in but the loose wheels, the dingoes who park their brains with their gum, the squirrels who can't find their nuts, the mechanics who always have a gear wheel left over.

The first was a big, blond roughneck named Kuissenen or something Finnish like that. He jammed his massive bottom in the customer's chair and planted two wide, horny hands on my desk and said he was a power-shovel operator, that he lived in Culver City, and the goddam woman who lived next door to him was trying to poison his dog. Every morning before he let the dog out for a run in the back yard he had to search the place from fence to fence for meatballs thrown over the potato vine from next door. He'd found nine of them so far and they were loaded with a greenish powder he knew was an arsenic weed-killer.

'How much to watch out and catch her at it?' He stared at me as unblinkingly as a fish in a tank.

'Why not do it yourself?'

'I got to work for a living, mister. I'm losing four twenty-five an hour just coming up here to ask.'

'Try the police?'

'I try the police. They might get around to it some time next year. Right now they're busy sucking up to MGM.'

'S.P.C.A.? The Tailwaggers?'

'What's them?'

I told him about the Tailwaggers. He was far from interested. He knew about S.P.C.A. The S.P.C.A. could take a running jump. They couldn't see nothing smaller than a horse.

'It says on the door you're an investigator,' he said truculently. 'Okay, go the hell out and investigate. Fifty bucks if you catch her.'

'Sorry,' I said. 'I'm tied up. Spending a couple of weeks hiding in a gopher hole in your back yard would be out of my line any-way – even for fifty bucks.'

He stood up glowering. 'Big shot,' he said. 'Don't need the dough, huh? Can't be bothered saving the life of a itty-bitty dog. Nuts to you, big shot.'

'I've got troubles too, Mr Kuissenen.'

'I'll twist her goddam neck if I catch her,' he said, and I didn't doubt he could have done it. He could have twisted the hind leg off an elephant. 'That's what makes it I want somebody else. Just because the little tyke barks when a car goes by the house. Sour-faced old bitch.'

He started for the door. 'Are you sure it's the dog she's trying to poison?' I asked his back.

'Sure I'm sure.' He was half-way to the door before the nickel dropped. He swung around fast then. 'Say that again, buster.'

I just shook my head. I didn't want to fight him. He might hit me on the head with my desk. He snorted and went out, almost taking the door with him.

The next cookie in the dish was a woman, not old, not young, not clean, not too dirty, obviously poor, shabby, querulous and stupid. The girl she roomed with – in her set any woman who works out is a girl – was taking money out of her purse. A dollar here, four bits there, but it added up. She figured she was out close to twenty dollars in all. She couldn't afford it. She couldn't afford to move either. She couldn't afford a detective. She thought I ought to be willing to throw a scare into the roommate just on the telephone like, not mentioning any names.

It took her twenty minutes or more to tell me this. She kneaded her bag incessantly while telling it.

'Anybody you know could do that,' I said.

'Yeah, but you bein' a dick and all.'

'I don't have a licence to threaten people I know nothing about.'

'I'm goin' to tell her I been in to see you. I don't have to say it's her. Just that you're workin' on it.'

'I wouldn't if I were you. If you mention my name she may call me up. If she does that, I'll tell her the facts.'

She stood up and slammed her shabby bag against her stomach. 'You're no gentleman,' she said shrilly.

'Where does it say I have to be?'

She went out mumbling.

After lunch I had Mr Simpson W. Edelweiss. He had a card to prove it. He was manager of a sewing machine agency. He was a small tired-looking man about forty-eight to fifty, small hands and feet, wearing a brown suit with sleeves too long, and a stiff white collar behind a purple tie with black diamonds on it. He sat on the edge of the chair without fidgeting and looked at me out of sad black eyes. His hair was black too and thick and rough without a sign of grey in it that I could see. He had a clipped moustache with a reddish tone. He could have passed for thirty-five if you didn't look at the backs of his hands.

'Call me Simp,' he said. 'Everybody else does. I got it coming. I'm a Jewish man married to a Gentile woman, twenty-four years of age, beautiful. She run away a couple of times before.'

He got out a photo of her and showed it to me. She might have been beautiful to him. To me she was a big, sloppy-looking cow of a woman with a weak mouth.

'What's your trouble, Mr Edelweiss? I don't do divorce business.' I tried to give him back the photo. He waved it away. 'The client is always mister to me,' I added. 'Until he has told me a few dozen lies anyway.'

He smiled. 'Lies I got no use for. It's not a divorce matter. I just want Mabel back again. But she don't come back until I find her. Maybe it's a kind of game with her.'

He told me about her, patiently, without rancour. She drank, she played around, she wasn't a very good wife by his standards, but he could have been brought up too strict. She had a heart as big as a house, he said, and he loved her. He didn't kid himself he was any dreamboat, just a steady worker bringing home the pay-cheque. They had a joint bank account. She had drawn it all out, but he was prepared for that. He had a pretty good idea who she had lit out with, and if he was right the man would clean her out and leave her stranded.

'Name of Kerrigan,' he said. 'Monroe Kerrigan. I don't aim to knock the Catholics. There is plenty of bad Jews too. This Kerrigan is a barber when he works. I ain't knocking barbers either. But a lot of them are drifters and horse players. Not real steady.'

'Won't you hear from her when she is cleaned out?'

'She gets awful ashamed. She might hurt herself.'

'It's a "Missing Persons" job, Mr Edelweiss. You should go down and make a report.'

'No. I'm not knocking the police, but I don't want it that way. Mabel would be humiliated.'

The world seemed to be full of people Mr Edelweiss was not knocking. He put some money on the desk.

'Two hundred dollars,' he said. 'Down payment. I'd rather do it my way.'

'It will happen again,' I said.

'Sure.' He shrugged and spread his hands gently. 'But twenty-four years old and me almost fifty. How could it be different? She'll settle down after a while. Trouble is, no kids. She can't have kids. A Jew likes to have a family. So Mabel knows that. She's humiliated.'

'You're a very forgiving man, Mr Edelweiss.'

'Well, I ain't a Christian,' he said. 'And I'm not knocking Christians, you understand. But with me it's a real. I don't just say it. I do it. Oh, I almost forgot the most important.'

He got out a picture postcard and pushed it across the desk after the money. 'From Honolulu she sends it. Money goes fast in Honolulu. One of my uncles had a jewellery business there. Retired now. Lives in Seattle.'

I picked the photo up again. 'I'll have to farm this one out,' I told him. 'And I'll have to have this copied.'

'I could hear you saying that, Mr Marlowe, before I got here. So I come prepared.' He took out an envelope and it contained five more prints. 'I got Kerrigan too, but only a snapshot.' He went into another pocket and gave me another envelope. I looked at Kerrigan. He had a smooth dishonest face that did not surprise me. Three copies of Kerrigan.

Mr Simpson W. Edelweiss gave me another card which had on it his name, his residence, his telephone number. He said he hoped it would not cost too much but that he would respond at once to any demand for further funds and he hoped to hear from me.

'Two hundred ought to pretty near do it if she's still in Honolulu,' I said. 'What I need now is a detailed physical description of both parties that I can put into a telegram. Height, weight, age, colouring, any noticeable scars or other identifying marks, what clothes she was wearing and had with her, and how much money was in the account she cleaned out. If you've been through this before, Mr Edelweiss, you will know what I want.'

'I got a peculiar feeling about this Kerrigan. Uneasy.'

I spent another half-hour milking him and writing things down. Then he stood up quietly, shook hands quietly, bowed and left the office quietly.

'Tell Mabel everything is fine,' he said as he went out.

It turned out to be routine. I sent a wire to an agency in Honolulu and followed it with an airmail containing the photos and whatever information I had left out of the wire. They found her working as a chambermaid's helper in a luxury hotel, scrubbing bathtubs and bathroom floors and so on. Kerrigan had done just what Mr Edelweiss expected, cleaned her out while she was asleep and skipped, leaving her stuck with the hotel bill. She pawned a ring which Kerrigan couldn't have taken without violence, and got enough out of it to pay the hotel but not enough to buy her way home. So Edelweiss hopped a plane and went after her.

He was too good for her. I sent him a bill for twenty dollars and the cost of a long telegram. The Honolulu agency grabbed the two hundred. With a portrait of Madison in my office safe I could afford to be underpriced.

So passed a day in the life of a P.I. Not exactly a typical day but not totally untypical either. What makes a man stay in it nobody knows. You don't get rich, you don't often have much fun. Sometimes you get beaten up or shot at or tossed into the jailhouse. Once in a long while you get dead. Every other month you decide to give it up and find some sensible occupation while you can still walk without shaking your head. Then the door buzzer rings and you open the inner door to the waiting-room and there stands a new face with a new problem, a new load of grief and a small piece of money.

'Come in, Mr Thingummy. What can I do for you?'

There must be a reason.

Three days later in the shank of the afternoon Eileen Wade called me up, and asked me to come round to the house for a drink the next evening. They were having a few friends in for cocktails. Roger would like to see me and thank me adequately. And would I please send in a bill?

'You don't owe me anything, Mrs Wade. What little I did I got paid for.'

'I must have looked very silly acting Victorian about it,' she said. 'A kiss doesn't seem to mean much nowadays. You will come, won't you?'

'I guess so. Against my better judgement.'

'Roger is quite well again. He's working.'

'Good.'

'You sound very solemn today. I guess you take life pretty seriously.'

'Now and then. Why?'

She laughed very gently and said good-bye and hung up. I sat there for a while taking life seriously. Then I tried to think of something funny so that I could have a great big laugh. Neither way worked, so I got Terry Lennox's letter of farewell out of the safe and reread it. It reminded me that I had never gone to Victor's for that gimlet he asked me to drink for him. It was just about the right time of day for the bar to be quiet, the way he would have liked it himself, if he had been around to go with me. I thought of him with a vague sadness and with a puckering bitterness too. When I got to Victor's I almost kept going. Almost, but not quite. I had too much of his money. He had made a fool of me but he had paid well for the privilege.

# Twenty-two

It was so quiet in Victor's that you almost heard the temperature drop as you came in at the door. On a bar stool a woman in a black tailormade, which couldn't at that time of year have

315

been anything but some synthetic fabric like orlon, was sitting alone with a pale greenish coloured drink in front of her and smoking a cigarette in a long jade holder. She had that fine-drawn, intense look that is sometimes neurotic, sometimes sex-hungry, and sometimes just the result of drastic dieting.

I sat down two stools away and the barkeep nodded to me, but didn't smile.

'A gimlet,' I said. 'No bitters.'

He put the little napkin in front of me and kept looking at me. 'You know something,' he said in a pleased voice. 'I heard you and your friend talking one night and I got me in a bottle of that Rose's Lime Juice. Then you didn't come back any more and I only opened it tonight.'

'My friend left town,' I said. 'A double if it's all right with you. And thanks for taking the trouble.'

He went away. The woman in black gave me a quick glance, then looked down into her glass. 'So few people drink them around here,' she said so quietly that I didn't realize at first she was speaking to me. Then she looked my way again. She had very large dark eyes. She had the reddest fingernails I had ever seen. But she didn't look like a pick-up and there was no trace of come-on in her voice. 'Gimlets, I mean.'

'A fellow taught me to like them,' I said.

'He must be English.'

'Why?'

'The lime juice. It's as English as boiled fish with that awful anchovy sauce that looks as if the cook had bled into it. That's how they got called limeys. The English – not the fish.'

'I thought it was more a tropical drink, hot weather stuff. Malaya or some place like that.'

'You may be right.' She turned away again.

The bartender set the drink in front of me. With the lime juice it has a sort of pale greenish-yellowish, misty look. I tasted it. It was both sweet and sharp at the same time. The woman in black watched me. Then she lifted her own glass towards me. We both drank. Then I knew hers was the same drink.

The next move was routine, so I didn't make it. I just sat there. 'He wasn't English,' I said after a moment. 'I guess may-be he had been there during the war. We used to come in here once in a while, early like now. Before the mob started boiling.'

'It's a pleasant hour,' she said. 'In a bar almost the only pleasant hour.' She emptied her glass. 'Perhaps I knew your friend,' she said. 'What was his name?'

I didn't answer her right away. I lit a cigarette and watched her tap the stub of hers out of the jade holder and fit another in its place. I reached across with a lighter. 'Lennox,' I said.

She thanked me for the light and gave me a brief searching glance. Then she nodded. 'Yes, I knew him very well. Perhaps a little too well.'

The barkeep drifted over and glanced at my glass. 'A couple more of the same,' I said. 'In a booth.'

I got down off the stool and stood waiting. She might or might not blow me down. I didn't particularly care. Once in a while in this much too sex-conscious country a man and a woman can meet and talk without dragging bedrooms into it. This could be it, or she could just think I was on the make. If so, the hell with her.

She hesitated, but not for long. She gathered up a pair of black gloves and a black suede bag with a gold frame and clasp and walked across into a corner booth and sat down without a word. I sat down across the small table.

'My name is Marlowe.'

'Mine is Linda Loring,' she said calmly. 'A bit of a sentimentalist, aren't you, Mr Marlowe?'

'Because I came in here to drink a gimlet? How about yourself?'

'I might have a taste for them.'

'So might I. But it would be a little too much coincidence.'

She smiled at me vaguely. She had emerald earrings and an emerald lapel pin. They looked like real stones because of the way they were cut – flat with bevelled edges. And even in the dim light of a bar they had an inner glow.

'So you're the man,' she said.

The bar waiter brought the drinks over and sat them down. When he went away I said: 'I'm a fellow who knew Terry Lennox, liked him and had an occasional drink with him. It was kind of a side deal, an accidental friendship. I never went to his home or knew his wife. I saw her once in a parking lot.'

'There was a little more to it than that, wasn't there?'

She reached for her glass. She had an emerald ring set in a nest of diamonds. Beside it a thin platinum band said she was married. I put her in the second half of the thirties, early in the second half.

'Maybe,' I said. 'The guy bothered me. He still does. How about you?'

She leaned on an elbow and looked up at me without any

particular expression. 'I said I knew him rather too well. Too well to think it mattered much what happened to him. He had a rich wife who gave him all the luxuries. All she asked in return was to be left alone.'

'Seems reasonable,' I said.

'Don't be sarcastic, Mr Marlowe. Some women are like that. They can't help it. It wasn't as if he didn't know in the beginning. If he had to get proud, the door was open. He didn't have to kill her.'

'I agree with you.'

She straightened up and looked hard at me. Her lip curled. 'So he ran away and, if what I hear is true, you helped him. I suppose you feel proud about that.'

'Not me,' I said. 'I just did it for the money.'

'That is not amusing, Mr Marlowe. Frankly I don't know why I sit here drinking with you.'

'That's easily changed, Mrs Loring.' I reached for my glass and dropped the contents down the hatch. 'I thought perhaps you could tell me something about Terry that I didn't know. I'm not interested in speculating why Terry Lennox beat his wife's face to a bloody sponge.'

'That's a pretty brutal way to put it,' she said angrily.

'You don't like the words? Neither do I. And I wouldn't be here drinking a gimlet if I believed he did anything of the sort.'

She stared. After a moment she said slowly: 'He killed himself and left a full confession. What more do you want?'

'He had a gun,' I said. 'In Mexico that might be enough excuse for some jittery cop to pour lead into him. Plenty of American police have done their killings the same way – some of them through doors that didn't open fast enough to suit them. As for the confession, I haven't seen it.'

'No doubt the Mexican police faked it,' she said tartly.

'They wouldn't know how, not in a little place like Otatoclan. No, the confession is probably real enough, but it doesn't prove he killed his wife. Not to me anyway. All it proves to me is that he didn't see any way out. In a spot like that a certain sort of man – you can call him weak or soft or sentimental if it amuses you – might decide to save some other people from a lot of very painful publicity.'

'That's fantastic,' she said. 'A man doesn't kill himself or deliberately get himself killed to save a little scandal. Sylvia was already dead. As for her sister and her father – they could take care of themselves very efficiently. People with enough money,

318

Mr Marlowe, can always protect themselves.'

'Okay, I'm wrong about the motive. Maybe I'm wrong all down the line. A minute ago you were mad at me. You want me to leave now – so you can drink *your* gimlet?'

Suddenly she smiled. 'I'm sorry. I'm beginning to think you are sincere. What I thought then was that you were trying to justify yourself, for more than Terry. I don't think you are, somehow.'

'I'm not. I did something foolish and I got the works for it. Up to a point anyway. I don't deny that his confession saved me a lot worse. If they had brought him back and tried him, I guess they would have hung one on me too. The least it would have cost me would have been far more money than I could afford.'

'Not to mention your licence,' she said dryly.

'Maybe. There was a time when any cop with a hangover could get me busted. It's a little different now. You get a hearing before a commissioner of the state licensing authority. Those people are not too crazy about the city police.'

She tasted her drink and said slowly: 'All things considered, don't you think it was best the way it was? No trial, no sensational headlines, no mud-slinging just to sell newspapers without the slightest regard for truth or fair play or for the feelings of innocent people.'

'Didn't I just say so? And you said it was fantastic.'

She leaned back and put her head against the upper curve of the padding on the back of the booth. 'Fantastic that Terry Lennox should have killed himself just to achieve that. Not fantastic that it was better for all parties that there should be no trial.'

'I need another drink,' I said, and waved at the waiter. 'I feel an icy breath on the back of my neck. Could you by any chance be related to the Potter family, Mrs Loring?'

'Sylvia Lennox was my sister,' she said simply. 'I thought you would know.'

The waiter drifted over and I gave him an urgent message. Mrs Loring shook her head and said she didn't want anything more. When the waiter took off I said:

'With the hush old man Potter – excuse me, Mr Harlan Potter – put on this affair, I would be lucky to know for sure that Terry's wife even had a sister.'

'Surely you exaggerate. My father is hardly that powerful, Mr Marlowe – and certainly not that ruthless. I'll admit he does have very old-fashioned ideas about his personal privacy. He never gives interviews even to his own newspapers. He is never photographed, he never makes speeches, he travels mostly by car or in his own plane with his own crew. But he is quite human for all that. He liked Terry. He said Terry was a gentleman twenty-four hours a day instead of for the fifteen minutes between the time the guests arrive and the time they feel their first cocktail.'

'He slipped a little at the end. Terry did.'

The waiter trotted up with my third gimlet. I tried it for flavour and then sat there with a finger on the edge of the round base of the glass.

'Terry's death was quite a blow to him, Mr Marlowe. And you're getting sarcastic again. Please don't. Father knew it would all look far too neat to some people. He would much rather Terry had just disappeared. If Terry had asked him for help, I think he would have given it.'

'Oh no, Mrs Loring. His own daughter had been murdered.'

She made an irritable motion and eyed me coldly.

'This is going to sound pretty blunt, I'm afraid. Father had written my sister off long ago. When they met he barely spoke to her. If he expressed himself, which he hasn't and won't, I feel sure he would be just as doubtful about Terry as you are. But once Terry was dead, what did it matter? They could have been killed in a plane crash or a fire or a highway accident. If she had to die, it was the best possible time for her to die. In another ten years she would have been a sex-ridden hag like some of these frightful women you see at Hollywood parties, or used to a few years back. The dregs of the international set.'

All of a sudden I got mad, for no good reason. I stood up and looked over the booth. The next one was still empty. In the one beyond a guy was reading a paper all by himself, quietly. I sat down with a bump, pushed my glass out of the way and leaned across the table. I had sense enough to keep my voice down.

'For hell's sake, Mrs Loring, what are you trying to sell me? That Harlan Potter is such a sweet, lovely character he wouldn't dream of using his influence on a political D.A. to drop the blanket on a murder investigation so that the murder was never really investigated at all? That he had doubts about Terry's guilt but didn't let anyone lift a finger to find out who was really the killer? That he didn't use the political power of his newspapers and his bank account and the nine hundred guys who would trip over their chins trying to guess what he wanted done before he knew himself? That he didn't arrange it so that a tame lawyer and nobody else, nobody from the D.A.'s office or the city cops, went down to Mexico to make sure Terry actually had put a slug in his head instead of being knocked off by some Indian with a hot gun just for kicks? Your old man is worth a hundred million bucks, Mrs Loring. I wouldn't know just how he got it, but I know damn well he didn't get it without building himself a pretty far-reaching organization. He's no softie. He's a hard, tough man. You've got to be in these days to make that kind of money. And you do business with some funny people. You may not meet them or shake hands with them, but they are there on the fringe doing business with you.'

'You're a fool,' she said angrily. 'I've had enough of you.'

'Oh sure. I don't make the kind of music you like to hear. Let me tell you something. Terry talked to your old man the night Sylvia died. What about? What did your old man say to him? "Just run on down to Mexico and shoot yourself, old boy. Let's keep this in the family. I know my daughter is a tramp and that any one of a dozen drunken bastards might have blown his top and pushed her pretty face down her throat for her. But that's incidental, old boy. The guy will be sorry when he sobers up. You've had it soft and now is the time you pay back. What we want is to keep the fair Potter name as sweet as mountain lilac. She married you because she needed a front. She needs it worse than ever now she's dead. And you're it. If you can get lost and stay lost, fine. But if you get found, you check out. See you in the morgue." '

'Do you really think,' the woman in black asked with dry ice in her voice, 'that my father talks like that?'

I leaned back and laughed unpleasantly. 'We could polish up the dialogue a little if that helps.'

She gathered her stuff together and slid along the seat. 'I'd like to give you a word of warning,' she said slowly and very carefully, 'a very simple word of warning. If you think my father is that kind of man and if you go around broadcasting the kind of thoughts you have just expressed to me, your career in this city in your business or in any business is apt to be extremely short and terminated very suddenly.'

'Perfect, Mrs Loring. Perfect. I get it from the law, I get it from the hoodlum element, I get it from the carriage trade. The words change, but the meaning is the same. Lay off. I came in here to drink a gimlet because a man asked me to. Now look at me. I'm practically in the boneyard.'

She stood up and nodded briefly. 'Three gimlets. Doubles. Perhaps you're drunk.'

I dropped too much money on the table and stood up beside

her. 'You had one and a half, Mrs Loring. Why even that much? Did a man ask you too, or was it all your own idea? Your own tongue got a little loose.'

'Who knows, Mr Marlowe? Who knows? Who really knows anything? There's a man over there at the bar watching us. Would it be anyone you know?'

I looked around, surprised that she had noticed. A lean dark character sat on the end stool nearest the door.

'His name is Chick Agostino,' I said. 'He's a gun toter for a gambling boy named Menendez. Let's knock him down and jump on him.'

'You certainly are drunk,' she said quickly and started to walk. I went after her. The man on the stool swung around and looked to his front. When I came abreast I stepped up behind him and reached in under both his arms quickly. Maybe I *was* a little drunk.

He swung around angrily and slid off the stool. 'Watch it, kiddo,' he snarled. Out of the corner of my eye I saw that she had stopped just inside the door to glance back.

'No guns, Mr Agostino? How reckless of you. It's almost dark. What if you should run into a tough midget?'

'Scram!' he said savagely.

'Aw, you stole that line from the New Yorker.'

His mouth worked but he didn't move. I left him and followed Mrs Loring out through the door into the space under the awning. A grey-haired coloured chauffeur stood there talking to the kid from the parking lot. He touched his cap and went off and came back with a flossy Cadillac limousine. He opened the door and Mrs Loring got in. He shut the door as though he was putting down the lid of a jewel box. He went around the car to the driver's seat.

She ran the window down and looked out at me, half smiling. 'Good night, Mr Marlowe. It's been nice – or has it?'

'We had quite a fight.'

'You mean you had – and mostly with yourself.'

'It usually is. Good night, Mrs Loring. You don't live around here, do you?'

'Not exactly. I live in Idle Valley. At the far end of the lake. My husband is a doctor.'

'Would you happen to know any people named Wade?'

She frowned. 'Yes, I know the Wades. Why?'

'Why do I ask? They're the only people in Idle Valley that I know.'

322

'I see. Well, good night again, Mr Marlowe.'

She leaned back in the seat and the Cadillac purred politely and slid away into the traffic along the Strip.

Turning, I almost bumped into Chick Agostino.

'Who's the doll?' he sneered. 'And next time you crack wise, be missing.'

'Nobody that would want to know you,' I said.

'Okay, bright boy. I got the licence number. Mendy likes to know little things like that.'

The door of a car banged open and a man about seven feet high and four feet wide jumped out of it, took one look at Agostino, then one long stride, and grabbed him by the throat with one hand.

'How many times I gotta tell you cheap hoods not to hang around where I eat?' he roared.

He shook Agostino and hurled him across the sidewalk against the wall. Chick crumpled up, coughing.

'Next time,' the enormous man yelled, 'I sure as hell put the blast on you, and believe me, boy, you'll be holding a gun when they pick you up.'

Chick shook his head and said nothing. The big man gave me a raking glance and grinned. 'Nice night,' he said and strolled into Victor's.

I watched Chick straighten himself out and regain some of his composure. 'Who's your buddy?' I asked him.

'Big Willie Magoon,' he said thickly. 'A vice squad bimbo. He thinks he's tough.'

'You mean he isn't sure?' I asked him politely.

He looked at me emptily and walked away. I got my car out of the lot and drove home. In Hollywood anything can happen, anything at all.


# Twenty-three


A low-slung Jaguar swept around the hill in front of me and slowed down so as not to bathe me in the granite dust from the half-mile of neglected paving at the entrance to Idle Valley. It seemed they wanted it left that way to discourage the Sunday drivers spoilt by drifting along on super-highways. I caught a glimpse of a bright scarf and a pair of sun goggles. A hand waved at me casually, neighbour to neighbour. Then the dust slid across the road and added itself to the white film already well spread over the scrub and the sunbaked grass. Then I was around the outcrop and the paving started up in proper shape and everything was smooth and cared for. Live oaks clustered towards the road, as if they were curious to see who went by, and sparrows with rosy heads hopped about pecking at things only a sparrow would think worth pecking at.

Then there were a few cottonwoods but no eucalyptus. Then a thick growth of Carolina poplars screening a white house. Then a girl walking a horse along the shoulder of the road. She had trousers on and a loud shirt and she was chewing on a twig. The horse looked hot but not lathered and the girl was crooning to him gently. Beyond a fieldstone wall a gardener was guiding a power lawn mower over a huge undulating lawn that ended far back in the portico of a Williamsburg Colonial mansion, the large *de luxe* size. Somewhere someone was playing left-handed exercises on a grand piano.

Then all this wheeled away and the glisten of the lake showed hot and bright and I began to watch numbers on gate-posts. I had seen the Wades' house only once and in the dark. It wasn't as big as it had looked by night. The driveway was full of cars, so I parked on the side of the road and walked in. A Mexican butler in a white coat opened the door for me. He was a slender, neat, good-looking Mexican and his coat fitted him elegantly and he looked like a Mexican who was getting fifty a week and not killing himself with hard work.

He said: '*Buenas tardes, señor,*' and grinned as if he had put one over. '*Su nombre de usted, por favor?*'

'Marlowe,' I said, 'and who are you trying to upstage, Candy? We talked on the phone, remember?'

He grinned and I went in. It was the same old cocktail party, everybody talking too loud, nobody listening, everybody hanging on for dear life to a mug of the juice, eyes very bright, cheeks flushed or pale and sweaty according to the amount of alcohol consumed and the capacity of the individual to handle it. Then Eileen Wade materialized beside me in a pale blue something which did her no harm. She had a glass in her hand but it didn't look as if it was more than a prop.

'I'm so glad you could come,' she said gravely. 'Roger wants to see you in his study. He hates cocktail parties. He's working.'

'With this racket going on?'

'It never seems to bother him. Candy will get you a drink – or if you'd rather go to the bar—'

324

'I'll do that,' I said. 'Sorry about the other night.'

She smiled. 'I think you apologized already. It was nothing.'

'The hell it was nothing.'

She kept the smile long enough to nod and turn and walk away. I spotted the bar over in the corner by some very large french doors. It was one of those things you push around. I was half-way across the room, trying not to bump anybody, when a voice said: 'Oh, Mr Marlowe.'

I turned and saw Mrs Loring on a couch beside a prissy-looking man in rimless cheaters with a smear on his chin that might have been a goatee. She had a drink in her hand and looked bored. He sat still with his arms folded and scowled.

I went over there. She smiled at me and gave me her hand. 'This is my husband, Dr Loring. Mr Philip Marlowe, Edward.'

The guy with the goatee gave me a brief look and a still briefer nod. He didn't move otherwise. He seemed to be saving his energy for better things.

'Edward is very tired,' Linda Loring said. 'Edward is always very tired.'

'Doctors often are,' I said. 'Can I get you a drink, Mrs Loring. Or you, Doctor?'

'She's had enough,' the man said without looking at either of us. 'I don't drink. The more I see of people who do, the more glad I am that I don't.'

'Come back, little Sheba,' Mrs Loring said dreamily.

He swung around and did a take. I got away from there and made it to the bar. In the company of her husband Linda Loring seemed like a different person. There was an edge to her voice and a sneer in her expression which she hadn't used on me even when she was angry.

Candy was behind the bar. He asked me what I would drink.

'Nothing right now, thanks. Mr Wade wants to see me.'

'*Es muy occupado, Señor.* Very busy.'

I didn't think I was going to like Candy. When I just looked at him he added: 'But I go see. *De pronto, Señor.*'

He threaded his way delicately through the mob and was back in no time at all. 'Okay, chum, let's go,' he said cheerfully.

I followed him across the room the long way of the house. He opened a door, I went through, he shut it behind me, and a lot of the noise was dimmed. It was a corner room, big and cool and quiet, with french doors and roses outside and an air-conditioner set in a window to one side. I could see the lake, and I could see Wade lying flat out on a long, blond leather couch. A big bleached wood desk had a typewriter on it and there was a pile of yellow paper beside the typewriter.

'Good of you to come, Marlowe,' he said lazily. 'Park yourself. Did you have a drink or two?'

'Not yet.' I sat down and looked at him. He still looked a bit pale and pinched. 'How's the work going?'

'Fine, except that I get tired too quick. Pity a four-day drunk is so painful to get over. I often do my best work after one. In my racket it's so easy to tighten up and get all stiff and wooden. Then the stuff is no good. When it's good it comes easy. Anything you have read or heard to the contrary is a lot of mish-mash.'

'Depends who the writer is, maybe,' I said. 'It didn't come easy to Flaubert, and his stuff is good.'

'Okay,' Wade said, sitting up. 'So you have read Flaubert, so that makes you an intellectual, a critic, a savant of the literary world.' He rubbed his forehead. 'I'm on the wagon and I hate it. I hate everybody with a drink in his hand. I've got to go out there and smile at those creeps. Every damn one of them knows I'm an alcoholic. So they wonder what I'm running away from. Some Freudian bastard has made that a commonplace. Every ten-year-old knows it by now. If I had a ten-year-old kid, which God forbid, the brat would be asking me, "What are you running away from when you get drunk, daddy?"'

'The way I got it, all this was rather recent,' I said.

'It's got worse, but I was always a hard man with a bottle. When you're young and in hard condition you can absorb a lot of punishment. When you are pushing forty you don't snap back the same way.'

I leaned back and lit a cigarette. 'What did you want to see me about?'

'What do *you* think I'm running away from, Marlowe?'

'No idea. I don't have enough information. Besides, everybody is running away from something.'

'Not everybody gets drunk. What are *you* running away from? Your youth or a guilty conscience or the knowledge that you're a small-time operator in a small-time business?'

'I get it,' I said. 'You need somebody to insult. Fire away, chum. When it begins to hurt I'll let you know.'

He grinned and rumpled his thick curly hair. He speared his chest with a forefinger. 'You're looking right at a small-time operator in a small-time business, Marlowe. All writers are punks and I am one of the punkest. I've written twelve best-sellers, and if I ever finish that stack of magoozlum on the desk there I may possibly have written thirteen. And not a damn one of them worth the powder to blow it to hell. I have a lovely home in a highly restricted residential neighbourhood that belongs to a highly restricted multimillionaire. I have a lovely wife who loves me and a lovely publisher who loves me and I love me the best of all. I'm an egotistical son of a bitch, a literary prostitute or pimp – choose your own word – and an all-round heel. So what can you do for me?'

'Well, what?'

'Why don't you get sore?'

'Nothing to get sore about. I'm just listening to you hate yourself. It's boring but it doesn't hurt my feelings.'

He laughed roughly. 'I like you,' he said. 'Let's have a drink.'

'Not in here, chum. Not you and me alone. I don't care to watch you take the first one. Nobody can stop you and I don't guess anyone would try. But I don't have to help.'

He stood up. 'We don't have to drink in here. Let's go outside and glance at a choice selection of the sort of people you get to know when you make enough lousy money to live where they live.'

'Look,' I said. 'Shove it. Knock it off. They're no different from anybody else.'

'Yeah,' he said tightly, 'but they ought to be. If they're not, what use are they? They're the class of the county and they're no better than a bunch of truckdrivers full of cheap whisky. Not as good.'

'Knock it off,' I said again. 'You want to get boiled, get boiled. But don't take it out on a crowd that can get boiled without having to lie up with Dr Verringer or get loose in the head and throw their wives down the stairs.'

'Yeah,' he said, and he was suddenly calm and thoughtful. 'You pass the test, chum. How about coming to live here for a while? You could do me a lot of good just being here.'

'I don't see how.'

'But I do. Just by being here. Would a thousand a month interest you? I'm dangerous when I'm drunk. I don't want to be dangerous and I don't want to be drunk.'

'I couldn't stop you.'

'Try it for three months. I'd finish the damn book and then go far off for a while. Lie up some place in the Swiss mountains and get clean.'

'The book, huh? Do you have to have the money?'

'No. I just have to finish something I started. If I don't I'm through. I'm asking you as a friend. You did more than that for Lennox.'

I stood up and walked over close to him and gave him a hard stare. 'I got Lennox killed, mister. I got him killed.'

'Phooey. Don't go soft on me, Marlowe.' He put the edge of his hand against his throat. 'I'm up to here in the soft babies.'

'Soft?' I asked. 'Or just kind?'

He stepped back and stumbled against the edge of the couch, but didn't lose his balance.

'The hell with you,' he said smoothly. 'No deal. I don't blame you, of course. There's something I want to know, that I have to know. You don't know what it is and I'm not sure I know myself. All I'm positive of is that there *is* something, and I have to know it.'

'About who? Your wife?'

He moved his lips one over the other. 'I think it's about me,' he said. 'Let's go get that drink.'

He walked to the door and threw it open and we went out.

If he had been trying to make me uncomfortable, he had done a first-class job.

# Twenty-four

When he opened the door the buzz from the living-room exploded into our faces. It seemed louder than before, if possible. About two drinks louder. Wade said hello here and there and people seemed glad to see him. But by that time they would have been glad to see Pittsburgh Phil with his custom-built ice-pick. Life was just one great big vaudeville show.

On the way to the bar we came face to face with Dr Loring and his wife. The doctor stood up and stepped forward to face Wade. He had a look on his face that was almost sick with hatred.

'Nice to see you, Doctor,' Wade said amiably. 'Hi, Linda. Where have you been keeping yourself lately? No, I guess that was a stupid question. I—'

'Mr Wade,' Loring said in a voice that had a tremor to it, 'I have something to stay to you. Something very simple, and I hope very conclusive. Stay away from my wife.'

Wade looked at him curiously. 'Doctor, you're tired. And you don't have a drink. Let me get you one.'

'I don't drink, Mr Wade. As you very well know. I am here for one purpose and I have expressed that purpose.'

'Well, I guess I get your point,' Wade said, still amiable. 'And since you are a guest in my house, I have nothing to say except that I think you are a little off the beam.'

There had been a drop in the talk near by. The boys and girls were all ears. Big production. Dr Loring took a pair of gloves out of his pocket, straightened them, took hold of one by the finger and swung it hard against Wade's face.

Wade didn't bat an eye. 'Pistols and coffee at dawn?' he asked quietly.

I looked at Linda Loring. She was flushed with anger. She stood up slowly and faced the doctor.

'Dear God, what a ham you are, darling. Stop acting like a damn fool, will you, darling? Or would you rather stick around until somebody slaps *your* face?'

Loring swung around to her and raised the gloves. Wade stepped in front of him. 'Take it easy, Doc. Around here we only hit our wives in private.'

'If you are speaking for yourself, I am well aware of it,' Loring sneered. 'And I don't need lessons in manners from you.'

'I only take promising pupils,' Wade said. 'Sorry you have to leave so soon.' He raised his voice. 'Candy! *Que el Doctor Loring salga de aqui en el acto!*' He swung back to Loring. 'In case you don't know Spanish, Doctor, that means the door is over there.' He pointed.

Loring stared at him without moving. 'I have warned you, Mr Wade,' he said icily. 'And a number of people have heard me. I shall not warn you again.'

'Don't,' Wade said curtly. 'But if you do, make it on neutral territory. Gives me a little more freedom of action. Sorry, Linda. But you married him.' He rubbed his cheek gently where the heavy end of the glove had hit him. Linda Loring was smiling bitterly. She shrugged.

'We are leaving,' Loring said. 'Come, Linda.'

She sat down again and reached for her glass. She gave her husband a glance of quiet contempt. 'You are,' she said. 'You have a number of calls to make, remember.'

'You are leaving with me,' he said furiously.

She turned her back on him. He reached suddenly and took hold of her arm. Wade took him by the shoulder and spun him round.

'Take it easy, Doc. You can't win them all.'

'Take your hand off me!'

'Sure, just relax,' Wade said. 'I have a good idea, Doctor. Why don't you see a good doctor?'

Somebody laughed loudly. Loring tensed like an animal all set to spring. Wade sensed it and neatly turned his back and moved away. Which left Dr Loring holding the bag. If he went after Wade, he would look sillier than he looked now. There was nothing for him to do but leave, and he did it. He marched quickly across the room staring straight in front of him to where Candy was holding the door open. He went out. Candy shut the door, wooden-faced, and went back to the bar. I went over there and asked for some Scotch. I didn't see where Wade went. He just disappeared. I didn't see Eileen either. I turned my back on the room and let them sizzle while I drank my Scotch.

A small girl with mud-coloured hair and a band round her forehead popped up beside me and put a glass on the bar and bleated. Candy nodded and made her another drink.

The small girl turned to me. 'Are you interested in Communism?' she asked me. She was glassy-eyed and she was running a small red tongue along her lips as if looking for a crumb of chocolate. 'I think everyone ought to be,' she went on. 'But when you ask any of the men here they just want to paw you.'

I nodded and looked over my glass at her snub nose and sun-coarsened skin.

'Not that I mind too much if it's done nicely,' she told me, reaching for the fresh drink. She showed me her molars while she inhaled half of it.

'Don't rely on me,' I said.

'What's your name?'

'Marlowe.'

'With an "e" or not?'

'With.'

'Ah, Marlowe,' she intoned. 'Such a sad beautiful name.' She put her glass down damn nearly empty and closed her eyes and threw her head back and her arms out, almost hitting me in the eye. Her voice throbbed with emotion, saying:

*Was this the face that launch'd a thousand ships*
*And burnt the topless towers of Ilium?*
*Sweet Helen, make me immortal with a kiss.*

She opened her eyes, grabbed her glass and winked at me. 'You were pretty good in there, chum. Been writing any poetry lately?'

'Not very much.'

'You can kiss me if you like,' she said coyly.

A guy in a shantung jacket and an open-neck shirt came up behind her and grinned at me over the top of her head. He had short red hair and a face like a collapsed lung. He was as ugly a guy as I ever saw. He patted the top of the little girl's head.

'Come on, Kitten. Time to go home.'

She rounded on him furiously. 'You mean you got to water those goddamned tuberous begonias again?' she yelled.

'Aw listen, kitten—'

'Take your hands off me, you goddamned rapist,' she screamed and threw the rest of her drink in his face. The rest wasn't more than a teaspoonful and two lumps of ice.

'For Chrissake, baby, I'm your husband,' he yelled back, grabbing for a handkerchief and mopping his face. 'Get it? Your husband.'

She sobbed violently and threw herself into his arms. I stepped around them and got out of there. Every cocktail party is the same, even the dialogue.

The house was leaking guests out into the evening air now. Voices were fading, cars were starting, good-byes were bouncing around like rubber balls. I went to the french windows and out on to a flagged terrace. The ground sloped towards the lake which was as motionless as a sleeping cat. There was a short wooden pier down there with a rowboat tied to it by a white painter. Towards the far shore, which wasn't very far, a black water hen was doing lazy curves, like a skater. They didn't seem to cause as much as a shallow ripple.

I stretched out on a padded aluminium chaise and lit a pipe and smoked peacefully and wondered what the hell I was doing there. Roger Wade seemed to have enough control to handle himself if he really wanted to. He had done all right with Loring. I wouldn't have been too surprised if he had hung one on Loring's sharp little chin. He would have been out of line by the rules, but Loring was much farther out of line.

If the rules mean anything at all any more, they mean that you don't pick a roomful of people as the spot to threaten a man and hit him across the face with a glove when your wife is standing right beside you and you are practically accusing her of a little double time. For a man still shaky from a hard bout with the hard stuff Wade had done all right. He had done more than all right. Of course I hadn't seen him drunk. I didn't know what he would be like drunk. I didn't even know that he was an alcoholic. There's a big difference. A man who drinks too much on occasion is still the same man as he was sober. An alcoholic, a real alcoholic, is not the same man at all. You can't predict anything about him for sure except that he will be someone you never met before.

Light steps sounded behind me and Eileen Wade came across the terrace and sat down beside me on the edge of a chaise.

'Well, what did you think?' she asked quietly.

'About the gentleman with the loose gloves?'

'Oh no.' She frowned. Then she laughed. 'I hate people who make stagey scenes like that. Not that he isn't a fine doctor. He has played that scene with half the men in the valley. Linda Loring is no tramp. She doesn't look like one, talk like one, or behave like one. I don't know what makes Dr Loring behave as if she was.'

'Maybe he's a reformed drunk,' I said. 'A lot of them grow pretty puritanical.'

'It's possible,' she said, and looked towards the lake. 'This is a very peaceful place. One would think a writer would be happy here – if a writer is ever happy anywhere.' She turned to look at me. 'So you won't be persuaded to do what Roger asked.'

'There's no point in it, Mrs Wade. Nothing I could do. I've said all this before. I couldn't be sure of being around at the right time. I'd have to be around *all* the time. That's impossible, even if I had nothing else to do. If he went wild, for example, it would happen in a flash. And I haven't seen any indication that he does get wild. He seems pretty solid to me.'

She looked down at her hands. 'If he could finish his book, I think things would be much better.'

'I can't help him do that.'

She looked up and put her hands on the edge of the chaise beside her. She leaned forward a little. 'You can if he thinks you can. That's the whole point. Is it that you would find it distasteful to be a guest in our house and be paid for it?'

'He needs a psychiatrist, Mrs Wade. If you know one that isn't a quack.'

She looked startled. 'A psychiatrist? Why?'

I knocked the ashes out of my pipe and sat holding it, waiting for the bowl to get cooler before I put it away.

'You want an amateur opinion, here it is. He thinks he has a secret buried in his mind and he can't get at it. It may be a guilty secret about himself, it may be about someone else. He thinks that's what makes him drink, because he can't get at this thing. He probably thinks that whatever happened, happened while he was drunk and he ought to find it wherever people go when they're drunk – really bad drunk, the way he gets. That's a job for a psychiatrist. So far, so good. If that is wrong, then he gets drunk because he wants to or can't help it, and the idea about the secret is just his excuse. He can't write his book, or anyway can't finish it. Because he gets drunk. That is, the assumption seems to be that he can't finish his book because he knocks himself out by drinking. It could be the other way around.'

'Oh no,' she said. 'No. Roger has a great deal of talent. I feel quite sure that his best work is still to come.'

'I told you it was an amateur opinion. You said the other morning that he might have fallen out of love with his wife. That's something else that could go the other way around.'

She looked towards the house, then turned so that she had her back to it. I looked the same way. Wade was standing inside the doors, looking out at us. As I watched he moved behind the bar and reached for a bottle.

'There's no use interfering,' she said quickly. 'I never do. Never. I suppose you're right, Mr Marlowe. There just isn't anything to do but let him work it out of his system.'

The pipe was cool now and I put it away. 'Since we're groping around in the back of the drawer, how about that other way around?'

'I love my husband,' she said simply. 'Not as a young girl loves, perhaps. But I love him. A woman is only a young girl once. The man I loved then is dead. He died in the war. His name, strangely enough, had the same initials as yours. It doesn't matter now – except that sometimes I can't quite believe that he is dead. His body was never found. But that happened to many men.'

She gave me a searching look. 'Sometimes – not often, of course – when I go into a quiet cocktail lounge or the lobby of a good hotel at a dead hour, or along the deck of a liner early in the morning or very late at night, I think I may see him waiting for me in some shadowy corner.' She paused and dropped her eyes. 'It's very silly. I'm ashamed of it. We were very much in love – the wild, mysterious, improbable kind of love that never comes but once.'

She stopped talking and sat there half in a trance looking out over the lake. I looked back at the house again. Wade was standing just inside the open french doors with a glass in his hand. I looked back at Eileen. For her I wasn't there any more. I got up and went into the house. Wade stood there with the drink and the drink looked pretty heavy. And his eyes looked wrong.

'How you making out with my wife, Marlowe?' It was said with a twist of the mouth.

'No passes, if you mean it that way.'

'That's exactly the way I mean it. You got to kiss her the other night. Probably fancy yourself as a fast worker, but you're wasting your time, bud. Even if you had the right kind of polish.'

I tried to move around him but he blocked me with a solid shoulder. 'Don't hurry away, old man. We like you around. We get so few private dicks in our house.'

'I'm the one too many,' I said.

He hoisted the glass and drank from it. When he lowered it he leered at me.

'You ought to give yourself a little more time to build resistance,' I told him. 'Empty words, huh?'

'Okay, coach. Some little character builder, aren't you? You ought to have more sense than to try educating a drunk. Drunks don't educate, my friend. They disintegrate. And part of the process is a lot of fun.' He drank from the glass again, leaving it nearly empty. 'And part of it is damned awful. But if I may quote the scintillating words of the good Dr Loring, a bastardly bastard with a little black bag, stay away from my wife, Marlowe. Sure you go for her. They all do. You'd like to sleep with her. They all would. You'd like to share her dreams and sniff the rose of her memories. Maybe I would too. But there is nothing to share, chum – nothing, nothing, nothing. You're all alone in the dark.'

He finished his drink and turned the glass upside-down.

'Empty like that, Marlowe. Nothing there at all. I'm the guy that knows.'

He put the glass on the edge of the bar and walked stiffly to the foot of the stairs. He made about a dozen steps up, holding on to the rail, and stopped and leaned against it. He looked down at me with a sour grin.

'Forgive the corny sarcasm, Marlowe. You're a nice guy. I wouldn't want anything to happen to you.'

'Anything like what?'

'Perhaps she didn't get around yet to that haunting magic of her first love, the guy that went missing in Norway. You wouldn't want to be missing, would you, chum? You're my own special private eye. You find me when I'm lost in the savage splendour of Sepulveda Canyon.' He moved the palm of his hand in a circular motion on the polished wood banister. 'It would hurt me to the quick if you got lost yourself. Like that character who hitched up with the limeys. He got so lost a man sometimes wonders if he ever existed. You figure she could have maybe just invented him to have a toy to play with?'

'How would I know?'

He looked down at me. There were deep lines between his eyes now and his mouth was twisted with bitterness.

'How would anybody know? Maybe she don't know herself. Baby's tired. Baby been playing too long with broken toys. Baby wants to go bye-bye.'

He went on up the stairs. I stood there until Candy came in and started tidying up around the bar, putting glasses on a tray, examining bottles to see what was left, paying no attention to me. Or so I thought. Then he said:

'*Señor*. One good drink left. Pity to waste him.' He held up a bottle.

'You drink it.'

'*Gracias, señor, no me gusta. Un vaso de cerveza, no más.* A glass of beer is my limit.'

'Wise man.'

'One lush in the house is enough,' he said, staring at me. 'I speak good English, not?'

'Sure, fine.'

'But I think Spanish. Sometimes I think with a knife. The boss is my guy. He don't need any help, hombre. I take care of him, see.'

'A great job you're doing, punk.'

'*Hijo de la flauta*,' he said between his white teeth. He picked up a loaded tray and swung it up on the edge of his shoulder and the flat of his hand, bus boy style.

I walked to the door and let myself out, wondering how an expression meaning 'son of a flute' had come to be an insult in Spanish. I didn't wonder very long. I had too many other things to wonder about. Something more than alcohol was the matter with the Wade family. Alcohol was no more than a disguised reaction.

Later that night, between nine-thirty and ten, I called the Wades' number. After eight rings I hung up, but I had only just taken my hand off the instrument when it started to ring me. It was Eileen Wade.

'Someone just rang here,' she said. 'I had a sort of hunch it might be you. I was just getting ready to take a shower.'

'It was me, but it wasn't important, Mrs Wade. He seemed a little woolly-headed when I left – Roger did. I guess maybe I feel a little responsibility for him by now.'

'He's quite all right,' she said. 'Fast asleep in bed. I think Dr Loring upset him more than he showed. No doubt he talked a lot of nonsense to you.'

'He said he was tired and wanted to go to bed. Pretty sensible, I thought.'

'If that is all he said, yes. Well, good night and thank you for calling, Mr Marlowe.'

'I didn't say it was all he said. I said he said it.'

There was a pause, then: 'Everyone gets fantastic ideas once in a while. Don't take Roger too seriously, Mr Marlowe. After all his imagination is rather highly developed. Naturally it would be. He shouldn't have had anything to drink so soon after the last time. Please try to forget all about it. I suppose he was rude to you among other things.'

'He wasn't rude to me. He made quite a lot of sense. Your husband is a guy who can take a long, hard look at himself and see what is there. It's not a very common gift. Most people go through life using up half their energy trying to protect· a dignity they never had. Good night, Mrs Wade.'

She hung up and I set out the chess board. I filled a pipe, paraded the chessmen and inspected them for French shaves and loose buttons, and played a championship tournament game between Gortchakoff and Meninkin, seventy-two moves to a draw, a prize specimen of the irresistible force meeting the immovable object, a battle without armour, a war without blood, and as elaborate a waste of human intelligence as you could find anywhere outside an advertising agency.

# Twenty-five

Nothing happened for a week except that I went about my business which just then didn't happen to be very much business. One morning George Peters of The Carne Organization called me up and told me he had happened to be down Sepulveda Canyon way and had looked in on Dr Verringer's place just out of curiosity. But Dr Verringer was no longer there. Half a dozen teams of surveyors were mapping the tract for a subdivision. Those he spoke to had never even heard of Dr Verringer.

'The poor sucker got closed out on a trust deed,' Peters said. 'I checked. They gave him a grand for a quit claim just to save time and expense, and now somebody is going to make a million bucks a year, out of cutting the place up for residential property. That's the difference between crime and business. For business you gotta have capital. Sometimes I think it's the only difference.'

'A properly cynical remark,' I said, 'but big-time crime takes capital too.'

'And where does it come from, chum? Not from guys that hold up liquor stores. So long. See you soon.'

It was ten minutes to eleven on a Thursday night when Wade called me up. His voice was thick, almost gurgling, but I recognized it somehow. And I could hear short, hard, rapid breathing over the telephone.

'I'm in bad shape, Marlowe. Very bad. I'm slipping my anchor. Could you make it out here in a hurry?'

'Sure – but let me talk to Mrs Wade a minute.'

He didn't answer. There was a crashing sound, then a dead silence, then in a short while a kind of banging around. I yelled something into the phone without getting any answer. Time passed. Finally the light click of the receiver being replaced and the buzz of an open line.

In five minutes I was on the way. I made it in slightly over half an hour and I still don't know how. I went over the pass on wings and hit Ventura Boulevard with the light against me and made a left turn anyhow and dodged between trucks and generally made a damn fool of myself. I went through Encino at close to sixty with a spotlight on the outer edge of the parked cars so that it would freeze anyone with a notion to step out suddenly. I had the kind of luck you only get when you don't care. No cops, no sirens, no red flashers. Just visions of what might be happening in the Wade residence and not very pleasant visions. She was alone in the house with a drunken maniac, she was lying at the bottom of the stairs with her neck broken, she was behind a locked door and somebody was howling outside and trying to break it in, she was running down a moonlit road barefoot and a big buck Negro with a meat cleaver was chasing her.

It wasn't like that at all. When I swung the Olds into their driveway lights were on all over the house and she was standing in the open doorway with a cigarette in her mouth. I got out and walked over the flagstones to her. She had slacks on and a shirt with an open collar. She looked at me calmly. If there was any excitement around there I had brought it with me.

The first thing I said was as loony as the rest of my behaviour. 'I thought you didn't smoke.'

'What? No, I don't usually.' She took the cigarette out and dropped it and stepped on it. 'Once in a long while. He called Dr Verringer.'

It was a remote placid voice, a voice heard at night over water. Completely relaxed.

'He couldn't,' I said. 'Dr Verringer doesn't live there any more. He called me.'

'Oh really? I just heard him telephoning and asking someone to come in a hurry. I thought it must be Dr Verringer.'

'Where is he now?'

'He fell down,' she said. 'He must have tipped the chair too far back. He's done it before. He cut his head on something. There's a little blood, not much.'

'Well, that's fine,' I said. 'We wouldn't want a whole lot of blood. Where is he now, I asked you.'

She looked at me solemnly. Then she pointed. 'Out there somewhere. By the edge of the road or in the bushes along the fence.'

I leaned forward and peered at her. 'Chrissake, didn't you look?' I decided by this time that she was in shock. Then I looked back across the lawn. I didn't see anything but there was heavy shadow near the fence.

'No, I didn't look,' she said quite calmly. 'You find him. I've had all of it I can take. I've had more than I can take. You find him.'

She turned and walked back into the house, leaving the door open. She didn't walk very far. About a yard inside the door she just crumpled to the floor and lay there. I scooped her up and spread her out on one of the two big davenports that faced each other across a long, blond cocktail table. I felt her pulse. It didn't seem very weak or unsteady. Her eyes were closed and the lids were blue. I left her there and went back out.

He was there all right, just as she had said. He was lying on his side in the shadow of the hibiscus. He had a fast, thumping pulse and his breathing was unnatural. Something on the back of his head was sticky. I spoke to him and shook him a little. I slapped his face a couple of times. He mumbled but didn't come to. I dragged him up into a sitting position and dragged one of his arms over my shoulder and heaved him up with my back turned to him and grabbed for a leg. I lost. He was as heavy as a block of cement. We both sat down on the grass and I took a short breather and tried again. Finally I got him hoisted into a fireman's lift position and ploughed across the lawn in the direction of the open front door. It seemed about the same distance as a round trip to Siam. The two steps of the porch were ten feet high. I staggered over to the couch and went down on my knees and rolled him off. When I straightened up again my spine felt as if it was cracked in at least three places.

Eileen Wade wasn't there any more. I had the room to myself. I was too bushed at the moment to care where anybody was. I sat down and looked at him and waited for some breath. Then I looked at his head. It was smeared with blood. His hair was sticky with it. It didn't look very bad but you never know with a head wound.

Then Eileen Wade was standing beside me, quietly looking down at him with that same remote expression.

'I'm sorry I fainted,' she said. 'I don't know why.'

'I guess we'd better call a doctor.'

'I telephoned Dr Loring. He is my doctor, you know. He didn't want to come.'

'Try somebody else then.'

'Oh, he's coming,' she said. 'He didn't want to. But he's coming as soon as he can manage.'

'Where's Candy?'

'This is his day off. Thursday. The cook and Candy have Thursdays off. It's the usual thing around here. Can you get him up to bed?'

'Not without help. Better get a rug or blanket. It's a warm night, but cases like this get pneumonia very easily.'

She said she would get a rug. I thought it was damn nice of her. But I wasn't thinking very intelligently. I was too bushed from carrying him.

We spread a streamer rug over him and in fifteen minutes Dr Loring came, complete with starched collar and rimless cheaters and the expression of a man who has been asked to clean up after the dog got sick.

He examined Wade's head. 'A superficial cut and bruises,' he said. 'No chance of concussion. I should say his breath would indicate his condition rather obviously.'

He reached for his hat. He picked up his bag.

'Keep him warm,' he said. 'You might bathe his head gently and get rid of the blood. He'll sleep it off.'

'I can't get him upstairs alone, Doctor,' I said.

'Then leave him where he is.' He looked at me without interest. 'Good night, Mrs Wade. As you know, I don't treat alcoholics. Even if I did, your husband would not be one of my patients. I'm sure you understand that.'

'Nobody's asking you to treat him,' I said. 'I'm asking for some help to get him into his bedroom so that I can undress him.'

'And just who are you?' Dr Loring asked me freezingly.

'My name's Marlowe. I was here a week ago. Your wife introduced me.'

'Interesting,' he said. 'In what connection do you know my wife?'

'What the hell does that matter? All I want is—'

'I'm not interested in what you want,' he cut in on me. He turned to Eileen, nodded briefly, and started out. I got between him and the door and put my back to it.

'Just a minute, Doc. Must be a long time since you glanced at that little piece of prose called the Hippocratic Oath. This man called me on the phone and I live some way off. He sounded bad and I broke every traffic law in the state getting over here. I found him lying out on the ground and I carried him in here and believe me he isn't any bunch of feathers. The houseboy is away and there's nobody here to help me upstairs with Wade. How does it look to you?'

'Get out of my way,' he said between his teeth. 'Or I shall call the sheriff's sub-station and have them send over a deputy. As a professional man—'

'As a professional man you're a handful of flea dirt,' I said, and moved out of his way.

He turned red – slowly but distinctly. He choked on his own bile. Then he opened the door and went out. He shut it carefully. As he pulled it shut he looked in at me. It was as nasty a look as I ever got and as nasty a face as I ever saw.

When I turned away from the door Eileen was smiling.

'What's funny?' I snarled.

'You. You don't care what you say to people, do you? Don't you know who Dr Loring is?'

'Yeah – and I know what he is.'

She glanced at her wristwatch. 'Candy ought to be home

by now,' she said. 'I'll go and see. He has a room behind the garage.'

She went out through an archway and I sat down and looked at Wade. The great big writer man went on snoring. His face was sweaty but I left the rug over him. In a minute or two Eileen came back and she had Candy with her.

## Twenty-six

The Mex had on a black and white checked sport shirt, heavily pleated black slacks without a belt, two-tone black and white buckskin shoes, spotlessly clean. His thick black hair was brushed straight back and shining with some kind of hair oil or cream.

'*Señor*,' he said, and sketched a brief, sarcastic bow.

'Help Mr Marlowe carry my husband upstairs, Candy. He fell and hurt himself a little. I'm sorry to trouble you.'

'*De nada, señora*,' Candy said, smiling.

'I think I'll say good night,' she said to me. 'I'm tired out. Candy will get you anything you want.'

She went slowly up the stairs. Candy and I watched her.

'Some doll,' he said confidently. 'You stay the night?'

'Hardly.'

'*Es lástima*. She is very lonely, that one.'

'Get that gleam out of your eye, kid. Let's put this to bed.'

He looked sadly at Wade snoring on the couch. '*Pobrecito*,' he murmured as if he meant it. '*Borracho como una cuba*.'

'He may be drunk but he sure ain't little,' I said. 'You take the feet.'

We carried him and even for two he was as heavy as a lead coffin. At the top of the stairs we went along an open balcony past a closed door. Candy pointed to it with his chin.

'*La señora*,' he whispered. 'You knock very light maybe she let you in.'

I didn't say anything because I needed him. We went on with the carcass and turned in at another door and dumped him on the bed. Then I took hold of Candy's arm high up near the shoulder where dug-in fingers can hurt. I made mine hurt him. He winced a little and then his face set hard.

'What's your name, *cholo*?'

341

'Take your hand off me,' he snapped. 'And don't call me a *cholo*. I'm no wetback. My name is Juan Garcia de Soto y Soto-mayor. I am Chileno.'

'Okay, Don Juan. Just don't get out of line around here. Keep your nose and mouth clean when you talk about the people you work for.'

He jerked loose and stepped back, his black eyes hot with anger. His hand slipped inside his shirt and came out with a long thin knife. He balanced it by the point on the heel of his hand, hardly even glancing at it. Then he dropped the hand and caught the handle of the knife while it hung in the air. It was done very fast and without any apparent effort. His hand went up to shoulder height, then snapped forward and the knife sailed through the air and hung quivering in the wood of the window frame.

*'Cuidado, señor!'* he said with a sharp sneer. 'And keep your paws to yourself. Nobody fools with me.'

He walked lithely across the room and plucked the knife out of the wood, tossed it in the air, spun on his toes and caught it behind him. With a snap it disappeared under his shirt.

'Neat,' I said, 'but just a little on the gaudy side.'

He strolled up to me, smiling derisively.

'And it might get you a broken elbow,' I said. 'Like this.'

I took hold of his right wrist, jerked him off balance, swung to one side and a little behind him, and brought my bent fore-arm up under the back of his elbow joint. I bore down on it, using my forearm as a fulcrum.

'One hard jerk,' I said, 'and your elbow joint cracks. A crack is enough. You'd be out of commission as a knife thrower for several months. Make the jerk a little harder and you'd be through permanently. Take Mr Wade's shoes off.'

I let go of him and he grinned at me. 'Good trick,' he said. 'I will remember.'

He turned to Wade and reached for one of his shoes, then stopped. There was a smear of blood on the pillow.

'Who cut the boss?'

'Not me, chum. He fell and cut his head on something. It's only a shallow cut. The doctor has been here.'

Candy let out his breath slowly. 'You see him fall?'

'Before I got here. You like this guy, don't you?'

He didn't answer me. He took the shoes off. We got Wade undressed little by little and Candy dug out a pair of green and silver pyjamas. We got Wade into those and got him inside the bed and well covered up. He was still sweaty and still snoring. Candy looked down at him sadly, shaking his sleek head from side to side, slowly.

'Somebody's got to take care of him,' he said. 'I go change my clothes.'

'Get some sleep. I'll take care of him. I can call you if I need you.'

He faced me. 'You better take care of him good,' he said in a quiet voice. 'Very good.'

He went out of the room. I went into the bathroom and got a wet washcloth and a heavy towel. I turned Wade over a little and spread the towel on the pillow and washed the blood off his head gently so as not to start the bleeding again. Then I could see a sharp, shallow cut about two inches long. It was nothing. Dr Loring had been right that much. It wouldn't have hurt to stitch it but it probably was not really necessary. I found a pair of scissors and cut the hair away enough so that I could put on a strip of adhesive. Then I turned him on his back and washed his face. I guess that was a mistake.

He opened his eyes. They were vague and unfocused at first, then they cleared and he saw me standing beside the bed. His hand moved and went up to his head and felt the adhesive. His lips mumbled something, then his voice cleared up also.

'Who hit me? You?' His hand felt for the adhesive.

'Nobody hit you. You took a fall.'

'Took a fall? When? Where?'

'Wherever you telephoned from. You called me. I heard you fall. Over the wire.'

'I called you?' He grinned slowly. 'Always available, aren't you, fella? What time is it?'

'After one a.m.'

'Where's Eileen?'

'Gone to bed. She had it rough.'

He thought that over silently. His eyes were full of pain. 'Did I—' He stopped and winced.

'You didn't touch her as far as I know. If that's what you mean. You just wandered outdoors and passed out near the fence. Quit talking. Go to sleep.'

'Sleep,' he said quietly and slowly, like a child reciting its lesson. 'What would that be?'

'Maybe a pill would help. Got any?'

'In the drawer. Night table.'

I opened it and found a plastic bottle with red capsules in it.

Seconal, $1\frac{1}{2}$ grains. Prescription by Dr Loring. That nice Dr Loring. Mrs Roger Wade's prescription.

I shook two of them loose and put the bottle back and poured a glass of water from a Thermos jug on the night table. He said one capsule would be enough. He took it and drank some water and lay back and stared at the ceiling again. Time passed. I sat in a chair and watched him. He didn't seem to get sleepy. Then he said slowly:

'I remember something. Do me a favour, Marlowe. I wrote some crazy stuff I don't want Eileen to see. It's on top of the typewriter under the cover. Tear it up for me.'

'Sure. That all you remember?'

'Eileen is all right? Positive about that?'

'Yes. She's just tired. Let it ride, Wade. Stop thinking. I shouldn't have asked you.'

'Stop thinking, the man says.' His voice was a little drowsy now. He was talking as if to himself. 'Stop thinking, stop dreaming, stop loving, stop hating. Good night, sweet prince. I'll take that other pill.'

I gave it to him with some more water. He lay back again, this time with his head turned so that he could see me. 'Look, Marlowe, I wrote some stuff I don't want Eileen—'

'You told me already. I'll attend to it when you go to sleep.'

'Oh. Thanks. Nice to have you around. Very nice.'

Another longish pause. His eyelids were getting heavy.

'Ever kill a man, Marlowe?'

'Yes.'

'Nasty feeling, isn't it?'

'Some people like it.'

His eyes went shut all the way. Then they opened again, but they looked vague. 'How could they?'

I didn't answer. The eyelids came down again, very gradually, like a slow curtain in the theatre. He began to snore. I waited a little longer. Then I dimmed the light in the room and went out.

# Twenty-seven

I stopped outside Eileen's door and listened. I didn't hear any sound of movement inside, so I didn't knock. If she wanted to know how he was, it was up to her. Downstairs the living-room looked bright and empty. I put out some of the lights. From over near the front door I looked up at the balcony. The middle part of the living-room rose to the full height of the house walls and was crossed by open beams that also supported the balcony. The balcony was wide and edged on two sides by a solid railing which looked to be about three and a half feet high. The top and the uprights were cut square to match the cross beams. The dining-room was through a square arch closed off by double louvered doors. Above it I guessed there were servants' quarters. This part of the second floor was walled off so there would be another stairway reaching it from the kitchen part of the house. Wade's room was in the corner over his study. I could see the light from his open door reflected against the high ceiling and I could see the top foot of his doorway.

I cut all the lights except in one standing lamp and crossed to the study. The door was shut but two lamps were lit, a standing lamp at the end of the leather couch and a cowled desk lamp. The typewriter was on a heavy stand under this and beside it on the desk there was a disorderly mess of yellow paper. I sat in a padded chair and studied the layout. What I wanted to know was how he had cut his head. I sat in his desk chair with the phone at my left hand. The spring was set very weak. If I tilted back and went over, my head may have caught the corner of the desk. I moistened my handkerchief and rubbed the wood. No blood, nothing there. There was a lot of stuff on the desk, including a row of books between bronze elephants, and an old-fashioned square glass inkwell. I tried that without result. Not much point to it anyway, because if someone else had slugged him, the weapon didn't have to be in the room. And there wasn't anyone else to do it. I stood up and switched on the cornice lights. They reached into the shadowy corners and of course the answer was simple enough after all. A square metal waste-basket was lying on its side over against the wall, with paper spilt. It couldn't have walked there, so it had been thrown or kicked. I tried its sharp corners with my moistened handkerchief. I got the red-brown smear of blood this time. No mystery at all. Wade had fallen over and struck his head on the sharp corner of the waste-basket – a glancing blow most likely – picked himself up and booted the damn thing across the room. Easy.

Then he would have another quick drink. The drinking liquor was on the cocktail table in front of the couch. An empty bottle, another three-quarters full, a Thermos jug of water and a silver bowl containing water which had been ice cubes. There was only one glass and it was the large economy size.

Having taken his drink he felt a little better. He noticed the phone off the hook in a bleary sort of way and very likely didn't remember any more what he had been doing with it. So he just walked across and put it back in its cradle. The time had been just about right. There is something compulsive about a telephone. The gadget-ridden man of our age loves it, loathes it, and is afraid of it. But he always treats it with respect, even when he is drunk. The telephone is a fetish.

Any normal man would have said hello into the mouthpiece before hanging up, just to be sure. But not necessarily a man who was bleary with drink and had just taken a fall. It didn't matter anyhow. His wife might have done it, she might have heard the fall and the bang as the wastebasket bounced against the wall and come into the study. About that time the last drink would kick him in the face and he would stagger out of the house and across the front lawn and pass out where I had found him. Somebody was coming for him. By this time he didn't know who it was. Maybe the good Dr Verringer.

So far, so good. So what would his wife do? She couldn't handle him or reason with him and she might well be afraid to try. So she would call somebody to come and help. The servants were out, so it would have to be by the telephone. Well, she *had* called somebody. She had called that nice Dr Loring. I'd just assumed she called him after I got there. She hadn't said so.

From here on it didn't quite add up. You'd expect her to look for him and find him and make sure he wasn't hurt. It wouldn't hurt him to lie out on the ground on a warm summer night for a while. She couldn't move him. It had taken all I had to do that. But you wouldn't expect to find her standing in the open doorway smoking a cigarette, not knowing except very vaguely where he was. Or would you? I didn't know what she had been through with him, how dangerous he was in that condition, how much afraid she might be to go near him. 'I've had all of it I can take,' she had said to me when I arrived. 'You find him.' Then she had gone inside and pulled a faint.

It still bothered me, but I had to leave it at that. I had to assume that when she had been up against the situation often enough to know there was nothing she could do about it except to let it ride, then that would be what she would do. Just that. Let it ride. Let him die out there on the ground until somebody came around with the physical equipment to handle him.

It still bothered me. It bothered me also that she had checked out and gone into her own room while Candy and I got him upstairs to bed. She said she loved the guy. He was her husband, they had been married for five years, he was a very nice guy indeed when sober – those were her own words. Drunk he was something else, something to stay away from because he was dangerous. All right, forget it. But somehow it still bothered me. If she was really scared, she wouldn't have been standing there in the open door smoking a cigarette. If she was just bitter and withdrawn and disgusted, she wouldn't have fainted.

There was something else. Another woman, perhaps. Then she had only just found out. Linda Loring? Maybe. Dr Loring thought so and said so in a very public manner.

I stopped thinking about it and took the cover off the typewriter. The stuff was there, several loose sheets of typed yellow paper that I was supposed to destroy so Eileen wouldn't see them. I took them over to the couch and decided I deserved a drink to go with the reading-matter. There was a half-bath off the study. I rinsed the tall glass out and poured a libation and sat down with it to read. And what I read was really wild. Like this:


# Twenty-eight


'The moon's four days off the full and there's a square patch of moonlight on the wall and it's looking at me like a big blind milky eye, a wall eye. Joke. Goddam silly simile. Writers. Everything has to be like something else. My head is as fluffy as whipped cream but not as sweet. More similes. I could vomit just thinking about the lousy racket. I could vomit anyway. I probably will. Don't push me. Give me time. The worms in my solar plexus crawl and crawl and crawl. I would be better off in bed but there would be a dark animal underneath the bed and the dark animal would crawl around rustling and hump himself and bump the underside of the bed, then I would let out a yell that wouldn't make any sound except to me. A dream yell, a yell in a nightmare. There is nothing to be afraid of and I am not afraid because there is nothing to be afraid of, but just the same I was lying like that once in bed and the dark animal was doing it to me, bumping himself against the underside of the bed, and I had an orgasm. That disgusted me more than any other of the nasty things I have done.

'I'm dirty. I need a shave. My hands are shaking. I'm sweating. I smell foul to myself. The shirt under my arms is wet and on the chest and back. The sleeves are wet in the folds of the elbows. The glass on the table is empty. It would take both hands to pour the stuff now. I could get one out of the bottle maybe to brace me. The taste of the stuff is sickening. And it wouldn't get me anywhere. In the end I won't be able to sleep even and the whole world will moan in the horror of tortured nerves. Good stuff, huh, Wade? More.

'It's all right for the first two or three days and then it is negative. You suffer and you take a drink and for a little while it is better, but the price keeps getting higher and higher and what you get for it is less and less and then there is always the point where you get nothing but nausea. Then you call Verringer. All right, Verringer, here I come. There isn't any Verringer any more. He's gone to Cuba or he is dead. The queen has killed him. Poor old Verringer, what a fate, to die in bed with a queen – that kind of queen. Come on, Wade, let's get up and go places. Places where we haven't ever been and aren't ever going back to when we have been. Does this sentence make sense? No. Okay, I'm not asking any money for it. A short pause here for a long commercial.

'Well, I did it. I got up. What a man. I went over to the couch and here I am kneeling beside the couch with my hands down on it and my face in my hands, crying. Then I prayed and despised myself for praying. Grade Three drunk despising himself. What the hell are you praying to, you fool? If a well man prays, that's faith. A sick man prays and he is just scared. Nuts to prayer. This is the world you made and you make it all by yourself and what little outside help you got – well, you made that too. Stop praying, you jerk. Get up on your feet and take that drink. It's too late for anything else now.

'Well, I took it. Both hands. Poured it in the glass too. Hardly spilled a drop. Now if I can hold it without vomiting. Better add some water. Now lift it slow. Easy, not too much at a time. It gets warm. It gets hot. If I could stop sweating. The glass is empty. It's down on the table again.

'There's a haze over the moonlight but I set that glass down in spite of it, carefully, carefully, like a spray of roses in a tall thin vase. The roses nod their heads with dew. Maybe I'm a rose. Brother, have I got dew. Now to get upstairs. Maybe a short one straight for the journey. No? Okay, whatever you say. Take it upstairs when I get there. If I get there, something to look forward to. If I make it upstairs I am entitled to compensation. A token of regard from me to me. I have such a beautiful love for myself – and the sweet part of it – no rivals.

'Double space. Been up and came down. Didn't like it upstairs. The altitude makes my heart flutter. But I keep hitting these typewriter keys. What a magician is the subconscious. If only it would work regular hours. There was moonlight upstairs too. Probably the same moon. No variety about the moon. It comes and goes like the milkman and the moon's milk is always the same. The milk's moon is always – hold it, chum. You've got your feet crossed. This is no time to get involved in the case history of the moon. You got enough case history to take care of the whole damn valley.

'She was sleeping on her side without sound. Her knees drawn up. Too still I thought. You always make some sound when you sleep. Maybe not sleep, maybe just trying to sleep. If I went closer I would know. Might fall down too. One of her eyes opened – or did it? She looked at me or did she? No. Would have sat up and said, Are you sick, darling? Yes, I am sick, darling. But don't give it a thought, darling, because this sick is my sick and not your sick, and let you sleep still and lovely and never remember and no slime from me to you and nothing come near you that is grim and grey and ugly.

'You're a louse, Wade. Three adjectives, you lousy writer. Can't you even stream of consciousness you louse without getting it in three adjectives for Chrissake? I came downstairs again holding on to the rail. My guts lurched with the steps and I held them together with a promise. I made the main floor and I made the study and I made the couch and I waited for my heart to slow down. The bottle is handy. One thing you can say about Wade's arrangements the bottle is always handy. Nobody hides it, nobody locks it up. Nobody says, Don't you think you've had enough, darling? You'll make yourself sick, darling. Nobody says that. Just sleep on side softly like roses.

'I gave Candy too much money. Mistake. Should have started him with a bag of peanuts and worked up to a banana. Then a little real change, slow and easy, always keep him eager. You give him a big slug of the stuff to begin with and pretty soon he has a stake. He can live in Mexico for a month, live high wide and nasty, on what it costs here for a day. So when he gets that stake, what does he do? Well, does a man ever have enough money, if he thinks he can get more? Maybe it's all right. Maybe I ought to kill the shiny-eyed bastard. A good man died for me once, why not a cockroach in a white jacket?

'Forget Candy. There's always a way to blunt a needle. The other I shall never forget. It's carved on my liver in green fire.

'Better telephone. Losing control. Feel them jumping, jumping, jumping. Better call someone quick before the pink things crawl on my face. Better call, call, call. Call Sioux City Sue. Hello, Operator, give me Long Distance. Hello, Long Distance, get me Sioux City Sue. What's her number? No have number, just name, Operator. You'll find her walking along Tenth Street, on the shady side, under the tall corn trees with their spreading ears ... All right, Operator, all right. Just cancel the whole programme and let me tell you something, I mean, ask you something. Who's going to pay for all those snazzy parties Gifford is throwing in London, if you cancel my long distance call? Yeah, you think your job is solid. You think. Here, I better talk to Gifford direct. Get him on the line. His valet just brought in his tea. If he can't talk we'll send over somebody that can.

'Now what did I write that for? What was I trying not to think about? Telephone. Better telephone now. Getting very bad, very, very—'

That was all. I folded the sheets up small and pushed them down into my inside breast pocket behind the note case. I went over to the french doors and opened them wide and stepped out on to the terrace. The moonlight was a little spoiled. But it was summer in Idle Valley and summer is never quite spoiled. I stood there looking at the motionless, colourless lake and thought and wondered. Then I heard a shot.

# Twenty-nine

On the balcony two lighted doors were open now – Eileen's and his. Her room was empty. There was a sound of struggling from his and I came through the door in a jump to find her bending over the bed wrestling with him. The black gleam of a gun shot up into the air, two hands, a large male hand and a woman's small hand were both holding it, neither by the butt. Roger was sitting up in bed and leaning forward pushing. She was in a pale blue house coat, one of those quilted things, her hair was all over her face and now she had both hands on the gun and with a quick jerk she got it away from him. I was surprised that she had the strength, even dopey as he was. He fell back glaring and panting and she stepped away and bumped into me.

She stood there leaning against me, holding the gun with both hands pressed hard against her body. She was racked with panting sobs. I reached around her body and put my hand on the gun.

She spun round as if it took that to make her realize I was there. Her eyes widened and her body sagged against me. She let go of the gun. It was a heavy, clumsy weapon, a Webley double-action hammerless. The barrel was warm. I held her with one arm, dropped the gun in my pocket and looked past her head at him. Nobody said anything.

Then he opened his eyes and that weary smile played on his lips. 'Nobody's hurt,' he muttered. 'Just a wild shot into the ceiling.'

I felt her go stiff. Then she pulled away. Her eyes were focused and clear. I let her go.

'Roger,' she said in a voice not much more than a sick whisper, 'did it have to be that?'

He stared owlishly, licked his lip and said nothing. She went and leaned against the dressing-table. Her hand moved mechanically and threw the hair back from her face. She shuddered once from head to foot, shaking her head from side to side. 'Roger,' she whispered again. 'Poor Roger. Poor miserable Roger.'

He was staring straight up at the ceiling now. 'I had a nightmare,' he said slowly. 'Somebody with a knife was leaning over the bed. I don't know who. Looked a little like Candy. Couldn't have been Candy.'

'Of course not, darling,' she said softly. She left the dressing-table and sat down on the side of the bed. She put her hand out and began to stroke his forehead. 'Candy has gone to bed long ago. And why would Candy have a knife?'

'He's a Mex. They all have knives,' Roger said in the same remote impersonal voice. They like knives. And he doesn't like me.'

'Nobody likes you,' I said brutally.

She turned her head swiftly. 'Please – please don't talk like that. He didn't know. He had a dream—'

'Where was the gun?' I growled, watching her, not paying any attention to him.

'Night table. In the drawer.' He turned his head and met my

stare. There hadn't been any gun in the drawer, and he knew I knew it. The pills had been in there and some odds and ends, but no gun.

'Or under the pillow,' he added. 'I'm vague about it. I shot once' – he lifted a heavy hand and pointed – 'up there.'

I looked up. There seemed to be a hole in the ceiling plaster all right. I went where I could look up at it. Yes. The kind of a hole a bullet might make. From that gun it would go on through, into the attic. I went back close to the bed and stood looking down at him, giving him the hard eye.

'Nuts. You meant to kill yourself. You didn't have any nightmare. You were swimming in a sea of self-pity. You didn't have any gun in the drawer or under your pillow either. You got up and got the gun and got back into bed and there you were all ready to wipe out the whole messy business. But I don't think you had the nerve. You fired a shot not meant to hit anything. And your wife came running – that's what you wanted. Just pity and sympathy, pal. Nothing else. Even the struggle was mostly fake. She couldn't take a gun away from you if you didn't want her to.'

'I'm sick,' he said. 'But you could be right. Does it matter?'

'It matters like this. They'd put you in the psycho ward, and believe me, the people who run that place are about as sympathetic as Georgia chain gang guards.'

Eileen stood up suddenly. 'That's enough,' she said sharply. 'He *is* sick, and you know it.'

'He wants to be sick. I'm just reminding him of what it would cost him.'

'This is not the time to tell him.'

'Go on back to your room.'

Her blue eyes flashed. 'How dare you—'

'Go on back to your room. Unless you want me to call the police. These things are supposed to be reported.'

He almost grinned. 'Yeah, call the police,' he said, 'like you did on Terry Lennox.'

I didn't pay any attention to that. I was still watching her. She looked exhausted now, and frail, and very beautiful. The moment of flashing anger was gone. I put a hand out and touched her arm. 'It's all right,' I said. 'He won't do it again. Go back to bed.'

She gave him a long look and went out of the room. When the open door was empty of her I sat down on the side of the bed where she had been sitting.

'More pills?'

'No thanks. It doesn't matter whether I sleep. I feel a lot better.'

'Did I hit right about that shot? It was just a crazy bit of acting?'

'More or less,' he turned his head away. 'I guess I was light-headed.'

'Nobody can stop you from killing yourself, if you really want to. I realize that. So do you.'

'Yes.' He was still looking away. 'Did you do what I asked you – that stuff in the typewriter.'

'Uh huh. I'm surprised you remember. It's pretty crazy writing. Funny thing, it's clearly typed.'

'I can always do that – drunk or sober – up to a point anyway.'

'Don't worry about Candy,' I said. 'You're wrong about his not liking you. And I was wrong to say nobody did. I was trying to jar Eileen, make her mad.'

'Why?'

'She pulled one faint already tonight.'

He shook his head slightly. 'Eileen never faints.'

'Then it was a phony.'

He didn't like that either.

'What did you mean – a good man died for you?' I asked.

He frowned, thinking about it. 'Just rubbish. I told you I had a dream—'

'I'm talking about that guff you typed out.'

He looked at me now, turning his head on the pillow as if it had enormous weight. 'Another dream.'

'I'll try again. What's Candy got on you?'

'Shove it, Jack,' he said and closed his eyes.

I got up and closed the door. 'You can't run for ever, Wade. Candy could be a blackmailer, sure. Easy. He could even be nice about it – like you and lift your dough at the same time. What is it – a woman?'

'You believe that fool, Loring,' he said with his eyes closed.

'Not exactly. What about the sister – the one that's dead?'

It was a wild pitch in a sense but it happened to split the plate. His eyes snapped wide open. A bubble of saliva showed on his lips.

'Is that – why you're here?' he asked slowly, and in a whispering voice.

'You know better. I was invited. You invited me.'

His head rolled back and forth on the pillow. In spite of the seconal he was eaten up by his nerves. His face was covered with sweat.

'I'm not the first loving husband who has been an adulterer. Leave me alone, damn you. Leave me alone.'

I went into the bathroom and got a face towel and wiped his face off. I grinned at him sneeringly. I was the heel to end all heels. Wait until the man is down, then kick him and kick him again. He's weak. He can't resist or kick back.

'One of these days we'll get together on it,' I said.

'I'm not crazy,' he said.

'You just hope you're not crazy.'

'I've been living in hell.'

'Oh sure. That's obvious. The interesting point is why. Here – take this.' I had another seconal out of the night table and another glass of water. He got up on one elbow and grabbed for the glass and missed it by a good four inches. I put it in his hand. He managed to drink and swallow his pill. Then he lay back flat and deflated, his face drained of emotion. His nose had that pinched look. He could almost have been a dead man. He wasn't throwing anybody down any stairs tonight. Most likely not any night.

When his eyelids got heavy I went out of the room. The weight of the Webley was against my hip, dragging at my pocket. I started back downstairs again. Eileen's door was open. Her room was dark but there was enough light from the moon to frame her standing just inside the door. She called out something that sounded like a name, but it wasn't my name. I stepped close to her.

'Keep your voice down,' I said. 'He's gone back to sleep.'

'I always knew you would come back,' she said softly. 'Even after ten years.'

I peered at her. One of us was goofy.

'Shut the door,' she said in the same caressing voice. 'All these years I have kept myself for you.'

I turned and shut the door. It seemed like a good idea at the moment. When I faced her she was already falling towards me. So I caught her. I damn well had to. She pressed herself hard against me and her hair brushed my face. Her mouth came up to be kissed. She was trembling. Her lips opened and her teeth opened and her tongue darted. Then her hands dropped and jerked at something and the robe she was wearing came open, and underneath it she was as naked as September Morn but a darn sight less coy.

354

'Put me on the bed,' she breathed.

I did that. Putting my arms around her I touched bare skin, soft skin, soft, yielding flesh. I lifted her and carried her the few steps to the bed and lowered her. She kept her arms around my neck. She was making some kind of a whistling noise in her throat. Then she threshed about and moaned. This was murder. I was as erotic as a stallion. I was losing control. You don't get that sort of invitation from that sort of woman very often anywhere.

Candy saved me. There was a thin squeak and I swung around to see the doorknob moving. I jerked loose and jumped for the door. I got it open and barged out through it and the Mex was tearing along the hall and down the stairs. Half-way down he stopped and turned and leered at me. Then he was gone.

I went back to the door and shut it – from the outside this time. Some kind of weird noises were coming from the woman on the bed, but that's all they were now. Weird noises. The spell was broken.

I went down the stairs fast and crossed into the study and grabbed the bottle of Scotch and tilted it. When I couldn't swallow any more I leaned against the wall and panted and let the stuff burn in me until the fumes reached my brain.

It was a long time since dinner. It was a long time since anything that was normal. The whisky hit me hard and fast and I kept guzzling it until the room started to get hazy and the furniture was all in the wrong places and the lamplight was like wildfire or summer lightning. Then I was flat out on the leather couch, trying to balance the bottle on my chest. It seemed to be empty. It rolled away and thumped on the floor.

That was the last incident of which I took any precise notice.


# Thirty

A shaft of sunlight tickled one of my ankles. I opened my eyes and saw the crown of a tree moving gently against a hazed blue sky. I rolled over and leather touched my cheek. An axe split my head. I sat up. There was a rug over me. I threw that off and got my feet on the floor. I scowled at a clock. The clock said a minute short of six-thirty.

I got up on my feet and it took character. It took will power.

355

It took a lot out of me, and there wasn't as much to spare as there once had been. The hard, heavy years had worked me over.

I ploughed across to the half bath and stripped off my tie and shirt and sloshed cold water in my face with both hands and sloshed it on my head. When I was dripping wet I towelled myself off savagely. I put my shirt and tie back on and reached for my jacket and the gun in the pocket banged against the wall. I took it out and swung the cylinder away from the frame and tipped the cartridges into my hand, five full, one just a blackened shell. Then I thought, what's the use, there are always more of them. So I put them back where they had been before and carried the gun into the study and put it away in one of the drawers of the desk.

When I looked up Candy was standing in the doorway, spick and span in his white coat, his hair brushed back and shining black, his eyes bitter.

'You want some coffee?'

'Thanks.'

'I put the lamps out. The boss is okay. Asleep. I shut his door. Why you get drunk?'

'I had to.'

He sneered at me. 'Didn't make her, huh? Got tossed out on your can, shamus.'

'Have it your own way.'

'You ain't tough this morning, shamus. You ain't tough at all.'

'Get the goddam coffee,' I yelled at him.

'*Hijo de la puta!*'

In one jump I had him by the arm. He didn't move. He just looked at me contemptuously. I laughed and let go of his arm.

'You're right, Candy. I'm not tough at all.'

He turned and went out. In no time at all he was back with a silver tray and a small silver pot of coffee on it and sugar and cream and a neat triangular napkin. He set it down on the cocktail table and removed the empty bottle and the rest of the drinking materials. He picked another bottle off the floor.

'Fresh. Just made,' he said, and went out.

I drank two cups black. Then I tried a cigarette. It was all right. I still belonged to the human race. Then Candy was back in the room again.

'You want breakfast?' he asked morosely.

'No, thanks.'

'Okay, scram out of here. We don't want you around.'

'Who's we?'

He lifted the lid of a box and helped himself to a cigarette. He lit it and blew smoke at me insolently.

'I take care of the boss,' he said.

'You making it pay?'

He frowned, then nodded. 'Oh yes. Good money.'

'How much on the side – for not spilling what you know?'

He went back to Spanish. '*No entiendido.*'

'You understand all right. How much you shake him for? I bet it's not more than a couple of yards.'

'What's that? Couple of yards?'

'Two hundred bucks.'

He grinned. 'You give me couple of yards, shamus. So I don't tell the boss you come out of her room last night.'

'That would buy a whole busload of wetbacks like you.'

He shrugged that off. 'The boss gets pretty rough when he blows his top. Better pay up, shamus.'

'Pachuco stuff,' I said contemptuously. 'All you're touching is the small money. Lots of men play around when they're lit. Anyhow she knows all about it. You don't have anything to sell.'

There was a gleam in his eye. 'Just don't come round any more, tough boy.'

'I'm leaving.'

I stood up and walked around the table. He moved enough to keep facing towards me. I watched his hand but he evidently wasn't wearing a knife this morning. When I was close enough I slapped a hand across his face.

'I don't get called a son of a whore by the help, greaseball. I've got business here and I come around whenever I feel like it. Watch your lip from now on. You might get pistol-whipped. That pretty face of yours would never look the same again.'

He didn't react at all, not even to the slap. That and being called a greaseball must have been deadly insults to him. But this time he just stood there wooden-faced, motionless. Then without a word he picked up the coffee tray and carried it out.

'Thanks for the coffee,' I said to his back.

He kept going. When he was gone I felt the bristles on my chin, shook myself and decided to be on my way. I had had a skinful of the Wade family.

As I crossed the living-room Eileen was coming down the stairs in white slacks and open-toed sandals and a pale blue shirt. She looked at me with complete surprise. 'I didn't know you were here, Mr Marlowe,' she said, as though she hadn't seen me for a week, and at that time I had just dropped in for tea.

'I put his gun in the desk,' I said.

'Gun?' Then it seemed to dawn on her. 'Oh, last night was a little hectic, wasn't it? But I thought you had gone home.'

I walked over closer to her. She had a thin gold chain around her neck and some kind of fancy pendant in gold and blue on white enamel. The blue enamelled part looked like a pair of wings, but not spread out. Against these there was a broad white enamel and gold dagger that pierced a scroll. I couldn't read the words. It was some kind of military emblem.

'I got drunk,' I said. 'Deliberately and not elegantly. I was a little lonely.'

'You didn't have to be,' she said, and her eyes were as clear as water. There wasn't a trace of guile in them.

'A matter of opinion,' I said. 'I'm leaving now and I'm not sure I'll be back. You heard what I said about the gun?'

'You put it in his desk. It might be a good idea to put it somewhere else. But he didn't really mean to shoot himself, did he?'

'I can't answer that. But next time he might.'

She shook her head. 'I don't think so. I really don't. You were a wonderful help last night, Mr Marlowe. I don't know how to thank you.'

'You made a pretty good try.'

She got pink. Then she laughed. 'I had a very curious dream in the night,' she said slowly, looking off over my shoulder. 'Someone I used to know was here in the house. Someone who had been dead for ten years.' Her fingers went up and touched the gold and enamel pendant. 'That's why I am wearing this today. He gave it to me.'

'I had a curious dream myself,' I said. 'But I'm not telling mine. Let me know how Roger gets on and if there is anything I can do.'

She lowered her eyes and looked into mine. 'You said you were not coming back.'

'I said I wasn't sure. I may have to come back. I hope I won't. There is something very wrong in this house. And only part of it came out of a bottle.'

She stared at me, frowning. 'What does that mean?'

'I think you know what I'm talking about.'

She thought it over carefully. Her fingers were still touching the pendant gently. She let out a slow patient sigh. 'There's always another woman,' she said quietly. 'At some time or other. It's not necessarily fatal. We're talking at cross purposes, aren't we? We are not even talking about the same thing, perhaps.'

'Could be,' I said. She was still standing on the steps, the third step from the bottom. She still had her fingers on the pendant. She still looked like a golden dream. 'Especially if you have in mind that the other woman is Linda Loring.'

She dropped her hand from the pendant and came down one more step of the stairs.

'Dr Loring seems to agree with me,' she said indifferently. 'He must have some source of information.'

'You said he had played that scene with half the males in the valley.'

'Did I? Well – it was the conventional sort of thing to say at the time.' She came down another step.

'I haven't shaved,' I said.

That startled her. Then she laughed. 'Oh, I wasn't expecting you to make love to me.'

'Just what did you expect of me, Mrs Wade – in the beginning, when you first persuaded me to go hunting? Why me – what have I got to offer?'

'You kept faith,' she said quietly. 'When it couldn't have been very easy.'

'I'm touched. But I don't think that was the reason.'

She came down the last step and then she was looking up at me. 'Then what was the reason?'

'Or if it was – it was a damn poor reason. Just about the worst reason in the world.'

She frowned a tiny frown. 'Why?'

'Because what I did – this keeping faith – is something even a fool doesn't do twice.'

'You know,' she said lightly, 'this is getting to be a very enigmatic conversation.'

'You're a very enigmatic person, Mrs Wade. So long and good luck and if you really care anything about Roger, you'd better find him the right kind of doctor – and quick.'

She laughed again. 'Oh, that was a mild attack last night. You ought to see him in a bad one. He'll be up and working by this afternoon.'

'Like hell he will.'

'But believe me he will. I know him so well.'

I gave her the last shot right in the teeth and it sounded pretty nasty.

'You don't really want to save him, do you? You just want to look as if you are trying to save him.'

'That,' she said deliberately, 'was a very beastly thing to say to me.'

She stepped past me and walked through the dining-room doors and then the big room was empty and I crossed to the front door and let myself out. It was a perfect summer morning in that bright secluded valley. It was too far from the city to get any smog and cut off by the low mountains from the dampness of the ocean. It was going to be hot later, but in a nice refined exclusive sort of way, nothing brutal like the heat of the desert, not sticky and rank like the heat of the city. Idle Valley was a perfect place to live. Perfect. Nice people with nice homes, nice cars, nice horses, nice dogs, possibly even nice children.

But all a man named Marlowe wanted from it was out. And fast.


# Thirty-one


I went home and showered and shaved and changed clothes and began to feel clean again. I cooked some breakfast, ate it, washed up, swept the kitchen and the service porch, filled a pipe and called the phone answering service. I shot a blank. Why go to the office? There would be nothing there but another dead moth and another layer of dust. In the safe would be my portrait of Madison. I could go down and play with that, and with the five crisp hundred-dollar bills that still smelt of coffee. I could do that, but I didn't want to. Something inside me had gone sour. None of it really belonged to me. What was it supposed to buy? How much loyalty can a dead man use? Phooey. I was looking at life through the mists of a hangover.

It was the kind of morning that seems to go on forever. I was flat and tired and dull and the passing minutes seemed to fall into a void, with a soft whirring sound, like spent rockets. Birds chirped in the shrubbery outside and the cars went up and down Laurel Canyon Boulevard endlessly. Usually I wouldn't even hear them. But I was brooding and irritable and mean and over-sensitive. I decided to kill the hangover.

Ordinarily I was not a morning drinker. The Southern California climate is too soft for it. You don't metabolize fast enough. But I mixed a tall cold one this time and sat in an easy-chair with my shirt open and pecked at a magazine, reading a crazy story about a guy that had two lives and two psychiatrists, one was human and one was some kind of insect in a hive. The guy kept going from one to the other and the whole thing was as crazy as a crumpet, but funny in an off-beat sort of way. I was handling the drink carefully, a sip at a time, watching myself.

It was about noon when the telephone rang and the voice said:

'This is Linda Loring. I called your office and your phone service told me to try your home. I'd like to see you.'

'Why?'

'I'd rather explain that in person. You go to your office from time to time, I suppose.'

'Yeah. From time to time. Is there any money in it?'

'I hadn't thought of it that way. But I have no objection, if you want to be paid. I could be at your office in about an hour.'

'Goody.'

'What's the matter with you?' she asked sharply.

'Hangover. But I'm not paralysed. I'll be there. Unless you'd rather come here.'

'Your office would suit me better.'

'I've got a nice quiet place here. Dead-end street, no near neighbours.'

'The implication does not attract me – if I understand you.'

'Nobody understands me, Mrs Loring. I'm enigmatic. Okay, I'll struggle down to the coop.'

'Thank you so much.' She hung up.

I was slow getting down there because I stopped on the way for a sandwich. I aired out the office and switched on the buzzer and poked my head through the communicating door and she was there already, sitting in the same chair where Mendy Menendez had sat and looking through what could have been the same magazine. She had a tan garbardine suit on today and she looked pretty elegant. She put the magazine aside, gave me a serious look and said:

'Your Boston fern needs watering. I think it needs repotting too. Too many air roots.'

I held the door open for her. The hell with the Boston fern. When she was inside and I had let the door swing shut I held the customer's chair for her and gave the office the usual once-over. I got around to my side of the desk.

'You're establishment isn't exactly palatial,' she said. 'Don't you even have a secretary?'

'It's a sordid life, but I'm used to it.'

'And I shouldn't think very lucrative,' she said.

'Oh I don't know. Depends. Want to see a portrait of Madison?'

'A what?'

'A five-thousand-dollar bill. Retainer. I've got it in the safe.' I got up and started over there. I spun the knob and opened it and unlocked a drawer inside, opened an envelope and dropped it in front of her. She stared at it in something like amazement.

'Don't let the office fool you,' I said. 'I worked for an old boy one time that would cash in at about twenty millions. Even your old man would say hello to him. His office was no better than mine, except he was a bit deaf and had that sound proofing stuff on the ceiling. On the floor brown linoleum, no carpet.'

She picked the portrait of Madison up and pulled it between her fingers and turned it over. She put it down again.

'You got this from Terry, didn't you?'

'Gosh, you know everything, don't you, Mrs Loring?'

She pushed the bill away from her, frowning. 'He had one. He carried it on him ever since he and Sylvia were married the second time. He called it his mad money. It was not found on his body.'

'There could be other reasons for that.'

'I know. But how many people carry a five-thousand-dollar bill around with them? How many who could afford to give you that much money would give it to you in this form?'

It wasn't worth answering. I just nodded. She went on brusquely:

'And what were you supposed to do for it, Mr Marlowe? Or would you tell me? On that last ride down to Tijuana he had plenty of time to talk. You made it very clear the other evening that you didn't believe his confession. Did he give you a list of his wife's lovers so that you might find a murderer among them?'

I didn't answer that either, but for different reasons.

'And would the name of Roger Wade appear on that list by any chance?' she asked harshly. 'If Terry didn't kill his wife, the murderer would have to be some violent and irresponsible man, a lunatic or a savage drunk. Only that sort of man could, to use your own repulsive phrase, beat her face into a bloody sponge. Is that why you are making yourself so very useful to the Wades – a regular mother's helper who comes on call to nurse him when he is drunk, to find him when he is lost, to bring him home when he is helpless?'

'Let me set you right on a couple of points, Mrs Loring. Terry may or may not have given me that beautiful piece of engraving. But he gave me no list and mentioned no names. There was nothing he asked me to do except what you seem to feel sure I did do, drive him to Tijuana. My getting involved with the Wades was the work of a New York publisher who is desperate to have Roger Wade finish his book, which involves him fairly sober, which in turn involves finding out if there is any special trouble that makes him get drunk. If there is and it can be found out, then the next step would be an effort to remove it. I say effort, because the chances are you couldn't do it. But you could try.'

'I could tell you in one simple sentence why he gets drunk,' she said contemptuously. 'That anaemic blonde showpiece he's married to.'

'Oh I don't know,' I said. 'I wouldn't call her anaemic.'

'Really? How interesting.' Her eyes glittered.

I picked up my portrait of Madison. 'Don't chew too long on that one, Mrs Loring. I am not sleeping with the lady. Sorry to disappoint you.'

I went over to the safe and put my money away in the locked compartment. I shut the safe and spun the dial.

'On second thoughts,' she said to my back, 'I doubt very much that anyone is sleeping with her.'

I went back and sat on the corner of the desk. 'You're getting bitchy, Mrs Loring. Why? Are you carrying a torch for our alcoholic friend?'

'I hate remarks like that,' she said bitingly. 'I hate them. I suppose that idiotic scene my husband made makes you think you have the right to insult me. No, I am not carrying a torch for Roger Wade. I never did – even when he was a sober man who behaved himself. Still less now that he is what he is.'

I flopped into my chair, reached for a matchbox and stared at her. She looked at her watch.

'You people with a lot of money are really something,' I said. 'You think anything you choose to say, however nasty, is perfectly all right. You can make sneering remarks about Wade and his wife to a man you hardly know, but if I hand you back a little change, that's an insult. Okay, let's play it low down. Any drunk will eventually turn up with a loose woman. Wade is a drunk, but you're not a loose woman. That's just a casual suggestion your high-bred husband drops to brighten up a cocktail party. He doesn't mean it, he's just saying it for laughs.

So we rule you out, and look for a loose woman elsewhere. How far do we have to look, Mrs Loring – to find one that would involve you enough to bring you down here trading sneers with me? It has to be somebody rather special, doesn't it – otherwise why should you care?'

She sat perfectly silent, just looking. A long half minute went by. The corners of her mouth were white and her hands were rigid on her garbardine bag that matched her suit.

'You haven't exactly wasted your time, have you?' she said at last. 'How convenient that this publisher should have thought of employing you! So Terry named no names to you! Not a name. But it really didn't matter, did it, Mr Marlowe? Your instinct was unerring. May I ask what you propose to do next?'

'Nothing.'

'Why, what a waste of talent! How can you reconcile it with your obligation to your portrait of Madison? Surely there must be something you can do.'

'Just between the two of us,' I said, 'you're getting pretty corny. So Wade knew your sister. Thanks for telling me, however indirectly. I already guessed it. So what? He's just one of what was most likely a fairly rich collection. Let's leave it there. And let's get around to why you wanted to see me. That kind of got lost in the shuffle, didn't it?'

She stood up. She glanced at her watch once more. 'I have a car downstairs. Could I prevail upon you to drive home with me and drink a cup of tea?'

'Go on,' I said. 'Let's have it.'

'Do I sound so suspicious? I have a guest who would like to make your acquaintance.'

'The old man?'

'I don't call him that,' she said evenly.

I stood up and leaned across the desk. 'Honey, you're awful cute sometimes. You really are. Is it all right if I carry a gun?'

'Surely you're not afraid of an old man.' She wrinkled her lip at me.

'Why not? I'll bet you are – plenty.'

She sighed. 'Yes, I'm afraid I am. I always have been. He can be rather terrifying.'

'Maybe I'd better take two guns,' I said, then wished I hadn't.

# Thirty-two

It was the damnedest-looking house I ever saw. It was a square, grey box three stories high, with a mansard roof, steeply sloped and broken by twenty or thirty double dormer windows with a lot of wedding-cake decorations around them and between them. The entrance had double stone pillars on each side but the cream of the joint was an outside spiral staircase with a stone railing, topped by a tower room from which there must have been a view the whole length of the lake.

The motor yard was paved with stone. What the place really seemed to need was a half-mile of poplar-lined driveway and a deer park and a wild garden and a terrace on three levels and a few hundred roses outside the library window and a long green vista from every window ending in forest and silence and quiet emptiness. What it had was a wall of fieldstone around a comfortable ten or fifteen acres, which is a fair hunk of real estate in our crowded little country. The driveway was lined with a cypress hedge trimmed round. There were all sorts of ornamental trees in clumps here and there and they didn't look like California trees. Imported stuff. Whoever built that place was trying to drag the Atlantic seaboard over the Rockies. He was trying hard, but he hadn't made it.

Amos, the middle-aged coloured chauffeur, stopped the Caddy gently in front of the pillared entrance, hopped out and came around to hold the door open for Mrs Loring. I got out first and helped him hold it. I helped her get out. She had hardly spoken to me since we got into the car in front of my building. She looked tired and nervous. Maybe this idiotic hunk of architecture depressed her. It would have depressed a laughing jackass and made it coo like a mourning dove.

'Who built this place?' I asked her. 'And who was he mad at?'

She finally smiled. 'Hadn't you seen it before?'

'Never been this far into the valley.'

She walked me over to the other side of the driveway and pointed up. 'The man who built it jumped out of that tower-room and landed about where you are standing. He was a French count named La Tourelle and, unlike most French counts, he had a lot of money. His wife was Ramona Desborough who was not exactly threadbare herself. In the silent picture days she made thirty thousand a week. La Tourelle built this place for their home. It's supposed to be a miniature of the Château de Blois. You know that, of course.'

'Like the back of my hand,' I said. 'I remember now. It was one of those Sunday paper stories once. She left him and he killed himself. There was some kind of queer will, too, wasn't there?'

She nodded. 'He left his ex-wife a few millions for carfare and tied up the rest in a trust. The estate was to be kept on just as it was. Nothing was to be changed, the dining-table was to be laid in style every night, and nobody was to be allowed inside the grounds except the servants and the lawyers. The will was broken, of course. Eventually the estate was carved up to some extent and when I married Dr Loring my father gave it to me for a wedding present. It must have cost him a fortune merely to make it fit to live in again. I loathe it. I always have.'

'You don't have to stay here, do you?'

She shrugged in a tired sort of way. 'Part of the time, at least. One of his daughters has to show him some sign of stability. Dr Loring likes it here.'

'He would. Any guy who could make the kind of scene he made at Wade's house ought to wear spats with his pyjamas.'

She arched her eyebrows. 'Why, thank you for taking such an interest, Mr Marlowe. But I think enough has been said on that subject. Shall we go in? My father doesn't like to be kept waiting.'

We crossed the driveway again and went up the stone steps and half of the big double doors swung open noiselessly and an expensive and very snooty-looking character stood aside for us to enter. The hallway was bigger than all the floor space in the house I was living in. It had a tessellated floor and there seemed to be stained-glass windows at the back, and if there had been any light coming through them I might have been able to see what else was there. From the hallway we went through some more double carved doors into a dim room that couldn't have been less than seventy feet long. A man was sitting there waiting, silent. He stared at us coldly.

'Am I late, father?' Mrs Loring asked hurriedly. 'This is Mr Philip Marlowe. Mr Harlan Potter.'

The man just looked at me and moved his chin down about half an inch.

'Ring for tea,' he said. 'Sit down, Mr Marlowe.'

I sat down and looked at him. He looked at me like an entomologist looking at a beetle. Nobody said anything. There was complete silence until the tea came. It was put down on a huge silver tray on a Chinese table. Linda sat at the table and poured.

'Two cups,' Harlan Potter said. 'You can have your tea in another room, Linda.'

'Yes, Father. How do you like your tea, Mr Marlowe?'

'Any way at all,' I said. My voice seemed to echo off into the distance and get small and lonely.

She gave the old man a cup and then gave me a cup. Then she stood up silently and went out of the room. I watched her go. I took a sip of tea and got a cigarette out.

'Don't smoke, please. I am subject to asthma.'

I put the cigarette back in the pack. I stared at him. I don't know how it feels to be worth a hundred millions or so, but he didn't look as if he was having any fun. He was an enormous man, all of six feet five and built to scale. He wore a grey tweed suit with no padding. His shoulders didn't need any. He wore a white shirt and a dark tie and no display handkerchief. A spectacle case showed in the outside breast pocket. It was black, like his shoes. His hair was black, too, no grey at all. It was brushed sideways across his skull in a MacArthur sweep. And I had a hunch there was nothing under it but bare skull. His eyebrows were thick and black. His voice seemed to come from a long way off. He drank his tea as if he hated it.

'It will save time, Mr Marlowe, if I put my position before you. I believe you are interfering in my affairs. If I am correct, I propose to stop it.'

'I don't know enough about your affairs to interfere in them, Mr Potter.'

'I disagree.'

He drank some more tea and put the cup aside. He leaned back in the big chair he was sitting in and took me to pieces with his hard grey eyes.

'I know who you are, naturally. And how you make your living – if you make one – and how you became involved with Terry Lennox. It has been reported to me that you helped Terry get out of the country, that you have doubts about his guilt, and that you have since made contact with a man who was known to my dead daughter. For what purpose has not been explained to me. Explain it.'

'If the man has a name,' I said, 'name it.'

He smiled very slightly but not as if he was falling for me. 'Wade. Roger Wade. Some sort of writer, I believe. A writer, they tell me, of rather prurient books which I should not be interested to read. I further understand that this man is a dangerous alcoholic. That may have given you a strange notion.'

'Maybe you had better let me have my own notions, Mr Potter. They are not important, naturally, but they're all I have. First, I do not believe Terry killed his wife, because of the way it was done and because I don't think he was that kind of man. Second, I didn't make contact with Wade. I was asked to live in his house and do what I could to keep him sober while he finished a job of writing. Third, if he is a dangerous alcoholic, I haven't seen any sign of it. Fourth, my first contact was at the request of his New York publisher and I didn't at that time have any idea that Roger Wade even knew your daughter. Fifth, I refused this offer of employment and then Mrs Wade asked me to find her husband who was away somewhere taking a cure. I found him and took him home.'

'Very methodical,' he said dryly.

'I'm not finished being methodical, Mr Potter. Sixth – I think that's the correct number – you or someone on your instructions sent a lawyer named Sewell Endicott to get me out of jail. He didn't say who sent him, but there wasn't anyone else in the picture. Seventh, when I got out of jail a hoodlum named Mendy Menendez pushed me around and warned me to keep my nose clean and gave me a song and dance about how Terry had saved his life and the life of a gambler at Las Vegas named Randy Starr. The story could be true for all I know. Menendez pretended to be sore that Terry hadn't asked him for help getting to Mexico and had asked a punk like me instead. He, Menendez, could have done it two ways from the jack by lifting one finger, and done it much better.'

'Surely,' Harlan Potter said with a bleak smile, 'you are not under the impression that I number Mr Menendez and Mr Starr among my acquaintances.'

'I wouldn't know, Mr Potter. A man doesn't make your kind of money in any way I can understand. The next person to warn me off the courthouse lawn was your daughter, Mrs Loring. We met by accident at a bar and we spoke because we were both drinking gimlets, Terry's favourite drink, but an uncommon one around here. I didn't know who she was until she told me. I told her a little of how I felt about Terry and she gave me the idea that I would have a short, unhappy career if I got you mad. Are you mad, Mr Potter?'

'When I am,' he said coldly, 'you will not have to ask me. You will be in no uncertainty about it.'

'What I thought. I've been kind of expecting the goon squad to drop around, but they haven't shown so far. I haven't been bothered by the cops either. I could have been. I could have been given a rough time. I think all you wanted, Mr Potter, was quiet. Just what have I done to disturb you?'

He grinned. It was a sour kind of grin, but it was a grin. He put his long, yellow fingers together and crossed a leg over his knee and leaned back comfortably.

'A pretty good pitch, Mr Marlowe, and I have let you make it. Now you listen to me. You are exactly right in thinking all I want is quiet. It's quite possible that your connection with the Wades may be incidental, accidental, and coincidental. Let it remain so. I am a family man in an age when it means almost nothing. One of my daughters married a Bostonian prig and the other made a number of foolish marriages, the last being with a complaisant pauper who allowed her to live a worthless and immoral life until he suddenly and for no good reason lost his self-control and murdered her. You think that impossible to accept because of the brutality with which it was done. You are wrong. He shot her with a Mauser automatic, the very gun he took with him to Mexico. And after he shot her he did what he did in order to cover the bullet wound. I admit the brutality of this, but remember the man had been in a war, had been badly wounded, had suffered a great deal and seen others suffer. He may not have intended to kill her. There may have been some sort of scuffle, since the gun belonged to my daughter. It was a small but powerful gun, 7.65 mm calibre, a model called PPK. The bullet went completely through her head and lodged in the wall behind a chintz curtain. It was not found immediately and the fact was not published at all. Now let us consider the situation.' He broke off and stared at me. 'Are you very badly in need of a cigarette?'

'Sorry, Mr Potter. I took it out without thinking. Force of habit.' I put the cigarette back for the second time.

'Terry had just killed his wife. He had ample motive from the rather limited police point of view. But he also had an excellent defence – that it was her gun in her possession and that he tried to take it away from her and failed and she shot herself with it. A good trial lawyer could have done a lot with that. He would probably have been acquitted. If he had called me up then, I would have helped him. But by making the murder a brutal affair to cover the traces of the bullet, he made it impossible. He had to run away and even that he did clumsily.'

'He certainly did, Mr Potter. But he called you up in Pasadena first, didn't he? He told me he did.'

The big man nodded. 'I told him to disappear and I would still see what I could do. I didn't want to know where he was. That was imperative. I could not hide a criminal.'

'Sounds good, Mr Potter.'

'Do I detect a note of sarcasm? No matter. When I learned the details there was nothing to be done. I could not permit the sort of trial that kind of killing would result in. To be frank, I was very glad when I learned that he had shot himself in Mexico and left a confession.'

'I can understand that, Mr Potter.'

He beetled his eyebrows at me. 'Be careful, young man. I don't like irony. Can you understand now that I cannot tolerate any further investigation of any sort by any person? And why I have used all my influence to make what investigation there was as brief as possible and as little publicized as possible?'

'Sure – if you're convinced he killed her.'

'Of course he killed her. With what intent is another matter. It is no longer important. I am not a public character and I do not intend to be. I have always gone to a great deal of trouble to avoid any kind of publicity. I have influence but I don't abuse it. The District Attorney of Los Angeles County is an ambitious man who has too much good sense to wreck his career for the notoriety of the moment. I see a glint in your eye, Marlowe. Get rid of it. We live in what is called a democracy, rule by the majority of the people. A fine ideal if it could be made to work. The people elect, but the party machines nominate, and the party machines to be effective must spend a great deal of money. Somebody has to give it to them, and that somebody whether it be an individual, a financial group, a trade union or what have you, expects some consideration in return. What I and people of my kind expect is to be allowed to live our lives in decent privacy. I own newspapers, but I don't like them. I regard them as a constant menace to whatever privacy we have left. Their constant yelping about a free press means, with a few honourable exceptions, freedom to peddle scandal, crime, sex, sensationalism, hate, innuendo, and the political and financial uses of propaganda. A newspaper is a business out to make money through advertising revenue. That is predicated on its circulation and you know what the circulation depends on.'

I got up and walked around my chair. He eyed me with cold attention. I sat down again. I needed a little luck. Hell, I needed it in carload lots.

'Okay, Mr Potter, what goes from here?'

He wasn't listening. He was frowning at his own thoughts. 'There's a peculiar thing about money,' he went on. 'In large quantities it tends to have a life of its own, even a conscience of its own. The power of money becomes very difficult to control. Man has always been a venal animal. The growth of populations, the huge cost of wars, the incessant pressure of confiscatory taxation – all these things make him more and more venal. The average man is tired and scared, and a tired, scared man can't afford ideals. He has to buy food for his family. In our time we have seen a shocking decline in both public and private morals. You can't expect quality from people whose lives are a subjection to a lack of quality. You can't have quality with mass production. You don't want it because it lasts too long. So you substitute styling, which is a commercial swindle intended to produce artificial obsolescence. Mass production couldn't sell its goods next year unless it made what it sold this year look unfashionable a year from now. We have the whitest kitchens and the most shining bathrooms in the world. But in the lovely white kitchen the average American housewife can't produce a meal fit to eat, and the lovely shining bathroom is mostly a receptacle for deodorants, laxatives, sleeping pills, and the products of that confidence racket called the cosmetic industry. We make the finest packages in the world, Mr Marlowe. The stuff inside is mostly junk.'

He took out a large white handkerchief and touched his temples with it. I was sitting there with my mouth open, wondering what made the guy tick. He hated everything.

'It's a little too warm for me in these parts,' he said, 'I'm used to a cooler climate. I'm beginning to sound like an editorial that has forgotten the point it wanted to make.'

'I got your point all right, Mr Potter. You don't like the way the world is going so you use what power you have to close off a private corner to live in as near as possible to the way you remember people lived fifty years ago before the age of mass production. You've got a hundred million dollars and all it has bought you is a pain in the neck.'

He pulled the handkerchief taut by two opposite corners, then crumpled it into a ball and stuffed it in a pocket.

'And then?' he asked shortly.

'That's all there is, there isn't any more. You don't care who murdered your daughter, Mr Potter. You wrote her off as a bad job long ago. Even if Terry Lennox didn't kill her, and the real murderer is still walking around free, you don't care. You wouldn't want him caught, because that would revive the scandal and there would have to be a trial and his defence would blow your privacy as high as the Empire State Building. Unless, of course, he was obliging enough to commit suicide, before there was any trial. Preferably in Tahiti or Guatemala or the middle of the Sahara Desert. Anywhere the County would hate the expense of sending a man to verify what had happened.'

He smiled suddenly, a big rugged smile with a reasonable amount of friendliness in it.

'What do you want from me, Marlowe?'

'If you mean how much money, nothing. I didn't ask myself here. I was brought. I told the truth about how I met Roger Wade. But he did know your daughter and he does have a record of violence, although I haven't seen any of it. Last night the guy tried to shoot himself. He's a haunted man. He has a massive guilt complex. If I happened to be looking for a good suspect, he might do. I realize he's only one of many, but he happens to be the only one I've met.'

He stood up and standing up he was really big. Tough too. He came over and stood in front of me.

'A telephone call, Mr Marlowe, would deprive you of your licence. Don't fence with me. I won't put up with it.'

'Two telephone calls and I'd wake up kissing the gutter – with the back of my head missing.'

He laughed harshly. 'I don't operate that way. I suppose in your quaint line of business it is natural for you to think so. I've given you too much of my time. I'll ring for the butler to show you out.'

'Not necessary,' I said, and stood up myself. 'I came here and got told. Thanks for the time.'

He held his hand out. 'Thank you for coming. I think you're a pretty honest sort of fellow. Don't be a hero, young man. There's no percentage in it.'

I shook hands with him. He had a grip like a pipe wrench. He smiled at me benignantly now. He was Mr Big, the winner, everything under control.

'One of these days I might be able to throw some business your way,' he said. 'And don't go away thinking that I buy politicians or law enforcement officers. I don't have to. Good-bye, Mr Marlowe. And thank you again for coming.'

He stood there and watched me out of the room, I had my hand on the front door when Linda Loring popped out of a shadow somewhere.

'Well?' she asked me quietly. 'How did you get on with Father?'

'Fine. He explained civilization to me. I mean how it looks to him. He's going to let it go on for a little while longer. But it better be careful and not interfere with his private life. It it does, he's apt to make a phone call to God and cancel the order.'

'You're hopeless,' she said.

'Me? I'm hopeless? Lady, take a look at your old man. Compared with him I'm a blue-eyed baby with a brand-new rattle.'

I went on out and Amos had the Caddy there waiting. He drove me back to Hollywood. I offered him a buck but he wouldn't take it. I offered to buy him the poems of T. S. Eliot. He said he already had them.


# Thirty-three


A week went by and I heard nothing from the Wades. The weather was hot and sticky and the acid sting of the smog had crept as far west as Beverly Hills. From the top of Mulholland Drive you could see it levelled out all over the city, a groundlike mist. When you were in it you could taste it and smell it and it made your eyes smart. Everybody was griping about it. In Pasadena, where the stuffy millionaires holed up after Beverly Hills was spoiled for them by the movie crowd, the city fathers screamed with rage. Everything was the fault of the smog. If the canary wouldn't sing, if the milkman was late, if the Pekinese had fleas, if an old coot in a starched collar had a heart attack on the way to church, that was the smog. Where I lived it was usually clear in the early morning and nearly always at night. Once in a while a whole day would be clear, nobody quite knew why.

It was on a day like that – it happened to be a Thursday – that Roger Wade called me up. 'How are you? This is Wade.' He sounded fine.

'Fine, and you?'

'Sober, I'm afraid. Scratching a hard buck. We ought to have a talk. And I think I owe you some dough.'

'Nope.'

'Well, how about lunch today? Could you make it here some-where around one?'

'I guess so. How's Candy?'

'Candy?' He sounded puzzled. He must have blacked out plenty that night. 'Oh, he helped you put me to bed that night.'

'Yeah. He's a helpful little guy – in spots. And Mrs Wade?'

'She's fine too. She's in town shopping today.'

We hung up and I sat and rocked in my swivel chair. I ought to have asked him how the book was going. Maybe you always ought to ask a writer how the book is going. And then again maybe he gets damned tired of that question.

I had another call in a little while, a strange voice.

'This is Roy Ashterfelt. George Peters told me to call you up, Marlowe.'

'Oh yes, thanks. You're the fellow that knew Terry Lennox in New York. Called himself Marston then.'

'That's right. He was sure on the sauce. But it's the same guy all right. You couldn't very well mistake him. Out here I saw him in Chasen's one night with his wife. I was with a client. The client knew them. Can't tell you the client's name, I'm afraid.'

'I understand. It's not very important now, I guess. What was his first name?'

'Wait a minute while I bite my thumb. Oh yeah, Paul. Paul Marston. And there was one thing more, if it interests you. He was wearing a British Army Service badge. Their version of the ruptured duck.'

'I see. What happened to him?'

'I don't know. I came west. Next time I saw him he was here too – married to Harlan Potter's somewhat wild daughter. But you know all that.'

'They're both dead now. But thanks for telling me.'

'Not at all. Glad to help. Does it mean anything to you?'

'Not a thing,' I said, and I was a liar. 'I never asked him about himself. He told me once he had been brought up in an orphan-age. Isn't it just possible you made a mistake?'

'With that white hair and that scarred face, brother? Not a chance. I won't say I never forget a face, but not that one.'

'Did he see you?'

'If he did, he didn't let on. Hardly expect him to in the cir-cumstances. Anyhow he might not have remembered me. Like I said he was always pretty well lit back in New York.'

I thanked him some more and he said it was a pleasure and we hung up.

I thought about it for a while. The noise of the traffic outside the building on the boulevard made an unmusical *obbligato* to my thinking. It was too loud. In summer in hot weather everything is too loud. I got up and shut the lower part of the window and called Detective-Sergeant Green at Homicide. He was obliging enough to be in.

'Look,' I said, after the preliminaries, 'I heard something about Terry Lennox that puzzles me. A fellow I know used to know him in New York under another name. You check his war record?'

'You guys never learn,' Green said harshly. 'You just never learn to stay on your own side of the street. The matter is closed, locked up, weighted with lead and dropped in the ocean. Get it?'

'I spent part of an afternoon with Harlan Potter last week. At his daughter's house in Idle Valley. Want to check?'

'Doing what?' he asked sourly. 'Supposing I believe you.'

'Talking things over. I was invited. He likes me. Incidentally, he told me the girl was shot with a Mauser 7.65 mm, Model PPK. That news to you?'

'Go on.'

'Her own gun, chum. Makes a little difference, maybe. But don't get me wrong. I'm not looking into any dark corners. This is a personal matter. Where did he get that wound?'

Green was silent. I heard a door close in the background. Then he said quietly: 'Probably in a knife fight south of the border.'

'Aw hell, Green, you had his prints. You sent them to Washington like always. You got a report back – like always. All I asked was something about his service record.'

'Who said he had one?'

'Well, Mendy Menendez for one. Seems Lennox saved his life one time and that's how he got the wound. He was captured by the Germans and they gave him the face he had.'

'Menendez, huh? You believe that son of a bitch? You got a hole in your own head. Lennox didn't have any war record. Didn't have any record of any kind under any name. You satisfied?'

'If you say so,' I said. 'But I don't see why Menendez would bother to come up here and tell me a yarn and warn me to keep my nose clean on account of Lennox was a pal of him and Randy

Starr in Vegas and they didn't want anybody fooling around. After all Lennox was already dead.'

'Who knows what a hoodlum figures?' Green asked bitterly. 'Or why? Maybe Lennox was in a racket with them before he married all that money and got respectable. He was a floor manager at Starr's place in Vegas for a while. That's where he met the girl. A smile and a bow and a dinner jacket. Keep the customers happy and keep an eye on the house players. I guess he had class for the job.'

'He had charm,' I said. 'They don't use it in the police business. Much obliged, Sergeant. How is Captain Gregorius these days?'

'Retirement leave. Don't you read the papers?'

'Not the crime news, Sergeant. Too sordid.'

I started to say good-bye but he chopped me off. 'What did Mr Money want with you?'

'We just had a cup of tea together. A social call. He said he might put some business my way. He also hinted – just hinted, not in so many words – that any cop that looked cross-eyed at me would be facing a grimy future.'

'He don't run the police department,' Green said.

'He admits it. Doesn't even buy commissioners or D.A.s, he said. They just kind of curl up in his lap when he's having a doze.'

'Go to hell,' Green said and hung up in my ear.

A difficult thing, being a cop. You never know whose stomach it's safe to jump up and down on.


# Thirty-four


The stretch of broken-paved road from the highway to the curve of the hill was dancing in the noon heat and the scrub that dotted the parched land on both sides of it was flour-white with granite dust by this time. The weedy smell was almost nauseating. A thin, hot, acrid breeze was blowing. I had my coat off and my sleeves rolled up, but the door was too hot to rest an arm on. A tethered horse dozed wearily under a clump of live oaks. A brown Mexican sat on the ground and ate something out of a newspaper. A tumbleweed rolled lazily across the road and came to rest against a piece of granite outcrop, and a lizard that had been there an instant before disappeared without seeming to move at all.

Then I was around the hill on the blacktop and in another country. In five minutes I turned into the driveway of the Wades' house, parked and walked across the flagstones and rang the bell. Wade answered the door himself, in a brown and white checked shirt with short sleeves, pale blue denim slacks and house slippers. He looked tanned and he looked good. There was an ink stain on his hand and a smear of cigarette ash on one side of his nose.

He led the way into his study and parked himself behind his desk. On it there was a thick pile of yellow typescript. I put my coat on a chair and sat on the couch.

'Thanks for coming, Marlowe. Drink?'

I got that look on my face you get when a drunk asks you to have a drink. I could feel it. He grinned.

'I'll have a coke,' he said.

'You pick up fast,' I said. 'I don't think I want a drink right now. I'll take a coke with you.'

He pressed something with his foot and after a while Candy came. He looked surly. He had a blue shirt on and an orange scarf and no white coat. Two-tone black and white shoes, elegant high-waisted gabardine pants.

Wade ordered the cokes. Candy gave me a hard stare and went away.

'Book?' I said, pointing to the stack of paper.

'Yeah. Stinks.'

'I don't believe it. How far along?'

'About two-thirds of the way – for what it's worth. Which is damn little. You know how a writer can tell when he's washed up?'

'Don't know anything about writers.' I filled my pipe.

'When he starts reading his old stuff for inspiration. That's absolute. I've got five hundred pages of typescript here, well over a hundred thousand words. My books run long. The public likes long books. The damn fool public thinks if there's a lot of pages there must be a lot of gold. I don't dare read it over. And I can't remember half of what's in it. I'm just plain scared to look at my own work.'

'You look good yourself,' I said. 'From the other night I wouldn't have believed it. You've got more guts than you think you have.'

'What I need right now is more than guts. Something you

don't get by wishing for it. A belief in yourself. I'm a spoiled writer who doesn't believe any more. I have a beautiful home, a beautiful wife and a beautiful sales record. But all I really want is to get drunk and forget.'

He leaned his chin in his cupped hands and stared across the desk.

'Eileen said I tried to shoot myself. Was it that bad?'

'You don't remember?'

He shook his head. 'Not a damn thing except that I fell down and cut my head. And after a while I was in bed. And you were there. Did Eileen call you?'

'Yeah. Didn't she say?'

'She hasn't been talking to me very much this last week. I guess she's had it. Up to here.' He put the edge of one hand against his neck just under his chin. 'That show Loring put on here didn't help any.'

'Mrs Wade said it meant nothing.'

'Well, she would, wouldn't she? It happened to be the truth, but I don't suppose she believed it when she said it. The guy is just abnormally jealous. You have a drink or two with his wife in the corner and laugh a little and kiss her good-bye and right off he assumes you are sleeping with her. One reason being that he isn't.'

'What I like about Idle Valley,' I said, 'is that everybody is living just a comfortable, normal life.'

He frowned and then the door opened and Candy came in with two cokes and glasses and poured the cokes. He set one in front of me without looking at me.

'Lunch in half an hour,' Wade said, 'and where's the white coat?'

'This my day off,' Candy said, deadpan. 'I ain't the cook, boss.'

'Cold cuts or sandwiches and beer will do,' Wade said. 'The cook's off today, Candy. I've got a friend to lunch.'

'You think he is your friend?' Candy sneered. 'Better ask your wife.'

Wade leaned back in his chair and smiled at him. 'Watch your lip, little man. You've got it soft here. I don't often ask a favour of you, do I?'

Candy looked down at the floor. After a moment he looked up and grinned. 'Okay, boss. I put the white coat on. I get the lunch, I guess.'

He turned softly and went out. Wade watched the door close. Then he shrugged and looked at me.

'We used to call them servants. Now we call them domestic help. I wonder how long it will be before we have to give them breakfast in bed. I'm paying the guy too much money. He's spoiled.'

'Wages – or something on the side?'

'Such as what?' he asked sharply.

I got up and handed him some folded yellow sheets. 'You'd better read it. Evidently you don't remember asking me to tear it up. It was in your typewriter, under the cover.'

He unfolded the yellow pages and leaned back to read them. The glass of coke fizzed unnoticed on the desk in front of him. He read slowly, frowning. When he came to the end he refolded the sheets and ran a finger along the edge.

'Did Eileen see this?' he asked carefully.

'I wouldn't know. She might have.'

'Pretty wild, isn't it?'

'I liked it. Especially the part about a good man dying for you.'

He opened the paper again and tore it into long strips viciously and dumped the strips into his waste-basket.

'I suppose a drunk will write or say or do anything,' he said slowly. 'It's meaningless to me. Candy's not blackmailing me. He likes me.'

'Maybe you'd better get drunk again. You might remember what you meant. You might remember a lot of things. We've been through this before – that night when the gun went off. I suppose the seconal blanked you out too. You sounded sober enough. But now you pretend not to remember writing that stuff I just gave you. No wonder you can't write your book, Wade. It's a wonder you can stay alive.'

He reached sideways and opened a drawer of his desk. His hand fumbled in it and came up with a three-decker cheque-book. He opened it and reached for a pen.

'I owe you a thousand dollars,' he said quietly. He wrote in the book. Then on the counterfoil. He tore the cheque out, came around the desk with it and dropped it in front of me. 'Is that all right?'

I leaned back and looked up at him and didn't touch the cheque and didn't answer him. His face was tight and drawn. His eyes were deep and empty.

'I suppose you think I killed her and let Lennox take the rap,' he said slowly. 'She was a tramp all right. But you don't beat a woman's head in just because she's a tramp. Candy knows I went there sometimes. The funny part of it is I don't think he would tell. I could be wrong, but I don't think so.'

'Wouldn't matter if he did,' I said. 'Harlan Potter's friends wouldn't listen to him. Also, she wasn't killed with that bronze thing. She was shot through the head with her own gun.'

'She maybe had a gun,' he said almost dreamily. 'But I didn't know she had been shot. It wasn't published.'

'Didn't know or didn't remember?' I asked him. 'No, it wasn't published.'

'What are you trying to do to me, Marlowe?' His voice was still dreamy, almost gentle. 'What do you want me to do? Tell my wife. Tell the police? What good would it do?'

'You said a good man died for you.'

'All I meant was that if there had been any real investigation I might have been identified as one – but only one – of the possible suspects. It would have finished me in several ways.'

'I didn't come here to accuse you of a murder, Wade. What's eating you is that you're not sure yourself. You have a record of violence to your wife. You black out when you're drunk. It's no argument to say you don't beat a woman's head in just because she's a tramp. That is exactly what somebody did do. And the guy who got credit for the job seemed to me a lot less likely than you.'

He walked to the open french windows and stood looking out at the shimmer of heat over the lake. He didn't answer me. He hadn't moved or spoken a couple of minutes later when there was a light knock at the door and Candy came in wheeling a tea wagon, with a crisp white cloth, silver-covered dishes, a pot of coffee and two bottles of beer.

'Open the beer, boss?' he asked Wade's back.

'Bring me a bottle of whisky.' Wade didn't turn around.

'Sorry, boss. No whisky.'

Wade spun around and yelled at him, but Candy didn't budge. He looked down at the cheque lying on the cocktail table and his head twisted as he read it. Then he looked up at me and hissed something between his teeth. Then he looked at Wade.

'I go now. This my day off.'

He turned and went. Wade laughed.

'So I get it myself,' he said sharply, and went.

I lifted one of the covers and saw some neatly trimmed three-cornered sandwiches. I took one and poured some beer and ate the sandwich standing up. Wade came back with a bottle and a glass. He sat down on the couch and poured a stiff jolt and sucked it down. There was the sound of a car going away from the house, probably Candy leaving by the service driveway. I took another sandwich.

'Sit down and make yourself comfortable,' Wade said. 'We have all afternoon to kill.' He had a glow on already. His voice was vibrant and cheerful. 'You don't like me, do you, Marlowe?'

'That question has already been asked and answered.'

'Know something? You're a pretty ruthless son of a bitch. You'd do anything to find what you want. You'd even make love to my wife while I was helpless drunk in the next room.'

'You believe everything that knife-thrower tells you?'

He poured some more whisky into his glass and held it up against the light. 'Not everything, no. A pretty colour whisky is, isn't it? To drown in a golden flood – that's not so bad. "To cease upon the midnight with no pain." How does that go on? Oh, sorry, you wouldn't know. Too literary. You're some kind of a dick, aren't you? Mind telling me why you're here?'

He drank some more whisky and grinned at me. Then he spotted the cheque lying on the table. He reached for it and read it over his glass.

'Seems to be made out to somebody named Marlowe. I wonder why, what for? Seems I signed it. Foolish of me. I'm a gullible chap.'

'Stop acting,' I said roughly. 'Where's your wife?'

He looked up politely. 'My wife will be home in due course. No doubt by that time I shall be passed out and she can entertain you at her leisure. The house will be yours.'

'Where's the gun?' I asked suddenly.

He looked blank. I told him I had put it in his desk. 'Not there now, I'm sure,' he said. 'You may search if it pleases you. Just don't steal any rubber bands.'

I went to the desk and frisked it. No gun. That was something. Probably Eileen had hidden it.

'Look, Wade, I asked you where your wife was. I think she ought to come home. Not for my benefit, friend, for yours. Somebody has to look out for you, and I'll be goddamned if it's going to be me.'

He stared vaguely. He was still holding the cheque. He put his glass down and tore the cheque across, then again and again, and let the pieces fall to the floor.

'Evidently the amount was too small,' he said. 'Your services come very high. Even a thousand dollars *and* my wife fail to satisfy you. Too bad, but I can't go any higher. Except on this.' He patted the bottle.

'I'm leaving,' I said.

'But why? You wanted me to remember. Well – here in the bottle is my memory. Stick around, pal. When I get lit enough I'll tell you about all the women I have murdered.'

'All right, Wade. I'll stick around for a while. But not in here. If you need me, just smash a chair against the wall.'

I went out and left the door open. I walked across the big living-room and out to the patio and pulled one of the chaises into the shadow of the overhang and stretched out on it. Across the lake there was a blue haze against the hills. The ocean breeze had begun to filter through the low mountains to the west. It wiped the air clean and it wiped away just enough of the heat. Idle Valley was having a perfect summer. Somebody had planned it that way. Paradise Incorporated, and also Highly Restricted. Only the nicest people. Absolutely no Central Europeans. Just the cream, the top-drawer crowd, the lovely, lovely people. Like the Lorings and the Wades. Pure gold.


# Thirty-five


I lay there for half an hour trying to make up my mind what to do. Part of me wanted to let him get good and drunk and see if anything came out. I didn't think anything much would happen to him in his own study in his own house. He might fall down again but it would be a long time. The guy had capacity. And somehow a drunk never hurts himself very badly. He might get back his mood of guilt. More likely, this time he would just go to sleep.

The other part of me wanted to get out and stay out, but this was the part I never listened to. Because if I ever had I would have stayed in the town where I was born and worked in the hardware store and married the boss's daughter and had five kids and read them the funny paper on Sunday morning and smacked their heads when they got out of line and squabbled with the wife about how much spending money they were to get and what programmes they could have on the radio or TV set. I might even have got rich – small-town rich, an eight-room house, two cars in the garage, chicken every Sunday and the *Reader's Digest* on the living-room table, the wife with a cast-iron permanent and me with a brain like a sack of Portland cement. You take it, friend. I'll take the big, sordid, dirty, crooked city.

I got up and went back to the study. He was just sitting there staring at nothing, the Scotch bottle more than half empty, a loose frown on his face and a dull glitter in his eyes. He looked at me like a horse looking over a fence.

'What d'you want?'

'Nothing. You all right?'

'Don't bother me. I have a little man on my shoulder telling me stories.'

I got another sandwich off the tea wagon and another glass of beer. I munched the sandwich and drank the beer, leaning against his desk.

'Know something?' he asked suddenly, and his voice suddenly seemed much more clear. 'I had a male secretary once. Used to dictate to him. Let him go. He bothered me sitting there waiting for me to create. Mistake. Ought to have kept him. Word would have got around I was a homo. The clever boys that write book reviews because they can't write anything else would have caught on and started giving me the build-up. Have to take care of their own, you know. They're all queers, every damn one of them. The queer is the artistic arbiter of our age, chum. The pervert is the top guy now.'

'That so? Always been around, hasn't he?'

He wasn't looking at me. He was just talking. But he heard what I said.

'Sure, thousands of years. And especially in all the great ages of art. Athens, Rome, the Renaissance, the Elizabethan Age, the Romantic Movement in France – loaded with them. Queers all over the place. Ever read *The Golden Bough*? No, too long for you. Shorter version though. Ought to read it. Proves our sexual habits are pure convention – like wearing a black tie with a dinner jacket. Me. I'm a sex writer, but with frills and straight.'

He looked up at me and sneered. 'You know something? I'm a liar. My heroes are eight feet tall and my heroines have callouses on their bottoms from lying in bed with their knees up. Lace and ruffles, swords and coaches, elegance and leisure, duels and gallant death. All lies. They used perfume instead of soap, their teeth rotted because they never cleaned them, their fingernails smelled of stale gravy. The nobility of France urinated against the walls in the marble corridors of Versailles, and when you finally got several sets of underclothes off the lovely marquise the first thing you noticed was that she needed a bath. I ought to write it that way.'

'Why don't you?'

He chuckled. 'Sure, and live in a five-room house in Compton – if I was that lucky.' He reached down and patted the whisky bottle. 'You're lonely, pal. You need company.'

He got up and walked fairly steadily out of the room. I waited, thinking about nothing. A speedboat came racketing down the lake. When it came in sight I could see that it was high out of the water on its step and towing a surfboard with a husky, sunburnt lad on it. I went over to the french doors and watched it make a sweeping turn. Too fast, the speedboat almost turned over. The surfboard rider danced on one foot trying to hold his balance, then went shooting off into the water. The speedboat drifted to a stop and the man in the water came up to it in a lazy crawl, then went back along the tow rope and rolled himself on to the surfboard.

Wade came back with another bottle of whisky. The speedboat picked up and went off into the distance. Wade put his fresh bottle down beside the other. He sat down and brooded.

'Christ, you're not going to drink all that, are you?'

He squinted his eyes at me. 'Take off, buster. Go on home and mop the kitchen floor or something. You're in my light.' His voice was thick again. He had taken a couple in the kitchen, as usual.

'If you want me, holler.'

'I couldn't get low enough to want you.'

'Yeah, thanks. I'll be around until Mrs Wade comes home. Ever hear of anybody named Paul Marston?'

His head came up slowly. His eyes focused, but with effort, I could see him fighting for control. He won the fight – for the moment. His face became expressionless.

'Never did,' he said carefully, speaking very slowly. 'Who's he?'

The next time I looked in on him he was asleep, with his mouth open, his hair damp with sweat, and reeking of Scotch. His lips were pulled back from his teeth in a loose grimace and the furred surface of his tongue looked dry.

One of the whisky bottles was empty. A glass on the table had about two inches in it and the other bottle was about three-quarters full. I put the empty on the tea wagon and rolled it out of the room, then went back to close the french doors and turn the slats of the blinds. The speedboat might come back and wake him. I shut the study door.

I wheeled the tea wagon out to the kitchen, which was blue

and white and large and airy and empty. I was still hungry. I ate another sandwich and drank what was left of the beer, then poured a cup of coffee and drank that. The beer was flat but the coffee was still hot. Then I went back to the patio. It was quite a long time before the speedboat came tearing down the lake again. It was almost four o'clock when I heard its distant roar swell into an ear-splitting howl of noise. There ought to be a law. Probably was and the guy in the speedboat didn't give a damn. He enjoyed making a nuisance of himself, like other people I was meeting. I walked down to the edge of the lake.

He made it this time. The driver slowed just enough on the turn and the brown lad on the surfboard leaned far out against the centrifugal pull. The surfboard was almost out of the water, but one edge stayed in and then the speedboat straightened out and the surfboard still had a rider and they went back the way they had come and that was that. The waves stirred up by the boat came charging in towards the shore of the lake at my feet. They slapped hard against the piles of the short landing and jumped the tied boat up and down. They were still slapping it around when I turned back to the house.

As I reached the patio I heard a bell chiming from the direction of the kitchen. When it sounded again I decided that only the front door would have chimes. I crossed to it and opened it.

Eileen Wade was standing there looking away from the house. As she turned she said: 'I'm sorry, I forgot my key.' Then she saw me. 'Oh – I thought it was Roger or Candy.'

'Candy isn't here. It's Thursday.'

She came in and I shut the door. She put a bag down on the table between the two davenports. She looked cool and also distant. She pulled off a pair of white pigskin gloves.

'Is anything wrong?'

'Well, there's a little drinking being done. Not bad. He's asleep on the couch in his study.'

'He called you?'

'Yes, but not for that. He asked me to lunch. I'm afraid he didn't have any himself.'

'Oh.' She sat down slowly on a davenport. 'You know, I completely forgot it was Thursday. The cook's away too. How stupid.'

'Candy got the lunch before he left. I guess I'll blow now. I hope my car wasn't in your way.'

She smiled. 'No. There was plenty of room. Won't you have some tea? I'm going to have some.'

'All right.' I didn't know why I said that. I didn't want any tea. I just said it.

She slipped off a linen jacket. She hadn't worn a hat. 'I'll just look in and see if Roger is all right.'

I watched her cross to the study door and open it. She stood there a moment and closed the door and came back.

'He's still asleep. Very soundly. I have to go upstairs for a moment. I'll be right down.'

I watched her pick up her jacket and gloves and bag and go up the stairs and into her room. The door closed. I crossed to the study with the idea of removing the bottle of hooch. If he was still asleep, he wouldn't need it.


# Thirty-six

The shutting of the french doors had made the room stuffy and the turning of the venetian blinds had made it dim. There was an acrid smell in the air and there was too heavy a silence. It was not more than sixteen feet from the door to the couch and I didn't need more than half of that to know a dead man lay on that couch.

He was on his side with his face to the back of the couch, one arm crooked under him and the forearm of the other lying almost across his eyes. Between his chest and the back of the couch there was a pool of blood and in that pool lay the Webley Hammerless. The side of his face was a smeared mask.

I bent over him, peering at the edge of the wide-open eye, the bare and gaudy arm, at the inner curve of which I could see the puffed and blackened hole in his head from which the blood oozed still.

I left him like that. His wrist was warm but there was no doubt he was quite dead. I looked around for some kind of note or scribble. There was nothing but the pile of script on the desk. They don't leave notes. The typewriter was uncovered on its stand. There was nothing in that. Otherwise everything looked natural enough. Suicides prepare themselves in all sorts of ways, some with liquor, some with elaborate champagne dinners. Some in evening clothes, some in no clothes. People have killed themselves on the tops of walls, in ditches, in bathrooms, in the water, over the water, on the water. They have hanged themselves in barns and gassed themselves in garages. This one looked simple.

I hadn't heard the shot but it must have gone off when I was down by the lake watching the surfboard rider make his turn. There was plenty of noise. Why that should have mattered to Roger Wade I don't know. Perhaps it hadn't. The final impulse had coincided with the run of the speedboat. I didn't like it, but nobody cared what I liked.

The torn strips of the cheque were still on the floor but I left them. The torn strips of that stuff he had written that other night were in the wastebasket. These I did not leave. I picked them out and made sure I had them all and stuffed them into my pocket. The basket was almost empty, which made it easy. No use wondering where the gun had been. There were too many places to hide it in. It could have been in a chair or in the couch, under one of the cushions. It could have been on the floor, behind the books, anywhere.

I went out and shut the door. I listened. From the kitchen, sounds. I went out there. Eileen had a blue apron on and the kettle was just beginning to whistle. She turned the flame down and gave me a brief, impersonal glance.

'How do you like your tea, Mr Marlowe?'

'Just out of the pot as it comes.'

I leaned against the wall and got a cigarette out just to have something to do with my fingers. I pinched and squeezed it and broke it in half and threw one half on the floor. Her eyes followed it down. I bent and picked it up. I squeezed the two halves together into a little ball.

She made the tea. 'I always take cream and sugar,' she said over her shoulder. 'Strange, when I drink my coffee black. I learned tea drinking in England. They were using saccharine instead of sugar. When the war came they had no cream, of course.'

'You lived in England?'

'I worked there. I stayed all through the Blitz. I met a man – but I told you about that.'

'Where did you meet Roger?'

'In New York.'

'Married there?'

She swung around, frowning. 'No, we were not married in New York. Why?'

'Just talking while the tea draws.'

She looked out of the window over the sink. She could see down to the lake from there. She leaned against the edge of the drainboard and her fingers fiddled with a folded tea towel.

'It has to be stopped,' she said, 'and I don't know how. Perhaps he'll have to be committed to an institution. Somehow I can't quite see myself doing that. I'd have to sign something, wouldn't I?'

She turned around when she asked that.

'He could do it himself,' I said. 'That is, he could have up to now.'

The tea timer rang its bell. She turned back to the sink and poured the tea from one pot into another. Then she put the fresh pot on the tray she had already fixed up with cups. I went over and got the tray and carried it to the table between the two davenports in the living-room. She sat down opposite me and poured two cups. I reached for mine and set it down in front of me for it to cool. I watched her fix hers with two lumps of sugar and the cream. She tasted it.

'What did you mean by that last remark?' she asked suddenly. 'That he could have up to now – committed himself to some institution, you meant, didn't you?'

'I guess it was a wild pitch. Did you hide the gun I told you about? You know, the morning after he made that play upstairs.'

'Hide it?' she repeated, frowning. 'No. I never do anything like that. I don't believe in it. Why are you asking?'

'And you forgot your house keys today?'

'I told you I did.'

'But not the garage key. Usually in this kind of house the outside keys are mastered.'

'I don't need a key for the garage,' she said sharply. 'It opens by a switch. There's a relay switch inside the front door you push up as you go out. Then another switch beside the garage operates that door. Often we leave the garage open. Or Candy goes out and closes it.'

'I see.'

'You are making some rather strange remarks,' she said with acid in her voice. 'You did the other morning.'

'I've had some rather strange experiences in this house. Guns going off in the night, drunks lying out on the front lawn and doctors coming that won't do anything. Lovely women wrapping their arms around me and talking as if they thought I was someone else, Mexican houseboys throwing knives. It's a pity about that gun. But you don't really love your husband, do you? I guess I said that before too.'

She stood up slowly. She was as calm as a custard, but her violet eyes didn't seem quite the same colour, nor of quite the same softness. Then her mouth began to tremble.

'Is – is something – wrong in there?' she asked very slowly, and looked towards the study.

I barely had time to nod before she was running. She was at the door in a flash. She threw it open and darted in. If I expected a wild scream I was fooled. I didn't hear anything. I felt lousy. I ought to have kept her out and eased into that corny routine about bad news, prepare yourself, won't you sit down, I'm afraid something serious has happened. Blah, blah, blah. And when you have worked your way through it you haven't saved anybody a thing. Often enough you have made it worse.

I got up and followed her into the study. She was kneeling beside the couch with his head pulled against her breast, smearing herself with his blood. She wasn't making a sound of any kind. Her eyes were shut. She was rocking back and forth on her knees as far as she could, holding him tight.

I went back out and found a telephone and a book. I called the sheriff's sub-station that seemed to be nearest. Didn't matter, they'd relay it by radio in any case. Then I went out to the kitchen and turned the water on and fed the strips of yellow paper from my pocket down the electric garbage grinder. I dumped the tea leaves from the other pot after it. In a matter of seconds the stuff was gone. I shut off the water and switched off the motor. I went back to the living-room and opened the front door and stepped outside.

There must have been a deputy cruising close by because he was there in about six minutes. When I took him into the study she was still kneeling by the couch. He went over to her at once.

'I'm sorry, ma'am. I understand how you must feel, but you shouldn't be touching anything.'

She turned her head, then scrambled to her feet. 'It's my husband. He's been shot.'

He took his cap off and put it on the desk. He reached for the telephone.

'His name is Roger Wade,' she said in a high brittle voice. 'He's the famous novelist.'

'I know who he is, ma'am,' the deputy said and dialled.

She looked down at the front of her blouse. 'May I go upstairs and change this?'

'Sure.' He nodded to her and spoke into the phone, then hung up and turned. 'You say he's been shot. That mean somebody else shot him?'

'I think this man murdered him,' she said without looking at me, and went quickly out of the room.

The deputy looked at me. He got a note-book out. He wrote something in it. 'I better have your name,' he said casually, 'and address. You the one called in?'

'Yes.' I told him my name and address.

'Just take it easy until Lieutenant Ohls gets here.'

'Bernie Ohls?'

'Yeah. You know him?'

'Sure. I've known him a long time. He used to work out of the D.A.'s office.'

'Not lately,' the deputy said. 'He's Assistant Chief of Homicide, working out of the L.A. Sheriff's Office. You a friend of the family, Mr Marlowe?'

'Mrs Wade didn't make it sound that way.'

He shrugged and half-smiled. 'Just take it easy, Mr Marlowe. Not carrying a gun, are you?'

'Not today.'

'I better make sure.' He did. He looked towards the couch then. 'In spots like this you can't expect the wife to make much sense. We better wait outside.'

# Thirty-seven

Ohls was a medium-sized thick man with short-cropped, faded, blond hair and faded blue eyes. He had stiff white eyebrows and in the days before he stopped wearing a hat you were always a little surprised when he took it off – there was so much more head than you expected. He was a hard, tough cop with a grim outlook on life but a very decent guy underneath. He ought to have made captain years ago. He had passed the examination among the top three half a dozen times. But the Sheriff didn't like him and he didn't like the Sheriff.

He came down the stairs rubbing the side of his jaw. Flash-lights had been going off in the study for a long time. Men had gone in and out. I had just sat in the living-room with a plain-clothes dick and waited.

Ohls sat down on the edge of a chair and dangled his hands. He was chewing on an unlit cigarette. He looked at me brood-ingly.

'Remember the old days when they had a gate house and a private police force in Idle Valley?'

I nodded. 'And gambling also.'

'Sure. You can't stop it. This whole Valley is still private property. Like Arrowhead used to be, and Emerald Bay. Long time since I was on a case with no reporters jumping around. Somebody must have whispered in Sheriff Peterson's ear. They kept it off the teletype.'

'Real considerate of them,' I said. 'How is Mrs Wade?'

'Too relaxed. She must of grabbed some pills. There's half a dozen kinds up there – even demerol. That's bad stuff. Your friends don't have a lot of luck lately, do they? They get dead.'

I didn't have anything to say to that.

'Gunshot suicides always interest me,' Ohls said loosely. 'So easy to fake. The wife says you killed him. Why would she say that?'

'She doesn't mean it literally.'

'Nobody else was here. She says you knew where the gun was, knew he was getting drunk, knew he had fired off the gun the other night when she had to fight with him to get the gun away from him. You were there that night too. Don't seem to help much, do you?'

'I searched his desk this afternoon. No gun. I'd told her where it was and to put it away. She says now she didn't believe in that sort of thing.'

'Just when would "now" be?' Ohls asked gruffly.

'After she came home and before I phoned the sub-station.'

'You searched the desk. Why?' Ohls lifted his hands and put them on his knees. He was looking at me indifferently, as if he didn't care what I said.

'He was getting drunk. I thought it just as well to have the gun somewhere else. But he didn't try to kill himself the other night. It was just show-off.'

Ohls nodded. He took the chewed cigarette out of his mouth, dropped it into a tray and put a fresh one in place of it.

'I quit smoking,' he said. 'Got me coughing too much. But the goddam things still ride me. Can't feel right without one in my mouth. You supposed to watch the guy when he's alone?'

'Certainly not. He asked me to come out and have lunch. We talked and he was kind of depressed about his writing not going well. He decided to hit the bottle. Think I should have taken it away from him?'

'I'm not thinking yet. I'm just trying to get a picture. How much drinking did you do?'

'Beer.'

'It's your tough luck you were here, Marlowe. What was the cheque for? The one he wrote and signed and tore up?'

'They all wanted me to come and live here and keep him in line. All means himself, his wife, and his publisher, a man named Howard Spencer. He's in New York, I guess. You can check with him. I turned it down. Afterwards she came to me and said her husband was off on a toot and she was worried and would I find him and bring him home. I did that. Next thing I knew I was carrying him in off his front lawn and putting him to bed. I didn't want any part of it, Bernie. It just kind of grew up around me.'

'Nothing to do with the Lennox case, huh?'

'Aw, for Pete's sake. There isn't any Lennox case.'

'How true,' Ohls said dryly. He squeezed his kneecaps. A man came in at the front door and spoke to the other dick, then came across to Ohls.

'There's a Dr Loring outside, Lieutenant. Says he was called. He's the lady's doctor.'

'Let him in.'

The dick went back and Dr Loring came in with his neat black bag. He was cool and elegant in a tropical worsted suit. He went past me without looking at me.

'Upstairs?' he asked Ohls.

'Yeah – in her room.' Ohls stood up. 'What you give her that demerol for, Doc?'

Dr Loring frowned at him. 'I prescribe for my patient as I think proper,' he said coldly. 'I am not required to explain why. Who says I gave Mrs Wade demerol?'

'I do. The bottle's up there with your name on it. She's got a regular drugstore in her bathroom. Maybe you don't know it, Doc, but we have a pretty complete exhibit of the little pills downtown. Bluejays, redbirds, yellow jackets, goofballs and all the rest of the list. Demerol's about the worst of the lot. That's the stuff Goering lived on, I heard somewhere. Took eighteen a day when they caught him. Took the army doctors three months to cut him down.'

'I don't know what these words mean,' Dr Loring said frigidly.

'You don't? Pity. Bluejays are sodium amytal. Redbirds are seconal. Yellow jackets are nembutal. Goofballs are one of the barbiturates laced with benzedrine. Demerol is a synthetic narcotic that is very habit-forming. You just hand 'em out, huh? Is the lady suffering from something serious?'

'A drunken husband can be a very serious complaint indeed for a sensitive woman,' Dr Loring said.

'You didn't get around to him, huh? Pity. Mrs Wade's upstairs, Doc. Thanks for the time.'

'You are impertinent, sir. I will report you.'

'Yeah, do that,' Ohls said. 'But before you report me, do something else. Keep the lady clear in her head. I've got questions to ask.'

'I shall do exactly what I think best for her condition. Do you know who I am, by any chance? And just to make matters clear, Mr Wade was not my patient. I don't treat alcoholics.'

'Just their wives, huh?' Ohls snarled at him. 'Yeah, I know who you are, Doc. I'm bleeding internally with panic. The name is Ohls. Lieutenant Ohls.'

Dr Loring went on up the stairs. Ohls sat down again and grinned at me.

'You got to be diplomatic with this kind of people,' he said.

A man came out of the study and came up to Ohls. A thin serious-looking man with glasses and a brainy forehead.

'Lieutenant.'

'Shoot.'

'The wound is contact, typically suicidal, with a good deal of distention from gas pressure. The eyes are exophthalmic from the same cause. I don't think there will be any prints on the outside of the gun. It's been bled on too freely.'

'Could it be homicide if the guy was asleep or passed out drunk?' Ohls asked him.

'Of course, but there's no indication of it. The gun's a Webley Hammerless. Typically, this gun takes a very stiff pull to cock it, but a very light pull to discharge it. The recoil explains the position of the gun. I see nothing against suicide so far. I expect a high figure on alcoholic concentration. If it's high enough' – the man stopped and shrugged meaningly – 'I might be inclined to doubt suicide.'

'Thanks. Somebody call the coroner?'

The man nodded and went away. Ohls yawned and looked at his watch. Then he looked at me.

'You want to blow?'

'Sure, if you'll let me. I thought I was a suspect.'

'We might oblige you later on. Stick around where you can be found, that's all. You were a dick once, you know how they go. Some you got to work fast before the evidence gets away from you. This one is just the opposite. If it was homicide, who wanted him dead? His wife? She wasn't here. You? Fine, you had the house to yourself and knew where the gun was. A perfect set-up. Everything but a motive, and we might perhaps give some weight to your experience. I figure if you wanted to kill a guy, you could maybe do it a little less obviously.'

'Thanks, Bernie. I could at that.'

'The help wasn't here. They're out. So it must have been somebody that just happened to drop by. That somebody had to know where Wade's gun was, had to find him drunk enough to be asleep or passed out, and had to pull the trigger when that speedboat was making enough noise to drown the shot, and had to get away before you came back into the house. That I don't buy on any knowledge I have now. The only person who had the means and opportunity was the one guy who wouldn't have used them – for the simple reason he *was* the one guy who had them.'

I stood up to go. 'Okay, Bernie. I'll be home all evening.'

'There's just one thing,' Ohls said musingly. 'This man Wade was a big-time writer. Lots of dough, lots of reputation. I don't go for his sort of crap myself. You might find nicer people than his characters in a whorehouse. That's a matter of taste and none of my business as a cop. With all this money he had a beautiful home in one of the best places to live in in the county. He had a beautiful wife, lots of friends, and no troubles at all. What I want to know is what made all that so tough that he had to pull a trigger? Sure as hell something did. If you know, you better get ready to lay it on the line. See you.'

I went to the door. The man on the door looked back at Ohls, got the sign and let me out. I got into my car and had to edge over on the lawn to get around the various official cars that jammed the driveway. At the gate another deputy looked me over but didn't say anything. I slipped my dark glasses on and drove back towards the main highway. The road was empty and peaceful. The afternoon sun beat down on the manicured lawns and the large, roomy, expensive houses behind them.

A man not unknown to the world had died in a pool of blood in a house in Idle Valley, but the lazy quiet had not been disturbed. So far as the newspapers were concerned it might have happened in Tibet.

At a turn of the road the walls of two estates came down to the shoulder and a dark green sheriff's car was parked there. A deputy got out and held up his hand. I stopped. He came to the window.

'May I see your driver's licence, please?'

I took out my wallet and handed it to him open.

'Just the licence, please. I'm not allowed to touch your wallet.'

I took it out and gave it to him. 'What's the trouble?'

He glanced into my car and handed me back my licence.

'No trouble,' he said. 'Just a routine check. Sorry to have troubled you.'

He waved me on and went back to the parked car. Just like a cop. They never tell you why they are doing anything. That way you don't find out they don't know themselves.

I drove home, bought myself a couple of cold drinks, went out to dinner, came back, opened the windows and my shirt and waited for something to happen. I waited a long time. It was nine o'clock when Bernie Ohls called up and told me to come in and not stop on the way to pick any flowers.

# Thirty-eight

They had Candy in a hard chair against the wall of the Sheriff's anteroom. He hated me with his eyes as I went by him into the big square room where Sheriff Petersen held court in the middle of a collection of testimonials from a grateful public to his twenty years of faithful public service. The walls were loaded with photographs of horses and Sheriff Petersen made a personal appearance in every photograph. The corners of his carved desk were horses' heads. His inkwell was a mounted, polished horse's hoof and his pens were planted in the mate to it filled with white sand. A gold plate on each of these said something or other about a date. In the middle of a spotless desk blotter lay a bag of Bull Durham and a pack of brown cigarette papers. Petersen rolled his own. He could roll one with one hand on horseback and often did, especially when leading a parade on a big white horse with a Mexican saddle loaded with beautiful Mexican silverwork. On horseback he wore a flat-crowned Mexican sombrero. He rode beautifully and his horse always knew exactly when to be quiet, when to act up so that the Sheriff with his calm, inscrutable smile could bring the horse back under control with one hand. The Sheriff had a good act. He had a handsome hawk-like profile, getting a little saggy under the chin by now, but he knew how to hold his head so it wouldn't show too much.

395

He put a lot of hard work into having his picture taken. He was in his middle fifties and his father, a Dane, had left him a lot of money. The Sheriff didn't look like a Dane, because his hair was dark and his skin was brown and he had the impassive poise of a cigar store Indian and about the same kind of brains. But nobody had ever called him a crook. There had been crooks in his department and they had fooled him as well as they had fooled the public, but none of the crookedness rubbed off on Sheriff Petersen. He just went right on getting elected without even trying, riding white horses at the head of parades, and questioning suspects in front of cameras. That's what the captions said. As a matter of fact he never questioned anybody. He wouldn't have known how. He just sat at his desk looking sternly at the suspect, showing his profile to the camera. The flash bulbs would go off, the camera men would thank the Sheriff deferentially, and the suspect would be removed not having opened his mouth, and the Sheriff would go home to his ranch in the San Fernando Valley. There he could always be reached. If you couldn't reach him in person, you could talk to one of his horses.

Once in a while, come election time, some misguided politician would try to get Sheriff Petersen's job, and would be apt to call him things like The Guy With The Built-In Profile or The Ham That Smokes Itself, but it didn't get him anywhere. Sheriff Petersen just went right on getting re-elected, a living testimonial to the fact that you can hold an important public office for ever in our country with no qualifications for it but a clean nose, a photogenic face, and a close mouth. If on top of that you look good on a horse, you are unbeatable.

As Ohls and I went in Sheriff Petersen was standing behind his desk and the camera boys were filing out by another door. The Sheriff had his white stetson on. He was rolling a cigarette. He was all set to go home. He looked at me sternly.

'Who's this?' he asked in a rich baritone voice.

'Name's Philip Marlowe, Chief,' Ohls said. 'Only person in the house when Wade shot himself. You want a picture?'

The Sheriff studied me. 'I don't think so,' he said, and turned to a big, tired-looking man with iron-grey hair. 'If you need me, I'll be at the ranch, Captain Hernandez.'

'Yes, sir.'

Petersen lit his cigarette with a kitchen match. He lit it on his thumbnail. No lighters for Sheriff Petersen. He was strictly a roll-your-own-and-light-'em-with-one-hand-type.

He said good night and went out. A deadpan character with hard black eyes went with him, his personal bodyguard. The door closed. When he was gone Captain Hernandez moved to the desk and sat in the Sheriff's enormous chair and a stenotype operator in the corner moved his stand out from the wall to get elbow room. Ohls sat at the end of the desk and looked amused.

'All right, Marlowe,' Hernandez said briskly. 'Let's have it.'

'How come I don't get my photo taken?'

'You heard what the Sheriff said.'

'Yeah, but why?' I whined.

Ohls laughed. 'You known damn well why.'

'You mean on account of I'm tall, dark and handsome and somebody might look at me?'

'Cut it,' Hernandez said coldly. 'Let's get on with your statement. Start from the beginning.'

I gave it to them from the beginning: my interview with Howard Spencer, my meeting with Eileen Wade, her asking me to find Roger, my finding him, her asking me to the house, what Wade asked me to do and how I found him passed out near the hibiscus bushes and the rest of it. The stenotype operator took it down. Nobody interrupted me. All of it was true. The truth and nothing but the truth. But not quite all the truth. What I left out was my business.

'Nice,' Hernandez said at the end. 'But not quite complete.' This was a cool, competent, dangerous guy, this Hernandez. Somebody in the Sheriff's office had to be. 'The night Wade shot off the gun in his bedroom you went into Mrs Wade's room and were in there for some time with the door shut. What were you doing in there?'

'She called me in and asked me how he was.'

'Why shut the door?'

'Wade was half asleep and I didn't want to make any noise. Also the houseboy was hanging around with his ear out. Also she asked me to shut the door. I didn't realize it was going to be important.'

'How long were you in there?'

'I don't know. Three minutes maybe.'

'I suggest you were in there a couple of hours,' Hernandez said coldly. 'Do I make myself clear?'

I looked at Ohls. Ohls didn't look at anything. He was chewing on an unlighted cigarette as usual.

'You are misinformed, Captain.'

'We'll see. After you left the room you went downstairs to the study and spent the night on the couch. Perhaps I should say the rest of the night.'

'It was ten minutes to eleven when he called me at home. It was long past two o'clock when I went into the study for the last time that night. Call it the rest of the night if you like.'

'Get the house boy in here,' Hernandez said.

Ohls went out and came back with Candy. They put Candy in a chair. Hernandez asked him a few questions to establish who he was and so on. Then he said:

'All right, Candy – we'll call you that for convenience – after you helped Marlowe put Roger Wade to bed, what happened?'

I knew what was coming more or less. Candy told his story in a quiet, savage voice with very little accent. It seemed as if he could turn that on and off at will. His story was that he had hung around downstairs in case he was wanted again, part of the time in the kitchen where he got himself some food, part of the time in the living-room. While in the living-room sitting in a chair near the front door he had seen Eileen Wade standing in the door of her room and he had seen her take her clothes off. He had seen her put a robe on with nothing under it and he had seen me go into her room and I had shut the door and stayed in there a long time, a couple of hours, he thought. He had gone up the stairs and listened. He had heard the bed springs making sounds. He had heard whispering. He made his meaning very obvious. When he had finished he gave me a corrosive look and his mouth was twisted tight with hatred.

'Take him out,' Hernandez said.

'Just a minute,' I said. 'I want to question him.'

'I ask the questions here,' Hernandez said sharply.

'You don't know how, Captain. You weren't there. He's lying and he knows it and I know it.'

Hernandez leaned back and picked up one of the Sheriff's pens. He bent the handle of the pen. It was long and pointed and made of stiffened horsehair. When he let go of the point it sprang back.

'Shoot,' he said at last.

I faced Candy. 'Where were you when you saw Mrs Wade take her clothes off?'

'I was sitting down in a chair near the front door,' he said in a surly tone.

'Between the front door and the two facing davenports?'

'What I said.'

'Where was Mrs Wade?'

'Just inside the door of her room. The door was open.'

'What light was there in the living-room?'

'One lamp. Tall lamp what they call a bridge lamp.'

'What light was on the balcony?'

'No light. Light in her bedroom.'

'What kind of light in her bedroom?'

'Not much light. Night table lamp, maybe.'

'Not a ceiling light?'

'No.'

'After she took her clothes off – standing just inside the door of her room, you said – she put on a robe. What kind of robe?'

'Blue robe. Long thing like a house-coat. She tie it with a sash.'

'So if you hadn't actually seen her take her clothes off you wouldn't know what she had on under the robe?'

He shrugged. He looked vaguely worried. '*Si*. That's right. But I see her take her clothes off.'

'You're a liar. There isn't any place in the living-room from which you could see her take her clothes off right bang in her doorway, much less inside her room. She would have to come out to the edge of the balcony. If she had done that she would have seen you.'

He just glared at me. I turned to Ohls. 'You've seen the house. Captain Hernandez hasn't – or has he?'

Ohls shook his head slightly. Hernandez frowned and said nothing.

'There is no spot in that living-room, Captain Hernandez, from which he could see even the top of Mrs Wade's head – even if he was standing up – and he says he was sitting down – provided she was as far back as her own doorway or inside it. I'm four inches taller than he is and I could only see the top foot of an open door when I was standing just inside the front door of the house. She would have to come out to the edge of the balcony for him to see what he says he saw. Why would she do that? Why would she undress in her doorway even? There's no sense to it.'

Hernandez just looked at me. Then he looked at Candy. 'How about the time element?' he asked softly, speaking to me.

'That's his word against mine. I'm talking about what can be proved.'

Hernandez spat Spanish at Candy too fast for me to understand. Candy just stared at him sulkily.

'Take him out,' Hernandez said.

Ohls jerked a thumb and opened the door. Candy went out. Hernandez brought out a box of cigarettes, stuck one on his lip and lit it with a gold lighter.

Ohls came back into the room. Hernandez said calmly: 'I just told him that if there was an inquest and he told that story on the stand, he'd find himself doing a one to three up in Q for perjury. Didn't seem to impress him much. It's obvious what's eating him. An old-fashioned case of hot pants. If he'd been around and we had any reason to suspect murder, he'd make a pretty good pigeon – except that he would have used a knife. I got the impression earlier that he felt pretty bad about Wade's death. Any questions you want to ask, Ohls?'

Ohls shook his head. Hernandez looked at me and said: 'Come back in the morning and sign your statement. We'll have it typed out by then. We ought to have a P.M. report by ten o'clock, preliminary anyway. Anything you don't like about this set-up, Marlowe?'

'Would you mind rephrasing the question? The way you put it suggests there might be something I do like about it.'

'Okay,' he said wearily. 'Take off. I'm going home.'

I stood up.

'Of course I never did believe that stuff Candy pulled on us,' he said. 'Just used it for a corkscrew. No hard feelings, I hope.'

'No feelings at all, Captain. No feelings at all.'

They watched me go out and didn't say good night. I walked down the long corridor to the Hill Street entrance and got into my car and drove home.

No feelings at all was exactly right. I was as hollow and empty as the spaces between the stars. When I got home I mixed a stiff one and stood by the open window in the living-room and sipped it and listened to the ground swell of the traffic on Laurel Canyon Boulevard and looked at the glare of the big, angry city hanging over the shoulder of the hills through which the boulevard had been cut. Far off the banshee wail of police or fire sirens rose and fell, never for very long completely silent. Twenty-four hours a day somebody is running, somebody else is trying to catch him. Out there in the night of a thousand crimes people were dying, being maimed, cut by flying glass, crushed against steering wheels or under heavy car tyres. People were hungry, sick, bored, desperate with loneliness or remorse or fear, angry, cruel, feverish, shaken by sobs. A city no worse than others, a city rich and vigorous and full of pride, a city lost and beaten and full of emptiness.

It depends on where you sit and what your own private score is. I didn't have one. I didn't care.

I finished the drink and went to bed.


# Thirty-nine


The inquest was a flop. The Coroner sailed into it before the medical evidence was complete, for fear the publicity would die on him. He needn't have worried. The death of a writer – even a loud writer – is not news for long, and that summer there was too much to compete. A king abdicated and another was assassinated. In one week three large passenger planes crashed. The head man of a big wire service was shot to pieces in Chicago in his own automobile. Twenty-four convicts were burnt to death in a prison fire. The Coroner of Los Angeles County was out of luck. He was missing the good things in life.

As I left the stand I saw Candy. He had a bright, malicious grin on his face – I had no idea why – and as usual he was dressed just a little too well, in a cocoa-brown garbardine suit with a white nylon shirt and a midnight blue bow tie. On the witness stand he was quiet and made a good impression. Yes, the boss had been pretty drunk lately a lot of times. Yes, he had helped put him to bed the night the gun went off upstairs. Yes, the boss had demanded whisky before he, Candy, left on the last day, but he had refused to get it. No, he didn't know anything about Mr Wade's literary work, but he knew the boss had been discouraged. He kept throwing it away and then getting it out of the wastebasket again. No, he had never heard Mr Wade quarrelling with anyone. And so on. The Coroner milked him but it was thin stuff. Somebody had done a good coaching job on Candy.

Eileen Wade wore black and white. She was pale and spoke in a low, clear voice which even the amplifier could not spoil. The Coroner handled her with two pairs of velvet gloves. He talked to her as if he had trouble keeping the sobs out of his voice. When she left the stand he stood up and bowed and she gave him a faint fugitive smile that nearly made him choke on his saliva.

She almost passed me without a glance on the way out, then at the last moment turned her head a couple of inches and nodded very slightly, as if I was somebody she must have met somewhere a long time ago, but couldn't quite place in her memory.

Outside on the steps, when it was all over, I ran into Ohls. He was watching the traffic down below, or pretending to.

'Nice job,' he said without turning his head. 'Congratulations.'

'You did all right on Candy.'

'Not me, kid. The D.A. decided the sexy stuff was irrelevant.'

'What sexy stuff was that?'

He looked at me then. 'Ha, ha, ha,' he said. 'And I don't mean you.' Then his expression got remote. 'I been looking at them for too many years. It wearies a man. This one came out of the special bottle. Old private stock. Strictly for the carriage trade. So long, sucker. Call me when you start wearing twenty-dollar shirts. I'll drop around and hold your coat for you.'

People eddied around us going up and down the steps. We just stood there. Ohls took a cigarette out of his pocket and looked at it and dropped it on the concrete and ground it to nothing with his heel.

'Wasteful,' I said.

'Only a cigarette, pal. It's not a life. After a while maybe you marry the girl, huh?'

'Shove it.'

He laughed sourly. 'I been talking to the right people about the wrong things,' he said acidly. 'Any objections?'

'No objections, Lieutenant,' I said, and went on down the steps. He said something behind me but I kept going.

I went over to a cornbeef joint on Flower. It suited my mood. A rude sign over the entrance said: 'Men only. Dogs and Women Not Admitted.' The service inside was equally polished. The waiter who tossed your food at you needed a shave and deducted his tip without being invited. The food was simple but very good and they had a brown Swedish beer which could hit as hard as a martini.

When I got back to the office the phone was ringing. Ohls said: 'I'm coming by your place. I've got things to say.'

He must have been at or near the Hollywood sub-station because he was in the office inside twenty minutes. He planted himself in the customer's chair and crossed his legs and growled:

'I was out of line. Sorry. Forget it.'

'Why forget it? Let's open up the wound.'

'Suits me. Under the hat, though. To some people you're a wrong gee. I never knew you to do anything too crooked.'

'What was the crack about twenty-dollars shirts?'

'Aw hell, I was just sore,' Ohls said. 'I was thinking of old man

Potter. Like he told a secretary to tell a lawyer to tell District Attorney Springer to tell Captain Hernandez you were a personal friend of his.'

'He wouldn't take the trouble.'

'You met him. He gave you time.'

'I met him, period. I didn't like him, but perhaps it was only envy. He sent for me to give me some advice. He's big and he's tough and I don't know what else. I don't figure he's a crook.'

'There ain't no clean way to make a hundred million bucks,' Ohls said. 'Maybe the head man thinks his hands are clean but somewhere along the line guys got pushed to the wall, nice little businesses got the ground cut from under them and had to sell out for nickels, decent people lost their jobs, stocks got rigged on the market, proxies got bought up like a pennyweight of old gold, and the five per centers and the big law firms got paid hundred grand fees for beating some law the people wanted but the rich guys didn't, on account of it cut into their profits. Big money is big power and big power gets used wrong. It's the system. Maybe it's the best we can get, but it still ain't my Ivory Soap deal.'

'You sound like a Red,' I said, just to needle him.

'I wouldn't know,' he said contemptuously. 'I ain't been investigated yet. You liked the suicide verdict, didn't you?'

'What else could it be?'

'Nothing else, I guess.' He put his hard blunt hands on the desk and looked at the big brown freckles on the backs of them. 'I'm getting old. Keratosis, they call those brown spots. You don't get them until you're past fifty. I'm an old cop and an old cop is an old bastard. I don't like a few things about this Wade death.'

'Such as?' I leaned back and watched the tight sun wrinkles around his eyes.

'You get so you can smell a wrong set-up, even when you know you can't do a damn thing about it. Then you just sit and talk like now. I don't like that he left no note.'

'He was drunk. Probably just a sudden crazy impulse.'

Ohls lifted his pale eyes and dropped his hands off the desk. 'I went through his desk. He wrote letters to himself. He wrote and wrote and wrote. Drunk or sober he hit that typewriter. Some of it is wild, come of it kind of funny, and some of it is sad. The guy had something on his mind. He wrote all around it but he never quite touched it. That guy would have left a two-page letter if he knocked himself off.'

'He was drunk,' I said again.

'With him that didn't matter,' Ohls said wearily. 'The next thing I don't like is he did it there in that room and left his wife to find him. Okay, he was drunk. I still don't like it. The next thing I don't like is he pulled the trigger just when the noise of that speedboat could drown out the shot. What difference would it make to him? More coincidence, huh? More coincidence still that the wife forgot her door keys on the help's day off and had to ring the bell to get into the house.'

'She could have walked around to the back,' I said.

'Yeah, I know. What I'm talking about is a situation. Nobody to answer the door but you, and she said on the stand she didn't know you were there. Wade wouldn't have heard the bell if he had been alive and working in his study. His door is sound-proofed. The help was away. That was Thursday. That she forgot. Like she forgot her keys.'

'You're forgetting something yourself, Bernie. My car was in the driveway. So she knew I was there – or that somebody was there – before she rang the bell.'

He grinned. 'I forgot that, didn't I? All right, here's the picture. You were down at the lake, the speedboat was making all that racket – incidentally it was a couple of guys from Lake Arrowhead just visiting, had their boat on a trailer – Wade was asleep in his study or passed out, somebody took the gun out of his desk already, and she knew you had put it there because you told her that other time. Now suppose she didn't forget her keys, that she goes into the house, looks across and sees you down at the water, looks into the study and sees Wade asleep, knows where the gun is, gets it, waits for the right moment, plugs him, drops the gun where it was found, goes back outside the house, waits a little while for the speedboat to go away, and then rings the doorbell and waits for you to open it. Any objections?'

'With what motive?'

'Yeah,' he said sourly. 'That knocks it. If she wanted to slough the guy, it was easy. She had him over a barrel, habitual drunk, record of violence to her. Plenty alimony, nice fat property settlement. No motive at all. Anyhow the timing was too neat. Five minutes earlier and she couldn't have done it, unless you were in on it.'

I started to say something but he put his hand up. 'Take it easy. I'm not accusing anybody, just speculating. Five minutes later and you get the same answer. She had ten minutes to pull it off.'

'Ten minutes,' I said irritably, 'that couldn't possibly have been foreseen, much less planned.'

He leaned back in the chair and sighed. 'I know. You've got all the answers. I've got all the answers. And I still don't like it. What the hell were you doing with these people anyway? The guy writes you a cheque for a grand, then tears it up. Got mad at you, you say. You didn't want it, anyway, wouldn't have taken it, you say. Maybe. Did he think you were sleeping with his wife?'

'Lay off, Bernie.'

'I didn't ask were you, I asked did he think you were.'

'Same answer.'

'Okay, try this. What did the Mex have on him?'

'Nothing that I know of.'

'The Mex has too much money. Over fifteen hundred in the bank, all kinds of clothes, a brand new Chevvy.'

'Maybe he peddles dope,' I said.

Ohls pushed himself up out of the chair and scowled down at me.

'You're an awful lucky boy, Marlowe. Twice you've slid out from under a heavy one. You could get over-confident. You were pretty helpful to those people and you didn't make a dime. You were pretty helpful to a guy named Lennox too, the way I hear it. And you didn't make a dime out of that one either. What do you do for eating money, pal? You got a lot saved up so you don't have to work any more?'

I stood up and walked around the desk and faced him. 'I'm a romantic, Bernie. I hear voices crying in the night and I go see what's the matter. You don't make a dime that way. You got sense, you shut your windows and turn up more sound on the TV set. Or you shove down on the gas and get far away from there. Stay out of other people's troubles. All it can get you is the smear. The last time I saw Terry Lennox we had a cup of coffee together that I made myself here in this house, and we smoked a cigarette. So when I heard he was dead I went out to the kitchen and made some coffee and poured a cup for him and lit a cigarette for him, and when the coffee was cold and the cigarette was burned down I said good night to him. You don't make a dime that way. *You* wouldn't do it. That's why you're a good cop and I'm a private eye. Eileen Wade is worried about her husband, so I go out and find him and bring him home. Another time he's in trouble and calls me up and I go out and carry him in off the lawn and put him to bed, and I don't make a dime out of it. No percentage at all. No nothing, except sometimes I get my face pushed in or get tossed in the can or get threatened by some fast money boy like Mendy Menendez. But no money, not a dime. I've got a five-thousand-dollar bill in my safe but I'll never spend a nickel of it. Because there was something wrong with the way I got it. I played with it a little at first and I still get it out once in a while and look at it. But that's all – not a dime of spending money.'

'Must be a phony,' Ohls said dryly, 'except they don't make them that big. So what's your point with all this yap?'

'No point. I told you I was a romantic.'

'I heard you. And you don't make a dime at it. I heard that too.'

'But I can always tell a cop to go to hell. Go to hell, Bernie.'

'You wouldn't tell me to go to hell if I had you in the back room under the light, chum.'

'Maybe we'll find out about that some day.'

He walked to the door and yanked it open. 'You know something, kid? You think you're cute but you're just stupid. You're a shadow on the wall. I've got twenty years on the cops without a mark against me. I know when I'm being kidded and I know when a guy is holding out on me. The wise guy never fools anybody but himself. Take it from me, chum. I know.'

He pulled his head back out of the doorway and let the door close. His heels hammered down the corridor. I could still hear them when the phone on my desk started to sound. The voice said in that clear professional tone:

'New York is calling Mr Philip Marlowe.'

'I'm Philip Marlowe.'

'Thank you. One moment, please, Mr Marlowe. Here is your party.'

The next voice I knew. 'Howard Spencer, Mr Marlowe. We've heard about Roger Wade. It was a pretty hard blow. We haven't the full details, but your name seems to be involved.'

'I was there when it happened. He just got drunk and shot himself. Mrs Wade came home a little later. The servants were away – Thursday's the day off.'

'You were alone with him?'

'I wasn't with him. I was outside the house, just hanging around waiting for his wife to come home.'

'I see. Well, I suppose there will be an inquest.'

'It's all over, Mr Spencer. Suicide. And remarkably little publicity.'

'Really? That's curious.' He didn't exactly sound disappointed – more like puzzled and surprised. 'He was so well known. I should have thought – well, never mind what I thought. I guess I'd better fly out there, but I can't make it before the end of next week. I'll send a wire to Mrs Wade. There may be something I could do for her – and also about the book. I mean there may be enough of it so that we could get someone to finish it. I assume you did take the job after all.'

'No. Although he asked me to himself. I told him right out I couldn't stop him from drinking.'

'Apparently you didn't even try.'

'Look, Mr Spencer, you don't know the first damn thing about this situation. Why not wait until you do before jumping to conclusions? Not that I don't blame myself a little. I guess that's inevitable when something like this happens, and you're the guy on the spot.'

'Of course,' he said. 'I'm sorry I made that remark. Most uncalled for. Will Eileen Wade be at her home now – or wouldn't you know?'

'I wouldn't know, Mr Spencer. Why don't you just call her up?'

'I hardly think she would want to speak to anyone yet,' he said slowly.

'Why not? She talked to the Coroner and never batted an eye.'

He cleared his throat. 'You don't sound exactly sympathetic.'

'Roger Wade is dead, Spencer. He was a bit of a bastard and maybe a bit of a genius too. That's over my head. He was an egotistical drunk and he hated his own guts. He made me a lot of trouble and in the end a lot of grief. Why the hell should I be sympathetic?'

'I was talking about Mrs Wade,' he said shortly.

'So was I.'

'I'll call you when I get in,' he said abruptly. 'Good-bye.'

He hung up. I hung up. I stared at the telephone for a couple of minutes without moving. Then I got the phone book up on the desk and looked for a number.

# Forty

I called Sewell Endicott's office. Somebody said he was in court and would not be available until late in the afternoon. Would I care to leave my name? No.

I dialled the number of Mendy Menendez's joint on the Strip. It was called El Tapado this year, not a bad name either. In American Spanish that means buried treasure among other things. It had been called other names in the past, quite a few other names. One year it was just a blue neon number on a blank high wall facing south on the Strip, with its back against the hill and a driveway curving around one side out of sight of the street. Very exclusive. Nobody knew much about it except vice cops and mobsters and people who could afford thirty bucks for a good dinner and any amount up to fifty grand in the big quiet room upstairs.

I got a woman who didn't know from nothing. Then I got a captain with a Mex accent.

'You wish to speak with Mr Menendez? Who is calling?'

'No names, *amigo*. Private matter.'

'*Un momento, por favor.*'

There was a longish wait. I got a hard boy this time. He sounded as if he was talking through the slit in an armoured car. It was probably just the slit in his face.

'Talk it up. Who wants him?'

'The name's Marlowe.'

'Who's Marlowe?'

'This Chick Agostino?'

'No, this ain't Chick. Come on, let's have the password.'

'Go fry your face.'

There was a chuckle. 'Hold the line.'

Finally another voice said: 'Hello, cheapie. What's the time by you?'

'You alone?'

'You can talk, cheapie. I been looking over some acts for the floor show.'

'You could cut your throat for one.'

'What would I do for an encore?'

I laughed. He laughed. 'Been keeping your nose clean?' he asked.

'Haven't you heard? I got to be friends with another guy who suicided. They're going to call me the "Kiss-of-Death-Kid" from now on.'

'That's funny, huh?'

'No, it isn't funny. Also the other afternoon I had tea with Harlan Potter.'

'Nice going. I never drink the stuff myself.'

'He said for you to be nice to me.'

'I never met the guy and I don't figure to.'

'He casts a long shadow. All I want is a little information, Mendy. Like about Paul Marston.

'Never heard of him.'

'You said that too quick. Paul Marston was the name Terry Lennox used one time in New York before he came west.'

'So?'

'His prints were checked through the FBI files. No record. That means he never served in the Armed Forces.'

'So?'

'Do I have to draw you a picture? Either that foxhole yarn of yours was all spaghetti or it happened somewhere else.'

'I didn't say where it happened, cheapie. Take a kind word and forget the whole thing. You got told, you better stay told.'

'Oh sure. I do something you don't like and I'm swimming to Catalina with a streetcar on my back. Don't try to scare me, Mendy. I've been up against the pros. You ever been in England?'

'Be smart, cheapie. Things can happen to a guy in this town. Things can happen to big strong boys like Big Willie Magoon. Take a look at the evening paper.'

'I'll get one if you say so. It might even have my picture in it. What about Magoon?'

'Like I said – things can happen. I wouldn't know how except what I read. Seems Magoon tried to shake down four boys in a car with Nevada plates. Was parked right by his house. Nevada plates with big numbers like they don't have. Must have been some kind of a rib. Only Magoon ain't feeling funny, what with both arms in casts, and his jaw wired in three places, and one leg in high traction. Magoon ain't tough any more. It could happen to you.'

'He bothered you, huh? I saw him bounce your boy Chick off the wall in front of Victor's. Should I ring up a friend in the Sheriff's office and tell him?'

'You do that, cheapie,' he said very slowly. 'You do that.'

'And I'll mention that at the time I was just through having a drink with Harlan Potter's daughter. Corroborative evidence, in a sense, don't you think? You figure to smash her up too?'

'Listen to me careful, cheapie—'

'Were you ever in England, Mendy? You and Randy Starr and Paul Marston or Terry Lennox or whatever his name was? In the British Army perhaps? Had a little racket in Soho and got hot and figured the Army was a cooling-off spot?'

'Hold the line.'

I held it. Nothing happened except that I waited and my arm got tired. I switched the receiver to the other side. Finally he came back.

'Now listen careful, Marlowe. You stir up that Lennox case and you're dead. Terry was a pal and I got feelings too. So you got feelings. I'll go along with you just this far. It was a commando outfit. It was British. It happened in Norway, one of those islands off the coast. They got a million of them. November 1942. Now will you lie down and rest that tired brain of yours?'

'Thank you, Mendy. I will do that. Your secret is safe with me. I'm not telling it to anybody but the people I know.'

'Buy yourself a paper, cheapie. Read and remember. Big tough Willie Magoon. Beat up in front of his own house. Boy, was he surprised when he come out of the ether!'

He hung up. I went downstairs and bought a paper and it was just as Menendez had said. There was a picture of Big Willie Magoon in his hospital bed. You could see half his face and one eye. The rest of him was bandages. Seriously but not critically injured. The boys had been very careful about that. They wanted him to live. After all he was a cop. In our town the mobs don't kill a cop. They leave that to the juveniles. And a live cop who has been put through the meat grinder is a much better advertisement. He gets well eventually and goes back to work. But from that time on something is missing – the last inch of steel that makes all the difference. He's a walking lesson that it is a mistake to push the racket boys too hard – especially if you are on the vice squad and eating at the best places and driving a Cadillac.

I sat there and brooded about it for a while and then I dialled the number of the Carne Organization and asked for George Peters. He was out. I left my name and said it was urgent. He was expected in about five-thirty.

I went over to the Hollywood Public Library and asked questions in the reference room, but couldn't find what I wanted. So I had to go back for my Olds and drive downtown to the Main Library. I found it there, in a smallish, red-bound book published in England. I copied what I wanted from it and drove home. I called the Carne Organization again. Peters was still out, so I asked the girl to re-route the call to me at home.

I put the chess board on the coffee table and set out a problem called The Sphinx. It is printed on the end-papers of a book on chess by Blackburn, the English chess wizard, probably the most dynamic chess player who ever lived, although he wouldn't get to first base in the cold war type of chess they play nowadays. The Sphinx is an eleven-mover and it justifies its name. Chess problems seldom run to more than four or five moves. Beyond that the difficulty of solving them rises in almost geometrical progression. An eleven-mover is sheer unadulterated torture.

Once in a long while when I feel mean enough I set it out and look for a new way to solve it. It's a nice quiet way to go crazy. You don't even scream, but you come awfully close.

George Peters called me at five-forty. We exchanged pleasantries and condolences.

'You've got yourself in another jam, I see,' he said cheerfully. 'Why don't you try some quiet business like embalming?'

'Takes too long to learn. Listen, I want to become a client of your agency, if it doesn't cost too much.'

'Depends what you want done, old boy. And you'd have to talk to Carne.'

'No.'

'Well, tell me.'

'London is full of guys like me, but I wouldn't know one from the other. They call them private inquiry agents. Your outfit would have connections. I'd just have to pick a name at random and probably get hornswoggled. I want some information that should be easy enough to get, and I want it quick. Must have it before the end of next week.'

'Spill.'

'I want to know something about the war service of Terry Lennox or Paul Marston, whatever name he used. He was in the Commandos over there. He was captured wounded in November 1942 in a raid on some Norwegian island. I want to know what outfit he was posted from and what happened to him. The War Office will have all that. It's not secret information, or I wouldn't think so. Let's say a question of inheritance is involved.'

'You don't need a P.I. for that. You could get it direct. Write them a letter.'

'Shove it, George. I might get an answer in three months. I want one in five days.'

'You have a thought there, pal. Anything else?'

411

'One thing more. They keep all their vital records over there in a place they call Somerset House. I want to know if he figures there in any connection – birth, marriage, naturalization, anything at all.'

'Why?'

'What do you mean, why? Who's paying the bill?'

'Suppose the names don't show?'

'Then I'm stuck. If they do, I want certified copies of anything your man turns up. How much you soaking me?'

'I'll have to ask Carne. He may thumb it out altogether. We don't want the kind of publicity you get. If he lets me handle it, and you agree not to mention the connection, I'd say three hundred bucks. Those guys over there don't get much by dollar standards. He might hit us for ten guineas, less than thirty bucks. On top of that any expenses he might have. Say fifty bucks altogether and Carne wouldn't open a file for less than two-fifty.'

'Professional rates.'

'Ha, ha. He never heard of them.'

'Call me, George. Want to eat dinner?'

'Romanoff's?'

'All right,' I growled, 'if they'll give me a reservation – which I doubt.'

'We can have Carne's table. I happen to know he's dining privately. He's a regular at Romanoff's. It pays off in the upper brackets of the business. Carne is a pretty big boy in this town.'

'Yeah, sure. I know somebody – and know him personally – who could lose Carne under his little fingernail.'

'Good work, kid. I always knew you would come through in the clutch. See you about seven o'clock in the bar at Romanoff's. Tell the head thief you're waiting for Colonel Carne. He'll clear a space around you so you don't get elbowed by any riff-raff like screenwriters or television actors.'

'See you at seven,' I said.

We hung up and I went back to the chess board. But the Sphinx didn't seem to interest me any more. In a little while Peters called me back and said it was all right with Carne provided the name of their agency was not connected with my problems. Peters said he would get a night letter off to London at once.

# Forty-one

Howard Spencer called me on the following Friday morning. He was at the Ritz-Beverly and suggested I drop over for a drink in the bar.

'Better make it in your room,' I said.

'Very well, if you prefer it. Room 828. I've just talked to Eileen Wade. She seems quite resigned. She has read the script Roger left and says she thinks it can be finished off very easily. It will be a good deal shorter than his other books, but that is balanced by the publicity value. I guess you think we publishers are a pretty callous bunch. Eileen will be home all afternoon. Naturally she wants to see me and I want to see her.'

'I'll be over in half an hour, Mr Spencer.'

He had a nice roomy suite on the west side of the hotel. The living-room had tall windows opening on a narrow, iron-railed balcony. The furniture was upholstered in some candy-striped material and that with the heavily flowered design of the carpet gave it an old-fashioned air, except that everything you could put a drink down on had a plate-glass top and there were nineteen ashtrays spotted around. A hotel room is a pretty sharp indication of the manners of the guests. The Ritz-Beverly wasn't expecting them to have any.

Spencer shook hands.

'Sit down,' he said. 'What will you drink?'

'Anything or nothing. I don't have to have a drink.'

'I fancy a glass of Amontillado. California is poor drinking country in the summer. In New York you can handle four times as much for one half the hangover.'

'I'll take a rye whisky sour.'

He went to the phone and ordered. Then he sat down on one of the candy-striped chairs and took off his rimless glasses to polish them on a handkerchief. He put them back on, adjusted them carefully and looked at me.

'I take it you have something on your mind. That's why you wanted to see me up here rather than in the bar.'

'I'll drive you out to Idle Valley. I'd like to see Mrs Wade too.'

He looked a little uncomfortable. 'I'm not sure that she wants to see you,' he said.

'I know she doesn't. I can get in on your ticket.'

'That would not be very diplomatic of me, would it?'

'She tell you she didn't want to see me?'

'Not exactly, not in so many words.' He cleared his throat. 'I get the impression that she blames you for Roger's death.'

'Yeah. She said that right out – to the deputy who came the afternoon he died. She probably said it to the Sheriff's homicide lieutenant that investigated the death. She didn't say it to the Coroner, however.'

He leaned back and scratched the inside of his hand with a finger, slowly. It was just a sort of doodling gesture.

'What good would it do for you to see her, Marlowe? It was a pretty dreadful experience for her. I imagine her whole life had been pretty dreadful for some time. Why make her live it over? Do you expect to convince her that you didn't miss out a little?'

'She told the deputy I killed him.'

'She couldn't have meant that literally. Otherwise—'

The door buzzer rang. He got up to go to the door and open it. The room service waiter came in with the drinks and put them down with as much flourish as if he were serving a seven-course dinner. Spencer signed the check and gave him four bits. The guy went away. Spencer picked up his glass of sherry and walked away as if he didn't want to hand me my drink. I let it stay where it was.

'Otherwise what?' I asked him.

'Otherwise she *would* have said something to the Coroner, wouldn't she?' He frowned at me. 'I think we are talking nonsense. Just what did you want to see me about?'

'You wanted to see me.'

'Only,' he said coldly, 'because when I talked to you from New York you said I was jumping to conclusions. That implied to me that you had something to explain. Well, what is it?'

'I'd like to explain it in front of Mrs Wade.'

'I don't care for the idea. I think you had better make your own arrangements. I have a great regard for Eileen Wade. As a businessman I'd like to salvage Roger's work if it can be done. If Eileen feels about you as you suggest I can't be the means of getting you into her house. Be reasonable.'

'That's all right,' I said. 'Forget it. I can get to see her without any trouble. I just thought I'd like to have somebody along with me as a witness.'

'Witness to what?' he almost snapped at me.

'You'll hear it in front of her or you won't hear it at all.'

'Then I won't hear it at all.'

I stood up. 'You're probably doing the right thing, Spencer.

You want that book of Wade's – if it can be used. And you want to be a nice guy. Both laudable ambitions. I don't share either of them. The best of luck to you and good-bye.'

He stood up suddenly and started towards me. 'Now just a minute, Marlowe. I don't know what's on your mind but you seem to take it hard. Is there some mystery about Roger Wade's death?'

'No mystery at all. He was shot through the head with a Webley Hammerless revolver. Didn't you see a report of the inquest?'

'Certainly.' He was standing close to me now and he looked bothered. 'What was in the eastern papers and a couple of days later a much fuller account in the Los Angeles paper. He was alone in the house, although you were not far away. The servants were away, Candy and the cook, and Eileen had been uptown shopping and arrived home just after it happened. At the moment it happened a very noisy motor boat on the lake drowned the sound of the shot, so that even you didn't hear it.'

'That's correct,' I said. 'Then the motor-boat went away, and I walked back from the lake edge up to the house, heard the doorbell ringing and opened it to find Eileen Wade had forgotten her keys. Roger was already dead. She looked into the study from the doorway, thought he was asleep on the couch, went out to the kitchen to make some tea. A little later than she did I also looked into the study, noticed there was no sound of breathing, and found out why. In due course I called the law.'

'I see no mystery,' Spencer said quietly, all the sharpness gone from his voice. 'It was Roger's own gun, and only the week before he had shot it off in his own room. You found Eileen struggling to get it away from him. His state of mind, his behaviour, his depression over his work – all that was brought out.'

'She told you the stuff is good. Why would he be depressed over it?'

'That's just her opinion, you know. It may be very bad. Or he may have thought it worse than it was. Go on. I'm not a fool. I can see there is more.'

'The homicide dick who investigated the case is an old friend of mine. He's a bulldog and a bloodhound and an old wise cop. He doesn't like a few things. Why did Roger leave no note – when he was a writing fool? Why did he shoot himself in such a way as to leave the shock of discovery to his wife? Why did he bother to pick the moment when I couldn't hear the gun go off? Why did she forget her house keys so that she had to be let into the house? Why did she leave him alone on the day the help got off? Remember, she said she didn't know I would be there. If she did, those two cancel out.'

'My God,' Spencer bleated, 'are you telling me the damn fool cop suspects Eileen?'

'He would if he could think of a motive.'

'That's ridiculous. Why not suspect you? You had all afternoon. There could have been only a few minutes when she could have done it – and she had forgotten her house keys.'

'What motive could I have?'

He reached back and grabbed my whisky sour and swallowed it whole. He put the glass down carefully and got a handkerchief out and wiped his lips and his fingers where the chilled glass had moistened them. He put the handkerchief away. He stared at me.

'Is the investigation still going on?'

'Couldn't say. One thing is sure. They know by now whether he had drunk enough hooch to pass him out. If he had, there may still be trouble.'

'And you want to talk to her,' he said slowly, 'in the presence of a witness.'

'That's right.'

'That means only one of two things to me, Marlowe. Either you are badly scared or you think she ought to be.'

I nodded.

'Which one?' he asked grimly.

'I'm not scared.'

He looked at his watch. 'I hope to God you're crazy.'

We looked at each other in silence.


# Forty-two

North through Coldwater Canyon it began to get hot. When we topped the rise and started to wind down towards the San Fernando Valley it was breathless and blazing. I looked sideways at Spencer. He had a vest on, but the heat didn't seem to bother him. He had something else to bother him a lot more. He looked straight ahead through the windshield and said nothing. The Valley had a thick layer of smog nuzzling down on it. From above it looked like a ground mist and then we were in it and it jerked Spencer out of his silence.

416

'My God, I thought Southern California had a climate,' he said. 'What are they doing – burning old truck tyres?'

'It'll be all right in Idle Valley,' I told him soothingly. 'They get an ocean breeze in there.'

'I'm glad they get something besides drunk,' he said. 'From what I've seen of the local crowd in the rich suburbs I think Roger Wade made a tragic mistake in coming out here to live. A writer needs stimulation – and not the kind they bottle. There's nothing around here but one great suntanned hangover. I'm referring to the upper crust people of course.'

I turned off and slowed down for the dusty stretch to the entrance of Idle Valley, then hit the paving again and in a little while the ocean breeze made itself felt, drifting down through the gap in the hills at the far end of the lake. High sprinklers revolved over the big, smooth lawns and the water made a swishing sound as it licked at the grass. By this time most of the well-heeled people were away somewhere else. You could tell by the shuttered look of the houses and the way the gardener's truck was parked smack in the middle of the driveway. Then we reached the Wades' place and I swung through the gateposts and stopped behind Eileen's Jaguar. Spencer got out and marched solidly across the flagstones to the portico of the house. He rang the bell and the door opened almost at once. Candy was there in the white jacket and the dark, good-looking face and the sharp black eyes. Everything was in order.

Spencer went in. Candy gave me a brief look and neatly shut the door in my face. I waited and nothing happened. I leaned on the bell and heard the chimes. The door swung wide and Candy came out snarling.

'Beat it! Turn blue. You want a knife in the belly?'

'I came to see Mrs Wade.'

'She don't want any part of you.'

'Out of my way, peasant. I got business here.'

'Candy!' It was her voice, and it was sharp.

He gave me a final scowl and backed into the house. I went in and shut the door. She was standing at the end of one of the facing davenports, and Spencer was standing beside her. She looked like a million. She had white slacks on, very high-waisted, and a white sport shirt with half sleeves, and a lilac-coloured handkerchief budding from the pocket over her left breast.

'Candy is getting rather dictatorial lately,' she said to Spencer. 'It's so good to see you, Howard. And so nice of you to come all this way. I didn't realize you were bringing someone with you.'

'Marlowe drove me out,' Spencer said. 'Also he wanted to see you.'

'I can't imagine why,' she said coolly. Finally she looked at me, but not as if not seeing me for a week had left an emptiness in her life. 'Well?'

'It's going to take a little time,' I said.

She sat down slowly. I sat down on the other davenport. Spencer was frowning. He took his glasses off and polished them. That gave him a chance to frown more naturally. Then he sat on the other end of the davenport from me.

'I was sure you would come in time for lunch,' she told him, smiling.

'Not today, thanks.'

'No? Well, of course if you are too busy. Then you just want to see that script.'

'If I may.'

'Of course. Candy! Oh, he's gone. It's on the desk in Roger's study. I'll get it.'

Spencer stood up. 'May I get it?'

Without waiting for an answer he started across the room. Ten feet behind her he stopped and gave me a strained look. Then he went on. I just sat there and waited until her head came around and her eyes gave me a cool impersonal stare.

'What was it you wanted to see me about?' she asked curtly.

'This and that. I see you are wearing that pendant again.'

'I often wear it. It was given to me by a very dear friend a long time ago.'

'Yeah. You told me. It's a British military badge of some sort, isn't it?'

She held it out at the end of the thin chain. 'It's a jeweller's reproduction of one. Smaller than the original and in gold and enamel.'

Spencer came back across the room and sat down again and put a thick pile of yellow paper on the corner of the cocktail table in front of him. He glanced at it idly, then his eyes were watching Eileen.

'Could I look at it a little closer?' I asked her.

She pulled the chain around until she could unfasten the clasp. She handed the pendant to me, or rather she dropped it in my hand. Then she folded her hands in her lap and just looked curious. 'Why are you so interested? It's the badge of a regiment called the Artists Rifles, a Territorial Regiment. The man who gave it to me was lost soon afterwards. At Andalsnes in Norway, in the spring of that terrible year – 1940.' She smiled and made a brief gesture with one hand. 'He was in love with me.'

'Eileen was in London all through the Blitz,' Spencer said in an empty voice. 'She couldn't get away.'

We both ignored Spencer. 'And you were in love with him,' I said.

She looked down and then raised her head and our glances locked. 'It was a long time ago,' she said. 'And there was a war. Strange things happen.'

'There was a little more to it than that, Mrs Wade. I guess you forget how much you opened up about him. "The wild mysterious improbable kind of love that never comes but once." I'm quoting you. In a way you're still in love with him. It's darn nice of me to have the same initials. I suppose that had something to do with your picking me out.'

'His name was nothing like yours,' she said coldly. 'And he is dead, dead, dead.'

I held the gold and enamel pendant out to Spencer. He took it reluctantly. 'I've seen it before,' he muttered.

'Check me on the design,' I said. 'It consists of a broad dagger in white enamel with a gold edge. The dagger points downwards and the flat of the blade crosses in front of a pair of upward-curling blue enamel wings. Then it crosses in back of a scroll. On the scroll are the words: WHO DARES WIN.'

'That seems to be correct,' he said. 'What makes it important?'

'She says it's a badge of the Artists Rifles, a Territorial outfit. She says it was given to her by a man who was in that outfit and was lost in the Norwegian campaign with the British Army in the spring of 1940 at Andalsnes.'

I had their attention. Spencer watched me steadily. I wasn't talking to the birds and he knew it. Eileen knew it too. Her tawny eyebrows were crimped in a puzzled frown which could have been genuine. It was also unfriendly.

'This is a sleeve badge,' I said. 'It came into existence because the Artists Rifles were made over or attached or seconded or whatever the correct term is into a Special Air Service Outfit. They had originally been a Territorial Regiment of infantry. This badge didn't even exist until 1947. Therefore nobody gave it to Mrs Wade in 1940. Also, no Artists Rifles were landed at Andalsnes in Norway in 1940. Sherwood Foresters and Leicestershires, yes. Both Territorial. Artists Rifles, no. Am I being nasty?'

Spencer put the pendant down on the coffee table and pushed it slowly across until it was in front of Eileen. He said nothing.

'Do you think I wouldn't know?' Eileen asked me contemptuously.

'Do you think the British War Office wouldn't know?' I asked her right back.

'Obviously there must be some mistake,' Spencer said mildly.

I swung around and gave him a hard stare. 'That's one way of putting it.'

'Another way of putting it is that I am a liar,' Eileen Wade said icily. 'I never knew anyone named Paul Marston, never loved him or he me. He never gave me a reproduction of his regimental badge, he was never missing in action, he never existed. I bought this badge myself in a shop in New York where they specialize in imported British luxuries, things like leather goods, hand-made brogues, regimental and school ties and cricket blazers, knick-knacks with coats of arms on them and so on. Would an explanation like that satisfy you, Mr Marlowe?'

'The last part would. Not the first. No doubt somebody told you it was an Artists Rifles badge and forgot to mention what kind, or didn't know. But you did know Paul Marston and he did serve in that outfit, and he was missing in action in Norway. But it didn't happen in 1940, Mrs Wade. It happened in 1942 and he was in the Commandos then, and it wasn't at Andalsnes, but on a little island off the coast where the Commando boys pulled a fast raid.'

'I see no need to be so hostile about it,' Spencer said in an executive sort of voice. He was fooling with the yellow sheets in front of him now. I didn't know whether he was trying to stooge for me or was just sore. He picked up a slab of yellow script and weighed it on his hand.

'You going to buy that stuff by the pound?' I asked him.

He looked startled, then he smiled a small difficult smile.

'Eileen had a pretty rough time in London,' he said. 'Things get confused in one's memory.'

I took a folded paper out of my pocket. 'Sure,' I said. 'Like who you got married to. This is a certified copy of a marriage certificate. The original came from Caxton Hall Register Office. The date of the marriage is August 1942. The parties named are Paul Edward Marston and Eileen Victoria Sampsell. In a sense Mrs Wade is right. There was no such person as Paul Edward Marston. It was a fake name because in the army you have to get permission to get married. The man faked an identity. In the army he had another name. I have his whole army history. It's a wonder to me that people never seem to realize that all you have to do is ask.'

Spencer was very quiet now. He leaned back and stared. But not at me. He stared at Eileen. She looked back at him with one of those faint, half-deprecatory, half-seductive smiles women are so good at.

'But he was dead, Howard. Long before I met Roger. What could it possibly matter? Roger knew all about it. I never stopped using my unmarried name. In the circumstances I had to. It was on my passport. Then after he was killed in action—' she stopped and drew a slow breath and let her hand fall slowly and softly to her knee. 'All finished, all done for, all lost.'

'You're sure Roger knew?' he asked her slowly.

'He knew something,' I said. 'The name Paul Marston had a meaning for him. I asked him once and he got a funny look in his eyes. But he didn't tell me why.'

She ignored that and spoke to Spencer.

'Why, of course Roger knew all about it.' Now she was smiling at Spencer patiently as if he was being a little slow on the take. The tricks they have.

'Then why lie about the dates?' Spencer asked dryly. 'Why say the man was lost in 1940 when he was lost in 1942. Why wear a badge that he couldn't have given you and make a point of saying that he did give it to you?'

'Perhaps I was lost in a dream,' she said softly. 'Or a nightmare, more accurately. A lot of my friends were killed in the bombing. When you said good night in those days you tried not to make it sound like good-bye. But that's what it often was. And when you said good-bye to a soldier – it was worse. It's always the kind and gentle ones that get killed.'

He didn't say anything. I didn't say anything. She looked down at the pendant lying on the table in front of her. She picked it up and fitted it to the chain around her neck again and leaned back composedly.

'I know I haven't any right to cross-examine you, Eileen,' Spencer said slowly. 'Let's forget it. Marlowe made a big thing out of the badge and the marriage certificate and so on. Just for a moment I guess he had me wondering.'

'Mr Marlowe,' she told him quietly, 'makes a big thing out of trifles. But when it comes to a really big thing – like saving a man's life – he is out by the lake watching a silly speedboat.'

'And you never saw Paul Marston again,' I said.

'How could I when he was dead?'

'You didn't know he was dead. There was no report of his death from the Red Cross. He might have been taken prisoner.'

She shuddered suddenly. 'In October 1942,' she said slowly, 'Hitler issued an order that all Commando prisoners were to be turned over to the Gestapo. I think we all know what that meant. Torture and a nameless death in some Gestapo dungeon.' She shuddered again. Then she blazed at me: 'You're a horrible man. You want me to live that over again, to punish me for a trivial lie. Suppose someone you loved had been caught by those people and you knew what had happened, what must have happened to him or her? Is it so strange that I tried to build another kind of memory — even a false one?'

'I need a drink,' Spencer said. 'I need a drink badly. May I have one?'

She clapped her hands and Candy drifted up from nowhere as he always did. He bowed to Spencer.

'What you like to drink, Señor Spencer?'

'Straight Scotch, and plenty of it,' Spencer said.

Candy went over in the corner and pulled the bar out from the wall. He got a bottle up on it and poured a stiff jolt into a glass. He came back and set it down in front of Spencer. He started to leave again.

'Perhaps, Candy,' Eileen said quietly, 'Mr Marlowe would like a drink too.'

He stopped and looked at her, his face dark and stubborn.

'No thanks,' I said. 'No drink for me.'

Candy made a snorting sound and walked off. There was another silence. Spencer put down half of his drink. He lit a cigarette. He spoke to me without looking at me.

'I'm sure Mrs Wade or Candy could drive me back to Beverly Hills. Or can I get a cab. I take it you've said your piece.'

I refolded the certified copy of the marriage licence. I put it back in my pocket.

'Sure that's the way you want it?' I asked him.

'That's the way everybody wants it.'

'Good.' I stood up. 'I guess I was a fool to try to play it this way. Being a big-time publisher and having the brains to go with it — if it takes any — you might have assumed I didn't come out here just to play the heavy. I didn't revive ancient history or spend my own money to get the facts just to twist them around somebody's neck. I didn't investigate Paul Marston be-cause the Gestapo murdered him, because Mrs Wade was wearing the wrong badge, because she got mixed up on her dates, because she married him in one of those quickie wartime marriages. When I started investigating him I didn't know any of those things. All I knew was his name. Now how do you suppose I knew that?'

'No doubt somebody told you,' Spencer said curtly.

'Correct, Mr Spencer. Somebody who knew him in New York after the war and later on saw him out here in Chasen's with his wife.'

'Marston is a pretty common name,' Spencer said and sipped his whisky. He turned his head sideways and his right eyelid drooped a fraction of an inch. So I sat down again. 'Even Paul Marstons could hardly be unique. There are nineteen Howard Spencers in the Greater New York area telephone directories, for instance. And four of them are just plain Howard Spencer with no middle initial.'

'Yeah. How many Paul Marstons would you say had had one side of their faces smashed by a delayed-action mortar shell and showed the scars and marks of the plastic surgery that repaired the damage?'

Spencer's mouth fell open. He made some kind of heavy breathing sound. He got out a handkerchief and tapped his temples with it.

'How many Paul Marstons would you say had saved the lives of a couple of tough gamblers named Mendy Menendez and Randy Starr on that same occasion? They're still around, they've got good memories. They can talk when it suits them. Why ham it up any more, Spencer? Paul Marston and Terry Lennox were the same man. It can be proved beyond any shadow of a doubt.'

I didn't expect anyone to jump six feet into the air and scream and nobody did. But there is a kind of silence that it almost as loud as a shout. I had it. I had it all around me, thick and hard. In the kitchen I could hear water run. Outside on the road I could hear the dull thump of a folded newspaper hit the drive-way, then the light, inaccurate whistling of a boy wheeling away on his bicycle.

I felt a tiny sting on the back of my neck. I jerked away from it and swung around. Candy was standing there with his knife in his hand. His dark face was wooden but there was something in his eyes I hadn't seen before.

'You are tired, *amigo*,' he said softly. 'I fix you a drink, no?'

'Bourbon on the rocks, thanks,' I said.

'*De pronto, señor.*'

423

He snapped the knife shut, dropped it into the side pocket of his white jacket and went softly away.

Then at last I looked at Eileen. She sat leaning forward, her hands clasped tightly. The downward tilt of her face hid her expression if she had any. And when she spoke her voice had the lucid emptiness of that mechanical voice on the telephone that tells you the time, and if you keep listening, which people don't because they have no reason to, it will keep on telling you the passing seconds for ever, without the slightest change of inflection.

'I saw him once, Howard. Just once. I didn't speak to him at all. Nor he to me. He was terribly changed. His hair was white and his face – it wasn't quite the same face. But of course I knew him, and of course he knew me. We looked at each other. That was all. Then he was gone out of the room and the next day he was gone from her house. It was at the Lorings I saw him – and her. One afternoon, late. You were there, Howard. And Roger was there. I suppose you saw him too.'

'We were introduced,' Spencer said. 'I knew who he was married to.'

'Linda Loring told me he just disappeared. He gave no reason. There was no quarrel. Then after a while that woman divorced him. And still later I heard she found him again. He was down and out. And they were married again. Heaven knows why. I suppose he had no money and it didn't matter to him any more. He knew that I was married to Roger. We were lost to each other.'

'Why?' Spencer asked.

Candy put my drink in front of me without a word. He looked at Spencer and Spencer shook his head. Candy drifted away. Nobody paid any attention to him. He was like the prop man in a Chinese play, the fellow that moves things around on the stage and the actors and audience alike behave as if he wasn't there.

'Why?' she repeated. 'Oh, you wouldn't understand. What we had was lost. It could never be recovered. The Gestapo didn't get him after all. There must have been *some* decent Nazis who didn't obey Hitler's order about the Commandos. So he survived, he came back. I used to pretend to myself that I would find him again, but as he had been, eager, young and unspoiled. But to find him married to that redheaded whore – that was disgusting. I already knew about her and Roger. I have no doubt Paul did too. So did Linda Loring, who is a bit of a tramp her-

424

self, but not completely so. They all are in that set. You ask me why I didn't leave Roger and go back to Paul. After he had been in her arms and Roger had been in those same willing arms? No thank you. I need a little more inspiration than that. Roger I could forgive. He drank, he didn't know what he was doing. He worried about his work and he hated himself because he was just a mercenary hack. He was a weak man, unreconciled, frustrated, but understandable. He was just a husband. Paul was either much more or he was nothing. In the end he was nothing.'

I took a swig of my drink. Spencer had finished his. He was scratching at the material of the davenport. He had forgotten the pile of paper in front of him, the unfinished novel of the very much finished popular author.

'I wouldn't say he was nothing,' I said.

She lifted her eyes and looked at me vaguely and dropped them again.

'Less than nothing,' she said, with a new note of sarcasm in her voice. 'He knew what she was, he married her. Then because she was what he knew she was he killed her. And then ran away and killed himself.'

'He didn't kill her,' I said, 'and you know it.'

She came upright with a smooth motion and stared at me blankly. Spencer let out a noise of some kind.

'Roger killed her,' I said, 'and you also know that.'

'Did he tell you?' she asked quietly.

'He didn't have to. He did give me a couple of hints. He would have told me or someone in time. It was tearing him to pieces not to.'

She shook her head slightly. 'No, Mr Marlowe. That was not why he was tearing himself to pieces. Roger didn't know he had killed her. He had blacked out completely. He knew something was wrong and he tried to bring it to the surface, but he couldn't. The shock had destroyed his memory of it. Perhaps it would have come back and perhaps in the last moments of his life it did come back. But not until then. Not until then.'

Spencer said in a sort of growl: 'That sort of thing just doesn't happen, Eileen.'

'Oh yes, it does,' I said. 'I know of two well-established instances. One was a blackout drunk who killed a woman he picked up in a bar. He strangled her with a scarf she was wearing fastened with a fancy clasp. She went home with him and what went on then is not known except that she got dead and when the law caught up with him he was wearing the fancy clasp on his own tie and he didn't have the faintest idea where he got it.'

'Never?' Spencer asked. 'Or just at the time?'

'He never admitted it. And he's not around any more to be asked. They gassed him. The other case was a head wound. He was living with a rich pervert, the kind that collects first editions and does fancy cooking and has a very expensive secret library behind a panel in the wall. The two of them had a fight. They fought all over the house, from room to room, the place was a shambles and the rich guy eventually got the low score. The killer, when they caught him, had dozens of bruises on him and a broken finger. All he knew for sure was that he had a headache and he couldn't find his way back to Pasadena. He kept circling around and stopping to ask directions at the same service station. The guy at the service station decided he was nuts and called the cops. Next time around they were waiting for him.'

'I don't believe that about Roger,' Spencer said. 'He was no more psycho than I am.'

'He blacked out when he was drunk,' I said.

'I was there. I *saw* him do it,' Eileen said calmly.

I grinned at Spencer. It was some kind of grin, not the cheery kind probably, but I could feel my face doing its best.

'She's going to tell us about it,' I told him. 'Just listen. She's going to tell us. She can't help herself now.'

'Yes, that is true,' she said gravely. 'There are things no one likes to tell about an enemy, much less about one's own husband. And if I have to tell them publicly on a witness stand, you are not going to enjoy it, Howard. Your fine, talented, ever so popular and lucrative author is going to look pretty cheap. Sexy as all get out, wasn't he? On paper, that is. And how the poor fool tried to live up to it! All that woman was to him was a trophy. I spied on them. I should be ashamed of that. One has to say these things. I am ashamed of nothing. I saw the whole nasty scene. The guest house she used for her amours happens to be a nice secluded affair with its own garage and entrance on a side street, a dead end, shaded by big trees. The time came, as it must to people like Roger, when he was no longer a satisfactory lover. Just a little too drunk. He tried to leave but she came out after him screaming and stark naked, waving some kind of small statuette. She used language of a depth of filth and depravity I couldn't attempt to describe. Then she tried to hit him with the statuette. You are both men and you must know that nothing shocks a man quite so much as to hear a supposedly refined woman use the language of the gutter and the public urinal. He was drunk, he had had sudden spells of violence, and he had one then. He tore the statuette out of her hand. You can guess the rest.'

'There must have been a lot of blood,' I said.

'Blood?' She laughed bitterly. 'You should have seen him when he got home. When I ran for my car to get away he was just standing there looking down at her. Then he bent and picked her up in his arms and carried her into the guest house. I knew then that the shock had partially sobered him. He got home in about an hour. He was very quiet. It shook him when he saw me waiting. But he wasn't drunk then. He was dazed. There was blood on his face, on his hair, all over the front of his coat. I got him into the lavatory off the study and got him stripped and cleaned off enough to get him upstairs into the shower. I put him to bed. I got an old suitcase and went downstairs and gathered up the bloody clothes and put them in the suitcase. I cleaned the basin and the floor and then I took a wet towel out and made sure his car was clean. I put it away and got mine out. I drove with the suitcase full of bloody clothes and towels.'

She stopped. Spencer was scratching at the palm of his left hand. She gave him a quick glance and went on.

'While I was away he got up and drank a lot of whisky. And the next morning he didn't remember a single thing. That is, he didn't say a word about it or behave as if he had anything on his mind but a hangover. And I said nothing.'

'He must have missed the clothes,' I said.

She nodded. 'I think he did eventually – but he didn't say so. Everything seemed to happen at once about that time. The papers were full of it, then Paul was missing, and then he was dead in Mexico. How was I to know that would happen? Roger was my husband. He had done an awful thing, but she was an awful woman. And he hadn't known what he was doing. Then almost as suddenly as it began the papers dropped it. Linda's father must have had something to do with that. Roger read the papers, of course, and he made just the sort of comments one would expect from an innocent bystander who had just happened to know the people involved.'

'Weren't you afraid?' Spencer asked her quietly.

'I was sick with fear, Howard. If he remembered, he would probably kill me. He was a good actor – most writers are – and perhaps he already knew and was just waiting for a chance. But

427

I couldn't be sure. He might – just might – have forgotten the whole thing permanently. And Paul was dead.'

'If he never mentioned the clothes that you had dumped in the reservoir, that proved he suspected something,' I said. 'And remember, in that stuff he left in the typewriter the other time – the time he shot the gun off upstairs and I found you trying to get away from him – he said a good man had died for him.'

'He said that?' Her eyes widened just the right amount.

'He wrote it – on the typewriter. I destroyed it, he asked me to. I supposed you had already seen it.'

'I never read anything he wrote in his study.'

'You read the note he left the time Verringer took him away. You even dug something out of the wastebasket.'

'That was different,' she said coolly. 'I was looking for a clue to where he might have gone.'

'Okay,' I said and leaned back. 'Is there any more?'

She shook her head slowly, with a deep sadness. 'I suppose not. At the very last, the afternoon he killed himself, he may have remembered. We'll never know. Do we want to know?'

Spencer cleared his throat. 'What was Marlowe supposed to do in all this? It was your idea to get him here. You talked me into that, you know.'

'I was terribly afraid. I was afraid of Roger and I was afraid *for* him. Mr Marlowe was Paul's friend, almost the last person to see him who knew him. Paul might have told him something. I had to be sure. If he was dangerous, I wanted him on my side. If he found out the truth, there might still be some way to save Roger.'

Suddenly and for no reason that I could see Spencer got tough. He leaned forward and pushed his jaw out.

'Let me get this straight, Eileen. Here was a private detective who was already in bad with the police. They'd had him in jail. He was supposed to have helped Paul – I call him that because you do – jump the country, to Mexico. That's a felony, if Paul was a murderer. So if he found out the truth and could clear himself, he would just sit on his hands and do nothing. Was that your idea?'

'I was afraid, Howard. Can't you understand that? I was living in the house with a murderer who might be a maniac. I was alone with him a large part of the time.'

'I understand that,' Spencer said, still tough. 'But Marlowe didn't take it on, and you were still alone. Then Roger fired the gun off and for a week after that you were alone. Then Roger killed himself and very conveniently it was Marlowe who was alone that time.'

'That is true,' she said. 'What of it? Could I help it?'

'All right,' Spencer said. 'Is it just possible you thought Marlowe might find the truth and with the background of the gun going off once already just kind of hand it to Roger and say something like, "Look, old man, you're a murderer and I know it and your wife knows it. She's a fine woman. She has suffered enough. Not to mention Sylvia Lennox's husband. Why not do the decent thing and pull the trigger and everybody will assume it was a case of too much wild drinking? So I'll stroll down by the lake and smoke a cigarette, old man. Good luck and goodbye. Oh, here's the gun. It's loaded and it's all yours."'

'You're getting horrible, Howard. I didn't think anything of the sort.'

'You told the deputy Marlowe had killed Roger. What was that supposed to mean?'

She looked at me briefly, almost shyly. 'I was very wrong to say that. I didn't know what I was saying.'

'Maybe you thought Marlowe had shot him,' Spencer suggested calmly.

Her eyes narrowed. 'Oh no, Howard. Why? Why would he do that? That's an abominable suggestion.'

'Why?' Spencer wanted to know. 'What's abominable about it? The police had the same idea. And Candy gave them a motive. He said Marlowe was in your room for two hours the night Roger shot a hole in the ceiling – after Roger had been put to sleep with pills.'

She flushed to the roots of her hair. She stared at him dumbly.

'And you didn't have any clothes on,' Spencer said brutally. 'That's what Candy told them.'

'But at the inquest—' she began to say in a shattered kind of voice. Spencer cut her off.

'The police didn't believe Candy. So he didn't tell it at the inquest.'

'Oh.' It was a sigh of relief.

'Also,' Spencer went on coldly, 'the police suspected you. They still do. All they need is a motive. Looks to me like they might be able to put one together now.'

She was up on her feet. 'I think you had both better leave my house,' she said angrily. 'The sooner, the better.'

'Well, did you or didn't you?' Spencer asked calmly, not

moving except to reach for his glass and find it empty.

'Did I or didn't I what?'

'Shoot Roger?'

She was standing there staring at him. The flush had gone. Her face was white and tight and angry.

'I'm just giving you the sort of thing you'd get in court.'

'I was out. I had forgotten my keys. I had to ring to get into the house. He was dead when I got home. All that is known. What has got into you, for God's sake?'

He took a handkerchief out and wiped his lips. 'Eileen, I've stayed in this house twenty times. I've never known that front door to be locked during the day time. I don't say you shot him. I just asked you. And don't tell me it was impossible. The way things worked out it was easy.'

'I shot my own husband?' she asked slowly and wonderingly.

'Assuming,' Spencer said in the same indifferent voice, 'that he *was* your husband. You had another when you married him.'

'Thank you, Howard. Thank you very much. Roger's last book, his swan song, is there in front of you. Take it and go. And I think you had better call the police and tell them what you think. It will be a charming ending to our friendship. Most charming. Good-bye, Howard. I am very tired and I have a headache. I'm going to my room and lie down. As for Mr Marlowe – and I suppose he put you up to all this – I can only say to him that if he didn't kill Roger in a literal sense, he certainly drove him to his death.'

She turned to walk away. I said sharply: 'Mrs Wade, just a moment. Let's finish the job. No sense in being bitter. We are all trying to do the right thing. That suitcase you threw into the Chatsworth Reservoir – was it heavy?'

She turned and stared at me. 'It was an old one, I said. Yes, it was very heavy.'

'How did you get it over the high wire fence around the reservoir?'

'What? The fence?' She made a helpless gesture. 'I suppose in emergencies one has an abnormal strength to do what has to be done. Somehow or other I did it. That's all.'

'There isn't any fence,' I said.

'Isn't any fence?' She repeated it dully, as if it didn't mean anything.

'And there was no blood on Roger's clothes. And Sylvia Lennox wasn't killed outside the guest house, but inside it on the bed. And there was practically no blood, because she was already dead – shot dead with a gun – and when the statuette was used to beat her face to a pulp, it was beating a dead woman. And the dead, Mrs Wade, bleed very little.'

She curled her lip at me contemptuously. 'I suppose you were there,' she said scornfully.

Then she went away from us.

We watched her go. She went up the stairs slowly, moving with calm elegance. She disappeared into her room and the door closed softly but firmly behind her. Silence.

'What was that about the wire fence?' Spencer asked me vaguely. He was moving his head back and forth. He was flushed and sweating. He was taking it gamely but it wasn't easy for him to take.

'Just a gag,' I said. 'I've never been close enough to the Chatsworth Reservoir to know what it looks like. Maybe it has a fence around it, maybe not.'

'I see,' he said unhappily. 'But the point is she didn't know either.'

'Of course not. She killed both of them.'

# Forty-three

Then something moved softly and Candy was standing at the end of the couch looking at me. He had his switch knife in his hand. He pressed the button and the blade shot out. He pressed the button and the blade went back into the handle. There was a sleek glitter in his dark eyes.

'Millon de perdones, Señor,' he said. 'I was wrong about you. She killed the boss. I think I—' he stopped and the blade shot out again.

'No.' I stood up and held my hand out. 'Give me the knife, Candy. You're just a nice Mexican houseboy. They'd hang it on to you and love it. Just the kind of smoke screen that would make them grin with delight. You don't know what I'm talking about. But I do. They fouled it up so bad that they couldn't straighten it out now if they wanted to. And they don't want to. They'd blast a confession out of you so quick you wouldn't even have time to tell them your full name. And you'd be sitting on your fanny up in San Quentin with a life sentence three weeks from Tuesday.'

'I tell you before I am not a Mexican. I am Chileno from Vina del Mar near Valparaiso.'

'The knife, Candy. I know all that. You're free. You've got money saved. You've probably got eight brothers and sisters back home. Be smart and go back where you came from. This job here is dead.'

'Lots of jobs,' he said quietly. Then he reached out and dropped the knife into my hand. 'For you I do this.'

I dropped the knife into my pocket. He glanced up towards the balcony. '*La señora* – what do we do now?'

'Nothing. We do nothing at all. The *señora* is very tired. She has been living under a great strain. She doesn't want to be disturbed.'

'We've got to call the police,' Spencer said grittily.

'Why?'

'Oh my God, Marlowe – we have to.'

'Tomorrow. Pick up your pile of unfinished novel and let's go.'

'We've got to call the police. There is such a thing as law.'

'We don't have to do anything of the sort. We haven't enough evidence to swat a fly with. Let the law enforcement people do their own dirty work. Let the lawyers work it out. They write the laws for other lawyers to dissect in front of other lawyers called judges so that other judges can say the first judges were wrong and the Supreme Court can say the second lot were wrong. Sure there's such a thing as law. We're up to our necks in it. About all it does is make business for lawyers. How long do you think the big-shot mobsters would last if the lawyers didn't show them how to operate?'

Spencer said angrily: 'That has nothing to do with it. A man was killed in this house. He happened to be an author and a very successful and important one, but that has nothing to do with it either. He was a man and you and I know who killed him. There's such a thing as justice.'

'Tomorrow.'

'You're just as bad as she is if you let her get away with it. I'm beginning to wonder about you a little, Marlowe. You could have saved his life if you had been on your toes. In a sense you did let her get away with it. And for all I know this whole performance this afternoon has been just that – a performance.'

'That's right. A disguised love scene. You could see Eileen is crazy about me. When things quiet down we may get married. She ought to be pretty well fixed. I haven't made a buck out of the Wade family yet. I'm getting impatient.'

He took his glasses off and polished them. He wiped perspiration from the hollows under his eyes, replaced the glasses and looked at the floor.

'I'm sorry,' he said. 'I've taken a pretty stiff pinch this afternoon. It was bad enough to know Roger had killed himself. But this other version makes me feel degraded – just knowing about it.' He looked up at me. 'Can I trust you?'

'To do what?'

'The right thing – whatever it is.' He reached down and picked up the pile of yellow script and tucked it under his arm. 'No, forget it. I guess you know what you are doing. I'm a pretty good publisher but this is out of my line. I guess what I really am is just a goddam stuffed shirt.'

He walked past me and Candy stepped out of his way, then went quickly to the front door and held it open. Spencer went out past him with a brief nod. I followed. I stopped beside Candy and looked into his dark shining eyes.

'No tricks, *amigo*,' I said.

'The *señora* is very tired,' he said quietly. 'She has gone to her room. She will not be disturbed. I know nothing, *señor. No me acuerdo de nada ... A sus ordones, señor.*'

I took the knife out of my pocket and held it out to him. He smiled.

'Nobody trusts me, but I trust you, Candy.'

'*Lo mismo, señor. Muchas gracias.*'

Spencer was already in the car. I got in and started it and backed down the driveway and drove him back to Beverly Hills. I let him out at the side entrance of the hotel.

'I've been thinking all the way back,' he said as he got out. 'She must be a little insane. I guess they'd never convict her.'

'They won't even try,' I said. 'But she doesn't know that.'

He struggled with the batch of yellow paper under his arm, got it straightened out and nodded to me. I watched him heave open the door and go on in. I eased up on the brake and the Olds slid out from the white curb, and that was the last I saw of Howard Spencer.

I got home late and tired and depressed. It was one of those nights when the air is heavy and the night noises seem muffled and far away. There was a high, misty, indifferent moon. I walked the floor, played a few records and hardly heard them. I seemed to hear a steady ticking somewhere, but there wasn't anything in the house to tick. The ticking was in my head. I was a one-man death watch.

I thought of the first time I had seen Eileen Wade and the

second and the third and the fourth. But after that something in her got out of drawing. She no longer seemed quite real. A murderer is always unreal once you know he is a murderer. There are people who kill out of hate or fear or greed. There are the cunning killers who plan and expect to get away with it. There are the angry killers who do not think at all. And there are the killers who are in love with death, to whom murder is a remote kind of suicide. In a sense they are all insane, but not in the way Spencer meant it.

It was almost daylight when I finally went to bed.

The jangle of the telephone dragged me up out of a black well of sleep. I rolled over on the bed, fumbled for slippers and realized that I hadn't been asleep for more than a couple of hours. I felt like a half-digested meal eaten in a greasy spoon joint. My eyes were stuck together and my mouth was full of sand. I heaved up on the feet and lumbered into the living-room and pulled the phone off the cradle and said into it: 'Hold the line.'

I put the phone down and went into the bathroom and hit myself in the face with some cold water. Outside the window something went snip, snip, snip. I looked out vaguely and saw a brown, expressionless face. It was the once-a-week Jap gardener I called Hard-Hearted Harry. He was trimming the tecoma – the way a Japanese gardener trims your tecoma. You ask him four times and he says, 'next week', and then he comes by at six o'clock in the morning and trims it outside your bedroom window.

I rubbed my face dry and went back to the telephone.

'Yeah?'

'This is Candy, *Señor*.'

'Good morning, Candy.'

*'La señora es muerta.'*

Dead. What a cold, black, noiseless word it is in any language. The lady is dead.

'Nothing you did, I hope.'

'I think the medicine. It is called demerol. I think forty, fifty in the bottle. Empty now. No dinner last night. This morning I climb up on the ladder and look in the window. Dressed just like yesterday afternoon. I break the screen open. *La señora es muerta. Frio como agua de nieve.'*

Cold as ice-water. 'You call anybody?'

'Si. *El Doctor Loring*. He call the cops. Not here yet.'

'Dr Loring, huh? Just the man to come too late.'

'I don't show him the letter,' Candy said.

'Letter to who?'

'Señor Spencer.'

'Give it to the police, Candy. Don't let Dr Loring have it. Just the police. And one more thing, Candy. Don't hide anything, don't tell them any lies. We were there. Tell the truth. This time the truth and all the truth.'

There was a little pause. Then he said: *Sí.* I catch. *Hasta la vista, amigo.*' He hung up.

I dialled the Ritz-Beverly and asked for Howard Spencer.

'One moment, please. I'll give you the desk.'

A man's voice said: 'Desk speaking. May I help you?'

'I asked for Howard Spencer. I know it's early, but it's urgent.'

'Mr Spencer checked out last evening. He took the eight o'clock plane to New York.'

'Oh, sorry. I didn't know.'

I went out to the kitchen to make coffee – yards of coffee. Rich, strong, bitter, boiling hot, ruthless, depraved. The life-blood of tired men.

It was a couple of hours later that Bernie Ohls called me.

'Okay, wise guy,' he said. 'Get down here and suffer.'


# Forty-four


It was like the other time except that it was day and we were in Captain Hernandez's office and the Sheriff was up in Santa Barbara opening Fiesta Week. Captain Hernandez was there and Bernie Ohls and a man from the Coroner's office and Dr Loring, who looked as if he had been caught performing an abortion, and a man named Lawford, a Deputy from the D.A.'s office, a tall, gaunt, expressionless man whose brother was vaguely rumoured to be a boss of the numbers racket in the Central Avenue district.

Hernandez had some handwritten sheets of note-paper in front of him, flesh-pink paper, deckle-edged, and written on with green ink.

'This is informal,' Hernandez said, when everybody was as comfortable as you can get in hard chairs. 'No stenotype or recording equipment. Say what you like. Dr Weiss represents the Coroner who will decide whether an inquest is necessary. Dr Weiss?'

He was fat, cheerful and looked competent. 'I think no inquest,' he said. 'There is every surface indication of narcotic poisoning. When the ambulance arrived the woman was still breathing very faintly and she was in a deep coma and all the reflexes were negative. At that stage you don't save one in a hundred. Her skin was cold and respiration would not be noticed without close examination. The houseboy thought she was dead. She died approximately an hour after that. I understand the lady was subject to occasional violent attacks of bronchial asthma. The demerol was prescribed by Dr Loring as an emergency measure.'

'Any information or deduction about the amount of demerol taken, Dr Weiss?'

'A fatal dose,' he said, smiling faintly. 'There is no quick way of determining that without knowing the medical history, the acquired or natural tolerance. According to her confession she took twenty-three hundred milligrams, four or five times the minimal lethal dose for a non-addict.' He looked questioningly at Dr Loring.

'Mrs Wade was not an addict,' Dr Loring said coldly. 'The prescribed dose would be one or two fifty-milligram tablets. Three or four during a twenty-four hour period would be the most I'd permit.'

'But you gave her fifty at a whack,' Captain Hernandez said. 'A pretty dangerous drug to have around in that quantity, don't you think? How bad was this bronchial asthma, Doctor?'

Dr Loring smiled contemptuously. 'It was intermittent, like all asthma. It never amounted to what we term *status asthmaticus*, an attack so severe that the patient seems in danger of suffocating.'

'Any comment, Dr Weiss?'

'Well,' Dr Weiss said slowly, 'assuming the note didn't exist and assuming we had no other evidence of how much of the stuff she took, it could be an accidental overdose. The safety margin isn't very wide. We'll know for sure tomorrow. You don't want to suppress the note, Hernandez, for Pete's sake?'

Hernandez scowled down at his desk. 'I was just wondering. I didn't know narcotics were standard treatment for asthma. Guy learns something every day.'

Loring flushed. 'An emergency measure, I said, Captain. A doctor can't be everywhere at once. The onset of an asthmatic flare-up can be very sudden.'

Hernandez gave him a brief glance and turned to Lawford.

'What happens to your office, if I give this letter to the press?'

The D.A.'s Deputy glanced at me emptily. 'What's this guy doing here, Hernandez?'

'I invited him.'

'How do you know he won't repeat everything said in here to some reporter?'

'Yeah, he's a great talker. You found that out. The time you had him pinched.'

Lawford grinned, then cleared his throat. 'I've read that purported confession,' he said carefully. 'And I don't believe a word of it. You've got a background of emotional exhaustion, bereavement, some use of drugs, the strain of wartime life in England under bombing, this clandestine marriage, the man coming back here, and so on. Undoubtedly she developed a feeling of guilt and tried to purge herself of it by a sort of transference.'

He stopped and looked around, but all he saw was faces with no expression. 'I can't speak for the D.A. but my own feeling is that your confession would be no grounds to seek an indictment even if the woman had lived.'

'And having already believed one confession you wouldn't care to believe another that contradicted the first one,' Hernandez said caustically.

'Take it easy, Hernandez. Any law-enforcement agency has to consider public relations. If the papers printed that confession we'd be in trouble. That's for sure. We've got enough eager beaver reformer groups around just waiting for that kind of chance to stick a knife into us. We've got a Grand Jury that's already jittery about the working over your vice squad lieutenant got last week.'

Hernandez said: 'Okay, it's your baby. Sign the receipt for me.'

He shuffled the pink deckle-edged pages together and Lawford leaned down to sign a form. He picked up the pink pages, folded them, put them in his breast pocket and walked out.

Dr Weiss stood up. He was tough, good-natured, unimpressed. 'We had the last inquest on the Wade family too quick,' he said. 'I guess we won't bother to have this one at all.'

He nodded to Ohls and Hernandez, shook hands formally with Loring, and went out. Loring stood up to go, then hesitated.

'I take it that I may inform a certain interested party that there will be no further investigation of this matter?' he said stiffly.

'Sorry to have kept you away from your patients so long, Doctor.'

'You haven't answered my question,' Loring said sharply. 'I'd better warn you—'

'Get lost, Jack,' Hernandez said.

Dr Loring almost staggered with shock. Then he turned and fumbled his way rapidly out of the room The door closed and it was a half-minute before anybody said anything. Hernandez shook himself and lit a cigarette. Then he looked at me.

'Well?' he said.

'Well what?'

'What are you waiting for?'

'This is the end, then? Finished? Kaput?'

'Tell him, Bernie.'

'Yeah, sure it's the end,' Ohls said. 'I was all set to pull her in for questioning. Wade didn't shoot himself. Too much alcohol in his brain. But like I told you, where was the motive? Her confession could be wrong in details, but it proves she spied on him. She knew the layout of the guest house in Encino. The Lennox frail had taken both her men from her. What happened in the guest house is just what you want to imagine. One question you forgot to ask Spencer. Did Wade own a Mauser PPK? Yeah, he owned a small Mauser automatic. We talked to Spencer already today on the phone. Wade was a blackout drunk. The poor unfortunate bastard either thought he had killed Sylvia Lennox or he actually had killed her or else he had some reason to know his wife had. Either way he was going to lay it on the line eventually. Sure, he'd been hitting the hooch long before, but he was a he-guy married to a beautiful nothing. The Mex knows all about it. The little bastard knows damn near everything. That was a dream girl. Some of her was here and now, but a lot of her was there and then. If she ever got hot pants, it wasn't for her husband. Get what I'm talking about?'

I didn't answer him.

'Damn near made her yourself, didn't you?'

I gave him the same no answer.

Ohls and Hernandez both grinned sourly. 'Us guys aren't exactly brainless,' Ohls said. 'We knew there was something in that story about taking her clothes off. You out-talked him and he let you. He was hurt and confused and he liked Wade and he wanted to be sure. When he got sure he'd have used his knife. This was a personal matter with him. He never snitched on Wade. Wade's wife did, and she deliberately fouled up the issue just to confuse Wade. It all adds. In the end I guess she was scared of him. And Wade never threw her down any stairs. That was an accident. She tripped and the guy tried to catch her. Candy saw that too.'

'None of it explains why she wanted me around.'

'I could think of reasons. One of them is old stuff. Every cop has run into it a hundred times. You were the loose end, the guy that helped Lennox escape, his friend, and probably to some extent his confidant. What did he know and what did he tell you? He took the gun that had killed her and he knew it had been fired. She could have thought he did it for her. That made her think he knew she had used it. When he killed himself she was sure. But what about you? You were still the loose end. She wanted to milk you, and she had the charm to use, and a situation ready-made for an excuse to get next to you. And if she needed a fall guy, you were it. You might say she was collecting fall guys.'

'You're imputing too much knowledge to her,' I said.

Ohls broke a cigarette in half and started chewing on one half. The other half he stuck behind his ear.

'Another reason is she wanted a man, a big, strong guy that could crush her in his arms and make her dream again.'

'She hated me,' I said. 'I don't buy that one.'

'Of course,' Hernandez put in dryly. 'You turned her down. But she would have got over that. And then you blew the whole thing up in her face with Spencer listening in.'

'You two characters been seeing any psychiatrists lately?'

'Jesus,' Ohls said, 'hadn't you heard? We got them in our hair all the time these days. We've got two of them on the staff. This ain't police business any more. It's getting to be a branch of the medical racket. They're in and out of jail, the courts, the interrogation rooms. They write reports fifteen pages long on why some punk of a juvenile held up a liquor store or raped a schoolgirl or peddled tea to the senior class. Ten years from now guys like Marty and me will be doing Rorschach tests and word associations instead of chin-ups and target practice. When we go out on a case we'll carry little black bags with portable lie detectors and bottles of truth serum. Too bad we didn't grab the four hard monkeys that poured it on Big Willie Magoon. We might have been able to unmaladjust them and make them love their mothers.'

'Okay for me to blow?'

'What are you not convinced about?' Hernandez asked, snapping a rubber band.

'I'm convinced. The case is dead. She's dead, they're all dead.

A nice smooth routine all round. Nothing to do but go home and forget it ever happened. So I'll do that.'

Ohls reached the half-cigarette from behind his ear, looked at it as if wondering how it got there, and tossed it over his shoulder.

'What are you crying about?' Hernandez said. 'If she hadn't been fresh out of guns she might have made it a perfect score.'

'Also,' Ohls said grimly, 'the telephone was working yesterday.'

'Oh sure,' I said. 'You'd have some running and what you would have found would have been a mixed-up story that admitted nothing but a few silly lies. This morning you have what I suppose is a full confession. You haven't let me read it, but you wouldn't have called in the D.A. if it was just a love note. If any real solid work had been done on the Lennox case at the time, somebody would have dug up his war record and where he got wounded and all the rest of it. Somewhere along the line a connection with the Wades would have turned up. Roger Wade knew who Paul Marston was. So did another P.I. I happened to get in touch with.'

'It's possible,' Hernandez admitted, 'but that isn't how police investigations work. You don't fool around with an open-shut case, even if there's no heat on to get it finalized and forgotten. I've investigated hundreds of homicides. Some are all of a piece, neat, tidy and according to the book. Most of them make sense here, don't make sense there. But when you get motive, means, opportunity, flight, a written confession, and a suicide immediately afterwards, you leave it lay. No police department in the world has the men or the time to question the obvious. The only thing against Lennox being a killer was that somebody thought he was a nice guy who wouldn't have done it and that there were others who could equally well have done it. But the others didn't take it on the lam, didn't confess, didn't blow their brains out. He did. And as for being a nice guy I figure sixty to seventy per cent of all the killers that end up in the gas chamber or the hot seat or on the end of a rope are people the neighbours thought were just as harmless as a Fuller Brush salesman. Just as harmless and quiet and well bred as Mrs Roger Wade. You want to read what she wrote in that letter? Okay, read it. I've got to go down the hall.'

He stood up and pulled a drawer open and put a folder on the top of the desk. 'There are five photostats in here, Marlowe. Don't let me catch you looking at them.'

440

He started for the door and then turned his head and said to Ohls: 'You want to talk to Peshorek with me?'

Ohls nodded and followed him out. When I was alone in the office I lifted the cover of the file folder and looked at the white on black photostats. Then touching only the edges I counted them. There were six, each of several pages clipped together. I took one and rolled it up and slipped it into my pocket. Then I read over the next one in the pile. When I had finished I sat down and waited. In about ten minutes Hernandez came back alone. He sat down behind his desk again, tallied the photostats in the file folder and put the file back in his desk.

He raised his eyes and looked at me without any expression. 'Satisfied?'

'Lawford know you have those?'

'Not from me. Not from Bernie. Bernie made them himself. Why?'

'What would happen if one got loose?'

He smiled unpleasantly. 'It won't. But if it did, it wouldn't be anybody in the Sheriff's office. The D.A. has photostat equipment too.'

'You don't like District Attorney Springer too well, do you, Captain?'

He looked surprised. 'Me? I like everybody, even you. Get the hell out of here. I've got work to do.'

I stood up to go. He said suddenly: 'You carry a gun these days?'

'Part of the time.'

'Big Willie Magoon carried two. I wonder why he didn't use them.'

'I guess he figured he had everybody scared.'

'That could be it,' Hernandez said casually. He picked up a rubber band and stretched it between his thumbs. He stretched it farther and farther. Finally with a snap it broke. He rubbed his thumb where the loose end had snapped back against it. 'Anything can be stretched too far,' he said. 'No matter how tough he looks. See you around.'

I went out of the door and got out of the building fast. Once a patsy, always a patsy.

# Forty-five

Back in my dog house on the sixth floor of the Cahuenga Building I went through my regular double play with the morning mail. Mail slot to desk to wastebasket, Tinkers to Evers to Chance. I blew a clear space on the top of the desk and unrolled the photostat on it. I had rolled it so as not to make creases.

I read it over again. It was detailed enough and reasonable enough to satisfy any open mind. Eileen Wade had killed Terry's wife in a fit of jealous fury, and later, when the opportunity was set up, she had killed Roger because she was sure he knew. The gun fired into the ceiling of his room that night had been part of the set-up. The unanswered and for ever unanswerable question was why Roger Wade had stood still and let her put it over. He must have known how it would end. So he had written himself off and didn't care. Words were his business, he had words for almost everything, but none for this.

'I have forty-six demerol tablets left from my last prescription,' she wrote. 'I now intend to take them all and lie down on the bed. The door is locked. In a very short time I shall be beyond saving. This, Howard, is to be understood. What I write is in the presence of death. Every word is true. I have no regrets – except possibly that I could not have found them together and killed them together. I have no regrets for Paul whom you have heard called Terry Lennox. He was the empty shell of the man I loved and married. He meant nothing to me. When I saw him that afternoon for the only time after he came back from the war – at first I didn't even know him. Then I did and he knew me at once. He should have died young in the snow of Norway, my lover that I gave to death. He came back a friend of gamblers, the husband of a rich whore, a spoiled and ruined man, and probably some kind of a crook in his past life. Time makes everything mean and shabby and wrinkled. The tragedy of life, Howard, is not that the beautiful things die young, but that they grow old and mean. It will not happen to me. Goodbye, Howard.'

I put the photostat in the desk and locked it up. It was time for lunch but I wasn't in the mood. I got the office bottle out of the deep drawer and poured a slug and then got the phone book off the hook at the desk and looked up the number of the *Journal*. I dialled it and asked the girl for Lonnie Morgan.

'Mr Morgan doesn't come in until around four o'clock. You might try the Press Room at the City Hall.'

I called that. And I got him. He remembered me well enough. 'You've been a pretty busy guy, I heard.'

'I've got something for you, if you want it. I don't think you want it.'

'Yeah? Such as?'

'A photostat of a confession of two murders.'

'Where are you?'

I told him. He wanted more information. I wouldn't give him any over the phone. He said he wasn't on a crime beat. I said he was still a newspaper man and on the only independent paper in the city. He still wanted to argue.

'Where did you get this whatever it is? How do I know it's worth my time?'

'The D.A.'s office has the original. They won't release it. It breaks open a couple of things they hid behind the ice-box.'

'I'll call you. I have to check with the brass.'

We hung up. I went down to the drugstore and ate a chicken salad sandwich and drank some coffee. The coffee was over-strained and the sandwich was as full of rich flavour as a piece torn off an old shirt. Americans will eat anything if it is toasted and held together with a couple of toothpicks and has lettuce sticking out of the sides, preferably a little wilted.

At three-thirty or so Lonnie Morgan came in to see me. He was the same long, thin, wiry piece of tired and expressionless humanity as he had been the night he drove me home from the jailhouse. He shook hands listlessly and rooted in a crumpled pack of cigarettes.

'Mr Sherman – that's the Managing Editor – said I could look you up and see what you have.'

'It's off the record unless you agree to my terms.' I unlocked the desk and handed him the photostat. He read the four pages rapidly and then again more slowly. He looked very excited – about as excited as a mortician at a cheap funeral.

'Gimme the phone.'

I pushed it cross the desk. He dialled, waited, and said: 'This is Morgan. Let me talk to Mr Sherman.' He waited and got some other female and then got his party and asked him to ring back on another line.

He hung up and sat holding the telephone in his lap with the forefinger pressing the button down. It rang again and he lifted the receiver to his ear.

'Here it is, Mr Sherman.'

He read slowly and distinctly. At the end there was a pause. Then, 'One moment, sir.' He lowered the phone and glanced across the desk. 'He wants to know how you got hold of this.'

I reached across the desk and took the photostat away from him. 'Tell him it's none of his goddam business how I got hold of it. Where is something else. The stamp on the back of the pages shows that.'

'Mr Sherman, it's apparently an official document of the Los Angeles Sheriff's office. I guess we could check its authenticity easy enough. Also there's a price.'

He listened some more and then said: 'Yes, sir. Right here.' He pushed the phone across the desk. 'Wants to talk to you.'

It was a brusque authoritative voice. 'Mr Marlowe, what are your terms? And remember the *Journal* is the only paper in Los Angeles which would even consider touching this matter.'

'You didn't do much on the Lennox case, Mr Sherman.'

'I realize that. But at that time it was purely a question of scandal for scandal's sake. There was no question of who was guilty. What we have now, if your document is genuine, is something quite different. What are your terms?'

'You print the confession in full in the form of a photographic reproduction. Or you don't print it at all.'

'It will be verified. You understand that?'

'I don't see how, Mr Sherman. If you ask the D.A. he will either deny it or give it to every paper in town. He'd have to. If you ask the Sheriff's office they will put it up to the D.A.'

'Don't worry about that, Mr Marlowe. We have ways. How about your terms?'

'I just told you.'

'Oh. You don't expect to be paid?'

'Not with money.'

'Well, you know your own business, I suppose. May I have Morgan again?'

I gave the phone back to Lonnie Morgan.

He spoke briefly and hung up. 'He agrees,' he said. 'I take that photostat and he checks it. He'll do what you say. Reduced to half size it will take about half of page IA.'

I gave him back the photostat. He held it and pulled at the tip of his long nose. 'Mind my saying I think you're a damn fool?'

'I agree with you.'

'You can still change your mind.'

'Nope. Remember that night you drove me home from the City Bastille? You said I had a friend to say good-bye to. I've never really said good-bye to him. If you publish this photostat, that will be it. It's been a long time – a long, long time.'

'Okay, chum.' He grinned crookedly. 'But I still think you're a damn fool. Do I have to tell you why?'

'Tell me anyway.'

'I know more about you than you think. That's the frustrating part of newspaper work. You always know so many things you can't use. You get cynical. If this confession is printed in the *Journal*, a lot of people will be sore. The D.A., the Coroner, the Sheriff's crowd, an influential and powerful private citizen named Potter, and a couple of toughies called Menendez and Starr. You'll probably end up in the hospital or in jail again.'

'I don't think so.'

'Think what you like, pal. I'm telling you what *I* think. The D.A. will be sore because he dropped a blanket on the Lennox case. Even if the suicide and confession of Lennox made him look justified, a lot of people will want to know how Lennox, an innocent man, came to make a confession, how he got dead, did he really commit suicide or was he helped, why was there no investigation into the circumstances, and how come the whole thing died so fast. Also, if he has the original of this photostat he will think he has been double-crossed by the Sheriff's people.'

'You don't have to print the identifying stamp on the back.'

'We don't. We're pals with the Sheriff. We think he's a straight guy. We don't blame him because he can't stop guys like Menendez. Nobody can stop gambling as long as its legal in all forms in some places and legal in some forms in all places. You stole this from the Sheriff's office. I don't know how you got away with it. Want to tell me?'

'No.'

'Okay. The Coroner will be sore because he buggered up the Wade suicide. The D.A. helped him with that too. Harlan Potter will be sore because something is reopened that he used a lot of power to close up. Menendez and Starr will be sore for reasons I'm not sure of, but I know you got warned off. And when those boys get sore at somebody he gets hurt. You're apt to get the treatment Big Willie Magoon got.'

'Magoon was probably getting too heavy for his job.'

'Why?' Morgan drawled. 'Because those boys have to make it stick. If they take the trouble to tell you to lay off, you lay off. If you don't and they let you get away with it they look weak. The hard boys that run the business, the big wheels, the board of directors, don't have any use for weak people. They're dangerous. And then there's Chris Mady.'

'He just about runs Nevada, I heard.'

'You heard right, chum. Mady is a nice guy but he knows what's right for Nevada. The rich hoodlums that operate in Reno and Vegas are very careful not to annoy Mr Mady. If they did, their taxes would go up fast and their police co-operation would go down the same way. Then the top guys back east would decide some changes were necessary. An operator who can't get along with Chris Mady ain't operating correctly. Get him the hell out of there and put somebody else in. Getting him out of there means only one thing to them. Out in a wooden box.'

'They never heard of me,' I said.

Morgan frowned and whipped an arm up and down in a meaningless gesture. 'They don't have to. Mady's estate on the Nevada side of Tahoe is right next to Harlan Potter's estate. Could be they say hello once in a while. Could be some character that is on Mady's payroll hears from another guy on Potter's payroll that a punk named Marlowe is buzzing too loud about things that are not any of his business. Could be that this passing remark gets passed on down to where the phone rings in some apartment in L.A. and a guy with large muscles gets a hint to go out and exercise himself and two or three of his friends. If somebody wants you knocked off or smashed, the muscle men don't have to have it explained why. It's mere routine to them. No hard feelings at all. Just sit still while we break your arm. You want this back?'

He held out the photostat.

'You know what I want,' I said.

Morgan stood up slowly and put the photostat in his inside pocket. 'I could be wrong,' he said. 'You may know more about it than I do. I wouldn't know how a man like Harlan Potter looks at things.'

'With a scowl,' I said. 'I've met him. But he wouldn't operate with a goon squad. He couldn't reconcile it with his opinion of how he wants to live.'

'For my money,' Morgan said sharply, 'stopping a murder investigation with a phone call and stopping it by knocking off the witnesses is just a question of method. And both methods stink in the nostrils of civilization. See you around – I hope.'

He drifted out of the office like something blown by the wind.

# Forty-six

I drove out to Victor's with the idea of drinking a gimlet and sitting around until the evening edition of the morning papers was on the street. But the bar was crowded and it wasn't any fun. When the barkeep I knew got around to me he called me by name.

'You like a dash of bitters in it, don't you?'

'Not usually. Just for tonight two dashes of bitters.'

'I haven't seen your friend lately. The one with the green ice.'

'Neither have I.'

He went away and came back with the drink. I pecked at it to make it last, because I didn't feel like getting a glow on. Either I would get really stiff or stay sober. After a while I had another of the same. It was just past six when the kid with the papers came into the bar. One of the barkeeps yelled at him to beat it, but he managed one quick round of the customers before a waiter got hold of him and threw him out. I was one of the customers. I opened up the *Journal* and glanced at page 1A. They had made it. It was all there. They had reversed the photostat by making it black on white and by reducing it in size they had fitted it into the top half of the page. There was a short brusque editorial on another page. There was a half-column by Lonnie Morgan with a by-line, on still another page.

I finished my drink and left and went to another place to eat dinner and then drove home.

Lonnie Morgan's piece was a straightforward factual recapitulation of the facts and happenings involved in the Lennox case and the 'suicide' of Roger Wade – the facts as they had been published. It added nothing, deduced nothing, imputed nothing. It was clear, concise, business-like reporting. The editorial was something else. It asked questions – the kind a newspaper asks of public officials when they are caught with jam on their faces.

About nine-thirty the telephone rang and Bernie Ohls said he would drop by on his way home.

'Seen the *Journal*?' he asked coyly, and hung up without waiting for an answer.

When he got there he grunted about the steps and said he would drink a cup of coffee if I had one. I said I would make some. While I made it he wandered around the house and made himself very much at home.

'You live pretty lonely for a guy that could get himself disliked,' he said. 'What's over the hill in back?'

'Another street. Why?'

'Just asking. Your shrubbery needs pruning.'

I carried some coffee into the living-room and he parked himself and sipped it. He lit one of my cigarettes and puffed at it for a minute or two, then put it out. 'Getting so I don't care for the stuff,' he said. 'Maybe it's the TV commercials. They make you hate everything they try to sell. God, they must think the public is a halfwit. Every time some jerk in a white coat with a stethoscope hanging around his neck holds up some toothpaste or a pack of cigarettes or a bottle of beer or a mouthwash or a jar of shampoo or a little box of something that makes a fat wrestler smell like mountain lilac I alway make a note never to buy any. Hell, I wouldn't buy the product even if I liked it. You read the *Journal*, huh?'

'A friend of mine tipped me off. A reporter.'

'You got friends?' he asked wonderingly. 'Didn't tell you how they got hold of the material, did they?'

'No. And in this state he doesn't have to tell you.'

'Springer is hopping mad. Lawford, the deputy D.A. that got the letter this morning, claims he took it straight to his boss, but it makes a guy wonder. What the *Journal* printed looks like a straight reproduction from the original.'

I sipped coffee and said nothing.

'Serves him right,' Ohls went on. 'Springer ought to have handled it himself. Personally I don't figure it was Lawford that leaked. He's a politician too.' He stared at me woodenly.

'What are you here for, Bernie? You don't like me. We used to be friends – as much as anybody can be friends with a tough cop. But it soured a little.'

He leaned forward and smiled – a little wolfishly. 'No cop likes it when a private citizen does police work behind his back. If you had connected up Wade and the Lennox for me the time Wade got dead I'd have made out. If you have connected up Mrs Wade and this Terry Lennox I'd have had her in the palm of my hand – alive. If you had come clean from the start Wade might be still alive. Not to mention Lennox. You figure you're a pretty smart monkey, don't you?'

'What would you like me to say?'

'Nothing. It's too late. I told you a wise guy never fools anybody but himself. I told you straight and clear. So it didn't take. Right now it might be smart for you to leave town. Nobody likes you and a couple of guys that don't like people do something about it. I had the word from a stoolie.'

'I'm not that important, Bernie. Let's stop snarling at each other. Until Wade was dead you didn't even enter the case. After that it didn't seem to matter to you and to the Coroner or to the D.A. or to anybody. Maybe I did some things wrong. But the truth came out. You could have had her yesterday afternoon – with what?'

'With what you had to tell us about her.'

'Me? With the police work I did behind your back?'

He stood up abruptly. His face was red. 'Okay, wise guy. She'd have been alive. We could have booked her on suspicion. You *wanted* her dead, you punk, and you know it.'

'I wanted her to take a good, long, quiet look at herself. What she did about it was her business. I wanted to clear an innocent man. I didn't give a good goddam how I did it and I don't now. I'll be around when you feel like doing something about me.'

'The hard boys will take care of you, buster. I won't have to bother. You think you're not important enough to bother them. As a P.I. named Marlowe, check. You're not. As a guy who was told where to get off and blew a raspberry in their faces publicly in a newspaper, that's different. That hurts their pride.'

'That's pitiful,' I said. 'Just thinking about it makes me bleed internally, to use your own expression.'

He went across to the door and opened it. He stood looking down the redwood steps and at the trees on the hill across the way and up the slope at the end of the street.

'Nice and quiet here,' he said. 'Just quiet enough.'

He went on down the steps and got into his car and left. Cops never say good-bye. They're always hoping to see you again in the line-up.

# Forty-seven

For a short time the next day things looked like getting lively. District-Attorney Springer called an early press conference and delivered a statement. He was the big, florid, black-browed, prematurely grey-haired type that always does so well in politics.

'I have read the document which purports to be a confession by the unfortunate and unhappy woman who recently took her life, a document which may or may not be genuine, but which, if genuine, is obviously the product of a disordered mind. I am willing to assume that the *Journal* published this document in good faith, in spite of its many absurdities and inconsistencies, and these I shall not bore you with enumerating. If Eileen Wade wrote these words, and my office in conjunction with the staff of my respected coadjutor, Sheriff Petersen, will soon determine whether or no she did, then I say to you that she did not write them with a clear head nor with a steady hand. It is only a matter of weeks since the unfortunate lady found her husband wallowing in his own blood, spilled by his own hand. Imagine the shock, the despair, the utter loneliness which must have followed so sharp a disaster! And now she has joined him in the bitterness of death. Is anything to be gained by disturbing the ashes of the dead? Anything, my friends, beyond the sale of a few copies of a newspaper which is badly in need of circulation? Nothing, my friends, nothing. Let us leave it at that. Like Ophelia in that great dramatic masterpiece called *Hamlet*, by the immortal William Shakespeare, Eileen Wade wore her rue with a difference. My political enemies would like to make much of that difference, but my friends and fellow voters will not be deceived. They know that this office has long stood for wise and mature law-enforcement, for justice tempered with mercy, for solid, stable and conservative government. The *Journal* stands for I know not what, and for what it stands I do not much or greatly care. Let the enlightened public judge for itself.'

The *Journal* printed this guff in its early edition (it was a round-the-clock newspaper) and Henry Sherman, the Managing Editor, came right back at Springer with a signed comment.

'Mr District-Attorney Springer was in good form this morning. He is a fine figure of a man and he speaks with a rich baritone voice that is a pleasure to listen to. He did not bore us with any facts. Any time Mr Springer cares to have the authenticity of the document in question proved to him, the *Journal* will be most happy to oblige. We do not expect Mr Springer to take any action to reopen cases which have been officially closed with his sanction or under his direction, just as we do not expect Mr Springer to stand on his head on the tower of the City Hall. As Mr Springer so aptly phrases it, is anything to be gained by disturbing the ashes of the dead? Or, as the *Journal* would prefer to phrase it less elegantly, is anything to be gained by finding out who committed a murder when the murderee is already dead? Nothing, of course, but justice and truth.

'On behalf of the late William Shakespeare, the *Journal* wishes to thank Mr Springer for his favourable mention of *Hamlet*, and for his substantially, although not exactly, correct allusion to Ophelia. "You must wear your rue with a difference" was not said of Ophelia but by her, and just what she meant has never been very clear to our less erudite minds. But let that pass. It sounds well and helps to confuse the issue. Perhaps we may be permitted to quote, also from that officially approved dramatic production known as *Hamlet*, a good thing that happened to be said by a bad man:

' "And where the offence is let the great axe fall." '

Lonnie Morgan called me up about noon and asked me how I liked it. I told him I didn't think it would do Springer any harm.

'Only with the eggheads,' Lonnie Morgan said, 'and they already had his number. I meant what about you?'

'Nothing about me. I'm just sitting here waiting for a soft buck to rub itself against my cheek.'

'That wasn't exactly what I meant.'

'I'm still healthy. Quit trying to scare me. I got what I wanted. If Lennox was still alive he could walk right up to Springer and spit in his eye.'

'You did it for him. And by this time Springer knows that. They got a hundred ways to frame a guy they don't like. I don't figure what made it worth your time. Lennox wasn't that much man.'

'What's that got to do with it?'

He was silent for a moment. Then he said: 'Sorry, Marlowe. Shut my big mouth. Good luck.'

We hung up after the usual good-byes.


About two in the afternoon Linda Loring called me. 'No names, please,' she said. 'I've just flown in from that big lake up north. Somebody up there is boiling over something that was in the *Journal* last night. My almost ex-husband got it right between the eyes. The poor man was weeping when I left. He flew up to report.'

'What do you mean, almost ex-husband?'

'Don't be stupid. For once father approves. Paris is an excellent place to get a quiet divorce. So I shall soon be leaving to go there. And if you have any sense left you could do worse than spend a little of that fancy engraving you showed me going a long way off yourself.'

'What's it got to do with me?'

'That's the second stupid question you've asked. You're not fooling anyone but yourself, Marlowe. Do you know how they shoot tigers?'

'How would I?'

'They tie a goat to a stake and then hide out in a blind. It's apt to be rough on the goat. I like you. I'm sure I don't know why, but I do. I hate the idea of your being the goat. You tried so hard to do the right thing – as you saw it.'

'Nice of you,' I said. 'If I stick my neck out and it gets chopped, it's still my neck.'

'Don't be a hero, you fool,' she said sharply. 'Just because someone we knew chose to be a fall guy, you don't have to imitate him.'

'I'll buy you a drink if you're going to be around long enough.'

'Buy me one in Paris. Paris is lovely in the fall.'

'I'd like to do that too. I hear it was even better in the spring. Never having been there I wouldn't know.'

'The way you're going you never will.'

'Good-bye, Linda. I hope you find what you want.'

'Good-bye,' she said coldly. 'I always find what I want. But when I find it, I don't want it any more.'

She hung up. The rest of the day was a blank. I ate dinner and left the Olds at an all-night garage to have the brake linings checked. I took a cab home. The street was empty as usual. In the wooden mailbox was a free soap coupon. I went up the steps slowly. It was a soft night with a little haze in the air. The trees on the hill hardly moved. No breeze. I unlocked the door and pushed it part way open and then stopped. The door was about ten inches open from the frame. It was dark inside, there was no sound. But I had the feeling that the room beyond was not empty. Perhaps a spring squeaked faintly or I caught the gleam of a white jacket across the room. Perhaps on a warm, still night like this the room beyond the door was not warm enough, but still enough. Perhaps there was a drifting smell of man on the air. And perhaps I was just on edge.

I stepped sideways off the porch on to the ground and leaned down against the shrubbery. Nothing happened. No light went on inside, there was no movement anywhere that I heard. I had a gun in a belt holster on the left side, butt forward, a short-barrelled Police .38. I jerked it out and it got me nowhere. The silence continued. I decided I was a damn fool. I straightened up and lifted a foot to go back to the front door, and then a car turned the corner and came fast up the hill and stopped almost without sound at the foot of my steps. It was a big black sedan with the lines of a Cadillac. It could have been Linda Loring's car, except for two things. Nobody opened a door and the windows on my side were all shut tight. I waited and listened, crouched against the bush and there was nothing to listen to and nothing to wait for. Just a dark car motionless at the foot of my redwood steps, with the windows closed. If its motor was still running I couldn't hear it. Then a big red spotlight clicked on and the beam struck twenty feet beyond the corner of the house. And then very slowly the big car backed until the spotlight could swing across the front of the house, across the hood and up.

Policemen don't drive Gadillacs. Cadillacs with red spotlights belong to the big boys, mayors and police commissioners, perhaps District Attorneys. Perhaps hoodlums.

The spotlight traversed. I went down flat, but it found me just the same. It held on me. Nothing else. Still the car door didn't open, still the house was silent and without light.

Then a siren growled in low pitch just for a second or two and stopped. And then at last the house was full of lights and a man in a white dinner-jacket came out to the head of the steps and looked sideways along the wall and the shrubbery.

'Come on it, cheapie,' Menendez said with a chuckle. 'You've got company.'

I could have shot him with no trouble at all. Then he stepped back and it was too late – even if I could have done it. Then a window went down at the back of the car and I could hear the thud as it opened. Then a machine pistol went off and fired a short burst into the slope of the bank thirty feet away from me.

'Come on in, cheapie,' Menendez said again from the doorway. 'There just ain't anywhere else to go.'

So I straightened up and went and the spotlight followed me accurately. I put the gun back in the holster on my belt. I stepped up on to the small redwood landing and went in through the door and stopped just inside. A man was sitting across the room with his legs crossed and a gun resting sideways on his thigh. He looked rangy and tough and his skin had that dried-out look of people who live in sun-bleached climates. He was wearing a dark brown gabardine type windbreaker and the zipper was open almost to his waist. He was looking at me and neither his eyes nor the gun moved. He was as calm as an adobe wall in the moonlight.

# Forty-eight

I looked at him too long. There was a brief half-seen move at my side and a numbing pain in the point of my shoulder. My whole arm went dead to the fingertips. I turned and looked at a big mean-looking Mexican. He wasn't grinning, he was just watching me. The forty-five in his brown hand dropped to his side. He had a moustache and his head bulged with oily black hair brushed up and back and over and down. There was a dirty sombrero on the back of his head and the leather chin strap hung loose in two strands down the front of a stitched shirt that smelled of sweat. There is nothing tougher than a tough Mexican, just as there is nothing gentler than a gentle Mexican, nothing more honest that an honest Mexican and above all nothing sadder than a sad Mexican. This guy was one of the hard boys. They don't come any harder anywhere.

I rubbed my arm. It tingled a little but the ache was still there and the numbness. If I had tried to pull a gun I should probably have dropped it.

Menendez held his hand out towards the slugger. Without seeming to look he tossed the gun and Menendez caught it. He stood in front of me now and his face glistened. 'Where would you like it, cheapie?' His black eyes danced.

I just looked at him. There was no answer to a question like that.

'I asked you a question, cheapie.'

I wet my lips and asked one back. 'What happened to Agostino? I thought he was your gun handler.'

'Chick went soft,' he said gently.

'He was always soft – like his boss.'

The man in the chair flicked his eyes. He almost but not quite smiled. The tough boy who had paralysed my arm neither moved nor spoke. I knew he was breathing. I could smell that.

'Somebody bump into your arm, cheapie?'

'I tripped over an enchilada.'

Negligently, not quite looking at me even, he slashed me across the face with the gun barrel.

'Don't get gay with me, cheapie. You're out of time for all that. You got told and you got told nice. When I take the trouble to call around personally and tell a character to lay off – he lays off. Or else he lays down and don't get up.'

I could feel a trickle of blood down my cheek. I could feel

454

the full numbing ache of the blow in my cheekbone. It spread until my whole head ached. It hadn't been a hard blow, but the thing he used was hard. I could still talk and nobody tried to stop me.

'How come you do your own slugging, Mendy? I thought that was coolie labour for the sort of boys that beat up Big Willie Magoon.'

'It's the personal touch,' he said softly, 'on account of I had personal reasons for telling you. The Magoon job was strictly business. He got to thinking he could push me around – me that bought his clothes and his cars and stocked his safe deposit box and paid off the trust deed on his house. These vice squad babies are all the same. I even paid school bills for his kid. You'd think the bastard would have some gratitude. So what does he do? He walks into my private office and slaps me around in front of the help.'

'On account of why?' I asked him, in the vague hope of getting him mad at somebody else.

'On account of some lacquered chippie said we used loaded dice. Seems like the bim was one of his sleepy time gals. I had her put out of the club – with every dime she brought in with her.'

'Seems understandable,' I said. 'Magoon ought to know no professional gambler plays crooked games. He doesn't have to. But what have I done to you?'

He hit me again, thoughtfully. 'You made me look bad. In my racket you don't tell a guy twice. Not even a hard number. He goes out and does it, or you ain't got control. You ain't got control, you ain't in business.'

'I've got a hunch that there's a little more to it than that,' I said. 'Excuse me if I reach for a handkerchief.'

The gun watched me while I got one out and touched the blood on my face.

'A two-bit peeper,' Menendez said slowly, 'figures he can make a monkey out of Mendy Menendez. He can get me laughed at. He can get me the big razzoo – me, Menendez. I ought to use a knife on you, cheapie. I ought to cut you into slices of raw meat.'

'Lennox was your pal,' I said, and watched his eyes. 'He got dead. He got buried like a dog without even a name over the dirt where they put his body. And I had a little something to do with proving him innocent. So that makes you look bad, huh? He saved your life and he lost his, and that didn't mean a thing to you. All that means anything to you is playing the big shot. You didn't give a hoot in hell for anybody but yourself. You're not big, you're just loud.'

His face froze and he swung his arm back to slug me a third time with the power behind it. His arm was still going back when I took a half-step forward and kicked him in the pit of the stomach.

I didn't think, I didn't plan, I didn't figure my chances or whether I had any. I just got enough of his yap and I ached and bled and maybe I was just a little punch drunk by this time.

He jack-knifed, gasping, and the gun fell out of his hand. He groped for it wildly, making strained sounds deep in his throat. I put a knee into his face. He screeched.

The man in the chair laughed. That staggered me. Then he stood up and the gun in his hand came up with him.

'Don't kill him,' he said mildly. 'We want to use him for live bait.'

Then there was movement in the shadows of the hall and Ohls came through the door, blank-eyed, expressionless and utterly calm. He looked down at Menendez. Menendez was kneeling with his head on the floor.

'Soft,' Ohls said. 'Soft as mush.'

'He's not soft,' I said. 'He's hurt. Any man can be hurt. Was Big Willie Magoon soft?'

Ohls looked at me. The other man looked at me. The tough Mex at the door hadn't made a sound.

'Take that goddam cigarette out of your face,' I snarled at Ohls. 'Either smoke it or leave it alone. I'm sick of watching you. I'm sick of you, period. I'm sick of cops.'

He looked surprised. Then he grinned.

'That was a nasty plant, kiddo,' he said cheerfully. 'You hurt bad? Did the nasty mans hit your facey-wacey? Well, for my money you had it coming and it was damn useful that you had.' He looked down at Mendy. Mendy had his knees under him. He was climbing out of a well, a few inches at a time. He breathed gaspingly.

'What a talkative lad he is,' Ohls said, 'when he doesn't have three shysters with him to button his lip.'

He jerked Menendez to his feet. Mendy's nose was bleeding. He fumbled the handkerchief out of his white dinner jacket and held it to his nose. He said no word.

'You got crossed up, sweetheart,' Ohls told him carefully. 'I ain't grieving a whole lot over Magoon. He had it coming. But he was a cop and punks like you lay off cops – always and for ever.'

Menendez lowered the handkerchief and looked at Ohls. He looked at me. He looked at the man who had been sitting in the chair. He turned slowly and looked at the tough Mex by the door. They all looked at him. There was nothing in their faces. Then a knife shot into view from nowhere and Mendy lunged for Ohls. Ohls side-stepped and took him by the throat with one hand and chopped the knife out of his hand with ease, almost indifferently. Ohls spread his feet and straightened his back and bent his legs slightly and lifted Menendez clear off the floor with one hand holding his neck. He walked him across the floor and pinned him against the wall. He let him down, but didn't let go of his throat.

'Touch me with one finger and I'll kill you,' Ohls said. 'One finger.' Then he dropped his hands.

Mendy smiled at him scornfully, looked at his handkerchief and refolded it to hide the blood. He held it to his nose again. He looked down at the gun he had used to hit me. The man from the chair said loosely: 'Not loaded, even if you could grab it.'

'A cross,' Mendy said to Ohls. 'I heard you the first time.'

'You ordered three muscles,' Ohls said. 'What you got was three deputies from Nevada. Somebody in Vegas don't like the way you forget to clear with them. The somebody wants to talk to you. You can go along with the deputies or you can go downtown with me and get hung on the back of the door by a pair of handcuffs. There's a couple of boys down there would like to see you close up.'

'God help Nevada,' Mendy said quietly, looking around again at the tough Mex by the door. Then he crossed himself quickly and walked out of the front door. The tough Mex followed him. Then the other one, the dried-out desert type, picked up the gun and the knife and went out too. He shut the door. Ohls waited motionless. There was a sound of doors banging shut, then a car went off into the night.

'You sure those mugs were deputies?' I asked Ohls.

He turned as if surprised to see me there. 'They had stars,' he said shortly.

'Nice work, Bernie. Very nice. Think he'll get to Vegas alive, you cold-hearted son of a bitch?'

I went to the bathroom and ran cold water and held a soaked towel against my throbbing cheek. I looked at myself in the glass. The cheek was puffed out of shape and bluish and there were jagged wounds on it from the force of the gun barrel hitting against the cheekbone. There was a discoloration under my left eye too. I wasn't going to be beautiful for a few days.

Then Ohls's reflection showed behind me in the mirror. He was rolling his damn unlighted cigarette along his lips, like a cat teasing a half-dead mouse, trying to get it to run away just once more.

'Next time don't try to outguess the cops,' he said gruffly. 'You think we let you steal that photostat just for laughs? We had a hunch Mendy would come gunning for you. We put it up to Starr cold. We told him we couldn't stop gambling in the county, but we could make it tough enough to cut way into the take. No mobster beats up a cop, not even a bad cop, and gets away with it in our territory. Starr convinced us he had nothing to do with it, that the outfit was sore about it and Menendez was going to get told. So when Mendy called for a squad of out-of-town hard boys to come and give you the treatment, Starr sent him three guys he knew, in one of his own cars, at his own expense. Starr is a police commissioner in Vegas.'

I turned around and looked at Ohls. 'The coyotes out in the desert will get fed tonight. Congratulations. Cop business is wonderful, uplifting, idealistic work, Bernie. The only thing wrong with cop business is the cops that are in it.'

'Too bad for you, hero,' he said with a sudden cold savagery. 'I could hardly help laughing when you walked into your own parlour to take your beating. I got a rise out of that, kiddo. It was a dirty job and it had to be done dirty. To make these characters talk you got to give them a sense of power. You ain't hurt bad, but we had to let them hurt you some.'

'So sorry,' I said. 'So very sorry you had to suffer like that.'

He shoved his taut face at me. 'I hate gamblers,' he said in a rough voice, 'I hate them the way I hate dope pushers. They pander to a disease that is every bit as corrupting as dope. You think those palaces in Reno and Vegas are just for harmless fun? Nuts, they're for the little guy, the something-for-nothing sucker, the lad that stops off with his pay envelope in his pocket and loses the week-end grocery money. The rich gambler loses forty grand and laughs it off and comes back for more. But the rich gambler don't make the big racket, pal. The big steal in is dimes and quarters and half dollars and once in a while a buck or even a five-spot. The big racket money comes in like water from the pipe in your bathroom, a steady stream that never stops flowing. Any time anybody wants to knock off a professional gambler that's for me. I like it. And any time a state government takes money from gambling and calls it taxes, that government is helping to keep the mobs in business. The barber or the beauty parlour girl puts two bucks on the nose. That's for the Syndicate, that's what really makes the profits. The people want an honest police force, do they? What for? To protect the guys with courtesy cards? We got legal horse tracks in this state, we got them all year round. They operate honest and the state gets its cut, and for every dollar laid at the track there's fifty laid with the bookies. There's eight or nine races on a card and in half of them, the little ones nobody notices, the fix can be in any time somebody says so. There's only one way a jock can win a race, but there's twenty ways he can lose one, with a steward at every eighth pole watching, and not able to do a damn thing about it if the jock knows his stuff. That's legal gambling, pal, clean honest business, state approved. So it's right, is it? Not by my book, it ain't. Because it's gambling and it breeds gamblers, and when you add it all up there's one kind of gambling – the wrong kind.'

'Feel better?' I asked him, putting some white iodine on my wounds.

'I'm an old tired beat-up cop. All I feel is sore.'

I turned around and stared at him. 'You're a damn good cop, Bernie, but just the same you're all wet. In one way cops are all the same. They all blame the wrong things. If a guy loses his pay-cheque at a crap table, stop gambling. If he gets drunk, stop liquor. If he kills somebody in a car crash, stop making automobiles. If he gets pinched with a girl in a hotel room, stop sexual intercourse. If he falls downstairs, stop building houses.'

'Aw shut up!'

'Sure, shut me up. I'm just a private citizen. Get off it, Bernie. We don't have mobs and crime syndicates and goon squads because we have crooked politicians and their stooges in the City Hall and the legislatures. Crime isn't a disease, it's a symptom. Cops are like a doctor that gives you aspirin for a brain tumour, except that the cop would rather cure it with a blackjack. We're a big, rough, rich, wild people and crime is the price we pay for it, and organized crime is the price we pay for organization. We'll have it with us a long time. Organized crime is just the dirty side of the sharp dollar.'

'What's the clean side?'

'I never saw it. Maybe Harlan Potter could tell you. Let's have a drink.'

'You looked pretty good walking in that door,' Ohls said.

'You looked better when Mendy pulled the knife on you.'

'Shake,' he said, and put his hand out.

We had the drink and he left by the back door, which he had jimmied to get in, having dropped by the night before for scouting purposes. Back doors are a soft touch if they open out and are old enough for the wood to have dried and shrunk. You knock the pins out of the hinges and the rest is easy. Ohls showed me a dent in the frame when he left to go back over the hill to where he had left his car on the next street. He could have opened the front door almost as easily but that would have broken the lock. It would have shown up too much.

I watched him climb through the trees with the beam of a torch in front of him and disappear over the rises. I locked the door and mixed another mild drink and went back to the living-room and sat down. I looked at my watch. It was still early. It only seemed a long time since I had come home.

I went to the phone and dialled the operator and gave her the Lorings' phone number. The butler asked who was calling, then went to see if Mrs Loring was in. She was.

'I was the goat all right,' I said, 'but they caught the tiger alive. I'm bruised up a little.'

'You must tell me about it sometime.' She sounded about as far away as if she had got to Paris already.

'I could tell you over a drink – if you had time.'

'Tonight? Oh, I'm packing my things to move out. I'm afraid that would be impossible.'

'Yes, I can see that. Well, I just thought you might like to know. It was kind of you to warn me. It had nothing at all to do with your old man.'

'Are you sure?'

'Positive.'

'Oh. Just a minute.' She was gone for a time, then she came back and sounded warmer. 'Perhaps I could fit a drink in. Where?'

'Anywhere you say. I haven't a car tonight, but I can get a cab.'

'Nonsense I'll pick you up, but it will be an hour or longer. What is the address there?'

I told her and she hung up and I put the porch light on and then stood in the open door inhaling the night. It had got much cooler.

I went back in and tried to phone Lonnie Morgan but couldn't reach him. Then just for the hell of it I put in a call to the Terrapin Club at Las Vegas, Mr Randy Starr. He probably wouldn't take it. But he did. He had a quiet, competent, man-of-affairs voice.

'Nice to hear from you, Marlowe. Any friend of Terry's is a friend of mine. What can I do for you?'

'Mendy is on his way.'

'On his way where?'

'To Vegas, with the three goons you sent after him in a big black Caddy with a red spotlight and siren. Yours, I presume?'

He laughed. 'In Vegas, as some newspaper guy said, we use Cadillacs for trailers. What's this all about?'

'Mendy staked out here in my house with a couple of hard boys. His idea was to beat me up – putting it low – for a piece in the paper he seemed to think was my fault.'

'Was it your fault?'

'I don't own any newspapers, Mr Starr.'

'I don't own any hard boys in Cadillacs, Mr Marlowe.'

'They were deputies maybe.'

'I couldn't say. Anything else?'

'He pistol-whipped me. I kicked him in the stomach and used my knee on his nose. He seemed dissatisfied. All the same I hope he gets to Vegas alive.'

'I'm sure he will, if he started this way. I'm afraid I'll have to cut this conversation short now.'

'Just a second, Starr. Were you in on that caper at Otatoclan – or did Mendy work it alone?'

'Come again?'

'Don't kid, Starr. Mendy wasn't sore at me for why he said – not to the point of staking out in my house and giving me the treatment he gave Big Willie Magoon. Not enough motive. He warned me to keep my nose clean and not to dig into the Lennox case. But I did, because it just happened to work out that way. So he did what I've just told you. So there was a better reason.'

'I see,' he said slowly and still mildly and quietly. 'You think there was something not quite kosher about how Terry got dead? That he didn't shoot himself, for instance, but someone else did?'

'I think the details would help. He wrote a confession which was false. He wrote a letter to me which got mailed. A waiter or hop in the hotel was going to sneak it out and mail it for him. He was holed up in the hotel and couldn't get out. There was a big bill in the letter and the letter was finished just as a knock came at his door. I'd like to know who came into the room.'

'Why?'

'If it had been a bellhop or a waiter, Terry would have added a line to the letter and said so. If it was a cop, the letter wouldn't have been mailed. So who was it – and why did Terry write that confession?'

'No idea, Marlowe. No idea at all.'

'Sorry I bothered you, Mr Starr.'

'No bother, glad to hear from you. I'll ask Mendy if he has any ideas.'

'Yeah – if you ever see him again – alive. If you don't – find out anyway. Or somebody else will.'

'You?' His voice hardened now, but it was still quiet.

'No. Mr Starr. Not me. Somebody that could blow you out of Vegas without taking a long breath. Believe me, Mr Starr. Just believe me. This is strictly on the level.'

'I'll see Mendy alive. Don't worry about that, Marlowe.'

'I figured you knew all about that. Good night, Mr Starr.'


# Forty-nine

When the car stopped out front and the door opened I went out and stood at the top of the steps to call down. But the middle-aged coloured driver was holding the door for her to get out. Then he followed her up the steps carrying a small overnight case. So I just waited.

She reached the top and turned to the driver: 'Mr Marlowe will drive me to my hotel, Amos. Thank you for everything. I'll call you in the morning.'

'Yes, Mrs Loring. May I ask Mr Marlowe a question?'

'Certainly, Amos.'

He put the overnight case down inside the door and she went in past me and left us.

' "I grow old ... I grow old ... I shall wear the bottoms of my trousers rolled." What does that mean, Mr Marlowe?'

'Not a bloody thing. It just sounds good.'

He smiled. 'That is from the Love Song of J. Alfred Prufrock. Here's another one. "In the room the women come and go Talking of Michael Angelo." Does that suggest anything to you, sir?'

'Yeah – it suggests to me that the guy didn't know very much about women.'

'My sentiments exactly, sir. Nonetheless I admire T. S. Eliot very much.'

'Did you say "nonetheless"?'

'Why, yes I did, Mr Marlowe. Is that incorrect?'

'No, but don't say it in front of a millionaire. He might think you were giving him the hotfoot.'

He smiled sadly. 'I shouldn't dream of it. Have you had an accident, sir?'

'Nope. It was planned that way. Good night, Amos.'

'Good night, sir.'

He went back down the steps and I went back into the house. Linda Loring was standing in the middle of the living-room looking around her.

'Amos is a graduate of Howard University,' she said. 'You don't live in a very safe place – for such an unsafe man, do you?'

'There aren't any safe places.'

'Your poor face. Who did that to you?'

'Mendy Menendez.'

'What did you do to him?'

'Nothing much. Kicked him a time or two. He walked into a trap. He's on his way to Nevada in the company of three or four tough Nevada deputies. Forget him.'

She sat down on the davenport.

'What would you like to drink?' I asked. I got a cigarette box and held it out to her. She said she didn't want to smoke. She said anything would do to drink.

'I thought of champagne,' I said. 'I haven't any ice bucket, but it's cold. I've been saving it for years. Two bottles. Cordon Rouge. I guess it's good. I'm no judge.'

'Saving it for what?' she asked.

'For you.'

She smiled, but she was still staring at my face. 'You're all cut.' She reached her fingers up and touched my cheek lightly. 'Saving it for me? That's not very likely. It's only a couple of months since we met.'

'Then I was saving it until we met. I'll go get it.' I picked up her overnight bag and started across the room with it.

'Just where are you going with that?' she asked sharply.

'It's an overnight bag, isn't it?'

'Put it down and come back here.'

I did that. Her eyes were bright and at the same time they were sleepy.

'This is something new,' she said slowly. 'Something quite new.'

'In what way?'

'You've never laid a finger on me. No passes, no suggestive remarks, no pawing, no nothing. I thought you were tough, sarcastic, mean, and cold.'

'I guess I am – at times.'

'Now I'm here and I suppose without preamble, after we have had a reasonable quantity of champagne you plan to grab me and throw me on the bed. Is that it?'

'Frankly,' I said, 'some such idea did stir at the back of my mind.'

'I'm flattered, but suppose I don't want it that way? I like you. I like you very much. But it doesn't follow that I want to go to bed with you. Aren't you rather jumping to conclusions – just because I happen to bring an overnight bag with me?'

'Could be I made an error,' I said. I went and got her overnight bag and put it back by the front door. 'I'll get the champagne.'

'I didn't mean to hurt your feelings. Perhaps you would rather save the champagne for some more auspicious occasion.'

'It's only two bottles,' I said. 'A really auspicious occasion would call for a dozen.'

'Oh, I see,' she said, suddenly angry. 'I'm just to be a fill-in until someone more beautiful and attractive comes along. Thank you so very much. Now you've hurt my feelings, but I suppose it's something to know that I'm safe here. If you think a bottle of champagne will make a loose woman out of me, I can assure you that you are very much mistaken.'

'I admitted the mistake already.'

'The fact that I told you I was going to divorce my husband and that I had Amos drop me by here with an overnight bag doesn't make me as easy as all that,' she said, still angry.

'Damn the overnight bag!' I growled. 'The hell with the overnight bag! Mention it again and I'll thrown the damn thing down the front steps. I asked you to have a drink. I'm going out to the kitchen to get the drink. That's all. I hadn't the least idea of getting you drunk. You don't want to go to bed with me. I understand perfectly. No reason why you should. But we can still have a glass or two of champagne, can't we? This doesn't have to be a wrangle about who is going to get seduced and when and where and on how much champagne.'

'You don't have to lose your temper,' she said, flushing.

'That's just another gambit,' I snarled. 'I know fifty of them and I hate them all. They're all phony and they all have a sort of leer at the edges.'

She got up and came over close to me and ran the tips of her fingers gently over the cuts and swollen places on my face. 'I'm sorry. I'm a tired and disappointed woman. Please be kind to me. I'm no bargain to anyone.'

'You're not tired and you're no more disappointed than most people are. By all the rules you ought to be the same sort of shallow, spoiled, promiscuous brat your sister was. By some miracle you're not. You've got all the honesty and a large part of the guts in your family. You don't need anyone to be kind to you.'

I turned and walked out of the room down the hall to the kitchen and got one of the bottles of champagne out of the icebox and popped the cork and filled a couple of shallow goblets quickly and drank one down. The sting of it brought tears to my eyes, but I emptied the glass. I filled it again. Then I put the whole works on a tray and carted it into the living-room.

She wasn't there. The overnight bag wasn't there. I put the tray down and opened the front door. I hadn't heard any sound of its opening and she had no car. I hadn't heard any sound at all.

Then she spoke from behind me. 'Idiot, did you think I was going to run away?'

I shut the door and turned. She had loosened her hair and she had tufted slippers on her bare feet and a silk robe the colour of a sunset in a Japanese print. She came towards me slowly with a sort of unexpectedly shy smile. I held a glass out to her. She took it, took a couple of sips of the champagne, and handed it back.

'It's very nice,' she said. Then, very quietly and without a trace of acting or affectation, she came into my arms and pressed her mouth against mine and opened her lips and her teeth. The tip of her tongue touched mine. After a long time she pulled her head back but kept her arms around my neck. She was starry-eyed.

'I meant to all the time,' she said. 'I just had to be difficult. I don't know why. Just nerves perhaps. I'm not really a loose woman at all. Is that a pity?'

'If I had thought you were I'd have made a pass at you the first time I met you in the bar at Victor's.'

She shook her head slowly and smiled. 'I don't think so. That's why I am here.'

'Perhaps not that night,' I said. 'That night belonged to something else.'

'Perhaps you don't ever make passes at women in bars.'

'Not often. The light's too dim.'

'But a lot of women go to bars just to have passes made at them.'

'A lot of women get up in the morning with the same idea.'

'But liquor is an aphrodisiac – up to a point.'

'Doctors recommend it.'

'Who said anything about doctors? I want my champagne.'

I kissed her some more. It was light, pleasant work.

'I want to kiss your poor cheek,' she said, and did. 'It's burning hot,' she said.

'The rest of me is freezing.'

'It is not. I want my champagne.'

'Why?'

'It'll get flat if we don't drink it. Besides I like the taste of it.'

'All right.'

'Do you love me very much? Or will you if I go to bed with you?'

'Possibly.'

'You don't have to go to bed with me, you know. I don't absolutely insist on it.'

'Thank you.'

'I want my champagne.'

'How much money have you got?'

'Altogether? How would I know? About eight million dollars.'

'I've decided to go to bed with you.'

'Mercenary,' she said.

'I paid for the champagne.'

'The hell with the champagne,' she said.


# Fifty

An hour later she stretched out a bare arm and tickled my ear and said:

'Would you consider marrying me?'

'It wouldn't last six months.'

'Well, for God's sake,' she said, 'suppose it didn't. Wouldn't it be worth it? What do you expect from life – full coverage against all possible risks?'

'I'm forty-two years old. I'm spoiled by independence. You're spoiled a little – not too much – by money.'

'I'm thirty-six. It's no disgrace to have money and no disgrace to marry it. Most of those who have it don't deserve it and don't know how to behave with it. But it won't be long. We'll have another war and at the end of that nobody will have any money – except the crooks and the chisellers. We'll all be taxed to nothing, the rest of us.'

I stroked her hair and wound some of it around my finger. 'You may be right.'

'We could fly to Paris and have a wonderful time.' She raised herself on her elbow and looked down at me. I could see the shine in her eyes but I couldn't read her expression. 'Do you have something against marriage?'

'For two people in a hundred it's wonderful. The rest just work at it. After twenty years all the guy has left is a work bench in the garage. American girls are terrific. American wives take in too damn much territory. Besides—'

'I want some champagne.'

'Besides,' I said, 'it would be just an incident to you. The first divorce is the only tough one. After that it's merely a problem in economics. No problem to you. Ten years from now you might pass me on the street and wonder where the hell you had seen me before. If you noticed me at all.'

'You self-sufficient, self-satisfied, self-confident, untouchable bastard. I want some champagne.'

'This way you will remember me.'

'Conceited too. A mass of conceit. Slightly bruised at the moment. You think I'll remember you? No matter how many men I marry or sleep with, you think I'll remember you? Why should I?'

'Sorry. I overstated my case. I'll get you some champagne.'

'Aren't we sweet and reasonable?' she said sarcastically. 'I'm a rich woman, darling, and I shall be infinitely richer. I could buy you the world if it were worth buying. What have you now? An empty house to come home to, with not even a dog or cat, a small stuffy office to sit in and wait. Even if I divorced you I'd never let you go back to that.'

'How would you stop me? I'm no Terry Lennox.'

'Please. Don't let's talk about him. Nor about that golden icicle, the Wade woman. Nor about her poor drunken, sunken husband. Do you want to be the only man who turned me down? What kind of pride is that? I've paid you the greatest compliment I know how to pay. I've asked you to marry me.'

'You paid me a greater compliment.'

She began to cry. 'You fool, you utter fool!' Her cheeks were wet. I could feel the tears on them. 'Suppose it lasted six months or a year or two years. What would you have lost except the dust on your office desk and the dirt on your venetian blinds and the loneliness of a pretty empty kind of life?'

'You still want some champagne?'

'All right.'

I pulled her close and she cried against my shoulder. She wasn't in love with me and we both knew it. She wasn't crying over me. It was just time for her to shed a few tears.

Then she pulled away and I got out of bed and she went into the bathroom to fix her face. I got the champagne. When she came back she was smiling.

'I'm sorry I blubbered,' she said. 'In six months from now I won't even remember your name. Bring it into the living-room. I want to see the lights.'

I did what she said. She sat on the davenport as before. I put the champagne in front of her. She looked at the glass but didn't touch it.

'I'll introduce myself?' I said. 'We'll have a drink together.'

'Like tonight?'

'It won't ever be like tonight again.'

She raised her glass of champagne, drank a little of it slowly, turned her body on the davenport and threw the rest in my face. Then she began to cry again. I got a handkerchief out and wiped my face off and wiped hers for her.

'I don't know why I did that,' she said. 'But for God's sake don't say I'm a woman and a woman never knows why she does anything.'

I poured some more champagne into her glass and laughed at her. She drank it slowly and then turned the other way and fell across my knees.

'I'm tired,' she said. 'You'll have to carry me this time.'

After a while she went to sleep.

In the morning she was still asleep when I got up and made coffee. I showered and shaved and dressed. She woke up then. We had breakfast together. I called a cab and carried her overnight case down the steps.

We said good-bye. I watched the cab out of sight. I went back up the steps and into the bedroom and pulled the bed to pieces and remade it. There was a long dark hair on one of the pillows. There was a lump of lead at the pit of my stomach.

The French have a phrase for it. The bastards have a phrase for everything and they are always right.

To say good-bye is to die a little.


# Fifty-one


Sewell Endicott said he was working late and I could drop around in the evening about seven-thirty.

He had a corner office with a blue carpet, a red mahogany desk with carved corners, very old and obviously very valuable, the usual glass-front bookshelves of mustard-yellow legal books, the usual cartoons by Spy of famous English judges, and a large portrait of Justice Oliver Wendell Holmes on the south wall, alone. Endicott's chair was quilted black leather. Near him was an open roll-top desk jammed with papers. It was an office no decorator had had a chance to pansy up.

He was in his shirtsleeves and he looked tired, but he had that kind of face. He was smoking one of his tasteless cigarettes. Ashes from it had fallen on his loosened tie. His limp black hair was all over the place.

He stared at me silently after I sat down. Then he said: 'You're a stubborn son of a bitch, if ever I met one. Don't tell me you're still digging into that mess.'

'Something worries me a little. Would it be all right now if I assumed you were representing Mr Harlan Potter when you came to see me in the birdcage?'

He nodded. I touched the side of my face gently with my fingertips. It was all healed up and the swelling was gone, but one of the blows must have damaged a nerve. Part of the cheek was still numb. I couldn't let it alone. It would get all right in time.

'And that when you went to Otatoclan you were temporarily deputized as a member of the D.A.'s staff?'

'Yes, but don't rub it in, Marlowe. It was a valuable connection. Perhaps I gave it too much weight.'

'Still is, I hope.'

He shook his head. 'No. That's finished. Mr Potter does his legal business through San Francisco, New York and Washington firms.'

'I guess he hates my guts – if he thinks about it.'

Endicott smiled. 'Curiously enough, he put all the blame on his son-in-law, Dr Loring. A man like Harlan Potter has to blame somebody. He couldn't possibly be wrong himself. He felt that if Loring hadn't been feeding the woman dangerous drugs, none of it would have happened.'

'He's wrong. You saw Terry Lennox's body in Otatoclan, didn't you?'

'I did indeed. In the back of a cabinet-maker's shop. They have no proper mortuary there. He was making the coffin too. The body was ice-cold. I saw the wound in the temple. There's no question of identity, if you had any ideas along those lines.'

'No, Mr Endicott, I didn't, because in his case it could hardly be possible. He was disguised a little though, wasn't he?'

'Face and hands darkened, hair dyed black. But the scars were still obvious. And the fingerprints, of course, were easily checked from things he had handled at home.'·

'What kind of police force do they have down there?'

'Primitive. The *jefe* could just about read and write. But he knew about fingerprints. It was hot weather, you know. Quite hot.' He frowned and took his cigarette out of his mouth and dropped it negligently into an enormous black basalt sort of receptacle. 'They had to get ice from the hotel,' he added. 'Plenty of ice.' He looked at me again. 'No embalming there. Things have to move fast.'

'You speak Spanish, Mr Endicott?'

'Only a few words. The hotel manager interpreted.' He smiled. 'A well-dressed smoothie, that fellow. Looked tough, but he was very polite and helpful. It was all over in no time.'

'I had a letter from Terry. I guess Mr Potter would know about it. I told his daughter, Mrs Loring. I showed it to her. There was a portrait of Madison in it.'

'A what?'

'Five-thousand-dollar bill.'

He raised his eyebrows. 'Really. Well, he could certainly afford it. His wife gave him a cool quarter of a million the second time they were married. I've an idea he meant to go to Mexico to live anyhow – quite apart from what happened. I don't know what happened to the money. I wasn't in on that.'

'Here's the letter, Mr Endicott, if you care to read it.'

I took it out and gave it to him. He read it carefully, the way lawyers read everything. He put it down on the desk and leaned back and stared at nothing.

'A little literary, isn't it?' he said quietly. 'I wonder why he did it?'

Killed himself, confessed, or wrote me the letter?'

'Confessed and killed himself, of course,' Endicott said sharply. 'The letter is understandable. At least you got a reasonable recompense for what you did for him – and since.'

'The mailbox bothers me,' I said. 'Where he says there was a mailbox on the street under his window and the hotel waiter was going to hold his letter up before he mailed it, so Terry could see that it was mailed.'

Something in Endicott's eyes went to sleep. 'Why?' he asked indifferently. He picked another of his filtered cigarettes out of a square box. I held my lighter across the desk for him.

'They wouldn't have one in a place like Otatoclan,' I said.

'Go on.'

'I didn't get it at first. Then I looked the place up. It's a mere village. Population say ten or twelve hundred. One street partly paved. The *jefe* has a Model A Ford as an official car. The post office is in the corner of a store, the chanceria, the butcher shop. One hotel, a couple of cantinas, no good roads, a small airfield. There's hunting around there in the mountains – lots of it. Hence the airfield. Only decent way to get there.'

'Go on. I know about the hunting.'

'So there's a mailbox on the street. Like there's a race-course and a dog-track and a golf-course and a *jai alai fronton* and park with a coloured fountain and a bandstand.'

'Then he made a mistake,' Endicott said coldly. 'Perhaps it was something that looked like a mailbox to him – say a trash receptacle.'

I stood up. I reached for the letter and refolded it and put it back in my pocket.

'A trash receptacle,' I said. 'Sure, that's it. Painted with the Mexican colours, green, white, red, and a sign on it stencilled in large clear print: KEEP OUR CITY CLEAN. In Spanish, of course. And lying around it seven mangy dogs.'

'Don't get cute, Marlowe.'

'Sorry if I let my brains show. Another small point I have already raised with Randy Starr. How come the letter got mailed at all? According to the letter the method was prearranged. So somebody told him about the mailbox. So somebody lied. So somebody mailed the letter with five grand in it just the same. Intriguing, don't you agree?'

He puffed smoke and watched it float away.

'What's your conclusion – and why ring Starr in on it?'

'Starr and a heel named Menendez, now removed from our midst, were pals of Terry in the British Army. They are wrong gees in a way – I should say in almost every way – but they still have room for personal pride and so on. There was a cover-up here engineered for obvious reasons. There was another sort of cover-up in Otatoclan, for entirely different reasons.'

'What's your conclusion?' he asked me again and much more sharply.

'What's yours?'

He didn't answer me. So I thanked him for his time and left.

He was frowning as I opened the door, but I thought it was an honest frown of puzzlement. Or maybe he was trying to remember how it looked outside the hotel and whether there was a mailbox there.

It was another wheel to start turning – no more. It turned for a solid month before anything came up.

Then on a certain Friday morning I found a stranger waiting for me in my office. He was a well-dressed Mexican or Suramericano of some sort. He sat by the open window smoking a brown cigarette that smelled strong. He was tall and very slender and very elegant, with a neat dark moustache and dark hair, rather longer than we wear it, and a fawn-coloured suit of some loosely woven material. He wore those green sun-glasses. He stood up politely.

'Señor Marlowe?'

'What can I do for you?'

He handed me a folded paper. '*Un aviso de parte del Señor Starr en Las Vegas, señor. Habla Ud. español?*'

'Yeah, but not fast. English would be better.'

'English then,' he said. 'It is all the same to me.'

I took the paper and read it. 'This introduces Cisco Maioranos, a friend of mine. I think he can fix you up. S.'

'Let's go inside, Señor Maioranos,' I said.

I held the door open for him. He smelled of perfume as he went by. His eyebrows were awfully damned dainty too. But he probably wasn't as dainty as he looked because there were knife scars on both sides of his face.

# Fifty-two

He sat down in the customer's chair and crossed his knees. 'You wish certain information about Señor Lennox, I am told.'

'The last scene only.'

'I was there at the time, *señor*. I had a position in the hotel.' He shrugged. 'Unimportant and of course temporary. I was the day clerk.' He spoke perfect English but with a Spanish rhythm. Spanish – American Spanish that is – has a definite rise and fall which to an American ear seems to have nothing to do with the meaning. It's like the swell of the ocean.

'You don't look the type,' I said.

'One has difficulties.'

'Who mailed the letter to me?'

He held out a box of cigarettes. 'Try one of these.'

I shook my head. 'Too strong for me. Colombian cigarettes I like. Cuban cigarettes are murder.'

He smiled faintly, lit another pill himself, and blew smoke. The guy was so goddam elegant he was beginning to annoy me.

'I know about the letter, *señor*. The *mozo* was afraid to go up to the room of this Señor Lennox after the *guarda* was posted. The cop or dick, as you say. So I myself took the letter to the *correo*. After the shooting, you understand.'

'You ought to have looked inside. It had a large piece of money in it.'

'The letter was sealed,' he said coldly. '*El honor no se mueve de lado como les congrejos.* That is, honour does not move side-wise like a crab, *señor.*'

'My apologies. Please continue.'

'Señor Lennox had a hundred-peso note in his left hand when I went into the room and shut the door in the face of the *guarda*. In his right hand was a pistol. On the table before him was the letter. Also another paper which I did not read. I refused the note.'

'Too much money,' I said, but he didn't react to the sarcasm.

'He insisted. So I took the note finally and gave it to the mozo later. I took the letter out under the napkin on the tray from the previous service of coffee. The dick looked hard at me. But he said nothing. I was half-way down the stairs when I heard the shot. Very quickly I hid the letter and ran back upstairs. The dick was trying to kick the door open. I used my key. Señor Lennox was dead.'

He moved his fingertips gently along the edge of the desk and sighed. 'The rest no doubt you know.'

'Was the hotel full?'

'Not full, no. There were half a dozen guests.'

'Americans?'

'Two *Americanos del Norte*. Hunters.'

'Real Gringos or just transplanted Mexicans?'

He drew a fingertip slowly along the fawn-coloured cloth above his knee. 'I think one of them could well have been of Spanish origin. He spoke border Spanish. Very inelegant.'

'They go near Lennox's room at all?'

He lifted his head sharply but the green cheaters didn't do a thing for me. 'Why should they, *señor*?'

I nodded. 'Well, it was damn nice of you to come in here and tell me about it, Señor Maioranos. Tell Randy I'm ever so grateful, will you?'

'*No hay de que, señor*. It is nothing.'

'And later on, if he has time, he could send me somebody who knows what he is talking about.'

'*Señor?*' His voice was soft, but icy. 'You doubt my word?'

'You guys are always talking about honour. Honour is the cloak of thieves – sometimes. Don't get mad. Sit quiet and let me tell it another way.'

He leaned back superciliously.

'I'm only guessing, mind. I could be wrong. But I could be right too. These two Americanos were there for a purpose. They came in on a plane. They pretended to be hunters. One of them was named Menendez, a gambler. He registered under some other name or not. I wouldn't know. Lennox knew they were there. He knew why. He wrote me that letter because he had a guilty conscience. He had played me for a sucker and he was too nice a guy for that to rest easy on him. He put the bill – five thousand dollars it was – in the letter because he had a lot of money and he knew I hadn't. He also put in a little off-beat hint which might or might not register. He was the kind of guy who always wants to do the right thing but somehow winds up doing something else. You say you took the letter to the *correo*. Why didn't you mail it in the box in front of the hotel?'

'The box, *señor*?'

'The mailbox. The *cajón cartero*, you call it, I think.'

He smiled. 'Otatoclan is not Mexico City, *señor*. It is a very primitive place. A street mailbox in Otatoclan? No one there would understand what it was for. No one would collect letters from it.'

I said: 'Oh. Well, skit it. You did not take any coffee on any tray up to Señor Lennox's room, Señor Maioranos. You did not go into the room past the dick. But the two Americanos did go in. The dick was fixed, of course. So were several other people. One of the Americanos slugged Lennox from behind. Then he took the Mauser pistol and opened up one of the cartridges and took out the bullet and put the cartridge back in the breech. Then he put this gun to Lennox's temple and pulled the trigger. It made a nasty-looking wound, but it did not kill him. Then he was carried out on a stretcher covered up and well hidden. Then when the American lawyer arrived, Lennox was doped and packed in ice and kept in a dark corner of the *carpinteria* where the man was making a coffin. The American lawyer saw Lennox there, he was ice cold, in a deep stupor and there was a bloody blackened wound in his temple. He looked plenty dead. The next day the coffin was buried with stones in it. The American lawyer went home with the fingerprints and some kind of document which was a piece of cheese. How do you like that, Señor Maioranos?'

He shrugged. 'It would be possible, *señor*. It would require money and influence. It would be possible, perhaps, if this Señor Menendez was closely related to important people in Otatoclan, the *alcalde*, the hotel proprietor and so on.'

'Well, that's possible, too. It's a good idea. It would explain why they picked a remote little place like Otatoclan.'

He smiled quickly. 'Then Señor Lennox may still be alive, no?'

'Sure. The suicide had to be some kind of fake to back up the confession. It had to be good enough to fool a lawyer who had been a District Attorney, but it would make a very sick monkey out of the current D.A. if it backfired. This Menendez is not as tough as he thinks he is, but he was tough enough to pistol-whip me for not keeping my nose clean. So he had to have reasons. If the fake got exposed, Menendez would be right in the middle of an international stink. The Mexicans don't like crooked police work any more than we do.'

'All that is possible, *señor*, as I very well know. But you accused me of lying. You said I did not go into the room where Señor Lennox was and get his letter.'

'You were already in there, chum – writing the letter.'

He reached up and took the dark glasses off. Nobody can change the colour of a man's eyes.

'I suppose it's a bit too early for a gimlet,' he said.

# Fifty-three

They had done a wonderful job on him in Mexico City, but why not? Their doctors, technicians, hospitals, painters, architects, are as good as ours. Sometimes a little better. A Mexican cop invented the paraffin test for powder nitrates. They couldn't make Terry's face perfect but they had done plenty. They had even changed his nose, taken out some bone and made it look flatter, less Nordic. They couldn't eliminate every trace of a scar, so they put a couple on the other side of his face too. Knife scars are not uncommon in Latin countries.

'They even did a nerve graft up here,' he said, and touched what had been the bad side of his face.

'How close did I come?'

'Close enough. A few details wrong, but they are not important. It was a quick deal and some of it was improvised and I didn't know myself just what was going to happen. I was told to do certain things and to leave a clear trail. Mendy didn't like my writing to you, but I held out for that. He undersold you a little. He never noticed the bit about the mailbox.'

'You knew who killed Sylvia?'

He didn't answer me directly. 'It's pretty tough to turn a woman in for murder – even if she never meant much to you.'

'It's a tough world. Was Harlan Potter in on all this?'

He smiled again. 'Would he be likely to let anyone know that? My guess is not. My guess is he thinks I am dead. Who would tell him otherwise – unless you did?'

'What I'd tell him you could fold into a blade of grass. How's Mendy these days – or is he?'

'He's doing all right. In Acapulco. He slipped by because of Randy. But the boys don't go for rough work on cops. Mendy's not as bad as you think. He has a heart.'

'So has a snake.'

'Well, what about that gimlet?'

I got up without answering him and went to the safe. I spun the knob and got out the envelope with the portrait of Madison in it and the five C notes that smelled of coffee. I dumped the lot out on the desk and then picked up the five C notes.

'These I keep. I spent all of it on expenses and research. The portrait of Madison I enjoyed playing with. It's all yours now.'

I spread it on the edge of the desk in front of him. He looked at it but didn't touch it.

'It's yours to keep,' he said. 'I've got plenty. You could have let things lie.'

'I know. After she killed her husband and got away with it she might have gone on to better things. He was of no real importance, of course. Just a human being with blood and a brain and emotions. He knew what happened too and he tried pretty hard to live with it. He wrote books. You may have heard of him.'

'Look, I couldn't very well help what I did,' he said slowly. 'I didn't want anyone to get hurt. I wouldn't have had a dog's chance up here. A man can't figure every angle that quick. I was scared and I ran. What should I have done?'

'I don't know.'

'She had a mad streak. She might have killed him anyway.'

'Yeah, she might.'

'Well, thaw out a little. Let's go have a drink somewhere where it's cool and quiet.'

'No time right now, Señor Maioranos.'

'We were pretty good friends once,' he said unhappily.

'Were we? I forget. That was two other fellows, seems to me. You permanently in Mexico?'

'Oh yes. I'm not here legally even. I never was. I told you I was born in Salt Lake City. I was born in Montreal. I'll be a Mexican national pretty soon now. All it takes is a good lawyer. I've always liked Mexico. It wouldn't be much risk going to Victor's for that gimlet.'

'Pick up your money, Señor Maioranos. It has too much blood on it.'

'You're a poor man.'

'How would you know?'

He picked the bill up and stretched it between his thin fingers and slipped it casually into an inside pocket. He bit his lip with the very white teeth you can have when you have a brown skin.

'I couldn't tell you any more than I did that morning you drove me to Tijuana. I gave you a chance to call the law and turn me in.'

'I'm not sore at you. You're just that kind of guy. For a long time I couldn't figure you at all. You had nice ways and nice qualities, but there was something wrong. You had standards and you lived up to them but they were personal. They had no relation to any kind of ethics or scruples. You were a nice guy because you had a nice nature. But you were just as happy with mugs or hoodlums as with honest men. Provided the hoodlums

477

spoke fairly good English and had fairly acceptable table manners. You're a moral defeatist. I think maybe the war did it and again I think maybe you were born that way.'

'I don't get it,' he said. 'I really don't. I'm trying to pay you back and you won't let me. I couldn't have told you any more than I did. You wouldn't have stood for it.'

'That's as nice a thing as was ever said to me.'

'I'm glad you like something about me. I got in a bad jam. I happened to know the sort of people who know how to deal with bad jams. They owed me for an incident that happened long ago in the war. Probably the only time in my life I ever did the right thing quick like a mouse. And when I needed them, they delivered. And for free. You're not the only guy in the world that has no price tag, Marlowe.'

He leaned across the desk and snapped at one of my cigarettes. There was an uneven flush on his face under the deep tan. The scars showed up against it. I watched him spring a fancy gas cartridge lighter loose from a pocket and light the cigarette. I got a whiff of perfume from him.

'You bought a lot of me, Terry. For a smile and a nod and a wave of the hand and a few quiet drinks in a quiet bar here and there. It was nice while it lasted. So long, *amigo*. I won't say good-bye. I said it to you when it meant something. I said it when it was sad and lonely and final.'

'I came back too late,' he said. 'These plastic jobs take time.'

'You wouldn't have come at all if I hadn't smoked you out.'

There was suddenly a glint of tears in his eyes. He put his dark glasses back on quickly.

'I wasn't sure about it,' he said. 'I hadn't made up my mind. They didn't want me to tell you anything. I just hadn't made up my mind.'

'Don't worry about it, Terry. There's always somebody around to do it for you.'

'I was in the Commandos, bud. They don't take you if you're just a piece of fluff. I got badly hurt and it wasn't any fun with those Nazi doctors. It did something to me.'

'I know all that, Terry. You're a very sweet guy in a lot of ways. I'm not judging you. I never did. It's just that you're not here any more. You're long gone. You've got nice clothes and perfume and you're as elegant as a fifty-dollar whore.'

'That's just an act,' he said almost desperately.

'You get a kick out of it, don't you?'

His mouth dropped in a sour smile. He shrugged an expressive Latin shrug.

'Of course. An act is all there is. There isn't anything else. In here' – he tapped his chest with the lighter – 'there isn't anything. I've had it, Marlowe. I had it long ago. Well – I guess that winds things up.'

He stood up. I stood up. He put out a lean hand. I shook it.

'So long, Señor Maioranos. Nice to have known you – however briefly.'

'Good-bye.'

He turned and walked across the floor and out. I watched the door close. I listened to his steps going away down the imitation marble corridor. After a while they got faint, then they got silent. I kept on listening anyway. What for? Did I want him to stop suddenly and turn and come back and talk me out of the way I felt? Well, he didn't. That was the last I saw of him.

I never saw any of them again – except the cops. No way has yet been invented to say good-bye to them.

# Playback

to
**Jean and Helga**
without whom this book would
never have been written

# One

The voice on the telephone seemed to be sharp and peremptory, but I didn't hear too well what it said – partly because I was only half-awake and partly because I was holding the receiver upside down. I fumbled it around and grunted.

'Did you hear me? I said I was Clyde Umney, the lawyer.'

'Clyde Umney, the lawyer. I thought we had several of them.'

'You're Marlowe, aren't you?'

'Yeah. I guess so.' I looked at my wrist watch. It was 6.30 a.m., not my best hour.

'Don't get fresh with me, young man.'

'Sorry, Mr Umney. But I'm not a young man. I'm old, tired and full of no coffee. What can I do for you, sir?'

'I want you to meet the Super Chief at eight o'clock, identify a girl among the passengers, follow her until she checks in somewhere, and then report to me. Is that clear?'

'No.'

'Why not?' he snapped.

'I don't know enough to be sure I could accept the case.'

'I'm Clyde Um—'

'Don't,' I interrupted. 'I might get hysterical. Just tell me the basic facts. Perhaps another investigator would suit you better. I never was an FBI man.'

'Oh. My secretary, Miss Vermilyea, will be at your office in half an hour. She will have the necessary information for you. She is very efficient. I hope you are.'

'I'm more efficient when I've had breakfast. Have her come here, would you?'

'Where is here?'

I gave him the address of my place on Yucca Avenue, and told him how she would find it.

'Very well,' he said grudgingly, 'but I want one thing very clear. The girl is not to know she is being followed. This is

485

very important. I am acting for a very influential firm of Washington attorneys. Miss Vermilyea will advance you some expense money and pay you a retainer of $250. I expect a high degree of efficiency. And let's not waste time talking.'

'I'll do the best I can, Mr Umney.'

He hung up. I struggled out of bed, showered, shaved and was nuzzling my third cup of coffee when the door bell rang.

'I'm Miss Vermilyea, Mr Umney's secretary,' she said in a rather chintzy voice.

'Please come in.'

She was quite a doll. She wore a white belted raincoat, no hat, a well-cherished head of platinum hair, bootees to match the raincoat, a folding plastic umbrella, a pair of blue-grey eyes that looked at me as if I had said a dirty word. I helped her off with her raincoat. She smelled very nice. She had a pair of legs – so far as I could determine – that were not painful to look at. She wore night-sheer stockings. I stared at them rather intently, especially when she crossed her legs and held out a cigarette to be lighted.

'Christian Dior,' she said, reading my rather open mind. 'I never wear anything else. A light, please.'

'You're wearing a lot more today,' I said, snapping a lighter for her.

'I don't greatly care for passes this early in the morning.'

'What time would suit you, Miss Vermilyea?'

She smiled rather acidly, inventoried her handbag and tossed me a manila envelope. 'I think you'll find everything you need in this.'

'Well – not quite everything.'

'Get on with it, you goof. I've heard all about you. Why do you think Mr Umney chose you? He didn't. I did. And stop looking at my legs.'

I opened the envelope. It contained another sealed envelope and two cheques made out to me. One, for $250, was marked 'Retainer, as an advance against fees for professional services'. The other was for $200 and was marked 'Advance to Philip Marlowe for necessary expenses'.

'You will account for the expenses to me, in exact detail,' Miss Vermilyea said. 'And buy your own drinks.'

The other envelope I didn't open – not yet. 'What makes Umney think I'll take a case I know nothing about?'

'You'll take it. You're not asked to do anything wrong. You have my word for that.'

'What else do I have?'

'Oh, we might discuss that over a drink some rainy evening, when I'm not too busy.'

'You've sold me.'

I opened the other envelope. It contained a photograph of a girl. The pose suggested a natural ease, or a lot of experience in being photographed. It showed darkish hair which might possibly have been red, a wide, clear forehead, serious eyes, high cheekbones, nervous nostrils and a mouth which was not giving anything away. It was a fine-drawn, almost a taut face, and not a happy one.

'Turn it over,' Miss Vermilyea said.

On the back there was clearly typed material.

'Name: Eleanor King. Height five feet four inches. Age about 29. Hair dark reddish-brown, thick, with a natural wave. Erect carriage, low, distinct voice, well-dressed but not overdressed. Conservative make-up. No visible scars. Characteristic mannerisms: habit of moving her eyes without moving her head when entering a room. Scratches palm of right hand when tense. Left-handed but adept in concealing it. Plays fast tennis, swims and dives beautifully, holds her liquor. No convictions, but prints on file.'

'Been in the coop,' I said, looking up at Miss Vermilyea.

'I have no information beyond what is there. Just follow your instructions.'

'No name, Miss Vermilyea. At twenty-nine a dish like this would almost certainly have been married. There's no mention of a wedding ring or any other jewels. That makes me wonder.'

She glanced at her watch. 'Better do your wondering at the Union Station. You haven't much time.' She stood up. I helped her on with her white raincoat and opened the door.

'You came in your own car?'

'Yes.' She went halfway out and turned. 'There's one thing I like about you. You don't paw. And you have nice manners – in a way.'

'It's rotten technique – to paw.'

'And there's one thing I don't like about you. Guess what it is.'

'Sorry. No idea – except that some people hate me for being alive.'

'I didn't mean that.'

I followed her down the steps and opened her car door for her. It was a cheap job, a Fleetwood Cadillac. She nodded briefly and slid down the hill.

I went back up and loaded a few things into an overnight bag, just in case.

# Two

There was nothing to it. The Super Chief was on time, as it almost always is, and the subject was as easy to spot as a kangaroo in a dinner jacket. She wasn't carrying anything but a paperback which she dumped in the first trash can she came to. She sat down and looked at the floor. An unhappy girl, if ever I saw one. After a while she got up and went to the book rack. She left it without picking anything out, glanced at the big clock on the wall and shut herself in a telephone booth. She talked to someone after putting a handful of silver into the slot. Her expression didn't change at all. She hung up and went to the magazine rack, picked up a *New Yorker*, looked at her watch again, and sat down to read.

She was wearing a midnight blue tailor-made suit with a white blouse showing at the neck and a big sapphire blue lapel pin which would probably have matched her earrings, if I could see her ears. Her hair was a dusky red. She looked like her photograph, but a little taller than I expected. Her dark blue ribbon hat had a short veil hanging from it. She was wearing gloves.

After a while she moved across the arches outside of which the taxis wait. She looked left at the coffee shop, turned and went into the main waiting-room, glanced at the drugstore and news-stand, the information booth, and the people sitting on the clean wooden benches. Some of the ticket windows were open, some not. She wasn't interested in them. She sat down again and looked up at the big clock. She pulled off her right glove and set her wrist watch, a small plain platinum toy without jewels. Mentally I put Miss Vermilyea beside her. She didn't look soft or prissy or prudish, but she made the Vermilyea look like a pick-up.

She didn't stay long sitting down this time, either. She got up and strolled. She went out into the patio and came back and went into the drugstore and stayed some time at the paperbook rack. Two things were obvious. If anyone was going to meet her, the date hadn't been for train time. She looked like a girl waiting between trains. She went into the coffee shop. She sat down at one of the plastic top tables, read the menu, and then started to read her book. A waitress came with the inevitable glass of ice water, and the menu. The subject gave an order. The waitress went away, the subject went on reading her book. It was about nine-fifteen.

I went out through the arches to where a redcap was waiting by the taxi starter. 'You work the Super Chief?' I asked him.

'Yeah. Part of it.' He glanced without too deep interest at the buck I was teasing with my fingers.

'I was expecting someone on the Washington–San Diego through car. Anybody get off?'

'You mean get off permanent, baggage and all?'

I nodded.

He thought about it, studying me with intelligent chestnut eyes. 'One passenger got off,' he said at last. 'What your friend look like?'

I described a man. Someone who looked something like Edward Arnold. The redcap shook his head.

'Can't help you, mister. What got off don't look like that at all. Your friend probably still on the train. They don't have to get off the through car. She gets hitched on to Seventy-Four. Leaves here eleven-thirty. The train ain't made up yet.'

'Thanks,' I said, and gave him the dollar. The subject's baggage was still on the train, which was all I wanted to know.

I went back to the coffee shop and looked in through the glass wall.

Subject was reading her paperback and toying with coffee and a snail. I moved over to a phone booth and called a garage I knew well and asked them to send somebody for my car if I didn't call again by noon. They'd done this often enough to have a spare key on hand. I went out to the car and got my overnight bag out of it and into a two-bit locker. In the enormous waiting-room, I bought a round trip to San Diego and trotted back to the coffee shop once again.

Subject was in place, but no longer alone. A guy was across the table from her smiling and talking, and one look was enough to show that she knew him and regretted it. He was California from the tips of his port wine loafers to the buttoned and tieless brown and yellow check shirt inside his rough cream sports jacket. He was about six feet one, slender, with a thin conceited face and too many teeth. He was twisting a piece of paper in his hand.

The yellow handkerchief in his outside breast pocket sprayed out like a small bunch of daffodils. And one thing was as clear as distilled water. The girl didn't want him there.

He went on talking and twitching the paper. Finally he shrugged and got up from his chair. He reached over and ran a fingertip down her cheek. She jerked back. Then he opened the twisted paper and laid it carefully down in front of her. He waited, smiling.

Her eyes went down to it very, very slowly. Her eyes held on it. Her hand moved to take it, but his was quicker. He put it away in his pocket, still smiling. Then he took out one of these pocket notebooks with perforated pages, and wrote something with a clip pen and tore the sheet out and put that down in front of her. That she could have. She took it, read it, put it in her purse. At last she looked at him. And at last she smiled at him. My guess was that it took quite an effort. He reached across to pat her hand, then walked away from the table and out.

He shut himself in a phone booth, dialled, and talked for quite a while. He came out, found himself a redcap and went with the redcap to a locker. Out came a light oyster white suitcase and a matching overnight case. The redcap carried them through the doors to the parking lot and followed him to a sleek two-toned Buick Roadmaster, the solid top convertible type that isn't convertible. The redcap put the stuff in behind the tipped seat, took his money, went away. The guy in the sports coat and yellow handkerchief got in and backed his car out and then stopped long enough to put on dark glasses and light a cigarette. After that he was gone. I wrote down the licence number and went back into the station.

The next hour was three hours long. The girl left the coffee shop and read her book in the waiting-room. Her mind wasn't on it. She kept turning back to see what she had read. Part of the time she didn't read at all, just held the book and looked at nothing. I had an early morning edition of the evening paper and behind it I watched her and added up what I had in my head. None of it was solid fact. It just helped to pass the time.

The guy who had sat at the table with her had come off the train, since he had baggage. It could have been her train and he could have been the passenger that got off her car. Her attitude made it pretty clear that she didn't want him around, and his that that was too bad but if she would glance at his piece of paper she would change her mind. And apparently she did. Since this happened after they got off the train when it could have happened more quietly before, then it followed that he didn't have his piece of paper on the train.

At this point the girl got up abruptly and went to the news-stand and came back with a packet of cigarettes. She tore it open and lit one. She smoked awkwardly as if she wasn't used to it, and while she smoked her attitude seemed to change, to become more flashy and hard, as if she was deliberately vulgarizing herself for some purpose. I looked at the wall clock. Ten-forty-seven. I went on with my thinking.

The twist of paper had looked like a newspaper clipping. She had tried to grab it, he hadn't let her. Then he had written some words on a piece of blank paper and given them to her and she had looked at him and smiled. Conclusion: the dreamboat had something on her and she had to pretend to like it.

Next point was that earlier on he had left the station and gone somewhere, perhaps to get his car, perhaps to get the clipping, perhaps anything you like. That meant he wasn't afraid that she would run out on him, and that reinforced the idea that he hadn't at that time disclosed everything he was holding up his sleeve but had disclosed some of it. Could be he wasn't sure himself. Had to check. But now having shown her his hole card he had gone off in a Buick with his baggage.

Therefore he was no longer afraid of losing her. Whatever held them together was strong enough to keep on holding them.

At eleven-five I tossed all this out of the window and started with a fresh premise. I got nowhere. At eleven-ten the public address system said Number Seventy-Four on Track Eleven was now ready to receive passengers for Santa Ana, Oceanside, Del Mar and San Diego. A bunch of people left the waiting-room, including the girl. Another bunch was already going through the gate. I watched her through and went back to the phone booths. I dropped my dime and dialled the number of Clyde Umney's office.

Miss Vermilyea answered by giving the phone number only.

'This is Marlowe. Mr Umney in?'

Her voice was formal saying: 'I'm sorry, Mr Umney is in court. May I take a message?'

'Am in contact and leaving by train for San Diego, or some intermediate stop. Can't tell which yet.'

'Thank you. Anything else?'

'Yeah, the sun's shining and our friend is no more on the lam than you are. She ate breakfast in the coffee shop which has a glass wall towards the concourse. She sat in the waiting-room with a hundred and fifty other people. And she could have stayed on the train out of sight.'

'I have all that, thank you. I'll get it to Mr Umney as soon as possible. You have no firm opinion then?'

'I have one firm opinion. That you're holding out on me.'

Her voice changed abruptly. Somebody must have left the office. 'Listen, chum, you were hired to do a job. Better do it and do it right. Clyde Umney draws a lot of water in this town.'

'Who wants water, beautiful? I take mine straight with a beer chaser. I might make sweeter music if I was encouraged.'

'You'll get paid, shamus – if you do a job. Not otherwise. Is that clear?'

'That's the nicest thing you ever said to me, sweetheart. Goodbye now.'

'Listen, Marlowe,' she said with sudden urgency. 'I didn't

mean to be rough with you. This is very important to Clyde Umney. If he doesn't come though, he might lose a very valuable connection. I was just sounding off.'

'I liked it, Vermilyea. It did things to my subconscious. I'll call in when I can.'

I hung up, went through the gate, down the ramp, walked about from here to Ventura to get to Track Eleven and climbed aboard a coach that was already full of the drifting cigarette smoke that is so kind to your throat and nearly always leaves you with one good lung. I filled and lit a pipe and added to the general frowst.

The train pulled out, dawdled interminably through the yards and the back stretches of East LA, picked up a little speed and made its first stop at Santa Ana. Subject did not get off. At Oceanside and Del Mar the same. At San Diego I hopped off quickly, chartered a cab, and then waited eight minutes outside the old Spanish station for the redcaps to come out with the baggage. Then the girl came out too.

She didn't take a cab. She crossed the street and rounded the corner to a U-Drive outfit and after a longish interval came out again looking disappointed. No driver's licence, no U-Drive. You'd think she would have known that.

She took a cab this time and it did a U-turn and started north. Mine did the same. I had a little difficulty with my driver about the tail job.

'That's something you read about in books, mister. We don't do it in Dago.'

I passed him a fin and the four by two and a half photostat of my licence. He looked them over, both of them. He looked off up the block.

'Okay, but I report it,' he said. 'The dispatcher may report it to the Police Business Office. That's the way it is here, chum.'

'Sounds like the kind of city I ought to live in,' I said. 'And you've lost the tail. He turned left two blocks ahead.'

The driver handed me back my wallet. 'Lost my left eye,' he said tensely. 'What you think a two-way radiophone is for?' He picked it up and talked into it.

He turned left at Ash Street to Highway 101 and we merged with the traffic and kept going at a peaceable forty I stared at the back of his head.

'You don't have a worry in the world,' the driver told me over his shoulder. 'This five is on top of the fare, huh?'

'Right. And why don't I have a worry in the world?'

'The passenger's going to Esmeralda. That's twelve miles north of here on the ocean front. Destination, unless changed *en route* – and if it is I'll get told – a motel hotel joint called the Rancho Descansado. That's Spanish for relax, take it easy.'

'Hell, I didn't need a cab at all,' I said.

'You got to pay for the service, mister. We ain't buying groceries giving it away.'

'You Mexican?'

'We don't call ourselves that, mister. We call ourselves Spanish-Americans. Born and raised in the USA. Some of us don't hardly speak Spanish any more.'

'*Es gran lastima,*' I said. '*Una lengua muchissima hermosa.*'

He turned his head and grinned. '*Tiene Vd. razon, amigo. Estoy muy bien de acuerdo.*'

We went on to Torrance Beach, through there and swung out towards the point. From time to time the hackie talked into his radiophone. He turned his head enough to speak to me again.

'You want to keep out of sight?'

'What about the other driver? Will he tell his passenger she's being tailed?'

'He ain't been told hisself. That's why I asked you.'

'Pass him and get there ahead, if you can. That's five more on the top.'

'A cinch. He won't even see me. I can rib him later on over a bottle of Tecate.'

We went through a small shopping centre, then the road widened and the houses on one side looked expensive and not new, while the houses on the other side looked very new and still not cheap. The road narrowed again and we were in a twenty-five-mile zone. My driver cut to the right, wound through some narrow streets, jumped a stop sign, and before I had had time to size up where we were going, we were sliding down into a canyon with the Pacific glinting off to the left beyond a wide, shallow beach with two lifeguard stations on open metal towers. At the bottom of the canyon the driver started to turn in through the gates, but I stopped him. A large sign, gold script on a green background, said: 'El Rancho Descansado'.

'Get out of sight,' I said. 'I want to make sure.'

He swung back on the highway, drove fast down beyond the end of the stucco wall, then cut into a narrow winding road on the far side and stopped. A gnarled eucalyptus with a divided trunk hung over us. I got out of the cab, put dark glasses on, strolled down to the highway and leaned against a bright red jeep with the name of a service station painted on it. A cab came down the hill and turned into the Rancho Descansado. Three minutes passed. The cab came out empty and turned back up the hill. I went back to my driver.

'Cab No. 423,' I said. 'That check?'

'That's your pigeon. What now?'

'We wait. What's the layout over there?'

'Bungalows with car ports. Some single, some double. Office in a small one down front. Rates pretty steep in season. This is slack time around here. Half price probably and plenty of room.'

'We wait five minutes. Then I check in, drop my suitcase, and look for a car to rent.'

He said that was easy. In Esmeralda there were three places that rented cars, time and mileage, any make you wanted.

We waited the five minutes. It was now just past three o'clock. I was empty enough to steal the dog's dinner.

I paid my driver off, watched him leave, and went across the highway and into the office.

# Three

I leaned a polite elbow on the counter and looked across at the happy-faced young guy in the polka-dotted bow tie. I looked from him to the girl at the small PBX against the side wall. She was an outdoorsy type with shiny make-up and a horse's tail of medium blonde hair sticking out at the back of her noodle. But she had nice large soft eyes and when they looked at the clerk they glistened. I looked back at him and choked back a snarl. The girl at the PBX swung her horse tail in an arc and put the eye on me also.

'I'd be glad to show you what we have vacant, Mr Marlowe,' the young guy said politely. 'You can register later, if you decide to stay here. About how long would you be likely to want accommodations?'

'Only as long as she does,' I said. 'The girl in the blue suit. She just registered. Using what name I wouldn't know.'

He and the PBX girl stared at me. Both their faces had the same expression of distrust mixed with curiosity. There are a hundred ways of playing this scene. But this was a new one for me. In no city hotel in the world would it work. It might work here. Mostly because I didn't give a damn.

'You don't like that, do you?' I said.

He shook his head slightly. 'At least you're frank about it.'

'I'm tired of being cagey. I'm worn out with it. Did you notice her ring finger?'

'Why no, I didn't.' He looked at the PBX girl. She shook her head and kept her eyes on my face.

'No wedding ring,' I said. 'Not any more. All gone. All broken up. All the years – ah, the hell with it. I've followed her all the way from – well, never mind where. She won't even speak to me. What am I doing here? Making a damn fool of myself.' I turned away quickly and blew my nose. I had their attention. 'I'd better go somewhere else,' I said, turning back.

'You want to make it up and she won't,' the PBX girl said quietly.

'Yes.'

'I'm sympathetic,' the young guy said. 'But you know how it is, Mr Marlowe. A hotel has to be very careful. These situations can lead to anything – even shootings.'

'Shootings?' I looked at him with wonder. 'Good God, what sort of people do that?'

He leaned both arms on the desk. 'Just what would you like to do, Mr Marlowe?'

'I'd like to be near her – in case she needs me. I wouldn't speak to her. I wouldn't even knock at her door. But she would know I was there and she'd know why. I'd be waiting. I'll always be waiting.'

The girl loved it now. I was up to my neck in the soft corn. I took a deep, slow breath and shot for the grand prize. 'And I don't somehow like the look of the guy who brought her here,' I said.

'Nobody brought her here – except a cab driver,' the clerk said. But he knew what I meant all right.

The PBX girl half smiled. 'He doesn't mean that, Jack. He means the reservation.'

Jack said, 'I kind of gathered as much, Lucille. I'm not so dumb.' Suddenly he brought a card out from the desk and put it down in front of me. A registration card. Across the corner diagonally was written the name Larry Mitchell. In a very different writing in the proper places: (Miss) Betty Mayfield, West Chatham, New York. Then in the top left-hand corner in the same writing as Larry Mitchell a date, a time, a price, a number.

'You're very kind,' I said. 'So she's gone back to her maiden name. It's legal, of course.'

'Any name is legal, if there's no intent to defraud. You would like to be next door to her?'

I widened my eyes. Maybe they glistened a little. Nobody ever tried harder to make them glisten.

'Look,' I said, 'it's damn nice of you. But you can't do it.

I'm not going to make any trouble, but you can't be sure. It's your job if I pulled anything.'

'Okay,' he said. 'I've got to learn some day. You look all right to me. Just don't tell anybody.' He took the pen from its cup and held it out. I signed my name with an address on East Sixty-first Street, New York City.

Jack looked at it. 'That's near Central Park, isn't it?' he asked idly.

'Three blocks and a bit,' I said. 'Between Lexington and Third Avenue.'

He nodded. He knew where it was. I was in. He reached for a key.

'I'd like to leave my suitcase here,' I said, 'and go get something to eat and maybe rent a car, if I can. You could have it put in the room for me?'

Sure. He could do that for me easy. He took me outside and pointed up through a grove of saplings. The cottages were all over shingled, white with green roofs. They had porches with railings. He showed me mine through the trees. I thanked him. He started back in and I said, 'Look, there's one thing. She may check out when she knows.'

He smiled. 'Of course. Nothing we can do about that, Mr Marlowe. Lots of our guests only stay a night or two – except in summer. We don't expect to be filled up this time of year.'

He went on into the office cottage and I heard the girl say to him: 'He's kind of cute, Jack – but you shouldn't have done it.'

I heard his answer too. 'I hate that guy Mitchell – even if he is a pal of the owner.'

# Four

The room was bearable. It had the usual concrete couch, chairs without cushions, a small desk against the front wall, a walk-in closet with a built-in chest, a bathroom with a Hollywood bath and neon shaving lights beside the mirror over the basin, a small kitchenette with a refrigerator and a white stove, a three-burner electric. In a wall cupboard over the sink enough dishes and stuff. I got some ice cubes and made myself a drink with the bottle from my suitcase, sipped it and sat in a chair listening, leaving the windows shut and the Venetian blinds dark. I heard nothing next door, then I heard the toilet flush. Subject was in residence. I finished the drink, killed a cigarette and studied the wall heater on the party wall. It consisted of two long frosted bulbs in a metal box. It didn't look as if it would throw out much heat, but in the closet there was a plug-in fan heater with a thermostat and a three-way plug, which made it 220 volts. I slipped off the chromium grille guard of the wall heater and twisted out the frosted bulbs. I got a doctor's stethoscope out of my suitcase and held it against the metal backing and listened. If there was another similar heater back against it in the next room, and there almost certainly would be, all I had between the two rooms was a metal panel and some insulation, probably a bare minimum of that.

I heard nothing for a few minutes, then I heard a telephone being dialled. The reception was perfect. A woman's voice said: 'Esmeralda 4-1499 please.'

It was a cool, contained voice, medium pitch, very little expression in it except that it sounded tired. It was the first time I had heard her voice in all the hours I had been following her.

There was a longish pause, then she said: 'Mr Larry Mitchell, please.'

Another pause, but shorter. Then: 'This is Betty Mayfield,

at the Rancho Descansado.' She pronounced the 'a' in Descansado wrong. Then, 'Betty Mayfield, I said. Please don't be stupid. Do you want me to spell it for you?'

The other end had things to say. She listened. After a while she said: 'Apartment 12C. You ought to know. You made the reservation . . . Oh. I see . . . Well, all right. I'll be here.'

She hung up. Silence. Complete silence. Then the voice in there said slowly and emptily: 'Betty Mayfield, Betty Mayfield, Betty Mayfield. Poor Betty. You were a nice girl once – long ago.'

I was sitting on the floor on one of the striped cushions with my back to the wall. I got up carefully, laid the stethoscope down on the cushion and went to lie on the day bed. After a while he would arrive. She was in there waiting for him, because she had to. She'd had to come there for the same reason. I wanted to know what it was.

He must have been wearing crêpe soles because I didn't hear anything until the buzzer sounded next door. Also, he hadn't driven his car up to the cottage. I got down on the floor and went to work with the stethoscope.

She opened the door, he came in and I could imagine the smile on his face as he said: 'Hello, Betty. Betty Mayfield is the name, I believe. I like it.'

'It was my name originally.' She closed the door.

He chuckled. 'I suppose you were wise to change it. But how about the initials on your luggage?'

I didn't like his voice any better than his smile. It was high and cheerful, almost bubbly with sly good humour. There was not quite a sneer in it, but close enough. It made me clamp my teeth.

'I suppose,' she said dryly, 'that was the first thing you noticed.'

'No, baby. *You* were the first thing I noticed. The mark of a wedding ring but no wedding ring was the second. The initials were only the third.'

'Don't call me "baby", you cheap blackmailer,' she said with a sudden muted fury.

It didn't faze him in the least. 'I may be a blackmailer, honey, but' – another conceited chuckle – 'I'm certainly not cheap.'

She walked, probably away from him. 'Do you want a drink? I see you have a bottle with you.'

'It might make me lascivious.'

'There's only one thing about you I'm afraid of, Mr Mitchell,' the girl said coolly. 'Your big loose mouth. You talk too much and you like yourself too well. We'd better understand each other. I like Esmeralda. I've been here before and I always wanted to come back. It's nothing but sheer bad luck that you live here and that you were on the train that was taking me here. It was the worst kind of luck that you should have recognized me. But that's all it is – bad luck.'

'Good luck for me, honey,' he drawled.

'Perhaps,' she said, 'if you don't put too much pressure on it. If you do, it's liable to blow up in your face.'

There was a brief silence. I could see them in my imagination, staring at each other. His smile might be getting a little nervous, but not much.

'All I've got to do,' he said quietly, 'is pick up the phone and call the San Diego papers. You want publicity? I can arrange it for you.'

'I came here to get rid of it,' she said bitterly.

He laughed. 'Sure, by an old coot of a judge falling to pieces with senile decay, and in the only State in the Union – and I've checked on that – where it could happen after the jury said otherwise. You've changed your name twice. If your story got printed out here – and it's a pretty good story, honey – I guess you'd have to change your name again – and start travelling a little more. Gets kind of tiresome, doesn't it?'

'That's why I'm here,' she said. 'That's why you're here. How much do you want? I realize it will only be a down payment.'

'Have I said anything about money?'

'You will,' she said. 'And keep your voice down.'

'The cottage is all yours, honey. I walked around it before

I came in. Doors closed, windows shut, blinds drawn, car ports empty. I can check with the office, if you're nervous. I've got friends around here – people you need to know, people who can make life pleasant for you. Socially this is a tough town to break into. And it's a damn' dull town if you're on the outside looking in.'

'How did *you* get in, Mr Mitchell?'

'My old man is a big shot in Toronto. We don't get on and he won't have me around home. But he's still my old man and he's still the real thing, even if he does pay me to stay away.'

She didn't answer him. Her steps went away. I heard her in the kitchen making the usual sounds connected with getting ice out of a tray of cubes. The water ran, the steps came back.

'I'd like one myself,' she said. 'Perhaps I've been rude to you. I'm tired.'

'Sure,' he said equably. 'You're tired.' A pause. 'Well, here's to when you're not tired. Say about seven-thirty this evening at The Glass Room. I'll pick you up. Nice place for dinner. Dancing. Quiet. Exclusive, if that means anything any more. Belongs to the Beach Club. They don't have a table unless they know you. I'm among friends there.'

'Expensive?' she asked.

'A little. Oh yes – and that reminds me. Until my monthly cheque comes in, you could let me have a couple of dollars.' He laughed. 'I'm surprised at myself. I did mention money after all.'

'A couple of dollars?'

'A couple of hundred would be better.'

'Sixty dollars is all I have – until I can open an account or cash some travellers' cheques.'

'You can do that at the office, baby.'

'So I can. Here's fifty. I don't want to spoil you, Mr Mitchell.'

'Call me Larry. Be human.'

'Should I?' Her voice had changed. There was a hint of invitation in it. I could imagine the slow smile of pleasure on his face. Then I guessed from the silence that he had grabbed her and she had let him. Finally her voice was a little muffled, saying:

'That's enough, Larry. Be nice now and run along. I'll be ready at seven-thirty.'

'One more for the road.'

In a moment the door opened and he said something I didn't catch. I got up and went to the window and took a careful look through the slats of the blind. A flood light was turned on in one of the tall trees. Under it I saw him stroll off up the slope and disappear. I went back to the heater panel and for a while I heard nothing and wasn't sure what I was listening for. But I knew soon enough.

There was quick movement back and forth, the sound of drawers being pulled open, the snap of a lock, the bump of a lifted lid against something.

She was packing up to leave.

I screwed the long, frosted bulbs back into the heater and replaced the grille and put the stethoscope back in my suitcase. The evening was getting chilly. I slipped my jacket on and stood in the middle of the floor. It was getting dark and no light on. I just stood there and thought it over. I could go to the phone and make a report and by that time she could be on her way in another cab to another train or plane to another destination. She could go anywhere she liked, but there would always be a dick to meet the train if it meant enough to the big, important people back in Washington. There would always be a Larry Mitchell or a reporter with a good memory. There would always be the little oddness to be noticed and there would always be somebody to notice it. You can't run away from yourself.

I was doing a cheap, sneaky job for people I didn't like, but – that's what you hire out for, chum. They pay the bills, you dig the dirt. Only this time I could taste it. She didn't look like a tramp and she didn't look like a crook. Which meant only that she could be both with more success than if she had.

# Five

I opened the door and went along to the next and pushed the little buzzer. Nothing moved inside. There was no sound of steps. Then came the click of a chain set in the groove and the door opened a couple of inches on light and emptiness. The voice said from behind the door: 'Who is it?'

'Could I borrow a cup of sugar?'

'I haven't any sugar.'

'Well how about a couple of dollars until my cheque comes in?'

More silence. Then the door opened to the limit of the chain and her face edged into the opening and shaded eyes stared out at me. They were just pools in the dark. The flood-light set high in the tree glinted on them obliquely.

'Who are you?'

'I'm your next door neighbour. I was having a nap and voices woke me. The voices spoke words. I was intrigued.'

'Go somewhere else and be intrigued.'

'I could do that, Mrs King – pardon me, Miss Mayfield – but I'm not sure you'd want me to.'

She didn't move and her eyes didn't waver. I shook a cigarette out of a packet and tried to push up the top of my Zippo with my thumb and rotate the wheel. You should be able to do it one-handed. You can too, but it's an awkward process. I made it at last and got the cigarette going, yawned, and blew smoke out through my nose.

'What do you do for an encore?' she asked.

'To be strictly kosher I should call LA and tell the party who sent me. Maybe I could be talked out of it.'

'God,' she said fervently, 'two of them in one afternoon. How lucky can a girl get?'

'I don't know,' I said. 'I don't know anything. I think I've been played for a sucker, but I'm not sure.'

'Wait a minute.' She shut the door in my face. She wasn't gone long. The chain came out of the groove inside and the door came open.

I went in slowly and she stepped back and away from me. 'How much did you hear? And shut the door, please.'

I shut it with my shoulder and leaned against it.

'The tag end of a rather nasty conversation. The walls here are as thin as a hoofer's wallet.'

'You in show business?'

'Just the opposite of show business. I'm in the hide-and-seek business. My name is Philip Marlowe. You've seen me before.'

'Have I?' She walked away from me in little cautious steps and went over by her open suitcase. She leaned against the arm of a chair. 'Where?'

'Union Station in LA. We waited between trains, you and I. I was interested in you. I was interested in what went on between you and Mr Mitchell – that's his name, isn't it? I didn't hear anything and I didn't see much because I was outside the coffee shop.'

'So what interested you, you great big lovable something or other?'

'I've just told you part of it. The other thing that interested me was how you changed after your talk with him. I watched you work at it. It was very deliberate. You made yourself over into just another flip, hard-boiled modern cutie. Why?'

'What was I before?'

'A nice quiet, well-bred girl.'

'That was the act,' she said. 'The other was my natural personality. Which goes with something else.' She brought a small automatic up from her side.

I looked at it. 'Oh guns,' I said. 'Don't scare me with guns. I've lived with them all my life. I teethed on an old Derringer, single-shot, the kind the river-boat gamblers used to carry. As I got older I graduated to a lightweight sporting rifle, then a .303 target rifle and so on. I once made a bull at nine hundred yards with open sights. In case you don't know, the whole target looks the size of a postage stamp at nine hundred yards.'

'A fascinating career,' she said.

'Guns never settle anything,' I said. 'They are just a fast curtain to a bad second act.'

She smiled faintly and transferred the gun to her left hand. With her right she grabbed the edge of her blouse at the collar line and with a quick decisive motion tore it to the waist.

'Next,' she said, 'but there's no hurry about it, I turn the gun in my hand like this' – she put it back in her right hand, but held it by the barrel – 'I slam myself on the cheekbone with the butt. I do a beautiful bruise.'

'And after that,' I said, 'you get the gun into its proper position and release the safety catch and pull the trigger, just about the time I get through the lead column in the Sports Section.'

'You wouldn't get halfway across the room.'

I crossed my legs and leaned back and lifted the green glass ashtray from the table beside the chair and balanced it on my knee and held the cigarette I was smoking between the first and second fingers of my right hand.

'I wouldn't get any of the way across the room. I'd be sitting here like this, quite comfortable and relaxed.'

'But slightly dead,' she said. 'I'm a good shot and it isn't nine hundred yards.'

'Then you try to sell the cops your account of how I tried to attack you and you defended yourself.'

She tossed the gun into her suitcase and laughed. It sounded like a genuine laugh with real amusement in it.

'Sorry,' she said. 'You sitting there with your legs crossed and a hole in your head and me trying to explain how I shot you to defend my honour – the picture makes me a little light-headed.'

She dropped into a chair and leaned forward with her chin cupped in a hand, the elbow propped on her knee, her face taut and drained, her dark red hair framing it too luxuriantly, so that her face looked smaller than it should have.

'Just what are you doing to me, Mr Marlowe? Or is it the other way around – what I can do for you in return for you not doing anything at all?'

'Who is Eleanor King? What was she in Washington, DC? Why did she change her name somewhere along the way and have the initials taken off her bag? Odds and ends like that are what you could tell me. You probably won't.'

'Oh, I don't know. The porter took the initials off my things. I told him I had had a very unhappy marriage and was divorced and had been given the right to resume my unmarried name. Which is Elizabeth or Betty Mayfield. That could all be true, couldn't it?'

'Yeah. But it doesn't explain Mitchell.'

She leaned back and relaxed. Her eyes stayed watchful. 'Just an acquaintance I made along the way. He was on the train.'

I nodded. 'But he came down here in his own car. He made the reservation here for you. He's not liked by the people here, but apparently he is a friend of someone with a lot of influence.'

'An acquaintance on a train or a ship sometimes develops very quickly,' she said.

'So it seems. He even touched you for a loan. Very fast work. And I got the impression you didn't care for him too well.'

'Well,' she said. 'So what? But as a matter of fact I'm crazy about him.' She turned her hand over and looked down at it. 'Who hired you, Mr Marlowe, and for what?'

'A Los Angeles lawyer, acting on instructions from back east. I was to follow you and check you in somewhere. Which I did. But now you're getting ready to move out. I'm going to have to start over again.'

'But with me knowing you're there,' she said shrewdly. 'So you'll have a much harder job of it. You're a private detective of some sort, I gather.'

I said I was. I had killed my cigarette some time back. I put the ashtray back on the table and stood up.

'Harder for me, but there are lots of others, Miss Mayfield.'

'Oh, I'm sure there are, and all such nice little men. Some of them are even fairly clean.'

'The cops are not looking for you. They'd have had you

508

easily. It was known about your train. I even got a photo of you and a description. But Mitchell can make you do just what he wants. Money isn't all he'll want.'

I thought she flushed a little, but the light didn't strike her face directly. 'Perhaps so,' she said. 'And perhaps I don't mind.'

'You mind.'

She stood up suddenly and came near me. 'You're in a business that doesn't pay fortunes, aren't you?'

I nodded. We were very close now.

'Then what would it be worth to you to walk out of here and forget you ever saw me?'

'I'd walk out of here for free. As for the rest, I have to make a report.'

'How much?' She said it as if she meant it. 'I can afford a substantial retainer. That's what you call it, I've heard. A much nicer word than blackmail.'

'It doesn't mean the same thing.'

'It could. Believe me, it can mean just that – even with some lawyers and doctors. I happen to know.'

'Tough break, huh?'

'Far from it, shamus. I'm the luckiest girl in the world. I'm alive.'

'I'm on the other side. Don't give it away.'

'Well, what do you know' she drawled. 'A dick with scruples. Tell it to the seagulls, buster. On me it's just confetti. Run along now, Mr PI Marlowe, and make that little old phone call you're so anxious about. I'm not restraining you.'

She started for the door, but I caught her by the wrist and spun her around. The torn blouse didn't reveal any startling nakedness, merely some skin and part of a brassiere. You'd see more on the beach, far more, but you wouldn't see it through a torn blouse.

I must have been leering a little, because she suddenly curled her fingers and tried to claw me.

'I'm no bitch in heat,' she said between tight teeth. 'Take your paws off me.'

I got the other wrist and started to pull her closer. She tried to knee me in the groin, but she was already too close. Then she went limp and pulled her head back and closed her eyes. Her lips opened with a sardonic twist to them. It was a cool evening, maybe even cold down by the water. But it wasn't cold where I was.

After a while she said with a sighing voice that she had to dress for dinner.

I said: 'Uh-huh.'

After another pause she said it was a long time since a man had unhooked her brassiere. We did a slow turn in the direction of one of the twin day beds. They had pink and silver covers on them. The little odd things you notice.

Her eyes were open and quizzical. I studied them one at a time because I was too close to see them together. They seemed well-matched.

'Honey,' she said softly, 'you're awful sweet, but I just don't have the time.'

I closed her mouth for her. It seems that a key slid into the door from the outside, but I wasn't paying too close attention. The lock clicked, the door opened, and Mr Larry Mitchell walked in.

We broke apart. I turned and he looked at me droopy-eyed, six feet one and tough and wiry.

'I thought to check at the office,' he said, almost absently. '12B was rented this afternoon, very soon after this was occupied. I got faintly curious, because there are a lot of vacancies here at the moment. So I borrowed the other key. And who is this hunk of beef, baby?'

'She told you not to call her "baby", remember?'

If that meant anything to him, he didn't show it. He swung a knotted fist gently at his side.

The girl said: 'He's a private eye named Marlowe. Somebody hired him to follow me.'

'Did he have to follow you as close as all that? I seem to be intruding on a beautiful friendship.'

She jerked away from me and grabbed the gun out of her suitcase. 'What we've been talking is money,' she told him.

'Always a mistake,' Mitchell said. His colour was high and his eyes too bright. 'Especially in that position. You won't need the gun, honey.'

He poked at me with a straight right, very fast and well sprung. I stepped inside it, fast, cool and clever. But the right wasn't his meal ticket. He was a lefty, too. I ought to have noticed that at the Union Station in LA. Trained observer, never miss a detail. I missed him with a right hook and he didn't miss with his left.

It snapped my head back. I went off balance just long enough for him to lunge sideways and lift the gun out of the girl's hand. It seemed to dance through the air and nestle in his left hand.

'Just relax,' he said. 'I know it sounds corny, but I could drill you and get away with it. I really could.'

'Okay,' I said thickly. 'For fifty bucks a day I don't get shot. That costs seventy-five.'

'Please turn around. It would amuse me to look at your wallet.'

I lunged for him, gun and all. Only panic could have made him shoot and he was on his home field and nothing to panic about. But it may be that the girl wasn't so sure. Dimly at the extreme edge of vision I saw her reach for the whisky bottle on the table.

I caught Mitchell on the side of the neck. His mouth yapped. He hit me somewhere, but it wasn't important. Mine was the better punch, but it didn't win the wrist watch, because at that moment an army mule kicked me square on the back of my brain. I went zooming out over a dark sea and exploded in a sheet of flame.

# Six

The first sensation was that if anybody spoke harshly to me I should burst out crying. The second, that the room was too small for my head. The front of the head was a long way from the back, the sides were an enormous distance apart, in spite of which a dull throbbing beat from temple to temple. Distance means nothing nowadays.

The third sensation was that somewhere not far off an insistent whining noise went on. The fourth and last was that ice water was running down my back. The cover of a day bed proved that I had been lying on my face, if I still had one. I rolled over gently and sat up and a rattling noise ended in a thump. What rattled and thumped was a knotted towel full of melting ice cubes. Somebody who loved me very much had put them on the back of my head. Somebody who loved me less had bashed in the back of my skull. It could have been the same person. People have moods.

I got up on my feet and lunged for my hip. The wallet was there in the left pocket, but the flap was unbuttoned. I went through it. Nothing was gone. It had yielded its information, but that was no secret any more. My suitcase stood open on the stand at the foot of the day bed. So I was home in my own quarters.

I reached a mirror and looked at the face. It seemed familiar. I went to the door and opened it. The whining noise was louder. Right in front of me was a fattish man leaning against the railing. He was a middle-sized fat man and the fat didn't look flabby. He wore glasses and large ears under a dull grey felt hat. The collar of his top-coat was turned up. His hands were in the pockets of his coat. The hair that showed at the sides of his head was battleship grey. He looked durable. Most fat men do. The light from the open door behind me bounced back from his glasses. He had a small pipe in his mouth, the kind they call a toy bulldog. I was still foggy but something about him bothered me.

'Nice evening,' he said.

'You want something?'

'Looking for a man. You're not him.'

'I'm alone in here.'

'Right,' he said. 'Thanks.' He turned his back on me and leaned his stomach against the railing of the porch.

I went along the porch to the whining noise. The door of 12c was wide open and the lights were on and the noise was a vacuum cleaner being operated by a woman in a green uniform.

I went in and looked the place over. The woman switched off the vacuum and stared at me. 'Something you wanted?'

'Where's Miss Mayfield?'

She shook her head.

'The lady who had this apartment,' I said.

'Oh, that one. She checked out. Half an hour ago.' She switched the vacuum on again. 'Better ask at the office,' she yelled through the noise. 'This apartment is on change.'

I reached back and shut the door. I followed the black snake of the vacuum cord over to the wall and yanked the plug out. The woman in the green uniform stared at me angrily. I went over and handed her a dollar bill. She looked less angry.

'Just want to phone,' I said.

'Ain't you got a phone in your room?'

'Stop thinking,' I said. 'A dollar's worth.'

I went to the phone and lifted it. A girl's voice said: 'Office. Your order, please.'

'This is Marlowe. I'm very unhappy.'

'What?... Oh yes, Mr Marlowe. What can we do for you?'

'She's gone. I never even got to talk to her.'

'Oh, I'm sorry, Mr Marlowe,' she sounded as if she meant it. 'Yes, she left. We couldn't very well—'

'She say where to?'

'She just paid up and left, sir. Quite suddenly. No forwarding address at all.'

'With Mitchell?'

'I'm sorry, sir. I didn't see anyone with her.'

'You must have seen something. How did she leave?'

'In a taxi. I'm afraid—'

'All right. Thank you.' I went back to my own apartment.

The middle-sized fat man was sitting comfortably in a chair with his knees crossed.

'Nice of you to drop in,' I said. 'Anything in particular I could do for you?'

'You could tell me where Larry Mitchell is.'

'Larry Mitchell?' I thought it over carefully. 'Do I know him?'

He opened a wallet and extracted a card. He struggled to his feet and handed it to me. The card read: 'Goble and Green, Investigators, 310 Prudence Building, Kansas City, Missouri'.

'Must be interesting work, Mr Goble.'

'Don't get funny with me, buster. I get annoyed rather easy.'

'Fine. Let's watch you get annoyed. What do you do – bite your moustache?'

'I ain't got no moustache, stupid.'

'You could grow one. I can wait.'

He got up on his feet much more rapidly this time. He looked down at his fist. Suddenly a gun appeared in his hand. 'You ever get pistol-whipped, stupid?'

'Breeze off. You bore me. Mudheads always bore me.'

His hand shook and his face turned red. Then he put the gun back in the shoulder holster and wobbled towards the door.

'You ain't through with me,' he snarled over his shoulder.

I let him have that one. It wasn't worth topping.

# Seven

After a while I went down to the office.

'Well, it didn't work,' I said. 'Does either one of you happen to have noticed the cab driver who took her away?'

'Joe Harms,' the girl said promptly. 'You ought to maybe find him at the stand halfway up Grand. Or you could call the office. A pretty nice guy. He made a pass at me once.'

'And missed by from here to Paso Robles,' the clerk sneered.

'Oh, I don't know. You didn't seem to be there.'

'Yeah,' he sighed. 'You work twenty hours a day trying to put enough together to buy a home. And by the time you have, fifteen other guys have been smooching your girl.'

'Not this one,' I said. 'She's just teasing you. She glows every time she looks at you.'

I went out and left them smiling at each other.

Like most small towns, Esmeralda had one main street from which in both directions its commercial establishments flowed gently for a short block or so and then with hardly a change of mood became streets with houses where people lived. But unlike most small California towns it had no false fronts, no cheesy billboards, no drive-in hamburger joints, no cigar counters or poolrooms, and no street corner toughs to hang around in front of them. The stores on Grand Street were either old and narrow but not tawdry or else well modernized with plate glass and stainless steel fronts and neon lighting in clear crisp colours. Not everybody in Esmeralda was prosperous, not everybody was happy, not everybody drove a Cadillac, a Jaguar or a Riley, but the percentage of obviously prosperous living was very high, and the stores that sold luxury goods were as neat and expensive-looking as those in Beverly Hills and far less flashy. There was another small difference too. In Esmeralda what was old was also clean and sometimes quaint. In other small towns what is old is just shabby.

I parked midway of the block and the telephone office was right in front of me. It was closed of course, but the entrance was set back and in the alcove which deliberately sacrificed money space to style were two dark green phone booths, like sentry boxes. Across the way was a pale buff taxi, parked diagonally to the kerb in slots painted red. A grey-haired man sat in it reading the paper. I crossed to him.

'You Joe Harms?'

He shook his head. 'He'll be back after a while. You want a cab?'

'No, thanks.'

I walked away from him and looked in at a store window. There was a checked brown and beige sports shirt in the window which reminded me of Larry Mitchell. Walnut brogues, imported tweeds, ties, two or three, and matching shirts for them set out with plenty of room to breathe. Over the store the name of a man who was once a famous athlete. The name was in script, carved and painted in relief against a redwood background.

A telephone jangled and the cab driver got out of the taxi and went across the sidewalk to answer it. He talked, hung up, got in his cab and backed out of the slot. When he was gone, the street was utterly empty for a minute. Then a couple of cars went by, then a good-looking, well-dressed coloured boy and his prettied-up cutie came strolling the block looking in at the windows and chattering. A Mexican in a green bell-hop's uniform drove up in somebody's Chrysler New Yorker – it could be his for all I knew – went into the drugstore and came out with a carton of cigarettes. He drove back towards the hotel.

Another beige cab with the name Esmeralda Cab Company tooled around the corner and drifted into the red slot. A big bruiser with thick glasses got out and checked on the wall phone, then got back into his cab and pulled a magazine out from behind his rear view mirror.

I strolled over to him and he was it. He was coatless and had his sleeves rolled up past the elbows, although this was no Bikini suit weather.

'Yeah. I'm Joe Harms.' He stuck a pill in his kisser and lit it with a Ronson.

'Lucille down at the Rancho Descansado thought maybe you'd give me a little information.' I leaned against his cab and gave him my big warm smile. I might as well have kicked the kerbing.

'Information about what?'

'You picked up a fare this evening from one of their cottages. Number 12c. A tallish girl with reddish hair and a nice shape. Her name's Betty Mayfield but she probably didn't tell you that.'

'Mostly they just tell me where they want to go. Quaint isn't it?' He blew a lungful of smoke at his windshield and watched it flatten out and float around in the cab. 'What's the pitch?'

'Girl friend walked out on me. We had a little argument. All my fault. I'd like to tell her I'm sorry.'

'Girl friend got a home somewhere?'

'A long way from here.'

He knocked ash from his cigarette by flicking his little finger at it still in his mouth.

'Could be she planned it that way. Could be she don't want you to know where she went. Could be you were lucky at that. They can drop the arm on you for shacking up in a hotel in this town. I'll admit it has to be pretty flagrant.'

'Could be I'm a liar,' I said, and got a business card out of my wallet. He read it and handed it back.

'Better,' he said. 'Some better. But it's against the company rules. I'm not driving this hack just to build muscle.'

'A five interest you? Or is that against the rules too?'

'My old man owns the company. He'd be pretty sore if I was on the chisel. Not that I don't like money.'

The phone on the wall jangled. He slid out of the cab and went over to it in about three long strides. I just stood planted, gnawing my lip. He talked and came back and stepped into the cab and was sitting behind the wheel all in one motion.

'Have to blow,' he said. 'Sorry. I'm kind of behind schedule.

Just got back from Del Mar. The seven-forty-seven to LA makes a flag stop there. Most people from here go that way.'

He started his motor and leaned out of the cab to drop his cigarette in the street.

I said, 'Thanks.'

'For what?' He backed out and was gone.

I looked at my watch again. Time and distance checked. It was all of twelve miles to Del Mar. It would take almost an hour to ferry someone to Del Mar and drop him or her off at the railroad station and turn around and come back. He had told me in his own way. There was no point in telling me at all unless it meant something.

I watched him out of sight and then crossed the street to the booths outside the telephone company's office. I left the booth door open and dropped my dime and dialled the big O.

'I'd like to make a collect call to West Los Angeles, please.' I gave her a Bradshaw number. 'Person to person, Mr Clyde Umney. My name is Marlowe and I'm calling from Esmeralda 4-2673, a pay phone.'

She got him a lot quicker than it took me to tell her all that. He came on sharp and quick.

'Marlowe? It's about time you reported in. Well – let's have it.'

'I'm in San Diego. I've lost her. She slipped away while I was taking a nap.'

'I just knew I'd picked a smart cookie,' he said unpleasantly.

'It's not as bad as it sounds, Mr Umney. I have a rough idea where she went.'

'Rough ideas are not good enough for me. When I hire a man I expect him to deliver exactly what I order. And just what do you mean by a rough idea?'

'Would it be possible for you to give me some notion of what this is all about, Mr Umney? I grabbed it off kind of quick on account of meeting the train. Your secretary gave me a lot of personality but very little information. You want me to be happy in my work, don't you, Mr Umney?'

'I gathered that Miss Vermilyea told you all there is to

know,' he grumbled. 'I am acting at the request of an important law firm in Washington. Their client desires to remain anonymous for the present. All you have to do is to trace this party to a stopping place, and by stopping place I do not mean a rest room or a hamburger stand. I mean a hotel, apartment house or perhaps the home of someone she knows. That's all. How much simpler do you want it?'

'I'm not asking for simplicity, Mr Umney. I'm asking for background material. Who the girl is, where she came from, what she's supposed to have done to make this job necessary.'

'Necessary?' he yapped at me. 'Who the hell are you to decide what is necessary? Find that girl, pin her down, and phone me her address. And if you expect to be paid, you better do it damn quick. I'll give you until ten o'clock tomorrow morning. After that I'll make other arrangements.'

'Okay, Mr Umney.'

'Where are you exactly and what is your telephone number?'

'I'm just kind of wandering around. I got hit on the head with a whisky bottle.'

'Well, that's too bad,' he said acidly. 'I presume you had already emptied the bottle.'

'Oh, it might have been worse, Mr Umney. It might have been *your* head. I'll call you around ten a.m. at your office. Don't worry about anybody losing anybody. There's two other guys working the same side of the street. One's a local boy named Mitchell and the other is a Kansas City shamus name of Goble. He carries a gun. Well, good night, Mr Umney.'

'Hold it!' he roared. 'Wait a minute! What does that mean – two other operatives?'

'You asking me what it means? I'm the guy that asked you. Looks like you only got a piece of the job.'

'Hold it! Hold it right there!' There was a silence. Then in a steady voice that didn't bluster any more: 'I'll call Washington the first thing in the morning, Marlowe. Excuse me if I sounded off. It begins to look as though I am entitled to a little more information about this project.'

'Yeah.'

'If you make contact again, call me here. At any hour. Any hour at all.'

'Yeah.'

'Good night, then.' He hung up.

I put the phone back on the hook and took a deep breath. My head still ached but the dizziness was gone. I breathed in the cool night air laced with sea fog. I pushed out of the booth and looked across the street. The old guy who had been in the taxi slot when I arrived was back again. I strolled across and asked him how to get to The Glass Room, which was where Mitchell had promised to take Miss Betty Mayfield to dinner – whether she liked it or not. He told me, I thanked him, re-crossed the empty street and climbed into my rented car, and started back the way I had come.

It was still possible that Miss Mayfield had grabbed the seven-forty-seven for Los Angeles or some way station. It was a lot more likely that she had not. A cab driver taking a fare to the station doesn't stick around to watch the fare get on the train. Larry Mitchell wouldn't be that easy to shake. If he had enough on her to make her come to Esmeralda, he had enough on her to keep her there. He knew who I was and what I was doing. He didn't know why, because I didn't know myself. If he had half a brain, and I gave him credit for a good deal more, he would have to assume I could trace her movements as far as a taxi took her. The first guess I was working on was that he would have driven to Del Mar, parked his big Buick somewhere in the shadows, and waited for her taxi to drive up and unload. When it turned around and started back, he would pick her up and drive her back to Esmeralda. The second guess I was working on was that she wouldn't tell him anything he didn't already know. I was a Los Angeles private eye, unknown parties had hired me to follow her, I had done so and then made the mistake of trying to get too close. That would bother him because it suggested he didn't have the field to himself. But if his information, whatever it was, came from a press clipping, he could hardly expect to have it to himself for ever. Anybody with enough interest and enough patience could turn it up in time. Anybody with enough reason to hire a private dick probably knew it already. And that in turn meant that whatever kind of bite he planned to put on Betty Mayfield, financial or amatory or both, would have to be put on fast.

A third of a mile down the canyon a small illuminated sign with an arrow pointing seawards said in script: *THE GLASS ROOM*. The road wound down between cliffside houses with warm lights in the windows, manicured gardens, stucco walls and one or two of fieldstone or brick inset with tiles in the Mexican tradition.

I drove down the last curve of the last hill and the smell of raw seaweed filled my nostrils and the fog-veiled lights of The Glass Room swelled to amber brightness and the sound of dance music drifted across the paved parking lot. I parked with the sea growling out of sight almost at my feet. There was no attendant. You just locked your car and went in.

A couple of dozen cars, no more. I looked them over. One hunch at least had paid off. The Buick Roadmaster solid top bore a licence number I had in my pocket. It was parked almost at the entrance and next to it in the very last space near the entrance was a pale green and ivory Cadillac convertible with oyster white leather seats, a plaid travelling rug thrown over the front seat to keep it dry, and all the gadgets a dealer could think of, including two enormous spotlights with mirrors on them, a radio aerial almost long enough for a tuna boat, a folding chrominum luggage rack to help out the boot if you wanted to travel far and in style, a sun visor, a prism reflector to pick up traffic lights obscured by the visor, a radio with enough knobs on it for a control panel, a cigarette lighter into which you dropped your cigarette and it smoked it for you, and various other trifles which made me wonder how long it would be before they installed radar, sound-recording equipment, a bar, and an anti-aircraft battery.

All this I saw by the light of a clip-on flash. I moved it to the licence holder and the name was Clark Brandon, Hotel Casa del Poniente, Esmeralda, California.

# Eight

The entrance lobby was on a balcony which looked down over the bar and a dining-room on two levels. A curving, carpeted staircase led down to the bar. Nobody was upstairs but the hat-check girl and an elderly party in a phone booth whose expression suggested that nobody better fool with him.

I went down the stairs to the bar and tucked myself in a small curved space that commanded a view of the dance floor. One side of the building was an enormous glass window. Outside of it was nothing but fog, but on a clear night with a moon low over the water it would have been sensational. A three-piece Mexican band was making the kind of music a Mexican band always makes. Whatever they play, it all sounds the same. They always sing the same song, and it always has nice open vowels and a drawn-out, sugary lilt, and the guy who sings it always strums on a guitar and has a lot to say about *amor*, *mi corazon*, a lady who is 'linda' but very hard to convince, and he always has too long and too oily hair and when he isn't making with the love stuff he looks as if his knife work in an alley would be efficient and economical.

On the dance floor half a dozen couples were throwing themselves around with the reckless abandon of a night watchman with arthritis. Most of them were dancing cheek to cheek, if dancing is the word. The men wore white tuxedos and the girls wore bright eyes, ruby lips, and tennis or golf muscles. One couple was not dancing cheek to cheek. The guy was too drunk to keep time and the girl was too busy not getting her pumps walked on to think of anything else. I needn't have worried about losing Miss Betty Mayfield. She was there and with Mitchell, but far from happy. Mitchell's mouth was open, he was grinning, his face was red and shiny, and his eyes had that glazed look. Betty was holding her head as far as she could get away from him without breaking her neck. It was very obvious that she had had about all of Mr Larry Mitchell that she could take.

A Mexican waiter in a short green jacket and white pants with a green stripe down the side came up and I ordered a double Gibson and asked if I could have a club sandwich where I was. He said, '*Muy bien, señor*,' smiled brightly, and disappeared.

The music stopped, there was desultory clapping. The orchestra was deeply moved, and played another number. A dark-haired headwaiter who looked like a road company Herbert Marshall circulated among the tables, offering his intimate smile and stopping here and there to polish an apple. Then he pulled out a chair and sat down opposite a big, handsome, Irish-type character with grey in his hair and just enough of it. He seemed to be alone. He wore a dark dinner jacket with a maroon carnation in the lapel. He looked like a nice guy if you didn't crowd him. At that distance and in that light I couldn't tell much more, except that if you did crowd him, you had better be big, fast, tough and in top condition.

The headwaiter leaned forward and said something and they both looked towards Mitchell and the Mayfield girl. The captain seemed concerned, the big guy didn't seem to care much one way or another. The headwaiter got up and left. The big guy fitted a cigarette into a holder and a waiter popped a lighter at him as if he had been waiting all evening for the opportunity. The big guy thanked him without looking up.

My drink came and I grabbed it and drank. The music stopped and stayed stopped. The couples divided and strolled back to their tables. Larry Mitchell still had hold of Betty. He was still grinning. Then he began to pull her close. He put his hand behind her head. She tried to shake him off. He pulled harder and pushed his flushed face down on hers. She struggled but he was too strong for her. He chewed her face some more. She kicked him. He jerked his head up, annoyed.

'Let go of me, you drunken slob,' she said breathlessly but very distinctly.

His face got a nasty look. He grabbed her arms hard enough to bruise her and slowly using his strength he pulled her tight against his body and held her there. People looked hard, but nobody moved.

'Whassa matta, baby, you no love poppa no more?' he inquired loudly and thickly.

I didn't see what she did to him with her knee but I could guess and it hurt him. He pushed her away and his face went savage. Then he hauled off and slapped her across the mouth, forehand and backhand. The red showed on her skin at once. She stood quite still. Then in a voice the whole joint could hear she said clearly and slowly:

'Next time you do that, Mr Mitchell – be sure to wear a bullet-proof vest.'

She turned and walked away. He just stood there. His face had gone glistening white – whether from pain or rage I couldn't tell. The headwaiter walked softly up to him and murmured something with an inquiring lift of the eyebrow.

Mitchell brought his eyes down and looked at the man. Then without a word he walked right through him and the headwaiter had to stagger out of his way. Mitchell followed Betty, and on the way he bumped a man in a chair and didn't stop to apologize. Betty was sitting down now at a table against the glass wall right next to the big dark guy in the dinner jacket. He looked at her. He looked at Mitchell. He took his cigarette holder out of his mouth and looked at that. His face was quite expressionless.

Mitchell reached the table. 'You hurt me, sweetness,' he said thickly but loudly. 'I'm a bad man to hurt. Catch on? Very bad. Want to apologize?'

She stood up, jerked a wrap off the back of the chair and faced him.

'Shall I pay the check, Mr Mitchell – or will you pay it with what you borrowed from me?'

His hand went back for another swing at her face. She didn't move. The guy at the next table did. He came up on his feet in one smooth movement and grabbed Mitchell's wrist.

'Take it easy, Larry. You've got a skin full.' His voice was cool, almost amused.

Mitchell jerked his wrist loose and spun around. 'Stay out of this, Brandon.'

'Delighted, old man. I'm not in it. But you'd better not slug the lady again. They don't often throw people out of here – but it could happen.'

Mitchell laughed angrily. 'Why don't you go spit in your hat, mister?'

The big man said softly, 'Take it easy, Larry, I said. I won't say it again.'

Mitchell glared at him. 'Okay, see you later,' he said in a sulky voice. He started off and stopped. 'Much later,' he added, half turning. Then he went out – unsteadily but quickly, looking at nothing.

Brandon just stood there. The girl just stood there. She looked uncertain about what to do next.

She looked at him. He looked at her. He smiled, just polite and easy-going, no come on. She didn't smile back.

'Anything I could do?' he asked. 'Drop you anywhere?' Then he half turned his head. 'Oh, Carl.'

The headwaiter came up to him quickly.

'No check,' Brandon said. 'You know, in the circumstances —'

'Please,' the girl said sharply. 'I don't want other people paying my bills.'

He shook his head slowly. 'Custom of the house,' he said. 'Nothing to do with me personally. But may I send you a drink?'

She looked at him some more. He had what it took all right. 'Send?' she asked.

He smiled politely. 'Well, bring then – if you care to sit down.'

And this time he pulled out the chair at his own table. And she sat down. And at that moment, not a second before, the headwaiter signalled the orchestra and they began to play another number.

Mr Clark Brandon seemed to be the sort of man who got what he wanted without raising his voice.

After a while my club sandwich came. It was nothing to brag about, but eatable. I ate it. I stuck around for half an hour. Brandon and the girl seemed to be doing all right. They were both quiet. After a while they danced. Then I left and sat in the car outside and smoked. She could have seen me although she didn't show it. I knew Mitchell hadn't. He had turned too quickly up the stairs, he had been too mad to see anything.

About ten-thirty Brandon came out with her and they got into the Cadillac convertible with the top down. I followed it away without trying to hide because the way they went would be the way anybody would go back to the downtown part of Esmeralda. Where they went was to the Casa del Poniente, and Brandon drove down the ramp to the garage.

There was only one thing more to find out. I parked in the side lot and went through the lobby to the house phones.

'Miss Mayfield, please. Betty Mayfield.'

'One moment, please' – slight pause – 'Oh yes, she just checked in. I'm ringing the room, sir.'

Another and much longer pause.

'I'm sorry, Miss Mayfield's room does not answer.'

I thanked her and hung up. I beat it out of there fast in case she and Brandon should get off at the lobby.

I went back to my rented chariot, and poked my way along the canyon through the fog to the Rancho Descansado. The cottage where the office was seemed to be locked up and empty. A single hazy light outside showed the position of a night bell. I groped my way up to 12c, tucked the car in the car port, and yawned my way into my room. It was cold and damp and miserable. Someone had been in and taken the striped cover off the day bed and removed the matching pillowcases.

I undressed and put my curly head on the pillow and went to sleep.

# Nine

A tapping sound awoke me. It was very light but it was also persistent. I had the feeling that it had been going on a long time and that it had very gradually penetrated my sleep. I rolled over and listened. Somebody tried the door and then the tapping started again. I glanced at my wrist watch. The faint phosphorescence showed it was past three o'clock. I got up on my feet and moved over to my suitcase and reached down into it for the gun. I went over to the door and opened it a crack.

A dark figure in slacks stood there. Some kind of windbreaker also. And a dark scarf knotted around the head. It was a woman.

'What do you want?'

'Let me in – quickly. Don't put any light on.'

So it was Betty Mayfield. I pulled the door back and she slid in like a wisp of the fog. I shut the door. I reached for my bathrobe and pulled it on.

'Anybody else outside?' I asked. 'There's nobody next door.'

'No. I'm alone.' She leaned against the wall and breathed quickly. I fumbled my pen flash out of my coat and poked a small beam around and found the heater switch. I shone the little light on her face. She blinked away from it and raised a hand. I put the light down on the floor and trailed it over to the windows and shut them both and lowered and turned the blind. Then I went back and switched on the lamp.

She let out a gasp, then said nothing. She was still leaning against the wall. She looked as if she needed a drink. I went out to the kitchenette and poured some whisky into a glass and carried it to her. She waved it away, then changed her mind and grabbed the glass and emptied it.

I sat down and lit a cigarette, the always mechanical reaction that gets so boring when someone else does it. Then I just sat there and looked at her and waited.

Our eyes met across great gulfs of nothing. After a while she reached slowly into the slanted pocket of the windbreaker and pulled out the gun.

'Oh no,' I said. 'Not that again.'

She looked down at the gun. Her lip twitched. She wasn't pointing it anywhere. She pushed herself away from the wall and crossed to lay the gun down at my elbow.

'I've seen it,' I said. 'We're old friends. Last time I saw it Mitchell had it. So?'

'That's why I knocked you out. I was afraid he would shoot you.'

'That would have fouled up all his plans – whatever his plans were.'

'Well, I couldn't be sure. I'm sorry. Sorry I hit you.'

'Thanks for the ice cubes,' I said.

'Aren't you going to look at the gun?'

'I have looked at it.'

'I walked all the way over here from the Casa. I'm staying there now. I – I moved in this afternoon.'

'I know. You took a taxi to the Del Mar station to catch an evening train and then Mitchell picked you up there and drove you back. You had dinner together and danced and there was a little ill-feeling. A man named Clark Brandon took you back to the hotel in his convertible.'

She stared. 'I didn't see you there,' she said finally, in a voice that was thinking of other things.

'I was in the bar. While you were with Mitchell you were too busy getting your face slapped and telling him to wear a bullet-proof vest next time he came around. Then at Brandon's table you sat with your back to me. I left before you did and waited outside.'

'I'm beginning to think you *are* a detective,' she said quietly. Her eyes went to the gun again. 'He never gave it back to me,' she said. 'Of course I couldn't prove that.'

'That means you'd like to be able to.'

'It might help a little. It probably wouldn't help quite enough. Not when they found out about me. I guess you know what I'm talking about.'

'Sit down and stop grinding your teeth.'

She moved slowly to a chair and sat down on the edge and leaned forward. She stared at the floor.

'I know there's something to find out,' I said. 'Because Mitchell found it out. So I could find it out too – if I tried. Anyone could who knows there is something to find. I don't know at this moment. All I was hired to do was to keep in touch and report back.'

She looked up briefly. 'And you've done that?'

'I reported in,' I said after a pause. 'I'd lost contact at the time. I mentioned San Diego. He'd get that from the operator anyway.'

'You'd lost contact,' she repeated dryly. 'He must think a lot of you, whoever he is.' Then she bit her lip. 'I'm sorry. I didn't mean to say that. I'm trying to make up my mind about something.'

'Take your time,' I said. 'It's only twenty past three a.m.'

'Now *you're* sneering.'

I looked toward the wall heater. It didn't show a thing, but there seemed to be a lessening of the chill if no more. I decided I needed a drink. I went out to the kitchen and got it. I put it down, poured some more and came back.

She had a small imitation leather folder in her hand now. She showed it to me.

'I have $5,000 in American Express cheques in this – one hundred dollar size. How far would you go for five grand, Marlowe?'

I took a sip of whisky. I thought about it with a judicial expression. 'Assuming a normal rate of expenses, that would buy me full time for several months. That is, if I happened to be for sale.'

She tapped on the chair arm with the folder. I could see that her other hand was almost pulling her kneecap off.

'You're for sale all right,' she said. 'And this would be

merely a down payment. I can buy big. I've got more money than you ever dreamed of. My last husband was so rich that it was pitiful. I got a cool half million dollars out of him.'

She put a hard-boiled sneer on her face and gave me plenty of time to get used to it.

'I take it I wouldn't have to murder anybody?'

'You wouldn't have to murder anybody.'

'I don't like the way you say that.'

I looked sideways at the gun that I hadn't so far laid a finger on. She had walked over from the Casa in the middle of the night to bring it to me. I didn't have to touch it. I stared at it. I bent over and sniffed it. I still didn't have to touch it, but I knew I was going to.

'Who's wearing the bullet?' I asked her. The cold in the room had got into my blood. It ran ice water.

'Just one bullet? How did you know?'

I picked up the gun then. I slipped the magazine out, looked at it, slipped it back. It snapped home in the butt.

'Well, it could have been two,' I said. 'There are six in the magazine. This gun holds seven. You could jack one into the chamber and then add another to the magazine. Of course you could fire the whole supply and then put six in the magazine.'

'We're just talking, aren't we?' she said slowly. 'We don't quite want to say it in plain words.'

'All right. Where is he?'

'Lying across a chaise on the balcony of my room. All the rooms on that side have balconies. They have concrete walls across them, and the end walls – between the rooms or suites, that is – are slanted outwards. I guess a steeplejack or a mountain climber might get around one of the end walls, but not carrying a weight. I'm on the twelfth floor. There's nothing any higher but the penthouse floor.' She stopped and frowned, then made a sort of helpless gesture with the hand that had been squeezing her kneecap. 'This is going to sound a little corny,' she went on. 'He could only have got there through my room. And I didn't let him through my room.'

'But you're sure he's dead?'

'Quite sure. Quite dead. Stone cold dead. I don't know when it happened. I didn't hear a sound. Something woke me all right. But it wasn't any sound like a shot. Anyhow he was already cold. So I don't know what woke me. And I didn't get up right away, I just lay there, thinking. I didn't go back to sleep, so after a while I put the light on and got up and walked around and smoked. Then I noticed the fog was gone and it was moonlight. Not down on the ground, but up there on my floor. I could still see fog down below when I went out on the balcony. It was damned cold. The stars seemed enormous. I stood there near the wall for quite a while before I even saw him. I guess that sounds pretty corny too – or pretty unlikely. I can't imagine the police taking it very seriously – even at first. And afterwards – well, just take it this way. I haven't a chance in a million – unless I get help.'

I stood up, tossed down what whisky was left in the glass and walked over to her.

'Let me tell you two or three things. First off, you're not taking this with normal reactions. You're not icy cool, but you're too cool. No panic, no hysteria, no nothing. You're fatalistic. Next, I heard the entire conversation between you and Mitchell this afternoon. I took those bulbs out' – I pointed to the wall heater – 'and used a stethoscope against the partition at the back. What Mitchell had on you was a knowledge of who you were, and that knowledge was something that if published could drive you into another switch of names and another dodge to some other town somewhere. You said you were the luckiest girl in the world because you were alive. Now a man is dead on your balcony, shot with your gun, and the man of course is Mitchell. Right?'

She nodded. 'Yes, it's Larry.'

'And you didn't kill him, you say. And the cops would hardly believe that even at first, you say. And later on not at all. My guess is that you've been there before.'

She was still looking up at me. She came slowly to her feet. Our faces were close, we stared hard into each other's eyes. It didn't mean a thing.

'Half a million dollars is a lot of money, Marlowe. You're not too hard to take. There are places in the world where you and I could have a beautiful life. In one of those tall apartment houses along the ocean front in Rio. I don't know how long it would last, but things can always be arranged, don't you think?'

I said: 'What a lot of different girls you are. Now you're making like a moll. When I first saw you, you were a quiet well-bred little lady. You didn't like dreamboats like Mitchell making a pitch at you. Then you bought yourself a packet of cigarettes and smoked one as if you hated it. Then you let him cuddle you – after you got down here. Then you tore your blouse at me ha, ha, ha, cynical as a Park Avenue pet after her butter and egg man goes home. Then you let me cuddle you. Then you cracked me on the head with a whisky bottle. Now you're talking about a beautiful life in Rio. Which one of you would have her head on the next pillow when I woke up in the morning?'

'Five thousand dollars down. And a lot more to come. The police wouldn't give you five toothpicks. If you think different, you have a telephone.'

'What do I do for the five grand?'

She let her breath out slowly as if a crisis was past. 'The hotel is built almost on the edge of the cliff. At the foot of the wall there's only a narrow walk, very narrow. Below the cliffs are rocks and the sea. It's almost high tide. My balcony hangs right over all that.'

I nodded. 'Are there fire stairs?'

'From the garage. They start just beside the basement elevator landing, which is up two or three steps from the garage floor. But it's a long hard climb.'

'For five grand I'd climb it in a diver's suit. Did you come out through the lobby?'

'Fire stairs. There's an all-night man in the garage but he was asleep in one of the cars.'

'You said Mitchell is lying on a chaise. Is there a lot of blood?'

She winced. 'I – I didn't notice. I suppose there must be.'

'You didn't notice? You went near enough to find out he was stone cold dead. Where was he shot?'

'Nowhere that I saw. It must have been under him.'

'Where was the gun?'

'It was lying on the floor of the porch – beside his hand.'

'Which hand?'

She widened her eyes slightly. 'Does it matter? I don't know which hand. He's sort of lying across the chaise with his head hanging on one side and his legs on the other. Do we have to keep on talking about it?'

'All right,' I said. 'I don't know a damn' thing about the tides and currents around here. He might wash up on the beach tomorrow and he might not show up for two weeks. Assuming, of course, we bring it off. If it's a long time they may not even find out he was shot. Then I guess there's some possibility that he won't be found at all. Not much, but some. There are barracuda in these waters, and other things.'

'You certainly do a thorough job of making it revolting,' she said.

'Well, I had a running start. Also I was thinking if there was any chance of suicide. Then we'd have to put the gun back. He was left-handed, you know. That's why I wanted to know which hand.'

'Oh. Yes, he was left-handed. You're right. But not suicide. Not that smirking, self-satisfied gentleman.'

'Sometimes a man kills the dearest thing he loves, they say. Couldn't it be himself?'

'Not this character,' she said briefly and finally. 'If we are very lucky, they will probably think he fell off the balcony. God knows he was drunk enough. And by that time I'll be in South America. My passport is still valid.'

'In what name is your passport?'

She reached out and drew her fingertips down my cheek. 'You'll know all about me soon enough. Don't be impatient. You'll know all the intimate things about me. Can't you wait a little?'

'Yeah. Start getting intimate with those American Express cheques. We have another hour or two of darkness and more than that of fog. You play with the cheques while I get dressed.'

I reached into my jacket and gave her a fountain pen. She sat down near the light and began to sign them with the second signature. Her tongue peeped out between her teeth. She wrote slowly and carefully. The name she wrote was Elizabeth Mayfield.

So the switch of names had been planned before she left Washington.

While I dressed I wondered if she was really foolish enough to think I'd help her dispose of a body.

I carried the glasses out to the kitchenette and scooped the gun up on the way. I let the swing door close and slipped the gun and the magazine into the tray under the broiler of the stove. I rinsed out the glasses and wiped them off. I went back into the living-room and threw my clothes on. She didn't even look at me.

She went on signing the cheques. When she had finished, I took the folder of cheques and flipped them over one by one, checking the signatures. The big money meant nothing to me. I shoved the folder into my pocket, put the lamp out and moved to the door. I opened it and she was beside me. She was close beside me.

'Sneak out,' I said. 'I'll pick you up on the highway just above where the fence ends.'

She faced me and leaned a little towards me. 'Can I trust you?' she asked softly.

'Up to a point.'

'You're honest at least. What happens if we don't get away with it? If somebody reported a shot, if he has been found, if we walk in on that and the place is full of policemen?'

I just stood there with my eyes on her face and didn't answer her.

'Just let me guess,' she said very softly and slowly. 'You'll sell me out fast. And you won't have any five thousand dollars.

534

Those cheques will be an old newspaper. You won't dare cash a single one of them.'

I still didn't say anything.

'You son of a bitch.' She didn't raise her voice even a semitone. 'Why did I ever come to you?'

I took her face between my hands and kissed her on the lips. She pulled away.

'Not for that,' she said. 'Certainly not for that. And one more small point. It's terribly small and unimportant, I know. I've had to learn that. From expert teachers. Long, hard, painful lessons and a lot of them. It just happens that I really didn't kill him.'

'Maybe I believe you.'

'Don't bother to try,' she said. 'Nobody else will.'

She turned and slid along the porch and down the steps. She flitted off through the trees. In thirty feet the fog hid her.

I locked up and got into the rent car and drove it down the silent driveway past the closed office with the light over the night bell. The whole place was hard asleep, but trucks were rumbling up through the canyon with building materials and oil and the big closed-up jobs with and without trailers, full of anything and everything that a town needs to live on. The fog lights were on and the trucks were slow and heavy up the hill.

Fifty yards beyond the gate she stepped out of the shadows at the end of the fence and climbed in. I switched on my headlights. Somewhere out on the water a foghorn was moaning. Upstairs in the clear reaches of the sky a formation of jets from North Island went over with a whine and a whoosh and a bang of the shock wave and were gone in less time than it took me to pull the lighter out of the dash and light a cigarette.

The girl sat motionless beside me, looking straight ahead and not speaking. She wasn't seeing the fog or the back of a truck we were coming up behind. She wasn't seeing anything. She was just sitting there frozen in one position, stony with despair, like somebody on the way to be hanged.

Either that or she was the best little scene stealer I had come across in a long, long time.

# Ten

The Casa del Poniente was set on the edge of the cliffs in about seven acres of lawn and flower beds, with a central patio on the sheltered side, tables set out behind a glass screen, and a trellised walk leading through the middle of it to an entrance. There was a bar on one side, a coffee shop on the other, and at each end of the building black-top parking lots partly hidden behind six-foot hedges of flowering shrubs. The parking lots had cars in them. Not everyone bothered to use the basement garage, although the damp salt air down there is hard on chromium.

I parked in a spot near the garage ramp and the sound of the ocean was very close and you could feel the drifting spray and smell it and taste it. We got out and moved over to the garage entrance. A narrow raised walk edged the ramp. A sign hung midway of the entrance said: Descend in Low Gear. Sound Horn. The girl grabbed me by the arm and stopped me.

'I'm going in by the lobby. I'm too tired to climb the stairs.'

'Okay. No law against it. What's the room number?'

'Twelve twenty-four. What do we get if we're caught?'

'Caught doing what?'

'You know what. Putting – putting it over the balcony wall. Or somewhere.'

'I'd get staked out on an anthill. I don't know about you. Depends what else they have on you.'

'How can you talk like that before breakfast?'

She turned and walked away quickly. I started down the ramp. It curved as they all do and then I could see a glassed-in cubbyhole of an office with a hanging light in it. A little farther down and I could see that it was empty. I listened for sounds of somebody doing a little work on a car, water in a wash rack, steps, whistling, any little noise to indicate where the night man was and what he was doing. In a basement garage you can hear a very small noise indeed. I heard nothing.

I went on down and was almost level with the upper end of the office. Now by stooping I could see the shallow steps up into the basement elevator lobby. There was a door marked: To Elevator. It had glass panels and I could see light beyond it, but little else.

I took three more steps and froze. The night man was looking right at me. He was in a big Packard sedan in the back seat. The light shone on his face and he wore glasses and the light shone hard on the glasses. He was leaning back comfortably in the corner of the car. I stood there and waited for him to move. He didn't move. His head was against the car cushions. His mouth was open. I had to know why he didn't move. He might be just pretending to be asleep until I got out of sight. When that happened he would beat it across to the phone and call the office.

Then I thought that was silly. He wouldn't have come on the job until evening and he couldn't know all the guests by sight. The sidewalk that bordered the ramp was there to walk on. It was almost four a.m. In an hour or so it would begin to get light. No hotel prowler would come around that late.

I walked straight over to the Packard and looked in on him. The car was shut up tight, all windows. The man didn't move. I reached for the door handle and tried to open the door without noise. He still didn't move. He looked like a very light-coloured man. He also looked asleep and I could hear him snoring even before I got the door open. Then I got it full in the face – the honeyed reek of well-cured marijuana. The guy was out of circulation, he was in the valley of peace, where time is slowed to a standstill, where the world is all colours and music. And in a couple of hours from now he wouldn't have a job, even if the cops didn't grab him and toss him into the deep freeze.

I shut the car door again and crossed to the glass-panelled door. I went through into a small, bare elevator lobby with a concrete floor and two blank elevator doors and beside them, opening on a heavy door closer, the fire stairs. I pulled that open and started up. I went slowly. Twelve storeys and a basement take a lot of stairs. I counted the fire doors as I passed them because they were not numbered. They were heavy and solid and grey like the concrete of the steps. I was sweating and out of breath when I pulled open the door to the twelfth corridor. I prowled along to Room 1224 and tried the knob. It was locked, but almost at once the door was opened, as if she had been waiting just behind it. I went in past her and flopped into a chair and waited to get some breath back. It was a big, airy room with french windows opening on a balcony. The double bed had been slept in or arranged to look that way. Odds and ends of clothing on chairs, toilet articles on the dresser, luggage. It looked about twenty bucks a day, single.

She turned the night latch in the door. 'Have any trouble?'

'The night man was junked to the eyes. Harmless as a kitten.' I heaved myself out of the chair and started across to the french doors.

'Wait!' she said sharply. I looked back at her. 'It's no use,' she said. 'Nobody could do a thing like that.'

I stood there and waited.

'I'd rather call the police,' she said. 'Whatever it means for me.'

'That's a bright idea,' I said. 'Why ever didn't we think of it before?'

'You'd better leave,' she said. 'There's no need for you to be mixed up in it.'

I didn't say anything. I watched her eyes. She could hardly keep them open. It was either delayed shock or some kind of dope. I didn't know which.

'I swallowed two sleeping pills,' she said, reading my mind. 'I just can't take any more trouble tonight. Go away from here. Please. When I wake I'll call room service. When the waiter comes I'll get him out on the balcony somehow and he'll find – whatever he'll find. And I won't know a damn' thing about it.' Her tongue was getting thick. She shook herself and rubbed hard against her temples. 'I'm sorry about the money. You'll have to give it back to me, won't you?'

I went over close to her. 'Because if I don't you'll tell them the whole story?'

'I'll have to,' she said drowsily. 'How can I help it? They'll get it out of me. I'm – I'm too tired to fight any more.'

I took hold of her arm and shook her. Her head wobbled. 'Quite sure you only took two capsules?'

She blinked her eyes open. 'Yes. I never take more than two.'

'Then listen. I'm going out there and have a look at him. Then I'm going back to the Rancho. I'm going to keep your money. Also I have your gun. Maybe it can't be traced to me but— Wake up! Listen to me!' Her head was rolling sideways again. She jerked straight and her eyes widened, but they looked dull and withdrawn. 'Listen. If it can't be traced to you, it certainly can't be traced to me. I'm working for a lawyer and my assignment is you. The travellers' cheques and the gun will go right where they belong. And your story to the cops won't be worth a wooden nickel. All it will do is to help to hang you. Understand that?'

'Ye-es,' she said. 'And I don't g-give a damn.'

'That's not you talking. It's the sleeping medicine.'

She sagged forward and I caught her and steered her over to the bed. She flopped on it any old way. I pulled her shoes off and spread a blanket over her and tucked her in. She was asleep at once. She began to snore. I went into the bathroom and groped around and found a bottle of nembutal on the shelf. It was almost full. It had a prescription number and a date on it. The date was a month old, the drugstore was in Baltimore. I dumped the yellow capsules out into my palm and counted them. There were forty-seven and they almost filled the bottle. When they take them to kill themselves, they take them all – except what they spill, and they nearly always spill some. I put the pills back in the bottle and put the bottle in my pocket.

I went back and looked at her again. The room was cold. I turned the radiator on, not too much. And finally at long last I opened the french doors and went out on the balcony. It was as cold as hell out there. The balcony was about twelve by fourteen feet, with a thirty-inch wall across the front and a low iron railing sprouting out of that. You could jump off easy enough, but you couldn't possibly fall off accidentally. There were two aluminium patio chaises with padded cushions, two arm-chairs of the same type. The dividing wall to the left stuck out the way she had told me. I didn't think even a steeplejack could get around the projection without climbing tackle. The wall at the other end rose sheer to the edge of what must be one of the penthouse terraces.

Nobody was dead on either of the chaises, nor on the floor of the balcony, nor anywhere at all. I examined them for traces of blood. No blood. No blood on the balcony. I went along the safety wall. No blood. No signs of anything having been heaved over. I stood against the wall and held onto the metal railing and leaned out as far as I could lean. I looked straight down the face of the wall to the ground. Shrubs grew close to it, then a narrow strip of lawn, then a flatstone footpath, then another strip of lawn and then a heavy fence with more shrubs growing against that. I estimated the distance. At that height it wasn't easy, but it must have been at least thirty-five feet. Beyond the fence the sea creamed on some half-submerged rocks.

Larry Mitchell was about half an inch taller than I was but weighed about fifteen pounds less, at a rough guess. The man wasn't born who could heave a hundred and seventy-five pound body over that railing and far enough out to fall into the ocean. It was barely possible that a girl wouldn't realize that, just barely possible, about one-tenth of one per cent possible.

I opened the french door and went through and shut it and crossed to stand beside the bed. She was still sound asleep. She was still snoring. I touched her cheek with the back of my hand. It was moist. She moved a little and mumbled. Then she sighed and settled her head into the pillow. No stertorous breathing, no deep stupor, no coma, and therefore no overdose.

She had told me the truth about one thing, and about damned little else.

I found her bag in the top drawer of the dresser. It had a zipper pocket at the back. I put her folder of travellers' cheques in it and looked through it for information. There was some crisp folding money in the zipper pocket, a Santa Fe timetable, the folder her ticket had been in and the stub of the railroad ticket and the Pullman reservation. She had had Bedroom E on Car 19, Washington, DC, to San Diego, California. No letters, nothing to identify her. That would be locked up in the luggage. In the main part of the bag was what a woman carries, a lipstick, a compact, a change purse, some silver, and a few keys on a ring with a tiny bronze tiger hanging from it. A packet of cigarettes that seemed just about full but had been opened. A match book with one match used. Three handkerchiefs with no initials, a packet of emery boards, a cuticle knife, and some kind of eyebrow stuff, a comb in a leather case, a little round jar of nail polish, a tiny address book. I pounced on that. Blank, not used at all. Also in the bag were a pair of sun glasses with spangled rims in a case, no name on the case; a fountain pen, a small gold pencil, and that was all. I put the bag back where I had found it. I went over to the desk for a piece of hotel stationery and an envelope.

I used the hotel pen to write: 'Dear Betty: So sorry I couldn't stay dead. Will explain tomorrow. Larry.'

I sealed the note in the envelope, wrote *Miss Betty Mayfield* on it, and dropped it where it might be if it had been pushed under the door.

I opened the door, went out, shut the door, went back to the fire stairs, then said out loud: 'The hell with it,' and rang for the elevator. It didn't come. I rang again and kept on ringing. Finally it came up and a sleepy-eyed young Mexican opened the doors and yawned at me, then grinned apologetically. I grinned back and said nothing.

There was nobody at the desk, which faced the elevators. The Mexican parked himself in a chair and went back to sleep before I had taken six steps. Everybody was sleepy but

Marlowe. He works around the clock, and doesn't even collect.

I drove back to the Rancho Descansado, saw nobody awake there, looked longingly at the bed, but packed my suitcase – with Betty's gun in the bottom of it – put twelve bucks in an envelope and on the way out put that through the slot in the office door, with my room key.

I drove to San Diego, turned the rent car in, and ate breakfast at a joint across from the station. At seven-fifteen I caught the two-car diesel job that makes the run to LA nonstop and pulls in at exactly ten a.m.

I rode home in a taxi and shaved and showered and ate a second breakfast and glanced through the morning paper. It was near on eleven o'clock when I called the office of Mr Clyde Umney, the lawyer.

He answered himself. Maybe Miss Vermilyea hadn't got up yet.

'This is Marlowe. I'm home. Can I drop around?'

'Did you find her?'

'Yeah. Did you call Washington?'

'Where is she?'

'I'd like to tell you in person. Did you call Washington?'

'I'd like your information first. I have a very busy day ahead.' His voice was brittle and lacked charm.

'I'll be there in half an hour.' I hung up fast and called the place where my Olds was.

# Eleven

There are almost too many offices like Clyde Umney's office. It was panelled in squares of combed plywood set at right angles one to the other to make a checker-board effect. The lighting was indirect, the carpeting wall to wall, the furniture blond, the chairs comfortable, and the fees probably exorbitant. The metal window frames opened outwards and there was a small but neat parking lot behind the building, and every slot in it had a name painted on a white board. For some reason Clyde Umney's stall was vacant, so I used it. Maybe he had a chauffeur drive him to his office. The building was four storeys high, very new, and occupied entirely by doctors and lawyers.

When I entered, Miss Vermilyea was just fixing herself for a hard day's work by touching up her platinum blonde coiffure. I thought she looked a little the worse for wear. She put away her hand mirror and fed herself a cigarette.

'Well, well. Mr Hard Guy in person. To what may we attribute this honour?'

'Umney's expecting me.'

'*Mister* Umney to you, buster.'

'Boydie-boy to you, sister.'

She got raging in an instant. 'Don't call me "sister", you cheap gumshoe!'

'Then don't call me buster, you very expensive secretary. What are you doing tonight? And don't tell me you're going out with four sailors again.'

The skin around her eyes turned whiter. Her hand crisped into a claw around a paperweight. She just didn't heave it at me. 'You son of a bitch!' she said somewhat pointedly. Then she flipped a switch on her talk box and said to the voice: 'Mr Marlowe is here, Mr Umney.'

Then she leaned back and gave me the look. 'I've got

friends who could cut you down so small you'd need a step-ladder to put your shoes on.'

'Somebody did a lot of hard work on that one,' I said. 'But hard work's no substitute for talent.'

Suddenly we both burst out laughing. The door opened and Umney stuck his face out. He gestured me in with his chin, but his eyes were on the platinum girl.

I went in and after a moment he closed the door and went behind his enormous semi-circular desk, with a green leather top and just piles and piles of important documents on it. He was a dapper man, very carefully dressed, too short in the legs, too long in the nose, too sparse in the hair. He had limpid brown eyes which, for a lawyer, looked very trustful.

'You making a pass at my secretary?' he asked me in a voice that was anything but limpid.

'Nope. We were just exchanging pleasantries.'

I sat down in the customer's chair and looked at him with something approaching politeness.

'She looked pretty mad to me.' He squatted in his executive-vice-president-type chair and made his face tough.

'She's booked up for three weeks,' I said. 'I couldn't wait that long.'

'Just watch your step, Marlowe. Lay off. She's private property. She wouldn't give you the time of day. Besides being a lovely piece of female humanity, she's as smart as a whip.'

'You mean she can type and take dictation as well?'

'As well as what?' He reddened suddenly. 'I've taken enough lip from you. Just watch your step, very carefully. I have enough influence around this town to hang a red light on you. Now let me have your report and make it short and to the point.'

'You talk to Washington yet?'

'Never mind what I did or didn't do. I want your report as of right now. The rest is my business. What's the present location of the King girl?' He reached for a nice sharp pencil and a nice clean pad. Then he dropped the pencil and poured himself a glass of water from a black and silver thermos jug.

'Let's trade,' I said. 'You tell me why you want her found and I'll tell you where she is.'

'You're my employee,' he snapped. 'I don't have to give you any information whatsoever.' He was still tough but beginning to shred a little around the edge.

'I'm your employee if I want to be, Mr Umney. No cheque has been cashed, no agreement has been made.'

'You accepted the assignment. You took an advance.'

'Miss Vermilyea gave me a cheque for $250 as an advance, and another cheque for $200 for expenses. But I didn't bank them. Here they are.' I took the two cheques out of my pocketbook and laid them on the desk in front of him. 'Better keep them until you make up your mind whether you want an investigator or a yes man, and until I make up my mind whether I was offered a job or was being suckered into a situation I knew nothing about.'

He looked down at the cheques. He wasn't happy. 'You've already had expenses,' he said slowly.

'That's all right, Mr Umney. I had a few dollars saved up – and the expenses are deductible. Also I've had fun.'

'You're pretty stubborn, Marlowe.'

'I guess, but I have to be in my business. Otherwise I wouldn't be in business. I told you the girl was being black-mailed. Your Washington friends must know why. If she's a crook, fine. But I have to get told. And I have an offer you can't match.'

'For more money you are willing to switch sides?' he asked angrily. 'That would be unethical.'

I laughed. 'So I've got ethics now. Maybe we're getting somewhere.'

He took a cigarette out of a box and lit it with a pot-bellied lighter that matched the thermos and the pen set.

'I still don't like your attitude,' he growled. 'Yesterday I didn't know any more than you did. I took it for granted that a reputable Washington law firm would not ask me to do anything against legal ethics. Since the girl could have been arrested without difficulty, I assumed it was some sort of domestic mix-up, a runaway wife or daughter, or an important but reluctant witness who was already outside the jurisdiction where she could be subpoenaed. That was just guessing. This morning things are a little different.'

He got up and walked to the big window and turned the slats of the blinds enough to keep the sun off his desk. He stood there smoking, looking out, then came back to the desk and sat down again.

'This morning,' he went on slowly and with a judicious frown, 'I talked to my Washington associates and I am informed that the girl was confidential secretary to a rich and important man – I'm not told his name – and that she absconded with certain important and dangerous papers from his private files. Papers that might be damaging to him if made public. I'm not told in what way. Perhaps he has been fudging his tax returns. You never know these days.'

'She took this stuff to blackmail him?'

Umney nodded. 'That is the natural assumption. They had no value to her otherwise. The client, Mr A. we will call him, didn't realize that the girl had left until she was already in another state. He then checked his files and found that some of his material was gone. He was reluctant to go to the police. He expects the girl to go far enough away to feel safe and from that point to start negotiations with him for the return of the material at a heavy price. He wants to peg her down somewhere without her knowing it, walk in and catch her off balance and especially before she contacts some sharp lawyer, of whom I regret to say there are far too many, and with the sharp lawyer works out a scheme that would make her safe from prosecution. Now you tell me someone is blackmailing her. On what grounds?'

'If your story stood up, it could be because he is in a position to spoil her play,' I said. 'Maybe he knows something that could hang a pinch on her without opening up the other box of candy.'

'You say if the story stood up,' he snapped. 'What do you mean by that?'

'It's as full of holes as a sink strainer. You're being fed a line, Mr Umney. Where would a man keep material like the important papers you mention – if he had to keep them at all? Certainly not where a secretary could get them. And unless he missed the stuff before she left, how did he get her followed to the train? Next, although she took a ticket to California, she could have got off anywhere. Therefore she would have to be watched on the train, and if that was done, why did someone need me to pick her up here? Next, this, as you tell it, would be a job for a large agency with nationwide connections. It would be idiotic to take a chance on one man. I lost her yesterday. I could lose her again. It takes a bare minimum of six operatives to do a standard tail job in any sizable place, and that's just what I mean – a bare minimum. In a really big city you'd need a dozen. An operative has to eat and sleep and change his shirt. If he's tailing by car he has to be able to drop a man while he finds a place to park. Department stores and hotels may have half a dozen entrances. But all this girl does is hang around Union Station here for three hours in full view of everybody. And all your friends in Washington do is mail you a picture, call you on the phone, and then go back to watching television.'

'Very clear,' he said. 'Anything else?' His face was deadpan now.

'A little. Why – if she didn't expect to be followed – would she change her name? Why if she did expect to be followed would she make it so easy? I told you two other guys were working the same side of the street. One is a Kansas City private detective named Goble. He was in Esmeralda yesterday. He knew just where to go. Who told him? I had to follow her and bribe a taxi driver to use his R/T outfit to find out where her cab was going so that I wouldn't lose her. So why was I hired?'

'We'll come to that,' Umney said curtly. 'Who was the other party you say was working the same side of the street?'

'A playboy named Mitchell. He lives down there. He met the girl on the train. He made a reservation for her in Esmeralda.

They're just like that' – I held up two touching fingers – 'except that she hates his guts. He's got something on her and she is afraid of him. What he has on her is a knowledge of who she is, where she came from, what happened to her there, and why she is trying to hide under another name. I overheard enough to know that, but not enough to give me exact information.'

Umney said acidly: 'Of course the girl was covered on the train. Do you think you are dealing with idiots? You were nothing more than a decoy – to determine whether she had any associates. On your reputation – such as it is – I relied on you to grandstand just enough to let her get wise to you. I guess you know what an open shadow is.'

'Sure. One that deliberately lets the subject spot him, then shake him, so that another shadow can pick him up when he thinks he is safe.'

'You were it.' He grinned at me contemptuously. 'But you still haven't told me where she is.'

I didn't want to tell him, but I knew I'd have to. I had up to a point accepted the assignment, and giving him back his money was only a move to force some information out of him.

I reached across the desk and picked up the $250 cheque. 'I'll take this as payment in full, expenses included. She is registered as Miss Betty Mayfield at the Casa del Poniente in Esmeralda. She is loaded with money. But of course your expert organization must know all this already.'

I stood up. 'Thanks for the ride, Mr Umney.'

I went out and shut his door. Miss Vermilyea looked up from a magazine. I heard a faint muffled click from somewhere in her desk.

'I'm sorry I was rude to you,' I said. 'I didn't get enough sleep last night.'

'Forget it. It was a stand-off. With a little practice I might get to like you. You're kind of cute in a low-down sort of way.'

'Thanks,' I said and moved to the door. I wouldn't say she looked exactly wistful, but neither did she look as hard to get as a controlling interest in General Motors.

I turned back and closed the door.

'I guess it's not raining tonight, is it? There was something we might have discussed over a drink, if it had been a rainy night. And if you had not been too busy.'

She gave me a cool, amused look. 'Where?'

'That would be up to you.'

'Should I drop by your place?'

'It would be damn' nice of you. That Fleetwood might help my credit standing.'

'I wasn't exactly thinking of that.'

'Neither was I.'

'About six-thirty perhaps. And I'll take good care of my nylons.'

'I was hoping you would.'

Our glances locked. I went out quickly.

# Twelve

At half-past six the Fleetwood purred to the front door and I had it open when she came up the steps. She was hatless. She wore a flesh-coloured coat with the collar turned up against her platinum hair. She stood in the middle of the living-room and looked around casually. Then she slipped the coat off with a lithe movement and threw it on the davenport and sat down.

'I didn't really think you'd come,' I said.

'No. You're the shy type. You knew darned well I'd come. Scotch and soda, if you have it.'

'I have it.'

I brought the drinks and sat down beside her, but not close enough for it to mean anything. We touched glasses and drank.

'Would you care to go to Romanoffs for dinner?'

'And then what?'

'Where do you live?'

'West Los Angeles. A house on a quiet old street. It happens to belong to me. I asked you, and then what, remember?'

'That would be up to you, naturally.'

'I thought you were a tough guy. You mean I don't have to pay for my dinner?'

'I ought to slap your face for that crack.'

She laughed suddenly and stared at me over the edge of her glass.

'Consider it slapped. We had each other a bit wrong. Romanoffs could wait a while, couldn't it?'

'We could try West Los Angeles first.'

'Why not here?'

'I guess this will make you walk out on me. I had a dream here once, a year and a half ago. There's still a shred of it left. I'd like it to stay in charge.'

She stood up quickly and grabbed her coat. I managed to help her on with it.

'I'm sorry,' I said, 'I should have told you that before.'

She swung around with her face close to mine, but I didn't touch her.

'Sorry that you had a dream and kept it alive? I've had dreams too, but mine died. I didn't have the courage to keep them alive.'

'It's not quite like that. There was a woman. She was rich. She thought she wanted to marry me. It wouldn't have worked. I'll probably never see her again. But I remember.'

'Let's go,' she said quietly. 'And let's leave the memory in charge. I only wish I had one worth remembering.'

On the way down to the Cadillac I didn't touch her either. She drove beautifully. When a woman is a really good driver she is just about perfect.

# Thirteen

The house was on a curving, quiet street between San Vincente and Sunset Boulevard. It was set far back and had a long driveway and the entrance to the house was at the back with a small patio in front of it. She unlocked the door and switched on lights all over the house and then disappeared without a word. The living-room had nicely mixed furniture and a feeling of comfort. I stood waiting until she came back with two tall glasses. She had taken her coat off.

'You've been married, of course,' I said.

'It didn't take. I got this house and some money out of it, but I wasn't gunning for anything. He was a nice guy, but we were wrong for each other. He's dead now – plane crash – he was a jet pilot. Happens all the time. I know a place between here and San Diego that is full of girls who were married to jet pilots when they were alive.'

I took a single sip of my drink and put it down.

I lifted her glass out of her hand and put it down too.

'Remember yesterday morning when you told me to stop looking at your legs?'

'I seem to remember.'

'Try and stop me now.'

I took hold of her and she came into my arms without a word. I picked her up and carried her and somehow found the bedroom. I put her down on the bed. I peeled her skirt up until I could see the white thighs above her long, beautiful nylon-clad legs. Suddenly she reached up and pulled my head down against her breast.

'Beast! Could we have a little less light?'

I went to the door and switched the light off in the room. There was still a glow from the hall. When I turned she was standing by the bed as naked as Aphrodite fresh from the Aegean. She stood there proudly and without either shame or enticement.

'Damn it,' I said. 'When I was young you could undress a girl slowly. Nowadays she's in the bed while you're struggling with your collar button.'

'Well, struggle with your goddamn collar button.'

She pulled the bed-covers back and lay on the bed shamelessly nude. She was just a beautiful naked woman completely unashamed of being what she was.

'Satisfied with my legs?' she asked.

I didn't answer.

'Yesterday morning,' she said, half dreamily, 'I said there was something about you I liked – you didn't paw – and something I didn't like. Know what it was?'

'No.'

'That you didn't make me do this then.'

'Your manner hardly encouraged it.'

'You're supposed to be a detective. Please put out all the lights now.'

Then very soon in the dark she was saying, Darling, darling, darling in that very special tone of voice a woman uses only in those special moments. Then a slow, gentle relaxing, a peace, a quietness.

'Still satisfied with my legs?' she asked dreamily.

'No man ever would be. They would haunt him, no matter how many times he made love to you.'

'You bastard. You complete bastard. Come closer.'

She put her head on my shoulder and we were very close now.

'I don't love you,' she said.

'Why would you? But let's not be cynical about it. There are sublime moments – even if they are only moments.'

I felt her tight and warm against me. Her body surged with vitality. Her beautiful arms held me tight.

And again in the darkness that muted cry, and then again the slow quiet peace.

'I hate you,' she said with her mouth against mine. 'Not

for this, but because perfection never comes twice and with us it came too soon. And I'll never see you again and I don't want to. It would have to be for ever or not at all.'

'And you acted like a hard-boiled pick-up who had seen too much of the wrong side of life.'

'So did you. And we were both wrong. And it's useless. Kiss me harder.'

Suddenly she was gone from the bed almost without sound or movement.

After a little while the light went on in the hallway and she stood in the door in a long wrapper.

'Goodbye,' she said calmly. 'I'm calling a taxi for you. Wait out in front for it. You won't see me again.'

'What about Umney?'

'A poor frightened jerk. He needs someone to bolster his ego, to give him a feeling of power and conquest. I give it to him. A woman's body is not so sacred that it can't be used – especially when she has already failed at love.'

She disappeared. I got up and put my clothes on and listened before I went out. I heard nothing. I called out, but there was no answer. When I reached the sidewalk in front of the house the taxi was just pulling up. I looked back. The house seemed completely dark.

No one lived there. It was all a dream. Except that someone had called the taxi. I got into it and was driven home.

# Fourteen

I left Los Angeles and hit the super-highway that now by-passed Oceanside. I had time to think.

From San Onofre to Oceanside were eighteen miles of divided six-lane super-highway dotted at intervals with the carcasses of wrecked, stripped, and abandoned cars tossed against the high bank to rust until they were hauled away. So I started thinking about why I was going back to Esmeralda. The case was all backwards and it wasn't my case anyway. Usually a PI gets a client who, for too little money, wants too much information. You get it or you don't, depending on circumstances. The same with your fee. But once in a while you get the information and too much else, including a story about a body on a balcony which wasn't there when you went to look. Common sense says go home and forget it, no money coming in. Common sense always speaks too late. Common sense is the guy who tells you you ought to have had your brakes relined last week before you smashed a front end this week. Common sense is the Monday morning quarterback who could have won the ball game if he had been on the team. But he never is. He's high up in the stands with a flask on his hip. Common sense is the little man in a grey suit who never makes a mistake in addition. But it's always somebody else's money he's adding up.

At the turn-off I dipped down into the canyon and ended up at the Rancho Descansado. Jack and Lucille were in their usual positions. I dropped my suitcase and leaned on the desk.

'Did I leave the right change?'

'Yes, thanks,' Jack said. 'And now you want the room back, I suppose.'

'If possible.'

'Why didn't you tell us you were a detective?'

'Now, what a question.' I grinned at him. 'Does a detective ever tell anyone he's a detective? You watch TV, don't you?'

'When I get a chance. Not too often here.'

'You can always tell a detective on TV. He never takes his hat off. What do you know about Larry Mitchell?'

'Nothing,' Jack said stiffly. 'He's a friend of Brandon's. Mr Brandon owns this place.'

Lucille said brightly: 'Did you find Joe Harms all right?'

'Yes, thanks.'

'And did you—?'

'Uh-huh.'

'Button the lip, kid,' Jack said tersely. He winked at me and pushed the key across the counter. 'Lucille has a dull life, Mr Marlowe. She's stuck here with me and a PBX. And an itty-bitty diamond ring – so small I was ashamed to give it to her. But what can a man do? If he loves a girl, he'd like it to show on her finger.'

Lucille held her left hand up and moved it around to get a flash from the little stone. 'I hate it,' she said. 'I hate it like I hate the sunshine and the summer and the bright stars and the full moon. That's how I hate it.'

I picked up the key and my suitcase and left them. A little more of that and I'd be falling in love with myself. I might even give myself a small, unpretentious diamond ring.

# Fifteen

The house phone at the Casa del Poniente got no reply from Room 1224. I walked over to the desk. A stiff-looking clerk was sorting letters. They are always sorting letters.

'Miss Mayfield is registered here, isn't she?' I asked.

He put a letter in a box before he answered me. 'Yes, sir. What name shall I say?'

'I know her room number. She doesn't answer. Have you seen her today?'

He gave me a little more of his attention, but I didn't really send him. 'I don't think so.' He glanced over his shoulder. 'Her key is out. Would you care to leave a message?'

'I'm a little worried. She wasn't well last night. She could be up there sick, not able to answer the phone. I'm a friend of hers. Marlowe's the name.'

He looked me over. His eyes were wise eyes. He went behind a screen in the direction of the cashier's office and spoke to somebody. He came back in a short time. He was smiling.

'I don't think Miss Mayfield is ill, Mr Marlowe. She ordered quite a substantial breakfast in her room. And lunch. She has had several telephone calls.'

'Thanks a lot,' I said. 'I'll leave a message. Just my name and that I'll call back later.'

'She might be out in the grounds or down on the beach,' he said. 'We have a warm beach, well sheltered by a breakwater.' He glanced at the clock behind him. 'If she is, she won't be there much longer. It's getting cool by now.'

'Thanks. I'll be back.'

The main part of the lobby was up three steps and through an arch. There were people in it just sitting, the dedicated hotel lounge sitters, usually elderly, usually rich, usually doing nothing but watching with hungry eyes. They spend their lives that way. Two old ladies with severe faces and purplish permanents were struggling with an enormous jigsaw puzzle set out on a specially built king size card table. Farther along there was a canasta game going – two women, two men. One of the women had enough ice on her to cool the Mojave Desert and enough make-up to paint a steam yacht. Both women had cigarettes in long holders. The men with them looked grey and tired, probably from signing cheques. Farther along, still sitting where they could look out through the glass, a young couple were holding hands. The girl had a diamond and emerald sparkler and a wedding ring which she kept touching with her fingertips. She looked a little dazed.

I went out through the bar and poked around in the gardens. I went along the path that threaded the cliff top and had no trouble picking out the spot I had looked down on the night before from Betty Mayfield's balcony. I could pick it out because of the sharp angle.

The bathing beach and small, curved breakwater were a hundred yards along. Steps led down to it from the cliff. People were lying around on the sand. Some in swim suits or trunks, some just sitting there on rugs. Kids ran around screaming. Betty Mayfield was not on the beach.

I went back into the hotel and sat in the lounge.

I sat and smoked. I went to the news-stand and bought an evening paper and looked through it and threw it away. I strolled by the desk. My note was still in box 1224. I went to the house phones and called Mr Mitchell. No answer. I'm sorry. Mr Mitchell does not answer his telephone.

A woman's voice spoke behind me: 'The clerk said you wanted to see me Mr Marlowe,' she said. 'Are you Mr Marlowe?'

She looked as fresh as a morning rose. She was wearing dark green slacks and saddle shoes and a green windbreaker over a white shirt with a loose Paisley scarf around that. A bandeau on her hair made a nice wind-blown effect.

The bell captain was hanging out his ear six feet away. I said:

'Miss Mayfield?'

'I'm Miss Mayfield.'

'I have the car outside. Do you have time to look at the property?'

She looked at her wrist watch. 'Ye-es, I guess so,' she said. 'I ought to change pretty soon, but – oh, all right.'

'This way, Miss Mayfield.'

She fell in beside me. We walked across the lobby. I was getting to feel quite at home there. Betty Mayfield glanced viciously at the two jigsaw puzzlers.

'I hate hotels,' she said. 'Come back here in fifteen years and you would find the same people sitting in the same chairs.'

'Yes, Miss Mayfield. Do you know anybody named Clyde Umney?'

She shook her head. 'Should I?'

'Helen Vermilyea? Ross Goble?'

She shook her head again.

'Want a drink?'

'Not now, thanks.'

We came out of the bar and went along the walk and I held the door of the Olds for her. I backed out of the slot and pointed it straight up Grand Street towards the hills. She slipped dark glasses with spangled rims on her nose. 'I found the travellers' cheques,' she said. 'You're a queer sort of detective.'

I reached in my pocket and held out her bottle of sleeping pills. 'I was a little scared last night,' I said. 'I counted these but I didn't know how many had been there to start with. You said you took two. I couldn't be sure you wouldn't rouse up enough to gulp a handful.'

She took the bottle and stuffed it into her windbreaker. 'I had quite a few drinks. Alcohol and barbiturates make a bad combination. I sort of passed out. It was nothing else.'

'I wasn't sure. It takes a minimum of thirty-five grains of that stuff to kill. Even then it takes several hours. I was in a tough spot. Your pulse and breathing seemed all right but maybe they wouldn't be later on. If I called a doctor, I might have to do a lot of talking. If you had taken an overdose, the homicide boys would be told, even if you snapped out of it. They investigate all suicide attempts. But if I guessed wrong, you wouldn't be riding with me today. And where would I be then?'

'It's a thought,' she said. 'I can't say I'm going to worry about it terribly. Who are these people you mentioned?'

'Clyde Umney's the lawyer who hired me to follow you – on instructions from a firm of attorneys in Washington, DC. Helen Vermilyea is his secretary. Ross Goble is a Kansas City private eye who says he is trying to find Mitchell.' I described him to her.

Her face turned stony. 'Mitchell? Why should he be interested in Larry?'

I stopped at the corner of Fourth and Grand for an old coot in a motorized wheel chair to make a left turn at four miles an hour. Esmeralda is full of the damn' things.

'Why should he be looking for Larry Mitchell?' she asked bitterly. 'Can't anybody leave anybody else alone?'

'Don't tell me anything,' I said. 'Just keep on asking me questions to which I don't know the answers. It's good for my inferiority complex. I told you I had no more job. So why am I here? That's easy. I'm groping for that five grand in travellers' cheques again.'

'Turn left at the next corner,' she said, 'and we can go up into the hills. There's a wonderful view from up there. And a lot of very fancy homes.'

'The hell with them,' I said.

'It's also very quiet up there.' She picked a cigarette out of the packet clipped to the dash and lit it.

'That's two in two days,' I said. 'You're hitting them hard. I counted your cigarettes last night too. And your matches. I went through your bag. I'm kind of snoopy when I get roped in on a phoney like that one. Especially when the client passes out and leaves me holding the baby.'

She turned her head to stare at me. 'It must have been the dope and the liquor,' she said. 'I must have been a little off base.'

'Over at the Rancho Descansado you were in great shape. You were hard as nails. We were going to take off for Rio and live in luxury. Apparently also in sin. All I had to do was get rid of the body. What a let-down! No body.'

She was still staring at me, but I had to watch my driving. I made a boulevard stop and a left turn. I went along another dead end street with old streetcar tracks still in the paving.

'Turn left up the hill at that sign. That's the high school down there.'

'Who fired the gun and what at?'

She pressed her temples with the heels of her hands. 'I guess *I* must have. I must have been crazy. Where is it?'

'The gun? It's safe. Just in case your dream came true, I might have to produce it.'

We were climbing now. I set the pointer to hold the Olds in third. She watched that with interest. She looked around her at the pale leather seats and the gadgets.

'How can you afford an expensive car like this? You don't make a lot of money, do you?'

'They're all expensive nowadays, even the cheap ones. Fellow might as well have one that can travel. I read somewhere that a dick should always have a plain, dark, inconspicuous car that nobody would notice. The guy had never been to LA. In LA to be conspicuous you would have to drive a flesh-pink Mercedes-Benz with a sun porch on the roof and three pretty girls sun-bathing.'

She giggled.

'Also,' I laboured the subject, 'it's good advertising. Maybe I dreamed I was going to Rio. I could sell it there for more than it set me back new. On a freighter it wouldn't cost too much to ferry.'

She sighed. 'Oh, stop teasing me about that. I don't feel funny today.'

'Seen your boy friend around?'

She sat very still. 'Larry?'

'You got others?'

'Well – you might have meant Clark Brandon, although I

hardly know him. Larry was pretty drunk last night. No – I haven't seen him. Perhaps he's sleeping it off.'

'Doesn't answer his phone.'

The road forked. One white line curved to the left. I kept straight on, for no particular reason. We passed some old Spanish houses built high on the slope and some very modern houses built downhill on the other side. The road passed these and made a wide turn to the right. The paving here looked new. The road ran out to a point of land and a turning circle. There were two big houses facing each other across the turning circle. They were loaded with glass brick and their seaward windows were green glass. The view was magnificent. I looked at it for all of three seconds. I stopped against the end kerb and cut the motor and sat. We were about a thousand feet up and the whole town was spread out in front of us like a forty-five degree air photo.

'He might be sick,' I said. 'He might have gone out. He might even be dead.'

'I told you—' She began to shake. I took the stub of the cigarette away from her and put it in the ash tray. I ran the car windows up and put an arm around her shoulders and pulled her head down on my shoulder. She was limp, unresisting: but she still shook.

'You're a comfortable man,' she said. 'But don't rush me.'

'There's a pint in the glove compartment. Want a snort?'

'Yes.'

I got it out and managed to pull the metal strip loose with one hand and my teeth. I held the bottle between my knees and got the cap off. I held it to her lips. She sucked some in and shuddered. I recapped the pint and put it away.

'I hate drinking from the bottle,' she said.

'Yeah. Unrefined. I'm not making love to you, Betty. I'm worried. Anything you want done?'

She was silent for a moment. Then her voice was steady, saying: 'Such as what? You can have those cheques back. They were yours. I gave them to you.'

'Nobody gives anybody five grand like that. It makes no

562

sense. That's why I came back down from LA. I drove up there early this morning. Nobody goes all gooey over a character like me and talks about having half a million dollars and offers me a trip to Rio and a nice home complete with all the luxuries. Nobody drunk or sober does that because she dreamed a dead man was lying out on her balcony and would I please hurry around and throw him off into the ocean. Just what did you expect me to do when I got there – hold your hand while you dreamed?'

She pulled away and leaned in the far corner of the car. 'All right, I'm a liar. I've always been a liar.'

I glanced at the rear view mirror. Some kind of a small, dark car had turned into the road behind and stopped. I couldn't see who or what was in it. Then it swung hard right against the kerbing and backed and made off the way it had come. Some fellow took the wrong road and saw it was a dead end.

'While I was on the way up those damn' fire stairs,' I went on, 'you swallowed your pills and then faked being awfully terribly sleepy and then after a while you actually did go to sleep – I think. Okay, I went out on the balcony. No stiff. No blood. If there had been, I might have managed to get him over the top of the wall. Hard work, but not impossible, if you know how to lift. But six trained elephants couldn't have thrown him far enough to land in the ocean. It's thirty-five feet to the fence and you'd have to throw him so far out that he would clear the fence. I figure an object as heavy as a man's body would have to be thrown a good fifty feet outwards to clear the fence.'

'I told you I was a liar.'

'But you didn't tell me why. Let's be serious. Suppose a man had been dead on your balcony. What would you expect me to do about it? Carry him down the fire stairs and get him into the car I had and drive off into the woods somewhere and bury him? You do have to take people into your confidence once in a while when bodies are lying around.'

'You took my money,' she said tonelessly. 'You played up to me.'

'That way I might find out who was crazy.'

'You found out. You should be satisfied.'

'I found out nothing – not even who you are.'

She got angry. 'I told you I was out of my mind,' she said in a rushing voice. 'Worry, fear, liquor, pills – why can't you leave me alone? I told you I'd give you back that money. What more do you want?'

'What do I do for it?'

'Just take it.' She was snapping at me now. 'That's all. Take it and go away. Far, far away.'

'I think you need a good lawyer.'

'That's a contradiction in terms,' she sneered. 'If he was good, he wouldn't be a lawyer.'

'Yeah. So you've had some painful experience along those lines. I'll find out in time, either from you or some other way. But I'm still being serious. You're in trouble. Apart from what happened to Mitchell, if anything, you're in enough trouble to justify hiring yourself a lawyer. You changed your name. So you had reasons. Mitchell was putting the bite on you. So *he* had reasons. A firm of Washington attorneys is looking for you. So *they* have reasons. And their client has reasons to have them looking for you.'

I stopped and looked at her as well as I could see her in the freshly darkening evening. Down below, the ocean was getting a lapis lazuli blue that somehow failed to remind me of Miss Vermilyea's eyes. A flock of seagulls went south in a fairly compact mass but it wasn't the kind of tight formation North Island is used to. The evening plane from LA came down the coast with its port and starboard lights showing, and then the winking light below the fuselage went on and it swung out to sea for a long, lazy turn into Lindbergh Field.

'So you're just a shill for a crooked lawyer,' she said nastily, and grabbed for another of my cigarettes.

'I don't think he's very crooked. He just tries too hard. But that's not the point. You can lose a few bucks to him without screaming. The point is something called privilege. A licensed investigator doesn't have it. A lawyer does, provided his concern is with the interests of a client who has retained him. If the lawyer hires an investigator to work in those interests, then the investigator has privilege. That's the only way he can get it.'

'You know what you can do with your privilege,' she said. 'Especially as it was a lawyer that hired you to spy on me.'

I took the cigarette away from her and puffed on it a couple of times and handed it back.

'It's all right, Betty. I'm no use to you. Forget I tried to be.'

'Nice words, but only because you think I'll pay you more to be of use to me. You're just another of them. I don't want your damn' cigarette either.' She threw it out of the window. 'Take me back to the hotel.'

I got out of the car and stamped on the cigarette. 'You don't do that in the California hills,' I told her. 'Not even out of season.' I got back into the car and turned the key and pushed the starter button. I backed away and made the turn and drove back up the curve to where the road divided. On the upper level where the solid white line curved away a small car was parked. The car was lightless. It could have been empty.

I swung the Olds hard the opposite way from the way I had come, and flicked my headlights on with the high beam. They swept the car as I turned. A hat went down over a face, but not quick enough to hide the glasses, the fat broad face, the out-jutting ears, of Mr Ross Goble of Kansas City.

The lights went on past and I drove down a long hill with lazy curves. I didn't know where it went except that all roads around there led to the ocean sooner or later. At the bottom there was a T-intersection. I swung to the right and after a few blocks of narrow street I hit the boulevard and made another right turn. I was now driving back towards the main part of Esmeralda.

She didn't speak again until I got to the hotel. She jumped out quickly when I stopped.

'If you'll wait here, I'll get the money.'

'We were tailed,' I said.

565

'What—?' She stopped dead, with her head half turned.

'Small car. You didn't notice him unless you saw my lights brush him as I made the turn at the top of the hill.'

'Who was it?' Her voice was tense.

'How would I know? He must have picked us up here, therefore he'll come back here. Could he be a cop?'

She looked back at me, motionless, frozen. She took a slow step, and then she rushed at me as if she was going to claw my face. She grabbed me by the arms and tried to shake me. Her breath came whistling.

'Get me out of here. Get me out of here, for the love of Christ. Anywhere. Hide me. Get me a little peace. Somewhere where I can't be followed, hounded, threatened. He swore he would do it to me. He'd follow me to the ends of the earth, to the remotest island of the Pacific—'

'To the crest of the highest mountain, to the heart of the loneliest desert,' I said. 'Somebody's been reading a rather old-fashioned book.'

She dropped her arms and let them hang limp at her side.

'You've got as much sympathy as a loan shark.'

'I'll take you nowhere,' I said. 'Whatever it is that's eating you, you're going to stay put and take it.'

I turned and got into the car. When I looked back, she was already half way to the bar entrance, walking with quick strides.

# Sixteen

If I had any sense, I would pick up my suitcase and go back home and forget all about her. By the time she made up her mind which part she was playing in which act of which play, it would probably be too late for me to do anything about it except maybe get pinched for loitering in the post office.

I waited and smoked a cigarette. Goble and his dirty little jaloppy ought to show up and slip into a parking lot almost any moment. He couldn't have picked us up anywhere else, and since he knew that much he couldn't have followed us for any reason except to find out where we went.

He didn't show. I finished the cigarette, dropped it overboard, and backed out. As I turned out of the driveway towards the town, I saw his car on the other side of the street, parked left hand to the kerb. I kept going, turned right at the boulevard and took it easy so he wouldn't blow a gasket trying to keep up. There was a restaurant about a mile along called The Epicure. It had a low roof, and a red brick wall to shield it from the street and it had a bar. The entrance was at the side. I parked and went in. It wasn't doing any business yet. The barkeep was chatting with the captain and the captain didn't even wear a dinner jacket. He had one of those high desks where they keep the reservation book. The book was open and had a list of names in it for later in the evening. But it was early now. I could have a table.

The dining-room was dim, candle-lit, divided by a low wall into two halves. It would have looked crowded with thirty people in it. The captain shoved me in a corner and lit my candle for me. I said I would have a double Gibson. A waiter came up and started to remove the place setting on the far side of the table. I told him to leave it, a friend might join me. I studied the menu, which was almost as large as the dining-room. I could have used a flashlight to read it, if I had been curious. This was about the dimmest joint I was ever in. You could be sitting at the next table from your mother and not recognize her.

The Gibson arrived. I could make out the shape of the glass and there seemed to be something in it. I tasted it and it wasn't too bad. At that moment Goble slid into the chair across from me. In so far as I could see him at all, he looked about the same as he had looked the day before. I went on peering at the menu. They ought to have printed it in braille.

Goble reached across for my glass of ice water and drank. 'How you making out with the girl?' he asked casually.

'Not getting anywhere. Why?'

'Whatcha go up on the hill for?'

'I thought maybe we could neck. She wasn't in the mood. What's your interest? I thought you were looking for some guy named Mitchell.'

'Very funny indeed. Some guy named Mitchell. Never heard of him, I believe you said.'

'I've heard of him since. I've seen him. He was drunk. Very drunk. He damn' near got himself thrown out of a place.'

'Very funny,' Goble said, sneering. 'And how did you know his name?'

'On account of somebody called him by it. That would be *too* funny, wouldn't it?'

He sneered. 'I told you to stay out of my way. I know who you are now. I looked you up.'

I lit a cigarette and blew smoke in his face. 'Go fry a stale egg.'

'Tough, huh,' he sneered. 'I've pulled the arms and legs off bigger guys than you.'

'Name two of them.'

He leaned across the table, but the waiter came up.

'I'll have bourbon and plain water,' Goble told him. 'Bonded stuff. None of that bar whisky for me. And don't try to fool me. I'll know. And bottled water. The city water here is terrible.'

The waiter just looked at him.

'I'll have another of these,' I said, pushing my glass.

'What's good tonight?' Goble wanted to know. 'I never

bother with these billboards.' He flicked a disdainful finger at the menu.

'The *plat du jour* is meat loaf,' the waiter said nastily.

'Hash with a starched collar,' Goble said. 'Make it meat loaf.'

The waiter looked at me. I said the meat loaf was all right with me. The waiter went away. Goble leaned across the table again, after first taking a quick look behind him and on both sides.

'You're out of luck, friend,' he said cheerfully. 'You didn't get away with it.'

'Too bad,' I said. 'Get away with what?'

'You're bad out of luck, friend. Very bad. The tide was wrong or something. Abalone fisher – one of those guys with frog feet and rubber masks – stuck under a rock.'

'The abalone fisher stuck under a rock?' A cold, prickly feeling crawled down my back. When the waiter came with the drinks, I had to fight myself not to grab for mine.

'Very funny, friend.'

'Say that again and I'll smash your goddamn glasses for you.' I snarled.

He picked up his drink and sipped it, tasted it, thought about it, nodded his head.

'I came out here to make money,' he mused. 'I didn't nowise come out to make trouble. Man can't make money making trouble. Man can make money keeping his nose clean. Get me?'

'Probably a new experience for you,' I said. 'Both ways. What was that about an abalone fisher?' I kept my voice controlled, but it was an effort.

He leaned back. My eyes were getting used to the dimness now. I could see that his fat face was amused.

'Just kidding,' he said. 'I don't know any abalone fishers. Only last night I learned how to pronounce the word. Still don't know what the stuff is. But things are kind of funny at that. I can't find Mitchell.'

'He lives at the hotel.' I took some more of my drink, not too much. This was no time to dive into it.

'I know he lives at the hotel, friend. What I don't know is where he is at right now. He ain't in his room. The hotel people ain't seen him around. I thought maybe you and the girl had some ideas about it.'

'The girl is screwy,' I said. 'Leave her out of it. And in Esmeralda they don't say "ain't seen". That Kansas City dialect is an offence against public morals here.'

'Shove it, Mac. When I want to get told how to talk English I won't go to no beat-up California peeper.' He turned his head and yelled: 'Waiter!'

Several faces looked at him with distaste. The waiter showed up after a while and stood there with the same expression as the customers.

'Hit me again,' Goble said, snapped a finger at his glass.

'It is not necessary to yell at me,' the waiter said. He took the glass away.

'When I want service,' Goble yelped at his back, 'service is what I want.'

'I hope you like the taste of wood alcohol,' I told Goble.

'Me and you could get along,' Goble said indifferently, 'if you had any brains.'

'And if you had any manners and were six inches taller and had a different face and another name and didn't act like you thought you could lick your weight in frog spawn.'

'Cut the doodads and get back to Mitchell,' he said briskly. 'And to the dish you was trying to fumble up the hill.'

'Mitchell is a man she met on a train. He had the same effect on her that you have on me. He created in her a burning desire to travel in the opposite direction.'

It was a waste of time. The guy was as invulnerable as my great-great-grandfather.

'So,' he sneered, 'Mitchell to her is just a guy she met on a train and didn't like when she got to know him. So she ditched him for you? Convenient you happened to be around.'

The waiter came with the food. He set it out with a flourish. Vegetables, salad, hot rolls in a napkin.

'Coffee?'

I said I'd rather have mine later. Goble said yes and wanted to know where his drink was. The waiter said it was on the way – by slow freight, his tone suggested. Goble tasted his meat loaf and looked surprised. 'Hell, it's good,' he said. 'What with so few customers I thought the place was a bust.'

'Look at your watch,' I said. 'Things don't get moving until much later. It's that kind of town. Also, it's out of season.'

'Much later is right,' he said, munching. 'An awful lot later. Two, three in the a.m. sometimes. People go calling on their friends. You back at the Rancho, friend?'

I looked at him without saying anything.

'Do I have to draw you a picture, friend? I work long hours when I'm on a job.'

I didn't say anything.

He wiped his mouth. 'You kind of stiffened up when I said that about the guy stuck under a rock. Or could I be wrong?'

I didn't answer him.

'Okay, clam up,' Goble sneered. 'I thought maybe we could do a little business together. You got the physique and you take a good punch. But you don't know nothing about nothing. You don't have what it takes in my business. Where I come from you got to have brains to get by. Out here you just got to get sunburned and forget to button your collar.'

'Make me a proposition,' I said between my teeth.

He was a rapid eater even when he talked too much. He pushed his plate away from him, drank some of his coffee and got a toothpick out of his vest.

'This is a rich town, friend,' he said slowly. 'I've studied it. I've boned up on it. I've talked to guys about it. They tell me it's one of the few spots left in our fair green country where the dough ain't quite enough. In Esmeralda you got to belong, or you're nothing. If you want to belong and get asked around and get friendly with the right people you got to have class. There's a guy here made five million fish in the rackets back in Kansas City. He bought up property, subdivided, built houses, built some of the best properties in town. But he didn't belong to the Beach Club because he didn't get asked.

So he bought it. They know who he is, they touch him big when they got a fund-raising drive, he gets service, he pays his bills, he's a good, solid citizen. He throws big parties but the guests come from out of town unless they're moochers, no-goods, the usual trash you always find hopping about where there's money. But the class people of the town? He's just a nigger to them.'

It was a long speech and while he made it he glanced at me casually from time to time, glanced around the room, leaned back comfortably in his chair and picked at his teeth.

'He must be breaking his heart,' I said. 'How did they find out where his dough came from?'

Goble leaned across the small table. 'A big shot from the Treasury Department comes here for a vacation every spring. Happened to see Mr Money and know all about him. He spread the word. You think it's not breaking his heart? You don't know these hoods that have made theirs and gone respectable. He's bleeding to death inside, friend. He's found something he can't buy with folding money and it's eating him to a shell.'

'How did you find out all this?'

'I'm smart. I get around. I find things out.'

'All except one,' I said.

'Just what's that?'

'You wouldn't know if I told you.'

The waiter came up with Goble's delayed drink and took dishes away. He offered the menu.

'I never eat dessert,' Goble said. 'Scram.'

The waiter looked at the toothpick. He reached over and deftly flicked it out from between Goble's fingers. 'There's a Men's Room here, chum,' he said. He dropped the toothpick into the ashtray and removed the ashtray.

'See what I mean?' Goble said to me. 'Class.'

I told the waiter I would have a chocolate sundae and some coffee. 'And give this gentleman the check,' I added.

'A pleasure,' the waiter said. Goble looked disgusted. The waiter drifted. I leaned across the table and spoke softly.

'You're the biggest liar I've met in two days. And I've met a few beauties. I don't think you have any interest in Mitchell. I don't think you ever saw or heard of him until yesterday when you got the idea of using him as a cover story. You were sent here to watch a girl and I know who sent you – not who hired you, but who had it done. I know why she is being watched and I know how to fix it so that she won't be watched. If you've got any high cards, you'd better play them right away quick. Tomorrow could be too late.'

He pushed his chair back and stood up. He dropped a folded and crimped bill on the table. He looked me over coolly.

'Big mouth, small brain,' he said. 'Save it for Thursday when they set the trash cans out. You don't know from nothing, friend. My guess is you never will.'

He walked off with his head thrust forward belligerently.

I reached across for the folded and crimped bill Goble had dropped on the table. As I expected it was only a dollar. Any guy who would drive a jaloppy that might be able to do forty-five miles an hour downhill would eat in joints where the eighty-five cent dinner was something for a wild Saturday night.

The waiter slid over and dumped the check on me. I paid up and left Goble's dollar in the plate.

'Thanks,' the waiter said. 'That guy's a real close friend of yours, huh?'

'The operative word is close,' I said.

'The guy might be poor,' the waiter said tolerantly. 'One of the choice things about this town is that the people who work here can't afford to live here.'

There were all of twenty people in the place when I left and the voices were beginning to bounce down off the low ceiling.

# Seventeen

The ramp down to the garage looked just the same as it had
looked at four o'clock in the morning, but there was a swishing
of water audible as I rounded the curve. The glassed-in
cubicle office was empty. Somewhere somebody was washing
a car, but it wouldn't be the attendant. I crossed to the door
leading into the elevator lobby and held it open. The buzzer
sounded behind me in the office. I let the door close and stood
outside it waiting and a lean man in a long white coat came
around the corner. He wore glasses, had a skin the colour of
cold oatmeal and hollow, tired eyes. There was something
Mongolian about his face, something south-of-the-border,
something Indian, and something darker than that. His black
hair was flat on a narrow skull.

'Your car, sir? What name, please?'

'Mr Mitchell's car in? The two-tone Buick hard-top?'

He didn't answer right away. His eyes went to sleep. He
had been asked that question before.

'Mr Mitchell took his car out early this morning.'

'How early?'

He reached for a pencil that was clipped to his pocket over
the stitched on scarlet-script with the hotel name. He took
the pencil out and looked at it.

'Just before seven o'clock. I went off at seven.'

'You work a twelve-hour shift? It's only a little past seven
now.'

He put the pencil back in his pocket. 'I work an eight-hour
shift but we rotate.'

'Oh. Last night you worked eleven to seven.'

'That's right.' He was looking past my shoulder at something far away. 'I'm due off now.'

I got out a packet of cigarettes and offered him one.

He shook his head.

574

'I'm only allowed to smoke in the office.'

'Or in the back of a Packard sedan.'

His right hand curled, as if around the haft of a knife.

'How's your supply? Needing anything?'

He stared.

'You should have said "Supply of what?" ' I told him.

He didn't answer.

'And I would have said I wasn't talking about tobacco,' I went on cheerfully. 'About something cured with honey.'

Our eyes met and locked. Finally he said softly: 'You a pusher?'

'You snapped out of it real nice, if you were in business at seven a.m. this morning. Looked to me like you would be out of circulation for hours. You must have a clock in your head – like Eddie Arcaro.'

'Eddie Arcaro,' he repeated. 'Oh yes, the jockey. Has a clock in his head, has he?'

'So they say.'

'We might do business,' he said remotely. 'What's your price?'

The buzzer sounded in the office. I had heard the elevator in the shaft subconsciously. The door opened and the couple I had seen holding hands in the lobby came through. The girl had on an evening dress and the boy wore a tux. They stood side by side, looking like two kids who had been caught kissing. The attendant glanced at them and went off and a car started and came back. A nice new Chrysler convertible. The guy handed the girl in carefully, as if she was already pregnant. The attendant stood holding the door. The guy came around the car and thanked him and got in.

'Is it very far to The Glass Room?' he asked diffidently.

'No, sir.' The attendant told them how to get there.

The guy smiled and thanked him and reached in his pocket and gave the attendant a dollar bill.

'You could have your car brought around to the entrance, Mr Preston. All you have to do is call down.'

'Oh, thanks, but this is fine,' the guy said hurriedly. He

started carefully up the ramp. The Chrysler purred out of sight and was gone.

'Honeymooners,' I said. 'They're sweet. They just don't want to be stared at.'

The attendant was standing in front of me again with the same flat look in his eyes.

'But there's nothing sweet about us,' I added.

'If you're a cop, let's see the buzzer.'

'You think I'm a cop?'

'You're some kind of nosy bastard.' Nothing he said changed the tone of his voice at all. It was frozen in B Flat. Johnny One-Note.

'I'm all of that. I agreed. 'I'm a private star. I followed somebody down here last night. You were in a Packard right over there' – I pointed – 'and I went over and opened the door and sniffed the weed. I could have driven four Cadillacs out of here and you wouldn't have turned over in bed. But that's your business.'

'The price today,' he said. 'I'm not arguing about last night.'

'Mitchell left by himself?'

He nodded.

'No baggage?'

'Nine pieces. I helped him load it. He checked out. Satisfied?'

'You checked with the office?'

'He had his bill. All paid up and receipted.'

'Sure. And with that amount of baggage a hop came with him naturally.'

'The elevator kid. No hops on until seven-thirty. This was about one a.m.'

'Which elevator kid?'

'A Mex kid we call Chico.'

'You're not Mex?'

'I'm part Chinese, part Hawaiian, part Filipino, and part nigger. You'd hate to be me.'

'Just one more question. How in hell do you get away with it? The muggles, I mean.'

He looked around. 'I only smoke when I feel extra special

low. What the hell's it to you? What the hell's it to anybody? Maybe I get caught and lose a crummy job. Maybe I get tossed in a cell. Maybe I've been in one all my life, carry it round with me. Satisfied?' He was talking too much. People with unstable nerves are like that. One moment monosyllables, next moment a flood. The low, tired monotone of his voice went on.

'I'm not sore at anybody. I live. I eat. Sometimes I sleep. Come around and see me some time. I live in a flea bag in an old frame cottage on Polton's Lane, which is really an alley. I live right behind the Esmeralda Hardware Company. The toilet's in a shed. I wash in the kitchen, at a tin sink. I sleep on a couch with broken springs. Everything there is twenty years old. This is a rich man's town. Come and see me. I live on a rich man's property.'

'There's a piece missing from your story about Mitchell,' I said.

'Which one?'

'The truth.'

'I'll look under the couch for it. It might be a little dusty.'

There was the rough noise of a car entering the ramp from above. He turned away and I went through the door and rang for the elevator. He was a queer duck, the attendant, very queer. Kind of interesting, though. And kind of sad, too. One of the sad, one of the lost.

The elevator was a long time coming and before it came I had company waiting for it. Six foot three inches of handsome, healthy male named Clark Brandon. He was wearing a leather windbreaker and a heavy roll-collar blue sweater under it, a pair of beat-up Bedford cord breeches, and the kind of high laced boots that field engineers and surveyors wear in rough country. He looked like the boss of a drilling crew. In an hour from now, I had no doubt he would be at The Glass Room in a dinner suit and he would look like the boss of that too, and perhaps he was. Plenty of money, plenty of health and plenty of time to get the best out of both, and wherever he went he would be the owner.

He glanced at me and waited for me to get into the elevator when it came. The elevator kid saluted him respectfully. He nodded. We both got off at the lobby. Brandon crossed to the desk and got a big smile from the clerk – a new one I hadn't seen before – and the clerk handed him a fistful of letters. Brandon leaned against the end of the counter and tore the envelopes open one by one and dropped them into a waste-basket beside where he was standing. Most of the letters went the same way. There was a rack of travel folders there. I picked one off and lit a cigarette and studied the folder.

Brandon had one letter that interested him. He read it several times. I could see that it was short and handwritten on the hotel stationery, but without looking over his shoulder that was all I could see. He stood holding the letter. Then he reached down into the basket and came up with the envelope. He studied that. He put the letter in his pocket and moved along the desk. He handed the clerk the envelope.

'This was handed in. Did you happen to see who left it? I don't seem to know the party.'

The clerk looked at the envelope and nodded. 'Yes, Mr Brandon, a man left it just after I came on. He was a middle-aged fat man with glasses. Grey suit and topcoat and grey felt hat. Not a local type. A little shabby. A nobody.'

'Did he ask for me?'

'No, sir. Just asked me to put the note in your box. Anything wrong, Mr Brandon?'

'Look like a goof?'

The clerk shook his head. 'He just looked what I said. Like a nobody.'

Brandon chuckled. 'He wants to make me a Mormon bishop for fifty dollars. Some kind of nut, obviously.' He picked the envelope up off the counter and put it in his pocket. He started to turn away, then said: 'Seen Larry Mitchell around?'

'Not since I've been on, Mr Brandon. But that's only a couple of hours.'

'Thanks.'

Brandon walked across to the elevator and got in. It was a

different elevator. The operator grinned all over his face and said something to Brandon. Brandon didn't answer him or look at him. The kid looked hurt as he whooshed the doors shut. Brandon was scowling. He was less handsome when he scowled.

I put the travel folder back in the rack and moved over to the desk. The clerk looked at me without interest. His glance said I was not registered there. 'Yes, sir?'

He was a grey-haired man who carried himself well.

'I was just going to ask for Mr Mitchell, but I heard what you said.'

'The house phones are over there.' He pointed with his chin. 'The operator will connect you.'

'I doubt it.'

'Meaning what?'

I pulled my jacket open to get at my letter case. I could see the clerk's eyes freeze on the rounded butt of the gun under my arm. I got the letter case out and pulled a card.

'Would it be convenient for me to see your house man? If you have one.'

He took the card and read it. He looked up. 'Have a seat in the main lobby, Mr Marlowe.'

'Thank you.'

He was on the phone before I had done a complete turn away from the desk. I went through the arch and sat against the wall where I could see the desk. I didn't have very long to wait.

The man had a hard, straight back and a hard, straight face, with the kind of skin that never tans but only reddens and pales out again. His hair was almost pompadour and mostly reddish-blond. He stood in the archway and let his eyes take in the lobby slowly. He didn't look at me any longer than at anybody else. Then he came over and sat down in the next chair to me. He wore a brown suit and a brown and yellow bow tie, His clothes fitted him nicely. There were fine blond hairs on his cheeks high up. There was a grace note of grey in his hair.

'My name's Javonen,' he said without looking at me. 'I know yours. Got your card in my pocket. What's your trouble?'

'Man named Mitchell, I'm looking for him. Larry Mitchell.'

'You're looking for him, why?'

'Business. Any reason why I shouldn't look for him?'

'No reason at all. He's out of town. Left early this morning.'

'So I heard. It puzzled me some. He only got home yesterday. On the Super Chief. In LA he picked up his car and drove down. Also, he was broke. Had to make a touch for dinner money. He ate dinner at The Glass Room with a girl. He was pretty drunk – or pretended to be. It got him out of paying the check.'

'He can sign his cheques there,' Javonen said indifferently. His eyes kept flicking around the lobby as if he expected to see one of the canasta players yank a gun and shoot his partner or one of the old ladies at the big jigsaw puzzle start pulling hair. He had two expressions – hard and harder. 'Mr Mitchell is well known in Esmeralda.'

'Well, but not favourably,' I said.

He turned his head and gave me a bleak stare. 'I'm an assistant manager here, Mr Marlowe. I double as security officer. I can't discuss the reputation of a guest of the hotel with you.'

'You don't have to. I know it. From various sources. I've observed him in action. Last night he put the bite on somebody and got enough to blow town. Taking his baggage with him, is my information.'

'Who gave this information to you?' He looked tough asking that.

I tried to look tough not answering it. 'On top of that I'll give you three guesses,' I said. 'One, his bed wasn't slept in last night. Two, it was reported to the office some time today that his room had been cleaned out. Three, somebody on your night staff won't show for work tonight. Mitchell couldn't get all his stuff out without help.'

Javonen looked at me, then prowled the lobby again with

his eyes. 'Got something that proves you are what the card reads? Anyone can have a card printed.'

I got my wallet out and slipped a small photostat of my licence from it and passed it over. He glanced at it and handed it back. I put it away.

'We have our own organization to take care of skip-outs,' he said. 'They happen – in any hotel. We don't need your help. And we don't like guns in the lobby. The clerk saw yours. Somebody else could see it. We had a stick-up attempted here nine months ago. One of the heist guys got dead. I shot him.'

'I read about it in the paper,' I said. 'It scared me for days and days.'

'You read some of it. We lost four or five thousand dollars worth of business the week following. People checked out by the dozen. You get my point?'

'I let the clerk see my gun butt on purpose. I've been asking for Mitchell all day and all I got was the run-around. If the man checked out, why not say so? Nobody had to tell me he had jumped his bill.'

'Nobody said he jumped his bill. His bill, Mr Marlowe, was paid in full. So where does that leave you?'

'Wondering why it was a secret he had checked out.'

He looked contemptuous. 'Nobody said that either. You don't listen good. I said he was out of town on a trip. I said his bill was paid in full. I didn't say how much baggage he took. I didn't say he had given up his room. I didn't say that what he took was all he had ... Just what are you trying to make out of all this?'

'Who paid his bill?'

His face got a little red. 'Look, buster, I told you *he* paid it. In person, last night, in full and a week in advance as well. I've been pretty patient with you. Now you tell me something. What's your angle?'

'I don't have one. You've talked me out of it. I wonder why he paid a week in advance.'

Javonen smiled – very slightly. Call it a down payment on a smile. 'Look, Marlowe, I put in five years in Military Intelligence. I can size up a man – like for instance the guy we're talking about. He pays in advance because we feel happier that way. It has a stabilizing influence.'

'He ever pay in advance before?'

'God damn it . . .!'

'Watch yourself,' I cut in. 'The elderly gent with the walking stick is interested in your reactions.'

He looked halfway across the lobby to where a thin, old, bloodless man sat in a very low, round-backed, padded chair, with his chin on gloved hands and the gloved hands on the crook of a stick. He stared unblinkingly in our direction.

'Oh, him,' Javonen said. 'He can't even see this far. He's eighty years old.'

He stood up and faced me. 'Okay, you're clammed,' he said quietly. 'You're a private op, you've got a client and instructions. I'm only interested in protecting the hotel. Leave the gun home next time. If you have questions, come to me. Don't question the help. It gets told around and we don't like it. You wouldn't find the local cops friendly if I suggested you were being troublesome.'

'Can I buy a drink in the bar before I go?'

'Keep your jacket buttoned.'

'Five years in Military Intelligence is a lot of experience,' I said looking up at him admiringly.

'It ought to be enough.' He nodded briefly and strolled away through the arch, back straight, shoulders back, chin in, a hard, lean, well set-up piece of man. A smooth operator. He had milked me dry – of everything that was printed on my business card.

Then I noticed that the old party in the low chair had lifted a gloved hand off the crook of his stick and was curving a finger at me. I pointed a finger at my chest and looked the question. He nodded, so over I went.

He was old, all right, but a long way from feeble and a long way from dim. His white hair was neatly parted, his nose was long and sharp and veined, his faded-out blue eyes were still keen, but the lids drooped wearily over them. One ear held the plastic button of a hearing aid, greyish-pink like his ear. The suede gloves on his hands had the cuffs turned back. He wore grey spats over polished black shoes.

'Pull up a chair, young man.' His voice was thin and dry and rustled like bamboo leaves.

I sat down beside him. He peered at me and his mouth smiled. 'Our excellent Mr Javonen spent five years in Military Intelligence, as no doubt he told you.'

'Yes, sir. CIC, a branch of it.'

'Military Intelligence is an expression which contains an interior fallacy. So you are curious about how Mr Mitchell paid his bill?'

I stared at him. I looked at the hearing aid. He tapped his breast pocket. 'I was deaf long before they invented these things. As the result of a hunter baulking at a fence. It was my own fault. I lifted him too soon. I was still a young man. I couldn't see myself using an ear trumpet, so I learned to lip-read. It takes a certain amount of practice.'

'What about Mitchell, sir?'

'We'll come to him. Don't be in a hurry.' He looked up and nodded.

A voice said, 'Good evening, Mr Clarendon.' A bellhop went by on his way to the bar. Clarendon followed him with his eyes.

'Don't bother with that one,' he said. 'He's a pimp. I have spent many, many years in lobbies, in lounges and bars, on porches, terraces and ornate gardens in hotels all over the world. I have outlived everyone in my family. I shall go on being useless and inquisitive until the day comes when the stretcher carries me off to some nice airy corner room in a hospital. The starched white dragons will minister to me. The bed will be wound up, wound down. Trays will come with that awful loveless hospital food. My pulse and temperature will be taken at frequent intervals and invariably when I am dropping off to sleep. I shall lie there and hear the rustle of the starched skirts, the slurring sound of the rubber shoe soles on the aseptic floor, and see the silent horror of the doctor's smile. After a while they will put the oxygen tent over me and draw the screens around the little white bed and I shall, without even knowing it, do the one thing in the world no man ever has to do twice.'

He turned his head slowly and looked at me. 'Obviously, I talk too much. Your name, sir?'

'Philip Marlowe.'

'I am Henry Clarendon IV. I belong to what used to be called the upper classes. Groton, Harvard, Heidelberg, the Sorbonne. I even spent a year at Upsala. I cannot clearly remember why. To fit me for a life of leisure, no doubt. So you are a private detective. I do eventually get around to speaking of something other than myself, you see.'

'Yes, sir.'

'You should have come to me for information. But of course you couldn't know that.'

I shook my head. I lit a cigarette, first offering one to Mr Henry Clarendon IV. He refused it with a vague nod.

'However, Mr Marlowe, it is something you should have certainly learned. In every luxury hotel in the world there will be half a dozen elderly idlers of both sexes who sit around and stare like owls. They watch, they listen, they compare notes, they learn everything about everyone. They have nothing else to do, because hotel life is the most deadly of all forms of boredom. And no doubt I'm boring you equally.'

'I'd rather hear about Mitchell, sir. Tonight at least, Mr Clarendon.'

'Of course. I'm egocentric, and absurd, and I prattle like a schoolgirl. You observe that handsome dark-haired woman over there playing canasta? The one with too much jewellery and the heavy gold trim on her glasses?'

He didn't point or even look. But I picked her out. She had an overblown style and she looked just a little hard-boiled. She was the one with the ice, the paint.

'Her name is Margo West. She is seven times a divorcee. She has stacks of money and reasonably good looks, but she can't hold a man. She tries too hard. Yet she's not a fool. She

584

would have an affair with a man like Mitchell, she would give him money and pay his bills, but she would never marry him. They had a fight last night. Nevertheless I believe she may have paid his bill. She often has before.'

'I thought he got a cheque from his father in Toronto every month. Not enough to last him, huh?'

Henry Clarendon IV gave me a sardonic smile. 'My dear fellow, Mitchell has no father in Toronto. He gets no monthly cheque. He lives on women. That is why he lives in a hotel like this. There is always some rich and lonely female in a luxury hotel. She may not be beautiful or very young, but she has other charms. In the dull season in Esmeralda, which is from the end of the race meet at Del Mar until about the middle of January, the pickings are very lean. Then Mitchell is apt to travel – Majorca or Switzerland if he can make it, to Florida or one of the Caribbean islands if he is not in rich funds. This year he had poor luck. I understand he only got as far as Washington.'

He brushed a glance at me. I stayed deadpan polite, just a nice, youngish guy (by his standards) being polite to an old gentleman who liked to talk.

'Okay,' I said. 'She paid his hotel bill, maybe. But why a week in advance?'

He moved one gloved hand over the other. He tilted his stick and followed it with his body. He stared at the pattern in the carpet. Finally he clicked his teeth. He had solved the problem. He straightened up again.

'That would be severance pay,' he said dryly. 'The final and irrevocable end of the romance. Mrs West, as the English say, had had it. Also, there was a new arrival in Mitchell's company yesterday, a girl with dark red hair. Chestnut red, not fire red or strawberry red. What I saw of their relationship seemed to me a little peculiar. They were both under some sort of strain.'

'Would Mitchell blackmail a woman?'

He chuckled. 'He would blackmail an infant in a cradle. A man who lives on women always blackmails them, although the word may not be used. He also steals from them when he can get his hands on any of their money. Mitchell forged two cheques with Margo West's name. That ended the affair. No doubt she has the cheques. But she won't do anything about it except keep them.'

'Mr Clarendon, with all due respect, how in hell would you know all these things?'

'She told me. She cried on my shoulder.' He looked towards the handsome, dark-haired woman. 'She does not at the moment look as if I could be telling the truth. Nevertheless I am.'

'And why are you telling it to me?'

His face moved into a rather ghastly grin. 'I have no delicacy. I should like to marry Margo West myself. It would reverse the pattern. Very small things amuse a man of my age. A humming bird, the extraordinary way a strellitzia bloom opens. Why at a certain point in its growth does the bud turn at right angles? Why does the bud split so gradually and why do the flowers emerge always in a certain exact order, so that the sharp, unopened end of the bud looks like a bird's beak and the blue and orange petals make a bird of paradise? What strange deity made such a complicated world when presumably he could have made a simple one? Is he omnipotent? How could he be? There's so much suffering and almost always by the innocent. Why will a mother rabbit trapped in a burrow by a ferret put her babies behind her and allow her throat to be torn out? Why? In two weeks more she would not even recognize them. Do you believe in God, young man?'

It was a long way around, but it seemed I had to travel it. 'If you mean an omniscient and omnipotent God who intended everything exactly the way it is, no.'

'But you should, Mr Marlowe. It is a great comfort. We all come to it in the end because we have to die and become dust. Perhaps for the individual that is all, perhaps not. There are grave difficulties about the after-life. I don't think I should really enjoy a heaven in which I shared lodgings with a Congo pygmy or a Chinese coolie or a Levantine rug peddler or even a Hollywood producer. I'm a snob, I suppose, and the remark is in bad taste. Nor can I imagine a heaven presided over by a benevolent character in a long white beard locally known as God. These are foolish conceptions of very immature minds. But you may not question a man's religious beliefs however idiotic they may be. Of course I have no right to assume that I shall go to heaven. Sounds rather dull, as a matter of fact. On the other hand how can I imagine a hell in which a baby that died before baptism occupies the same degraded position as a hired killer or a Nazi death camp commandant or a member of the Politburo? How strange it is that man's finest aspirations, dirty little animal that he is, his finest actions also, his great and unselfish heroism, his constant daily courage in a harsh world – how strange that these things should be so much finer than his fate on this earth. That has to be somehow made reasonable. Don't tell me that honour is merely a chemical reaction or that a man who deliberately gives his life for another is merely following a behaviour pattern. Is God happy with the poisoned cat dying alone in convulsions behind the billboard? Is God happy that life is cruel and that only the fittest survive? The fittest for what? Oh no, far from it. If God were omnipotent and omniscient in any literal sense, he wouldn't have bothered to make the universe at all. There is no success where there is no possibility of failure, no art without the resistance of the medium. Is it blasphemy to suggest that God has his bad days when nothing goes right, and that God's days are very, very long?'

'You're a wise man, Mr Clarendon. You said something about reversing the pattern.'

He smiled faintly. 'You thought I had lost the place in the overlong book of my words. No, sir, I had not. A woman like Mrs West almost always ends up marrying a series of pseudo-elegant fortune hunters, tango dancers with handsome side-burns, skiing instructors with beautiful blond muscles, faded French and Italian aristocrats, shoddy princelings from the Middle East, each worse than the one before. She might even in her extremity marry a man like Mitchell. If she married me, she would marry an old bore, but at least she would marry a gentleman.'

'Yeah.'

He chuckled. 'The monosyllable indicates a surfeit of Henry Clarendon IV. I don't blame you. Very well, Mr Marlowe, why are you interested in Mitchell? But I suppose you can't tell me.'

'No, sir, I can't. I'm interested in knowing why he left so soon after coming back, who paid his bill for him and why, if Mrs West or, say, some well-heeled friend like Clark Brandon paid for him, it was necessary to pay a week in advance as well.'

His thin, worn eyebrows curved upwards. 'Brandon could easily guarantee Mitchell's account by lifting the telephone. Mrs West might prefer to give him the money and have him pay the bill himself. But a week in advance? Why would our Javonen tell you that? What does it suggest to you?'

'That there's something about Mitchell the hotel doesn't want known. Something that might cause the sort of publicity they hate.'

'Such as?'

'Suicide and murder are the sort of things I mean. That's just by way of example. You've noticed how the name of a big hotel is hardly ever mentioned when one of the guests jumps out of a window? It's always a mid-town or a down-town hotel or a well known, exclusive hotel – something like that. And if it's rather a high-class place, you never see any cops in the lobby, no matter what happened upstairs.'

His eyes went sideways and mine followed his. The canasta table was breaking up. The dolled-up and well-iced woman called Margo West strolled off towards the bar with one of the men, her cigarette holder sticking out like a bowsprit.

'So?'

'Well,' I said, and I was working hard, 'if Mitchell keeps his room on the records, whatever room he had—'

'Four-eighteen,' Clarendon put in calmly. 'On the ocean side. Fourteen dollars a day out of season, eighteen in season.'

'Not exactly cheap for a guy on his uppers. But he still has it, let's say. So whatever happened, he's just away for a few days. Took his car out, put his luggage in around seven a.m. this morning. A damn' funny time to leave when he was as drunk as a skunk late last night.'

Clarendon leaned back and let his gloved hands hang limp. I could see that he was getting tired. 'If it happened that way, wouldn't the hotel prefer to have you think he had left for good? Then you'd have to search for him somewhere else. That is, if you really are searching for him.'

I met his pale stare. He grinned.

'You're not making very good sense to me, Mr Marlowe. I talk and talk, but not merely to hear the sound of my voice. I don't hear it naturally in any case. Talking gives me an opportunity to study people without seeming altogether rude. I have studied you. My intuition, if such be the correct word, tells me that your interest in Mitchell is rather tangential. Otherwise you would not be so open about it.'

'Uh-huh. Could be,' I said. It was a spot for a paragraph of lucid prose. Henry Clarendon IV would have obliged. I didn't have a damn' thing more to say.

'Run along now,' he said. 'I'm tired. I'm going up to my room and lie down a little. A pleasure to have met you, Mr Marlowe.' He got slowly to his feet and steadied himself with the stick. It was an effort. I stood up beside him.

'I never shake hands,' he said. 'My hands are ugly and painful. I wear gloves for that reason. Good evening. If I don't see you again, good luck.'

He went off, walking slowly and keeping his head erect. I could see that walking wasn't any fun for him. The two steps up from the main lobby to the arch were made one at a time, with a pause in between. His right foot always moved first. The cane bore down hard beside his left. He went out through the arch and I watched him move towards an elevator. I decided Mr Henry Clarendon IV was a pretty smooth article.

I strolled along to the bar. Mrs Margo West was sitting in the amber shadows with one of the canasta players. The waiter was just setting drinks before them. I didn't pay too much attention because farther along in a little booth against the wall was someone I knew better. And alone.

She had the same clothes on except that she had taken the bandeau off her hair and it hung loose around her face.

I sat down. The waiter came over and I ordered. He went away. The music from the invisible record player was low and ingratiating.

She smiled a little. 'I'm sorry I lost my temper,' she said. 'I was very rude.'

'Forget it. I had it coming.'

'Were you looking for me in here?'

'Not especially.'

'Were you – oh, I forgot.' She reached for her bag and put it in her lap. She fumbled in it and then passed something rather small across the table, something not small enough for her hand to hide that it was a folder of travellers' cheques. 'I promised you these.'

'No.'

'Take them, you fool! I don't want the waiter to see.'

I took the folder and slipped it into my pocket. I reached into my inside pocket and got out a small receipt book. I entered the counterfoil and then the body of the receipt. 'Received from Miss Betty Mayfield, Hotel Casa del Poniente, Esmeralda, California, the sum of $5,000 in American Express Company travellers' cheques of $100 denomination, countersigned by the owner, and remaining her property, subject to her demand at any time until a fee is arranged with, and an employment accepted by me, the undersigned.'

I signed this rigmarole and held the book for her to see it.

'Read it and sign your name in the lower left-hand corner.'

She took it and held it close to the light.

'You make me tired,' she said. 'Whatever are you trying to spring?'

'That I'm on the level and you think so.'

She took the pen I held out and signed and gave the stuff back to me. I tore out the original and handed it to her. I put the book away.

The waiter came and put my drink down. He didn't wait to be paid. Betty shook her head at him. He went away.

'Why don't you ask me if I have found Larry?'

'All right. Have you found Larry, Mr Marlowe?'

'No. He had skipped the hotel. He had a room on the fourth floor on the same side as your room. Must be fairly nearly under it. He took nine pieces of luggage and beat it in his Buick. The house peeper, whose name is Javonen – he calls himself an assistant manager and security officer – is satisfied that Mitchell paid his bill and even a week in advance for his room. He has no worries. He doesn't like me, of course.'

'Does somebody?'

'You do – five thousand dollars' worth.'

'Oh, you *are* an idiot. Do you think Mitchell will come back?'

'I told you he paid a week in advance.'

She sipped her drink quietly. 'So you did. But that could mean something else.'

'Sure. Just spitballing, for example, I might say it could mean that he didn't pay his bill, but someone else did. And that the someone else wanted time to do something – such as getting rid of that body on your balcony last night. That is, if there was a body.'

'Oh, stop it!'

She finished her drink, killed her cigarette, stood up and left me with the check. I paid it and went back through the lobby, for no reason that I could think of. Perhaps by pure instinct. And I saw Goble getting into the elevator. He seemed to have a rather strained expression. As he turned he caught my eye, or seemed to, but he gave no sign of knowing me. The elevator went up.

I went out to my car and drove back to the Rancho Descansado. I lay down on the couch and went to sleep. It had been a lot of day. Perhaps if I had a rest and my brain cleared, I might have some faint idea of what I was doing.

# Eighteen

An hour later I was parked in front of the hardware store. It wasn't the only hardware store in Esmeralda, but it was the only one that backed on the alley called Polton's Lane. I walked east and counted the stores. There were seven of them to the corner, all shining with plate glass and chromium trim. On the corner was a dress shop with mannequins in the windows, scarves and gloves and costume jewellery laid out under the lights. No prices showing. I rounded the corner and went south. Heavy eucalyptus trees grew out of the sidewalk. They branched low down and the trunks looked hard and heavy, quite unlike the tall, brittle stuff that grows around Los Angeles. At the far corner of Polton's Lane there was an automobile agency. I followed its high, blank wall, looking at broken crates, piles of cartons, trash drums, dusty parking spaces, the back yard of elegance. I counted the buildings. It was easy. No questions to ask. A light burned in the small window of a tiny frame cottage that had long ago been somebody's simple home. The cottage had a wooden porch with a broken railing. It had been painted once, but that was in the remote past before the shops swallowed it up. Once it may even have had a garden. The shingles of the roof were warped. The front door was a dirty mustard yellow. The window was shut tight and needed hosing off. Behind part of it hung what remained of an old roller blind. There were two steps up to the porch, but only one had a tread. Behind the cottage and halfway to the loading platform of the hardware store there was what had presumably been a privy. But I could see where a water pipe cut through the sagging side. A rich man's improvements on a rich man's property. A one-unit slum.

I stepped over the hollow place where a step should have been and knocked on the door. There was no bell push. Nobody answered. I tried the knob. Nobody had locked the door. I pushed it open and went in. I had that feeling. I was going to find something nasty inside.

A bulb burned in a frayed lamp crooked on its base, the paper shade split. There was a couch with a dirty blanket on it. There was an old cane chair, a Boston rocker, a table covered with a smeared oilcloth. On the table spread out beside a coffee cup was a copy of *El Diario*, a Spanish language newspaper, also a saucer with cigarette stubs, a dirty plate, a tiny radio which emitted music. The music stopped and a man began to rattle off a commercial in Spanish. I turned it off. The silence fell like a bag of feathers. Then the clicking of an alarm clock from beyond a half-open door. Then the clank of a small chain, a fluttering sound and a cracked voice said rapidly: *'Quien es? Quien es? Quien es?'* This was followed by the angry chattering of monkeys. Then silence again.

From a big cage over in the corner the round, angry eye of a parrot looked at me. He sidled along the perch as far as he could go.

*'Amigo,'* I said.

The parrot let out a screech of insane laughter.

'Watch your language, brother,' I said.

The parrot crabwalked to the other end of the perch and pecked into a white cup and shook oatmeal from his beak contemptuously. In another cup there was water. It was messy with oatmeal.

'I bet you're not even housebroken,' I said.

The parrot stared at me and shuffled. He turned his head and stared at me with his other eye. Then he leaned forward and fluttered his tail feathers and proved me right.

*'Necio!'* he screamed. *'Fuera!'*

Somewhere water dripped from a leaky faucet. The clock ticked. The parrot imitated the ticking amplified.

I said: 'Pretty Polly.'

*'Hijo de la chingada,'* the parrot said.

I sneered at him and pushed the half-open door into what there was of a kitchen. The linoleum on the floor was worn through to the boards in front of the sink. There was a rusty three-burner gas stove, an open shelf with some dishes and the alarm clock, a riveted hot-water tank on a support in the corner, the antique kind that blows up because it has no safety valve. There was a narrow rear door, closed, with a key in the lock, and a single window, locked. There was a light bulb hanging from the ceiling. The ceiling above it was cracked and stained from roof leaks. Behind me the parrot shuffled aimlessly on his perch and once in a while let out a bored croak.

On the zinc drainboard lay a short length of black rubber tubing, and beside that a glass hypodermic syringe with the plunger pushed home. In the sink were three long, thin, empty tubes of glass with tiny corks near them. I had seen such tubes before.

I opened the back door, stepped to the ground and walked to the converted privy. It had a sloping roof, about eight feet high in front, less than six at the back. It opened outwards, being too small to open any other way. It was locked but the lock was old. It did not resist me much.

The man's scuffed toes almost touched the floor. His head was up in the darkness inches from the two by four that held up the roof. He was hanging by a black wire, probably a piece of electric light wire. The toes of his feet were pointed down as if they reached to stand on tiptoe. The worn cuffs of his khaki denim pants hung below his heels. I touched him enough to know that he was cold enough so that there was no point in cutting him down.

He had made very sure of that. He had stood by the sink in his kitchen and knotted the rubber tube around his arm, then clenched his fist to make the vein stand out, then shot a syringe full of morphine sulphate into his blood stream. Since all three of the tubes were empty, it was a fair guess that one of them had been full. He could not have taken in less than enough. Then he had laid the syringe down and released the knotted tube. It wouldn't be long, not a shot directly into the blood stream. Then he had gone out to his privy and stood on the seat and knotted the wire around his throat. By that time he would be dizzy. He could stand there and wait until his knees went slack and the weight of his body took care of the rest. He would know nothing. He would already be asleep.

I closed the door on him. I didn't go back into the house. As I went along the side towards Polton's Lane, that handsome residential street, the parrot inside the shack heard me and screeched 'Quien es? Quien es? Quien es?'

Who is it? Nobody, friend. Just a footfall in the night.

I walked softly, going away.

# Nineteen

I walked softly, in no particular direction, but I knew where I would end up. I always did. At the Casa del Poniente. I climbed back into my car on Grand and circled a few blocks aimlessly, and then I was parked as usual in a slot near the bar entrance. As I got out I looked at the car beside mine. It was Goble's shabby, dark little jaloppy. He was as adhesive as a band-aid.

At another time I would have been racking my brains for some idea of what he was up to, but now I had a worse problem. I had to go to the police and report the hanging man. But I had no notion what to tell them. Why did I go to his house? Because, if he was telling the truth, he had seen Mitchell leave early in the morning. Why was that of significance? Because I was looking for Mitchell myself. I wanted to have a heart-to-heart talk with him. About what? And from there on I had no answers that would not lead to Betty Mayfield, who she was, where she came from, why she changed her name, what had happened back in Washington, or Virginia or wherever it was, that made her run away.

I had five thousand dollars of her money in travellers' cheques in my pocket, and she wasn't even formally my client. I was stuck, but good.

I walked over to the edge of the cliff and listened to the sound of the surf. I couldn't see anything but the occasional gleam of a wave breaking out beyond the cove. In the cove the waves don't break, they slide in politely, like floorwalkers. There would be a bright moon later, but it hadn't checked in yet.

Someone was standing not far away, doing what I was doing. A woman. I waited for her to move. When she moved I would know whether I knew her. No two people move in just the same way, just as no two sets of fingerprints match exactly.

I lit a cigarette and let the lighter flare in my face, and she was beside me.

'Isn't it about time you stopped following me around?'

'You're my client. I'm trying to protect you. Maybe on my seventieth birthday someone will tell me why.'

'I didn't ask you to protect me. I'm not your client. Why don't you go home – if you have a home – and stop annoying people?'

'You're my client – five thousand dollars worth. I have to do something for it – even if it's no more than growing a moustache.'

'You're impossible. I gave you the money to let me alone. You're impossible. You're the most impossible man I ever met. And I've met some dillies.'

'What happened to that tall, exclusive apartment house in Rio? Where I was going to lounge around in silk pyjamas and play with your long, lascivious hair, while the butler set out the Wedgwood and the Georgian silver with that faint dishonest smile and those delicate gestures, like a pansy hair stylist fluttering around a screen star?'

'Oh, shut up!'

'Wasn't a firm offer, huh? Just a passing fancy, or not even that. Just a trick to make me slaughter my sleeping hours and trot around looking for bodies that weren't there.'

'Did anybody ever give you a swift poke in the nose?'

'Frequently, but sometimes I make them miss.'

I grabbed hold of her. She tried to fight me off, but no fingernails. I kissed the top of her head. Suddenly she clung to me and turned her face up.

'All right. Kiss me, if it's any satisfaction to you. I suppose you would rather have this happen where there was a bed.'

'I'm human.'

'Don't kid yourself. You're a dirty, low-down detective. Kiss me.'

I kissed her. With my mouth close to hers I said: 'He hanged himself tonight.'

She jerked away from me violently. 'Who?' she asked in a voice that could hardly speak.

'The night garage attendant here. You may never have seen him. He was on mesca, tea, marijuana. But tonight he shot himself full of morphine and hanged himself in the privy behind his shack in Polton's Lane. That's an alley behind Grant Street.'

She was shaking now. She was hanging on to me as if to keep from falling down. She tried to say something, but her voice was just a croak.

'He was the guy that said he saw Mitchell leave with his nine suitcases early this morning. I wasn't sure I believed him. He told me where he lived and I went over this evening to talk to him some more. And now I have to go to the cops and tell them. And what do I tell them without telling them about Mitchell and from then on about you?'

'Please – please – *please* leave me out of it,' she whispered. 'I'll give you more money. I'll give you all the money you want.'

'For Pete's sake. You've already given me more than I'd keep. It isn't money I want. It's some sort of understanding of what the hell I'm doing and why. You must have heard of professional ethics. Some shreds of them still stick to me. Are you my client?'

'Yes. I give up. They all give up to you in the end, don't they?'

'Far from it. I get pushed around plenty.'

I got the folder of travellers' cheques out of my pocket and put a pencil flash on them and tore out five. I refolded it and handed it to her. 'I've kept five hundred dollars. That makes it legal. Now tell me what it's all about.'

'No. You don't have to tell anybody about that man.'

'Yes, I do. I have to go to the cop house just about now. I have to. And I have no story to tell them that they won't bust open in three minutes. Here, take your goddamn cheques – and if you ever push them at me again, I'll smack your bare bottom.'

She grabbed the folder and tore off into the darkness to the hotel. I just stood there and felt like a damn' fool. I don't know how long I stood there, but finally I stuffed the five cheques into my pocket and went wearily back to my car and started off to the place where I knew I had to go.

# Twenty

A man named Fred Pope who ran a small motel had once told me his views on Esmeralda. He was elderly, talkative, and it always pays to listen. The most unlikely people sometimes drop a fact or two that means a lot in my business.

'I been here thirty years,' he said. 'When I come here I had dry asthma. Now I got wet asthma. I recall when this town was so quiet dogs slept in the middle of the boulevard and you had to stop your car, if you had a car, and get out and push them out of the way. The bastards just sneered at you. Sundays it was like you was already buried. Everything shut up as tight as a bank vault. You could walk down Grand Street and have as much fun as a stiff in the morgue. You couldn't even buy a pack of cigarettes. It was so quiet you could of heard a mouse combin' his whiskers. Me and my old woman – she's been dead fifteen years now – used to play cribbage in a little place we had down on the street that goes along the cliff, and we'd listen in case something exciting would happen – like an old geezer taking a walk and tapping with a cane. I don't know if the Hellwigs wanted it that way or whether old man Hellwig done it out of spite. In them years he didn't live here. He was a big shot in the farm equipment business.'

'More likely,' I said, 'he was smart enough to know that a place like Esmeralda would become a valuable investment in time.'

'Maybe,' Fred Pope said. 'Anyhow, he just about created the town. And after a while he come to live here – up on the hill in one of them great big stucco houses with tile roofs. Pretty fancy. He had gardens with terraces and big green lawns and flowering shrubs, and wrought-iron gates – imported from Italy, I heard, and Arizona fieldstone walks, and not just one garden, half a dozen. And enough land to keep the neighbours out of his hair. He drank a couple bottles of hooch a day and I heard he was a pretty rough customer. He had one daughter, Miss Patricia Hellwig. She was the real cream and still is.

'By that time Esmeralda had begun to fill up. At first it was a lot of old women and their husbands, and I'm tellin' you the mortician business was real good with tired old men that died and got planted by their loving widows. The goddam women last too long. Mine didn't.'

He stopped and turned his head away for a moment, before he went on.

'There was a streetcar from San Diego by then, but the town was still quiet – too quiet. Not hardly anybody got born here. Child-bearing was thought kind of too sexy. But the war changed all that. Now we got guys that sweat, and tough school kids in levis and dirty shirts, and artists and country club drunks and them little gifte shoppes that sell you a two-bit highball glass for eight-fifty. We got restaurants and liquor stores, but we still don't have no billboards or pool rooms or drive-ins. Last year they tried to put in a dime-in-the-slot telescope in the park. You ought to of heard the town council scream. They killed it for sure, but the place ain't no bird refuge any more. We got as smart stores as Beverly Hills. And Miss Patricia, she spent her whole life working like a beaver to give things to the town. Hellwig died five years ago. The doctors told him he would have to cut down on the booze or he wouldn't live a year. He cussed them out and said if he couldn't take a drink when he wanted to, morning, noon or night, he'd be damned if he'd take one at all. He quit – and he was dead in a year.

'The docs had a name for it – they always have – and I guess Miss Hellwig had a name for them. Anyway, they got bumped off the staff of the hospital and that knocked them loose from Esmeralda. It didn't matter a whole lot. We still got about sixty doctors here. The town's full of Hellwigs, some with other names, but all of the family one way or another. Some are rich and some work. I guess Miss Hellwig works harder than most. She's eighty-six now, but tough as a mule. She don't chew tobacco, drink, smoke, swear or use no make-up. She give the town the hospital, a private school, a library, an art centre, public tennis courts, and God knows what else. And she still gets driven in a thirty-year-old Rolls-Royce that's about as noisy as a Swiss watch. The mayor here is two jumps from a Hellwig, both downhill. I guess she built the municipal centre too, and sold it to the city for a dollar. She's some woman. Of course we got Jews here now, but let me tell you something. A Jew is supposed to give you a sharp deal and steal your nose, if you ain't careful. That's all bunk. A Jew enjoys trading; he likes business, but he's only tough on the surface. Underneath a Jewish businessman is usually real nice to deal with. He's human. If you want cold-blooded skinning, we got a bunch of people in this town now that will cut you down to the bone and add a service charge. They'll take your last dollar from you between your teeth and look at you like you stole it from them.'

# Twenty-one

The cop house was part of a long, modernistic building at the corner of Hellwig and Orcutt. I parked and went into it, still wondering how to tell my story, and still knowing I had to tell it.

The business office was small but very clean, and the duty officer on the desk had two sharp creases in his shirt, and his uniform looked as if it had been pressed ten minutes before. A battery of six speakers on the wall was bringing in police and sheriffs' reports from all over the county. A tilted plaque on the desk said the duty officer's name was Griddell. He looked at me the way they all look, waiting.

'What can we do for you, sir?' He had a cool, pleasant voice, and that look of discipline you find in the best ones.

'I have to report a death. In a shack behind the hardware store on Grand, on an alley called Polton's Lane, there's a man hanging in a sort of privy. He's dead. No chance to save him.'

'Your name, please?' He was already pressing buttons.

'Philip Marlowe. I'm a Los Angeles private detective.'

'Did you notice the number of this place?'

'It didn't have one that I could see. But it's right smack behind the Esmeralda Hardware Company.'

'Ambulance call, urgent,' he said into his mike. 'Possible suicide in a small house behind the Esmeralda Hardware Store. Man hanging in a privy behind the house.'

He looked at me. 'Do you know his name?'

I shook my head. 'But he was the night garage man at the Casa del Poniente.'

He flicked some sheets of a book. 'We know him. Has a record for marijuana. Can't figure how he held the job, but he may be off it now, and his sort of labour is pretty scarce here.'

A tall sergeant with a granite face came into the office, gave me a quick glance and went out. A car started.

The duty officer flicked a key on a small PBX. 'Captain, this is Griddell on the desk. A Mr Philip Marlowe has reported a death in Polton's Lane. Ambulance moving. Sergeant Green is on his way. I have two patrol cars in the vicinity.'

He listened for a moment, then looked at me. 'Captain Alessandro would like to speak to you, Mr Marlowe. Down the hall, last door on the right, please.'

He was on the mike again before I was through the swinging door.

The last door on the right had two names on it. Captain Alessandro in a plaque fastened to the wood, and Sergeant Green on a removable panel. The door was half open, so I knocked and went in.

The man at the desk was as immaculate as the desk officer. He was studying a card through a magnifying glass, and a tape recorder beside him was telling some dreary story in a crumpled, unhappy voice. The Captain was about six feet three inches tall and had thick, dark hair and a clear, olive skin. His uniform cap was on the desk near him. He looked up, cut off the tape recorder and put down the magnifying glass and the card.

'Have a seat, Mr Marlowe.'

I sat down. He looked at me for a moment without speaking. He had rather soft, brown eyes, but his mouth was not soft.

'I understand you know Major Javonen at the Casa.'

'I've met him, Captain. We are not close friends.'

He smiled faintly. 'That's hardly to be expected. He wouldn't enjoy private detectives asking questions in the hotel. He used to be in the CIC. We still call him Major. This is the politest goddamn town I was ever in. We are a goddam smooth bunch around here, but we're police just the same. Now how about this Ceferino Chang?'

'So that's his name. I didn't know.'

'Yes. We know him. May I ask what you are doing in Esmeralda?'

'I was hired by a Los Angeles attorney named Clyde Umney

to meet the Super Chief and follow a certain party until that party came to a stop somewhere. I wasn't told why, but Mr Umney said he was acting for a firm of Washington attorneys and he didn't know why himself. I took the job because there is nothing illegal in following a person, if you don't interfere with that person. The party ended up in Esmeralda. I went back to Los Angeles and tried to find out what it was all about. I couldn't, so I took what I thought was a reasonable fee, $250, and absorbed my own expenses. Mr Umney was not very pleased with me.'

The Captain nodded. 'That doesn't explain why you are here or what you have to do with Ceferino Chang. And since you are not now working for Mr Umney, unless you are working for another attorney you have no privilege.'

'Give me a break, if you can, Captain. I found out that the party I was following was being blackmailed, or there was an attempt at blackmail, by a man named Larry Mitchell. He lives or lived at the Casa. I have been trying to get in touch with him, but the only information I have is from Javonen and this Ceferino Chang. Javonen said he checked out, paid his bill, and a week in advance for his room. Chang told me he left at seven a.m. this morning with nine suitcases. There was something a bit peculiar about Chang's manner, so I wanted to have another talk with him.'

'How did you know where he lived?'

'He told me. He was a bitter man. He said he lived on a rich man's property, and he seemed angry that it wasn't kept up.'

'Not good enough, Marlowe.'

'Okay, I didn't think it was myself. He was on the weed. I pretended to be a pusher. Once in a while in my business a man has to do a good deal of faking.'

'Better. But there's something missing. The name of your client – if you have one.'

'Could it be in confidence?'

'Depends. We never disclose the names of blackmail victims, unless they come out in court. But if this party has committed or been indicted for a crime, or has crossed a state line to escape prosecution, then it would be my duty as an officer of the law to report her present whereabouts and the name she is using.'

'Her? So you know already. Why ask me? I don't know why she ran away. She won't tell me. All I know is she is in trouble and in fear, and that somehow Mitchell knew enough to make her say uncle.'

He made a smooth gesture with his hand and fished a cigarette out of a drawer. He stuck it in his big mouth but didn't light it.

He gave me another steady look.

'Okay, Marlowe. For now I'll let it lay. But if you dig anything up, here is where you bring it.'

I stood up. He stood up too and held his hand out.

'We're not tough. We just have a job to do. Don't get too hostile with Javonen. The guy who owns that hotel draws a lot of water around here.'

'Thanks, Captain. I'll try to be a nice little boy – even to Javonen.'

I went back along the hall. The same officer was on the desk. He nodded to me and I went out into the evening and got into my car. I sat with my hands tight on the steering wheel. I wasn't too used to cops who treated me as if I had a right to be alive. I was sitting there when the desk officer poked his head out of the door and called that Captain Alessandro wanted to see me again.

When I got back to Captain Alessandro's office, he was on the telephone. He nodded me to the customer's chair and went on listening and making quick notes in what looked like the sort of condensed writing that many reporters use. After a while he said: 'Thanks very much. We'll be in touch.'

He leaned back and tapped on his desk and frowned.

'That was a report from the sheriff's sub-station at Escondido. Mitchell's car has been found – apparently abandoned. I thought you might like to know.'

'Thanks, Captain. Where was this?'

'About twenty miles from here, on a county road that leads

to Highway 395, but is not the road a man would naturally take to get to 395. It's a place called Los Penasquitos Canyon. Nothing there but outcrop and barren land and a dry river bed. I know the place. This morning a rancher named Gates went by there with a small truck, looking for fieldstone to build a wall. He passed a two-tone Buick hardtop parked off the side of the road. He didn't pay much attention to the Buick, except to notice that it hadn't been in a wreck, so somebody just parked it there.

'Later on in the day, around four, Gates went back to pick up another load of fieldstone. The Buick was still there. This time he stopped and looked it over. No keys in the lock but the car wasn't locked up. No sign of any damage. Just the same Gates wrote down the licence number and the name and address on the registration certificate. When he got back to his ranch he called the sub-station at Escondido. Of course the deputies knew Los Penasquitos Canyon. One of them went over and looked at the car. Clean as a whistle. The deputy managed to trick the trunk open. Empty except for a spare tyre and a few tools. So he went back to Escondido and called in here. I've just been talking to him.'

I lit a cigarette and offered one to Captain Alessandro. He shook his head.

'Got any ideas, Marlowe?'

'No more than you have.'

'Let's hear them anyway.'

'If Mitchell had some good reason to get lost and had a friend who would pick him up – a friend nobody here knew anything about – he would have stored his car in some garage. That wouldn't have made anyone curious. There wouldn't be anything to make the garage curious. They would just be storing a car. Mitchell's suitcases would already have been in his friend's car.'

'So?'

'So there wasn't any friend. So Mitchell disappeared into thin air – with his nine suitcases – on a very lonely road that was hardly ever used.'

'Go on from there.' His voice was hard now. It had an edge to it. I stood up.

'Don't bully me, Captain Alessandro. I haven't done anything wrong. You've been very human so far. Please don't get the idea that I had anything to do with Mitchell's disappearance. I didn't – and still don't – know what he had on my client. I just know that she is a lonely and frightened and unhappy girl. When I know why, if I do manage to find out, I'll let you know or I won't. If I don't, you'll just have to throw the book at me. It wouldn't be the first time it's happened to me. I don't sell out – even to good police officers.'

'Let's hope it doesn't turn out that way, Marlowe. Let's hope.'

'I'm hoping with you, Captain. And thanks for treating me the way you have.'

I walked back down the corridor, nodded to the duty officer on the desk and climbed back into my car again. I felt twenty years older.

I knew – and I was pretty damn' sure Captain Alessandro knew too – that Mitchell wasn't alive, that he hadn't driven his car to Los Penasquitos Canyon, but somebody had driven him there, with Mitchell lying dead on the floor of the back seat.

There was no other possible way to look at it. There are things that are facts, in a statistical sense, on paper, on a tape recorder, in evidence. And there are things that are facts because they have to be facts, because nothing makes any sense otherwise.

# Twenty-two

It is like a sudden scream in the night, but there is no sound. Almost always at night, because the dark hours are the hours of danger. But it has happened to me also in broad daylight – that strange, clarified moment when I suddenly know something I have no reason for knowing. Unless out of the long years and the long tensions, and in the present case, the abrupt certainty that what bullfighters call 'the moment of truth' is here.

There was no other reason, no sensible reason at all. But I parked across from the entrance to the Rancho Descansado, and cut my lights and ignition, and then drifted about fifty yards downhill and pulled the brake back hard.

I walked up to the office. There was the small glow of light over the night bell, but the office was closed. It was only ten-thirty. I walked around to the back and drifted through the trees. I came on two parked cars. One was a Hertz rent car, as anonymous as a nickel in a parking meter, but by bending down I could read the licence number. The car next to it was Goble's little dark jaloppy. It didn't seem very long since it was parked by the Casa del Poniente. Now it was here.

I went on through the trees until I was below my room. It was dark, soundless. I went up the few steps very slowly and put my ear to the door. For a little while I heard nothing. Then I heard a strangled sob – a man's sob, not a woman's. Then a thin, low, cackling laugh. Then what seemed to be a hard blow. Then silence.

I went back down the steps and through the trees to my car. I unlocked the trunk and got out a tyre iron. I went back to my room as carefully as before – even more carefully. I listened again. Silence. Nothing. The quiet of the night. I reached out my pocket flash and flicked it once at the window, then slid away from the door. For several minutes nothing happened. Then the door opened a crack.

I hit it hard with my shoulder and smashed it wide open. The man stumbled back and then laughed. I saw the glint of his gun in the faint light. I smashed his wrist with the tyre iron. He screamed. I smashed his other wrist. I heard the gun hit the floor.

I reached back and switched the lights on. I kicked the door shut.

He was a pale-faced redhead with dead eyes. His face was twisted with pain, but his eyes were still dead. Hurt as he was, he was still tough.

'You ain't going to live long, boy,' he said.

'You're not going to live at all. Get out of my way.'

He managed to laugh.

'You've still got legs,' I said. 'Bend them at the knees and lie down – face down – that is, if you want a face.'

He tried to spit at me, but his throat choked. He slid down to his knees, holding his arms out. He was groaning now. Suddenly he crumpled. They're so goddam tough when they hold the stacked deck. And they never know any other kind of deck.

Goble was lying on the bed. His face was a mass of bruises and cuts. His nose was broken. He was unconscious and breathing as if half strangled.

The redhead was still out, and his gun lay on the floor near him. I wrestled his belt off and strapped his ankles together. Then I turned him over and went through his pockets. He had a wallet with $670 in it, a driver's licence in the name of Richard Harvest, and the address of a small hotel in San Diego. His pocketbook contained numbered cheques on about twenty banks, a set of credit cards, but no gun permit.

I left him lying there and went down to the office. I pushed the button of the night bell, and kept on pushing it. After a while a figure came down through the dark. It was Jack in a bathrobe and pyjamas. I still had the tyre iron in my hand.

He looked startled. 'Something the matter, Mr Marlowe?'

'Oh, no. Just a hoodlum in my room waiting to kill me. Just another man beaten to pieces on my bed. Nothing the matter at all. Quite normal around here, perhaps.'

'I'll call the police.'

'That would be awfully damn' nice of you, Jack. As you see, I am still alive. You know what you ought to do with this place? Turn it into a pet hospital.'

He unlocked the door and went into the office. When I heard him talking to the police I went back to my room. The redhead had guts. He had managed to get into a sitting position against the wall. His eyes were still dead and his mouth was twisted into a grin.

I went over to the bed. Goble's eyes were open.

'I didn't make it,' he whispered. 'Wasn't as good as I thought I was. Got out of my league.'

'The cops are on their way. How did it happen?'

'I walked into it. No complaints. This guy's a life-taker. I'm lucky. I'm still breathing. Made me drive over here. He cooled me, tied me up, then he was gone for a while.'

'Somebody must have picked him up, Goble. There's a rent car beside yours. If he had that over at the Casa, how did he get back there for it?'

Goble turned his head slowly and looked at me. 'I thought I was a smart cookie. I learned different. All I want is back to Kansas City. The little guys can't beat the big guys – not ever. I guess you saved my life.'

Then the police were there.

First two prowl car boys, nice, cool-looking, serious men in the always immaculate uniforms and the always deadpan faces. Then a big, tough sergeant who said his name was Sergeant Holzminder, and that he was the cruising sergeant on the shift. He looked at the redhead and went over to the bed.

'Call the hospital,' he said briefly, over his shoulder.

One of the cops went out to the car. The Sergeant bent down over Goble. 'Want to tell me?'

'The redhead beat me up. He took my money. Stuck a gun

into me at the Casa. Made me drive him here. Then he beat me up.'

'Why?'

Goble made a sighing sound and his head went lax on the pillow. Either he passed out again or faked it. The Sergeant straightened up and turned to me. 'What's your story?'

'I haven't any, Sergeant. The man on the bed had dinner with me tonight. We'd met a couple of times. He said he was a Kansas City PI. I never knew what he was doing here.'

'And this?' The Sergeant made a loose motion towards the redhead, who was still grinning a sort of unnatural epileptic grin.

'I never saw him before. I don't know anything about him, except that he was waiting for me with a gun.'

'That your tyre iron?'

'Yes, Sergeant.'

The other cop came back into the room and nodded to the Sergeant. 'On the way.'

'So you had a tyre iron,' the Sergeant said coldly. 'So why?'

'Let's say I just had a hunch someone was waiting for me here.'

'Let's try it that you didn't have a hunch, that you already knew. And knew a lot more.'

'Let's try it that you don't call me a liar until you know what you're talking about. And let's try it that you don't get so goddamn tough just because you have three stripes. And let's try something more. This guy may be a hood, but he still has two broken wrists, and you know what that means, Sergeant? He'll never be able to handle a gun again.'

'So we book you for mayhem.'

'If you say so, Sergeant.'

Then the ambulance came. They carried Goble out first and then the interne put temporary splints on the two wrists of the redhead. They unstrapped his ankles. He looked at me and laughed.

'Next time, pal, I'll think of something original – but you did all right. You really did.'

He went out. The ambulance doors clanged shut and the growling sound of it died. The Sergeant was sitting down now, with his cap off. He was wiping his forehead.

'Let's try again,' he said evenly. 'From the beginning. Like as if we didn't hate each other and were just trying to understand. Could we?'

'Yes, Sergeant. We could. Thanks for giving me the chance.'

# Twenty-three

Eventually I landed back at the cop house. Captain Alessandro had gone. I had to sign a statement for Sergeant Holzminder.

'A tyre iron, huh?' he said musingly. 'Mister, you took an awful chance. He could have shot you four times while you were swinging on him.'

'I don't think so, Sergeant. I bumped him pretty hard with the door. And I didn't take a full swing. Also, maybe he wasn't supposed to shoot me. I don't figure he was in business for himself.'

A little more of that, and they let me go. It was too late to do anything but go to bed, too late to talk to anyone. Just the same I went to the telephone company office and shut myself in one of the two neat, outdoor booths and dialled the Casa del Poniente.

'Miss Mayfield, please. Miss Betty Mayfield. Room 1224.'

'I can't ring a guest at this hour.'

'Why? You got a broken wrist?' I was a real tough boy tonight. 'Do you think I'd call if it wasn't an emergency?'

He rang and she answered in a sleepy voice.

'This is Marlowe. Bad trouble. Do I come there or do you come to my place?'

'What? What kind of trouble?'

'Just take it from me for just this once. Should I pick you up in the parking lot?'

'I'll get dressed. Give me a little time.'

I went out to my car and drove to the Casa. I was smoking my third cigarette and wishing I had a drink when she came quickly and noiselessly up to the car and got in.

'I don't know what this is all about,' she began, but I interrupted her.

'You're the only one that does. And tonight you're going to tell me. And don't bother getting indignant. It won't work again.'

I jerked the car into motion and drove fast through silent streets and then down the hill and into the Rancho Descansado and parked under the trees. She got out without a word and I unlocked my door and put the lights on.

'Drink?'

'All right.

'Are you doped?'

'Not tonight, if you mean sleeping pills. I was out with Clark and drank quite a lot of champagne. That always makes me sleepy.'

I made a couple of drinks and gave her one. I sat down and leaned my head back.

'Excuse me,' I said. 'I'm a little tired. Once in every two or three days I have to sit down. It's a weakness I've tried to get over, but I'm not as young as I was. Mitchell's dead.'

Her breath caught in her throat and her hand shook. She may have turned pale. I couldn't tell.

'Dead?' she whispered. 'Dead?'

'Oh, come off it. As Lincoln said, you can fool all the detectives some of the time, and some of the detectives all the time, but you can't—'

'Shut up! Shut up right now! Who the hell do you think you are?'

'Just a guy who has tried very hard to get where he could do you some good. A guy with enough experience and enough understanding to know that you were in some kind of jam. And wanted to help you out of it, with no help from you.'

'Mitchell's dead,' she said in a low, breathless voice. 'I didn't mean to be nasty. Where?'

'His car has been found abandoned in a place you wouldn't know. It's about twenty miles inland, on a road that's hardly used. A place called Los Penasquitos Canyon. A place of dead land. Nothing in his car, no suitcases. Just an empty car parked at the side of a road hardly anybody ever uses.'

She looked down at her drink and took a big gulp. 'You said he was dead.'

'It seems like weeks, but it's only hours ago that you came

over here and offered me the top half of Rio to get rid of his body.'

'But there wasn't – I mean, I must just have dreamed—'

'Lady, you came over here at three o'clock in the morning in a state of near-shock. You described just where he was and how he was lying on the chaise on your little porch. So I went back with you and climbed the fire stairs, using the infinite caution for which my profession is famous. And no Mitchell, and then you asleep in your little bed with your little sleeping pill cuddled up to you.'

'Get on with your act,' she snapped at me. 'I know how you love it. Why didn't *you* cuddle up to me? I wouldn't have needed a sleeping pill – perhaps.'

'One thing at a time, if you don't mind. And the first thing is that you were telling the truth when you came here. Mitchell *was* dead on your porch. But someone got his body out of there while you were over here making a sucker out of me. And somebody got him down to his car and then packed his suitcases and got them down. All this took time. It took more than time. It took a great big reason. Now who would do a thing like that – just to save you the mild embarrassment of reporting a dead man on your porch?'

'Oh, shut up!' She finished her drink and put the glass aside. 'I'm tired. Do you mind if I lie down on your bed?'

'Not if you take your clothes off.'

'All right – I'll take my clothes off. That's what you've been working up to, isn't it?'

'You might not like that bed. Goble was beaten up on it tonight – by a hired gun named Richard Harvest. He was really brutalized. You remember Goble, don't you? The fat sort of man in the little dark car that followed us up the hill the other night.'

'I don't know anybody named Goble. And I don't know anybody named Richard Harvest. How do you know all this? Why were they here – in your room?'

'The hired gun was waiting for me. After I heard about Mitchell's car I had a hunch. Even generals and other important people have hunches. Why not me? The trick is to know when to act on one. I was lucky tonight – or last night. I acted on the hunch. He had a gun, but I had a tyre iron.'

'What a big, strong, unbeatable man you are,' she said bitterly. 'I don't mind the bed. Do I take my clothes off now?'

I went over and jerked her to her feet and shook her. 'Stop your nonsense, Betty. When I want your beautiful white body, it won't be while you're my client. I want to know what you are afraid of. How the hell can I do anything about it, if I don't know? Only you can tell me.'

She began to sob in my arms.

Women have so few defences, but they certainly perform wonders with those they have.

I held her tight against me. 'You can cry and cry and sob and sob, Betty. Go ahead, I'm patient. If I wasn't that – well, hell, if I wasn't that—'

That was as far as I got. She was pressed tight to me, trembling. She lifted her face and dragged my head down until I was kissing her.

'Is there some other woman?' she asked softly, between my teeth.

'There have been.'

'But someone very special?'

'There was once, for a brief moment. But that's a long time ago now.'

'Take me. I'm yours – all of me is yours. Take me.'

# Twenty-four

A banging on the door woke me. I opened my eyes stupidly. She was clinging to me so tightly that I could hardly move. I moved her arms gently until I was free. She was still sound asleep.

I got out of bed and pulled a bathrobe on and went to the door; I didn't open it.

'What's the matter? I was asleep.'

'Captain Alessandro wants you at the office right away. Open the door.'

'Sorry, can't be done. I have to shave and shower and so on.'

'Open the door. This is Sergeant Green.'

'I'm sorry, Sergeant. I just can't. But I'll be along just as soon as I can make it.'

'You got a dame in there?'

'Sergeant, questions like that are out of line. I'll be there.'

I heard his steps go down off the porch. I heard someone laugh. I heard a voice say, 'This guy is really rich. I wonder what he does on his day off.'

I heard the police car going away. I went into the bathroom and showered and shaved and dressed. Betty was still glued to the pillow. I scribbled a note and put it on my pillow. 'The cops want me. I have to go. You know where my car is. Here are the keys.'

I went out softly and locked the door and found the Hertz car. I knew the keys would be in it. Operators like Richard Harvest don't bother about keys. They carry sets of them for all sorts of cars.

Captain Alessandro looked exactly as he had the day before. He would always look like that. There was a man with him, an elderly stony-faced man with nasty eyes.

Captain Alessandro nodded me to the usual chair. A cop in uniform came in and put a cup of coffee in front of me. He gave me a sly grin as he went out.

'This is Mr Henry Kinsolving of Westfield, Carolina, Marlowe. North Carolina. I don't know how he found his way out here, but he did. He says Betty Mayfield murdered his son.'

I didn't say anything. There was nothing for me to say. I sipped the coffee which was too hot, but good otherwise.

'Like to fill us in a little, Mr Kinsolving?'

'Who's this?' He had a voice as sharp as his face.

'A private detective named Philip Marlowe. He operates out of Los Angeles. He is here because Betty Mayfield is his client. It seems that you have rather more drastic ideas about Miss Mayfield than he has.'

'I don't have any ideas about her, Captain,' I said. 'I just like to squeeze her once in a while. It soothes me.'

'You like being soothed by a murderess?' Kinsolving barked at me.

'Well, I didn't know she was a murderess, Mr Kinsolving. It's all news to me. Would you care to explain?'

'The girl who calls herself Betty Mayfield – and that was her maiden name – was the wife of my son, Lee Kinsolving. I never approved of the marriage. It was one of those wartime idiocies. My son received a broken neck in the war and had to wear a brace to protect his spinal column. One night she got it away from him and taunted him until he rushed at her. Unfortunately, he had been drinking rather heavily since he came home, and there had been quarrels. He tripped and fell across the bed. I came into the room and found her trying to put the brace back on his neck. He was already dead.'

I looked at Captain Alessandro. 'Is this being recorded, Captain?'

He nodded. 'Every word.'

'All right, Mr Kinsolving. There's more, I take it.'

'Naturally. I have a great deal of influence in Westfield. I own the bank, the leading newspaper, most of the industry. The people of Westfield are my friends. My daughter-in-law was arrested and tried for murder and the jury brought in a verdict of guilty.'

'The jury were all Westfield people, Mr Kinsolving?'

'They were. Why shouldn't they be?'

'I don't know, sir. But it sounds like a one-man town.'

'Don't get impudent with me, young man.'

'Sorry, sir. Would you finish?'

'We have a peculiar law in our state, and I believe in a few other jurisdictions. Ordinarily the defence attorney makes an automatic motion for a directed verdict of not guilty and it is just as automatically denied. In my state the judge may reserve his ruling until after the verdict. The judge was senile. He reserved his ruling. When the jury brought in a verdict of guilty, he declared in a long speech that the jury had failed to consider the possibility that my son had in a drunken rage removed the brace from his neck in order to terrify his wife. He said that where there was so much bitterness anything was possible, and that the jury had failed to consider the possibility that my daughter-in-law might have been doing exactly what she said she was doing – trying to put the brace back on my son's neck. He voided the verdict and discharged the defendant.

'I told her that she had murdered my son and that I would see to it that she had no place of refuge anywhere on this earth. That is why I am here.'

I looked at the Captain. He looked at nothing. I said: 'Mr Kinsolving, whatever your private convictions, Mrs Lee Kinsolving, whom I know as Betty Mayfield, has been tried and acquitted. You have called her a murderess. That's a slander. We'll settle for a million dollars.'

He laughed almost grotesquely. 'You small-town nobody,' he almost screamed. 'Where I come from you would be thrown into jail as a vagrant.'

'Make it a million and a quarter,' I said. 'I'm not so valuable as your ex-daughter-in-law.'

Kinsolving turned on Captain Alessandro. 'What goes on here?' he barked. 'Are you all a bunch of crooks?'

'You're talking to a police officer, Mr Kinsolving.'

'I don't give a good goddamn what you are,' Kinsolving said furiously. 'There are plenty of crooked police.'

'It's a good idea to be sure – before you call them crooked,' Alessandro said, almost with amusement. Then he lit a cigarette and blew smoke and smiled through it.

'Take it easy, Mr Kinsolving. You're a cardiac case. Prognosis unfavourable. Excitement is very bad for you. I studied medicine once. But somehow I became a cop. The war cut me off, I guess.'

Kinsolving stood up. Spittle showed on his chin. He made a strangled sound in his throat. 'You haven't heard the last of this,' he snarled.

Alessandro nodded. 'One of the interesting things about police work is that you never hear the last of anything. There are always too many loose ends. Just what would you like me to do? Arrest someone who has been tried and acquitted, just because you are a big shot in Westfield, Carolina?'

'I told her I'd never give her any peace,' Kinsolving said furiously. 'I'd follow her to the end of the earth. I'd make sure everyone knew just what she was!'

'And what is she, Mr Kinsolving?'

'A murderess that killed my son and was let off by an idiot of a judge – that's what she is!'

Captain Alessandro stood up, all six feet three inches of him. 'Take off, buster,' he said coldly. 'You annoy me. I've met all kinds of punks in my time. Most of them have been poor, stupid backward kids. This is the first time I've come across a great, big, important man who was just as stupid and vicious as a fifteen-year-old delinquent. Maybe you own Westfield, North Carolina, or think you do. You don't own a cigar butt in my town. Get out before I put the arm on you for interfering with an officer in the performance of his duties.'

Kinsolving almost staggered to the door and groped for the knob, although the door was wide open. Alessandro looked after him. He sat down slowly.

'You were pretty rough, Captain.'

'It's breaking my heart. If anything I said makes him take another look at himself – oh well, hell!'

'Not his kind. Am I free to go?'

'Yes. Goble won't make charges. He'll be on his way back to Kansas City today. We'll dig up something on this Richard Harvest, but what's the use? We put him away for a while, and a hundred just like him are available for the same work.'

'What do I do about Betty Mayfield?'

'I have a vague idea that you've already done it,' he said, deadpan.

'Not until I know what happened to Mitchell.' I was just as deadpan as he was.

'All I know is that he's gone. That doesn't make him police business.'

I stood up. We gave each other those looks. I went out.

# Twenty-five

She was still asleep. My coming in didn't wake her. She slept like a little girl, soundlessly, her face at peace. I watched her for a moment, then lit a cigarette and went out to the kitchen. When I had put coffee on to percolate in the handsome, paper-thin, dime-store aluminium percolator provided by the management, I went back and sat on the bed. The note I had left was still on the pillow with my car keys.

I shook her gently and her eyes opened and blinked.

'What time is it?' she asked stretching her bare arms as far as she could. 'God, I slept like a log.'

'It's time for you to get dressed. I have some coffee brewing. I've been down to the police station – by request. Your father-in-law is in town, Mrs Kinsolving.'

She shot upright and stared at me without breathing.

'He got the brush, but good, from Captain Alessandro. He can't hurt you. Was that what all the fear was about?'

'Did he say – say what happened back in Westfield?'

'That's what he came here to say. He's mad enough to jump down his own throat. And what of it? You didn't, did you? Do what they said?'

'I did not.' Her eyes blazed at me.

'Wouldn't matter, if you had – now. But it wouldn't make me very happy about last night. How did Mitchell get wise?'

'He just happened to be there or somewhere nearby. Good heavens, the papers were full of it for weeks. It wasn't hard for him to recognize me. Didn't they have it in the papers here?'

'They ought to have covered it, if only because of the unusual legal angle. If they did, I missed it. The coffee ought to be ready now. How do you take it?'

'Black, please. No sugar.'

'Fine. I don't have any cream or sugar. Why did you call

yourself Eleanor King? No, don't answer that. I'm stupid. Old man Kinsolving would know your unmarried name.'

I went out to the kitchen and removed the top of the percolator, and poured us both a cup. I carried hers to her. I sat down in a chair with mine. Our eyes met and were strangers again.

She put her cup aside. 'That was good. Would you mind looking the other way while I gather myself together?'

'Sure.' I picked a paperback off the table and made a pretence of reading it. It was about some private eye whose idea of a hot scene was a dead, naked woman hanging from the shower rail with the marks of torture on her. By that time Betty was in the bathroom. I threw the paperback into the wastebasket, not having a garbage can handy at the moment. Then I got to thinking there are two kinds of women you can make love to. Those who give themselves so completely and with such utter abandonment, like Helen Vermilyea, that they don't even think about their bodies. And there are those who are self-conscious and always want to cover up a little. I remembered a girl in a story by Anatole France who insisted on taking her stockings off. Keeping them on made her feel like a whore. She was right.

When Betty came out of the bathroom she looked like a fresh-opened rose, her make-up perfect, her eyes shining, every hair exactly in place.

'Will you take me back to the hotel? I want to speak to Clark.'

'You in love with him?'

'I thought I was in love with you.'

'It was a cry in the night,' I said. 'Let's not try to make it more than it was. There's more coffee out in the kitchen.'

'No, thanks. Not until breakfast. Haven't you ever been in love? I mean enough to want to be with a woman every day, every month, every year?'

'Let's go.'

'How can such a hard man be so gentle?' she asked wonderingly.

'If I wasn't hard, I wouldn't be alive. If I couldn't ever be gentle, I wouldn't deserve to be alive.'

I held her coat for her and we went out to my car. On the way back to the hotel she didn't speak at all. When we got there and I slid into the now familiar parking slot, I took the five folded travellers' cheques out of my pocket and held them out to her.

'Let's hope it's the last time we pass these back and forth,' I said. 'They're wearing out.'

She looked at them, but didn't take them. 'I thought they were your fee,' she said rather sharply.

'Don't argue, Betty. You know very well that I couldn't take money from you.'

'After last night?'

'After nothing. I just couldn't take it. That's all. I haven't done anything for you. What are you going to do? Where are you going? You're safe now.'

'I've no idea. I'll think of something.'

'Are you in love with Brandon?'

'I might be.'

'He's an ex-racketeer. He hired a gunman to scare Goble off. The gunman was ready to kill me. Could you really love a man like that?'

'A woman loves a man. Not what he is. And he may not have meant it.'

'Goodbye, Betty. I gave it what I had, but it wasn't enough.'

She reached her hand out slowly and took the cheques. 'I think you're crazy. I think you're the craziest man I ever met.' She got out of the car and walked away quickly, as she always did.

# Twenty-six

I gave her time to clear the lobby and go up to her room, and then I went into the lobby myself and asked for Mr Clark Brandon on a house phone. Javonen came by and gave me a hard look, but he didn't say anything.

A man's voice answered. It was his all right.

'Mr Brandon, you don't know me, although we shared an elevator the other morning. My name is Philip Marlowe. I'm a private detective from Los Angeles, and I'm a friend of Miss Mayfield. I'd like to talk to you a little, if you'll give me the time.'

'I seem to have heard something about you, Marlowe. But I'm all set to go out. How about a drink around six this evening?'

'I'd like to get back to Los Angeles, Mr Brandon. I won't keep you long.'

'All right,' he said grudgingly. 'Come on up.'

He opened the door, a big, tall, very muscular man in top condition, neither hard nor soft. He didn't offer to shake hands. He stood aside, and I went in.

'You alone here, Mr Brandon?'

'Sure. Why?'

'I wouldn't want anyone else to hear what I have to say.'

'Well say it and get done.'

He sat in a chair and put his feet up on an ottoman. He flicked a gold lighter at a gold-tipped cigarette. Big deal.

'I first came down here on the instructions of a Los Angeles lawyer to follow Miss Mayfield and find out where she went, and then report back. I didn't know why and the lawyer said he didn't either, but that he was acting for a reputable firm of attorneys in Washington. Washington, DC.'

'So you followed her. So what?'

'So she made contact with Larry Mitchell, or he with her, and he had a hook of some sort into her.'

'Into a lot of women from time to time,' Brandon said coldly. 'He specialized in it.'

'He doesn't any more, does he?'

He stared at me with cool, blank eyes. 'What's that mean?'

'He doesn't do anything any more. He doesn't exist any more.'

'I heard he left the hotel and went off in his car. What's it to do with me?'

'You didn't ask me how I know he doesn't exist any more.'

'Look, Marlowe.' He flicked ash from his cigarette with a contemptuous gesture. 'It could be that I don't give a damn. Get to what concerns me, or else get out.'

'I also got involved down here, if involved is the word, with a man named Goble who said he was a private eye from Kansas City, and had a card which may or may not have proved it. Goble annoyed me a good deal. He kept following me around. He kept talking about Mitchell. I couldn't figure what he was after. Then one day at the desk you got an anonymous letter. I watched you read it over and over. You asked the clerk who left it. The clerk didn't know. You even picked the empty envelope out of the wastebasket. And when you went up in the elevator you didn't look happy.'

Brandon was beginning to look a little less relaxed. His voice had a sharper edge.

'You could get too nosy, Mr PI. Ever think of that?'

'That's a silly question. How else would I make a living?'

'Better get out of here while you can still walk.'

I laughed at him, and that really burned him. He shot to his feet and came striding over to where I was sitting.

'Listen, boy friend. I'm a pretty big man in this town. I don't get pushed around much by small-time operators like you. Out!'

'You don't want to hear the rest?'

'I said, out!'

I stood up. 'Sorry. I was prepared to settle this with you privately. And don't get the idea that I'm trying to put a bite on you – like Goble. I just don't do those things. But if you toss me out – without hearing me out – I'll have to go to Captain Alessandro. He'll listen.'

He stood glowering for a long moment. Then a curious sort of grin appeared on his face.

'So he'll listen to you. So what? I could get him transferred with one phone call.'

'Oh, no. Not Captain Alessandro. He's not brittle. He got tough with Henry Kinsolving this morning. And Henry Kinsolving isn't a man that's used to having anyone get tough with him, any place, any time. He just about broke Kinsolving in half with a few contemptuous words. You think you could get that guy to lay off? You should live so long.'

'Jesus,' he said, still grinning, 'I used to know guys like you once. I've lived here so long now I must have forgotten they still make them. Okay. I'll listen.'

He went back to the chair and picked another gold-tipped cigarette from a case and lit it. 'Care for one?'

'No thanks. This boy Richard Harvest – I think he was a mistake. Not good enough for the job.'

'Not nearly good enough, Marlowe. Not nearly. Just a cheap sadist. That's what comes of getting out of touch. You lose your judgement. He could have scared Goble silly without laying a finger on him. And then taking him over to your place – what a laugh! What an amateur! Look at him now. No good for anything any more. He'll be selling pencils. Would you care for a drink?'

'I'm not on that kind of terms with you, Brandon. Let me finish. In the middle of the night – the night I made contact with Betty Mayfield, and the night you chased Mitchell out of The Glass Room – and did it very nicely, I might add – Betty came over to my room at the Rancho Descansado. One of your properties, I believe. She said Mitchell was dead on a chaise on her porch. She offered me large things to do something about it. I came back over here and there was no man dead on her porch. The next morning the night garage man told me Mitchell had left in his car with nine suitcases. He'd paid his bill and a week in advance to hold his room. The same day his car was found abandoned in Los Penasquitos Canyon. No suitcases, no Mitchell.'

Brandon stared hard at me, but said nothing.

'Why was Betty Mayfield afraid to tell me what she was afraid of? Because she had been convicted of murder in Westfield, North Carolina, and then the verdict was reversed by the judge, who has that power in that state, and used it. But Henry Kinsolving, the father of the husband she was accused of murdering, told her he would follow her anywhere she went and see that she had no peace. Now she finds a dead man on her porch. And the cops investigate and her whole story comes out. She's frightened and confused. She thinks she couldn't be lucky twice. After all, a jury did convict her.'

Brandon said softly: 'His neck was broken. He fell over the end wall of my terrace. She couldn't have broken his neck. Come out here. I'll show you.'

We went out on the wide, sunny terrace. Brandon marched to the end wall and I looked down over it and I was looking straight down on a chaise on Betty Mayfield's porch.

'This wall isn't very high,' I said. 'Not high enough to be safe.'

'I agree,' Brandon said calmly. 'Now suppose he was standing like this' – he stood with his back against the wall, and the top of it didn't come very much above the middle of his thighs. And Mitchell had been a tall man too – 'and he goads Betty into coming over near enough so that he can grab her, and she pushes him off hard, and over he goes. And he just happens to fall in such a way – by pure chance – that his neck snaps. And that's exactly how her husband died. Do you blame the girl for getting in a panic?'

'I'm not sure I blame anybody, Brandon. Not even you.'

He stepped away from the wall and looked out to sea and was silent for a moment. Then he turned.

'For anything,' I said, 'except that you managed to get rid of Mitchell's body.'

'Now, how in hell could I do that?'

'You're a fisherman, among other things. I'll bet that right

629

here in this apartment you have a long, strong cord. You're a powerful man. You could get down to Betty's porch, you could put that cord under Mitchell's arms, and you have the strength to lower him to the ground behind the shrubbery. Then, already having his key out of his pocket, you could go to his room and pack up all his stuff, and carry it down to the garage, either in the elevator, or down the fire stairs. That would take three trips. Not too much for you. Then you could drive his car out of the garage. You probably knew the night-man was a doper and that he couldn't talk, if he knew you knew. This was in the small hours of the night. Of course the garage man lied about the time. Then you could drive the car as near as possible to where Mitchell's body was, and dump him into it, and drive off to Los Penasquitos Canyon.'

Brandon laughed bitterly. 'So I am in Los Penasquitos Canyon with a car and a dead man and nine suitcases. How do I get out of there?'

'Helicopter.'

'Who's going to fly it?'

'You. They don't check much on helicopters yet, but they soon will, because they are getting more and more numerous. You could have one brought to you in Los Penasquitos Canyon, having arranged in advance, and you could have had someone come along to pick up the pilot. A man in your position can do almost anything, Brandon.'

'And then what?'

'You loaded Mitchell's body and his suitcases into the helicopter and flew out to sea and set the helicopter hovering close to the water, and then you could dump the body and the suitcases, and drift on back to wherever the helicopter came from. A nice, clean, well-organized job.'

Brandon laughed raucously – too raucously. The laugh had a forced sound.

'You think I'd actually be idiot enough to do all this for a girl I had only just met?'

'Uh-uh. Think again, Brandon. You did it for you. You forget Goble. Goble came from Kansas City. Didn't *you*?'

'What if I did?'

'Nothing. End of the line. But Goble didn't come out here for the ride. And he wasn't looking for Mitchell, unless he already knew him. And between them, they figured they had a gold mine. You were the gold mine. But Mitchell got dead and Goble tried to go it alone, and he was a mouse fighting with a tiger. But would you want to explain how Mitchell fell off your terrace? Would you want an investigation of your background? What so obvious as for the police to think you had thrown Mitchell over the wall? And even if they couldn't prove it, where would you be in Esmeralda from then on?'

He walked slowly to the far end of the terrace and back. He stood in front of me, his expression completely blank.

'I could have you killed, Marlowe. But in some strange way in the years I have lived here, I don't seem to be that kind of guy any more. So you have me licked. I don't have any defence, except to have you killed. Mitchell was the lowest kind of man, a blackmailer of women. You could be right all along the line, but I wouldn't regret it. And it's just possible believe me, just possible that I, too, went out on a limb for Betty Mayfield. I don't expect you to believe it, but it *is* possible. Now, let's deal. How much?'

'How much for what?'

'For not going to the cops.'

'I already told you how much. Nothing. I just wanted to know what happened. Was I approximately right?'

'Dead right, Marlowe. Right on the nose. They may get me for it yet.'

'Maybe. Well, I'll take myself out of your hair now. Like I said – I want to get back to Los Angeles. Somebody might offer me a cheap job. I have to live, or do I?'

'Would you shake hands with me?'

'No. You hired a gun. That puts you out of the class of people I shake hands with. I might be dead today, if I hadn't had a hunch.'

'I didn't mean him to kill anyone.'

'You hired him. Goodbye.'

# Twenty-seven

I got out of the elevator and Javonen seemed to be waiting for me. 'Come into the bar,' he said. 'I want to talk to you.'

We went into the bar, which was very quiet at that hour. We sat at a corner table. Javonen said quietly: 'You think I'm a bastard, don't you?'

'No. You have a job. I have a job. Mine annoyed you. You didn't trust me. That doesn't make you a bastard.'

'I try to protect the hotel. Who do you try to protect?'

'I never know. Often, when I do know, I don't know how. I just fumble around and make a nuisance of myself. Often I'm pretty inadequate.'

'So I heard – from Captain Alessandro. If it's not too personal, how much do you make on a job like this?'

'Well, this was a little out of the usual line, Major. As a matter of fact, I didn't make anything.'

'The hotel will pay you five thousand dollars – for protecting its interests.'

'The hotel, meaning Mr Clark Brandon.'

'I suppose. He's the boss.'

'It has a sweet sound – five thousand dollars. A very sweet sound. I'll listen to it on my way back to Los Angeles.' I stood up.

'Where do I send the cheque, Marlowe?'

'The Police Relief Fund could be glad to have it. Cops don't make much money. When they get in trouble they have to borrow from the Fund. Yes, I think the Police Relief Fund would be very grateful to you.'

'But not you?'

'You were a major in the CIC. You must have had a lot of chances to graft. But you're still working. I guess I'll be on my way.'

'Listen, Marlowe. You're being a damn' fool. I want to tell you—'

632

'Tell yourself, Javonen. You have a captive audience. And good luck.'

I walked out of the bar and got into my car. I drove to the Descansado and picked up my stuff and stopped at the office to pay my bill. Jack and Lucille were in their usual positions. Lucille smiled at me.

Jack said: 'No bill, Mr Marlowe. I've been instructed. And we offer you our apologies for last night. But they're not worth much, are they?'

'How much would the bill be?'

'Not much. Twelve-fifty maybe.'

I put the money on the counter, Jack looked at it and frowned. 'I said there was no bill, Mr Marlowe.'

'Why not? I occupied the room.'

'Mr Brandon—'

'Some people never learn, do they? Nice to have known you both. I'd like a receipt for this. It's deductible.'

# Twenty-eight

I didn't do more than ninety back to Los Angeles. Well, perhaps I hit a hundred for a few seconds now and then. Back on Yucca Avenue I stuck the Olds in the garage and poked at the mail box. Nothing, as usual. I climbed the long flight of redwood steps and unlocked my door. Everything was the same. The room was stuffy and dull and impersonal as it always was. I opened a couple of windows and mixed a drink in the kitchen. I sat down on the couch and stared at the wall. Wherever I went, whatever I did, this was what I would come back to. A blank wall in a meaningless room in a meaningless house.

I put the drink down on a side table without touching it. Alcohol was no cure for this. Nothing was any cure but the hard inner heart that asked for nothing from anyone.

The telephone started to ring. I picked it up and said emptily: 'Marlowe speaking.'

'Is this Mr Philip Marlowe?'

'Yes.'

'Paris has been trying to reach you, Mr Marlowe. I'll call you back in a little while.'

I put the phone down slowly and I think my hand shook a little. Driving too fast, or not enough sleep.

The call came through in fifteen minutes: 'The party calling you from Paris is on the line, sir. If you have any difficulty, please flash your operator.'

'This is Linda. Linda Loring. You remember me, don't you, darling?'

'How could I forget?'

'How are you?'

'Tired – as usual. Just came off a very trying sort of case. How are you?'

'Lonely. Lonely for you. I've tried to forget you. I haven't been able to. We made beautiful love together.'

'That was a year and a half ago. And for one night. What am I supposed to say?'

'I've been faithful to you. I don't know why. The world is full of men. But I've been faithful to you.'

'I haven't been faithful to you, Linda. I didn't think I'd ever see you again. I didn't know you expected me to be faithful.'

'I didn't. I don't. I'm just trying to say that I love you. I'm asking you to marry me. You said it wouldn't last six months. But why not give it a chance? Who knows – it might last for ever. I'm begging you. What does a woman have to do to get the man she wants?'

'I don't know. I don't even know how she knows she wants him. We live in different worlds. You're a rich woman, used to being pampered. I'm a tired hack with a doubtful future. Your father would probably see to it that I didn't even have that.'

'You're not afraid of my father. You're not afraid of anyone. You're just afraid of marriage. My father knows a man when he sees one. Please, please, please. I'm at the Ritz. I'll send you a plane ticket at once.'

I laughed. 'You'll send *me* a plane ticket? What sort of guy do you think I am? I'll send *you* a plane ticket. And that will give you time to change your mind.'

'But, darling, I don't need you to send me a plane ticket. I have—'

'Sure. You have the money for five hundred plane tickets. But this one will be *my* plane ticket. Take it, or don't come.'

'I'll come, darling. I'll come. Hold me in your arms. Hold me close in your arms. I don't want to own you. Nobody ever will. I just want to love you.'

'I'll be here. I always am.'

'Hold me in your arms.'

The phone clicked, there was a buzzing sound, and then the line went dead.

I reached for my drink. I looked around the empty room – which was no longer empty. There was a voice in it, and a tall, slim, lovely woman. There was a dark head on the pillow in the bedroom. There was that soft, gentle perfume of a woman who presses herself tight against you, whose lips are soft and yielding, whose eyes are half-blind.

The telephone rang again. I said: 'Yes?'

'This is Clyde Umney, the lawyer. I don't seem to have had any sort of satisfactory report from you. I'm not paying you to amuse yourself. I want an accurate and complete account of your activities at once. I demand to know in full detail exactly what you have been doing since you returned to Esmeralda.'

'Having a little quiet fun – at my own expense.'

His voice rose to a sharp cackle. 'I demand a full report from you at once. Otherwise I'll see that you get bounced off your licence.'

'I have a suggestion for you, Mr Umney. Why don't you go kiss a duck?'

There were sounds of strangled fury as I hung up on him. Almost immediately the telephone started to ring again.

I hardly heard it. The air was full of music.

Raymond Chandler
# The Chandler Collection Volume 1 £2.95

**The Big Sleep, The Lady in the Lake, The Little Sister**

'In everything that can be called art there is a quality of redemption. It may be pure tragedy if it is high tragedy, and it may be pity and irony, and it may be the raucous laughter of the strong man. But down these mean streets a man must go who is not himself mean, who is neither tarnished nor afraid. The detective in this kind of story must be such a man. He is the hero, he is everything ... He is a relatively poor man or he would not be a detective at all. He is a common man or he could not go among common people. He has a sense of character or he would not know his job. He is a lonely man and his pride is that you will treat him as a proud man or be very sorry you ever saw him. He talks as the man of his age talks, that is with rude wit, a lively sense of the grotesque, a disgust for sham and a contempt for pettiness ... If there were enough like him, I think the world would be a very safe place to live in, and yet not too dull to be worth living in' RAYMOND CHANDLER, THE SIMPLE ART OF MURDER

Dashiell Hammett
# The Four Great Novels £3.95

**The Dain Curse, The Glass Key, The Maltese Falcon, Red Harvest**

'Hammett had seen the rotten underbelly of his country and wanted others to see it ... Not just the first of the tough school of crime-writing but the best' THE TIMES

'Hammett ... took murder out of the Venetian vase and dropped it into the alley. He was spare, frugal, hard-boiled, but he did over and over again what only the best writers can ever do at all' RAYMOND CHANDLER

'The genius of the American detective story' TIME OUT

'The America of Prohibition days, and over all is the stink of corruption and cordite and hard liquor' OXFORD TIMES

Nathaneal West
# The Complete Works of Nathaneal West £3.50

**The Dream Life of Balso Snell, Miss Lonelyhearts, A Cool Million, The Day of the Locust**

Increasingly recognized as the great precursor of the black comedy, Nathaneal West, who was killed in a car crash at the age of thirty-seven, wrote four novels. Here are his complete works in one volume – one of the most telling indictments of America ever written by an American.

'West was always an idiosyncratic writer ... his desire to mock, undercut, make art into a kind of comic strip with puppet-like agents ... was to prove his real resource ... He constructs his own surreal canvas, expressing a dream-like motion filled with extraordinary images – the dead horse in the swimming pool, the cock fight, and so on ... a speculative reminder that Thirties fiction was not solely an affair of reportage and protest fiction, but also of a new experimentalism' MALCOLM BRADBURY, THE MODERN AMERICAN NOVEL

F. Scott Fitzgerald
# The Price Was High Volume 1 £2.95

**last uncollected stories**

'The price was high, right up with Kipling, because there was one little drop of something, not blood, not a tear, not my seed, but me more intimately than these, in every story, it was the extra I had' – throughout the twenties and thirties, Scott Fitzgerald was widely known as a writer of short stories about his generation's defiance of convention, far more so than for the novels – *The Great Gatsby, Tender is the Night* – which ensured his immortality. The stories in this volume all bear the unmistakable stamp of Fitzgerald's genius, and make wonderfully entertaining reading.

'Testimony to the truth of Dorothy Parker's observation: although he could write a bad story, he could not write badly' ANTHONY BURGESS, OBSERVER

## Picador

| | | | |
|---|---|---|---|
| ☐ | **Burning Leaves** | Don Bannister | £2.50p |
| ☐ | **Making Love: The Picador Book of Erotic Verse** | edited by Alan Bold | £1.95p |
| ☐ | **The Tokyo-Montana Express** | Richard Brautigan | £2.50p |
| ☐ | **Bury My Heart at Wounded Knee** | Dee Brown | £3.95p |
| ☐ | **Cities of the Red Night** | William Burroughs | £2.50p |
| ☐ | **The Road to Oxiana** | Robert Byron | £2.50p |
| ☐ | **If on a Winter's Night a Traveller** | Italo Calvino | £2.50p |
| ☐ | **Auto Da Fé** | Elias Canetti | £3.95p |
| ☐ | **Exotic Pleasures** | Peter Carey | £1.95p |
| ☐ | **Chandler Collection Vol. 1** | Raymond Chandler | £2.95p |
| ☐ | **In Patagonia** | Bruce Chatwin | £2.50p |
| ☐ | **Sweet Freedom** | Anna Coote and Beatrix Campbell | £1.95p |
| ☐ | **Crown Jewel** | Ralph de Boissiere | £2.75p |
| ☐ | **Letters from Africa** | Isak Dinesen (Karen Blixen) | £3.95p |
| ☐ | **The Book of Daniel** | E. L. Doctorow | £2.50p |
| ☐ | **Debts of Honour** | Michael Foot | £2.50p |
| ☐ | **One Hundred Years of Solitude** | Gabriel García Márquez | £2.95p |
| ☐ | **Nothing, Doting, Blindness** | Henry Green | £2.95p |
| ☐ | **The Obstacle Race** | Germaine Greer | £5.95p |
| ☐ | **Meetings with Remarkable Men** | Gurdjieff | £2.95p |
| ☐ | **Roots** | Alex Haley | £3.50p |
| ☐ | **The Four Great Novels** | Dashiell Hammett | £3.95p |
| ☐ | **Growth of the Soil** | Knut Hamsun | £2.95p |
| ☐ | **When the Tree Sings** | Stratis Haviaras | £1.95p |
| ☐ | **Dispatches** | Michael Herr | £2.50p |
| ☐ | **Riddley Walker** | Russell Hoban | £2.50p |
| ☐ | **Stories** | Desmond Hogan | £2.50p |
| ☐ | **Three Trapped Tigers** | C. Cabrera Infante | £2.95p |
| ☐ | **Unreliable Memoirs** | Clive James | £1.95p |
| ☐ | **Man and His Symbols** | Carl Jung | £3.95p |
| ☐ | **China Men** | Maxine Hong Kingston | £2.50p |
| ☐ | **Janus: A Summing Up** | Arthur Koestler | £3.50p |
| ☐ | **Memoirs of a Survivor** | Doris Lessing | £2.50p |
| ☐ | **Albert Camus** | Herbert Lottman | £3.95p |
| ☐ | **The Road to Xanadu** | John Livingston Lowes | £1.95p |
| ☐ | **Zany Afternoons** | Bruce McCall | £4.95p |
| ☐ | **The Cement Garden** | Ian McEwan | £1.95p |
| ☐ | **The Serial** | Cyra McFadden | £1.75p |
| ☐ | **McCarthy's List** | Mary Mackey | £1.95p |
| ☐ | **Psychoanalysis: The Impossible Profession** | Janet Malcolm | £1.95p |
| ☐ | **Daddyji/Mamaji** | Ved Mehta | £2.95p |
| ☐ | **Slowly Down the Ganges** | Eric Newby | £2.95p |
| ☐ | **The Snow Leopard** | Peter Matthiessen | £2.95p |

| | | | |
|---|---|---|---|
| ☐ | **History of Rock and Roll** | ed. Jim Miller | £4.95p |
| ☐ | **Lectures on Literature** | Vladimir Nabokov | £3.95p |
| ☐ | **The Best of Myles** | Flann O' Brien | £2.95p |
| ☐ | **Autobiography** | John Cowper Powys | £3.50p |
| ☐ | **Hadrian the Seventh** | Fr. Rolfe (Baron Corvo) | £1.25p |
| ☐ | **On Broadway** | Damon Runyon | £3.50p |
| ☐ | **Midnight's Children** | Salman Rushdie | £3.50p |
| ☐ | **Snowblind** | Robert Sabbag | £1.95p |
| ☐ | **Awakenings** | Oliver Sacks | £3.95p |
| ☐ | **The Fate of the Earth** | Jonathan Schell | £1.95p |
| ☐ | **Street of Crocodiles** | Bruno Schultz | £1.25p |
| ☐ | **Poets in their Youth** | Eileen Simpson | £2.95p |
| ☐ | **Miss Silver's Past** | Josef Skvorecky | £2.50p |
| ☐ | **A Flag for Sunrise** | Robert Stone | £2.50p |
| ☐ | **Visitants** | Randolph Stow | £2.50p |
| ☐ | **Alice Fell** | Emma Tennant | £1.95p |
| ☐ | **The Flute-Player** | D. M. Thomas | £2.25p |
| ☐ | **The Great Shark Hunt** | Hunter S. Thompson | £3.50p |
| ☐ | **The Longest War** | Jacob Timerman | £2.50p |
| ☐ | **Aunt Julia and the Scriptwriter** | Mario Vargas Llosa | £2.95p |
| ☐ | **Female Friends** | Fay Weldon | £2.50p |
| ☐ | **No Particular Place To Go** | Hugo Williams | £1.95p |
| ☐ | **The Outsider** | Colin Wilson | £2.50p |
| ☐ | **Kandy-Kolored Tangerine-Flake Streamline Baby** | Tom Wolfe | £2.25p |
| ☐ | **Mars** | Fritz Zorn | £1.95p |

All these books are available at your local bookshop or newsagent, or can be ordered direct from the publisher. Indicate the number of copies required and fill in the form below

...............................................................................................................

Name.................................................................................................
(Block letters please)

Address.............................................................................................

_____

Send to CS Department, Pan Books Ltd, PO Box 40, Basingstoke, Hants
Please enclose remittance to the value of the cover price plus:
35p for the first book plus 15p per copy for each additional book ordered
to a maximum charge of £1.25 to cover postage and packing
Applicable only in the UK

While every effort is made to keep prices low, it is sometimes
necessary to increase prices at short notice. Pan Books reserve
the right to show on covers and charge new retail prices which
may differ from those advertised in the text or elsewhere